the

yadayada

Prayer Group

GETS ROLLING

the yada yada *Prayer Group* GETS ROLLING

a Novel

neta jackson

Published by
THOMAS NELSON™
Since 1798
www.thomasnelson.com

Published in Nashville, Tennessee. Thomas Nelson is a trademark of Thomas Nelson, Inc.

Published in association with the literary agency of Alive Communications, Inc., 7680 Goddard Street, Suite 200, Colorado Springs, CO 80920.

Thomas Nelson, Inc. titles may be purchased in bulk for educational, business, fundraising, or sales promotional use. For information, please e-mail SpecialMarkets@ThomasNelson.com.

Scripture quotations are taken from the following: THE HOLY BIBLE, NEW INTERNATIONAL VERSION®. Copyright © 1973, 1978, 1984 by International Bible Society. Used by permission of Zondervan Publishing House.

The Holy Bible, New Living Translation, copyright © 1996. Used by permission of Tyndale House Publishers, Inc., Wheaton, Illinois 60819. All rights reserved.

The New King James Version®. Copyright © 1982 by Thomas Nelson, Inc. Used by permission. All rights reserved.

The King James Version of the Bible. Public domain.

Selected song lyrics are taken from the following:

"I Go to the Rock" by Dottie Rambo, Copyright © 1977 John T. Benson Publishing Co. (ASCAP). All rights reserved.

"Knowing You" by Graham Kendrick, Copyright © 1993 Make Way Music, www.grahamkendrick.co.uk All rights reserved. International copyright secured. Used by permission.

This novel is a work of fiction. Any references to real events, businesses, organizations, and locales are intended only to give the fiction a sense of reality and authenticity. Any resemblance to actual persons, living or dead, is entirely coincidental.

Library of Congress Cataloging-in-Publication Data has been applied for.

Printed in the United States of America
07 08 09 10 11 RRD 5 4 3 2 1

To the Yada Yada Prayer Support Team . . .

Pam Sullivan

Karen Evans

Julia Pferdehirt

Janalee Croegaert

Cynthia Wilson

Sue Mitrovitch

Janelle Schneider

Becky Gansky

Jodee Vragel

Sherri Hopper

Dawn Ashby

who committed themselves to pray for the writing of every Yada Yada

novel, prayed me through writer's block and family crises,

rejoiced with me when I met my deadlines,

and encouraged me with e-mail prayers—

even though a few of these precious sisters are readers I've never met!

And to Terry-Ann Wilson,

bookstore owner in Essex, Ontario,

who provided the name for . . . well, you'll find out!

Prologue

A surge of energy flowed through the wire, a cocktail of adrenaline greedy for power. The Spark flexed, pushing at the cord that gripped its life force, holding it in, always holding it back, harnessing its urge to jump free, to feed, to grow . . .

"Girl! You be careful with that outlet. You got too many cords plugged in there."

"Nah. It's okay . . . look at that, will ya? The kids are gonna love those lights. Kinda skimpy though. We could use a few more strings."

"I dunno. Looks okay to me. What else we gonna put on it?"

"The kids can make stuff—paper chains, snowflakes. String popcorn. That's what I used to do as a kid."

"Ha. You were never a kid. Bet you never made one of them paper snowflakes, neither."

"You don't know what you talkin' about. Gimme a sheet of paper, I'll show you. Scissors. We got scissors anywhere?"

Constrained, the Spark quit struggling and resigned itself to keeping

the strings of Christmas lights lit on a meager diet of fifteen watts . . .
Jolted awake, the Spark gulped air frantically. Zzzzzt. Zzzzzt.

"Ow!"

"Mikey! You know you ain't s'posed to touch no electric cord."

"I jus' wanted ta turn the tree on. But it bited me!"

"Nuthin' bit you, stupid."

"Did too. Like *that*."

"Ow! Let go! I'm gonna tell Mama, an' she whip your butt good."

"But you dint believe me. Had to show you."

"You didn't have ta show me nuthin'. 'Sides, your fingernails all dirty! What if you broke my skin, huh? You gonna give me rabies!"

The Spark laid back down. Hunger nibbled at its belly, but there was nothing to feed on. Might as well sleep . . .

ON. OFF. On. Off. On. Off . . .

The Spark had nearly given up its quest for bigger and better things.

"When we gonna take down this tree? It's already past New Year's. We always took our tree down New Year's Day."

"What? Ain't you never heard of the Twelve Days of Christmas?"

"That's just a song. One of them counting songs, sing it over an' over till ya wanna puke."

"Nah, nah, it's for real. Christmas Day's just the beginning. Some churches got stuff goin' for weeks, before an' after. Saint Lucy, or somebody, wears candles in her hair and gives out real homemade pastries. And Boxing Day—don't know what that one is. Three Kings Day—that's in January when we really s'posed to give gifts like the Wise Men brought to baby Jesus."

"How do you know all this stuff?"

"Oh, I get around. Girl, just pour some more water in that bucket."

"What for? Tree's too dead. Ain't drinkin' up anymore. Next year when I'm outta here, I'm gonna get me one of them artificial trees. I'm tired of sweeping up all these needles."

"Ha. We used ta leave ours up till *all* the needles fell off."

"What? Your mama put up with that?"

"Nah. My grandma raised all six of us. And she didn't see too good. Here . . . plug in the tree an' dim the other lights. See? Still looks like we just put it up."

The familiar jolt. The Spark licked hopefully . . . and was rewarded. A small frayed piece of the cord. Just a taste. Sizzled on its tongue and disappeared.

"You smell somethin'? Somethin' hot?"

"Ha. Hope so. Maybe the heat's come back on."

The Spark laid low, nibbling its way along the frayed cord. The more it nibbled, the more its hunger grew. Urgent now, it smoldered and smoked, pushing its way into the dark. And then . . . tinder.

Fragrant. Green. Dry.

The Spark consumed the fallen pine needles, its hunger glowing into a small flame. But there was more. More! With utter abandon, the Spark became a blaze, leaping and crackling and climbing the brittle branches. Feeding and fueling, the Spark flashed into a full bonfire. Glorious light! Nothing could stop it now!

Feeling its power, the Spark—fat and full, dancing and darting— leaped from the charred tree to the overstuffed furniture, consuming the frayed fabric and matted stuffing, licking its way up the walls and across the ceiling, finally embracing the whole room in a fiery feast—

"Fire! Fire! Everybody out!"

"Oh my God! Oh, please God!"

"Keep low! Keep low! Don't take anything—just go! Go!"

"My baby! My baby! Where's—? I gotta go back! Let me go!"

Screams. Cries. Coughing and gagging.

"Mama! Maaaamaaaaa!"

"I got you! I got you! Run!"

1

Stepping over Willie Wonka's inert body sprawled on the floor, I groped in the shadows behind the Christmas tree for the electric cord, felt for the outlet, and plugged it in. Instantly, a glittering fairyland replaced the early morning gloom. Framed neatly by the bay window in the front room of our first-floor apartment, the six-foot fir tree we'd found at Poor Bob's Tree Lot winked and twinkled its multicolored minilights like little blessings.

Shivering, I pulled Denny's robe tighter around me and drank in the sight. If I had to choose between Christmas presents or a Christmas tree, I'd take the tree any day. Memories hung from every branch. Orange-juice-lid ornaments the kids made when they were in kindergarten bobbed nobly on the front branches. The ornaments we'd given both kids each year had multiplied until they actually filled up the tree. I smiled. That was a tradition I'd brought to our marriage from my family, who had carefully packed up *my* ornaments as a wedding present when I got married. As we would do when Josh and Amanda—

My smile faded. *Ack!* Didn't want to go *there.* I dreaded the Christmas our tree would be denuded of our kids' ornaments.

I heard the coffee gurgling its last gasps as the pot filled. Scurrying back to the kitchen as fast as the stiffness in my left leg would let me, I poured my first mug of the day and then settled into the recliner facing the glittering tree for a few quiet moments before our Saturday began. It had been a nice Christmas—nothing spectacular, but nice. Leslie Stuart, our upstairs neighbor and one of my Yada Yada sisters, had invited her parents to visit her for a few days—a Christmas miracle big enough to warrant a few angels singing, "Glory! Hallelujah!" if you asked me. We'd met the senior Stuarts briefly when they'd arrived at our shared two-flat on Christmas Eve, but we'd officially invited the three of them for supper tonight.

Which meant I had to get everything ready this morning, since Ruth and Ben Garfield had also asked us and the other Yada Yadas to their house for baby Isaac's *brit mila* this afternoon.

"Brit mila? What's that?" I'd blurted when Ruth called me the day before Christmas.

"Brit mila—the ritual circumcision ceremony. A newborn Jewish male is joined to the Jewish people on the eighth day. Read your Bible, Jodi."

I had ignored the dig. *"Don't they do that in the hospital nowadays? With Josh—"*

"Is your Josh Jewish? Didn't think so. So, are you coming?"

"Wait a minute. The twins were born almost a month ago. What happened to the eighth day?"

A long pause. Not like Ruth, who usually filled up gaps in conversation like rainwater flowing into sidewalk cracks. I had immediately regretted my blunt question and started to apologize, but Ruth had just sighed. *"Pediatrician said we had to wait. Preemies, you know. But . . ."* Her voice had brightened. *"All is well. Havah and Isaac came home from the hospital on their due date—last Saturday. So* this *Saturday is the 'official' eighth day. The eighth day of Hanukkah too. See? God is good."*

"All the time," I'd agreed. *"Sure, we'll be there."*

Should have checked with my family first.

"Mo-om," Amanda had wailed. *"That's gross! If they gotta do that circumcision thing, at least do it in private. Not with everybody gawking at that poor naked baby. He'll be so embarrassed when he's thirteen and we all say, 'My, how you've grown! I was at your circumcision.'"*

I had ignored her. Sixteen-year-olds are embarrassed by everything. But even Denny had blanched. *"Uh, I dunno, Jodi. I'm kinda squeamish. What if I faint?"*

Josh, however, was the only one with a real excuse. *"Sorry, Mom. We're doing a Christmas party at Manna House for the kids."*

Now it was Saturday. The Big Day for Ben and Ruth. I sipped the hot coffee, feeling its lingering warmth. The sky beyond the bay windows—more visible in winter through the bare tree branches lining our narrow street on Chicago's north side—had begun to lighten. *Well, God,* I thought, *this year is almost over, a new one about to begin. Didn't I tell You I could use some "dull and boring" last year about this time? What happened, huh?*

Huh. Fact was, it had been a tough year for the Yada Yada Prayer Group all the way around. Nonyameko's husband, Mark, beaten up after that racist rally . . . Chanda finding out she had breast cancer . . . Florida's boy arrested and locked up in the juvenile detention center . . . Avis's daughter ending up at the Manna House shelter for

3

abused and homeless women . . . Ruth—childless, on her third husband, and pushing fifty—discovering she was pregnant with *twins* . . . Josh, our firstborn, refusing to go to college and falling in love with an "older woman" . . .

Didn't I walk with you every step of the way? The Voice in my spirit spoke gently but firmly. *Have I brought you this far to leave you now?*

"Yes, Lord, thank You," I whispered. "And . . . I guess it's a good thing You don't show us everything that's going to happen ahead of time." Because if this coming year was anything like the last year and a half since I'd met the rest of the Yada Yadas at that Chicago Women's Conference, change was in the wind.

Just then, Willie Wonka wheezed noisily to his feet and pushed his wet nose into my lap, rear end wiggling impatiently. Translated: *I gotta go out—now.*

Yeah, well. Some things *never* change.

BY THE TIME THE THREE OF US Baxters squeezed into the Garfields' compact living room that afternoon, there wasn't much room to sit. Amanda—as I'd suspected—wouldn't dream of being left behind, though her face fell when she realized Delores and Ricardo Enriques had left all the kids at home. Amanda never missed an opportunity to show up when Delores's sixteen-year-old son José might be there.

I spied Ruth standing by the front window holding one of the twins; Delores, standing beside her, was patting the other twin over her shoulder. Had to be the boy. Even from across the room I could see the large red birthmark covering a third of the baby's face. I winced, not yet used to such a conspicuous raspberry.

I quickly counted Yada Yada noses. Besides Ruth and Delores, I spied Hoshi Takahashi and Nonyameko Sisulu-Smith sitting on the couch—but not Nony's husband, Mark, who was still recovering from his head injury. Yo-Yo Spencer, who'd been taken under the Garfields' wing when she got out of prison after doing time for forgery, perched on the arm of the couch . . . was that *it*? Only five of us? Well, six, counting myself. Where was everybody?

But I only had time to give the couch sitters a quick wave before a bearded man wearing a prayer shawl began to chant a prayer. Voices immediately hushed all around the cramped living room. This must be the *mohel*, who, according to Ruth, would perform the ceremony. *"An expert he is, trained to do the circumcision with minimal discomfort,"* she'd told us on the phone. Then she'd muttered, *"He'd better be."*

After the prayer, the *mohel* called out, "Kvatter!"

Heads turned as Ruth nodded to Delores. "Delores Enriques is *kvatterin*, the child's godmother," she announced with that stubborn tilt of her chin, daring anyone to disagree. My mouth dropped in delight, and I saw our Yada Yada sisters exchange astonished smiles as Delores, blushing up to her hair roots, tenderly cradled the little boy and made her way toward the other end of the room where she handed the baby to her husband, Ricardo.

"And Ricardo Enriques is *kvatter*, the child's godfather," Ruth announced.

Again, little gasps of surprise and pleasure circled the room. *Well, well,* I thought. *No one deserves it more than Delores; she stuck with Ruth through this pregnancy like white on rice.* But Ricardo. *That* was a surprise—though, sure, it made sense to have husband and wife be the godparents. They were hardly Jewish, though.

As Ricardo took the baby, the *mohel* with the prayer shawl said, "*Baruch haba*," while Ruth and several others responded, "May he who cometh be blessed." And then the *mohel* offered another prayer, mentioning God's covenant with Abraham, the sign of which was circumcision. ". . . and through Abraham's seed, all nations will be blessed." And we all said, "Amen."

The *mohel* took the baby from Ricardo Enriques and handed him to someone sitting in a straight-back chair. Craning my neck, I saw Ruth's husband, Ben—a brand-new daddy at sixty-something—take his tiny son and place him on a large pillow on his lap. Ruth, coming up behind me, muttered in my ear, "Huh. Would Ben let anyone else hold his only son for his *brit mila*? Lucy would let Charlie Brown kick the football first."

I had to stuff my fist against my mouth to keep from laughing.

"—Oh Lord, King of the universe," the *mohel* was praying once again, "who has sanctified us with Thy commandments, and commanded us concerning the rite of circumcision." And then there was murmuring and rustling. Backs closed in around Ben and the baby.

This is it! I thought, looking away. I steeled myself for—

A wail broke the hush in the room. Ruth was fanning herself big-time. I could hear Ben's growly voice soothing and shushing his child as the *mohel* finished his administrations. As Isaac's wail subsided, sighs of relief and whispers filled the room.

Then the *mohel* lifted his voice once more. "Creator of the universe, may it be Thy gracious will"—I leaned forward, trying to hear—"and give a pure and holy heart to *Yitzak*, to be called Isaac, the son of Ben and Ruth Garfield, who has just now been circumcised in honor of Thy great name. May his heart be wide open to comprehend Thy holy Law, that he may learn and teach, keep and fulfill Thy laws."

Ben's "Amen!" boomed out over all the others. I caught Denny's eye—and saw that he had his handkerchief out and was blowing his nose. At least he didn't faint.

"One moment, please," the *mohel* added, finishing the ritual and actually smiling. "Today we have a double privilege, the honor of blessing and naming Isaac's twin sister. Ruth, can you join us?"

Beaming now, Ruth elbowed her way to the *mohel* and surrendered the baby in her arms. The bearded man took her gently and then held her up for all to see. A pink headband circled the tiny head, the bow on top matching the just-woke-up rosy cheeks. An *ahh* seemed to squeeze from the room, like the sigh of an accordion. And then the *mohel* prayed, "Lord of the universe, who created us both male and female, we ask your blessing on this little girl, to be called Havah, which means *life*. Help her to grow in joy and understanding of your gift of life to all people, even as she herself is a gift to her parents."

Again we all cried, "Amen!" accompanied by much applause and laughter.

And like all Jewish festivities Ruth had introduced us to, the *brit mila* was soon followed by food—lots and lots of food, spread out on the dining room table like its own deli. I sidled up alongside Yo-Yo, who was filling her plate. "Hey, Yo-Yo," I grinned. "Wasn't that a neat ceremony?"

"Yeah. I guess." Yo-Yo shrugged inside the bulky cotton sweater she was wearing over her overalls and moved to the other side of the table.

I frowned. *What was that about?* But Yo-Yo ducked out and

headed for a seat, just as Ruth appeared with little Havah in her arms. Clucking ladies—clones of Ruth, I thought—gathered around, oohing and ahhing over the pretty child, passing her from hand to hand. "Two minutes older than Isaac, she is," Ruth bragged.

Ben, I noticed, anchored the straight-back chair in the other room with Isaac on the lap pillow, as if daring anyone to pluck away his son.

After urging platefuls of macaroons, rugelach, and mandel-bread on everyone—"Jewish biscotti, only better," Ruth said about the latter—Ruth followed several of us Yadas as we finally headed for the bedroom to retrieve our coats piled on the bed. "So," she said, "does this count as our Yada Yada meeting? Everybody in town was here—or else up to their eyeballs in family shtick."

Yada Yada normally met on second and fourth Sundays, and this was the last weekend of the year. But she had a point. Stu's parents were still here. Avis's daughter and grandbaby were "home" for the holidays. (Avis couldn't bear the thought of Rochelle and little Conny spending Christmas at the women's shelter, where they'd been since Rochelle left her abusive husband a month ago.) Becky Wallace probably had Little Andy for the holidays, and—

"What about Chanda's birthday?" Yo-Yo piped up. "She complained that we missed her birthday last year 'cause it falls between Christmas and New Year's."

"Do not worry about Chanda. She decided at the last minute to take the kids to Jamaica." Nony's cultured South African accent made it sound like the queen of England had gone abroad. "Since her sister moved back to the island, Chanda has been—how do you say it?—sick for home."

"Oh, *si*, Jamaica!" Delores closed her eyes dreamily. "Sunshine. Tropical breezes. No ice storms . . . Can't blame her. Every Chicago winter I get homesick for Mexico."

"Yeah, me too," Yo-Yo muttered. "And I've never been out of Illinois." We all laughed.

"So, we cancel?" Ruth pushed, handing out the last of our coats.

"Uh," I stalled. "If we don't meet tomorrow, it'll be *another* two weeks before we get together—practically a whole month since our last real meeting." Didn't we all need a lot of prayer going into the New Year?

"Excuse me." My husband poked his head (swathed in the overly long scarf my mother had knit him for Christmas) into our little huddle. "I hate to state the obvious, but why don't you Yadas just meet the next week? Try first and third Sundays for a while. Half of you were complaining about meeting second Sundays anyway."

Which was true. Now that Uptown Community Church and New Morning Christian had merged, half of us Yada Yadas were in the same church, and second Sundays already had a combined church potluck and business meeting until we ironed out all the bumps in the road.

But I whacked him with my glove anyway. "Isn't it a burden to be *right* all the time, Denny Baxter?"

2

The clock said 4:30 when we got home. Ack! Stu and her parents would show up for supper in less than two hours. Did I have time to finish supper and send an e-mail to Yada Yada suggesting the new time? Not that most of us looked at our e-mail on a regular basis, especially around holidays. I'd probably have to call people so they wouldn't show up at . . . whose turn was it, anyway?

I looked at the Yada Yada list taped inside one of the kitchen cupboards. Yo-Yo's turn to host next.

What was up with Yo-Yo, anyway? I thought, opening the fridge and pulling out the lasagna spinach roll-ups I'd made earlier that day. I thought she'd be all over those babies, as close as she and her brothers were to Ben and Ruth. But she'd seemed . . . indifferent. Never once saw her hold one of the twins or even talk to Ben and Ruth, except when Ruth cornered us about our next meeting. *Weird.*

Oh well. Maybe she just felt out of place. There had been a lot of people today at the *brit mila* I didn't know either.

While the oven was heating, I called up e-mail and typed a quickie to Yada Yada saying, "It has been suggested"—didn't have to say *who* suggested—"we (a) cancel our fourth-Sunday meeting tomorrow, and (b) consider changing our meeting times to first and third Sundays to avoid schedule conflicts at Uptown–New Morning Church. That would mean we could meet NEXT week, the first weekend of the New Year."

I frowned at the message. If anybody didn't like this, *I* was the one who was going to hear about it. How did I end up being the group secretary, anyway?

I could just hear Stu answer that one: *"Because you do it, Jodi. If you don't want the job, just say so!"*

But as a precaution, I signed it, "Ruth, Nony, Hoshi, Delores, Yo-Yo, and Jodi," and thumped the Send key. I was pretty sure no one would complain about canceling tomorrow. And I'd let Avis, our unflappable group leader, handle the other one. After all, didn't elementary school principals have to major in Scheduling Changes Diplomacy?

By the time our front doorbell rang—*Stu must be on her best behavior,* I snickered to myself; she usually came sailing through our back door without knocking—I'd dragged Amanda off the phone long enough to set the table, Denny had buttered some garlic bread, and I'd tossed together a green salad. While Denny was greeting Stu and her parents in the front hall, I was still wondering whether to put out wineglasses. We usually splurged on wine with Italian food. But *my* parents would die if I served wine, with or without Italian food. Any kind of alcohol was *verboten* in the little Bible church I grew up in.

Better not risk it. Should've checked with Stu first.

I scurried into the living room to greet our guests. The resemblance between Stu and her father was striking. Tall. Angular face. Strong nose. "Hi, Jodi," Stu said. "You met my folks the other day, right? Lester and Luann Stuart . . . Jodi Baxter."

I smiled and stuck out my hand. "I'm so happy you guys could come for supper." *Ack!* *"You guys"? Why did I say that? But what am I supposed to call them? Lester and Luann? Or is that too familiar? They're Stu's parents, for pity's sake. Should I call them Mr. and Mrs. Stuart?*

Stu's mother, a sixtyish woman with short blonde hair, smiled and shook my hand. "Mrs. Baxter. You are very kind to invite us. You and your husband have been so good to Leslie . . ."

Okay. That answered that.

Mr. Stuart presented a slim bottle of red wine with a fancy label. "I hope you can use this. A small token of our appreciation."

I smiled, trying not to giggle. *And that answered that.* Oh, right. They were Lutherans. Real wine at Communion.

Stu and I left Denny to small-talk with the Stuarts while we set out the food and added wineglasses to the table. "How's it going?" I whispered, climbing on the kitchen stool to get a basket for the garlic bread.

She idly twisted a long strand of her straight blonde hair. "Pretty good, I guess . . . well, okay, kind of weird. I mean, until Thanksgiving we hadn't even talked to each other for four years! But yesterday we went to the Museum of Science and Industry and had dinner at Bubba Gumps on Navy Pier. Not too bad if we keep busy."

"Bubba Gumps! I'm jealous." We'd never been to the popular seafood restaurant named after the boat in the *Forrest Gump* movie. I struck a match, lit the green tapers nestled in some fake holly in the center of our red holiday tablecloth, and dimmed our modest chandelier. Even in the candlelight, Stu's eyes carried a sadness that the holidays only intensified. "Can you . . . you know, talk about stuff?"

She snorted. "You mean about the abortion? The grandchild they don't have? They know about it, sure—we got it all out on the table at Thanksgiving. We all cried buckets. But now it's like a big elephant standing in my living room that we're all pretending isn't there. No one wants to bring it up."

I gave Stu a squeeze. "Give it time. I'm humbled by your courage, Stu. Took guts to break the ice after so many years."

The back door opened and slammed shut, letting in a surge of frigid air. "Yo! I'm home!" Josh announced, shrugging out of his winter jacket. "What's for—oh. Hi, Stu." Josh surveyed the candlelit table. "Whassup? We got company?"

I held up a warning finger. "Read my lips," I breathed. "Stu's parents are here. Go meet them. You are not surprised. You are pleased to meet them. You speak English." I raised my voice sweetly as he meekly headed for the living room. "Call everyone to the table, will you, Josh? Your sister too."

Stu snickered. "I'll get another plate. You forgot to set a place for him."

I rolled my eyes. "Huh. Never know when Josh will show up for dinner. We still get mail for him, so I think he still lives here." I was only half kidding.

But ten minutes later, as we passed around the lasagna roll-ups, I breathed a prayer of thanksgiving that Josh had showed up. He kept the conversation rolling with tales from the Christmas party at the Manna House women's shelter. Mrs. Stuart seemed especially interested.

"—and you should have seen the crazy decorations the kids made for the Christmas tree. Somebody donated a tree *after* Christmas, but hey. We went all out anyway. Paper chains out of magazine pages, newspaper snowflakes—even raided the kitchen for measuring spoons and tea balls. We tried to string popcorn, but most of it got eaten. Maybe ten or twelve lonely kernels got on the tree itself."

We all laughed, but I felt a twinge. *Sheesh.* I could've sent tons of colored construction paper. Why didn't he *ask?*

Stu's mother leaned forward, fork delicately held in her manicured hand. "And how did you happen to get involved in this charity, Josh?"

Josh had used the laughter to finish off a piece of garlic bread. He chewed thoughtfully. "Kind of a long story. But if you're coming to church tomorrow, you'll hear a little more. Edesa and I are recruiting volunteers."

"Edesa?" Mrs. Stuart asked sweetly. Josh's ears turned red.

"She's in our prayer group," I put in. "Also volunteers at Manna House."

I eyed Stu across the table. *Are you going to bring your parents to church?* Uptown Community had been "an interesting experience" when my parents had visited a year ago. But the Uptown–New Morning amalgamation? We hadn't yet ironed out all the booby traps inherent in merging two churches—one mostly white, one mostly black—in an unfinished new building smack-dab in the middle of a shopping mall. That might be a stretch for a couple in their sixties from a mainstream church in Indianapolis.

Stu must have read my mind. She slipped a grin and mouthed, *"Sure. Why not?"*

"ON SECOND THOUGHT," Stu murmured to me the next morning as we surveyed the rapidly filling storefront sanctuary at the Howard Street Shopping Center, "I forgot about these awful folding chairs. My dad will be squirming in no time."

New chairs were probably at the bottom of the list of things to be decided by our new congregation. "Maybe we could make a case that padded chairs are a necessary tool for shopping center evangelism," I murmured.

Stu rolled her eyes. "Ha. Good luck." She moved off to rejoin her parents. "Pastor Clark, Pastor Cobbs," I heard her say, "these are my parents, Lester and—"

"Hey, Jodi. How ya feel?" Florida Hickman peeled off her winter jacket and knit hat, shaking out the coppery corkscrew curls that nearly matched her skin. "Man, it's hot up in here."

I nodded. "Yep. Temps in the forties today. Not what you expect from a Chicago winter." Florida looked good but didn't sound like her usual high-octane self. "How was—"

"*I* wannit ta *snow.*" Nine-year-old Carla Hickman, hair done in matching corkscrews, folded her arms in a pout. "Daddy said I could build a snowman when we got us a house."

"Of *course* you want it to snow," I teased. "You're *nine.*" I'd made it through half a bumpy school year with Carla Hickman in my third-grade class at Bethune Elementary; maybe we'd make it through the rest of the year. I leaned down and whispered in her ear. "Tell you what. If it snows after school starts, we'll build a snowman in the playground, how about that?"

She cocked her head at me. "Cross your heart and hope to die?"

Might as well live recklessly. "Promise." I got a rare Carla-smile in return before she skipped off. I turned back to Florida. "So, how was Christmas in your new house?"

Florida sighed. "Decent, I guess. Carl got us a tree, tried to keep our spirits up on account of Carla and Cedric. An' it was fun havin' Becky and Little Andy with us."

Ah, yes. *Becky.* Ex-con Becky Wallace had moved out of Stu's apartment and into the Hickmans' upstairs studio back in November when she got off house arrest. Trying to make a home of her own so she could get custody of Little Andy.

"But . . ." Florida wagged her head. "My insides was all torn up, knowin' Chris is locked up at juvie." Then she brightened. "But God is good, know what I'm sayin'? Carl an' me got to go see him that evenin', an' we goin' again tonight. They don't let kids in, though. Oh, hey!" She waved across the room. "There's Nony an' Mark. Mark's lookin' good, don't ya think?" Florida made a bee-line for the Sisulu-Smith family.

The worship band and praise team were warming up, and Denny beckoned me to come sit down. But as I headed his way, I did a quick gander around the room to see if any other Yada Yada sisters were there . . . yep. Avis Johnson-Douglass and her husband, Peter, sat in the second row. Avis's daughter Rochelle sat beside her—a beauty, just like Avis, with that trim figure, smooth nutmeg skin, and fall of long, raven-colored, wavy hair. Two-year-old Conny was crawling all over his stepgranddaddy's lap. *Hm.* The Christmas visit must be going well.

My attention was diverted by Becky Wallace grabbing for Little Andy, who was chasing the Sisulu-Smith boys across the six-inch-high platform and dodging musicians—and I had to snicker when I saw Hoshi Takahashi, the Northwestern University student who lived with the Sisulu-Smith household, snag Marcus and Michael and march them to their parents. *Ha.* Mild-mannered Hoshi obviously didn't put up with any nonsense from her charges.

So that was Avis, Stu, me, Flo, Becky, Nony, Hoshi, and—wait a minute. Edesa Reyes just came in, getting a huge hug from our sixteen-year-old Amanda. I poked Denny. "Look. Edesa's here," I whispered. Even though seven of us from Yada Yada had ended up here after the Uptown–New Morning merge, Edesa was a member of *Iglesia del Espirito Santo* on the West Side, had been ever since she came to the States from Honduras on a student visa.

Denny nodded. "Yeah. Recruiting volunteers for Manna House, remember?"

Oh. Right. Josh had said . . . *Ack!* I twisted my head, trying to catch a glimpse of my son. *Did Josh wear those tattered jeans again?* It was one thing to sit at the back with the sound equipment and look like something that's been through a paper shredder, but to get up front—

Pastor Clark, our pastor from Uptown, and Pastor Cobbs, New Morning's pastor, both stepped onto the low platform to signal the beginning of the worship service. They made a funny pastoral team: salt and pepper, tall and short, widowed and married. And to be honest, Pastor Clark's quiet demeanor was usually no match for Pastor Cobb's vigorous style. But as Pastor Clark kept saying, *"God is doing a new thing."*

"Good morning, church!" Pastor Cobbs boomed.

"Good morning!" bounced back from all over the spacious room.

"Our hearts should be bursting with joy this morning, for this week we celebrated the birth of the Christ child—"

"Thank ya, Jesus!" "Praise God!" "Hallelujah!"

The congregation was definitely awake. I fully expected the worship band and praise team to swing into a rousing gospel version of "Joy to the World!"—the usual carol to kick off the Sunday after Christmas. But Pastor Cobbs simply started to sing from somewhere deep, slowly, majestically . . .

O come, let us adore Him

O come, let us adore Him

O come, let us adore Hi-im . . .

Chri-ist the Lord.

All the instruments were still except the saxophone, rich and resonant. I forgot about Josh's jeans. I forgot about Stu's parents and whether they were squirming on our awful folding chairs. The words pulled at my heart . . .

O come, let us adore Him . . .

We sang no verses, just the chorus, again and again . . . until I longed to get down on my knees, like the shepherds of old, and just worship the Christ, Immanuel, come to live among us . . .

But I didn't. Too chicken.

3

*T*he praise team finally wound up the time of worship with a get-down version of "Joy to the World," causing Sunday morning shoppers to peer in the windows. A few even stepped inside the door to listen, though they skittered back outside when Pastor Clark—wearing a skinny red tie that ran up and down his white shirt like a fever thermometer—stood up to welcome visitors and give announcements. "Don't forget our next business meeting and potluck on the second Sunday of the New Year—"

"What? No New Year's Eve service?" I whispered to Denny. He ignored me.

"—Also, volunteers from the Manna House women's shelter here in Chicago would like to bring an announcement. Josh? Edesa?" Pastor Clark waved them up.

I was relieved to see Josh was clad in a pair of jeans with no skin showing. Edesa, as usual, glowed like polished mahogany. She was the first Spanish-speaking black person I'd ever met. Even with all my textbook education about the ugly slave trade on both American continents, it had somehow eluded me that African descendants peppered South America too—until I met Edesa. Nationality: African Honduran.

But as the two of them stood up there in front of the whole church, my heart bounced back and forth between affection and anxiety. Josh, our eldest, was a recent high school graduate, with no plans—yet—to go to college; he wanted "life experience first." Edesa, three years older, had recently changed her study track to public health at UIC —and had been one of *my* Yada Yada prayer sisters ever since God threw the twelve of us together at that Chicago Women's Conference a year and a half ago.

Josh and Edesa. Everywhere I turned lately, they were doing some kind of youth group thing together. They'd helped chaperone a group of Uptown teens at the Cornerstone Music Festival last summer. Taken kids to Six Flags Great America. (Huh! In *my* book, nineteen-year-old Josh was still two hairs shy of being an adult.) Now they were volunteering at a homeless women's shelter, of all things!

Josh, of course, admired Edesa. Who didn't? The Honduran student was a vibrant young woman—one of the sweetest I'd ever met. Thoughtful. Caring. Like a daughter to Delores Enriques and her brood. Still, I nearly swallowed my tongue when, in a rare moment of vulnerability, my son had told me, *"Mom. I . . . love . . . Edesa Reyes."* And in an even rarer moment of motherly grace, I'd actually asked, *"Have you told her?"*

No. She'd never encouraged him that way, he said. They were "just friends."

Right.

"Buenos días, church!" Edesa's bright yellow sweater and yellow cloth headband added sunshine to the rather gray day outside. "I

22

bring you greetings from *Iglesia del Espirito Santo*, my home church on the West Side. I am delighted to be with you this morning—and I see many familiar faces here." She winked at Little Andy, who hid his face and giggled.

Josh picked it up. "Edesa and I are volunteers at Manna House, a women's shelter in Chicago, less than a year old." He sketched the beginnings of the shelter, "home" to two dozen women with children, more or less, who were homeless or—in some cases—victims of domestic abuse who needed a place of safety.

"Right now," Edesa said, "we have only one full-time paid staff member—our director. Our office manager is part-time. We desperately need more volunteers—especially on the weekends, to give the staff a break—including those who would be willing to spend one or two nights simply being *un amigo* to the women, doing activities with the *niños*, and simply being a 'presence.'" She smiled at the gaggle of kids on the front row. "But maybe the best thing would be to hear from one of the current residents."

Who? Rochelle? Only a few people here knew Rochelle was a "current resident" at Manna House. Wouldn't it be risky to go public? She didn't want Dexter to find her. Besides, I thought Rochelle was still so mad at Peter "You're Not My Dad" Douglass for sending her to a shelter when she showed up at their apartment a third time, I couldn't imagine she'd plug Manna House—not in front of her mom's new husband!

But Rochelle didn't move. Instead, Edesa took a letter from her pocket, unfolded it and began to read. "*To whom it may concern: To tell the truth, I never imagined that I would end up in a women's shelter. But I never imagined I'd be afraid of my husband either, so here I am . . .*"

23

Did Rochelle write the letter? Sounded like her story. She whispered something to Conny, as if not paying attention. Avis's eyes were closed, her lips moving soundlessly. Praying, no doubt.

"The shelter isn't much," Edesa read on. *"The space could use a lot of sprucing up."* Josh rolled his eyes in agreement; the kids on the front row giggled. *"But I'm so grateful the staff and volunteers have been there for me and my baby. They've loved on us, accepted us, given us legal help, and been a safe haven when we needed it most. Of course, we don't want to stay here forever! But for now, we are blessed. And if you can do anything to keep the shelter going, I know you will be blessed too."* Edesa looked up. "Signed by one of our residents."

The congregation clapped spontaneously. When the noise died down, Josh said, "Uh, I think that speaks for itself. We're hoping to get enough volunteers so your time would only be one weekend per month. So . . . if you have any questions, please talk to us after the service. We can give more details at that time."

Before Josh and Edesa went back to their seats, both Pastor Clark and Pastor Cobbs laid hands on them and prayed for this new shelter. I noticed Denny fishing in his pants pocket for a handkerchief and blowing his nose.

When the prayer was over, Josh and Edesa finally left the platform—and then suddenly Josh turned back. "As long as I have the floor—"

My head jerked up. *Uh-oh.* What was my unpredictable son going to do *now?*

"—we've had a tradition at Uptown Community on New Year's Day—"

Oh no. He's not going to bring that *up in the middle of a worship service!*

"—a Polar Bear Swim down at Loyola Beach. I know we're a 'new' church now, and all the old things are on the shelf till we get things decided, but, hey, just wanted to invite anyone, especially the teens and anyone young at heart—"

Oh, brother. He's actually inviting people to that crazy Polar Bear Swim right here in the middle of worship! And Stu's parents are visiting too! I saw a few New Morning adults shaking their heads. *Ack! What are people thinking!*

"—noon sharp, 'cause I know everybody's gonna stay up late the night before seeing the New Year in. So—" Whatever Josh said after that was drowned out by the whoops and enthusiastic catcalls of several teenagers, both black and white.

I was afraid to look at Pastor Cobbs's face. I mean, there was nothing remotely *spiritual* about a Polar Bear Swim! And we were the newbies in this church—after all, we *were* meeting in New Morning's new space, and—

Beside me, I felt Denny shaking. I looked at him, startled.

My husband had his head down, laughing silently.

"WHAT YOU SO UPTIGHT FOR, GIRL?" Florida rolled her eyes at me after church as we walked away from the coffee table, Styrofoam cups of hot, black liquid in our hands. "Thought you was gonna turn into a frog, the way your eyes bugged out when Josh did that Polar Bear thang." She grinned at me unsympathetically.

"I know, I know," I moaned. "It's just that . . ."

Just what, Jodi Baxter? said the Voice in my spirit. *Worried about what people will think? Hm, haven't we been there before, you and Me?*

Well, yeah, but—

And what's "unspiritual" about the Polar Bear Swim? After all, Scripture says, "Do all things to the glory of God."

Well, yeah, but—

Stop worrying about what people will think, Jodi, and start looking for the possibilities. Like your son.

Like my son. I looked around until I saw Josh—in the middle of a knot of kids, laughing and talking. Huh. I doubted they were signing up to be volunteers at Manna House. But just then I saw Pastor Cobbs thread his way through the mob of youthful bodies and shake Josh's hand. Josh's face lit up. Even from where I was standing, I heard him say, "That'd be great! Wow."

Nanoseconds later, Amanda, butterscotch hair falling out of a butterfly clip perched on the back of her head, bounced over to me. "Hey, Mom. Guess what? Pastor Cobb thinks the Polar Bear Swim thing is great. He encouraged all of us kids to invite other teenagers, then bring them back here to the church for hot chocolate and music and stuff. Cool, huh?" She bounced off. Amanda rarely waited for an actual dialogue.

I closed my eyes and shook my head. *Sheesh.* When was I ever going to learn that God was a whole lot bigger than me and all my ought-tos and fear factors and what-ifs? Was God giving me a word for the New Year?

Look for the possibilities, Jodi . . .

4

So once again I found myself standing on the beach on New Year's Day along with Stu, filling cups of hot chocolate for the shivering teenagers who had just come up out of the water after their mad dash into—and out of—Lake Michigan. The lake, which hugged the long eastern shore of Chicago like a wet, soggy blanket, rolled in unhindered. No ice this year; it'd been too warm. Not that I felt warm, standing on a beach in forty-degree weather, hunched inside my winter jacket, wishing I'd worn a sweatshirt underneath to cut the wind.

Clad in dry sweats over wet bathing suits, the teenagers piled into an assortment of minivans and cars and Uptown's old fifteen-passenger van, driven by—bless him—a beaming Pastor Clark. I waved good-bye as the cars headed back to our shopping center church, glad that Pastor Cobb, Pastor Clark, and Rick Reilly—Uptown's youth group leader before the merge—were going to take it from there.

"And that's that," Stu said, loading the two big Igloo coolers we'd lugged down to the beach. "Quite a few kids I'd never seen before. Our kids must have invited them . . ." She looked at me sideways. "Or was that the whole idea all along?"

"Maybe." I climbed into the passenger seat of her silver Celica, blowing on my hands, and waited for her to get in. "All I know is Pastor Cobbs jumped on the idea and saw it as a youth outreach . . . Turn on the heat, will ya?"

"Who's doing the food back at the church?" Stu steered the car up Sheridan Road until we came to Lunt Avenue, our street.

I shrugged inside my jacket. "Dunno. Rose Cobbs got on it"— I still wasn't used to calling her First Lady Cobbs, the term of respect New Morning members gave to their pastor's wife—"and asked somebody to do it. Say, did you get any feedback from your folks about their visit to our nameless church? Sheesh. Hope we do something about that soon. Can't keep calling it 'Uptown–New Morning' forever."

"Ha." Stu pulled into the alley behind our two-flat, hit the garage door opener, and drove in. "I think my folks were a little shell-shocked. You've gotta admit, we're not exactly a liturgical church."

We headed for the house through our tiny backyard, and parted as Stu turned up the back steps to her apartment. "Hey," she called back, "has anyone heard from Chanda? Are she and the kids back from Jamaica yet?"

I blinked. "Ack! Chanda! . . . No, I haven't heard if she's back, but school starts on Monday, so she's gotta get home this weekend. But it was her birthday yesterday—New Year's Eve, remember? She was complaining it never got celebrated because of all the holidays. We gotta do something for her at Yada Yada this weekend."

"Piece of cake—pun intended." Stu laughed. "I'll make a cake.

I think we should give Becky's lopsided creations a rest, don't you think? And you do your meaning-of-the-name thing, Jodi. Think you can dig up a meaning for Chanda?"

I made a face and unlocked our back door. Willie Wonka was whining on the other side. "Huh. It's not exactly 'Sue' or 'Mary,' but I'll give it a go. Oughta be interesting . . . okay, okay, Wonka. Come on out. Go pee. But hurry it up, will ya?"

As if the poor deaf dog could hear a thing I said.

"AH, THE MIRACLE OF THE INTERNET," I murmured, staring at the computer screen. I'd been trying for an hour to find the meaning of Chanda's name—putting off the job of taking down the Christmas tree, the major chore on my to-do list the Saturday after New Year's Day—but kept running into dead ends. It wasn't listed in any of the usual "Baby Name" sites; searching Jamaican names turned up nothing; ditto African-American. Finally, I'd just Googled "Chanda . . . name . . . meaning" . . . and there it was.

"CHANDA. Hindi, meaning 'dignified.'"

From the Hindi language? *Huh. Wonder where her Jamaican parents got that from?* I couldn't help smiling. Dear, funny, fussy Chanda was a lot of things, but "dignified" didn't come to mind. On the other hand, it was amazing the significance God seemed to squeeze from the meaning of our names—

"Mom?" Josh's voice behind me interrupted my thoughts. "You got a minute?"

"Sure." I suppressed a smile. My nineteen-year-old actually wanted to *talk* to me? I had sixty minutes!

Josh, dressed in a rumpled T-shirt and sweatpants that had

seen better days, sprawled into a dining room chair. He ran a hand over his tousled hair. "Well, we didn't get that many volunteers last Sunday at church . . . three, I think. A girl—well, young woman—named Karen somebody, and Mr. and Mrs. Meeks."

"Debra and Sherman Meeks? I mean, aren't they too old? Sherman's got asthma; he has to use an inhaler."

"Mom." Josh dialed up his patient voice. "Young, old—age doesn't matter. Anybody can volunteer if they've got the right heart. Which is why I wanted to talk to you. Edesa's going to ask again at your Yada Yada meeting tomorrow night, but I thought, if *you* volunteered, maybe some of the other Yadas would too. You gotta pass a background check, but no sweat." He must have seen my eyes widen, because he threw up his hands. "Only one weekend a month, I promise! You can bring your own sheets and pillow if you like."

If I *liked*? It hadn't even occurred to me to volunteer. I was blithely assuming others would, single people probably, without family responsibilities, without—

Think of the possibilities, Jodi.

The phone was ringing. "Uh . . . let me think about it, Josh. Okay?"

"Sure!" Josh unwound his body and hopped off the chair like a human Slinky. "Thanks, Mom." He grabbed the kitchen phone. "Baxters . . . Yeah, she's here." He handed me the receiver and headed for the refrigerator.

"Hello, this is—"

"Sista Jodee, is dat you? We back from Jamaica! Mi mama *so* happy to see de t'ree kids—first time to see de girls! An' dey got to play wit all dey cousins, an' swim in de ocean, an' milk a goat. Yah, a goat for true . . ."

Chanda giggled, giving me an opening. "So glad you had a

good trip, Chanda. We're all jealous, you know! But we missed you. Hey . . . are you coming to Yada Yada tomorrow? It's Yo-Yo's turn to host." If we were going to do this birthday thing, it'd be handy to know if she'd be there.

"Oh, *yah mon*. Such a good time we had. Got mi a nice tan too." She giggled again. *"Irie, mon!* Yah, mi be dere." And the phone went dead.

I blinked, still holding the receiver. Why in the world did Chanda want a tan? She was already brown! And was it my imagination, or had her Jamaican *patois* thickened up like chicken gravy?

IT SNOWED SIX INCHES THAT NIGHT, burying the Christmas tree we'd dragged out to the curb the day before. Our first real snow of the winter. But salt trucks and snowplows had cleared most of the major streets by the time Stu and I headed for Yo-Yo's apartment Sunday evening in her Celica. Stu cautiously navigated the slick side streets, while I balanced the cake carrier. We'd be lucky to get her three-layer red velvet cake there still layered.

"Sorry." Stu grimaced. "If I'd known it was going to snow, I'd have made brownies or something."

But somehow the two of us and the cake made it in one piece, and so did most everyone else. Everyone except Ruth.

"Aw," Chanda pouted, shrugging off her winter coat and boots and twirling to show off a bright turquoise-print Jamaican dress, which she filled out. "Mi wanted to see dem babies. What are dey—six weeks? Dey must be so big now!"

"Shoulda met at your house, then," Yo-Yo muttered. "Mine's probably not clean enough."

She was kidding, right? I tried to read her face with no luck.

But Adele Skuggs, who styled funky cuts on everybody else at Adele's Hair and Nails, shook her short, no frills, black-and-silver afro. "Don't think we'll see Ruth for a while—an' clean ain't got nothin' to do with it, Yo-Yo Spencer. MaDear always said, 'Got one, you on the run; got two, you make do; got three, there you be.' An' if you ask me, two at the same time probably *feels* like three."

"She should just leave 'em with Ben," Stu said. "He's the daddy. He can take a turn."

Adele snorted. "Yeah, right."

We all laughed. Yeah, it was a bit of a stretch imagining white-haired Ben Garfield juggling both babies by himself all evening.

By that time, we'd all found something resembling a place to sit—on Yo-Yo's salvaged-from-the-alley couch, a few mismatched table chairs, and the floor. But our first meeting of the New Year felt more like a party than a prayer meeting. Even Avis and Nony and Florida, all struggling with huge family challenges, just seemed glad to be there, their burdens a bit lighter in the company of sisters who knew and still cared. And, well, it *was* a party. We surprised Chanda with the red velvet cake, Adele had picked up a mixed bouquet of cut flowers, and I presented Chanda with the birthday card we'd all been secretly signing as people dribbled in.

Chanda beamed—until we cut the cake. "Dat cake! Why she so *red*?" Her eyes rounded, as if suspecting someone had bled into it. But Stu cut a huge bite from the slice on Chanda's paper plate and teased her into opening her mouth. And then . . . *"Mmm."* Chanda's eyes rolled back in blissful delight at the velvety chocolate taste.

Four enormous bites later, she handed her plate to Stu for a second slice and opened the card. I'd used a sheet of pale gold vellum and a pretty script font, trying to find something that expressed "dignified." But as she read silently, tiny frown lines pinched between her brows. She looked up. "Dis no joke? Me name mean 'dignified'?"

I nodded. "I looked for a name spelled C-H-A-N-D-A. It's Hindi."

"Hindi! What's dat?"

"India's official language—or one of them."

The frown deepened. "Oh." A pause. "Guess dat explains it."

Now I was surprised. I'd expected her to protest that she wasn't from India, that there had to be a mistake. But now we all looked at her, curious. "Explains what?" I blurted.

Chanda shrugged. "De mon from India, dey like Jamaica. One mon come, soon all de brothers and cousins come too. *Yah, mon.* All de family. Own all de jewelry stores, all de shops for tourists in town. Some peoples tink dey take all de jobs. But me mama, she 'ave a good friend . . ." Another shrug. "We kids called her Missus Siddhu. But mi tink Mama maybe name mi after she friend."

"Read the inside," I urged. I'd found a perfect quotation about *dignity* in *Bartlett's Quotations* and was feeling smug.

> *No race can prosper till it learns*
> *That there is as much dignity*
> *In tilling a field*
> *As in writing a poem.*
> *—Booker T. Washington*

I thought Chanda would be pleased, but her lip quivered. "You just making fun of mi. Mi know what you tink—Chanda some kind of fool, get rich quick, just a cleaning woman dressed in fancy clothes."

I started to protest, but Avis got up quickly, moved behind Chanda, resting both hands on her round shoulders, and began to pray. "Lord, Your Word says that You created us in *Your image.* That means Chanda has the stamp of God on her life, giving her a dignity that no one can take away from her. Help her to see herself as You see her, Lord—beautiful, dignified, worthy, noble, Your highest creation!"

Nony carried the prayer. "Yes, yes! And this is a special birthday, Father, because the breast cancer was found early and You have given our dear sister another year of life!—to praise You, serve You, and be a blessing to all of us, her sisters and her friends. Help her to hold her head up high, with dignity, for she is Your daughter, Your child, Your precious creation."

This was followed by a chorus of "Amen!" "Hallelujah!" and "Thank ya, *Je*sus!"

Chanda said nothing. But her eyes glistened as she fished in her bag for a tissue and blew her nose.

Resuming her seat, Avis said, "As long as we're praying, do we have other prayer requests? What about your boy, Florida? Has he had a hearing yet?"

Florida's forehead puckered. "Some good news. Peter Douglass—Carl works for Avis's husband, ya know—found a good defense lawyer who's gonna represent Chris pro bono. Says he believes Chris's story, that he just caught a ride with those gangbangers, didn't know nothin' about the robbery that was gonna go down. Smucker's the name." She rolled her eyes. "At least I ain't gonna forget his name."

The rest of us snickered. We weren't going to forget it either.

"But what's next?" Yo-Yo asked. "Chris had a prelim yet?"

Florida shook her head. "That's comin' up. But what worries me is, the perp that robbed that 7-Eleven was eighteen, is bein' charged as an adult. The state's attorney is hot to charge *all* those boys as adults, rather than juveniles." Tears collected, threatening to spill. "Chris only fourteen! If they find him guilty under that accountability law an' he goes to prison . . . oh, Jesus!" She buried her face in her hands.

"Uh . . ." Becky Wallace, our other ex-con, cleared her throat. "I'm not so good at prayin' out loud, but I'd like to pray for Chris." And she did, stumbling here and there, but asking God plain and simple to keep Florida's boy in the juvie system.

I thought we were going to close our prayer time, but Edesa waved her hand. "Sisters, Manna House needs our prayers. Not only prayers, it needs warm bodies—several more volunteers willing to give a day or two every month." She lowered her dark lashes a moment and leaned forward, clasping her hands. "I—I don't want to put pressure on anyone, but I'd like to ask if any of you would be willing to volunteer."

Ack. There it was again. I could hear Josh's voice in my ear. *"Mom, if you volunteered, maybe some of the other Yadas would too."* I looked around the room. *I don't need to go first—maybe several others will volunteer and that will be enough.* My eyes alighted on Avis. *Like Avis. Good grief, why not? She's got a daughter at the shelter, for heaven's sake!*

As if my thoughts had appeared on my forehead in an LED readout, Avis spoke up. "I've given it a lot of thought, since my own daughter and grandson are at Manna House. But to tell you the truth, I think that's why I *shouldn't* volunteer. It puts both Rochelle and me in an awkward position—and things are awkward enough. Maybe there is some other way I can help."

Becky Wallace waved her hand. "I'd like to volunteer. Could do it Saturday—Bagel Bakery's closed for Shabbat. But not Sunday. That's the day I get Little Andy."

"I dunno, Becky," Yo-Yo said. "You're still on parole. Might not go over so good with your PO. Better check it out."

The room was quiet. I knew Delores worked weekend shifts at the county hospital . . . Chanda had little kids at home . . . Nony's husband still needed nursing care . . . Saturday was the busiest day at Adele's Hair and Nails . . . even Stu had DCFS visits to make on the weekends . . .

That pretty much left me.

Think of the possibilities, Jodi.

The Voice within my spirit was surprisingly gentle. Beckoning. As if this wasn't something I *ought* to do, but a privilege, an adventure. The next step in the God-journey I was on—though I had to admit it felt more like a roller coaster than a mere step.

But I raised my hand. "Um, Edesa? I'd like to volunteer . . . I think."

5

Winter vacation slam-dunked to a finish by dropping temperatures to a mere five degrees Sunday night, and the ever-cheerful weather guy said Chicago could expect more snow and below-freezing temps all week. As I spooned hot oatmeal into bowls for the Baxter crew Monday morning, I batted my eyelashes at Denny. "Any chance I can get a ride to school on your way?" If flirting didn't work, I could always use the rod in my leg—left over from my car accident a year and a half ago—as an excuse.

"Me, too, Dad." Amanda flopped into a dining room chair, dropping her book bag on the floor. "It's *murder* out there. Wonka told me so, didn't ya, baby?" She scratched Willie Wonka's rump before dumping a mountain of brown sugar on her oatmeal.

"Hey!" Denny said, grabbing the sugar bowl.

Good, I thought. About time Denny did some of the nagging.

". . . Leave some for me!" he finished, matching her brown-sugar mountain granule for granule. I rolled my eyes. They were both hopeless.

Gulping his oatmeal, Denny glanced at his watch. As the new athletic director at West Rogers High School, he didn't like to be late. I knew dropping me off at Bethune Elementary a few blocks away was one thing; but Lane Tech College Prep was at least two or three miles out of his way—in rush-hour traffic on slick roads. But leave his little princess standing at a bus stop in weather like this? *Ha.* "Okay," he said. "Everybody in the car in three minutes."

So I got to school forty-five minutes early. Not a bad thing. I had time to organize my lessons for the day, hunt up chalk and erasers, which had somehow disappeared over Christmas vacation, and best of all, walk up and down the rows of desks, praying for my third-grade students by name.

The laminated names taped to each desk were a little dog-eared but still readable. "Lord, bless Abrianna this semester. Help me encourage her when she wants to give up, when she thinks she can't do it . . . and Caleb. Oh, Lord, he's so bright! But he needs a little humility too. The other kids tend to avoid him because of his bragging. I think he's lonely . . . Thank You for Mercedes, God. She is Your special creation, even though the kids tease her because of her weight. I've seen Big Mama, too, so it's no surprise . . . and Carla, Lord. That little girl's been through so much! Now her big brother's been arrested. When she lashes out, help me to remember that she's scared . . ."

Because of the cold weather, the kids lined up in the gym instead of on the playground when the bell rang. Carla was first in line, the pink fur of her jacket hood framing her dark eyes and creamy brown face. "Miz Baxter?" She tugged on my sweater. "Miz Baxter!"

Two boys started pushing at the back of the line, and the kids were standing so close to each other I was afraid they'd all go down like dominoes. "Lamar! Demetrius! Stop that!—not now, Carla."

By the time I'd herded the kids into our room, marshaled coats, boots, and mittens into the general vicinity of the coat pegs, and collected the take-home folders, I'd totally forgotten Carla's question. But she obviously hadn't. She appeared beside my desk, jiggling impatiently, but I held up my hand, palm out, as the office intercom came on and a fifth grader led the whole school—remotely—in the Pledge of Allegiance.

"—withlibertyan'justiceforall," Carla gushed. "Miz Baxter?"

"*What*, Carla?"

"You said if it snowed, we could build a snowman." She pointed a finger at the bank of windows running along the classroom wall, a miniature prosecutor pointing out the culprit in the courtroom.

"Oh, Carla." I had, hadn't I. What was I *thinking*?! I walked over to the windows, ignoring the noise level rising around me. The six inches of snow that fell on Sunday had been trampled Monday morning by the diehards who had started off "back to school" with a rousing snowball fight. "I don't know, honey . . . the playground is pretty much a mess."

Carla's eyes narrowed. "But you *promised*. Crossed your heart and hoped to die."

Right. I glanced at the thermometer outside the window. Nudging slowly upward, a whopping fifteen degrees now. Maybe we'd get more snow by the end of the day . . .

I leaned close to Carla's ear. "All right," I whispered. "We can try. But don't say anything to the other children, or the deal's off." Mention snowman making and I'd be nagged to death by short people all day.

At lunchtime, Carla blocked my way, arms folded, giving me The Look. I shook my head, stalling. What should I do? Keep Carla after school? Wait until the other kids had gone home?

My slower readers were parked on the Story Rug after lunch, plowing in jerks and starts through *Charlotte's Web*, when Carla yelled from her desk, "Look!" The telltale finger pointed toward the windows. A curtain of powdered-sugar snow sifted past the glass. "*Now* we can make a snowman!" she announced.

An immediate stampede to the windows ensued. "Yea!"

I took a deep breath and glanced at the clock. Two-ten. If I took my class outside to build snowmen before the last bell, other classes would probably hear them and mutiny. Even if I wasn't censured for ignoring the no-early-dismissal policy, the other teachers would be mad. But I couldn't keep all the children after school. After-school childcare buses would be waiting; parents would show up, impatient to drag their progeny off to violin lessons or ice hockey.

But I was reluctant to extinguish the eager anticipation shining in the eyes of the kids. Here in the city, how many of them had ever built a snowman? If we just plowed on with our reading lesson, this day would simply melt into the pool of all the other school days. But if we built a snowman, we'd create a childhood memory that might linger for years. A memory like . . .

I was in third grade, chewing on my pencil and trying to do my sheet of division problems, when my teacher tapped me on the shoulder. "Your father is here." I looked up, startled. Was something wrong? But he stood in the doorway, hat in hand, smiling. I grabbed my lunch box and followed him to the car; my two brothers were already slouched in the backseat. What was going on? They shrugged. Daddy was mum.

Didn't say a thing. Just drove to the Veterans Memorial Auditorium in Des Moines, surrounded by enormous billboards shouting, "CIRCUS!" with pictures of gold-and-black tigers jumping through flaming hoops and clowns in whiteface and bushy red hair.

It was one of those magic memories of childhood. Funny thing is, I don't remember much about the circus. What still makes me giggle is that Daddy took us out of school just to have fun . . .

"Everybody! Come to my desk. No talking." Wide-eyed, the children crowded around my desk. I'd never called them to come around my desk, all at the same time. Something was up and they knew it. I lowered my voice and we made plans. Wait another twenty minutes. Then *quietly* get on our coats and boots. *Silently* tiptoe down the hall and out to the playground, like mice creeping past a big cat. By then, I figured, there would only be ten minutes before the bell rang. By the time the other students or teachers heard us, it'd hardly be worth complaining about.

BY THREE-TEN, three lopsided snowmen stood in the school playground. Two were sightless, since we only found two small rocks to use for eyes. One had a branch sticking out of its side for an "arm." But all three wore brightly colored knit caps and scarves, donated by junior Good Samaritans who insisted the snowmen needed *something*. I'd have to rescue the hats and scarves before leaving the school grounds, but for now . . .

"They *bee-yoo-tee-ful*," Carla breathed. She was the last kid to leave.

I grinned. "Yep. But off you go. Cedric picking you up?"

She shook her head. "Nah. I walk by myself. Mama be home

soon." Her eyes lit up. "Maybe now Daddy help Cedric an' me build *another* snowman at home! We got us a backyard now, you know." She ran off, her backpack bumping on her rump like a loose saddle.

I stopped in at the school office, took off my gloves, and knocked on Avis's inner office door, which was slightly ajar. She was on the phone, dressed in black slacks, white silk blouse, and black-and-white costume jewelry, dark hair neatly wound into a French roll. She held up a finger to wait. I loitered by the bulletin board in the main office, reading the school lunch menu for January: chicken tenders with muffin, cheese or pepperoni pizza slice, peanut-butter sandwich with fruit cup, turkey hot dog on bun . . . until I heard her say, "All right . . . Thursday. Yes . . . me too. Bye."

I slipped into her office and closed the door, unzipping my down jacket. "I'm here to confess before you get a complaint."

She put down the phone and glanced in my direction.

"I took my class outside ten minutes before the last bell and we built snowmen. Guilty as charged." I grinned, fishing a tissue from my jacket pocket and swiping my still-icy nose. "Call it outdoor education."

"Jodi Baxter," she snapped. "What *are* you talking about?"

"Uh . . . snowmen." Her tone of voice caught me completely off guard. I thought Avis would be my ally in this minor flouting of school dismissal policy. "Took my kids outside before dismissal and . . ."

Her eyes wandered. I could tell I'd lost the connection. She was frowning at the phone. *Sheesh, Jodi.* I felt like slapping myself upside the head. I'd just blundered into her office, didn't even ask if it was a good time—and now that I thought about it, her last few words on the phone had sounded personal.

"Sorry, Avis. Uh . . . are you okay? Is something wrong?"

Avis sighed and sank down into her desk chair. "Yes. Maybe . . . I don't know, Jodi." She propped her elbows on the arms of the high-backed desk chair and pressed the tips of her fingers against her temples. "That was Rochelle . . ."

I waited.

She finally looked up at me and shook her head. "Just when I think God's answering our prayers, we get blindsided from a different direction."

This sounded like *Are-you-sitting-down?* news. I pulled up a cushioned chair.

"Manna House routinely asks residents to get HIV testing. No big deal. We knew that." Avis blew out another breath. Her voice dropped to a whisper. "Rochelle's came back positive."

6

ositive! But . . . I mean, how could . . ." I stopped, embarrassed. But my mind churned. Dexter was the one who'd been running around on his wife. Nobody would be surprised if *he* turned up HIV-positive. But sweet Rochelle? "Is that for sure?" I finished lamely. "I mean, isn't there such a thing as a false positive?"

Avis shrugged. "We can hope. Rochelle insists it's impossible, says she's never been unfaithful to Dexter. She's going back for a retest on Thursday. Wants me to go with her—though I'm not sure why. She won't get the results for another week." She smiled weakly. "But at this point, it's enough that she *wants* me to go."

"Oh, Avis." I could hardly imagine hearing that kind of news about my daughter. People with HIV were at risk for AIDS, and people with AIDS often died a terrible, lingering death. I suddenly felt like throwing up.

Avis took a deep breath, as if collecting herself. "So . . . what's this about a snowman?"

I snorted. "Nothing." Which was the truth. Here today, gone tomorrow. I reached for her hand across the desk; she put both of hers in mine. What could I say? If she were in my shoes, Avis would probably offer a comforting scripture or pray. But what did one pray in a situation like this? *Oh Lord, make it go away! Heal Rochelle! We know You're going to do it!* . . . I couldn't. The words seemed hollow. Dishonest. A cliché. I didn't know what God would do.

So all I offered was a whisper. "Oh Jesus. Help us." She squeezed my hands.

THE SNOWMEN MET A VIOLENT DEATH sometime before the first bell. Stomped on. Kicked to smithereens. Anger boiled in my gut as I surveyed the damage from my classroom window. "What kind of deranged person would destroy a kid's *snowman?*" I muttered.

Huh. I sounded like my mother. Mom Jennings just couldn't understand anyone who would talk back to a teacher or drop a candy wrapper on the ground, much less bump off a snowman. Her world was populated by hardworking men, dutiful women, and polite children—or she thought it ought to be.

I traced a frowny face in the fog on the window. No wonder I'd had such a hard time owning the fact that I was "just a sinner," like everyone else. Funny thing, it was such a relief not to be perfect. To know I could mess up and still be forgiven. To begin to understand what *grace* was all about. Yep. Jodi "Good Girl" Baxter had ugly thoughts, did things she regretted, didn't do things she should—

Ack! My hand flew to my mouth; I peered out the foggy window. Not only had the snowmen disappeared, but the hats and scarves they'd been wearing had too! I'd totally forgotten to bring them in before going home last night. *Blip*, right off my radar screen. And it was starting to snow again . . .

I pulled on the jacket and boots I'd just taken off and ran out to the playground. Most of the early birds were heading for the warm gym. But Bowie Garcia and Lamar Pearson stood looking at the lumps of snow that used to be snowmen, muttering dark threats. "Man, I find out who kicked our snowmen, I'm gonna pop 'em," Bowie said. He made his gloved hand into a pistol. "Pow! Pow!"

My own anger turned to alarm. But now wasn't the time to talk about "disproportionate response"—though, hm, it might be a good life lesson for my third graders. *"Snowmen can be remade; people can't."* Right now, my own forgetfulness was getting buried deeper in new snow.

Several of my other third graders appeared on the playground. "Oh no!" "Who did that?" Followed by a few nasty expletives they probably heard at home.

"Sorry about the snowmen, kids," I said. "But with this good snow, we'll be able to make bigger and better ones, whaddya say?" Their scowls slowly turned to grins. "But tell you what, how about a contest? Whoever finds one of those hats or scarves in the snow gets a bag of Skittles. For each one!"

WE FOUND TWO HATS AND ONE SCARF buried in the snow and I was out three bags of Skittles. The lost scarf belonged to Mercedes LaLuz and she shrieked. "My mama said she gonna *kill* me if I lose

47

another scarf!" Which hopefully was an overstatement. But to placate the situation, I brought in the handmade knit scarf my mother had made me and gave it to Mercedes the next morning.

Josh and Amanda thought the whole episode was hilarious. "I'll donate *my* scarf to your next snowman," Josh said, faking a straight face. "My sacrifice to a good cause." *Yeah, right.* He had yet to wear the overly long and rather garish scarf his grandmother had crocheted for *him.*

Ruth Garfield, on the other hand, was full of advice. She called midweek to ask how the first week back at school was going. With the phone cradled between my shoulder and ear, I moaned about the vandalized snowmen in the schoolyard while trying to fry up some hamburger and peel potatoes for a Baxter version of shepherd's pie.

"Vandals? A lesson from us you should take. Havah and Isaac's snowman—"

"*Havah and Isaac's* snowman?" I snickered so hard the phone lost its precarious perch and crashed to the floor. I snatched it up. "Oops. Sorry. Ruth, *what* are you talking about? Havah and Isaac are . . . what? Six weeks old? You didn't take them outside to—"

"Six-and-a-half. Very bright they are too. Looking around, taking in everything. Ben decides to make a snowman so the twins can see it from the front window—"

"*Ben* made a snowman? Ben 'I'm-Too-Old-to-Have-Kids' Garfield?" Now I was laughing out loud.

"What are you, my echo? Don't be a *shmo.* I'm trying to help you, Jodi Baxter. Ben knew the little *nudniks* on our block would knock over anything in the front yard, so he sprayed the snowman with the garden sprayer. Froze solid overnight. Any juvenile delinquent who tries to kick down *that* snowman is going home with a broken toe."

"Love it!" I hooted. I had visions of young thugs hopping around the schoolyard bawling like branded calves. But my ecstasy was short-lived. "On second thought, if we did that, the school would probably get sued for erecting 'dangerous structures' on public property."

"Humph," Ruth sniffed. "You could always melt the evidence— wait a minute."

In the background, I heard Ben yelling. A minute later, Ruth was back. "Blind as a bat, he is! Turning everything upside down looking for a pacifier. I show him, there it is, pinned right to Isaac's sleeper. Does he say thanks? No. Tells me, why don't you put it somewhere I can find it? Such a klutz."

"Uh-huh." I dumped the peeled potatoes into a pot of water and turned on the gas burner. Ruth plunged on, though she lowered her voice.

"But here's the good news. 'Ben,' I say, 'I want to go to Beth Yehudah services on Saturday.' So Ben considers. I see his brain working. If I go by myself, he's stuck with the twins all morning. If I *take* the twins, he'll worry I can't manage car, car seats, baby carriers, diaper bags all by myself. So he says, 'All right, all right, I'll drive you.'" I could hear the chuckle in her voice. "Once we get there, he'll have to help me take the baby carriers inside, and once he's inside . . ."

"Ruth! You're shameless!" But I laughed. The good people at Ruth's Messianic Jewish congregation would fall all over themselves, oohing and ahhing over the twins. A good number had been at Isaac's *brit mila* and baby naming. Proud daddy Ben would eat it

49

up and hang around, not wanting to miss a minute of adoration. "Well, that's one way to get Ben Garfield to church."

She sighed. "He might go to church more often if he could hang out with Denny or Peter Douglass or Carl Hickman or Mark Smith. He respects all those guys . . . wait a minute. All those Yada Yada husbands ended up at Uptown when it merged with Mark and Nony's church, didn't they! Maybe we ought to come visit you some Sunday . . ."

"That'd be great, Ruth! Just don't call it Uptown anymore. We're meeting in New Morning's new space, which makes it kind of awkward. Guess we need a new name in a hurry. We have a business meeting this Sunday to talk about it."

"Yachad," she said. An infant started wailing in the background. "What?"

"Yachad! A good name for your church."

"Yachad? What kind of name is that? What does it mean?"

The wailing was now a duet and rising in intensity.

"Yachad. It's Hebrew. Look it up—sorry. Feeding time. Talk to you later!"

IT WAS SATURDAY before I had time to "look it up," as Ruth ordered.

Almost a foot of snow fell that week, and my class and I tried to build some new snowmen during Thursday lunchtime. Kids from other classes joined us, which is probably why the new snowmen lasted *two* days. *Snowmen* was a bit of a misnomer, though; the hapless creations looked more like "snow bumps with eyes." This time I donated the black and red checkers from our old checkerboard at home for eyes, along with a bag of carrots from the Rogers Park Fruit Market for noses. Even bought a disposable camera and shot the whole roll.

I dipped into the school office Thursday afternoon to update Avis on Bethune Elementary's snowman project, but her inner office was dark. "Oh, Mrs. Douglass left at one o'clock," Ms. Ivy offered, fiddling with the temperamental photocopy machine. "Said she had an appointment."

Ouch. That's right. Rochelle's retest . . .

Almost decided not to call Avis about the retest. What was the point? They wouldn't know the results for a week anyway. But on Saturday morning—I still had two weeks until my turn came up to volunteer at Manna House, hallelujah!—as I stuffed laundry into the washing machine in the basement of our two-flat, it hit me: waiting is sometimes harder than knowing.

I called Avis on my next trip through the kitchen. Peter Douglass answered. "No, Avis isn't here. She drove down to Manna House to take Rochelle shopping."

Shopping. Yeah, I bet. More likely Rochelle needed some propping up. There was nothing in Peter's voice to indicate that Avis had told him about the HIV diagnosis, though. Maybe she was waiting for the second test; probably didn't want to get him all upset until they knew for sure. Or maybe it was Avis who needed propping up! Mother-daughter shopping could be a good emotional Novocain.

Peter's voice plowed into my thoughts. "I was just about to call your house anyway. Is that man of yours there?"

"Nope. Gone to a basketball game over at West Rogers High. Intramurals. You know Denny; he's got coaching in the blood."

"Yeah, well. Tell him to give me a call when he gets home."

I hung up, feeling a strange warmth. What was it—appreciation? Well, yes. But more than that. Feeling blessed . . .

My mind lingered on Avis's new husband as I trekked back down to the basement to change laundry loads. When Peter first started courting Avis, we Yada Yadas were like a bunch of schoolgirls. *"Ooo, girl, that man is fine!"* We started making her a wedding quilt before he even popped the question! Then . . . I started worrying that Peter might take Avis away from Uptown Community Church. He seemed uncomfortable being the only African-American male in the congregation; came only because his ladylove was a member and worship leader there. But when New Morning Christian Church, which was mostly black, started using our building for their worship services, Peter Douglass was one of the first people to articulate that "God had a reason."

Now, with the extraordinary decision to merge Uptown and New Morning, Peter had jumped in with both feet. "Thank You, Jesus!" I said, dumping a capful of detergent into the washing machine and pushing the Start button.

Hiking back up the basement stairs with a basket of hot, fluffy towels, however, I knew the blessing was bigger than just "not losing Avis." God not only brought Peter Douglass into Avis's life, courting and winning her after several years of widowhood—the first wedding I'd ever been to where the bride and groom "jumped the broom"!—but He'd brought Peter into our lives too. A seasoned businessman, Peter had not only found a job at Software Symphony for Carl Hickman, Florida's husband, but took Josh on, too, when our son decided *not* to go to college this year. But more than that, Peter and Denny seemed to respect each other, even though the two men couldn't be more different. Peter—serious, thoughtful, businesslike, always practical. Denny—the sports-crazy kid who never grew up. But it was Peter Denny had talked to when struggling with whether to take the job of athletic director at the high school. Peter who had said, *"It's not just about what you like to do. Where can you be the most influence on those kids' lives?"*

"Wonder what he wants to talk to Denny about?" I murmured, stepping over Willie Wonka's inert body at the top of the basement stairs. The dog opened one eye at me but didn't move. The dog rarely moved these days. Slowing down. Waaay down. *One of these days, I'm going to trip over that dog and kill myself.*

I set the basket of clean towels on the dining room table and began to fold. Maybe Peter wanted to talk to Denny about the men's breakfast next Saturday . . . or the church business meeting tomorrow. We were all supposed to come with ideas for a new church name—

"Yachad."

My telephone conversation with Ruth earlier that week popped into my head. Ruth had just thrown that word into the ring and told me to look it up. Not sure why I should bother. *What a weird name for a church.* Maybe it meant something in Hebrew. Might be a nice name for a Jewish synagogue or a Messianic congregation. But the hodgepodge that was Uptown–New Morning? *Nobody* would know what "Yachad" meant.

Still, curiosity got the better of me. I dumped a towel in mid-fold and booted up the computer. Took me a while to Google it, but finally I found it in an online Old Testament Hebrew lexicon. *"Yachad . . . "*

"Whoa!" I said. Then, "Wow." I moved my cursor to Print Current Page, typed in "20" copies, and hit Print.

7

So what did Peter Douglass want yesterday?" I had given Peter's message to Denny when he got home Saturday afternoon. They'd spent a good thirty minutes on the phone, with Denny saying stuff like, *"Yeah, I agree . . . Good point . . . Man, wish I knew . . . I'll see what I can find out."* I might as well have been Willie Wonka for all I learned from Denny's side of the conversation. I gave up and took the dog for walk, but even that didn't last long. Poor Wonka. Every time we found a cleared sidewalk, he'd lifted first one paw, then another, and looked at me with that pitiful rumpled brow. The salted sidewalks stung his cracked pads.

By the time we got back to the house (finally cutting through the alleys, which were *never* salted and *never* plowed, creating a mishmash of stuck cars like a destruction derby pileup), Denny was engrossed in a basketball game on TV. I knew I'd only get *"Huh?"* and *"Can it wait?"* if I tried to strike up a conversation while "da Bulls" were scoring. So I'd given up on curiosity and tackled a major molehill: what to take to the Second Sunday Potluck tomorrow.

Josh, who'd done a twenty-four-hour shift at Manna House, said he'd take the el and meet us at church this morning. Now I pulled the big bowl of hot calico beans out of the back of the mini-van and stood aside while Denny locked the car before following Amanda, who'd already disappeared into our "new" shopping center church. "You guys talked long enough," I added.

"Oh yeah." Denny took my arm to steady me as we mushed through the icy parking lot. "He's concerned about Carl. Seems depressed on the job. Can't blame the guy. I'd be depressed, too, if my kid was locked up in juvie. Anyway, Peter was trying to pick my brain about what we could do to support the Hickman family right now—or Chris for that matter. But the only visitors allowed at the JDC are parents or guardians—not even siblings."

Huh. And I thought they were hashing over new names for the church. "You come up with any ideas?"

"Peter thinks a bunch of guys need to be there for Carl on a regular basis. Let him vent his feelings, pray with him, get him out with the guys now and then—stuff like that. I mean, Florida has you Yada Yadas for support, but . . ."

I cringed. *Florida has you Yada Yadas for support.* It'd been a week since our last meeting at Yo-Yo's. Had I even called Florida this past week to see how she was doing? Had I called *anybody* except Avis—and I didn't get her even then. Ruth had called me, but . . .

Sheesh, Lord. You're so faithful! But I always seem to fall down on the job. It's hard being Your hands and feet in this Body You've put us in.

Denny held the glass door open as I carefully carried the hot beans inside and headed for the half-finished kitchen on the other side of the "sanctuary," trying not to bump into anyone.

I dunno, God. Maybe You can be there for a zillion people at once. But I'm only one person—with thirty kids on my job, two almost-grown teenagers at home, a prayer group of twelve sisters whose lives keep getting snarly like a dozen cats in a yarn shop. How am I supposed to—

"Yo, Jodi." Becky Wallace stood in front of me and peered into my face. "The kitchen's back that way. You planning on storin' that dish in the ladies washroom or something?"

I sighed and pushed back my paper plate. That morning's worship—get-down praise and a good word from the Word from dear Pastor Clark, who'd seemed energized by the congregational talk-back of "Amen!" and "That's right, brother!"—had satisfied my soul. The potluck—a glut of greens, macaroni and cheese, fried chicken, hot wings, calico beans, potato salad, and green salad—had satisfied my stomach.

Now it was time for the church business meeting. Would it satisfy my spirit?

Tables were pushed back, chairs replaced into rows, and cleanup left until later. I chafed at the rows of chairs. Wouldn't a circle, even several layers deep, be more welcoming? Maybe I'd work up the courage to suggest it next time.

Some of the younger teens took the little kids and babies into one of the back rooms, while most of the older teens, like Josh and Amanda, elected to stay in the meeting. Pastor Joe Cobbs opened the meeting with prayer.

"Father God." The fifty-something pastor's booming voice

always took me a bit off guard. "You led Your people across the Red Sea. You provided manna and meat in the wilderness. You gave them clothes that didn't wear out, even though they wandered around in that wilderness for forty years. You told them that if they followed Your commandments, You would make them into a great people. And then You brought them victorious into the Promised Land."

"That's right! That's right!"

"So, Father God. We *know* You are going to lead us through the deep waters we're facing—"

"Hallelujah! Jesus!"

"We *know* You are going to provide the ways and means to survive our challenges and be nourished along the way—"

"Jesus! Thank You!"

"And we *know* that if we listen to Your Word and obey the voice of Your Holy Spirit, You are going to make us into Your people, right here on Howard Street!"

By this time, people were on their feet, hands raised, shouting hallelujah, thanking God. Not exactly how most business meetings started, but the hope and confidence in the prayer squeezed the anxiety out of me. "Yes, Lord!" I cried, adding my voice to the hubbub. "We know You have a plan for us, to give us a future and a hope!"

Praying Scripture was still new for me, but thanks to Yada Yada, I was beginning to memorize more of God's promises, so that they came pouring out when we needed them. Like now.

Nonyameko must have had the same prompting, because as the general praises drifted to a hush, I heard her voice lift above the others. "'For I know the thoughts that I think toward you, says the Lord, thoughts of peace and not of evil, to give you a future and a hope. Then you will call upon Me and go and pray to Me, and I will listen to you. And you will seek Me and find Me, when you search for Me with all your heart.' God's Word from Isaiah chapter twenty-nine, verse eleven. Amen."

As we resumed our seats and took up the agenda, I was surprised at how quickly a number of potentially sticky issues were cared for. But the first recommendation oiled the gears: all decisions made today would take effect for one year, giving the congregation more experience with one another, at which time all decisions would be reviewed. That one passed unanimously. "Smart," Denny murmured. "Very smart."

Next, the double congregation affirmed that Pastor Joseph Cobbs and Pastor Hubert Clark were copastors, with mutual responsibility for teaching and preaching, but with a division of administrative oversight for the various ministries according to their gifts and strengths. (*"Hubert?"* Florida hissed in my ear from the row behind me. "No wonder that man keeps his given name under his hat!")

I wondered how we'd deal with the next level of leadership, though. We didn't know each other well enough to elect new elders from each previous church. But the current crop—three from Uptown and five from New Morning—was too many for a church our size, seemed to me. Peter Douglass cleared his throat and stood up.

"I realize I'm not a voting member of this congregation . . . yet." He smiled. "A fact I intend to change at the first opportunity." A burst of applause and laughter erupted. "But I'd like to make a suggestion about elders. Why don't the current elders from both congregations draw lots. Half would serve the first six months of this year; half would serve the second half. Then at the end of the year, we can have a new election."

A murmur rippled among the rows of chairs. But Peter held up a hand to continue. "That way, we honor our current elders, giving us the benefit of their experience as we begin this marriage." Several people laughed. "But it also gives an opportunity to raise up new leaders in the near future."

"Amen, brother!" More clapping.

Denny stood up. "I like that suggestion. But I have to confess, I don't know who we're talking about—from New Morning, at least. Could we have the current elders from Uptown and New Morning introduce themselves?"

More clapping. Pastor Clark introduced Uptown's current elders: Rick Reilly, Tom Fitzhugh, and David Brown. Pastor Cobbs said New Morning had deacons, not elders, but the function was probably similar. He called on Debra and Sherman Meeks, Carrie Walker, Rommel Custer, and Mark Smith to stand.

I beamed at the Meeks, who'd been so warm and welcoming from day one.

"Hallelujah!" Florida exclaimed behind me. "All right now!" Then I heard her hiss in my ear again. "They got *women* on they board!"

I watched as Nony's husband stood with the other deacons, gripping the back of the chair in front of him. The Northwestern University history professor whose head had been bashed in with a brick last summer was still a looker, in spite of the weight he'd lost during his convalescence. The black eye patch he wore over his left eye gave him a debonair, mysterious air—especially with that trim goatee outlining his chin. I poked Denny. "Did you know Mark was a deacon at New Morning?" I whispered.

He shrugged. "Not surprised."

But I saw Nony's face tilt upward, watching him, brows knit in concern.

Mark raised his hand. "Pastors? If I may say something?" He spoke clearly, just a tad slowly. Easy to miss if someone didn't know what he'd been through.

The room quieted. People leaned forward.

"I think Peter Douglass's suggestion is excellent, and under normal circumstances I would be glad to serve. But as you all know, I haven't been able to carry out my responsibilities for the last six months, and I think it best to step down at this time. God has brought me a very long way . . . but I also want to be realistic. I don't think I need to explain." He sat down. Nony put an arm across the back of his chair, resting it there.

Pastor Cobbs stroked his chin thoughtfully. "We could assign you to the second six months if that would make a difference, brother."

Mark just shook his head. My heart was aching. Why step down? Give the healing process another six months! Was stepping down accepting defeat?

But we moved on. Peter's suggestion became a motion, which was carried by the "ayes." Then and there, the seven remaining elder-deacons drew slips of paper, four of which had X's on them. Our first set of elders was Debra Meeks, Rommel Custer, Rick Reilly, and Tom Fitzhugh. The second set would be David Brown,

Sherman Meeks, Carrie Walker. I noticed no one said anything about the disproportionate number. Maybe Pastor Cobbs was leaving the position open on purpose, just in case . . .

The last item on the agenda was a new name for the church. Now I was getting excited. I fished the papers I'd printed out from my tote bag. Wasn't sure what the procedure for introducing new names would be, but I was ready. The pastors passed out a sheet with a few possibilities. All were a combination of the old names: *Uptown New Morning Church . . . New Morning Community Church . . . New Community Christian Church.*

The discussion was spirited.

"How we gonna decide whose name goes first?"

"Does it matter?"

"Sure it does. Uptown's been around twenty years. If we want people to know we're still around, the name ought to be in there somewhere."

"I like that 'New Community' one."

"We're not voting yet."

Becky Wallace waved her hand. "Uh, seems ta me we oughta come up with a new name. New church, new name." Her head swiveled at the murmurs that rippled around her. "Or maybe not. What do I know?" She shrank into her seat.

"Maybe the old names aren't important to *some* folks." A big woman eyed Becky over the top of her skinny reading glasses. "But for those of us who've been around awhile, the name is important. Preserves our history. It's part of our identity."

Murmurs of assent this time.

"Heh-heh-heh. This is like John Smith-Brown gettin' hitched to Mary Jones-White," a man cracked. "Whatcha gonna call the *next* generation? Smith-Brown-Jones-White?" That got a laugh—but I could tell the tension had risen.

Silence descended over the room. My insides were churning. Seemed like some combination of the old names would win the day. My idea was probably dumb anyway. Nobody else had mentioned any new names—

"Could I say something?" Avis Johnson-Douglass stood up, her Bible open. "I don't disagree about the importance of history, of celebrating our identities. But I find it interesting that God often gave a *new name* when He was doing something new in the lives of His people. Abram was changed to Abraham. Jacob was changed to Israel. Simon was changed to Peter. Oftentimes there was a prophetic quality to the new name—a promise of something new, something *God* was going to do. Here, let me read . . ."

My eyes widened. *Prophetic.* That was the word. That was what had excited me about Ruth's off-the-cuff suggestion.

Avis read from Revelation chapter three. "'He who overcomes, I will make him a pillar in the temple of My God, and he shall go out no more. I will write on him the name of My God and the name of the city of My God, the New Jerusalem, which comes down out of heaven from My God. And I will write on him *My new name.* He who has an ear, let him hear what the Spirit says to the churches.'" Avis closed her Bible. "I don't have a name to suggest, but Pastor Clark often says, 'God is doing a *new thing.*' A new wineskin, so to speak, for new wine. So I'd like to suggest we add some new names to this list. Something that expresses what God is doing among us. Or"—she smiled—"what God will do among us if we let Him."

I felt like shouting. *Thank you, Avis!* But I still hesitated. Didn't want to be the first one.

To my surprise, Hoshi Takahashi stood up. "Avis spoke my heart. Thank you, dear sister. I have a name to suggest: All Nations Church. Because we want people of all nations to be welcome here."

I saw a few heads bobbing, as well as a few frowns. But Hoshi's courage strengthened my own backbone. I stood up. "Thank you, Hoshi. I like your suggestion. But I also have a suggestion. You might think it sounds funny at first—I did. But the more I thought about it, the more I realized—"

"Just tell us the name, Jodi," Stu piped up.

For a moment, I felt flustered. "Okay. *Yachad.*" I heard a few snickers, so I rushed on. "*Yachad* is a Hebrew word, found in the Bible, which means 'together in unity' or 'in one accord.' It has the prophetic quality Avis was talking about. Like Jesus' prayer in John seventeen, when He asked God to make us one, just as He and the Father are One. That's our prayer for this merger, too, I think. I've got a page here explaining the meaning if anyone's interested."

I sat down, feeling the heat in my face. Comments flew all around me. "Yachad what? Yachad Community Church?" "Sounds like a mosque to me. We'd get a bunch of Muslims showing up." "So? Maybe that's good." "She said it's Hebrew, not Arabic." "Still, nobody would know what it means." "But people would ask and we could tell them—like a witness, you know." "I kinda like it." "I don't know . . ."

But a sense of peace lapped quietly at my frazzled nerves. In spite of the voices all around me, I heard a still, small Voice in my spirit. *Now let it go, Jodi. You planted the seed. You were obedient to speak the Word. Let it go.*

8

My watch said 3:10 by the time Josh pulled our minivan into the garage after the marathon worship, potluck, and business meeting. I groaned, shedding my coat as I dragged myself from the back door to the coat tree in the front hall. "I am *so* glad we changed Yada Yada off second Sundays. I just wanna chill tonight and go to bed early."

"Oh." Denny, following me to the front of the house, sounded disappointed. "I thought maybe we could go out or something, take advantage of a free Sunday night."

I locked eyes with him. "Why not Friday? Why not Saturday? Why wait till *Sunday*? We've both got to go to work tomorrow morning."

He tossed his London Fog with the flannel zip-in liner over the top of the coat tree, making it look like a football pileup. "Okay. Except we *didn't* go out Friday or Saturday this weekend, and now it's Sunday. Besides, you know Fridays are bad. A night game or something usually keeps me at school late."

"You're not coaching now, remember? You don't *have* to be at every game." I headed back to the kitchen. I needed a cup of hot tea.

"Whoa, whoa, whoa, what's that about?" Denny was right behind me. "I said I'd like to go out with my wife tonight, and now we're talking about my *job*? C'mon, Jodi."

Josh was standing at the refrigerator, pulling out bread, mayo, cheese, and lunchmeat, in spite of the fact we'd had a megapotluck only two hours ago. Irritated that I was sandwiched between my son and my husband, when what I really wanted was a cup of tea and a good book, I flipped on the gas under the teakettle. "Fine."

Denny stopped in the kitchen doorway. "Yeah. I know what 'fine' means. It means I haven't heard the last of this yet."

Josh stared at us, hands full of sandwich makings. "You two need a time-out?"

"Mind your own business, buster." I turned off the stove, marched out of the kitchen, and headed for the bedroom.

"So much for *yachad*!" Denny yelled after me.

I slammed the bedroom door behind me. Hot tears stung my eyes. What did he mean by *that*? That he wasn't going to vote for the name I suggested for the church, just because I didn't want to go out tonight? How mean was that!

Shedding my nylons, skirt, and sweater, I crawled under our wedding quilt in my slip and punched the pillow into submission. How did Denny and I end up fighting five minutes after coming home from church? Yeah, I'd been kind of nervous to nominate a name for the church . . . but nobody got upset at me. The pastors suggested we have a preliminary paper vote between all the names in two weeks, then a discussion and final vote of the top two at our next business meeting. That was cool. So why did I get all hot and bothered the minute we got home from church?

I had no idea. Still, it had already been a long day. Maybe I just needed a nap.

But as I lay in the bed, willing my churned up emotions to calm down, I heard Denny's comment again in my head: *"So much for yachad!"* . . . and I boiled up all over again, mad tears wetting the pillow. Maybe I had been short with Denny, but *that* was downright mean.

Jodi, My child. Are you sure? Denny may be a lot of things—but mean?

I listened. Was the Holy Spirit talking to me? I mean, it was like a thought in my head, and yet . . . more than a thought. Something deeper down, nudging my spirit.

It was true. Whatever faults Denny had—huh! *Clueless* came to mind—"mean" wasn't one of them. So what was he implying?

Now I was wide awake. I got out of bed, pulled on a robe, and quietly opened the door. Competing music came from behind Amanda's and Josh's closed bedroom doors. Down the hall, I could hear the TV . . .

I snuck into the dining room, found my Sunday tote bag I used to carry my Bible and other stuff, and pulled out one of the sheets I'd photocopied. *"Yachad . . . together in unity . . . in one accord."*

My eyes teared up again. That's what Denny meant. *So much for 'together in unity' . . . so much for being 'in one accord.'"* Touché. Yeah, it hurt—but he was right.

Darn it. I sighed. Why was I the one who always had to say I'm sorry? On the other hand, wasn't I learning that "I'm sorry" and

"Please forgive me" were steps toward healing and freedom? The sooner the better, before we made mountains out of molehills.

I sucked up my pride and headed for the living room.

DENNY NOT ONLY FORGAVE ME (as I knew he would), but said we could have a night "in," make something yummy like quesadillas after Amanda went to youth group, and just watch TV together. But as it turned out, every single station—we didn't have cable—was running specials on the "Presidential Primaries 2004" kicking off in high gear. Channel 2 . . . 5 . . . 7 . . . 11 . . . all blabbing opinions about the chances of the president's reelection. Followed by cozy magazine formats on the various candidates' backgrounds and dissecting their political careers (or lack thereof). Commentators nodded soberly at their monitors showing reporters in the field, following presidential wannabes like rock-star groupies. We even tried channels 32, 38, and 50, but only got a rerun of *The Good, the Bad, and the Ugly,* some big-haired TV evangelist I'd never heard of striding around a platform, and a motivational speaker talking about turning your money into millions. Yeah, right.

Denny finally jumped in the car and rented a video. We both fell asleep on the couch and had no idea how the movie ended, waking only when Amanda came in after being dropped off after youth group. Well, at least Denny and I had zoned out "in one accord."

If the kickoff of the presidential primaries had taken over our Sunday evening, it consumed the teachers' lounge at Mary MacLeod Bethune Elementary that week. No *yachad* here, though. A couple of the staff bellyached loudly about the current administration, complained about the war in Iraq dragging on when we'd been promised the US would be "in and out," and enumerated a long list of election promises from 2000, which still eluded fulfillment. A few defended the president. Most of us kept our mouths shut. In fact, I did my brave Jodi Baxter thing—I began avoiding the teachers' lounge altogether. Maybe I could return when the election was over next November.

Florida called me Tuesday evening while I was recording math homework scores in my grade book. "Jodi? Girl, I got a big favor to ask ya."

My mind was still calculating scores. *Lamar is falling too far behind . . . I need to get him some extra help . . .* "Uh, sure, Flo. What's up?"

"Chris got a hearing tomorrow down at the JDC, know what I mean? Smuckers, the new lawyer Peter Douglass lined up for us, he gonna try and get the charges thrown out. Says Chris don't have no priors, was just in the wrong place at the wrong time. All the other perps are two, three years older; the perp who pulled the job is gonna get tried as an adult. Smuckers says it's a long shot, but he wants to keep Chris out of adult court at all costs. This would be a prelim hearing; if it don't work out, then they schedule a hearing to decide whether he gets tried as a juvie or an adult."

She had my attention now. "Oh, Flo. Want me to get the Yada Yadas praying? I could send out an e-mail, make some calls—"

"Well, yeah. That too. But what I wanna ask is, can Carla come home from school with you tomorrow? The hearing's at two—but regardless of what happens, Smuckers says he wants to meet with Carl and me afterward. We both takin' the afternoon off work. Don't know when we get done. I'd feel better if I knew Carla had someplace ta go."

I hesitated. Teachers weren't supposed to take kids home—for obvious reasons. But given my personal relationship with Florida, this wasn't exactly a normal situation. How could I *not* be there for my friend? "Uh, sure! Not a problem."

Should I let the office know what was going on? Like, do it officially? I decided no. I'd write Avis a note and leave it in her box to cover my butt.

WHICH IS HOW Carla Hickman ended up at my house Wednesday after school, cooing over Willie Wonka while I made hot chocolate. Wonka, stretched out on the floor by the window radiator in the dining room, patiently put up with the child kissing his nose, stroking his silky ears, and yelling into the kitchen, "Isn't Willie Wonka a boy dog? How come he got those nipple things on his belly?"

I took two mugs of instant hot chocolate out of the microwave and brought them into the dining room. Carla hopped onto a chair and took a sip. "Eww. It's too hot!"

"Sorry 'bout that. I'll put some cold milk in it."

Carla seemed satisfied with the cooled-down chocolate but eyed me over the rim of her mug, her three wiry ponytails peeking out top and sides. "Got any cookies? My other mama always had cookies to go with hot chocolate."

I winced. How many times did Florida have to put up with *"My other mama always . . ."*? The Department of Child and Family Services had taken the Hickman kids into state custody and put them in foster care for five years. That was *before* Florida got "saved an' sober." Now the Hickmans were trying to put their family back together again. And they'd come a long way, praise Jesus! They'd found the missing Carla, whose files had somehow been "misplaced" in the DCFS system. Peter Douglass had offered Flo's husband a decent job at Software Symphony. They'd just moved out of a crowded apartment in the Edgewater district into a rented house here in Rogers Park. And Florida had been clean for six years now. Things had really been looking up . . .

Until Chris got arrested, hopping a ride after school with some gangbanger who "just happened" to rob a 7-Eleven at gunpoint while Chris waited outside in the car.

Carla was still waiting for an answer about the cookies. "Sorry, kiddo. Don't have any cookies—but tell you what. Why don't we make some? What kind do you like?"

Carla's eyes rounded. "Really? Can we make a whole bunch of cookies?" She hopped off her chair. "Oatmeal raisin chocolate chip! That's what I wanna make."

I did a mental run-through of the cupboards. *Oatmeal—check. Raisins—check. Chocolate chips—maybe.* I scrapped the idea of parking Carla in front of some kid video while I graded homework papers. "Let's do it." I headed for the kitchen, expecting Carla to follow me, but turned back to see her still standing by the dining room table. I paused at the doorway. "You okay?"

"It's my birthday Saturday," she blurted. "I'm gonna be ten."

"Why, that's right. Amanda and I came to your birthday party last year." *A party Florida would rather forget.* I wondered if there would be a party this year.

"Since we gonna make cookies, can we make enough to take to school on Friday? Ya know, like some of the other mamas do when they kids have birthdays?"

How easy to say, *"Sure. No problem."* But was it a problem? How would Florida feel if I stepped in and did her mama thing? Except, I reasoned, given everything going on at the Hickman household, I doubted cookies for Carla's third-grade classroom was on the priority list. Second problem. If my class found out the *teacher* made cookies for Carla, was I setting myself up to make cookies for *all* the kids' birthdays? If not, would I be accused of playing favorites?

But I grinned at Carla. Life was slippery; didn't fit neatly into all the pigeonholes. We had to take risks—if the risk was about love. "Tell you what. Sure, we'll make cookies you can take to class on Friday. On one condition." I leaned close to her ear. "You can't tell *anybody* at school that you made them at my house. Deal?"

WE FOUND HALF A BAG of chocolate chips—some lowlife chocolate fiend had snacked away the other half, and it wasn't Willie Wonka!—giving us enough goodies to make four dozen oatmeal-raisin-chocolate-chip cookies. Carla counted and recounted the cookies, making sure we saved enough so every kid in the class could have two, then insisted we leave those at my house. "Otherwise, they be gone by Friday," she said darkly. "Cedric eat 'em all his own self."

I wasn't sure they'd be any safer at my house, but I promised I'd guard them with my life—having to "cross my heart and hope to die" again.

Denny took the call saying Hickmans were home and could we bring Carla? "What happened at the hearing?" I asked him. Denny just shrugged and shook his head.

Men! Denny in particular was missing the curiosity gene.

Which is why I took Carla home. I mean, did the case get dropped or not? Probably not. Wouldn't whoever called have been praising God and yelling with joy if Chris's case had been thrown out?

Florida confirmed my fears, after sending Carla inside and closing the front door behind her, leaving us standing out on their front porch in thirty-degree weather. She lit a cigarette and blew smoke into the frosty air, eyes smoldering. "Judge turned down the petition. Said Smuckers could argue 'not guilty' at Chris's trial. So that's the next thing we facin'—another hearing to decide if he gets tried in juvie or in adult court. 'Cept they don' call it a trial in juvie—a *disposition* or somethin'. No jury either. Just the judge, decidin' my baby's whole life." She frowned at the cigarette. "Huh. Tryin' ta give up these things, but it ain't easy, not with all this crap goin' on."

I felt tongue-tied. *Sheesh!* What could I say? I blew on my hands to warm them, then thrust them back into my jacket pockets. "How can I pray, Flo?"

She sucked on the cigarette again and shook her head. "Don' really know, Jodi. Sometimes it feel like my prayers just bouncin' off the ceiling, know what I'm sayin'?" She flipped the cigarette stub into the darkness and sighed. "Maybe pray that Carl an' me, we can just keep hangin' on ta God's hand." She reached for the door handle. "Guess I'll see ya Sunday. Thanks for keepin' Carla."

I opened my mouth to ask if they were planning anything for Carla's birthday on Saturday, but the door closed abruptly behind her.

THE TV NEWS that night flashed the attractive face of a Palestinian woman who blew herself up along with four Israelis.

Watching the news felt like a punch to the stomach. *Oh God, not a woman!* I didn't understand the hatred that drove suicide bombers to throw their lives away to kill "the enemy." But a woman? Women were *life-givers!* Weren't we? Didn't women keep the world sane when all hell was breaking loose?

I felt so sick about it, I almost forgot to bring Carla's cookies to school on Friday—I'd "hidden" them upstairs in Stu's apartment to thwart the Baxter cookie monsters—but thankfully *she* remembered and dropped them off at the back door on her way to work. "Count 'em. They're all there." She grinned at me under her red felt beret and headed for the garage.

Monday would be a school holiday—Dr. Martin Luther King Jr.'s birthday—so we had a nice all-school program that Friday morning commemorating the civil rights leader. Back in our classroom, I mentioned that Carla Hickman *almost* shared a birthday with the famous African-American and had brought everyone a treat. Carla, true to her word, kept mum about the cookie origins, beamed happily as we sang "Happy Birthday" to her *and* to Dr. King, and only threatened to punch Lamar one time, when he started to help himself to the last four cookies, left over because two students were absent.

"Those cookies are for . . . for Miz Douglass, ain't that right, Miz Baxter?" Carla thrust the plastic container with the four orphan cookies at me. "You give 'em to her, okay?"

Which gave me a lovely excuse to drop into Avis's office at lunchtime, avoiding both the noisy cafeteria and the teachers' lounge with its nonstop droning TV. But the moment I saw the tightness in her face, the missing smile, I remembered. Rochelle was supposed to get results back yesterday from the HIV retest.

I shut the door to her office and sank into a chair. "Bad news?" I whispered.

Avis nodded. Sudden tears glistened in her eyes and she grabbed a tissue from the box on her desk. "No question. Rochelle tested positive for the HIV virus." The tears spilled and she blew her nose.

"Oh, Avis." I could barely grasp the reality of it. What did it mean? What was going to happen to Rochelle? Was there anything that could be done? How—

Avis stood up abruptly and paced behind her desk, then turned back to me, her voice low and intense. "I am *so angry*, Jodi! So angry I could spit. Do you know why? Rochelle says Dexter is the only man she's ever slept with, that she's been faithful to him from day one." The side of her mouth twisted slightly. "Well, she didn't say whether day one was *before* or *after* their wedding day . . . but I believe her. Which means . . ." Avis gulped for air, as if she couldn't breathe.

I watched pain and anger twist Avis's beautiful face into something almost terrifying.

"Which means," she finally breathed, "that *Dexter* is the one who infected her. That pretty-boy Don Juan has not only been abusing my daughter, but he's going to kill her too."

9

I was tempted to snuggle deeper under the covers the next morning when my inner alarm woke me up at six. Why couldn't my body clock tell the difference between weekdays and weekends? But the memory of Avis's muffled tears wetting my shoulder as we just held each other in her office the day before, got me out of bed and shuffling toward the kitchen to start the coffee. I needed some time alone to pray, to talk to God, to ask Him how in the world this made any sense!

Ten minutes later I was in the recliner in the front room where the Christmas tree had stood, flipping open my Bible in the glow of the floor lamp. Denny's warm robe and the hot coffee soothed my body, but I missed the glittering Christmas tree lights, as if cheer had been snuffed out from my spirit too.

The Psalms . . . that's what I needed. Good ol' King David somehow got away with ranting at God when *he* was upset. Yeah, Psalm 69—that was a good one. I'd pray it on Avis's and Rochelle's behalf. Maybe mine too. I took a breath and spoke aloud in the stillness, my mind paraphrasing the verses even as I read.

"God, it's Jodi here. This news about Rochelle feels like flood-waters rising clear up to their necks, about to drown them. Avis is sinking right now into the mud, unable to keep her feet on solid ground. She's overwhelmed, God! I'm sure she's worn out calling on You for help, calling until she has no voice left! She's looking for You, God—trying to understand why this is happening. Why aren't You answering?"

My eyes skimmed part of the chapter until I came to verse 13: "But I'm praying to You, O Lord, looking for Your favor. In Your great love, O God, answer me! Answer Avis! Answer Rochelle! Answer with your sure salvation. Rescue them, O God, from the muck. Don't let them sink! Don't let these floodwaters, this terrible disease, swallow them up! Don't just throw Rochelle's life away into a pit. Answer us, O Lord, out of the goodness of Your love! Answer quickly, because Avis and her family are in trouble, Lord, and it hurts—it hurts all of us who love them . . ."

I heard Denny clear his throat behind me. "Uh, sorry to interrupt, babe. Just want to let you know I'm heading over to the church. Going to pick up Carl on the way."

"What?" I squinted at my watch. "It's only six-forty! Doesn't men's breakfast start at eight o'clock?"

"Yeah." He came over to the recliner, bent down, and kissed my nose, smelling like mint toothpaste. "But Peter Douglass talked to Carl about the men at church praying for Chris, and for him and his family. Carl was kinda shy about it, said he'd rather do it with just a few guys he knows instead of the whole men's breakfast. So a few of us are getting together ahead of time to pray with Carl." I saw him grin in the glow of the lamplight. "I asked Ben Garfield to come. Said he would. Mark Smith is coming too."

"Really?" For a moment I forgot I was mad at God. "That's great!" I chuckled. "God's got Ben in His sights, for sure . . . oh! Let Wonka in, will you? He's been out there quite a while."

When the back door closed behind Denny a few minutes later, I squeezed my eyes shut. *Thank You, God. Thank You for reminding me that You are answering our prayers. Maybe not on our timeline, but we've been praying for Ben a long time, and there he is, joining the guys for a Jesus prayer meeting.* I giggled to myself. Knowing Ben, half the reason he'd agreed to come was probably to get out of the house for a couple of hours, escaping baby duty. But who cared? Didn't Ruth say Ben might go to church if he could hang out with Denny and the other Yada husbands?

On the way to the coffee pot for a refill, I passed the kitchen calendar and realized I had one other thing to be thankful for this morning. I still had a whole week before I had to show up for overnight duty at Manna House.

"HE *WHAT?*" I started laughing as Denny reported the morning's events while he threw stuff into a small duffle bag. "He brought *Isaac* to the prayer meeting?" I still couldn't get used to the image of white-haired Ben Garfield walking around with a baby in a baby carrier. Would wonders never cease?

"Yep. Fed him a bottle, burped him, put him to sleep over his shoulder. Gotta tell you, Jodi, that guy is nuts about that kid."

My grin faded. "Yeah. *Isaac.* Wish he paid that much attention to Havah. I think he overcompensates with Isaac because of that birthmark on his face."

Denny shrugged, hunting for his clipboard. "Don't worry

about it. They've got *twins*, remember? Makes sense for them to divvy up the childcare."

Yeah, maybe. But I pushed the thought aside, following Denny back into the kitchen. "How was the prayer time with Carl? Did he stay for the men's breakfast too?"

He rummaged in the refrigerator. "Yeah, it was great. Just five of us—Peter, Mark, Ben, me, and Carl. Well, and Isaac." He chuckled. "Gave Carl a chance to just talk about how he feels with his boy in lockup—he hides a lot of that, you know. He's scared, big-time . . . Jodi? We got any more bottles of water in here?"

I pulled one out of the refrigerator door, right in front of his nose.

"Oh. Thanks." He threw it in the duffle bag and shrugged into his down jacket. "But no, he didn't stay for the men's breakfast. Mostly because we all encouraged him to go home and take Carla out for breakfast for her birthday. Told him it was important not to neglect his other kids in his worry over Chris."

"Great idea!" Hopefully Ben Garfield would take the hint too.

Denny headed for the back door. "Varsity game's over by three. I should be home by four." Pulling open the door, he waggled his eyebrows at me. "Anything happening tonight I should know about? Or can we go out? See? I'm asking early."

"Hm. I'll think about it, see if I get any better offers . . . Just kidding! Close the door! No, wait." I pulled Denny back inside and shut the door. "Did Peter Douglass mention anything about Rochelle? I mean, did you guys pray for her too?" I had told Denny the news about the HIV test and how devastated Avis was.

He shook his head. "He didn't say anything, and I hesitated to ask. You said yourself you didn't know if Avis had told him yet. Look, I gotta go."

I leaned against the door after Denny left. I didn't get it. Avis was a strong woman. She knew how to lean on God front and center, especially since Conrad died and left her a widow. But this thing with Rochelle was tearing her up! She needed the support of her new husband. Maybe she had told him, and Peter just didn't want to bring it up, afraid it would take away from the focus on praying for the Hickmans.

"I dunno, Wonka," I muttered to the dog, stepping around his bulk as I headed for the basement to switch loads in the laundry. "I can't figure Avis out, sometimes. But guess it's not easy getting married in your fifties. Trying to merge your old family with your new one." Down in the basement, I pulled a load of whites out of the dryer and stuffed wet wash-and-wear into it. But I knew one thing—I was gonna get on her case. She couldn't keep this all bottled up inside. She needed support! And Rochelle did too.

"IT'S NOT THAT EASY, JODI." Avis spoke quietly into the phone. No tears now. "Rochelle isn't ready to tell the world. People . . . react funny when they find out you have HIV or AIDS. You know that."

I did know that. Did I want someone who was HIV-positive or had AIDS to check out my groceries? Handle my money at the bank? Teach my kid at school? It was hard to let go of the myths about how HIV could be transmitted when it got in-your-face personal.

"And the minute someone says they are HIV-positive," she went on, "everybody's thinking, 'Oh, are you gay?' Or, 'Must've been sleeping around, *tsk tsk*.'"

Exactly.

"But to defend herself, Rochelle would have to point the finger at Dexter—and she's not ready to do that. He hasn't even been tested yet."

"Why in the world would she want to protect *Dexter*?" The cad.

"I think"—her voice got tight—"she's hoping they could work it out, get back together. He is Conny's daddy, you know."

I stifled a snort, cradling the phone in my ear while I pulled a clean towel out of the laundry basket and started folding. When I could trust myself, I got to the point: "The thing is, Avis, how can Yada Yada pray for Rochelle and Conny—and you!—if you keep this a secret? In fact, did you tell Peter yet?"

A silent beat hung in the air. Then, "Yes. Yes, I did. Last night. He . . . didn't say much. Just held me and let me cry."

Well, good. That was a start. I glanced at the clock. Almost four. "I better go, Avis. Denny wants to go out tonight and I still gotta do something with this rag-mop hair. See you tomorrow at Yada Yada? We're meeting at . . ." I looked at the list posted on one of the kitchen cupboard doors. "Florida's house. Wait—do you think that's a good idea? I mean, what they're going through with Chris and all that?"

"Flo's not shy. She'd say something if it's not okay. Besides"—Avis's voice took on the old, familiar "everything's under control" tone—"didn't Becky say the next time Yada Yada met at the Hickmans, she wanted an apartment blessing for her squirrel's nest on the second floor? And seems like it's somebody's birthday . . . who did we celebrate last year in January? Not Chanda—we missed her last year. Somebody else . . ."

I groaned. Now I remembered. *Nony.* Why didn't we celebrate both Chanda and Nony at our last meeting? Well, I knew why we hadn't. Chanda needed her own celebration. But who was going to bake a cake *this* time? Get a card for all of us to sign? Why in the world didn't we *plan ahead* for this kind of stuff!

"Well, I'm not going to stay home tonight to pull it together," I sniffed, knowing I sounded like a snit.

TURNED OUT HOSHI TAKAHASHI had everything under control. She pulled me aside at worship on Sunday morning, said she had ordered a cake from the Bagel Bakery and Ruth and Yo-Yo were going to bring it. "You already did the meaning of Nony's name last year, correct?" she said softly. She smiled, dark eyes twinkling. "So this year I have a little surprise we can give her. Not exactly a birthday card, but something we can sign and give to her."

My snit melted. I even felt ashamed. Why had I gotten so aggravated, assuming that if I didn't do it, nobody would? But we really did need a birthday maven to make sure *somebody* was on top of the Yada Yada birthdays. I'd bring it up at Yada Yada tonight—

I smiled and shook my head. *There you go again, Jodi!*

Denny was laid back about me going off to Yada Yada Sunday evening. We'd had a great time the night before—went out to dinner at the Davis Street Fish Market in Evanston, tried *not* to talk about all the trials of various Yada Yada sisters, spent way too much money ("It's Jamaica Jerk Café next time," Denny groused good-naturedly), and laughed at my squeamish attempt to eat one of the oysters he'd ordered. We ended the evening with some behind-closed-doors hanky-panky, given that Amanda had a late-night babysitting job and Josh was "out."

I hitched a ride to Yada Yada with Stu, who seemed kind of quiet on the way over to Hickmans. Dirty ice and snow humped in ugly patches along the streets. It was time for a fresh snowfall to brighten up winter's gray rags. "You okay?" I said.

She shrugged. "Just tired. I might leave early. We'll see."

We arrived at the little frame house before Nony and Hoshi got there. But Becky Wallace beckoned us furtively into the Hickmans' narrow kitchen. A baby carrier on the floor contained baby Havah, sound asleep just under a pretty bakery cake on the counter. But Yo-Yo, Ruth, and Florida were crowded around a box lid on the other counter. My eyes widened. Sitting in the box lid were at least a dozen exquisite origami shapes folded from bright colored paper. A star, a butterfly, a rose, an owl . . .

"Hoshi smuggled 'em to me after church," Flo said. "Said we were supposed to each pick one and sign it for Nony."

"Hey. I like that frog on a lily pad." Yo-Yo picked it up. "Do we hafta give 'em *all* to Nony? Man, this is cool."

"Don't be a *shmo*, Yo-Yo," Ruth sniffed. "Sign the frog." She lifted the paper butterfly from the box. "This one I like. I will sign it from Havah and Isaac, one name on each wing."

Chanda called while others were still arriving. "All three of her kids got the flu," Flo announced when she hung up. "She said Adele ain't gonna make it either. MaDear's got the flu too. They had to put her in the hospital. Worried about pneumonia."

The prayer list for tonight was getting longer.

But Nony, wearing a blue-and-gold tunic over a black turtleneck and wide, black pants, was utterly delighted with the origami shapes and touched that we had remembered her birthday. I eyed Avis. *Ha.* If it weren't for Hoshi, we'd be up a creek without a paddle. I was touched by Hoshi's unselfish spirit, providing a gift for all of us to give Nony.

"So, Nony. How old are you? I wanna be like you when I grow up." Yo-Yo was serious. Ruth rolled her eyes and stuck a pacifier in Havah's mouth.

"I am thirty-eight this week," Nony admitted in her cultured South African accent. "Do you think I will know what I am supposed to do with my life by the time I am forty years?" Her tone was light, but I suspected her words betrayed a trace of frustration. Six months of playing nursemaid to her husband recovering from head trauma had sapped some of her fire.

After demolishing the bakery cake, we tromped upstairs to Becky Wallace's studio apartment at the back of the Hickmans' house. The two rooms—combination kitchen/living area plus a bedroom with a single bed for Becky and a youth bed for Little Andy—were somewhat bare but neat and clean. The closet-size bathroom even had a scented candle burning on the sink. Stu poked me and muttered in my ear, "Maybe she picked up some household tips living with me after all, you think?" Avis brought out her anointing oil, and we prayed that God would fill the apartment with His love, His laughter, His protection, His hope. The prayers didn't take long, but Becky sniffled and had to blow her nose.

Half our time was gone already, but back downstairs Avis led us in singing, "Jesus, Your Name is Power." I was gripped by the words, *"Jesus, Your name will break every stronghold . . ."*

We all sat quietly after the song, each one probably grappling with the words. Did I really believe Jesus had the power to break strongholds? Free every captive? Give life?

To my surprise, Avis broke the silence. "I've been singing this song in my heart all day," she said, "holding on to the words. Because, I confess, Satan seems to have established a stronghold in my family that threatens to devastate us."

Ten pairs of eyes stared at her.

"I . . . did ask Rochelle's permission to tell you this, but I'd like to ask that it not leave the room." And then Avis said it, flat out. "Rochelle has been diagnosed with HIV."

Shock and disbelief registered on every face, like freeze-frame photography. But Nony literally lifted right out of her seat, hands clenched toward the ceiling. "Nooo!" she wailed. "No! No! No!" Then she burst into tears.

10

I was startled by Nony's outburst, even though I'd had the same inner reaction when I first heard the news. But she practically flew to Avis, fell to her knees, and grasped Avis's hands in her own. "Oh, my sister! The devil is afoot, stealing the health of our own daughters, right under our noses. It is her husband, yes?"

Avis, slightly taken aback, nodded silently.

"O God, how long will the wicked be jubilant? They pour out arrogant words! Evildoers are full of boasting!" Nony's head was thrown back, eyes tightly closed, even as she still kneeled in front of Avis. I knew she had to be praying one of the psalms, but I didn't know which one. "They crush Your people, O Lord! They oppress Your inheritance—even one of our own precious daughters! They slay the widow and the alien; they murder the fatherless. They say, 'The Lord does not see; the God of Jacob pays no heed.'"

The rest of us reached out for one another's hands, making a circle as she prayed.

"O Lord God who avenges, shine forth! Rise up, O Judge of the earth; pay back to the proud what they deserve." With this, Nony's chin fell to her chest. She seemed spent. After a few moments, she got to her feet and returned to her chair. She looked around the circle. "Forgive me, my sisters. But you know that AIDS is killing my people in South Africa at a terrible rate, leaving thousands of orphans. It has troubled my spirit for years, and I have often felt God calling me to respond in some way. But Rochelle . . . Oh Jesus, Jesus, have mercy." Tears rolled down her smooth cheeks. "It is as if a spear has pierced my own child, child of my own body. That beautiful girl . . . Oh Jesus."

Avis's calm had been rattled by Nony's intense emotion, and she dabbed at her eyes with a tissue.

We moved on with our meeting, gathering prayer requests and covering each other with prayer and words of encouragement from Scripture. But as we hugged each other goodnight, I noticed that Nony's eyes had a new fire in them. If I had to guess, the call of God on her life was roaring in her ears.

AMANDA WAS ON THE PHONE in the kitchen when I got home, still wearing her jacket after getting home from youth group. "Why not?" she was saying. "It's a holiday! . . . José! You played with your father's mariachi band on Saturday! Why do you have to do it again tomor—" She rolled her eyes, leaning against the doorjamb between kitchen and dining room as she listened, totally ignoring me as I squeezed past. "So? That's in the evening! We could do something earlier in the day—go roller-skating or something . . .

What? . . . *Practice!* What do you need to practice for! . . . Fine! *Fine!*" Amanda slammed the phone into the wall set and stormed past me, heading for her room.

The door slam shook the whole house.

Denny poked his head into the dining room, where I was still standing with my coat on. "What was *that*?"

"Uh, a fight with José, I think. Did you pick her up from youth group?"

"Yeah. We just got home ten minutes ago. She was fine."

I sighed. Seemed like Amanda had inherited my ability to go from zero to eighty mood-wise when it came to reacting to the men in our lives.

I decided to ignore my daughter's little tiff. Let them work it out. I was tired. What I wanted to do was crawl into bed, turn on the electric blanket—if we had one, which we didn't; a hot water bottle would have to do—and read myself to sleep on a cold winter night. It was supposed to get down to seven degrees tonight. Even if it was a school holiday the next day, thanks to Dr. King . . .

But as I lay in bed, feet propped on the hot water bottle under the covers, trying to concentrate on my novel, I rather regretted that Amanda hadn't been able to talk José into going roller-skating tomorrow. I used to love to roller-skate—the "good Christian girl" alternative to going to dances when I was growing up. I'd gotten pretty good too. Skating backward, leaning around the corners, waltzing with my partner . . .

I smiled. Maybe I could talk Denny into going skating sometime. Wondered if Amanda and José would come with us . . . maybe Josh and Edesa too . . .

I closed my book. Okay, that was weird. Triple dating with your own teenagers.

Nah.

MAYBE IT WAS BECAUSE we only had four school days that week. Maybe it was because the president gave his State of the Union address on Tuesday, heating up the opinions dividing the school staff into liberal, moderate, conservative, or head-in-the-sand. Maybe it was because I had a lot on my mind, worried about my friends who seemed to have a *lot* on their plates. Not just Florida with her boy locked up on charges of armed robbery—and he hadn't even done the robbery! . . . Not just Avis, learning that her own precious daughter had been diagnosed with HIV . . . but Adele, too, worried about her ailing mother, who already suffered from dementia and was now in the hospital with pneumonia . . .

Whatever it was that stole my attention, suddenly it was Saturday. The *fourth* Saturday of January. The day I'd agreed to be an overnight volunteer at Manna House.

Hoo boy. I wasn't ready.

"Mom." Josh eyed me over the rim of his glass of orange juice as he slouched in the kitchen, backside propped against the counter, legs crossed at the ankle like an urban cowboy, arms folded except for the hand holding the glass. "It's going to be fine. You'll love it. The kids are great. Besides, the staff will give you a tour and an orientation the first time you volunteer."

"Uh-huh." I opened cupboards, doing a quick inventory so I could make a shopping list for Denny and Amanda. "Twenty-four hours, you say?"

"Well, give or take. They usually let us off a couple of hours early Sunday morning so we can get to church . . . There, see?" He slapped the counter. "The shelter needs a *van* so we can bring some of the women and kids to church! Know anybody who has a van they'd like to donate? They could get a tax write-off."

Had to admire Josh's dedication to Manna House. How my nineteen-year-old son got so immersed at a *women's shelter* still seemed odd to me. Although . . . Edesa Reyes had changed her college major to public health last year, and Manna House, a new and struggling shelter on Chicago's north side, was crying out for public health volunteers. And where Edesa was, you could pretty well count on Josh showing up too.

Oh Lord, I prayed silently as I stuffed sweats for sleeping, slacks and a sweater for Sunday, and my toothbrush into my backpack. *I hope You've got that "first love" thing under control.* At Josh's suggestion, I left all jewelry except for my wedding ring at home, along with my wallet and purse, tucking only my driver's license and ten bucks into my jeans pocket.

At least Josh was going with me. He and Edesa and one of the other new volunteers—Karen from church—were also scheduled for this weekend. We nobly took the elevated train down to Belmont so Denny could have the car. *Correction,* I thought, shivering inside my winter jacket while we waited on the platform at the Morse Avenue el station. *Denny already has the car over at school, leaving me no choice.*

I was a bit taken aback when Josh said, "Well, this is it," after getting off at the Belmont el stop and walking four or five blocks. We stood in front of a small, rather dilapidated, brick church building shoehorned between two larger buildings, complete with ancient stained-glass windows and a short steeple, badly in need of paint.

"Wow," I said. "You didn't tell me Manna House was housed in a *church*. Do they still—"

"Nope. Congregation moved out to the suburbs years ago. Some little Missionary Baptist Church met here for several years, I'm told, but it was mostly elderly people who couldn't meet the mortgage payments, so the bank foreclosed. Not sure how Manna House got hold of it."

Beside the warped and damaged wooden doors hung a church sign—the kind you could slide letters in to post worship times or change the name of the sermon each Sunday. Blank. "There's no sign that says Manna House. How would anyone know—"

"Because it's a safe house, Mom. We don't exactly want to advertise to every Tom, Dick, and Harry. C'mon." Josh took my arm and steered me around to a side door, located in a little gangway that measured five feet at best between the church and the ugly brick building next to it, which housed at quick glance a Korean grocery, a Pay-Day Loan, and a twenty-four-hour Laundromat on the street level, topped by five floors of apartments. *Who in the world would do their laundry at three in the morning?*

We went down five steps into a small stairwell, where Josh tapped a numeric code into the automatic lock and then opened the door. In spite of the almost clandestine entryway, I was pleasantly surprised by the brightly lit basement room, even more delighted by the bright, colorful walls—orange, yellow, and blue. A Christmas tree that had seen better days dominated one corner of the room, decorated with dozens of handmade decorations and strings of mismatched lights. Nearby, a teenage girl and two smaller boys—all African-American—played a noisy game of Ping-Pong. Several cozy sitting areas had been created with overstuffed couches, armchairs, and braided rugs, none of which matched, while another corner functioned as an office or reception area, complete with a large desk, computer, two large file drawers, and an overflowing wastebasket.

The young woman sitting at the desk looked up. "Jodi Baxter! *Hola!*" Edesa Reyes scurried from behind the desk to give me a big hug. Out of the corner of my eye, I saw Josh beaming at her. No wonder. Edesa's wide smile lit up her whole face, like gemstones laid out on velvety soft mahogany. As usual, her ebony curls bounced behind a sunny headband of three-inch cloth, tied at the base of her neck.

Edesa's eyes danced. "We are so excited to have you join our volunteers! And *I* get to give you the tour and the orientation." She motioned to the Ping-Pong players. "Mikey! Jeremy! Come here! I want you to meet someone. You too, Sabrina."

The two boys put down their paddles and ran over. The girl followed more slowly, seemingly indifferent, but she said hello, then flopped on one of the couches and flipped open an ancient issue of *Allure* magazine. But the boys, maybe eight and nine, tugged on Edesa's hands. "Let us give her the tour, Miz 'Desa!"

The younger boy, Mikey, looked suspiciously up at Josh. "Is that lady really your mama, Mr. Josh?"

"I dunno," he said with a straight face. "She and the guy she's married to let me sleep at their house, though."

I backhanded his shoulder. "Watch it, buddy."

The two boys nodded at each other knowingly. "Yeah, she his mama," they chorused in tandem.

Josh disappeared somewhere, lugging a bucket with tools in it, while Edesa and the two chatty boys gave me a tour of the building. Another brightly painted basement room was set up as a playroom, with tables and small chairs, large pads of newsprint clipped to painting easels, dolls and doll furniture, several potty chairs, and shelves of toys. Two heavyset white women with frowzy hair chatted in a corner while several children bounced around the room.

We passed an office door—locked—marked "Director," peeked into a kitchen where three women, two Latina and one black, were doing dishes at one end of the room, and another was wiping tables—six long ones with four chairs along each side.

"How many residents do you have?" I asked Edesa.

"Right now, twenty women and about that many *niños.*"

Where are they all? I wondered as the boys led us up some narrow stairs to the main floor. We peeked into the sanctuary, which was just that—a small sanctuary, complete with pews, platform, and a pulpit. In the dim light that made its way through the dusky stained-glass windows, I saw the shadowy form of someone sitting in a far pew.

"We use this as a prayer room," Edesa whispered. "Women can come here to be quiet, get away from the common rooms. We have a prayer meeting on Saturday mornings, and sometimes a music group or drama troupe lead worship service on Sunday evenings. No one could bear to turn it into a dormitory."

But finally we did get to the sleeping rooms both on the sanctuary floor and the second floor—what were once Sunday school rooms, I presumed, now containing six to eight bunks each. Edesa introduced me to every woman and child whose path we crossed, and I was greeted for the most part by friendly smiles. *Nametags would be helpful,* I thought ruefully, knowing I'd never remember all the names. Well, I'd just have to suck it up and keep asking until I learned a few. Mikey and Jeremy and Sabrina . . . at least that was a start.

Back in the basement common room, the two boys grabbed both my hands. "C'mon, Miz Jodi, play Ping-Pong with us!"

Edesa laughed. "Go ahead. We can show you where you'll sleep later."

I let the boys drag me away, but I called back over my shoulder, "I didn't see Rochelle. Is she here?"

Edesa looked at a sign-out book on the desk. "She's out. Avis often comes down on Saturday and they do lunch or go shopping or something with Conny." She gave me a meaningful look. "Rochelle's kind of fragile right now, because of . . . well, you know."

Yes, I knew. But I didn't have any time to dwell on it, because Jeremy and Mikey started slamming Ping-Pong balls at me from their end of the table. It'd been a long time since I'd played Ping-Pong—almost as long as my roller-skating days—but I was surprised at how quickly it came back. Laughing and giggling, we slammed the little white balls back and forth until Josh came tromping back through the room with a plastic pitcher and tried to pour water into the Christmas tree stand.

"Huh. Still full," Josh muttered.

"Okay, okay, that's enough," I told the little boys, raising my hands in surrender. I joined Josh at the Christmas tree and rubbed one of the branches between my fingers. Needles fell off like a spring rain.

"Josh," I hissed. "This tree is too dry. You really should take it down." The boys hovered nearby, so I didn't add, *It's a real fire hazard.*

He scratched his head, which sported another couple of inches of sandy growth. "Yeah, guess you're right. The kids keep begging us to leave it up, but . . . maybe we'll do it tonight, make a game out of it or something."

"Just don't tell them *I* suggested it," I whispered under my breath. "That's all I need my first weekend here is to be the Big Baddy."

11

$\mathcal{A}$vis, Rochelle, and Conny trudged in the side door, stamping snow off their boots, just as Mikey ran up and down the stairs ringing a bell for supper. I got a tired smile from Rochelle and a damp hug from little Conny, who wanted to show me the colorful "bug" he'd made at the Children's Museum at Navy Pier from different "bug parts." Avis, wearing a hat trimmed with fake fur that matched the collar of her hip-length winter jacket, bent down to get a good-bye hug and kiss from her grandson, but I butted in. "Why don't you stay for supper, Avis?—if that's okay," I amended hastily, realizing I had no idea what the rules might be about dinner guests.

"*Si, si!* The more, the merrier." Edesa laughed, grabbed Conny's hand, and headed for the kitchen/dining room.

"Thanks, but I need to get home. I told Peter I'd be home by dinner. Bye, baby! Grammy loves you!" She blew Conny a kiss.

Rochelle rolled her eyes, gave her mother a peck on the cheek, and disappeared in the direction of the washroom. I followed Avis to the door. "How's Rochelle?" That felt lame. How *should* some-one be who just found out she had HIV?

Avis glanced away, absently pulling on her gloves. "We've got an appointment at the HIV clinic next week. Conny needs to be tested. They strongly recommend that other family members come, too, to learn what the treatment options are. 'How to live with HIV,' as the brochure says." She sounded weary.

My mouth went dry. Surely not Conny too! I swallowed. "What about Dexter? Has Rochelle told him yet?"

Avis shook her head. "We're going to get some advice about that too. Peter thinks we should phone Dexter, tell him we need to talk, then all meet together. But . . ." Her mouth tightened. "Don't know if I can do that. Right now I just want to strangle him." Suddenly she pulled me into a tight embrace. "Thank you, Jodi. For being here. Knowing Rochelle and Conny are with you and Edesa and Josh this weekend helps. I just wish . . ."

She didn't finish. Just turned and disappeared out the door. Snow fell gently into the narrow stairwell, the monster flakes slid-ing down light beams cast by the hundred-watt bulb just outside the door. Behind me, a wobbly *a cappella* rendition of the Doxology floated from the dining room. I shut the door and scurried in that direction.

The other new volunteer—a young black woman named Karen, whom I'd seen at church—turned out to be the cook that night. She'd done a passable job making enchilada casseroles for forty-plus hungry appetites, along with a chopped salad and brownies for dessert. The director, a stocky white woman with cropped salt-and-pepper hair, wire rim glasses, and a firm handshake, dropped by in time for dessert and coffee, and to meet the new volunteers.

Karen and me, that is. She introduced herself as Liz Handley, but I noticed everyone else called her "Reverend Handley."

Okay, so I was curious. "Uh, Reverend Handley, do you pastor a church?"

She smiled, grabbed a passing kid, and gave her a tickle-hug. "This is my parish now." The child dissolved in laughter and pulled away.

For some reason, her comment put a lump in my throat. *"Whatever you do for the least of these, you do for Me."* Jesus had said that. And here I'd come, mentally dragging my feet and wishing I was anywhere but.

You're here, Jodi. Don't beat yourself up. Think of the possibilities . . .

Well, might as well start with the dirty dishes. Maybe the equivalent of "washing feet" here at the shelter. I joined the dish crew, drawn to a talkative young woman named Precious who had something to say about everything. "Gonna be a mild winter. All that global warmin', ya know . . . Man, wish I could get myself down to Houston to see them Panthers play at the Super Bowl. My people come from Carolina, ya know . . . Wait, wait! Girl, don't dry those dishes wit' *that*." She snatched the dishtowel from my hand. "Get that boilin' water off the stove, pour it over them dishes in the rack, then let 'em air dry. They be dry in a minute." She plunged her hands back into the soapy dishwater and tossed her braids—twenty or more skinny ropes hanging halfway down her back. "My grandma only got a third-grade education, but she taught me that much."

I complied, wondering how a woman named Precious—someone, somewhere, had loved this girl enough to call her "precious"—had ended up homeless in a women's shelter. "Do you have any kids?" I asked, stacking the hot, dry plates onto a rolling cart.

Precious jerked a thumb toward the common room, where we could hear the *whack, whack, whack* of a Ping-Pong game. "Sabrina. She's my girl. She fourteen."

I couldn't contain my surprise. "You don't seem old enough to have a teenager!"

She grimaced. "Yeah. Got myself pregnant, not much older than she be now." She busied herself scrubbing one of the casserole dishes. "Sure did want a better life for my baby, but . . ." For the first time since we'd started doing the dishes, Precious fell silent.

LATER THAT NIGHT, curled up in a lumpy comforter on a lower bunk in one of the Sunday-school-rooms-turned-dormitories, I listened to the assorted breathing in the other bunks. I'd asked if I could spend the night in Rochelle and Conny's room. In fact, while Josh was getting whupped by Mikey and Jeremy at the Ping-Pong table and Edesa played cards with other Manna House residents in the common room, I'd volunteered to read Conny a story and put him to bed. Rochelle shrugged and said sure, but stayed in the room with me buffing her nails. I read *Goodnight Moon*, which I'd tucked into my backpack at home, then tiptoed out after Conny fell asleep. I'd been hoping I could talk to Rochelle, get to know her a little better, but though she was friendly enough, she stayed distant. Probably because I was her mother's friend.

I was tired now, but sleep eluded me. I felt so out of place. So . . . homesick. I wanted my own pillow and my crisp sheets and my husband's comforting sprawl in the bed next to me. What a wimp I was! I had volunteered to stay here one measly night per month. Precious and her daughter, Sabrina . . . Mikey and Jeremy's mom, Margo . . . and the other women I'd met that night—Estelle and

Nikki and Bonny, to name just a few—didn't have that choice. Whether for six weeks or six months, this *was* home.

Oh God! Why did You put me here? What am I supposed to do?

The Voice in my spirit responded, *First things first, Jodi. You can start by praying for them. Pray for the women and the children by name. Precious ... Sabrina ... Estelle ...*

And so I did, picturing each one's face that I'd met that night. Mikey's delighted giggle when Josh let him plug in the Christmas tree lights one last time. Conny cuddling close to me while I read, *"Goodnight room ... Goodnight moon ..."* Precious dispensing her grandmother's dishwashing wisdom. Sabrina absorbed in *Allure* magazine's teenage fantasies, where no teenager was homeless or had to wear clothes from the Salvation Army. Estelle deftly knitting a bright blue sweater vest with skill and an eye for pattern and design. Each with her own story, stories I didn't know yet. But if Avis's daughter was just one example, how many others had been betrayed, abused, rejected? How many had turned to drugs or alcohol to dull the pain? How many dreamed of a day when they could sleep in their own bed. At home. Safe. Loved.

Oh God, help me to see these women as You see them. Like Precious, each one precious in Your sight ...

BLAAAT! BLAAAT! BLAAAT! Blaaat! ...

I groaned and turned over. Was it morning already?

Wait a minute. That wasn't my alarm clock—

"Fire! Fire! Everybody out! Now!"

I sat up, eyes wide in the dark. That was Josh's voice yelling from below!

Thudding feet on the stairs. "Oh my God! Oh, please God!"

I leaped out of bed, fishing for my gym shoes. I grabbed them and ran for the door. Smoke was drifting up the stairs.

"Keep low! Keep low! Don't take anything—just go! Go!"

"My baby! My baby! Where's—? I gotta go back! Let me go!"

Screams. Cries. Coughing and gagging. Bodies pushing down the stairs.

Edesa stood at the bottom of the stairs. "Go out the sanctuary door—*don't run*. Ladies! Don't run. Don't push. But hurry! Hurry!"

Wait. Was everybody out of the room? Where were Rochelle and Conny? I turned and started back up. Two bodies pushed past me on the stairs, knocking me against the railing. But I finally gained the top and practically fell into our sleeping room.

"Mama! Maaaamaaaaa!" Conny was sitting up in his bunk, screaming.

Rochelle sat on the edge of her bed, a dazed look on her face. "Rochelle!" I screamed. "It's a fire! We have to go!" I pulled at her arms. "Get up! Get up!"

She let me pull her up onto her feet. Bare feet. What was the matter with this girl? Had she taken a sleeping pill? Drugged herself?

"Maaaamaaaaa!" Conny screamed again.

I pushed Rochelle out the door toward the stairs and grabbed Conny into my arms, blanket and all. "I got you, I got you, sweetie." Putting the blanket over his head and pushing Rochelle ahead of me, we stumbled down the stairs.

FIVE MINUTES LATER I found myself standing outside the old church on the sidewalk in my wet socks, holding Conny wrapped in his blanket and staring at the smoke pouring from windows, doors, the steeple, and hundreds of other cracks in the structure. I vaguely remember Josh grabbing my arm. "Mom! Thank God you're okay. Is everybody out of your room? Yes? Good!" And then he disappeared again.

Why don't I hear any sirens? Didn't someone dial 9-1-1? I could do it. Where's my cell? . . . I shifted Conny to one hip and slapped at my sweatpants. No pockets. No cell phone. It was upstairs in my backpack, probably melting down into a glump of plastic and computer chips. That's when I realized I didn't have my shoes either. Hadn't I grabbed my shoes? Must have lost them when I went back for Conny and Rochelle.

I heard sirens then. Thank God! *Somebody* called the fire department.

Josh appeared again. I suddenly realized he was bare-chested and barefoot, wearing only sweatpants. Two inches of fresh snow were soaking through my socks, but Josh, Rochelle, and several others didn't even have socks. "Everybody, into the Laundromat," he croaked. "We have to count noses, make sure everybody's out." His voice didn't sound like Josh. Stretched with strain. Had he swallowed smoke?

Numbly we followed Josh, the only male among the herd of females and assorted children, into the Laundromat. *Oh, hallelujah, thank You, Jesus, for Laundromats that stay open all night!* My throat caught at the unexpected blessing. It was warm. It was dry. It was empty—no, an old gentleman in a rumpled golf hat sat in a corner, babysitting a tumbling dryer, staring at us as we came in. A clock on the wall said 1:40.

The bundle in my arms squirmed. "Mama!" I found Rochelle, who still seemed in shock, pushed her into one of the molded plastic chairs, and plonked Conny into her arms. Several fire trucks roared up outside. Men in big boots and heavy coats jumped off the pumper, grabbed axes, and ran for the church. Others grabbed huge, pythonlike hoses, and pulled them toward a fire hydrant. The long hook-and-ladder backed into place, beeping warnings.

"Listen up, everybody." Josh's voice was firm, though to my mother's eye, he looked like he was about to cry. "Is *anybody* missing? We have to know *now*. We have to tell the firemen if there's anybody inside. Estelle? Everybody out of your bedroom? Margo?"

"Precious! I don't see Precious or Sabrina!" someone cried.

"I saw 'em heading for the alley door. Couple others too."

Josh sprinted for the glass door of the Laundromat.

"Wait, son!" The old man in the corner moved with surprising speed from chair to door. He peeled off his faded jacket and pushed it at Josh, who wiggled his long arms into it. Then the man took off his shoes that had seen better days. "Good thing I got big feet," he chuckled.

Stuffing his bare feet into the old leather shoes, Josh flew out the door, laces undone. In two minutes, he was back, herding a small group of women and children who had been coming out of the alley on the far side of the Laundromat. Cheers went up from the crew crowded around the window, watching the drama outside.

We counted noses again. And again. I felt helpless, because I didn't know everyone and couldn't have said if anyone was missing. But Josh and Edesa and the others finally seemed satisfied. Everyone was out.

Several of the women broke down crying. Others shouted. "Praise Jesus!" Children clung to the closest adult. Someone muttered, "We sure is homeless now."

The fire chief pushed open the door of the Laundromat and

asked who was in charge. Edesa spoke up. "If you'll let me use your cell phone, I'll get our director down here."

Fifteen minutes later, Rev. Handley arrived. Shock at what she'd seen outside had tightened her face into a grim mask, but she quickly kicked into gear, huddling with the fire chief, Josh, Edesa, and Estelle, who at fifty-something seemed to be the senior resident of Manna House. I sank into a plastic chair and watched. The adrenaline of fear was wearing off and cold reality was settling in.

Manna House was gone. What were all these women and children going to do?

A mad started to build up inside my gut. I knew without asking where the fire had started. *That tinderbox Christmas tree.* I *knew* it was a fire hazard. Josh had known it too! I glared at his back, looking slightly silly with his long arms sticking out of that too-small jacket. He was still a kid. Nineteen. His good intentions outweighed his wisdom. But the director, that Rev. Handley—*she* was responsible too. She should have told them to throw it out weeks ago.

Estelle's voice rose above the rest. "Yessir, praise Jesus, every one of them smoke detectors was working. That's why we are all *here* and not in *there.*" She pointed dramatically in the direction of the burning building next door with her knitting needles. I stared at the wad of bright blue yarn clutched in her hand. . . and started to laugh. Estelle had run outside shoeless, coatless, and wearing nothing but a shapeless, flannel bag of a nightgown. She'd just lost every possession down to her toothbrush.

But Estelle had come out carrying her knitting!

12

*T*he fire chief clicked his cell phone shut. "People? Can you all hear me?" Sniffles quieted; murmurs died away. The old man pulled open the door of the big dryer so it would stop rumbling. "The Salvation Army will be here in thirty minutes with blankets, food, and some warm clothes. But their shelter is on overload tonight. We, uh, we'll try to find a place for you all to go, but for now just sit tight. It might take—"

"Uh, chief?" Josh glanced at me, as if he wanted confirmation. "I think I know a place we can take these women and children for the night."

My mind spun. *Of course!* "That's right." I got off my duff and joined my son. "Our church is only twenty minutes from here. But we need to make some calls . . ."

Rev. Handley mutely offered her cell phone to Josh. The old man—who gave his name as Rosco Harris—shuffled over with half a roll of quarters. His laundry money. "Pay phone over there." He pointed.

"Bless you," I whispered, giving him a hug. "You are definitely a Good Samaritan."

He waved it off. "Hey. I still got a roof over my head, lady."

I didn't know Pastor Cobbs's or Pastor Clark's numbers by heart and neither did Josh. So we started with the numbers we did have. Denny. Avis and Peter.

"Dad," I heard Josh say. "We're *okay* . . . yeah, she's okay too. Look, we need a place to take these women and children for the night. Could you call—"

The pay phone was ringing in my ear; then I heard someone pick up on the other end. I glanced at Rochelle, arms wrapped around Conny, rocking and crying silently in a corner of the brightly lit Laundromat. No, I was not going to ask Avis or Peter to make any calls. "Peter? It's Jodi Baxter. There's been a fire down here at Manna House. Everybody's okay. But you and Avis need to come *now*."

THE DOUGLASSES WERE THE FIRST TO ARRIVE. Peter jerked open the door of the Laundromat, searched faces, then strode to the corner where Rochelle and Conny still huddled. The big man knelt beside his stepdaughter and pulled her and the child in her lap into a big embrace. "Oh, Rochelle, baby." His voice, though muffled against Conny's blanket, was more like a groan. "I'm so sorry, baby . . . so sorry. I never should have—" His shoulders began to shake.

Avis also knelt beside her daughter and put her arms around them all. Some of the other women respectfully moved away, giving the little family a scrap of privacy.

Peter finally helped Rochelle to her feet, took Conny into his arms, and made for the door. Avis hesitated before following her husband and daughter out into the night. "Jodi? Edesa? Should we take anyone else?"

"No, no! Go." Edesa gently pushed her out the door. "We'll be fine. Others are coming."

The Douglasses had no sooner left than a Salvation Army van squeezed past the police barricades. A man and three women in navy blue uniforms quietly and efficiently carried in armloads of colorful fleece blankets, baskets of sweet rolls, jugs of hot coffee, and boxes overflowing with sweatshirts, hats, mittens, socks, children's boots, and adult gym shoes. In one way or another, all of us got fitted with something to keep body and soul together for the next few hours.

The clock on the wall said 2:45. My eyes burned with unshed tears.

While the Salvation Army people were gathering names, ages, and contact information for any relatives in the local area from the Manna House residents, Pastor Clark showed up, rail thin even in his bulky parka and big rubber boots. He asked no questions, just said, "The church van is around the corner. I can take fourteen people. Several other church members with minivans are coming. The Cobbses are over at the church, making calls and collecting blankets, food, and air mattresses."

I wanted to throw my arms around Pastor Clark and hug him. But Denny arrived, ashen-faced, unshaven. He looked terrible. He looked wonderful. He held me a long time. "You okay, babe?" he whispered into my hair. "You sure?" I nodded my head against his chest but couldn't speak.

Finally, he gently pushed me away. "Let me go see Josh, okay?"

I nodded again. For the first time I noticed Josh sitting in one of the ugly plastic chairs, elbows on his knees, head in his hands. Denny sat down next to him, stretched an arm across his son's bent shoulders, then . . . just sat without speaking. My heart ached as I watched my two men sharing a silent pain.

Edesa didn't sit. She joined Pastor Clark as he made his way from person to person, touching one. Hugging a child. Whispering something to another.

But within the next half hour, several other members from Uptown–New Morning Church arrived with minivans and SUVs, lined up just outside the barricades. Josh, Edesa, Karen, and I managed to park our feelings and assigned small groups of women and kids to the various cars, agreeing all would meet at the church building in the Howard Street shopping center. Rev. Handley said she'd stay with the Manna House residents until they got situated. Pastor Clark promised to stay in touch with the Salvation Army people, and we moved amoebalike out of the safety of the twenty-four-hour Laundromat into the night.

Most of the women, dead tired, wrapped in blankets and assorted sweatshirts, plodded silently behind their assigned driver toward the cars. But, like Lot's wife, I turned and looked back at the smoldering remains of Manna House. The stained-glass windows were broken. Smoke had blackened the outside bricks and still rose in stubborn ribbons from holes chopped into the roof. Leaking water from the hydrant and drips from the broken windows were turning into ghostly icicles. The wide sidewalk, steps into the church, and the front of the church itself glistened like sheets of ice.

Unlike Lot's wife, I didn't turn into a pillar of salt. But the image of the shelter—shattered, broken, no longer a refuge—burned itself into my spirit, especially as Precious and Sabrina, and Mikey, Jeremy, and Margo climbed into our Caravan for the trip up an empty Lake Shore Drive toward Howard Street. From somewhere in my memory, the words of the psalmist floated to my lips. "God is our refuge and strength," I murmured. "Our ever-present help in trouble."

"I know that one," Precious said from the back. "My grandma used ta say it. 'God is our refuge and strength, a very present help in trouble. Therefore, we will not fear, though the earth be removed, and though the mountains be carried into the midst of the sea. Though the waters roar, though the mountains shake . . .' Somethin' like that."

"Huh," Margo muttered from the third seat. "Don't say nothin' 'bout no fire."

"Yeah, but there's another one. Lord, Lord, my grandma knew 'em all! Somethin' 'bout passin' through the waters—"

"I said *fire*," Margo grumbled. "An' keep it down. Mikey's asleep."

Precious was not deterred. "I'm gettin' there. Mr. Denny, you know what one I'm getting' at?"

Denny kept his eyes on the drive as the tall streetlights passed over us like gentle waves. But I saw the tightness in his face soften slightly. "Uh, think so. The one that goes, 'When you pass through the waters, I will be with you; and through the rivers, they shall not overflow you . . .'" He glanced at me, as if asking for help.

Now I knew the scripture Precious was remembering. "'When you walk through the fire, you shall not be burned, nor shall the flames kindle upon you. For I am the Lord your God . . .'"

"Yeah." Precious blew out a long sigh. "That's the one."

PASTOR JOE COBBS and First Lady Rose cheerfully welcomed the stream of homeless women and children as if the shopping center church were always open at five in the morning with the temperatures outside hovering at fifteen degrees. A small crew of volunteers—I saw both Uptown and New Morning people among them—had stacked up the chairs in the large meeting room, and assorted "beds" had already been laid out. More blankets and air mattresses were in some of the back rooms used as Sunday school rooms. "Get some sleep," Rose Cobbs urged the bedraggled band, giving hugs to as many women and children as time allowed. "We'll be back at nine o'clock with breakfast."

Oh yes, God. Sleep... Suddenly I felt as if all my body parts might disconnect and clatter to the floor if I didn't lie down somewhere.

Pastor Cobbs pushed the church keys into Josh's hand and herded the drivers and other volunteers out the door. I hesitated. Rev. Handley was spreading blankets on the floor as a makeshift bed for herself. Should I leave? Could I live with myself if I did? After all, my twenty-four-hour volunteer stint wasn't up yet. But Pastor Cobbs tapped a finger on Denny's chest. "Brother Baxter, take your wife home. Reverend Handley, Josh, and Sister Reyes can stay with these people. But you'll both be more helpful sorting things out for these women if you go home and get some sleep."

I didn't protest. I didn't even look back this time as I numbly shuffled behind Denny across the icy parking lot to the car. But when I crawled into the front seat and Denny turned the heater on full blast for the one-mile trip to our house on Lunt Street, I cried all the way home.

13

*W*illie Wonka nosed my hand and whined. Blearily, I opened one eye and tried to focus on the bedside clock. Eight-thirty . . . *Eight-thirty!* No wonder Wonka was whining. I slid out of bed, groped for Denny's robe, and followed the dog to the back door, my eyes at slit-level, hoping I could remain half-asleep and fall back into bed.

Then it hit me. Rose Cobbs would be showing up at the church with breakfast for the fire victims at nine o'clock. *I should be there.* After all, I wasn't the only one short on sleep. *And Josh . . . how is he doing? Did he get any sleep at all?* I'd hardly spoken more than a few sentences to my son since the fire alarm went off. Frankly, I'd let him and Edesa shoulder the primary responsibility for the Manna House residents.

A pitiful whine from outside broke up my reverie. Stuffing my feet into a pair of clogs by the back door, I darted outside into air so brittle it felt like it would break and hauled the arthritic dog up the icy back steps and into the house. Then I stumbled toward the bathroom mumbling, "Sleep can come later . . . sleep can come later." But I had to admit, I felt worse now than I did before I fell into bed three hours ago.

A shower and a strong cup of coffee helped a little. But I pulled on my sweats from the night before. No way was I going to dress up for church. I was tempted to just take the car and let Denny and Amanda come later with Stu. But a call upstairs nixed that idea. Stu was headed out the door herself to pick up Little Andy Wallace on Chicago's west side.

Sheesh. She's still doing that? Why hasn't she asked—

"What's going on?" Stu demanded. I told her in twenty-five words or less. "A fire at Manna House! Why didn't you call me?"

"Later, Stu," I mumbled and hung up.

Reluctantly, I woke Denny and offered to come back and pick him up, but he gamely got out of bed. He even woke up Amanda with the promise that all she had to do was throw on her sweats. Fifteen minutes later, we all piled into the car with travel mugs of coffee—though we had to wait while Amanda doctored hers with lots of milk and sugar. "Cool," she said. "Wish we could dress like this every Sunday."

Her eyes widened when we pulled up in the shopping center parking lot and she saw the crowd of homeless women and children milling around inside the big open room we used as a sanctuary. True to their word, Pastor Joe and Rose Cobbs, along with Debra and Sherman Meeks, were handing out bagels with cream cheese, jam, hardboiled eggs, apple, and orange juice, while a crowd-size pot of coffee perked away in a corner. Several of the young children were still sleeping on blanket pallets in spite of the chatter among the adults, while others were sitting up and rubbing their eyes as bright daylight streamed into the room from the bank of windows along the front.

The director of Manna House, still grim-faced, and a representative from the Salvation Army were huddled in a far corner with Pastor Clark, comparing lists, frowning. Two women in Salvation Army uniforms were opening boxes of donated clothing and passing out jeans, sweats, tops, sweaters, and socks.

Taking her cue from Edesa, who was taking some of the children to the bathroom, Amanda pitched right in with the kids— getting them washed up, sitting them down with bagels and juice, cracking the hardboiled eggs while making little jokes. I greeted Precious and Estelle with a hug, then assigned myself to serving coffee as soon as the big pot stopped gurgling.

Josh was nowhere to be seen.

I snagged Edesa, but she shook her head. A moment later, little Mikey tugged on my sweatshirt. "You lookin' for Mr. Josh?" He pointed toward the parking lot. "He said he goin' for a walk."

Wearing what? I thought. He'd run out of the burning building with no shirt and bare feet. The last I'd seen him, he was still wearing the old man's coat and shoes . . .

We were still cleaning up after breakfast when people began arriving for our usual ten o'clock worship service. Mattresses and blankets still dotted the floor, the chairs had not been set up, and the room was full of strange women and children in an assortment of rumpled nightclothes.

"Come in, come in!" Pastor Cobbs beckoned the bewildered members of our Needing-a-New-Name Church into the warmth of the big room. "Grab a chair and a cup of coffee, or sit on the floor. Church is going to be somewhat different this morning."

The sound crew and musicians cleared a little area at the back and the front of the room for their equipment—and with extra hands, it didn't take long to stack the mattresses and blankets along one wall. The women and children from Manna House looked a bit overwhelmed as the room filled with men in suits and ties and women in dressy coats and high-heeled boots. Mothers drew their children close.

As folding chairs were set up at random, Pastor Cobbs took a handheld mic and explained the emergency situation as briefly as possible. "What we have here, brothers and sisters, is an opportunity for us to worship God not only in spirit but in truth. Let the Word of God speak for itself." He flipped open his Bible and searched for a passage. "In the Gospel of Luke, chapter three, John the Baptist said, 'Every tree that does not produce good fruit will be cut down and thrown into the fire.' So the people asked him, 'What shall we do then?' He answered and said to them, 'He who has two tunics'—make that two coats—'let him give to the one who has none; and he who has food, let him do likewise.'" More page flipping. "And in the book of Romans, chapter twelve, the apostle Paul said, 'Share with God's people who are in need. Practice hospitality.'"

Pastor Cobbs looked up from his Bible, and made his way to where Margo was sitting with Mikey in her lap. He lifted the little boy—still in his pajamas—into his arms. "But maybe the most important word of all was spoken by Jesus. 'Whatever you did for one of the least of these brothers and sisters of mine, you did for Me.'"

Sherman Meeks stood up. "All right, Pastor. Say it now."

Pastor Cobbs let Mikey get down. "Thank you, Brother

Meeks. What we need, church, are temporary homes for these women and children until the Salvation Army or another shelter can find a more permanent place for them. But while you're thinking about that, we're going to thank the Lord God Almighty—"

"Hallelujah! Oh, thank You, Jesus!" At first, I thought it was Florida, but then I saw Estelle on her feet, still in her nightgown with a worn sweater over it, arms lifted in praise and tears running down her cheeks.

Pastor Cobbs's voice caught. "That's right, sister. Let's thank the Lord God Almighty for all His goodness and mercy in saving every single life from that fire last night. Praise team, can you do 'We Bring a Sacrifice of Praise'?"

As voices joined in a hearty rendition of, *"We bring a sacrifice of praise into the house of the Lord!"* I saw Josh slip inside the double doors, blowing on his bare hands. I sidled over to him and slipped an arm around his waist. He was shivering.

I could've kicked myself. *Why didn't I bring some of his warm clothes from home? Socks! Boots! Gloves! His own coat, for heaven's sake.* Under cover of the music, I whispered, "Josh, honey. You're freezing. Let me take you home—"

He shook his head and pulled away from me. He looked down at his sockless feet, stuffed into the old, scuffed shoes. Then he said in a hoarse whisper, "The old man . . . I took his jacket and shoes. How . . ." His lip twitched. "How am I ever going to find him to give them back?"

BY THE TIME OUR UNUSUAL "WORSHIP SERVICE" was over, a table had been set up where Pastor Clark, Major Lewis from the

Salvation Army, and Liz Handley coordinated the matching process, assigning Manna House residents to the homes of various church members. Denny and I agreed to take Precious and her daughter Sabrina. Stu, grinning, said she'd take Estelle. Rochelle and Conny, of course, were already with Avis and Peter, who didn't make it to church that morning. Who could blame them?

I was surprised, though, when the Hickmans agreed to take Margo and her two boys. I pulled her aside. "Flo! You guys don't have to do this. With what you're going through with Chris, don't you guys have enough on your plate?"

"Like nobody else does? Look, girl, we got us an empty bedroom now, don't we? And them two little boys, they don't have *nothin'*. 'Sides, Becky Wallace said they mama could bunk up with her."

I backed off, feeling like I'd just had my mouth washed out with soap.

All the host families were told to remember that Manna House had been a "safe house" for several of these women and our homes needed to function in the same way. "Do not talk publicly with your coworkers or neighbors, even your extended families, about who you are hosting," Rev. Handley said. "Do not take any phone calls for your guests except from Major Lewis, Pastor Clark, or myself. If you have questions, feel free to call me at any time on my cell. One of us will let you know as soon as we have found more permanent shelter for the Manna House residents— hopefully within the week. If you have e-mail, we will send a daily report about our progress."

Josh insisted on taking Edesa home after dropping us off at home. I figured they needed to debrief after the stressful events of the past twelve hours, but he was home sooner than I expected.

He seemed relieved that his sister had already given up her room for Precious and Sabrina, turned down the sandwiches we'd thrown together for lunch, and disappeared into his room.

"I think we all need a nap," Denny said.

I lay beside Denny in the darkened bedroom, feeling awkward with strangers under my roof. I envied Stu and her guest room upstairs, beautifully decorated in muted green and rose. All we had was Amanda's bedroom, which looked like a geometric black-and-yellow puzzle with one thousand loose pieces, though at least I was able to put clean sheets on the double bed.

Today's the last Sunday of January . . . thank goodness Yada Yada isn't meeting on the fourth Sunday anymore! . . . but something was supposed to happen today . . . can't remember what . . . Oh, yeah.

"We didn't take the paper vote."

"*Huh?* What paper vote?" Denny's voice was muffled by his pillow.

"For the church name. We were going to take a paper vote today to narrow it down. Final vote at the next business meeting."

Denny raised his head an inch from the pillow, eyed me with a look that suggested I'd just entered a not-guilty-because-of-insanity plea, and turned over.

I GOT UP AT FIVE, worried that I wouldn't get any sleep that night if I napped too long. Under other circumstances, I would have told my family "you're on your own" for supper, but with two guests, I ransacked the cupboards and threw canned beans, chopped vegetables, a can of tomatoes, and macaroni into a soup pot that was supposed to resemble minestrone.

Precious, dressed in her "new" clothes from the Salvation Army boxes, raved over the soup, as chatty and bubbly as if there'd been no fire the night before. But Sabrina kept her eyes down, stirring the soup with her spoon and mostly nibbling crackers. She cringed warily every time Willie Wonka wandered through the dining room. I finally had to shut the dog in our bedroom.

"Um . . . what grade are you in, Sabrina?" Amanda asked.

"Ninth. But . . ." Sabrina shrugged. "Ain't got no school clothes now. An' don' know how I'd get there."

"Maybe you could wear something of mine." Amanda eyed her enviously. "Though you're smaller than me, lucky you."

Lucky you? I hoped the irony was lost on Sabrina.

"Hey! Let's go shopping tonight." Amanda brightened. "I've got some babysitting money—we could get one outfit at least. If we went to Target or A. J. Wright, anyway." She turned on Denny. "See why I need my license, Dad? Then you wouldn't have to drive us!"

Her father waggled his eyebrows. "You know the drill, kiddo. Finish driver's training, come up with your share of the insurance, *then* you get your license."

"What about youth group tonight?" I asked. "Maybe Sabrina would like to go."

Sabrina shook her head emphatically even before I finished. Amanda rolled her eyes. "Don't sweat it, Mom. Come on, Sabrina. I'll find you something to wear to the store."

Shopping. Huh. Why didn't I think of that? Surely Precious could use some more clothes—underwear, at least. "Precious, do you want to go with—?"

"Nah. Let them two go. Maybe 'nother day." She watched the girls disappear. "She sweet, your Amanda."

"Mm. She can be. Would you like some more soup?"

14

*T*he girls came home with a pair of fashion-faded jeans, bikini underwear, a bra, two clingy tops, and two pairs of socks. Denny pleaded no contest. "Uh, no way was I going to hang around women's intimate apparel."

"Dad got the shoes, though," Amanda said, giving him a hug. She didn't seem the least bothered that she'd just spent all her babysitting cash.

But as it turned out, Precious decided not to send Sabrina to school the next morning until she talked to Rev. Handley about train fare and figured out the route. Couldn't blame her. I'd probably do the same thing in her shoes. Still, I felt uncomfortable going to work the next morning, leaving two strangers in my house all day with only Willie Wonka on duty. And Sabrina still whimpered every time Wonka came within three feet.

Bethune Elementary office was in an uproar when I got to school. All the school computers had been shut down as a precaution against the MyDoom virus, supposedly wreaking havoc on millions of computers nationwide via the Internet. Teachers wanted lesson plans, now locked in the school's digital brain. The office staff wanted the weekly schedule, the lunchroom rotation list, and a flyer for the upcoming Fall Festival. "The Fall Festival isn't even on the Internet!" snapped Ms. Ivy, the chief school secretary.

But Tom Davis, second-grade teacher and the closest the school had to a computer guru, was adamant. "No one gets on a computer until we've blocked the virus."

I called Denny at his office. "Do we have virus protection against this MyDoom 'worm,' or whatever they call it?"

He sighed. "Just don't open any e-mails when you get home. I'll ask Peter what we should do. Or Josh. Maybe he knows."

Sabrina and Precious were both watching afternoon TV when I got home, Wonka zoned at their feet. Guess girl and dog had made their peace. Precious glanced up, then crowed as the contestant failed to win his round. "Girl, I knew that! They should get *me* up on that show!" But when the show ended, she bounced into the kitchen, where I was frowning at the open refrigerator, trying to think what to feed our expanded family. "Miz Estelle came down, said the Stuart lady invited us all upstairs for supper t'night. Nice of her, ain't it?"

Downright nice. I let the refrigerator door close with a sigh of relief.

Stu seemed almost giddy having company. She and Estelle had obviously hit it off big-time, laughing and joking. Josh, however, came upstairs reluctantly and excused himself from Stu's table early, saying he was going to do a search-and-destroy on our computer in case MyDoom was lurking somewhere.

"I think we're clean," he reported when the rest of us trooped downstairs half an hour later. "But I deleted all our incoming e-mails just in case one of them was infected."

"What?" I jerked a thumb at Precious and Sabrina. "Reverend Handley said they were going to keep us updated by e-mail! How are we supposed to know—"

"Mom." Irritation spiked Josh's voice. "These worms aren't pretty. Do you want us to be protected or not?" He stomped off to his room.

Denny and I exchanged glances. Why did I suspect this wasn't just about a computer virus? But I was frustrated too. I'd wanted to send an e-mail to the rest of Yada Yada, to tell them what had happened. Now I was going to have to make calls.

Sabrina had no homework—yet—but Denny hogged the TV for Monday night football, so the fourteen-year-old sprawled on Amanda's bed listening to CDs while Amanda did her calculus. I listened to the decibels shake the windows for two minutes before marching in and handing Sabrina a set of earphones. Amanda would thank me later.

Precious went back upstairs to Stu's apartment to hang out with Estelle while I spread out my February lesson plans on the dining room table. This was my third year at Bethune Elementary, which helped. I could build on my previous syllabus, tweaking as needed: introduce fractions and word problems using measurements in math . . . highlight "Main Idea" and "Fact vs. Opinion" in language arts . . . tackle early Illinois history, Abraham Lincoln, and Black History Month in social studies . . . construct simple machines and focus on home safety in science. Add test-taking skills somewhere—

"Mom?"

I looked up. Josh leaned against the dining room archway in his favorite pair of shredded jeans and a sweatshirt with the sleeves ripped off. His disheveled sandy hair hung over his ears and down his neck. I was beginning to think the bald look he used to sport was better.

"Got a minute?"

"Sure. Time for a tea break. Want some?"

He shook his head. I turned on the tea water and sat back down at the table.

Josh didn't look at me, just sank into a chair and hung one arm over the back. He sighed. "Okay. I deleted all our incoming e-mails, like I said. But . . . I did scan through some of the senders and subject headings. One was from the Manna House director—" He sucked in his breath and let it out. "Calling a meeting this coming Saturday to debrief about the fire."

I nodded. "Makes sense." Huh. I needed a meeting next Saturday like I needed sand in my shoes. "But . . . you didn't open the message."

He shook his head again. "Guess we should call to get the details."

I waited. He said nothing. Just fidgeted with his hands.

I cleared my throat. "So are you going to call, or do you want me to?"

"Oh. . . . Yeah, would you?" More fidgeting.

God, help me here! I'm not sure what's going on.

The Voice in my spirit said, *Just ask him, Jodi. He came to you. That was an invitation.*

I reached out and laid a hand on his. "Josh, what's going on? It's natural to feel upset after a fire like that. *I'm* upset! Everybody is. Just give yourself some time . . ."

He pulled his hands away, jaw muscles working. "It's—it's not that."

Oh, great, Jodi. You not only asked, you supplied your own answer. This time I kept my mouth shut.

Finally he sighed. "I don't want to go to that meeting Saturday. Because everyone wants to know what happened. And you and I"—he finally looked at me, eyes tortured—"we both know how that fire started. Mikey and Jeremy, they begged and begged me to keep the tree lights on one more time. So I gave in. And then . . ." His head sagged into his hands. "I forgot to turn them off. That fire's my fault, Mom. *My fault!*"

Josh's shoulders began to shake.

"Oh, Josh." My heart squeezed so hard I could hardly breathe. I got up and put my arms around my son. "Don't . . . don't cry. It's all right. Nobody's blaming you."

He jerked out of my embrace, nearly vaulting out of his chair. "That's not true! *Edesa* blames me. I can see it in her eyes! And she won't talk to me." With that, Josh strode out of the room and slammed his bedroom door.

I TOLD DENNY ABOUT MY TALK with Josh. He frowned. "I'll talk with him." But it wasn't easy. Josh left early for work, worked late, went out in the evening, or stayed holed up in his room. Not to mention that with two extra people in the house, juggling our schedules took extra energy and time.

Denny drove Precious and Sabrina to the Morse Avenue el station early the next morning so Sabrina could get to school on time. Had to hand it to Precious, who decided to take Sabrina and pick her up each day from school until they got resettled, rather than leave her daughter to navigate the new route on her own.

As for Yada Yada, I was sure Edesa would have called Delores first thing. But I finally managed to call Chanda to tell her about the fire, and she promised to call Adele and Yo-Yo. "Why you wait t'ree days to call mi?" Chanda scolded. But she seemed pleased that I called her first and asked her to call the others.

I called Ruth myself. Had to check on the twins, anyway.

"*Oy! Oy!* I read about that fire in the paper!" Ruth said. "An abandoned church, the paper said. Or maybe they said it no longer had a congregation. But they didn't mention Manna House. Rochelle and her little boy are okay? No one was hurt? Praise to Jehovah-Rohi, the Good Shepherd! You were there, Jodi? Gray hair it would give me! You need something to help you lighten up. Come to our party on Saturday."

She actually left space for me to speak. "Uh, what party, Ruth?"

"The twins' birthday party! They're two months old this week. Ben says, why wait a whole year to celebrate? Every month they change so much. Did you know, Jodi, that babies change more in the first year than—"

"Uh, sorry Ruth. I have to go to a meeting on Saturday. The volunteers and staff of Manna House."

"A meeting? Why? You were there two minutes, the place burns down, end of story. Come on, come to the party. You should see Havah lift her head, straight up on her arms. Like a gymnast she is!"

End of story . . . I wished. I hadn't even finished my volunteer training, so what did I have to contribute? I sighed. "I'd love to, Ruth. But I was there when the shelter burned down, so I better go."

STU POPPED IN Thursday night while Denny and I were doing dishes, looked into the dining room to make sure no one else was about, then leaned against the counter. "I'm thinking of asking Estelle to stay, to be my roommate. Housemate. Whatever." She liberated a cookie from the cookie jar. "Whaddya think?"

I stared at her. "Are you sure, Stu? It's only been a couple of months since Becky moved out. Weren't you looking for some peace and quiet?"

She nibbled on the cookie. "Yeah. But . . . I miss the company. Miss having someone there when I get home." She looked at Denny. "What do you think, Big Guy?"

He frowned. "How well do you know Estelle? I mean, she's been living in a shelter for some reason. No money. No job. Will you be giving her a free ride? How can she pay her share of the expenses?"

Stu rolled her eyes. "How well did I know Becky Wallace? At least Estelle never robbed me, isn't a drug addict, and isn't under house arrest. So far, we've hit it off great. She's got a great sense of humor. Like living with an older sister or favorite aunt."

"Sounds like you've made up your mind." I knew that sounded tart, so I softened. "Just give yourself a little time before committing yourself, Stu. Maybe invite her to stay for a few weeks as your guest, you know, to give her a breather from living in a shelter. You can decide to invite her longer if it works out."

"Huh. Now *that's* a good idea. Glad I talked to you guys . . . Oh, your phone's ringing." Stu bopped out the back door as quickly as she'd come.

The answering machine had kicked in by the time I found the cordless phone tucked between the couch cushions in the living room, where Precious and Sabrina were watching sitcoms on TV. "We're here! . . . Oh, hello, Reverend Handley. . . . Yes, she's here."

I handed the phone to Precious and headed back to the kitchen, but not before I heard her say, "Yeah, okay . . . That's good, I guess." A few minutes later, she showed up in the kitchen doorway. "Uh, Reverend Handley says Salvation Army has room in they shelter for Sabrina an' me, if y'all can take us down there Saturday morning." She shrugged. "Or we can take the el if that's too much trouble. We ain't got that much stuff."

"No trouble. Be glad to take you." Denny smiled as he turned on the dishwasher. "Glad something is getting worked out. Sabrina will be closer to school too."

"Yeah." Precious leaned against the kitchen doorjamb. "It's been nice here, y'all. Real nice. Someday me an' my girl gonna have a nice apartment like this. Just gotta get me a job, save up some money." She started to go, then turned back with a wry smile. "Heard Estelle might be stayin'. Lucky Estelle." And then she was gone.

I looked at Denny. Had Precious been hoping we'd let her stay permanently? Impossible. Completely impossible!

15

Chicago got a dump of snow that Thursday—an accumulation of five inches. My third graders wanted to build more snowmen. I rolled my eyes. "You're on your own, kiddos." A few diehards charged bravely into the playground at lunchtime, but they were back in five minutes. The high that day was only ten degrees above zero. Add the wind off the lake and it felt like tiny ice picks hammering away at your face.

Josh emerged from his hole Saturday morning to say he'd drive Precious and Sabrina to the Salvation Army shelter. Amanda also wanted to go along. We packed up as many warm clothes, boots, jackets, and blankets as we could find to fit the mother and daughter, using Pastor Cobbs's John-the-Baptist guideline: "If you have two coats, share with the one who has none." But our guests looked so forlorn as we hugged them good-bye that guilt nibbled away my smile. *Just washing your hands of it, aren't you, Jodi? You're glad they're gone. Now maybe things can get back to normal. But how would you like to be heading to a shelter with your teenage daughter for who knows how long?*

I stood in the kitchen long after the minivan disappeared down our icy alley. It was true. I felt relieved that they were gone. The week had gone smoothly enough, but it had been taxing having two extra people in the house—people whose life situation was so starkly different from ours. Homeless. Poor—no, not poor. *Destitute.* No relatives in Chicago to take them in. Sabrina's father had abandoned them long ago. Since then it had been hand to mouth, shelter to SRO "by the week," back to a shelter. Then the fire, wiping out everything but the clothes on their backs. Literally. Now another shelter.

Should we have invited them to stay, like Stu invited Estelle? Wait. Here I was wrestling with those questions in good old Jodi fashion. Stewing. Going around and around. I needed to pray. Didn't the Bible say we could ask God for wisdom?

I heard Denny turn on the shower; now was not a good time to wash the sheets from the "guest bed" anyway. Willie Wonka followed me stiffly as I grabbed my Bible and another cup of coffee, and settled into the peace and quiet of the living room. I reread the scriptures Pastor Cobbs had mentioned on Sunday morning: Luke 3:9–11; Romans 12:13; Matthew 25:40. Definitely stretched my comfort zone, but Scripture was clear: we needed to not just be "concerned" about the poor but give practical help. *Okay, Lord, what are You saying here?* I really didn't want to put it into words, but I gulped and prayed: *Were we supposed to ask Precious and Sabrina to stay?*

The Voice in my spirit seemed to speak right up. *Why are you assuming you have to fix it for Precious and Sabrina all by yourself, Jodi? You did what was needed: you gave them a place to stay until another could be found. You gave them food and clothing.*

Huh. Was that the Holy Spirit speaking to me, or just wishful thinking?

I know. But look at Stu. She's going the extra mile, asking Estelle to stay.

The Voice continued, *So? Are you Stu? Do you have room in your home for another grown woman and her almost grown teenager for the long haul?*

Well, no. Amanda had had to sleep on the couch all week. She was a good sport about it, but it wasn't a permanent solution.

Guilt isn't helpful, Jodi. Neither is overresponsibility. But that doesn't mean there isn't more you can do. Look for the possibilities, My daughter. And ask for My direction. Because My yoke is easy, and My burden is light.

"Jodi?" Denny poked his head into the living room, swathed in knit hat, long scarf, and several sweatshirt layers. "I think I'll jog over to the Hickmans'. Been wanting to talk to Carl about something. Give me some exercise too. Oh—when's your meeting?"

"One o'clock. At the church. Josh promised he'd be back in time to pick me up. I think he's going to pick up Edesa first while he's down that way. Isn't it too icy out there to jog?"

"I'll be fine." He came into the room, bent down, and kissed me on the lips. He smelled good. Irish Spring good. "Just one thing, Jodi. Don't feel like you have to take the world on your shoulders, just because this situation with Manna House presents a lot of needs. Whatever they ask you today, it's okay to think about it. Take time to pray about it. Talk about it with me. Okay? Promise?"

I nodded sheepishly. "Thanks. I needed that."

"What? The kiss or the lecture?"

I grabbed his shirt and pulled him closer, kissing him back. "Both. Believe me."

THE MANNA HOUSE MEETING started at one and ended at three. To my surprise, the group was small—just Rev. Handley and the other staff person, an African-American woman named Mabel, who served part time as office manager, resident coordinator, and volunteer organizer, plus the four volunteers who had been there that night: Josh, Edesa, Karen, and myself. I thought all the volunteers would be there to get hyped up about "what next."

The fire marshal showed up to report on the inspection. The fire had started in the basement, probably an electrical short, intensified, of course, by the dry Christmas tree. Josh kept his eyes down, his face pale. "But it was a fire waiting to happen," the fire marshal added, "Christmas tree or no Christmas tree. The wiring in that old building should have been totally replaced before getting a permit to use it as a shelter." He glared pointedly at Rev. Handley. "I'm not saying anything illegal happened here, but we are investigating who did the safety inspection for your permit and whether city negligence is an issue."

Rev. Handley nodded, visibly upset.

The verbal reports we had each given the night of the fire had been typed up. The marshal asked us to read them over and sign our names if we stood by our reports. I was afraid Josh would scrawl over his, *"It's all my fault!"* But like the rest of us, he read his report tersely, then signed.

The fire marshal stood up to leave. "You people are trying to do a good thing here. But if you manage to get a building and start up again, now you have a chance to do it right. That's what I want to say to you. No shortcuts. *Always* put safety first." He solemnly shook hands all around, then headed for his official car, parked like a red cherry in the snowy parking lot.

We all just looked at each other. Rev. Handley finally cleared her throat. "Well. Mabel and I will be meeting with the board to discuss the future of Manna House—or even if we have one. Right now, however, I want to commend each one of you volunteers for responding quickly and responsibly during the emergency. I've talked to all the residents, and they have nothing but praise for you four helping to get them all out of the building. Josh, I especially want to thank you for taking charge—"

"That's right!" I wanted to cry out. *"He did!"* But Josh was shaking his head miserably. I bit my lip, my throat tight, knowing my son was in pain.

Rev. Handley pursed her lips thoughtfully. "Son, I know you're beating yourself up because you turned on the Christmas tree lights that night. But all of us—myself included—knew that tree was nothing but dry kindling. We let cozy feelings—trying to create a homey atmosphere for Manna House residents—override our responsibility to put safety first. And you heard the marshal. All the electrical wiring was compromised. As director of Manna House, I take full responsibility for what happened."

I stared at the short, stocky woman with the salt-and-pepper cropped hair and wire-rimmed glasses. Admiration for her eased the tightness in my throat. She could so easily have dumped blame on someone else . . . on my son. She'd only been there briefly that night; wasn't anywhere around when the fire started. But she took responsibility without mincing around. *Huh. If only more leaders displayed that kind of leadership* . . .

Liz Handley sucked in a deep breath, hands on her knees. "We've learned something the hard way. But God in His mercy protected all lives . . ." The director seemed to have a hard time getting any more out.

"*Sí*. That is what is important." Edesa leaned over and gently touched the director's hand. "I think we should pray and thank our heavenly Father for His mercy." She didn't wait for confirmation but moved right into earnest prayer. "*Oh Dios, nuestro Padre, gracias por su misericordia!* . . ."

"YOU DIDN'T TALK ABOUT the future of Manna House? Nobody asked you to do anything?" Denny couldn't hide his surprise.

I shook my head. "That's all it was—a debriefing after the fire. Reverend Handley reported that all the residents have been moved to other shelters—except for a few, like Rochelle and Estelle, who are staying put—and then we just prayed for them all." I fished a sheet of paper out of my jeans pocket. "I asked for the list so I could continue to pray for them all. By name." I grinned at him impishly. "Didn't think I needed to talk to you or pray about praying."

Denny scratched his chin. "Uh-huh. Well then, guess I don't have to ask *you* if it's okay if I invite all the guys over here tomorrow afternoon for the Super Bowl. Twenty or thirty is all—"

"What?" I snatched a dishtowel and flipped him good. "You didn't!"

He threw up both hands. "Hey! Just kidding! Carl Hickman

and I both nixed our homes; our TVs aren't big enough. We're asking Mark Smith. They've got one of those monster screens in their family room."

"Wait just a cotton-pickin' minute." I opened the cupboard door where I kept the Yada Yada list. Tomorrow was February first. Super Bowl Sunday. *And* Yada Yada was supposed to meet . . . where? I ran my finger down the list.

Adele. Perfect. At least she didn't have a sports fanatic hogging the living room or hollow-leg teenagers emptying the food cupboards on Super Bowl Sunday like most of the rest of us.

RUTH AND YO-YO STRUGGLED out of the Garfields' big green Buick in front of Adele's apartment building, each one lugging a baby carrier, just as Stu and I parked across the street. "Where's Ben? Doesn't he usually drop you off?" I asked as we huddled in the small entryway of the apartment building, waiting for Adele to buzz us in.

Ruth rolled her eyes. "Does he usually let me drive? Never. But today, drop *him* off at the Sisulu-Smiths early, he says. Huh. Doesn't want to miss even one Super Bowl commercial, that's what."

"He was going to teach *me* to drive so I could get my license," Yo-Yo grumbled. "But that was B.B."

I started to ask what "B.B." meant, but I figured it out: *Before Babies.*

We had a good turnout that night, in spite of chilly temperatures. February had shuffled in like a hobo in dirty clothes—no exciting snowstorm, no cleansing thaw, just leftover piles of dirty snow along the plowed streets. I thought Stu might bring Estelle, but she said Estelle was busy sewing up some new clothes for herself from material Stu once bought but had never done anything with.

Rochelle didn't come with Avis either. Avis wasn't happy about leaving her and Conny alone on a weekend. "What if Dexter finds out where she is now? But Peter took himself off to the Super Bowl Bash at Nony's house, so someone had to stay with Conny. Rochelle said she'd love a quiet evening alone anyway." Avis shrugged. Seemed to me Avis's usually joyous face had a permanently strained look these days.

After the traumatic events of last weekend, it felt good to see my Yada Yada sisters chirping away like sparrows on a telephone wire. We teased Nony about leaving her lovely home at the mercy of the guys. She rolled her eyes and laughed. "I know, I know. But Mark was so excited, we managed to get rid of anything on the first floor that said 'Convalescent Lives Here.'"

But even as we attacked the banana bread Adele brought out right from the oven and passed the babies around, fussing over them like blithering idiots, something seemed amiss. Was someone missing? I counted noses, stopping at Edesa. It occurred to me that Josh had taken her home after the meeting yesterday and had *not* come right home. What was going on with those two? Well, that was neither here nor there right now. I finished going around the circle. All present and accounted for. *So what . . . ?* And then I realized what it was.

MaDear's wheelchair was empty.

16

*A*dele? Where's MaDear? Did your sister take her for the weekend?" Immediately heads turned, and the chatting and munching hushed to a whisper. Adele snorted. "My sister? That hussy? Don't know what's gotten into that girl! Sissy's so busy huntin' for a man, she's likely to forget MaDear's at her place and go dancin' all night." She jerked a thumb toward the small bedroom in the back. "Got MaDear in the bed. She's still gettin' over that pneumonia, you know. But don't know what I'm gonna do, y'all. I can't leave her here by herself all day. Gotta get her up an' take her to the shop." Adele sank into a chair and sighed from deep inside, like a slow leak in a truck tire. "Might have to put her in a nursing home. Hate to do it, though. My people take care of their own."

"Girl, I know what you sayin'," Flo agreed. "Just don't seem right, how we treat our elders these days. But I hear ya. Ya gotta do what ya gotta do."

Delores spoke up. "*Si.* But maybe we should pray that God would provide another way for Adele and MaDear."

Avis smiled. "Sounds like we're ready to begin our prayer time. Why don't we worship the Lord for a few minutes, get our focus right, before we gather up our other prayer concerns." She followed her own suggestion and led out with a familiar hymn . . .

> *My hope is built on nothing less*
> *Than Jesus' blood and righteousness!*
> *I dare not trust the sweetest frame,*
> *But wholly lean on Jesus' name.*

Even Becky and Yo-Yo, who didn't seem to know the words to the verse, picked up on the chorus:

> *On Christ the solid Rock I stand!*
> *All other ground is sinking sand;*
> *All other ground is sinking sand.*

We helped each other through the next few verses and heartily sang the chorus once more, followed by some spontaneous praise. "Thank ya, Jesus!—for being my Rock in the middle of this storm!" "*Sí! Sí! Dios,* You are the anchor we cling to." "Yeah. Thanks, Jesus, for keepin' me from drownin' in my own mess."

Some quarterback must have made a touchdown at Reliant Stadium in Houston just then, because people in the apartment above Adele started yelling and stomping their feet. "Or maybe they tryin' to drown *us* out," Becky smirked. We laughed.

Most of the prayer requests that night were updates on ongoing concerns. The Manna House fire and displaced residents . . . a second hearing coming up for Chris Hickman . . . Ricardo

Enriques still looking for a job . . . Becky groaning about the "loop-de-loops" DCFS was putting her through to regain custody of Little Andy . . . whether Stu should ask Estelle to be her housemate . . .

"Avis," Nony cut in, two furrows gathered between her brows. "What about your daughter? You are not sending her back to a shelter, are you? I am very concerned about Rochelle. This is a critical time for her, and the fire is one more trauma on top of everything else."

Avis shook her head. "Rochelle and Conny are going to stay with us for the indefinite future. In fact, Peter says he was wrong to send her away when she needed us most." She let slip a wry smile. "Kind of nice to see him grovel."

We all laughed again, even harder this time. How many of us had squirmed uncomfortably when Peter put his foot down but kept our mouths shut, not wanting to create more tension in Avis's new marriage?

A loud wail from one of the baby carriers joined the laughter. "Awake she is now," Ruth pouted. "Yo-Yo, see if Havah will fall back asleep if you walk her."

Yo-Yo didn't move. "Walk her yourself," she muttered.

My mouth nearly fell open. Ruth glared at Yo-Yo, but unbuckled the baby from the carrier and headed for Adele's hallway, murmuring, "Shh, shh, *mamela*. Don't pay any attention to that *nebbish*."

Avis did not seem to notice the interruption. "There is one piece of good news, sisters. The HIV clinic tested Conny, too, but"—her voice dropped to a choked whisper—"praise God! His test came back negative. We are so grateful!"

"Thank ya, *Jesus!*" Florida cried. Others joined in the praise while some looked shocked, as though they hadn't even considered that possibility.

When the room quieted, Nony leaned forward. "Avis, do you think Rochelle would be comfortable talking with me? I would very much like to help her get the help she needs to live with her HIV diagnosis. It is not hopeless, you know. But . . ."

"Thank you, Nony. I—I would appreciate that very much. Let me talk to her." Avis looked at her lap, absently twisting her wedding ring. "In fact, I think all three of us need some help to live with this diagnosis."

In the silence that followed, the only sound was Ruth jouncing the baby over her shoulder and muttering who-knows-what in Havah's tiny ear.

"Well." Avis raised her head and looked around, back to business. "Have we heard from everyone? Hoshi. You've been very quiet tonight. Is everything all right? How is your new semester going?"

Hoshi nodded, her straight hair falling like black silk over her shoulder. "It is very good. But hard. This is my last semester at Northwestern, you know."

Her last semester! How had that snuck up on us? I felt a sudden pang. Would Hoshi go back to Japan after graduation? Would Yada Yada lose her? And what would the Sisulu-Smith family do without her? She had been an incredible help to them during the difficult time of Mark's injury and convalescence.

" . . . but most of all, I would like prayer for Sara," she was saying.

My attention snapped back. Sara. "The girl in the sundress" who had caught my eye at the racist rally at Northwestern last spring, part of the White Pride group. The girl God had prodded me to pray for, even before I knew her name. The girl who had defied her racist friends and named the men who had attacked Mark Smith and left him for dead. The girl Hoshi had unknowingly befriended at Northwestern and brought to a Yada Yada meeting at the Sisulu-Smith home one night last fall, tearing the peace of that home to shreds and smashing the fragile friendship between the gentle Japanese student and the mixed-up white girl from Chicago's North Shore.

We all leaned forward. Even Ruth stopped jouncing the baby and tuned an ear.

"Sara transferred out of my history class, so I do not see her as often. But our walkways keep crossing anyway." Hoshi smiled. "Nony calls them 'divine appointments.'"

"Hallelujah, Jesus," Nony murmured.

"We had coffee at the student center last week, and I invited her once more to Yada Yada, at a different home this time. But . . ." Hoshi shook her head. "I do not think she will agree."

This was met with sympathetic murmurings. "Well, girl, you tried," Florida said.

"Yeah," Yo-Yo chimed in from her perch on a floor pillow. "That girl's a hard case. Maybe harder than me."

Hoshi's volume hiked up a notch or two. "I do not agree. It is not time to give up on Sara. Why has God put her in our way if He does not want to show her how much He loves her? Haven't we often said, 'God's ways are not our ways'?"

Whoa. Hoshi had some backbone!

Hoshi's voice softened. "I . . . there is a Christian student group on campus. I am going to ask Sara if she would like to attend. They share a meal together, then have a Bible study and discussion. She may say yes if I go with her. She's very lonely."

Delores Enriques patted Hoshi's hand. "We will pray that she will go with you."

Hoshi lowered her lashes. "There is only one thing. It meets on Sunday evenings."

"SUNDAY EVENINGS?" I groused to Stu as we walked from the garage to our back porch. Stu's lights were on upstairs, but my house was dark. "Do you think Hoshi will start going to this campus group rather than coming to Yada Yada?"

"Possibility, I guess." But I could tell Stu was distracted. "Adele said she has to take MaDear to the beauty shop with her, even when she's sick. But, you know, I wonder . . ." She ran up the back stairs and I heard her call out, "Estelle? How's the sewing going?" before the door shut.

I unlocked our door. Wonka rose stiffly from his post just inside the door to greet me, snuffling. Otherwise, the house was silent. So Amanda wasn't back yet from youth group. But surely the Super Bowl was over. Maybe Denny and Josh were giving rides home to some of the other guys.

I suddenly had an inkling of how Stu felt coming home every night to a dark house.

I shed my jacket and turned on the flame under the teakettle. Wonka just stood in the kitchen, whining faintly.

"What's the matter, Wonka? Want to go out?" But the dog was facing me, not the door. "Hungry?" I looked in the dog's bowl. Still full of kibbles. Hadn't been touched. How strange was that? "Just lonely, huh?" I scratched the dog's ears. "You don't like it when we all leave the house, do you?"

I glanced at the clock. Still had a couple of hours before bed. I should probably finish my lesson plans. February was Black History Month. I already had my class reading books about Mary McLeod Bethune, the inspiring African-American teacher our school was named after. But I felt weighted down by all the concerns we were carrying in Yada Yada. *MaDear's illness . . . Chris Hickman locked up at the JDC . . . Rochelle needing to "live with HIV," as Nony put it . . .*

I knew we were supposed to take our burdens to God and leave them there. But I still felt like I had sand in my gears. Maybe it was just the winter blues. While we had been sending up desperate prayers for our loved ones that evening, the guys had probably been laughing, cracking jokes, and yelling at their Super Bowl bash. Plain old fun.

That's what we Yadas needed! Some good old-fashioned *fun.*

I looked at the calendar in the kitchen, ignoring the whistle of the teakettle. Our next meeting in two weeks would meet upstairs at Stu's place. That Saturday was Valentine's Day . . . and the following Monday was a school holiday: President's Day. We should do something fun that weekend! Something everyone could do, not just the "couples" on Valentine's Day. But what? Something like . . .

I grinned. *That's it!*

"Wonka, old buddy," I said, as I plonked myself down in front of the computer and booted it up, "it's too bad you have four feet, because I don't think they make roller skates for dogs." A few minutes later, I was typing furiously.

To: Yada Yada
From: BaxterBears@wahoo.com
Re: A Roller Party

Sisters! Anybody up for some FUN in the midst of all
the serious stuff life throws at us? How about a roller-
skating party on Valentine's Day! That's a Saturday.
Bring the kids! Bring a friend! (Hoshi? Do you think
Sara might come?) Oh, yeah. We might even let the
guys come if they behave themselves and don't act like
a bunch of adolescent showoffs. So . . . what do you
think?

Love, Jodi

ALL THREE OF MY FAMILY MEMBERS looked at each other as
though sharing a terrible secret: Mom had gone completely off her
rocker. Denny backpedaled. "Uh, Jodi. It's been twenty years
since—"

"It's like riding a bike. You never forget!"

Amanda rolled her eyes. *"Kids* go roller skating, not . . . not *old*
people." She flounced off to her room.

"Watch it, kid. I could skate circles around you!" Denny called
after her.

Oh, so Denny was on my side now?

Josh shrugged noncommittally and hauled out the city phone
book. "Mom? You got a number for the Salvation Army?"

So much for roller-skating. "Uh, think I do." I flipped through our address book. "Who're you calling?" *None of my business, but so what?*

"Precious. She's gotta be bummed."

"What? You mean . . .?" Guilt over letting Precious and Sabrina go to the Salvation Army shelter popped up again and danced like a gremlin on my conscience.

"I *mean*"—Josh grinned wickedly—"the Carolina Panthers lost to the Patriots 29 to 32 tonight. I'm calling to rub it in."

THE FIRST WEEK OF FEBRUARY slogged its way across the city, with snow flurries upping the snow cover to about seven inches. At least it blanketed the dirt-encrusted ice clumps that made walking as treacherous as downhill skiing. Still dangerous, but not so ugly. One out of two wasn't bad. But I felt like a triathlon athlete every time I made it to and from school with no broken bones.

A couple of days in a row, I saw Estelle leaving with Stu in the morning. On the third day, I poked my head out the back door. "What's up with you two? Estelle going to work with you?"

Stu laughed. "Better than that! Estelle is taking care of MaDear at home so Adele doesn't have to take her to the shop."

Estelle, bundled against the cold, smiled big. "Ain't the Lord good? That MaDear is the sweetest thing. And Ms. Skuggs is paying me, too, so I can contribute to my room and board while I'm here."

I wouldn't have called forgetful, feisty MaDear "the sweetest thing," but I whooped, "Hallelujah!" anyway. "What a great idea! I'm so glad for Adele—and you, too, Estelle. Keep warm!" I quickly shut the door against the frigid air, then pulled it open again. "Stu! Did you get my e-mail about the roller-skating party?"

"Count me in!" she yelled back.

"Count me out!" laughed Estelle.

But as the week wore on, I got several more positive responses to the roller-skating party idea. Florida said she was game, also Cedric and Carla, but she couldn't vouch for Carl. Chanda and her tribe said they'd come, so did Becky, Yo-Yo, and Edesa. Delores said it depended on her work schedule, but she knew Ricardo had a gig that night. Well, that was a good start, so I Googled a list of roller rinks in the Chicago area and started making calls to find the closest rink. It didn't matter if everyone got on board. The rest of us could have fun.

But I was worried about Willie Wonka. I fed him in the morning as usual before leaving for school, but more often than not, when I came home from school, the bowl of kibbles had barely been touched.

"What's the matter, old boy?" I murmured, sitting down on the floor beside him and stroking his silky brown head. But all he did was lay his muzzle in my lap and look up at me with dark liquid eyes, whimpering softly.

17

*D*enny?" I said, wandering into the living room Friday night after Amanda had gone out babysitting. "I think we need to take Willie Wonka to the vet. He hasn't been eating, and he's been whimpering a lot. But I don't know what's wrong."

Denny put down the sports section. "I think he's just getting old, Jodi. What is he now—fifteen? sixteen? We got him when Amanda was still floor-scooting, mopping up dust bunnies better than Dial-a-Maid."

"Yeah. What were we *thinking*?" I sank down on the couch beside my husband. "A puppy and a baby—it was like having twins! Guess we can empathize with Ben and Ruth, huh?"

He chortled. "Yeah. Except both of their twins poop in diapers, not on the kitchen floor!"

We both started to laugh, remembering our attempts to house-break a two-month-old Lab—but the next moment I was feeling teary. "Amanda's grown up with Willie Wonka. Don't know what she'll do if he . . . if he . . ."

"Hey, we don't need to go there yet, babe. See what the vet says! Look at your mom. She's got arthritis and had a bad bout of pneumonia last year, but she's still chugging along."

Oh, great. Thanks, Denny. That's real helpful.

But I tried to be matter-of-fact when we loaded Willie Wonka into the back of the Dodge Caravan for the trip to the vet the next morning. "He's probably just getting old," I told Amanda when she got up that morning. "But we should let the vet check him out."

Amanda climbed into the back with the dog, crooning, "Poor baby. You don't feel so good? Don't worry. The doctor's going to make it all better. That's right. Don't be scared, Amanda's here . . ."

I gripped the steering wheel and headed for the animal hospital on McCormick Boulevard. I hardly knew how to pray. Dogs and people . . . we all had to die sometime. *But we're not ready to let Wonka go, God! Please let it be something the vet can fix.* I hated my next thought: *How much is this going to cost?* We barely had enough medical insurance to cover our family, much less the dog.

But maybe Denny was right. Wonka had been healthy up until now, except for going deaf and his joints getting stiff. We'd just have to see what the vet said.

"THE VET THINKS IT'S *CANCER*?" Denny's jaw dropped when I gave him the news.

"Might be cancer." I peeked down the hall, where Amanda had headed with the dog, and saw that her bedroom door was shut. I sank into a chair at the dining room table and wrapped my hands around the steaming cup of coffee Denny had poured. "He's got a growth in his abdomen about the size of a tennis ball. She can't

know if it's benign or malignant unless they do a biopsy and run a bunch of tests."

"And these tests—?"

I sighed. "Expensive. And if we want the tumor removed, well, they *could* do surgery. But . . ."

Denny's face sagged. "Yeah, I know. Mega bucks."

We sat at the dining room table in silence for several minutes, letting our coffee get cold. *Sheesh.* Made me mad that "what it cost" was even a consideration, if that's what Wonka needed! But God knew we didn't have a couple thousand dollars just sitting in the bank. Even Denny's raise barely covered cost of living increases.

Denny sighed. "So what did the vet recommend?"

I took a sip of the now-lukewarm coffee and made a face. "Well, I kinda expected her to push for the biopsy and then surgery if the tumor is malignant. That's how she makes her living, for Pete's sake! But she didn't really. Said it was a toss-up at Wonka's age. And surgery is, well, *surgery.* Always a risk. It's up to us, of course, she said. But I kinda got the feeling she thought making him comfortable and not doing anything drastic was a decent way to go. In fact . . ." I dug around in the tote bag I'd tossed on the table and pulled out a couple of pill containers. "She gave me some sample meds that will help with his arthritis pain. Also, something"—I squinted at the label of another bottle—"to help him digest his food easily. She recommended we give him a small amount of canned food twice a day rather than the dry kibbles, see if that helps." I shrugged. "She wrote a prescription for the meds and put it with his chart. She said we could take a few days to think about it and let her know."

Denny nodded, rubbing the back of his head. Proof positive he didn't know what to do. "Okay. Let's give it a few days." He pushed back his chair. "Want me to run to the store and get some canned dog food?"

I let slip a grin. "Sure. And while you're at it . . ." I handed him the grocery list I'd made out while sitting in the waiting room, surrounded by meowing cats in plastic carriers and dogs so nervous they were shedding all over me.

THE PHONE RANG THE NEXT MORNING while we were doing our usual Baxter hurry-scurry, trying to get out of the house in time to make it to church by ten o'clock. The caller ID said Chanda George. "Hey, Chanda, what's up?"

"So when you going to invite mi to dat new church?" she sniffed over the phone. "You got som'ting special coming up? Men's and Women's Day? Pastor's anniversary? Why you not let mi know?"

"Uh, if that's part of New Morning's traditions, I haven't heard about it yet. We're still trying to decide on a name! But if . . . wait a minute. Why don't you just come to visit today? It's the second Sunday of the month, and we have a potluck after service. That'd be fun to have you there. Except, we're having a business meeting after the potluck. It's like the Chicago Marathon: only the strong survive!" I snickered. "But don't worry. You can duck out at that point."

"*Dis day?* But you said *potluck.* Anyting I cook take at least half a day."

"Just come, Chanda. I'm bringing a taco salad—plenty for you too. Besides, they don't expect guests to bring food. It'll be fun to see the kids."

"Mm." She considered. "What dey wear to dat church? Maybe mi have to shop first."

I laughed, remembering the parade of hats at Paul and Silas Apostolic Baptist, where Chanda, Adele Skuggs, and MaDear were members. "Believe me, Chanda. *Anything* you have in your closet will be fine."

Well, almost anything. Chanda showed up at our shopping center sanctuary in a long red wool coat with a fur collar—probably real—and a fur-trimmed red hat. Underneath she wore a red wool suit, the skirt above the knees and tight around her ample hips, and black, high-heeled boots.

"Wow," I said, and turned my attention to Dia and Cheree, cute as catalog cherubs in matching taffeta frilly dresses, lacy ankle socks, and patent leather Mary Janes. Both of them clung shyly to their mother's hands while twelve-year-old Tom trailed behind, running a finger around his stiff shirt collar and tie. But when the children saw kids they knew—Cedric and Carla Hickman, Marcus and Michael Sisulu-Smith, and Little Andy Wallace—it didn't take long until they were running around with the rest of the rat pack.

As the praise band warmed up and we all found our seats on the folding chairs, I noticed Dia cuddling with Amanda, reaching up and twisting Amanda's butterscotch hair into little ringlets, coaxing a smile out of my teenager. I smiled too. I'd practically had to drag Amanda to church this morning; she'd wanted to stay with Willie Wonka. "He *needs* me, Mom!" But when he ate half the soft canned food we'd put in his dish that morning, I assured her he would be fine without her for a couple of hours.

We didn't have a choir swaying down the aisle like Paul and

Silas Apostolic Baptist did. Our preachers didn't wear black robes with Afro-centric stoles. We didn't have cushioned pews. But Chanda seemed to enjoy herself, throwing herself into the praise and worship as though she felt right at home. At one point, she leaned over to me and whispered, "Ooo, dat saxophone player is *fine.*" I wasn't sure if she meant his music, or if she noticed that he was young, good-looking, and dressed smart. "What dat mon's name? He from de islands. Uh-huh. Mi know it."

I had to admit I didn't know his name, but said I'd find out.

Pastor Clark preached that day. Well, "teached." I'd kind of hoped Pastor Cobbs would preach today, since his style would be closer to what Chanda was used to. But as Pastor Clark taught from the life of David, about how God prepared him to be a powerful warrior and a worshiper while he was still a nobody, out in the fields by himself, watching his father's sheep, Chanda nodded and called out, "Amen! Dat's right, Preacher." Young David, Pastor Clark pointed out, killed a lion and a bear when they threatened his sheep, never knowing that God was preparing him to slay giants. He learned to play the lute and sang praises to God when no one was watching, unaware that God was preparing him to soothe the king when he was troubled by evil spirits, and to write psalms that still inspire and comfort us today.

"What about you?" Pastor Clark said, looking around the room. "How is God preparing you in the situation you're in right now, because He has a bigger job for you down the road? Are you being faithful? Using your gifts *now*?"

Chanda leaned toward me again. "Now dat's some good teaching. But dese chairs . . . uh-uh. Dey *killing* my bottom."

I stifled a giggle. "Stu's started a Chair Fund. But it might be awhile."

Immediately after the service, tables were set up and I lost track of Chanda while helping to set out the food—the usual array of rice and beans, fried chicken, potato salad, greens, oxtails, macaroni and cheese, and my taco salad with lettuce, spiced hamburger, chopped tomatoes, onions, cheese, black olives, and crushed tortilla chips on top. The teenagers scarfed that up.

I looked around for Chanda, to be sure she and the kids got food, and saw her talking to the saxophone player. "His name is Oscar Frost," she smirked at me a few minutes later. "De mon has family in Kingston, like mi. Now what you tink about dat?"

Well, at least now I knew his name.

Chanda and kids scooted when the tables were pushed back and chairs lined up for the business meeting. "Mi coming back, dat for sure," she giggled suggestively, pulling the fur-trimmed red hat firmly down on her braided head. "You let mi know when dis church get itself some new chairs."

Pastor Cobbs called the business meeting to order and asked for the minutes from the last meeting to be read. Debra Meeks stood up with a notebook and read the items that had been approved: *Pastor Joe Cobbs and Pastor Hubert Clark to be copastors of the merger of Uptown Community Church and New Morning Christian Church . . . The combined elders from both churches would continue to serve for one year, half serving the first six months, the other half serving the following six months, with a new election in one year . . . However, Mark Smith had withdrawn from the elder board for medical reasons . . . The worship band would incorporate musicians from both churches . . . Current worship leaders would rotate for the next six months, then form new worship teams . . .*

Debra looked up. "Last item of business: Names for the church were still being accepted. We decided a paper vote would be taken in two weeks to whittle the list down to the top two; a final vote at the next business meeting—today."

Pastor Cobbs cleared his throat and grinned sheepishly. "As everyone knows, we had an emergency situation two weeks ago and never got that paper vote. What would people like to do— take a paper vote of the list of names today, and put off the final vote until the next meeting? Or . . . yes, Sister Florida?"

Florida bounced to her feet. "Don't mean to be pushy, Pastor, but I move we vote on a name *today*. Take two or three votes to narrow it down, I don't care. But calling this church by both names for even one more day be like that Chinese water torture you hear about. *I'm* 'bout to go crazy, know what I'm sayin'?" She sat down to general laughter and not a few hearty amens.

Pastor Cobbs was smiling too. "All in favor?" The ayes clearly carried. "All right. Let's get the list of suggested names passed out. Any discussion before we do the first paper vote?"

The discussion picked up right where we'd left off a month ago. "Seems like we ought to merge the two original names somehow." "Nah, we need a new name, like Sister Avis said." "Sister Jodi, could you tell us what that Hebrew word means again?" "Do we really want a name you have to explain to people all the time?" . . .

I tuned out the discussion, realizing it wasn't looking good for *Yachad*, and read down the list of possible names. *Wait a minute.* A new one had been added since last time. I looked up, about to ask about it, when Rick Reilly stood up.

"As you can see, a new proposal has been added. When we didn't take the paper vote a couple of weeks ago, the youth group said they'd like to come up with a suggestion. The pastors said fine since, technically, the floor was still open." He looked around at the teens. "Anyone want to explain it? Amanda?"

My daughter ducked her head, but several of the other teens hissed, "Go on, go on." She stood up, giggling with embarrassment.

"Well, like, it's kind of self-explanatory. SouledOut Christian Church . . . or maybe SouledOut Community Church. We couldn't decide. Somebody saw a bookstore with that name—SouledOut Christian Bookstore, or something like that—and we thought it would make a cool name for a church. You know, *souls* and *sold out*— like a double meaning, 'sold out for Jesus' and 'winning souls to Jesus.' But also kinda jazzy."

"You go, girl!" Florida crowed. The congregation laughed. Back at the soundboard, Josh grinned, as if proud of his sister. Flustered, Amanda sat down, her face bright red.

It only took one paper vote. "SouledOut Community Church" got over 50 percent of the vote the first time around. The teens were excited, shouting "Woo woo woo!" as they pumped their fists and then gathered into a spontaneous huddle, slapping hands and yelling, "SouledOut! SouledOut!" like a team ready to go into action on the court.

Amanda slipped over to me as I packed up my empty taco salad bowl. "Sorry, Mom. *Yachad* was kinda cool, too, but like, the whole teen group came up with—"

I gave her a quick hug. "Honey, it's fine! Really. It's a good name. Now go on, shoo, before I put you to work washing dishes."

I wanted her out of there before she saw the tears watering my eyes. Sure, I had a twinge of disappointment that the name I suggested got left in the dust. But that wasn't the reason I felt teary. Even though I'd barely had thirty minutes to get used to the new name, I realized something profound had just happened.

The *teenagers*—black and white—had suggested a name for *their* church.

The congregation *voted for* their name.

Could anything say louder to these young people, *"You are important. We respect your ideas. You contribute to our church"?*

And *SouledOut?* Wow, what a concept! "Oh God," I whispered under my breath, taking another swipe at the serving table I'd already cleaned, "let it be true for me too."

18

*C*uriosity got the better of me once we got home. "So, um, what name did you vote for, Denny?" He waggled a finger in front of my face. "Uh-uh-uh! No fair. We don't tell each other who we vote for in presidential elections. Why would I tell you how I voted at church?"

"Oh. So you didn't vote for *Yachad*." I caught the warning look in his eye. "Okay, okay, you don't have to tell me . . . *if* you go roller-skating with me on Valentine's Day."

He threw up his hands. "Jodi! That's practically blackmail! Are you sure you don't want me to take you out to a nice restaurant? Or go see a play or something? Something where the odds are in our favor for staying on our feet?"

I giggled. "Nope. Besides, this will be cheaper. *And* lots of fun." I grabbed his arm and pulled him close, rubbing noses with him. Eskimo kisses, we used to call them as kids. "Aw, c'mon, Denny. Otherwise I'll have to sit out all the 'couples skates' by myself—or end up skating with some dark-eyed lothario in tight leather pants."

Maybe it was the "tight leather pants" that did it, but I squeezed a reluctant promise from my hubby of twenty-one years to accompany me to the Super Skatium the following Saturday. I called some of the other Yada sisters to see if any of their guys were coming. Yo-Yo said her brothers wanted to know "Who else is comin'?"—meaning kids their age, which I couldn't tell her. My own kids had ignored the invitation so far. Florida said she was still working on Carl, but he might be more open to it if he knew Denny was going. "Kinda depends on how Chris's hearing on Wednesday turns out. An' I need another favor . . ."

"This Wednesday?" I peeked at our kitchen calendar. I'd written "FLO 38" in red marker across February 11. "But that's your birthday, Flo!"

She snorted in my ear. "Yeah. Some birthday present, huh? But if the judge doesn't assign Chris to adult court like those other perps, that'd be about the best birthday gift anyone could give me right now."

"You want me to take Carla home with me after school again?"

"Yeah. That's what I was gonna axe ya. Would give me some space to handle whatever comes down before I have to relate to the other kids."

"Oh, Florida." My heart ached for my friend. "Come on, let's pray about it. We gotta keep faith that God's gonna work this out. If Chris didn't do this—"

"*If*, Jodi?"

I stopped. Why did I say "if"? Well, I didn't *know*, did I? And Chris had been hanging out on the edges of the Black Disciples all year. Wasn't that why the Hickmans moved to Rogers Park from their old neighborhood? Only there wasn't any place in Chicago "safe" from gangs if you were looking for trouble. Wannabes like Chris got pressured into lots of petty crime—and some not so petty—just to prove they were "down" for their homeboys.

But Chris insisted he'd only hopped in the car for a ride home. Did I believe him? Would a judge believe him? If that's what happened, someone better tell him, "With friends like that, who needs enemies!"

I blew out a breath. "I'm sorry, Flo. Poor choice of words. Let's pray that God will give Chris favor with this judge and assign him to juvenile court."

"Yeah, Jodi." She sniffed. "Do that."

So I did, right there on the phone, prayed that God would be present at that hearing on Wednesday, prayed that Chris would not only be assigned to juvenile court, but that God would bring him out of the JDC and restore him to his family. "Oh Jesus! Put a hedge of protection around that boy while he's separated from his family! And when he comes out, Lord, give him honest opportunities to develop that artistic talent You've given him!"

Florida was silent when I finished. "Flo? You still there?"

"Yeah." Another silence. Then, "You really think Chris got him some talent?"

CARLA CAME HOME WITH ME after school on Wednesday. Willie Wonka, who seemed to have perked up on his new diet of canned dog food and two pricey prescriptions, lumbered to his feet when we came in the door and gave Carla a tail wag and a lick on the face, much to her delight.

Over hot chocolate and toast with cinnamon sugar, we plotted

159

the afternoon. "Can I make a card for my mommy? It's her birth-day today, but . . ." Carla's face fell. "I don't got no present for her."

I grinned. "You absolutely can make a card for your mom. Not only that—ta da!" I pulled a chocolate cake mix out of the cupboard. "And not only that . . ." I flashed her my recipe card for craft "salt dough."

For the next hour, we were busy mixing the cake, licking the bowl and the beaters, and making salt dough. Before I could warn her, Carla stuck her finger in the salt dough and popped it in her mouth. "Yuck!" Much spitting followed, while I tried not to laugh. But by the time the cake came out of the oven, Carla had crafted five rather lumpy napkin rings out of the salt dough on a cookie sheet, which we popped into the oven for twenty minutes while I scrounged in my craft supplies for poster paints, paint brushes, and a bottle of varnish.

Denny arrived home, gave me a passing peck on the cheek, and headed for the front room and the TV news. Right on his heels, Amanda dumped her jacket and school bag on the floor, gave Wonka his kissy-face greeting, and leaned over the dining room table. "Hey! Salt dough. Whatcha makin', Carla?"

Carla beamed and held up one of the brightly painted napkin rings. "See? It gots Chris's name on this one." She picked up another. "An' this purple-an'-pink one's for Mommy. See? M-O-M. For her birthday!"

"Cool." Amanda peered into the plastic bowl of dough. "Can I make something?" She scooped out a blob of dough and went to work.

I hid a smile as I disappeared into the kitchen to ice the cooled cake. If I had *asked* Amanda if she wanted to play with salt dough, she would have given me The Look, absolutely sure her mother still lived in the Dark Ages.

The phone rang. I barely got out a hello when Florida screeched in my ear. "Praise Jesus, Jodi! The attorney didn't even hafta make a big case. Judge looked at some papers, said somethin' like, 'This kid's got no priors . . . wasn't identified as the gunman . . . he's only fourteen . . . whatever the court decides at his disposition, there's no way I'm going to send this case to adult court.' Then he set a court date for April somethin', an' *bam*! That was it! Oh, hallelujah! Praise Jesus!" Florida's voice faded temporarily while she did some serious praising in the background. When she came back on the phone, she said, "Carl is so relieved, I might even get him to the roller rink on Saturday."

"That's great, Florida! See? God really answered our prayer!" But I was thinking, *April? That's two months away! If Chris was just in the wrong place at the wrong time and he's not guilty, they've still had him locked up for five months of his life.* But I didn't say any of that to Florida. One day at a time, and this day the news was good.

As we got cake, craft, and Carla ready for the half-mile ride home, she suddenly gave me a big hug. "I like third grade," she announced, grinning up at me. "I wish you could be my teacher next year too."

I was so surprised, it took me several seconds to find my voice. "That," I finally said, returning her hug, "is just about the nicest thing anyone's ever said to me."

AMANDA WAS PAINTING a couple of salt dough hearts when I got back from taking Carla home. "What are *you* making, Michelangelo?"

No answer. More delicate painting. Then she held up two hearts on key rings. "Which one do you like, Mom?"

One heart had delicate white flowers painted on the red background; the other had funky polka dots. Both had **AB + JE** in the center. I pointed to the one with flowers.

She lifted the polka dot heart. "I like this one. It's for José. You know, for Valentine's Day."

My choosing the one with flowers had probably sealed its fate. "That's nice."

"Yeah. But I'm gonna give it to him *after* the roller-skating party, in case he falls down or something and breaks it." She hopped up. "Thanks for the salt dough, Mom."

I watched her go and shook my head. By the time I figured out how to step with my teenagers, they'd be gone and I'd have to start all over learning a new dance. *Empty nest . . . adult kids . . . grandchildren . . .*

Whoa. Did she say roller-skating party?

AS IT TURNED OUT, Josh also decided to go roller-skating because Edesa was bringing the Enriques kids—including José, hence Amanda's change of heart—and he borrowed the church van to pick them up. I was hoping Ben Garfield would bring Yo-Yo Spencer and her brothers, but Ruth just snorted. "Skating, schmating. Broken necks we don't need, Jodi. Who would bring up Isaac and Havah?" So Denny and I picked up the Spencers and met the rest of our party at the Skatium for the four o'clock skate.

Had to admit, Chanda's Lexus and Stu's silver Celica seemed a bit overdressed for the parking lot full of five-year-old Hondas and Fords. Nony and Mark had declined, but they sent Marcus and Michael in their minivan with Hoshi, who also picked up the

Hickmans. I never did hear from Avis and Peter, but they didn't show. No surprise there. Couldn't really imagine Avis on roller skates—but given all they were dealing with right now, letting loose with a little undignified fun might've been just what they needed!

Oh, well, we had a good turnout anyway.

I felt almost giddy lacing up my rented roller skates. As Denny said, it'd been more than twenty years since I'd been to a skating rink! The live organ music was gone, replaced by an unseen DJ spinning unfamiliar CDs, stopping the music now and then to announce in a throaty voice, "All Skate" . . . "Ladies Choice" . . . "Couples Only" . . .

My first few times around the rink during All Skate, I had serious doubts about my declaration, *"It's like riding a bike! You never forget!"* Picking me up after a spill, Denny laughed and took my hand. "Come on." Hand in hand, I gradually found my "skate legs" and started to enjoy myself . . . until the DJ sent us off the rink saying, "Guys Only. Ladies, if you value your life, leave the floor . . ."

I didn't remember that one. But I clumped together with my Yada Yada sisters behind the railing, making irreverent comments about Pete Spencer, Josh, and José racing each other around the rink like a trio of speed demons. The DJ had even cut the music. We applauded the younger boys—Marcus and Michael Smith, Chanda's Tom, Cedric Hickman, and Yo-Yo's brother Jerry— holding their own against the tide of bigger teenage boys and twenty-somethings. Denny and Carl, meanwhile, wisely took the opportunity to duck over to the concession stand and get a Coke.

Another All Skate, then Couples Only. "It's Valentine's Day, lovers," the DJ smirked. "Get out on the floor and get your groooove on." The music wasn't exactly the good ol' sixties love songs we used to skate to, even in the late seventies and early eighties. In fact, I didn't recognize any of the music, if you could call it that. Mostly noise to my ears. But it was fun seeing Carl skating with Florida, nothing fancy, just hand in hand, grins on their faces. Denny took my left hand and put his right arm around my waist. I leaned against him, and we floated around the curves . . . *left, glide . . . right, glide . . .*

We passed Josh and Edesa skating together slowly—she'd said this was her first time ever. I didn't see Amanda and José on the floor, but didn't give it much thought. Didn't want to rush them, anyway.

I half-closed my eyes, aware of Denny's arm snug around my waist, pulling me gently along, holding me up without seeming to. No wonder the Bible said, *"Two are better than one . . ." Oh God, this is so much fun!*

When the Couples Skate was over, I took a break and joined a few other Yada Yadas sipping Cokes and munching on nachos. "Kinda surprised they playin' these kind of songs with all these little kids here," Yo-Yo was saying.

I blinked. What kind of songs?

Edesa nodded. "*Si.* The words make me feel ashamed."

"Uh," I stammered. "Have to admit, I can't understand the words. What's going on?"

Stu rolled her eyes knowingly. "Probably just as well, Jodi."

I sat down on a bench and tried to listen. Still didn't understand much . . . but by concentrating I caught enough to feel my face redden.

Good grief. My kids are here, listening to this crap? The other Yadas had brought their kids at *my* urging! I saw nine-year-old

Carla and Chanda's girls, Dia and Cheree, out on the floor, wiggling their behinds suggestively and giggling.

Edesa must have seen the shocked look on my face. "Do not be upset, Sister Jodi. You did not know. None of us thought about it. But if the other *mamacitas* don't mind, maybe it will be good to cut our time short."

I stood up. "Well, sure. But before we slink out of here with our tails between our legs, I'm going to talk to the DJ. This just isn't appropriate for a Family Skate."

I had to ask three different people before I found where the DJ was hidden behind his glass wall, and then had to wait while he announced, "Ladies Choice. This is Ladies Choice, gents, so suck in that gut and your Valentine just might ask you to skate." He punched a button and looked at the window where I gestured at him to open the door. "Yeah?"

My little talk lasted about sixty seconds. It did not go well.

"Look, lady. I play these songs all the time, and you're the first person who's complained about it. This is what the kids are listening to. It's what they want to hear. If you don't like it, take it up with the manager . . . Gotta go." The door shut in my face.

Ooo! Now my blood was up. I clumped my skates on the threadbare "carpet" back to my friends. The lights were down; Ladies Choice was still on the floor. I saw Chanda flash by hand in hand with a guy in his thirties, a pretty good skater. Becky had asked Carl Hickman, with Florida's blessing, I guessed. But to my surprise, Amanda was sitting on a bench, arms crossed, glaring at the darkened skating rink with the spinning colored lights flickering around the walls and ceiling. I squinted at the circling skaters.

A dark-haired Latina skated past, arm in arm with José Enriques. I darted a glance at Amanda. *Uh-oh.* Should I say anything? It was Ladies Choice, after all. The other girl had probably beaten her to it. But I knew she wouldn't want my sympathy, not in public anyway.

After the skate, I saw José make his way over to Amanda and plop down on the bench next to her, laughing, but she turned her face away, mouth pinched. For a few minutes, he seemed to be arguing with her, but finally he threw up his arms and left her alone.

I sighed. *Oh, Amanda.*

We didn't stay for the end of the Family Skate. Some of the younger set griped about it, until we reminded them we were heading for Giordano's for pizza and root beer. All twenty-six of us, adults and kids, crowded into Giordano's party room, generating a lot of laughter and happy bedlam.

Make that twenty-five. Amanda said she had a stomachache and wanted us to drop her off at home. No, she did *not* want us to bring her any pizza.

Denny and I didn't get home until after nine o'clock, after dropping off our passengers. Josh was still out, driving Edesa and the Enriques crew back to Little Village. The house was dark. Denny and I entered quietly, not wanting to disturb Amanda if she was asleep. I listened at her bedroom door.

Muffled sobs broke the silence.

I stood uncertainly in the hallway, wondering if I should go in. And that's when I saw it in the hallway, broken into pieces as if it had been stomped on.

The heart-shaped key ring Amanda had made for José for Valentine's Day.

19

*T*he next morning Amanda appeared briefly in her rumpled sleep shirt, hair tousled, mumbling that she didn't feel good and wasn't going to church. She disappeared back into her bedroom. "Let her be," Denny advised. "Timing is everything."

As we drove to church, I watched the gray streets go by without really seeing them. I felt badly for Amanda, but my feelings were mixed. She and José had been sweet on each other for over a year already, and they were only sixteen. A year ago this month José had come up with the big idea to throw a *quinceañera* for Amanda—a formal "coming out" fifteenth birthday party, a Mexican tradition, though by that time Amanda was fifteen-and-a-half. Delores's son was a sweet boy, but they were really too young to get serious with each other. Some distance wasn't a bad idea in my book.

"Hey. Look at that," Denny said, pulling into a parking space facing our shopping center church.

I looked up. Painted across the wide glass windows in a bold red script were the words: SOULEDOUT COMMUNITY CHURCH. A few early shoppers paused and read the sign before heading for the large Dominick's grocery store that anchored the shopping center. Well. There it was. The new name of our church. I smiled. *I think I like it.*

I found it hard to concentrate on worship that morning, though. Roller-skating had been fun, and fun was what we needed, but I also felt embarrassed, inviting my Yada Yada sisters and their families into a situation I hadn't really checked out, music-wise anyway. That language! I cringed just thinking about the few phrases I'd caught. A far cry from the sweet love songs of my parents' generation. Even rock and roll was tame by comparison. Made me mad that the DJ had blown me off, telling me to speak to the manager if I had a problem . . .

Hey. That was a thought. I could gripe . . . or I could do something about it. My brain started composing a strongly worded letter. Maybe I should start a petition—

A nudge in my spirit pulled me up short. *Jodi? Where are you? Did you come to worship Me today? Let's spend some time together . . .*

I squeezed my eyes shut. *I'm sorry, Lord. Yes, I want to worship You.* I pigeonholed the letter I'd been writing in my head and focused on the song the praise team was singing . . .

Knowing You, Jesus, knowing You . . . There is no greater thing . . .

The song was a new one to me, but easy to pick up. We sang it through two more times, and the words began to sink deeper into my spirit. How glad I was to be in a church where Jesus was "the main thing." It kept me centered.

The words of the song continued to whisper in my spirit all that afternoon as I worked on a card for Florida's birthday,

reviewed my lesson plans for the coming week, and composed a
letter to the roller rink manager.

Knowing You, Jesus . . . There is no greater thing . . .

I sat at the dining room table, chewing on the end of my pen.
How easy it was for me to be consumed with everyday busyness,
to fret over all the trouble around me, to spin my wheels even over
things I could do nothing about—and forget just to spend time in
God's presence. Hadn't the Holy Spirit already shown me there
was a difference between knowing *about* God and *knowing* God?
I'd started on the journey, but I knew how easy it was for me to get
distracted.

*Thank You, Father, for reminding me that Jesus made it possible for
me to have a relationship with You.* A relationship that meant taking time to soak up His Word, listen to His voice, rest in His
promises, play music that called me to worship . . .

I got up to put on a praise and worship CD, but the phone
rang. "Señora Baxter? Can I, uh, speak to Amanda?" José sounded
nervous.

"I'll see if she's awake, José. She didn't feel good today." Well,
that's what she'd said. And I needed to give Amanda an out if she
didn't want to talk to him.

I covered the mouthpiece and knocked gently on her bedroom
door. "Amanda? You awake? Phone for you." Then I added, "It's
José."

Silence. I was just about to walk away when the door opened a
crack and Amanda held her hand out for the phone. But not two
minutes later, I heard Amanda yell, "Fine! If that's the way you
want it, *don't* call me anymore!" and the phone came thumping
down the hall and cracked into the dining room archway.

The basketball game on television suddenly went mute and Denny appeared in the hallway. "What was *that?*"

I waved him back with my hand and headed for Amanda's door. "Amanda?" I knocked but this time didn't wait for an answer before going in. Amanda was sprawled on her bed, sobbing. A school picture of José had been torn in half and thrown on the floor. I sat down on the bed, pulled her head into my lap, and just let her cry.

DELORES ENRIQUES came to Yada Yada at Stu's that night, but if she knew that José and Amanda had had a huge fight, she didn't say anything. In fact, she pulled me aside and asked if Denny was home. When I nodded, she said, "Do you think it is all right if I talk to him a few minutes? *Mi Ricardo* . . ." She bit her lip. "I would very much like it if Denny invited him again to the men's breakfast at your church. He needs the support of other brothers, though he'd never admit it. In Mexico"—she pronounced it *Me-hi-co*—"humph." She rolled her eyes and slapped her motherly bosom. "Our men keep all their feelings locked up here."

I shooed her downstairs to our apartment, assuring her Denny wouldn't mind. She passed Nony, Avis, and Chanda, who were on the way up . . . and by the time Delores came back upstairs, most of the others had arrived. Becky was secretly putting candles on the birthday cake she'd made to celebrate Florida's birthday and managed to smuggle in, even though they'd both ridden over in Avis's car.

A beaming Estelle, clothed in her handmade top and pants, was introduced all around the circle as Stu's new housemate . . . until Stu stopped and frowned. "Ruth? Where's Yo-Yo? Isn't she coming tonight?"

We all looked at Ruth. For the past year and a half, the Garfields had been Yo-Yo's sole transportation to Yada Yada. Most anywhere, for that matter. But Ruth stared back blankly. "Um . . . well, we . . ."

"Ruth!" several voices chorused at once. "You *forgot* Yo-Yo?"

Ruth drew herself up. "So much to think about now to leave the house with twins."

"But you didn't bring the babies tonight, Ruth," Stu pointed out dryly.

"You noticed. Ben is taking care of both of them tonight by himself. A good father, he is!"

Stu unfolded herself from the wicker basket chair where she'd been sitting. "Well, I'm going to call the Good Daddy and tell him to go pick up Yo-Yo and get her over here. I can't believe you *forgot* Yo-Yo." Stu was clearly steamed.

"No," Ruth said.

"Excuse me?"

Ruth looked at her watch. "By now he will be back home feeding the twins. He can't take them out again! Feeding. Changing. Burping. Then two snowsuits. Two hats. Four mittens. Strapping them in the car seats . . . an hour it takes!"

"Fine. Then I'll go get her." Stu grabbed her purse and jacket and headed for the back door.

"Uh, Stu?" I called after her. "You're the hostess tonight."

Stu turned. "So? Estelle can be the hostess."

"At least call Yo-Yo first. Tell her you're coming."

Stu let that sink in, then nodded. But she was back in two minutes, frowning. "No answer. I left a message, told her to call here ASAP and we'd come get her." She flopped back into the basket

171

chair and busied her hands twisting her long hair into a single braid.

The silence was awkward. I wished Avis would say something or get the meeting started, but she seemed to be waiting. Ruth studied her hands, twisting her wedding ring. Finally, she sighed. "Oh, all right. We forgot. And I am sorry. I will call Yo-Yo and ask her to forgive us. *Oy!* At my age, when new information goes in the brain"—she tapped the side of her head—"something else falls out. Maybe she should call to remind us . . ."

I doubted if Yo-Yo would do that. One of *us* might have to call to remind them.

Nonyameko placed a hand on Ruth's arm. "We forgive you, Ruth." Nony darted a quick glance at Stu, as if to say, *Don't we, Stu?* "We know you did not forget on purpose. I am glad you are going to call Yo-Yo tonight. I'm sure she will understand." She leaned forward, as if shifting gears. "Hoshi is not here tonight, either, but"—she smiled—"no, I did not forget her. The good news is, young Sara agreed to go with her to the Christian campus group tonight—they call it ReJOYce—and Hoshi wants us to pray."

The bad news is, my brain filled in, *that takes Hoshi away from Yada Yada.* But I shook off the thought. Hoshi was doing a good thing. She had "looked for the possibilities" and found a way to befriend lonely, confused Sara.

Hoshi's prayer request via Nony opened up our prayer time, followed by praise and thanksgiving that Chris Hickman's case had *not* been sent to adult court, and more praise that Nony had helped Avis's daughter find a doctor who specialized in HIV cases. "Yes," Avis agreed gratefully. "We have an appointment to meet with him next week—all of us."

"Guess God's been busy since our last meeting," Adele said, slipping a grin. "Don't know if y'all know Estelle, here, has been comin' over to my house to stay with MaDear while I'm at work." Her grin widened, showing the little gap between her front teeth. "Have to say Estelle is one big blessing."

Estelle acted offended. "You talkin' about my *size?*" Which got a laugh around the circle, even from Stu. The last of the tension seemed to drain away.

We prayed and praised, and then Becky brought out her cake— in a nine-by-thirteen pan. "Why y'all didn't tell me this kind was so easy? Jodi had me makin' them layer cakes, always fallin' over." More laughter. We'd decided to bring individual cards for Florida this time, a virtual card shower, with inexpensive gifts—jar candles, a bookmark, candy bars. Becky gave her safety pins and rubber bands. "Why not?" she sniffed. "Seems like nobody can ever find a safety pin or rubber band when they need one. Well, now Flo can."

We whooped. "Good idea, Becky!"

Stu left the room to answer the phone, and we all looked at each other, thinking the same thing: *Yo-Yo returning her call.* But when Stu came back, she motioned to Avis. "For you."

Avis disappeared into the kitchen with the phone. When she returned, she quickly gathered up her Bible and purse. "I need to go home. Dexter called the house." She held up a hand, stifling the questions that rose to our lips. "Rochelle didn't think it was him at first because she didn't recognize the caller ID, but thank goodness, Peter had told her to not answer *any* calls until she knew for sure who it was, to let the person leave a message. But when she heard Dexter's voice leaving a message, she got very frightened." Avis slipped into her winter coat that Stu brought to her.

"Pray, sisters. He doesn't *know* Rochelle is staying with us, but he's obviously looking for her."

YO-YO STILL HADN'T CALLED by the time we left Stu's apartment. Nony, bless her, took Ruth home so Ben wouldn't have to bring the babies out again. Why Ruth didn't just drive herself over, I'd never understand. She'd done it two weeks ago when the Super Bowl started an hour before our Yada Yada meeting. But then again, there was a lot I didn't understand about Ruth and Ben's relationship. Despite Ben's growl and Ruth's ever-rolling eyes, it seemed like they were devoted to each other. And crazy about those babies.

Stu made Ruth promise she'd call Yo-Yo that evening and apologize. "I'm going to call Yo-Yo too," Stu muttered to me as Estelle and I helped her clean up the birthday cake crumbs and paper plates. "I'll let you know if I hear from her."

When I came down Stu's carpeted stairs and let myself in by our front door, the house was dark. *That's strange,* I thought, flipping on the hall light—

"Eek!" I screeched. Denny was leaning against the archway into the living room, arms folded, a long-stemmed rose in his teeth. "Denny Baxter! You scared me half to death. *What* are you doing?"

He took the rose out of his mouth and picked his teeth with the end of the stem. "It's still Valentine's weekend. Wanna go out on the town?"

"Now?" I glanced at my watch. Eight-thirty. I was in my jeans, my hair was a mess, my makeup faded. I didn't feel like sprucing up on the spur of the moment.

He waggled the rose at me. "Hate to tell you this, babe, but roller-skating with the Yada Yadas and their assorted offspring—plus fifty other shady characters, strangers all—did not cut it as a romantic Valentine rendezvous. Just you and me. And there's no school tomorrow. President's Day. We can sleep in."

He could sleep in. Willie Wonka always woke me at six-thirty, needing to go out, holiday or no holiday. And it was *cold* out there, hadn't he noticed? Frankly, I'd rather crawl into a nice warm bed about now. But I took the outstretched rose, my mind scrambling how to get out of this without hurting his feelings. "Oh, Denny, that's sweet. But could I take a rain check for tomorrow, when I have more time to get ready? Tonight isn't—"

"Didn't think so." He grinned. "Plan B." He took my hand. "This way, darlin'."

Now I was suspicious. He took that rejection too easily.

He opened our bedroom door. The lights were off, but candles flickered from both nightstands, our dressers, even on the floor. The quilt was turned back. Soft music played from the little FM radio we kept in the bedroom. Now it was my turn to grin. It was obvious what he'd had in mind all along . . .

But I tipped my head in the direction of Amanda's room. "Um, kids?"

"Gone," he murmured, brushing my hair to the side and nuzzling my neck. "Amanda got a call from the youth group, they're watching a movie tonight since there's no school tomorrow. Guess she decided that was better than moping around all evening . . . yeah, yeah, I checked. The movie's PG. Josh took her, said he'd hang around."

I stifled a snort. The car wasn't even here. What if I'd said, *Sure, let's go out tonight!* . . . but all I said now was, "Give me five minutes to jump in the shower, okay? Don't go anywhere."

"*Go* anywhere?" He was already peeling off his clothes. "I'm coming with you!"

20

*W*hen Willie Wonka woke me up the next morning, I stretched and yawned. Now *that* was a good night's sleep. Hadn't even heard Amanda and Josh come in! But Josh must have brought his sister home before curfew, because the alarm clock I'd set and left out in the hall had been shut off before midnight.

Might as well plan my day since I was the first one up. A school holiday in the middle of February was usually good for one thing: staying home and catching up on . . . whatever. Laundry. E-mail. Mending. Lesson plans.

Yeah, right. Today I was going to do minimal "ought-to" stuff and curl up in the living room with a cup of gourmet coffee and the gorgeously illustrated book my parents had given me for Christmas about gardening in flower boxes. After all, if students could sleep in until noon, why couldn't we teachers take a day off too? Even Josh had a day off from Software Symphony, though I had no idea why Peter Douglass closed his shop for President's Day . . . unless it was to coordinate with Avis's school holidays.

Then Denny announced he was going to school for a couple of hours to catch up on some work, but he'd be back in time to catch a few college games on TV. I refused to feel guilty. I'd play while he worked, then work while he played.

The book on flower boxes had me salivating. Perfect escapism for a snowy day in February. Besides, if I wanted flowers this spring, I was going to have to plant them myself. Now that Becky Wallace was no longer living with Stu on house arrest, we'd lost our resident gardener.

I ignored the kids when they got up, other than to yell into the kitchen that they had to clean up after themselves and to answer a plea where to find the electric griddle. I knew what that meant. Pancakes. Maybe French toast.

Back to my fantasy flower boxes . . .

But a few minutes later, I realized my coffee was cold. I wandered to the kitchen to get a refill and to see if Willie Wonka had touched his "special diet." So far, it had been iffy with the canned dog food, sometimes nibbling, other times giving it a sniff and wandering away with a sigh. Maybe I should call the vet again . . .

Amanda and Josh were still making their breakfast, stepping back and forth over Willie Wonka, who lay inert in the middle of the kitchen floor. "He said I was getting too *possessive*," Amanda was saying, spitfire in her voice. "Just 'cause I got upset when he skated with some other girl. Well, why shouldn't I? He didn't even *know* her!"

I stopped, uncertain whether to intrude.

"Sure you didn't overreact? Guys get squirmy when girls get demanding."

"Oh, thanks, big brother. Not you too."

"Hey. Hold on a minute. I just mean, do you two have an understanding that you're an official item? Can't date anyone else?"

"Well . . . not exactly. We're just friends. Special friends, though. At least I thought we were."

"Uh-huh." For a few moments, all I heard were dishes clattering.

"You really think I overreacted?" Amanda's voice was more contrite. "But I'd been planning to ask him to skate when it was Ladies Choice, then that . . . that hussy grabbed him first. And he was *enjoying* himself! Made me so mad." Her voice rose again. "And then *he* calls *me* and says maybe we should break things off, not call each other so much! The jerk! Who dissed who at the rink, huh? Tell me that!"

Now the dish banging got louder. Then a sigh. "But maybe I should call him, tell him I'm sorry for jumpin' on him. See if he wants to do anything this afternoon."

"Uh, know what, Mandy? I'd give him some space right now. Don't call. Don't beg. Don't chase him." Josh's tone was surprisingly empathetic. "Trust me on this one."

I looked at my empty coffee cup. Guessed a refill could wait. I turned to go back to the living room but heard sniffles from the kitchen, then Josh murmuring, "Aw, c'mere, bed head." The sniffles became muffled sobs. I peeked. Josh had pulled Amanda against his chest, letting her cry into his sweatshirt. "Know how you feel, kiddo. Loving somebody ain't as easy as it looks . . ."

I FELT SAD FOR AMANDA. A broken heart at sixteen. Wouldn't help to tell her that most adults looked back at their high school crushes and wondered, what was the big deal? But I wondered how Amanda would manage seeing José at school. After all, he'd transferred from Benito Juarez High School mostly because she was at Lane Tech. Well, because it was a college prep school too. But she didn't say anything all week. Spent most of her time at home doing homework or listening to music.

The phone stayed in its perch on the kitchen wall.

Denny came home Thursday night all excited, saying he wanted to talk to me. After supper, I loaded the dishwasher while he talked and waved a dishtowel around. He and Peter Douglass had been knocking heads about how best to support the Hickman family, and Pastor Cobb told them about a ministry called Captives Free Jail and Prison Ministry that needed volunteers to lead Bible studies at the JDC. "The girls' units are all staffed, but only about half the boys' units"—the dishtowel waved with enthusiasm— "meaning they need men to volunteer, the sooner the better."

"How does that support the Hickman family? I mean, can you request getting assigned to Chris's unit?"

He considered. "Hm. Probably not. But still, if we could get several Uptown . . . uh, I mean SouledOut brothers to volunteer, I think we could add another two or three Bible studies down there at the JDC. Whatever unit Chris is in, it'd be great if there was a Bible study going on, someone from outside to give kids like Chris friendship and prayer support." He shrugged. "We're going to try to get somebody from Captives Free to come talk about the jail and prison ministry at our men's breakfast this Saturday. Carl is pumped! Thinks it's a great idea."

"Can he volunteer? I mean, with a kid inside?"

Denny shrugged. "Doubt it. Still, I think it means a lot that we're talking about volunteering at the JDC . . . *because of* Chris, really."

I handed him a bowl that wouldn't fit inside the dishwasher. "So when are these Bible studies?"

"Thursday nights at seven—which means I'd probably go right from school." He held the dripping bowl in one hand, the towel in another. "Wouldn't get home till nine or ten. I know having dinner as a family is important, but now that the kids are older . . ."

I nodded, remembering something. "Isn't that how Ruth met Yo-Yo?—leading a Bible study for women at the Cook County Jail?" *Yo-Yo and Ruth . . . My mind rewound to the last Yada Yada meeting. What's going on between those two? Did Ruth ever apologize for forgetting to pick her up last Sunday? Stu was going to—*

"That's right!" Denny said. "Man, I forgot all about that. Want me to double-check if Captives Free needs female volunteers? Might be something the Yada Yadas could do down the road, now that Manna House is kaput."

"Hey!" I took the still-wet bowl and still-dry towel away from him. "Don't go volunteering me for anything just yet! Now git, Denny Boy. You're useless in here." A series of sharp raps at the back door saved him from getting snapped with the towel. "And by the way," I called after him, "don't forget to call Ricardo and ask him to come to the men's breakfast! Delores asked you, remember?"

I opened the back door. "Estelle! Come in, girl. It's cold out there." I pulled her in and shut the door. "Just getting back from Adele's?"

She nodded, hands jammed in the pockets of her long, second-hand coat, head wrapped in one of her knitted creations. "Can't stay. Just want to ask y'all to be prayin' for MaDear. She . . ." Estelle shook her head. "She's not doing well. My Lord. She's coughin' an' chokin' all the time. Adele was goin' to cancel her appointments tomorrow an' get her to the doc, but I told her I could take MaDear. We can go by taxi and let Adele know if she's needed. But main thing, we got to be prayin'."

"Sure. I'll let the other sisters know. Thanks, Estelle." I shut the door behind her, then leaned against it, my spirit sinking. Pneumonia again? Couldn't be good.

But maybe this was a good excuse to call Yo-Yo myself. I'd held off, giving Ruth or Stu a chance to connect, but I hadn't heard from anybody if they'd gotten hold of her. I dialed her number, let it ring . . . but then her voice-mail message kicked in: *"Yo, dude or dudette! Yo-Yo isn't home and neither are the Rug Rats. You know what to do at the beep."*

I smiled as the *beep* sounded. "Dudette yourself, Yo-Yo. This is Jodi. Missed you Sunday night." I almost apologized for Ruth forgetting her, then decided not to go there. "I wanted to let you know that MaDear isn't doing so good. Might be pneumonia again. Estelle's been taking care of her, is asking all the sisters to pray. Give me a call when you can, okay?"

I CALLED ADELE'S HAIR AND NAILS when I got home from school on Friday, but Takeisha, the other hairstylist, said Adele was at the hospital.

"They admitted MaDear?" I asked.

"Guess so. All I know is Ms. Adele got a call an' she flew out of here like her hair was on fire."

I called upstairs to see if Estelle was home. No answer. I didn't even know what hospital. St. Francis in south Evanston? That would be the closest. I started to hunt for the number, but for the life of me, I couldn't remember MaDear's real name. Everybody just called her MaDear. Started with an S . . . Sue? Sharon? Didn't sound right.

But Denny remembered. "Her name's Sally. Sally Skuggs." His run-in with MaDear a year and a half ago, when her demented mind mistook him for the man who'd lynched her big brother back in the forties, had affected him deeply. Denny asking her forgiveness for that terrible act had bonded the two of them in a deep, mysterious way.

We called St. Francis. Yes, a Sally Skuggs had been admitted to the ICU. No, they weren't allowing visitors. We hopped in our car anyway.

At St. Francis Hospital, we found our way through a maze of elevators and hallways to the ICU family waiting room. A few people gazed absently at the droning TV hanging high in the corner; others flipped through magazines or just sat. At first, I didn't recognize anyone; then I saw Estelle's knitted hat covering the face of a bulky woman dozing in a corner.

"Estelle?" I shook her shoulder. The hat fell off and her eyes popped open.

"Hey, there." She struggled to sit up. "You the second one to come by . . . that Georgia woman been here, maybe a half hour ago."

Georgia? "You mean Florida?"

"Guess that's it."

I grinned. *Well, good. Word was getting around.* "How's MaDear?"

Estelle shook her head. "Nobody's telling me anything." She lumbered to her feet, rubbing her cramped neck. "But I'll go to the desk, have them tell Adele you're here. Adele's sister in there too."

Sissy was here? "That's good." *I think.* Sometimes Adele talked as if having Sissy around was enough to drive *her* crazy.

A few minutes later, Adele came into the waiting room, still wearing her bright green T-shirt that proudly announced "Adele's Hair and Nails" in white script, a hospital face mask dangling by its strings around her neck. "Hey." She gave us each a tired hug. "Thanks for coming by. Florida was here a while ago. But they don't want any visitors right now 'cept family."

"That's okay," Denny said. We found seats together. Part of me desperately wanted to see MaDear, to kiss her leathery cheek with its childish freckles, wanted to ask if Adele could smuggle us in. But I bit it back. "What are the doctors saying?"

"Pneumonia. Again. Lungs all filled up. Mostly they're trying to keep her comfortable." She snorted. "You know what they say. Pneumonia is the old person's 'friend.' Meaning it's better to die of that than some long, drawn-out disease." Adele's face tightened and she clenched her fist. "But I want her to fight back! Beat this thing! That old woman in there, she's one ornery woman, drives me to distraction. But . . ." Her shoulders sagged, fighting back tears. ". . . don't know what I'd do without her."

We sat in silence for several minutes. Then I asked, "What can we do, Adele? Are you hungry? Do you need anything from home?"

Adele jerked a thumb in Estelle's direction. "You can take Ms. Angel of Mercy over there home. I haven't been able to get rid of her."

Estelle jammed the knit hat down over her head. "All right, all right. I'm goin'. But I'll be back tomorrow mornin'. Meantime, you better come up with another 'sistah' named Estelle right quick on that list of visitors. 'Cause I can sit with MaDear, but I can't cut no hair at your shop. If I did, you'd be out of business in twenty-four hours!"

*W*e played ring-around-the-rosey with the car the next morning. Denny left at six-thirty to pick up Ricardo Enriques for the prayer time some of the guys were having *before* the official men's breakfast at eight-thirty. On his way back, Denny swung past the house and picked me up a few minutes before seven-thirty so I could keep the car for a visit to the hospital that morning. When I dropped them off at the church, Peter Douglass's Lexus was just pulling in with Carl Hickman and Mark Smith inside.

Huh, I thought, as I watched our Yada Yada men unlock and enter the dimly lit storefront "sanctuary." *Mark still must not be able to drive after his head injury.* Even though the vicious beating had happened eight months ago, he still experienced occasional confusion and short blackouts—a frustration, Nony had once confided, that made him feel as if his ankles were shackled together and the key lost.

Oh God, forgive me, I prayed as I headed for the exit of the shopping center. *It's so easy to forget to keep praying for Mark. Please God, heal that man one hundred percent!* The driver of the car behind me honked angrily as I suddenly did a U-turn back into the parking lot. Might as well get my weekly groceries at Dominick's as long as I was here.

By nine-thirty, Estelle and I were in the elevator heading up to the ICU at St. Francis Hospital. We had stopped at Adele's apartment—using Estelle's key—and picked up a change of clothes for Adele, her toothbrush, a pillow and afghan, and her personal address book. Stu had sent along a basket of goodies: hand lotion, gel hand sanitizer, facial wipes, a small notebook and pen, trail mix to munch on, a small box of Fannie May chocolates, and breath mints. She'd wanted to come with us but had several DCFS visits to make that morning. "Tell Adele I'll be up there this afternoon!"

Strangely enough, the ICU waiting room was almost empty, except for a dark-skinned woman with bleached-blonde, straightened hair zonked out on one of the couches. Estelle and I went to "ICU Central"—the squared-off desk area with a visual shot of every ICU room—and asked a woman frowning at a computer screen if someone could let Adele Skuggs know she had, um, "family" here.

Five minutes later Adele met us in the waiting room. "Humph," she said, glaring at the sleeping woman on the couch. "That Sissy still 'sleep? She been there since midnight."

I blinked. That skinny wraith was Adele's *sister*? She looked like an aging hooker.

"No matter," Adele said, linking her arm into Estelle's. "Just as well she's out, 'cause *we* goin' *in*." She handed each of us a sterile face mask and marched us right past ICU Central and into a dimly lit room with its curtains pulled.

MaDear barely took up space in the bed. She was on a ventilator, breathing rhythmically, in and out, but even I could hear the raspy sound of each breath. For a moment, the room blurred because my eyes teared up. I grabbed the hospital-issue box of tissues from the adjustable tray table and mopped my face above the mask. If MaDear were awake, she'd probably tell me I looked like a raccoon with smeared mascara.

The thought made me smile. Estelle was talking quietly to Adele, asking questions. But I just reached out and held MaDear's bony hand, being careful not to disturb the IV tubes taped to her caramel-colored, paper-thin skin. Many of us in the Yada Yada prayer group had parents who lived far away, so we'd adopted MaDear—even though she hardly ever called any of us by our right name. Dementia had scrambled her mind, and she often confused us with cousins or neighbors from her girlhood back in Mississippi.

It didn't matter. We'd loved on her, taking her for "walks" in her wheelchair on nice days to get her out of Adele's shop, even "eldersitting" from time to time so Adele could get out for an evening. Now I held her fingers and thought about the big box of miscellaneous buttons that kept MaDear busy sorting them by color into an empty egg carton.

"Hang on, MaDear," I murmured, "hang on! Jesus, please let her stay with us a while longer."

On the way home, I had a little spat with God. *How are we supposed to pray for someone at the end of life? Huh?* Avis would say that as long as there's life, we pray for healing. After all, God is the Creator of life, not death! But, my mind argued (ignoring Estelle, who was humming quietly in the passenger seat of the Caravan), we all have to die sometime. Don't the preachers say at funerals,

"The Lord giveth, and the Lord taketh away"? And death is the only way we pass from this painful, imperfect life to our resurrected life—no tears, no pain, joy forever! Why keep MaDear here on earth with our desperate prayers, when she will have a clear mind and a whole body in heaven?

When I unlocked the back door and realized Willie Wonka's food had barely been touched that morning, the tears I'd been holding back spilled over. I sank down on the floor beside the old dog, stroking his soft head and letting him lick my hand.

Oh God! Why do dogs and people we love have to get old?

MOST OF YADA YADA STOPPED BY St. Francis Hospital at some point that day. Stu said she'd coordinate meals for Adele and MaDear as soon as they came home from the hospital. In the meantime, she lined up a few volunteers to take some non-hospital food to Adele and Sissy at least once a day: salads, homemade sandwiches, fruit—all the stuff one's body craves after two days of starchy cafeteria fare.

Denny had come home from the men's breakfast that morning with a form he had to fill out from the Cook County Sheriff's Department for a background check before he could sign up with Captives Free Jail and Prison Ministry. That night at supper he said, "At least six guys from SouledOut have volunteered, so that's three more Bible study teams. Assuming I pass the criminal background check"—he waggled his eyebrows—"I signed up to attend a training session next Saturday morning."

Josh helped himself to seconds of beef stew. "I dunno, Dad. Not if they count all the rules you broke in high school."

"Uh-uh. Nobody knows *I* hid the homecoming mascot to this day, bucko. Unless you're talking."

I pretended to ignore their sparring and got up from the table to look at the kitchen calendar. Next Saturday was blank, so I wrote in "Captives Free training a.m." But it was good to hear Josh joke with his dad. He'd been so glum ever since the fire.

After the kids excused themselves, Denny and I lingered at the table over cups of decaf hazelnut coffee. "How was the Bada-Boom Brotherhood this morning?" I grinned.

He groaned. "Don't say that out loud. It might stick." But he leaned toward me, eyes keen. "We had about an hour before the other guys showed up for the breakfast. Ricardo actually opened up, said how desperate he feels about finding a new job. He applied to a moving company that needs long-distance drivers, but it would mean days away from home, and he'd probably have to give up the mariachi band. It's a tough choice. But except for the restaurant gigs, he's been unemployed for over a year and a half."

I winced. *Give up the band?* That was the one sphere where Ricardo Enriques seemed to come alive. Even though he'd been a truck driver for years, he had the soul of a musician. But Delores's income from her job as pediatrics nurse at the county hospital was barely enough to keep the family of seven afloat.

"Peter had to twist Mark's arm to get him there, though. I'm worried about him, Jodi. Almost feels like he's giving up. Peter got in his face, told him he needs to kick self-pity to the curb and move forward. 'God brought you back from that coma for a reason!' he said."

I widened my eyes. "Whoa. How did Mark take that?"

"Humph. He didn't say much. But he listened. And we prayed

over him—yeah, literally. Carl rebuked Satan trying to *discourage* this man; made a point that the devil was *dissin'* God's man. He asked God to give Mark the courage to fight back, because Almighty God still wanted to use this man in a mighty way . . ." Denny wagged his head thoughtfully. "Never heard Carl Hickman pray like that before."

Wow. Neither had I. But I knew it was true. They say adversity will make or break you. Could the pain of his son be the making of Carl?

Denny collected our empty mugs and headed for the kitchen. "By the way," he said, lowering his voice. "What's with Amanda? She hardly said anything all through supper."

I sighed. "Still hurting because José broke up with her, I think. Maybe she needs some daddy-daughter time, you know, to assure her she's not ugly and unlovable. Mom can't tell her that. Takes a dad."

TEMPERATURES HAD BEEN RISING STEADILY all that last week of February, melting the ugly snow and leaving behind the trash it had collected in its frozen grip. By the time we arrived at the church on Sunday, the parking lot boasted a miniature lake from the melting mounds of ice that zealous snowplows had piled all around the edges, and the temperature was heading for the high fifties.

But all our laughing comments about getting out our swimsuits and wading to church died at the church door. My mouth dropped open. People stood in little groups, murmuring comments of wonder and delight as we surveyed an amazing sight.

New chairs.

Rows and rows of sturdy new chairs. Each one with an uphol-
stered padded seat and a padded back, with a rack underneath to
hold hymnals—not that we had hymnals—that could interlock
with other chairs to make a row of any size, or be used individually.

"Good color," I heard someone comment. "That tweedy material picks up the coral and salmon walls, even the blue trim."

"Where's Stu?" I whispered at Denny. "I had no idea the Chair
Fund had collected this much money. She didn't say a thing!" I spotted Stu and Estelle coming in just then and made a beeline in their
direction.

"Stu!" I exclaimed. "Why didn't you tell us you'd collected
enough money in the Chair Fund to do this! It's wonderful!"

But Stu's mouth and eyes were matching O's. "Uh-uh. Not *our*
Chair Fund. Last time I counted, we had about ninety-six dollars."

Pastor Cobbs and Pastor Clark had grins as wide as Cheshire
cats, watching as people tried out the chairs, breathing out sighs of
comfort and contentment.

"Okay, pastors," Sherman Meeks called out. "Let us in on the
secret. Where did these chairs come from?"

Both pastors laughed. "We don't know! That's the amazing
thing. A truck just pulled up yesterday with this address on their
lading bill—and what you see is what they unloaded. All they said
was, 'Sign here.' No bill. All paid for."

Now the room buzzed like a queen bee convention. What
anonymous person knew we needed chairs and had enough
money to give the church an outright gift? Had to be someone in
the congregation, didn't it? Heads were shaking everywhere.

"Come on, church, let's give God some praise!" Pastor Cobb
boomed.

Someone started to clap, and everyone joined in with spontaneous applause, punctuated with "Praise Jesus!" and "Hallelujah!" from all corners of the room. And just then my brain clicked and my eyes widened. I looked at Stu . . . and caught Avis and Florida looking at us. All of us nodded slightly, reading each other's thoughts.

We knew where these chairs came from.

Chanda George.

22

I called Chanda as soon as we got home from church. No answer. *Rats.* I'd forgotten that services at Paul and Silas Apostolic Baptist ran *late.* But I left a voice mail: "Nice try, Chanda. We know you're behind those new chairs that appeared out of nowhere at our church. Gotta say, a lot of weary bottoms thank you *very* much! Don't worry, we won't spill your secret. Maybe." I laughed and hung up.

Then I called back and got voice mail again. "Sorry, Chanda, almost forgot. Avis is suggesting that as many Yada Yadas as possible gather at St. Francis Hospital later this afternoon to pray for MaDear and Adele. See you there if you can make it!"

Next, I called Ruth with the same message. I heard one of the twins squalling in the background. She didn't commit, but thanked me for calling. I almost asked her to call Yo-Yo, but thought better of it and dialed her myself. No answer. *Oh, right. The Bagel Bakery is open on Sunday.* I dialed her work number and asked to speak to Yo-Yo.

Yo-Yo seemed subdued. "Real sorry to hear MaDear's doin' so bad," she said. "But don't think I can make it."

"What time do you get off work?"

"Ain't that. I don't have no way to get there."

"Yo-Yo! Just call the Garfields and see if Ruth's coming. Get a ride with them!"

Silence on the other end. Then, "I'll see what I can do."

I hung up, frustrated. This was getting ridiculous.

Stu, Estelle, and I rode together to the hospital later that afternoon, bringing a shopping bag full of raw veggies, dried fruit and nuts, and orange juice to help get Adele and Sissy through the long days and nights at the hospital. Edesa and Delores had come up by el. When we arrived, Delores was huddled with Adele, translating some of the medical gobbledygook so she could understand what was happening with MaDear. Avis picked up both Florida and Becky at the Hickmans.

Hoshi came in with Nonyameko, eliciting gleeful hugs from the Yadas who attended other churches and hadn't seen her that morning at SouledOut. "I have only missed one Yada Yada," the Japanese student protested. "Not a trip around the world."

"*Si, mi amiga,*" Delores beamed, "but missing one Yada Yada means we do not get to see you for several weeks! How is your last semester going?"

We chatted—too loudly, I thought—in the ICU waiting room as we waited for any others to arrive. To my surprise, Yo-Yo walked in. Alone.

"How did you get here?" I whispered, taking her parka and tossing it on the growing pile filling up two chairs.

The pixie-haired girl shrugged, hands in the pockets of her faded denim overalls. "Took a taxi. Wasn't too bad."

I opened my mouth to fuss at her, then shut it. Okay, so maybe it was good for Yo-Yo not to rely on the Garfield limo service all the time. Anyway, Ruth wasn't here; maybe she couldn't make it. Yo-Yo headed across the room to say "hey" to Adele, who was giving a rundown—for the millionth time, probably—about MaDear's condition and treatments.

Chanda blew in like Little Red Riding Hood—well, not *little*—in her red wool coat with the fur collar, matching hat, and leather boots with skinny heels. I noticed that none of the other SouledOut church members rushed to say anything to her about the new chairs—had they decided that "anonymous" *meant* anonymous?—but I sidled up to her and put on my sing-songy voice. "The new chairs were a big hit this morning."

"Chairs?" She dumped her coat and hat on top of the pile.

"Aw, come on, Chanda. Did you donate new chairs to our church or not?"

She tipped her nose in the air. "Amendment Five. Don't have to answer. Mi learn 'bout dat in citizenship class." Then she dropped her voice near my ear. "Did dat *fine* Oscar Frost like dose chairs?"

My mouth dropped open. "Chanda George! You didn't!" I rolled my eyes. "You ordered those chairs to impress the *saxophone player*?!" I was laughing now. "Don't forget the donor was 'anonymous.' How would he know?"

"Humph. Well den, no matter. Mi just asking." She flounced around the room, giving overzealous hugs.

Avis had just called us to gather around Adele for prayer when Ruth stole in, hair askew, lipstick crooked. "I know, I know, late I am. And I can't stay long. Ben is driving around with the twins in the car." She suddenly seemed aware of Yo-Yo in the circle. "Oh! Yo-Yo. What, you sprouted wings and flew? We could have . . ." Her voice trailed off and she seemed momentarily confused.

Avis wisely took the cue and began to pray as we grabbed hands, ignoring the sullen looks of the few others in the room. For several minutes, we all prayed at once in quiet voices. "Oh Jesus, we need You now" . . . "Come, Holy Spirit, Comforter, fill this place" . . . "We love You, Lord" . . . "Yes, Lord, yes!" . . . "Bless Your name, Father" . . . "You are Jehovah-Rapha, the God Who Heals!" . . .

Then Avis led out in a specific prayer for MaDear. "Father God, Your daughter Sally is fighting a tough battle right now. Sickness and pneumonia are ravaging her body. But life and death are in Your hands, Oh God. You created us to be whole, to be strong, to be about the business of the kingdom! Jesus raised up Peter's mother-in-law from her sickbed, so we know nothing is impossible for You. You can raise MaDear up out of that bed in the ICU and restore her body and her mind."

"Yes, Jesus!" and "Hallelujahs" from others rode under Avis's voice. I squirmed. Heal her mind too? MaDear's dementia was pretty far gone. On the other hand, Jesus *had* healed that crazy guy named Legion running naked among the tombs.

Oh Lord, I breathed silently, *I want to believe.* Could it actually be?

Nonyameko picked up after Avis. "Praise the Lord, O my soul; in my inmost being, I praise Your holy name. Praise the Lord, O my soul! We do not forget all Your benefits. For You are the One who forgives all our sins and heals all our diseases, who redeems our lives from the pit and crowns us with love and compassion, who satisfies our desires with good things so that our youth is renewed like the eagle's! . . ."

Even though I had heard Nony pray the psalms many times, I felt mesmerized as she prayed Psalm 103. *God forgives our sins and heals our diseases—yes! . . . God satisfies our desires with good things— yes! . . . He renews our "youth," giving us strength and energy to fly rather than plod—yes! . . .*

How true that is, I thought. *How easy to take for granted the many small miracles of forgiveness and healing happening daily in this very group, in my own life. Though*—I peeked at Ruth and Yo-Yo— *God knows we could use a few more.*

As the prayers ended, Avis asked Adele if a few could go into MaDear's room to anoint her with oil and lay hands on her. Adele nodded and marched resolutely out of the room with Avis and Florida in tow. I doubted whether any hospital staff would deny her.

I wanted to see MaDear again and would've asked, but I knew all of us couldn't go in there. Avis and Florida soon returned, saying that a doctor came in and wanted to talk with Adele about switching MaDear to another antibiotic. Florida shook her head. "They talkin' 'bout some kind of chest physiotherapy—somethin' to clear her lungs out, so she can breathe easier. Ain't a pretty sight. But . . ." She grinned. "We got her anointed and prayed over 'fore they chased us out."

We untangled the pile of coats and started to leave the ICU floor. While we waited for the Down elevator, I nudged Ruth. "Ruth," I murmured, "why does Ben always have to drive you? Especially if it means bundling the twins up and taking them out, or driving circles around the hospital. You drove to Yada Yada on Super Bowl Sunday—I saw you!"

Ruth grimaced. "So call me a criminal. What, they expect a mother of twins to remember to renew her license?" She rolled her eyes. "Ben, of course, conveniently 'forgot' my license had expired when he wanted to watch the Super Bowl with his buddies. But his mind is sharp as a fox now. 'Get your license! Get your license!' he says. How, I ask? I drive myself, I break the law, and who wants to take along a grumpy husband and my two little *oysters*"—she kissed her fingers twice, like a little blessing.

The elevator door slid open. Half the group crowded inside. "Yo-Yo, wait!" Ruth waved her hand. "If you want a ride—" But the door slid closed. We heard the car *whirr* and fade. She looked at me and frowned. "What *mishegoss* is that?"

TEMPERATURES DIPPED THAT WEEK back into the Ice Age, but at least no new snow. Still, I lusted for spring, when I could send my class full of Tiggers into the playground so they could *boing boing* outside rather than off the walls—sometimes literally.

I was shouting, "Caleb Levy! Sit down!" for the fourth time on Tuesday when my classroom door opened and Avis Douglass motioned to me. Embarrassed, I held up my finger and nodded that I'd be there in a moment, then marched to Caleb's desk and placed my hand firmly on his shoulder. "If you get out of your seat once more, young man," I murmured, "or if I hear your voice even once while I am speaking to Mrs. Douglass, you will sit in the principal's office the rest of the day. Understand?"

The boy gave a slight nod, bottom lip stuck out in a pout. *Like his ears,* I thought uncharitably, as I gave the class instructions to complete the math paper I'd just handed out. "In silence," I added before stepping out into the hallway.

Avis took a deep breath. "She's gone."

"Gone? You mean . . . Rochelle?" I couldn't fathom why.

Avis shook her head. "No. MaDear. She died this morning about six o'clock. I just got a call from Adele."

I took a step back, as if an invisible hand had slapped me. *Gone?* But . . . hadn't we just pounded heaven with our prayers Sunday night? How could she—

Avis touched my shoulder. "We can talk later. I know you need to get back to your class. But I thought you'd want to know sooner rather than later." She gave me a half smile, her eyes sad. She seemed weary. "God knows, Jodi. He's in control."

I watched her walk down the hall toward the school office, her usual erect posture slightly deflated. Was she saying that for my benefit? Or hers?

I tried to get a breath, but I seemed to have a slow leak, draining the energy out of my body. MaDear was gone? *Dead?* In my mind, I saw her wrinkled, arthritic hand gently stroking Denny's head when he'd knelt beside her and asked for her forgiveness that strange day two Christmases ago. The image sent a shudder through my body.

Couldn't go there . . . I had to get through the rest of the day.

I gulped another prayer. *God, this is hard. I know she's old and has to go sometime, but* . . . My whole body felt tied in knots; I shook myself, as if shaking would loosen up my neurons and make them function again.

I pulled open the door to my classroom and stepped inside.

Several pairs of eyes peeked at me guiltily, as if wondering if I'd caught them doing . . . whatever. I didn't care. What was a whisper behind hands or a doodle on the math paper or a booger under the desk, when a precious old woman, as much a fixture at Adele's Hair and Nails as the hair dryers and nail art and weekly chatter, was suddenly gone?

No, I couldn't go back to "class as usual." "Caleb?" I called.

The boy looked up, startled, mouth open, ready to protest, *"I didn't do anything!"*

"Would you like to choose a chapter book from the bookshelf for us to read? Everyone else, come to the Story Rug . . . That's right, just leave your math pages on your desk. We're going to get comfy and listen to a good book . . . *Encyclopedia Brown,* Caleb? Good choice."

AS WORD FLEW FROM PHONE TO PHONE, Stu's meal plan for MaDear's homecoming kicked into action, only the food now was for Adele and out-of-town relatives who started arriving the very next day. Estelle took herself over to Adele's apartment every morning that week and lit into cleaning the house, doing laundry, answering the phone, kicking out visitors so Adele could get some rest, helping Adele find MaDear's insurance papers, and in general holding things together at the Skuggs household so that Adele could fall apart.

Florida had dropped by to see Adele when a male cousin from Memphis—who'd just been told to take his feet off the coffee table—fussed at Adele: *"Baby, that maid o' yours is too bossy. You shouldn't let no maid talk to family like that."*

According to Florida, Adele had reared up and spit fire. *"Estelle is not a maid, and don't you forget it! She's family as much as you are, cousin—more so in my book. I see you makin' more work 'round here, 'stead of helpin' out."*

"Couldn't help myself," Florida had written in an e-mail to the Yada Yadas. *"I bust out laughing. Don't want to say Manna House burning down was a good thing, but the day Stu invited Estelle to move in was like a gift from the Wise Men."*

Estelle called from Adele's on Thursday to say that visitation was scheduled for one o'clock on Saturday at Paul and Silas Apostolic Baptist Church, the funeral would begin at two, and Adele wanted Denny to read the scripture during the service.

Denny scratched his chin nervously when I delivered the news. "Uh, I don't know, Jodi. I'm scheduled to do that Captives Free prison training Saturday."

"Denny!" I gaped at him. "You can't mean that's more important than showing up at MaDear's *funeral,* do you?"

"I didn't say that. It's just . . . let me get my information sheet." A moment later, he was back. "Okay." He blew out a breath. "The training is from eight to one. If I go straight from there to the church, I ought to make it in time for the funeral. Maybe even time to spare."

"Except that means you'll have the car," I grumbled. "How are we supposed to get there?"

The phone rang, cutting us off. "We'll figure it out," he called over his shoulder. ". . . Hello?" He listened for several moments. "Okay, *mi hermano.* That's good news. We'll be praying with you. *Adios.*"

Denny looked at me, a grin slowly deepening his side dimples.

"That was Ricardo. His job application was accepted by Midwest Movers. They only cover eight states—so most trips will only take two to three days, both ways."

I felt a pang. *Good news . . . and bad?* "What about his mariachi band?"

Denny shrugged slightly. "He doesn't know. José's going to fill in for him for now if he can't make it. But the good thing is, Jodi, Ricardo said he's taking the trucking job—band or no band— because he knows he has to put first things first. '*Mi familia,*' he said. 'They are most important.'"

23

*T*he day of MaDear's funeral dawned bright, clear, and cold—not a hard-edged, bitter cold, but softened by the sun, hinting at spring.

Still, I shivered inside my robe as I half-pushed, half-carried Willie Wonka up the back porch stairs after his morning pee. But the shiver seemed to come from deep inside, not just the snap in the air on my skin. "Come on, old boy," I murmured, shutting the door behind us and attaching a can of dog food to the electric can opener. "Eat some breakfast, will you? Gotta keep your strength up." For some reason, my eyes misted as I spooned half the can into Wonka's dog dish. "Eat . . . please eat," I whispered.

Willie Wonka looked up at me with his liquid brown eyes, then lowered his muzzle to the dish and nibbled.

"Good boy." I filled a mug with fresh coffee and settled into the recliner in the front room for some prayer time. But my Bible remained closed on my lap. Why did I feel so . . . low? As if Wonka's obvious decline and MaDear's death were pressing my spirit down into the mud. After all, I tried to reassure myself, Willie Wonka was still his loveable, sweet self, in spite of slowing down. *Waaay down.* But he didn't seem to be in pain, thanks to the meds the vet had given him. And MaDear had lived a long, full life. The last few years had been distorted by mental confusion, which had to have been stressful for MaDear herself, as well as Adele. Shouldn't we feel glad that the end was quick, without a long, painful illness?

With a twinge of guilt, I remembered how relieved I'd felt when my grandmother died. I was barely a teenager when she came to live with us in Des Moines. Gram had dominated our life with her complaints. The whole family had to tiptoe around *her* needs. My older brothers dealt with the Gram Invasion by staying out of the house as much as possible, hanging out with their friends. But as the only girl, I had to share my room with that impossible woman, who felt free to poke around in my dresser drawers when I was at school. I didn't shed a tear when she died. In fact, I would have shouted "*Hallelujah!*" if I'd been a hallelujah-shouting person then.

Was Adele feeling relieved that MaDear was gone? And guilty that she felt relieved?

At least Adele had treated her mother with compassion, bringing her mother as best she could into her life at Adele's Hair and Nails, giving her comforting things to do to keep her busy, like sorting the buttons from the old button jar and looking through old photos . . . old photos that brought up memories, both painful and sweet, even in MaDear's confused mind.

A tear slid down my face. "Oh God," I groaned, "forgive me for being such a selfish pig when I was a teenager, never once thinking about life from Gram's point of view. All I thought about was how she disrupted *my* life." For the first time ever, I wished I could hug my grandmother once more, ask her to tell me stories from her life as a girl, ask her to forgive me for not understanding what it meant to get old.

I blubbered for a few minutes, my feelings all mixed up because I'd loved MaDear more than my own grandmother. Finally, I mopped my face, blew my nose, and headed back to the kitchen, still feeling depressed. But I needed to get some laundry done so we'd have clean clothes for MaDear's funeral.

AS IT TURNED OUT, Denny got a ride with Peter Douglass to the Captives Free Jail and Prison Ministry training that morning, so we were able to take our minivan after all. Josh drove, looking like a Gap ad in a rumpled shirt and tie, his increasingly shaggy hair caught back in a small, sandy ponytail at the nape of his neck.

From shaved head to ponytail . . . didn't this boy-turning-man know about that lovely concept called moderation? I sighed and kept my mouth shut.

We picked up the Hickman family and Becky Wallace. That put eight in the car and we only had seven seatbelts. Carla and Cedric clamored to ride in the "way back," but I insisted on them having seatbelts. I finally allowed Amanda to ride back there and prayed all the way to Paul and Silas that no one would slam us in the rear.

Even when we found the church on Kedzie, we had to drive around a couple of blocks before we found a parking space. I had visited Paul and Silas Apostolic Baptist a year earlier with Yada

Yada, but this was a first for the rest of my family. I'd warned Amanda about the head coverings, but even though there was a basket available with the little "doilies," as Flo called them, for those without a hat, no one was offering them to the many guests coming that day. We waved at Avis and Peter Douglass across the foyer and caught a glimpse of Chanda George arriving with her children, but the foyer was too crowded to actually meet up.

After hanging up our coats in the coatroom, a female usher with white gloves handed us an order of service with a picture of a young Sally Rutherford Skuggs on the front, and directed us to join the long line moving along the far right aisle. I spotted Delores Enriques and Edesa Reyes in the line ahead of us. As the line approached the front of the church, people were greeting the family sitting in the front rows and paying their respects at the open casket, which was flanked by a lush garden of roses and white carnations. Most of the crowd was black—though after generations in America, "black" was hardly the word for the rich, rippling shades of brown and tan filling the church, from dark coffee bean to malted milk.

The line moved slowly. I had plenty of time to gape at the stylish women's suits and big hats—most of them silky black on black, or black with white or silver trim. I suddenly felt terribly underdressed in my ordinary blue-and-black print dress. I had a gorgeous black dress at home—the slinky black number Denny had bought for me two birthdays ago—but it was definitely *not* funeral-appropriate.

As the line inched along, I wondered how many of the women present that day had sat in one of the chairs at Adele's Hair and Nails getting cut, processed, permed, straightened, weaved, braided, or curled . . . laughing, chatting, *tsk-tsking* over somebody's child, or complaining loudly about the latest runaround with "the system." Knowing Adele, she had probably functioned as Mother Confessor to hundreds of women who knew she would listen, give a word or two of sympathy or encouragement, even pray for them, and keep her mouth shut.

"Excuse me . . . thank you . . . excuse me . . ." A familiar male voice interrupted my wandering thoughts as Denny squeezed into the line next to me. "Made it," he breathed into my ear. "Tie on straight?" I looked him up and down, grinned, and nodded.

We had almost reached the front. Watching what others did, I shook hands with the people in the front row, murmuring, "Hello. My name is Jodi Baxter. I'm a member of Adele's prayer group . . . you're Adele's aunt? I'm so sorry for your loss." This went on for five or six people and then I was toe to toe with Adele's overly made-up, bleached-blonde sister dabbing at her eyes. "Sissy? I'm Jodi Baxter, Adele's friend. We met briefly at the hospital." Sissy shook my hand limply, a hankie pressed to her nose.

Adele sat next to the aisle. A stylish black hat with a modest brim and a wide black ribbon around the crown hid her short, black-and-silver natural 'fro. She looked up at me, eyes sad but calm, and smiled, showing the tiny gap between her front teeth. "Jodi and Denny Baxter . . ." When Adele used both my first and last name, I never knew what to expect. To my surprise, she stood up and hugged us both before turning to Amanda and Josh, who were crowding on our heels. They got hugs too.

Then it was our turn at the casket. Two male ushers stood impassively on either side, each with one white-gloved hand behind his back. A shimmering white brocade covered the casket, as if the material had been sprayed on. A spray of pink and white roses with a pink ribbon that read "Dearest Mother" in gold script lay on the closed lower half. The upper half was open, lined with tinted pink crepe, shirred and thick and soft. I willed myself to step close and look at the body lying stiffly on the pillow . . .

MaDear? It didn't look like her. The spark of life that had lit up her glittering eyes, whether happy, sad, or angry, was gone. But the freckles dusting the yellowish cheeks were the same. I reached into the casket and brushed the back of my hand against her cold, waxy skin. "Good-bye, MaDear," I murmured, pushing the words past the lump in my throat. "See you in heaven. I loved you, you know."

I started to turn away but felt Denny's arm go around my waist and hold me there. His other hand gripped the casket. We stayed another long minute until the ushers sternly waved us on.

It took a long time for everyone to greet the family and pass by the casket, but the service finally started with the small organ belting out Tommy Dorsey's "Precious Lord, take my hand . . ." A procession of officials in black robes—pastors, ministers, and visiting pastors—walked slowly and solemnly down the two middle aisles. The choir, in dark green robes and bold, gold-brown-and-red Afro-centric stoles, slow-stepped in their wake. The pastors and ministers stood in a row across the platform while Paul and Silas's senior pastor, listed in the program as "Rev. Arthur B. Miles III," gave the invocation.

As the ministers took their seats, the choir launched into a spirited rendition of *"Some glad morning, when this life is o'er, I'll fly away . . ."* The choir swayed; people clapped. *"Just a few more weary days and then, I'll fly away . . ."*

The church quieted as a lanky man from the family row—

probably that Mississippi cousin—stood up and read the obituary printed on the back side of the program. "Born Sally Rutherford, August 2, 1923 in Tupelo, Mississippi, to a hardworking family that endured many hardships in the Jim Crow South . . . Married Emil Skuggs in 1942 . . . Moved to Chicago with two young daughters after the death of her husband, often working two jobs to give them an education . . . She is survived by a younger sister and brother and two loving daughters . . . and leaves a host of family and friends to celebrate her life and miss her physical presence."

My mind stuck on the words, *"endured many hardships."* How many in this congregation knew those hardships included the horrific lynching of her fifteen-year-old brother for being "too uppity" around white folks? Hardships, indeed.

The obituary was followed by a congregational hymn: *"Blessed assurance, Jesus is mine! Oh what a foretaste of glory divine . . ."* Halfway through the hymn, I glanced at my program and realized that the Scripture reading was next. Did Denny remember? Had he brought his Bible? I poked him and pointed it out in the program: *Psalm 27* on the left side, *Mr. Dennis Baxter* on the right. He nodded.

He seemed calm enough. I'd be a wreck about now if I had to get up in front of all these people, a white face in a sea of black, with half the women probably thinking, *"Who's that white chick, and why is she wearing that pathetic rag?"* Kinda funny that Adele had asked Denny to read the Scripture, though. Why not Avis or Nony or one of her other Yada Yada sisters?

". . . will be read by Mr. Dennis Baxter," Rev. Miles was saying. "Come on up here, brother." Well. At least it wasn't me, thank goodness. I gave Denny's back an encouraging smile as he made his way up the aisle, up the two carpeted platform steps, and made his way to the podium. He took a small Bible out of his inside suit coat pocket, glanced in Adele's direction with a brief smile, then began to read.

"Psalm 27 . . . The Lord is my light and my salvation, whom shall I fear? The Lord is the strength of my life; of whom shall I be afraid?" As my husband read the words of the psalm, I suddenly realized it was talking to me. My depression that morning had actually been fear. Fear of loss. Fear that I'd lost my chance to make it right with my grandmother. Fear that all the ongoing prayers we'd been praying in Yada Yada—for Florida's boy and Nony's husband and Avis's daughter and Becky fighting to get her parental rights back—would go unanswered, just like our prayer for MaDear's healing. Even my stupid fear a few minutes ago of what people here were thinking of me.

But what in heaven's name did I have to be afraid of? The *Lord* was the strength of my life—*and* Adele's, *and* MaDear's, *and* my family's, *and* of all my Yada Yada sisters and their families. Hadn't we seen God's hand in our lives again and again? Just like the psalmist had written: "*Though an army may encamp against me, my heart shall not fear . . . For in the time of trouble He shall hide me in His pavilion; in the secret place of His tabernacle He shall hide me; He shall set me high upon a rock.*"

As he neared the end of the psalm, Denny's voice grew stronger. "—I would have lost heart, unless I had believed that I would see the goodness of the Lord in the land of the living!" Denny closed his Bible and started to return to his seat. But Adele stood up, stepped in his way, and folded him in a long embrace.

Suddenly I realized why Adele had asked *Denny* to read that psalm at MaDear's funeral! It was her way of laying to rest that painful episode when MaDear's confused mind thought Denny was the white man who had lynched her brother decades ago in Mississippi. Two Christmases ago, Denny had bravely asked MaDear to forgive him for something he hadn't done, because the old lady needed closure. "And because somebody needs to," he had said. And MaDear had laid her hand on his head and forgiven him.

But I knew Adele still struggled with the tragedy that had torn her mother's family apart, and the not-always-subtle bigotry she still had to deal with, like being ignored by the cops when she went to the police station to get her jewelry back that Becky Wallace had stolen. Adele had many reasons to "lose heart"—and yet, in spite of everything, she still believed in "the goodness of the Lord in the land of the living."

That was the strength Adele brought to Yada Yada. That was the strength she gave to me: *"Whatever comes your way, Jodi, deal with it and go on . . . because God is our light and our salvation, and God is good."*

I saw Denny's lips form the words, *"Thank you,"* when Adele released him from her embrace. I touched his arm when he sat down, but he was busy fishing for his handkerchief and blowing his nose.

That's when I understood Adele had offered Denny closure too.

24

I tried to concentrate on the rest of the funeral service. One of the visiting ministers was reading a handful of "resolutions" from various congregations in Chicago and Tupelo, paying tribute to the life of Sally Rutherford Skuggs. They got a little long and repetitious, but my ears pricked up when Rev. Miles took the pulpit to preach the eulogy, using 1 Thessalonians 4:13–18 as his text.

"Brothers and sisters," he thundered, "even though we have to say farewell to our elder sister for a time, we are not full of sorrow like people who have no hope. No! Because we know something the world doesn't know—or chooses to ignore. And that is"—he paused dramatically—"the reality, the *fact*, brothers and sisters, of the resurrection from the dead."

Half the congregation was on its feet, shouting back to the preacher. "Yes!" "Tell the truth, Pastor!" "Praise Jesus!"

"If God the Father raised *Jesus* from the dead, then *we* who call on His name will *also* be raised from the dead, and we will be *reunited* with all the dead in Christ who have gone before us. Sister Adele, you *will* see your mother again, and she'll have a *new* body, one that sickness has not ravaged, and her mind will be *clear and sharp*—"

Now Adele was on her feet, practically dancing on the front row, hand in the air, tears running down her face. "Thank You, Jesus! Thank You! Thank You!"

Watching Adele, it suddenly occurred to me that I would see my grandmother again too. Not the decrepit creature I remembered—shuffling around the house, mumbling to herself—but a strong woman with a vigorous body and a quick mind. I stifled a giggle, thinking about Gram and MaDear matching wits in heaven. Maybe MaDear would tell Gram that I'd grown up a little, and I'd be coming too, one of these days, to tell her I was sorry and could we spend part of eternity getting to know each other again?

"—Then we who are still alive and remain on the earth will be caught up in the clouds to meet the Lord in the air and remain with Him forever. So comfort and encourage each other with these words."

The rest of the church was on its feet now as the organ punctuated the pastor's closing words. In the midst of the praise all around me, I whispered my own praise. *"Thank You for MaDear, Jesus, for giving me a second chance to love a 'grandma' these last two years."* The tears ran again and I used up half my travel packet of tissues mopping my face, probably smearing my mascara.

But my once-heavy spirit had reached zero gravity.

"MOM!" Amanda tugged on my arm as the pastor invited the congregation to go downstairs to the fellowship hall for the repast.

"Don't we drive out to the cemetery or something? I mean, don't they have to bury her?"

"—Please allow the family to leave and be served first," the pastor was saying.

"I think the body is going to be cremated and the ashes taken to Tupelo for burial," I whispered back.

Amanda's eyes widened. "You mean, *burn* her bod—!"

"Shh!" I hissed. "Later, okay?"

The closed casket remained at the front of the church as the family of Sally Rutherford Skuggs processed up the aisle and disappeared down the stairs to the fellowship hall. The ushers, crisp and unflappable, allowed each row to follow, starting near the front, and working toward the back.

When we finally nudged our way into the fellowship hall, we headed for the long row of tables at the other end loaded down with hot casseroles, salads, chicken, and cake. When Denny and I finally got our paper plates filled, we made our way through the noisy crowd to a table populated mostly by Yada Yada folks. Denny put his plate down on the end of the table where Peter Douglass and Carl Hickman were digging in.

"Anybody see Yo-Yo?" Becky said between munches on a piece of crispy fried chicken. "She told me yesterday at work that she was gonna try to come." She licked her fingers as the rest of us shook our heads.

"Guess we all used to Ruth and Ben takin' that girl wherever she needs ta go," Florida said, a forkful of beans and cornbread halfway to her mouth. "But I don't see Garfields, neither."

Becky shrugged. "Maybe one of the twins is sick or somethin'. If I had a car, I could pick up Yo-Yo. Could pick up Little Andy

215

on Sundays too—sure would be a lot easier. But . . . guess that ain't gonna happen for a while."

"Huh. You and me both, girl." Florida jabbed the plastic fork at Becky. "But we got us a *two*-car garage out back of our house, so I'm thinkin' God gonna fill it one o' these days. For both of us."

Becky sighed. "Yeah, but it ain't gonna happen on my part-time salary from the Bagel Bakery. Man! I need me a new job!"

As the chatter resumed around us, Florida leaned closer to me, her voice lowered. "What's with that boy of yours, Jodi, sittin' over there all by hisself? He look as miserable as a wet cat in a bubble bath."

I followed her glance and saw Josh parked in a metal folding chair against the wall, his tie and collar loosened, picking at his plate of food. He did look miserable. In fact, if I thought about it, Josh hadn't been himself since the night of the fire at Manna House. I said as much to Florida.

"He still blaming hisself for that? Ain't nobody else blamin' him that I know of. Girl, if we let our screwups dog our footsteps, we *all* be headin' down a dead-end street."

I snorted. "Tell me about it." Seemed like I had enough "screwups" the past couple of years to sink any "good Christian girl" on her way to sainthood. Maybe Denny and I should talk to Josh, find out what was going on . . .

Just then, I saw Estelle, large, round, and comforting, make her way to the chairs along the wall and sink down beside Josh. He gave her a polite nod, but in a few moments, she had him half-grinning in spite of himself and shaking his head as if trying not to laugh. Did that woman know how to work wonders, or what?

By this time, Nony, Hoshi, and Chanda joined the rest of us as we scooted chairs to make room, and Chanda waved at Edesa and Delores, who had just waded through the line for the first time. "Now, this what mi tinkin'," Chanda said, casting her eyes this way and that, as if making sure she wouldn't be overheard—though it was hard enough to hear ourselves talking face to face. She leaned in. "Now, we sistas know Adele be stubborn as old Billy Goat Gruff when it come to letting us know she need som'ting. So we gotta check on her wit'out letting her know we doing it. What you tink of dat idea?"

We all looked at her. "Think about *what* idea?" Stu said.

Chanda rolled her eyes. "Hair! Hair!" She grabbed her own braided extensions and shook them. "We all make appointments at Adele's Hair and Nails in de next two, t'ree weeks. Give us excuse to see how she doing!"

I FELT DRAINED by the time we got home around six, but I checked the kitchen calendar. Next Saturday would work for me. I could use a cut . . . maybe even a color. That'd be fun. Besides, Denny had wickedly pointed out a few gray hairs not two days ago, the jerk. Huh. I'd show him. Go blonde or something— maybe a redhead. Or get my hair cut *short*. Spiky, like Yo-Yo's. That'd freak him out.

Yeah, right, Jodi. You're as likely to go redhead or spiky-haired as get your navel pierced.

I wrote "Haircut?" on the first weekend in March, then flipped back to February. It'd been two weeks since Yada Yada met upstairs at Stu's apartment. Where were we meeting tomorrow? . . . "Wait a minute," I mumbled aloud. "Tomorrow is the fifth Sunday in

February. How did the shortest month of the year get a *fifth* Sunday?"

"Leap year, babe." Denny was raiding the refrigerator. "We've got an extra day to use up. Wanna do something?" I'd announced *no supper tonight* since we'd just eaten the equivalent of four Thanksgiving dinners at the repast. How could the man eat again?

I turned the calendar back to March. "Huh. Monday is General Pulaski Day. No school. Sheesh! Didn't we just have Presidents' Day off two weeks ago? How are kids going to learn anything if they keep shortening the school calendar!"

"Don't knock it, kiddo. Chicago's tip of the old *chapka* to its Polish son." Denny raised the can of Pepsi he'd found, as if making a toast. "One of the perks of working for the Chicago school system. A family holiday!"

"*Used* to be a family holiday," Josh grumbled, coming in the back door just then with a wheezing Willie Wonka. "I gotta work on Monday." He opened the refrigerator, not even bothering to shed his winter jacket. "We got anything in here to eat?"

Men. Didn't they ever outgrow the hollow-leg syndrome?

DENNY WAS GOING TO ASK AMANDA if she'd like to go out to a movie Sunday afternoon for some daddy-daughter time, but we scrapped that idea when Pastor Clark announced a leap year party for the youth that night at the church. "Your ticket to the party is to bring a friend who doesn't attend our church already," he said. A month ago, that would have been a no-brainer for Amanda. *José, who else?* But when we got home after church, she started wailing, "Who can I invite? I don't know anybody!"

Which might be another good reason the relationship with José had dialed down, I thought. Amanda needed a broader circle of friends.

"I just won't go!" she pouted. But with some prodding, Amanda finally called a couple of girls in her Spanish club at school who lived in Rogers Park—and to her surprise, both said they'd like to come. "Josh, can you drive me and pick them up? *Puh–leeease?*"

I didn't see that one coming. With Amanda out for the evening, I'd been hoping Denny and I could talk to Josh. Most days we passed each other like the proverbial ships in the night. On the other hand, might be a good thing for him to hang out with the youth at SouledOut tonight. For a while, he'd seemed ready to jump on board with Pastor Cobb's vision for youth; then Manna House had taken up all his free time. But now, he was bobbing around like a rubber ducky in a Jacuzzi . . .

"Do you know what's going on with Josh?" I asked Denny over hot cider and an appetizer called *Avacado con Salsa y Queso* at the Heartland Café later that evening.

He shook his head, dipping corn chips into the baked avocado. "Figured he just needed some time to sort things out after the fire."

"But that was five weeks ago! He seems so . . . deflated lately."

Denny pursed his lips. "Yeah. Know what you mean. He was so fired up about his volunteer work at Manna House. Of course, part of that was working with Edesa, but who knows where *that* relationship is going. Maybe he'd be ready to talk about going to school next year . . . what? Are you okay?"

A couple of corn chips had suddenly created a traffic jam in my throat. I took a swig of hot cider to wash them down. "Ohmigosh, Denny," I choked. "*School?* I'm sure the deadline has passed for renewing his application to the University of Illinois! Wasn't it

January first or something like that when he was sending out applications last year?" I pushed my mug and plate away. *Sheesh! Why didn't we get on his case a couple of months ago!* The thought of Josh hanging around the Baxter domicile another whole year, not doing much, made me lose my appetite.

I pressed my fingers against my temples. *Okay, okay. Old Jodi response or New Jodi?* I could freak out, or . . . I could pray, ask God for wisdom, talk to Josh, cool my jets, pray some more . . .

But for that, I needed time. I ordered another hot cider and changed the subject. "Denny, remember all that crappy music at the roller-skating rink? Still sticks in my craw, thinking of all those kids listening to that sleazy music every weekend. The DJ I talked to that night just blew me off."

He snorted. "Yeah. I remember."

"Well, I've been thinking about writing a letter to the manager, maybe sending a petition from those of us who were there that night, asking the rink to offer at least one skate time every weekend that's truly 'family friendly' . . . what do you think?"

He lifted his eyebrows. "What do *I* think?"

"Yeah." I could feel my face coloring. "I don't want to ride off on one of my 'good ideas' again without getting your input this time."

To his credit, Denny laughed. "Ah. The ol' lemonade stand syndrome." He cleaned out the bottom of the avocado dip with the last few chips. "A letter sounds good. Petition sounds good. But don't get your hopes up too high, Jodi. It would probably take a major boycott of the place to sway management to—"

He must have seen the light go on in my eyes because he suddenly threw up his hands. "Now, wait a minute. I was not *suggesting* a major boycott! I just meant . . ." He blew out a huge breath. "You know good and well what I meant."

25

*Y*eah. I knew what he meant. We'd gone to the rink *once*. It wasn't as if we were regular customers. But still, maybe the letter and petition would be worth a try. And maybe we'd go back sometime if they didn't have R-rated music to skate by.

So while Denny took Amanda on a daddy-daughter date to Walker Brothers Original Pancake House the next morning (their favorite breakfast haunt), I took advantage of the school holiday to compose a polite but assertive letter to the management of the Super Skatium about our experience on Valentine's Day.

"We brought a large group with us," I typed into the computer, *"including parents, children, teens, and singles, but our entire group left early because of the sexually explicit music, which we thought was highly inappropriate for a general audience that included children and young teens."* Then I suggested having at least one family-friendly skating session each weekend. *"If so,"* I concluded, *"we would be happy to patronize your establishment more often and encourage others to do the same."* Well, at least *once* more.

I read my letter over several times, then sent it by e-mail attachment to the other Yada Yadas who had gone to our "Valentine skate," asking what they thought about adding their names and addresses to the letter at our next meeting. I hit Send, not sure if anyone else had given the problem another thought after that night. But at least I wasn't jumping on my high horse this time and riding off in all directions.

That done, I was strongly tempted to find the book my parents had given me for Christmas and start planning flower boxes for the front and back porches this spring . . . but with a sigh I pulled out my school calendar and lesson plans to review. *Hm. March. Women's History Month.* What could I do this year besides the typical read-a-biography-and-report-on-it yawn?

And who to highlight? We'd already celebrated Mary McLeod Bethune, whose name graced our school, for Black History Month. I looked at the suggested reading list. Marie Curie, Jane Austen, Gwendolyn Brooks, Florence Nightingale, Clara Barton, Susan B. Anthony, Sojourner Truth, Amelia Earhart, Dr. Sally Ride . . . *Hm. Those last two would appeal to third graders. Airplanes and spaceships.*

I chewed the end of my pen. But what about courageous women like Gladys Aylward, an Englishwoman who became a Chinese citizen, ran an orphanage for abandoned children, and challenged the ancient ritual of binding little girls' feet—a painful custom that had kept women mincing on tiny feet for centuries. But what about the fact that Gladys was a Christian missionary too—did we have to hush that up? Could I include her name, or would the PC police come knocking on my door?

I decided to make up my own reading list and include some notable women of faith like Gladys Aylward, Mother Teresa, and Betty Greene, the World War II test pilot who helped to start Missionary Aviation Fellowship. And instead of book reports, maybe my third graders could pretend to be the person they chose and tell her story in first person. Boys could pretend to be newscasters reporting on a famous woman.

Excited, I turned the computer back on and started my list. But would it fly?

THE DRONING TV in the teachers' lounge made sure I kept abreast of the news that week, whether I wanted to or not. *John Kerry had virtually wrapped up the Democratic nomination for the presidential election . . . a space probe had discovered evidence of water on Mars . . . and suicide bombers had hit several Iraqi mosques, killing 170 Shiite worshipers.*

I was tempted to turn a deaf ear, but a nudge in my spirit said, *Pray, Jodi. Pray for the news . . .*

Avis was cautious but open to my revised list of "Notable Women Who Changed the World." "Add some Jewish and Muslim heroines to your list, Jodi, and I might be able to defend it if anyone raises questions."

Okay. That would take a little more research. Had to admit I was out of touch with most Middle Eastern history, in spite of America's war in Iraq. *But Jewish . . .* I was tempted to ask Avis how far back I could go in time. There was always Esther, the Jewish girl chosen by King Xerxes to be queen over all Persia in

400-something B.C.—who ended up putting her life on the line to save her people from total annihilation. The story was a great read, even in the Old Testament.

Just for fun, I Googled "Queen Esther" when I got home on Thursday to see what other interesting facts I could come up with—and discovered that *Purim,* the Jewish holiday celebrating Esther's courage, an ordinary woman God had put into the royal palace "for such a time as this," was only a few days away!

I called Ruth Garfield, all excited. "Ruth! Why didn't you tell us Purim was this month?"

"Did you ask?"

Argh. "How am I supposed to know if—! Never mind. We're celebrating Women's History Month at school, and I was wondering if you . . . would you come to my class one day next week and tell them about Purim and Queen Esther?"

A brief silence. "Me you're asking?"

"Yes, you, you goose! Please?"

"Love to, Jodi. I would. But . . ." She sighed. "I'm still criminal. Can't drive. And Ben is working part time. Who would take care of the babies?"

My mind spun like a top, sorting through possibilities. *Estelle. She'd love to take care of the twins.* "Leave it to me, Ruth. Just tell me a day that's good for you and I'll work out . . . something." I glanced at my kitchen calendar. "By the way, Yada Yada is supposed to meet at your house Sunday night. Still good for you?" And, I noticed, it was Ruth's birthday the day after . . . the Big Five-O.

"Sure. You come to me, anything works. What's that clicking sound?"

"Oh . . . call waiting. I think it's Denny's cell. Talk to you later." I pushed the Flash button. "Denny?"

"Hey, babe. Just want to remind you that tonight's my first time volunteering at the JDC. My team partner is Oscar Frost, you know, the guy who plays saxophone at church. Nice kid. He volunteered too. Anyway, might not be home till ten or so. Save some supper for me, okay? . . . What's so funny?"

All I could see in my mind was Chanda putting her hand on her hip and saying, "That *fine* Oscar Frost." I was trying so hard to stifle my giggles it came out snorting. "Nothing . . . tell you later . . . I'll pray for you, okay? I want to hear all about it."

But when I hung up the phone, I leaned against the counter and laughed aloud. Wait until I told Chanda who Denny's partner was for the JDC Bible studies. Or maybe I shouldn't. She'd bug Denny to death, wanting to know every little detail. What a hoot!

AS I DROVE TO ADELE'S HAIR AND NAILS Saturday morning, I noticed three young teens standing on a street corner, hunched inside their gray hooded sweatshirts, baggy jeans hanging half off their butts, as if waiting . . . for what? Would this trio end up at the JDC like too many other young men? Like . . . Chris Hickman? Kids with stressed-out families, kids with talent, wanting to belong, but hanging with the wrong friends, "catching a case."

Denny had come home Thursday night so wired we both got to bed late. "What a bunch of sharp kids, Jodi. Most of them polite, too, believe it or not. Not what I expected. Real leadership types, if pointed in the right direction. I came with six New Testaments that Captives Free provided—but at least four other guys begged me to get them one too. Talk about a ripe situation, getting to these kids before they get sentenced to prison—or go back out on the streets."

"Did you see Chris?"

He'd grinned big. "Oscar and I got assigned to his unit! Didn't know that till he showed up tonight, though. He acted a bit distant; maybe he was surprised to see us there. I was friendly but didn't acknowledge I knew him or his family. He stayed for the study."

Just seeing a familiar face must be encouraging, I thought, pushing open the door of Adele's Hair and Nails, setting off the little bell above the door. The sharp odor of hair relaxer snaked up my nose, making my eyes water. Or maybe it was just the difference between the chilly March wind outside and the moist, warm air inside the salon.

Or maybe because I knew MaDear would not be in the back room today, sorting her buttons.

"Jodi Baxter." Adele caught my eye in the wall mirror, as she stood behind the customer in the first chair. "I smell a conspiracy."

"Hi, Miz Baxter!" piped up a childish voice. Avis's grandson hopped off the couch in the waiting area and tugged on my jacket. "Grammy's over there." Conny pointed at the hair dryers halfway back in the narrow salon. "An' Mommy's getting her hair all pretty." The finger swung to the first chair.

The young woman in the chair also caught my eye in the mirror and gave a little smile. "Rochelle!" I said. "I didn't recognize you all covered up in Adele's plastic."

"Uh-huh." Adele went back to sectioning Rochelle's wet locks and rolling them up on squishy pink curlers. "Just coincidence, I suppose, that you and Avis and Rochelle 'just happened' to come in this morning. Stu and Estelle were here last night. Chanda's coming this afternoon . . ."

I laughed, stooping down to give Conny a hug. I shrugged out of my jacket and hung it up on the coat rack. "Guess we all need perking up with spring coming."

Conny ran to his mother. "I gotta *go!*" he whispered loudly, tugging on her arm.

"I'll take you, little man." I held out my hand to him. "Your mommy and grammy are kinda busy right now."

"Thanks, Mrs. Baxter." Rochelle smiled at me in the mirror. *Sheesh.* The girl was gorgeous, even with pink knobby curlers framing the deep golden glow of her skin.

"Hey. Call me Jodi. When I have grandkids, too, like your *mom*"—I cast a grin in Avis's direction, who couldn't hear a thing we were saying—"*then* you can call me Mrs. Baxter."

Conny frowned up at me under his mat of loose, dark curls, as if considering whether I could handle this major assignment. Then he gave me his hand, and we threaded our way down the middle aisle of Adele's salon, waving at Avis parked under one of the beehive hair dryers as we passed, heading for the cubbyhole bathroom that said, "Employees Only."

My heart squeezed tightly as we entered the back room, and I saw MaDear's empty wheelchair. On the floor beside the chair sat the jar of buttons and the empty egg carton she'd used for sorting—colors, sizes, memories . . .

"I gotta *go!*" Conny reminded me, tugging on my hand.

I turned on the light in the bathroom, pulled down his corduroy trousers and "big boy pants," and sat him on the toilet. "You okay?"

He waved me off. "I can do it myself."

"Okay." I grinned. "I'll be right here if you need me." I stepped outside, leaving the door open a crack.

Adele bustled into the back room. "You're in the chair next, Jodi . . . oh, he's not done. No problem. I wanted to give you something anyway."

She bent over with an *oof!* and picked up the jar of buttons. "Here." She thrust the jar into my hands. "I want you to have these. Kind of a thank you for all the times you came to 'play' with MaDear."

Tears sprang to my eyes. I brushed them away with the back of one hand. "Oh, Adele. I . . ." My voice got husky. "Thank you. It's the best memento you could've given me of your mom."

"Thought so. Well, come on up front when you—"

We both heard the bell tinkle up front, both heard the angry male voice bark, "Where is he, Rochelle? Where's my son?"

"Uh-oh." Adele moved so fast out of the back room, she seemed to be moving on roller skates. *My* feet, on the other hand, felt nailed to the floor.

Dexter!

Female voices. Avis . . . Adele . . . Rochelle . . . Then Dexter's voice, louder. "Fine! You don't want to come home. But you can't steal my son from me! Where—"

"Is that my daddy?" piped up a tiny voice from within the cubicle.

I darted into the bathroom, pulled the door shut behind me, and hooked the lock. "Hey, little guy. You done?" *Keep calm, Jodi. Keep calm.*

Conny swung his legs and shook his head.

I turned on the water in the sink, full blast. "Sometimes

running the water helps, did you know that? Say, do you know this song?" I held up my hands, thumb to finger, finger to thumb, and started to sing in a whisper voice. "Itsy, bitsy spider, went up the water spout. *Down* came the rain"—I wiggled my fingers like raindrops—"and *washed* the spider out . . ."

Conny giggled. I sang another nursery rhyme, and another, and another, all the while the water in the sink splashed and gurgled. Somewhere up front I could hear muffled shouting. I sang louder. Finally, the little boy slid off the stool. "All done."

"Yea! What a good boy." I washed his hands as slowly as possible, and then the moment I dreaded . . . opening the door. What was happening out there? Was Dexter still in the shop?

"Tell you what, buddy." I put my finger to my lips. "Let's play hide-and-seek. You stay here a minute, while I look for another hiding place, okay?"

He nodded, eyes bright. I listened at the door. I heard voices in the distance, but no one was in the back room. I risked unhooking the latch. "Shhh. Let me see if the coast is clear. Then we can find a new hiding place, okay?" Conny nodded again, crouching down low behind a large, twenty-four pack of toilet paper.

I unlocked the door, stepped out into the back room, and closed it softly behind me. I couldn't see the front of the salon from here, but I heard Adele's commanding voice: *"Out.* Out this *second,* or I call the police. Rochelle has a restraining order against you, and they'll slap your sorry butt in jail faster than you can say 'mama.'"

"Hey, I just happened to be out on the street, saw my lady in here—"

"Like hell you did! Avis, call the police . . . *OUT!"*

The bell over the door jangled. I heard Avis screech, "Lock it!"

The next moment, feet came flying and Avis and Rochelle burst into the back room.

I pointed to the bathroom. Rochelle jerked open the door and gathered Conny tightly in her arms. "Oh, baby, baby . . . are you all right?"

Conny squirmed. "Aw, you found us. Wanna play hide-an'-seek?"

26

I don't know who was more upset, Avis or Rochelle. Avis paced back and forth in the small back room, mouth tight, brow furrowed, arms crossed tightly across her middle, while Rochelle rocked a squirming Conny, who was much more interested in playing more hide-and-seek.

We heard banging on the glass door up front. A moment later Adele appeared in the back room. "Uh, Avis and Rochelle? You need to, uh . . . Jodi, can you . . .?"

I nodded, grabbed MaDear's button jar, and made up a counting game for Conny, sorting buttons into the egg carton cups. "Can you put *one* button in this cup? . . . Good job! How about two buttons in this one?" While he was busy, I peeked out front. Rochelle and Avis were talking to two uniformed police officers, one of them female.

Avis finally returned, a smile for Conny. "Hey. Can I play?" She turned to me. "Thanks, Jodi. The coast is clear, and Adele wants you in the chair. Rochelle's under the dryer. But I called Peter. He's coming to take them home, to make sure . . . you know."

I gave her a wordless hug, left her with Conny, and made my way to where Adele waited for me, plastic cape in one hand, the other on her hip. As I settled in the chair, she whipped the cape around my shoulders and muttered, "I'm gonna rename my shop."

A grin tickled my lips as I watched her in the mirror. "Change it to what?"

"Adele's Rescue Mission. Whaddya think?"

ROCHELLE WASN'T AT WORSHIP with Avis and Peter the next morning. Probably afraid to take Conny out of the house! Afraid that Dexter was going to find her and snatch her baby. But Avis was worship leader that morning, and her normally robust style seemed even more passionate as she read the call to worship from Psalm 139:

"Where can I go from your Spirit? Where can I flee from your presence? If I go up to the heavens, You are there! If I make my bed in the depths, You are there. If I rise on the wings of the dawn, if I settle on the far side of the sea, even there Your hand will guide me, Your right hand will hold me fast . . ."

She looked up from her fat Bible. "Think about it, church! When you leave your house in the morning, God's presence is there! When you crawl into bed at night, God is there. When you stop at the barbershop or the hair salon"—she closed her eyes, lifted a hand, and interrupted herself—"Oh, thank You, Jesus! Yes . . . God is already there."

I blew out a breath. Denny, who'd heard the story from me, squeezed my hand as the praise team followed the call to worship with a stand-and-clap version of the traditional gospel song,

"I Go to the Rock." The "fine" Oscar Frost really wailed on his saxophone as we leaned into the vamp: *When I need a shelter, when I need a friend, I go to the Rock!*"

My own spirit felt like it was going to go right through the roof as hands and voices lifted all over our storefront sanctuary, repeating the vamp. The experience yesterday at Adele's Hair and Nails had rattled my cage, too, giving me a tiny taste of what Rochelle must feel like all the time, never feeling safe, hovering like a mother hen over her chick, trying to protect it from the fox in the henhouse. But Jesus *had* protected Rochelle and Conny yesterday—using even a toddler's need to go potty as perfect timing. I wished Rochelle *had* come to worship that morning, to be reminded that, "*When I need a shelter, when I need a friend, I go to the Rock!*"

The whole service made me want to shout. I was so glad that SouledOut Community Church put Jesus the Solid Rock right at the center of its praise and worship and teaching. And knowing my own tendency to let everyday worries sift the sand under my feet, I probably needed that reminder *at least* once a week!

The Yada Yada sisters who attended SouledOut got our heads together after the service to see what we could do for Ruth's birthday that evening. "We could order a cake from the Bagel Bakery, ask Yo-Yo bring it," Stu suggested. "But do we want to do cards? A gift?"

Florida snorted. "Betcha anythang she'd appreciate a package of disposable diapers from each one of us."

Nonyameko frowned. "Oh no."

The rest of us chorused, "Oh, yes!" That would be the perfect gift for the mother of three-and-a-half-month-old twins! "Wrap 'em in the funny papers," Becky snickered.

As our huddle broke up, I slipped my arm around Hoshi Takahashi's slender waist and gave her a hug. "Can you come tonight?"

She shook her head, smiling apologetically. "I am sorry, Jodi. But Sara likes the ReJOYce campus group, so as long as she is willing to go, I think . . . no, I *know* God wants me to go with her. But . . ." Her silky black hair fell over one shoulder as she looked away. "I do miss you all."

"Oh, Hoshi. We miss you too. But you're right; you are doing the God-thing."

How long had Hoshi been a Christian? Two short years? And she'd already had to choose between Jesus and her Shinto family back in Tokyo. Her sturdy obedience to God's call put me to shame, and I'd been a Christian for decades. Supposedly.

Then she laughed. "I will send a package of *kami omutsu*—paper diapers—with Nony for the birthday queen. But you Americans are very strange!"

I CALLED YO-YO at the Bagel Bakery and told her we were all getting Ruth disposable diapers for her birthday, large or small package, didn't matter, whatever we could afford, and we'd pick her up if she didn't mind squishing into the back of Stu's car with me.

"Uh . . . Ruth's birthday? Where's Yada Yada meetin' tonight?"

"Ruth's house." I kept my voice light, even as a red flag poked up in my brain.

"Ah, I dunno, Jodi. Jerry, uh, he need some help with his homework when I get off work. Tell everyone 'hey' for me though."

She hung up before I could say we wanted to order a cake from the Bagel Bakery. *Sheesh.* What was that word Ruth sometimes used? . . . *Mishegoss.* Crazy behavior. Yeah. What in the world was that *mishegoss* all about!

With no special cake from the Bagel Bakery, Estelle, Stu, and I picked up a two-layer carrot cake from the grocery store—still cost almost fifteen bucks—when we picked up the disposable diapers. We gift-wrapped the diapers in the car on the way to the Garfields' house. Ha! The manufacturer should add to the car manual: *"The backseat of the Celica is not suitable for gift-wrapping."*

But backseat gymnastics aside, we were the first ones to pile through the front door of the Garfields' brick bungalow, squealing like teenagers when we saw the twins sitting in bouncy seats in the middle of the living room. Isaac and Havah were dressed in matching denim jeans and little T-shirts that said, "I'm the Brother" and "I'm the Sister," both waving noisy toys that didn't look like any rattles I'd ever seen. Ruth noticed our puzzled faces. *"Graggers* they are. Traditional noisemaker during Purim." She winked at me. "Your third graders will love 'em."

Ack! Should I have second thoughts about Ruth coming to my class?

"Ooo. I need a baby fix *bad,"* Estelle said. She reached out for Havah, then stopped and eyed Ruth. "May I?"

"Not if you've had a cold in the last two weeks!" Ben hollered from the next room.

"Don't mind him," Ruth sniffed. *"He's* the one with the cold. I made him stay away from the twins a whole week!"

I picked up and cuddled little Isaac, who looked at me solemnly with his big, dark eyes, the large red birthmark vivid on his otherwise perfect face. "You, little guy, are going to be a heartbreaker when you grow up." Though, knowing the cruelty of children, my heart ached, realizing the birthmark would invite teasing when he started school. I kissed his soft forehead, drinking in the clean smell of baby powder. But I didn't get to keep him long, as other Yada Yadas arrived and everyone wanted a "baby fix."

But we finally got started by bringing in our generic grocery store cake with five flaming candles—one for each decade—and bestowed a pile of wrapped packages on Ruth. She protested when she saw all the "gifts," but after unwrapping the first three and realizing what we'd done, she laughed with glee. "Diapers, Ben!" she yelled into the next room. "Enough diapers for another set of twins!"

If Ben responded, he was drowned out by gleeful laughter in the living room.

A few people had brought silly cards declaring, "Over the Hill!" and "Congratulations at the Half-Century Mark!" Opening one, Ruth took out a gift certificate, and her eyes widened at Chanda. "What are you, a stockholder at Talbots Kids?" Ruth *tsk-tsked* through her teeth. "Too much it is, Chanda."

Chanda shrugged one shoulder. "Not so much. Dem babies grow so fast, dey outta dey cloes in one minit."

The rest of us had fallen silent. Didn't we agree on bringing disposable diapers? What was Chanda trying to do, upstage the rest of us? I felt a poke in my side and heard Florida hiss, "We gotta rein that girl in."

Stu disappeared into the kitchen and returned with a plastic garbage bag, gathering up wrapping paper, newspaper comic pages, plastic forks, and paper plates with cake crumbs. Avis smiled. "I guess it's time to start our prayer time. 'Martha' has taken care of everything so now we can be 'Marys' and sit at Jesus' feet."

"Huh?" Becky Wallace looked bewildered. "Is that Stu's real name? Martha?"

The room dissolved in laughter. Becky's face colored. Finally Avis gasped, "That wasn't fair to you, Becky. I was referring to a story in the New Testament about two sisters, Mary and Martha. Martha was the efficient one, who made sure everything and everybody was taken care of. She fussed at Jesus, because Mary was ignoring the dishes and just sat at Jesus' feet, listening to him teach. But Jesus said Mary had chosen well."

"Hm," Stu grunted. "Always did think Martha got a bum rap."

Her comment was met with hoots and clapping. From the other room Ben shouted, "Hey! Pipe down in there! I can't hear the TV."

"Sisters, sisters." Avis held up both hands and quieted us down. "I did not mean to get us off track. And Stu, I did not mean to disparage your quick cleanup. I don't think Jesus belittled Martha's gift of service either. Only when she let her good deeds keep her from sitting at Jesus' feet, soaking up His words. So . . . let's just worship Him a few minutes before moving into our sharing time."

We sang a couple of quiet, worshipful songs, and I noticed that Isaac had fallen asleep over Delores's shoulder. Havah, cuddled in Adele's arms and sucking two fingers, was fast on her way out too. When it was time to share requests, Estelle piped up and said she needed a job. "But I loved caring for Adele's mother. I'd like to do more elder care. Does anyone know if I need to get certified or go to school or . . .?"

"I could find out for you," Stu said.

Florida pumped a hand in the air. "Somebody else's MaDear gonna be sayin' *thank ya, Jesus*, when you show up on her doorstep, Estelle."

That was followed by "Amen to that" and "That's right." Adele nodded, but she simply jounced baby Havah on her knees, as if she didn't trust herself to speak.

Avis glanced around the room. "Edesa? How can we pray for the future of Manna House? Are all the former residents cared for?"

I leaned forward. Josh had said next to nothing about Manna House for the past few weeks, and I'd hated to ask, not wanting to rub it in that the place had burned down. What *was* happening to the women's shelter?

"*Gracias*. Thank you for asking." Edesa, her dark curls pulled away from her high forehead, sighed. She seemed emotionally tired. "Yes, shelter has been found for all the residents—"

"*El Dios es bueno!*" Delores cried, beaming.

God is good, I translated mentally. Maybe I could learn Spanish after all.

"—but even before Manna House burned down," Edesa frowned, "the need for more shelter for homeless women was very great in this city. Manna House had to turn some away. Now . . . it, too, is gone." She shook her head sadly. "Maybe they will rebuild. The last I heard, the board wants to build a new building on the old site. But . . . where to get the money?"

"Could take a long time if you don't want government money," Stu murmured. "You need a foundation or something."

Edesa threw up a hand. "*Sí*. And in the meantime, our women bounce around from shelter to shelter, which are already overcrowded. It feels like too little, too late—but just pray, sisters. Just pray." She pressed her fingers against her eyes.

Avis cleared her throat. "We will pray, Edesa. And please include Rochelle in the prayers." She briefly shared Rochelle's close call at Adele's Hair and Nails the previous day. "Even though Peter is willing to have Rochelle and Conny continue staying with us, Rochelle says Dexter knows where we live. She's afraid that one day, somehow, he'll get in the building and take Conny from her when we aren't home. I don't know . . ." Avis massaged her hands with her long, tapered fingers, as if working the kinks out of her thoughts. "If she keeps the doors locked . . ."

"Dat girl can't live dat way, no how," Chanda sputtered. "Hiding behind locked doors? She need to come live wit me."

"What? Oh, no, Chanda, that's not what I was asking—"

"But dat *is* what mi a-sayin', Sista Avis. For true. Me new 'ouse is big, eh? Four bedrooms, but we only need t'ree. Dia an' Cheree, dey always end up sleepin' in de same bed anyway, don' like to sleep by demselves. Your grandbaby can sleep in Tom's room— he'd like dat. Tom never did like bein' de only mon in de 'ouse. Rochelle can have her own room, pay no money till she get a job. An dat Dexter mon, he don' know where we live. An' if he find out . . . " Chanda drew herself up, crossing her arms across her chest. "Dat mon have to get by *mi!*"

27

Chanda was serious. When our prayer meeting broke up, I saw her buttonhole Avis again. "It's very generous of you, Chanda," I heard Avis say. But she seemed flummoxed. "I—I'll have to talk to Rochelle. And Peter too."

"You do dat. You pray 'bout dat too."

Everyone else was bundling up in the foyer, talking all at once. *"Adios, mis hermanas!"* . . . "See you in two weeks!" . . . "Where are we meeting?" . . . "Chanda's house!" . . . "Anyone talk to Yo-Yo?" . . . "Yeah. Said she had to help her kid brother with homework tonight." . . . "Huh. I bet."

I hung back, wanting to double-check with Ruth about coming to my classroom this week to talk about Queen Esther and Purim. Estelle was willing to take care of the twins—but how to get Estelle *here* and Ruth to the *school* if Ben was working?

Florida grabbed my arm and pulled me aside as the others tromped out the front door. "Jodi. Whatchu doin' Saturday? Yo-Yo's day off, right? I think a couple of us sistahs oughta kidnap that girl, find out what's goin' on. She 'bout ready to slide right on outta Yada Yada."

"Good idea. Gotta check my calendar. It should be okay, though."

"Jodi!" Stu yelled from the sidewalk. "Are you coming? It's snowing!"

"Just a minute!" I yelled, waving out the door. A flurry of the white stuff sparkled in the light falling from the Garfields' front window. "*Sheesh*. She's right."

"Oh no!" Florida peeked over my shoulder and groaned. "It's *March*. It's not supposed to *snow*. I'll never get to sit outside on my white wicker porch furniture."

"It's snowing?" Chanda bustled up, pulling on her snazzy red coat and hat. "What crazy sista tinking 'bout sitting in she porch furniture?"

Becky, waiting for Florida, snorted. "Hickman, here. Except she don't *have* any wicker porch furniture."

"Humph. I can dream, can't I? . . . Oh, hey, Avis. We're riding with you, right?" Florida and Becky ducked out into the snow flurry with Avis. "Call me 'bout Saturday, Jodi!" Florida called back.

Chanda frowned at the snow. "Uh-uh-uh. Mi don' like to drive dat new car in snow. Dis might be a good time to soak up some Jamaica sunshine!"

"Don't worry, Chanda. It's not sticking. This won't last half an hour." Suddenly an idea tickled my brain. *Chanda*. Chanda had a car . . . and a license. And she wasn't working anymore, not since she'd won the lottery . . .

I WAS RIGHT. The snow was gone by the next morning. And Ruth was coming to my classroom! I was so excited on my way to school the next morning, I felt like a little kid humming along with Jiminy Cricket: *"Zip-a-dee-doo-dah, zip-a-dee-ay!"*

Spring was coming! A sure thing—in spite of today's temperature, which hovered in the low forties. *Hm,* I thought. *I ought to have that same kind of confidence in God's promises in the Bible. A sure thing—even if the circumstances don't look like it at the moment. Same God, isn't it? Spring Creator and Promise Giver?*

"Zip-a-dee-do-dah!" *Yikes!* Did I sing that out loud? Giggling, I gave up and warbled, ". . . wonderful feeling, wonderful day!" Not a typical "praise" song, but to me it was.

When I got to school, I told my class that in honor of Women's History Month, we were going to have a special visitor this week—Queen Esther of Persia. I saw Caleb Levy's eyes widen and his hand shot up. "I know that story! We just celebrated Purim this weekend!" He nodded knowingly at his classmates. "It's a Jewish holiday."

"That's right, Caleb. Queen Esther lived many centuries ago, but her story is told and retold every year right up to the present day."

By the time Ruth arrived on Wednesday, excitement was practically at fever pitch. She had told me she was going to tell the story of Queen Esther in first person, to make it come alive, but I had to grin when she came into the classroom dressed in a long gauzy gown, a "cloak" with a gold brocade trim down the front, and a thin silver crown on her head. My class gasped in unison as she came in.

Chanda—who'd picked up Estelle, dropped her off at the Garfields to take care of the twins, and brought Ruth to Bethune

Elementary—slipped into the room behind Ruth and sat down on a chair in the back of the room. She grinned at me and put a finger to her lips, as if promising she'd be quiet.

"An old woman I am now," Ruth began—a smart beginning, since she didn't exactly look young and beautiful as one always imagined Queen Esther—"but I will tell you how I came to be Queen of Persia, and why Almighty God put me in the palace."

Not one child cried, *"Foul! Separation of church and state!"* They were hanging on every word.

As I listened to her tell the familiar story—well, familiar to me—Ruth indeed seemed to transform into a majestic queen, keeping her story alive for future generations. "Well! When Queen Vashti ignored her husband, the king decided he needed a new queen. All the beautiful girls"—Ruth batted her eyelashes, setting off giggles all over the room— "were called to the palace, and one by one we were taken to see the king."

She didn't mention that each one spent the night and ended up in the king's harem. *Smooth move, Ruth.*

"But I—a Jewish girl who had been taken captive from my own country—found favor with the king and I became the new queen of Persia. But that didn't mean I was safe."

My students' mouths hung open as they listened to the story of Queen Esther's "Uncle Mordecai," actually Esther's older cousin, who wouldn't bow down to anyone but God, which made the king's chief adviser very angry. "This man's name was Haman. Can you say that?"

All the kids yelled, *"Haman!"*

"That name you must remember, because Haman was a very bad man. In Jewish homes, when the story of Queen Esther is told and Haman's name is mentioned, everyone boos and makes noise with a *gragger*—like this." Ruth reached into a bag she'd brought with her, and pulled out one of the noisemakers the twins had been waving the other night. She gave it to me with a smirk. "Here. We'll let your teacher rattle the *gragger*, and all the rest of you, *boo* whenever you hear Haman's name. Ready?"

"Boooo!" everyone yelled. I swung the *gragger* and grimaced. We'd be lucky to make it through Queen Esther without some teacher poking her head in and telling us to be quiet. But at least she'd brought only one of the noisemakers—not thirty!

Ruth took a deep breath. "Well. Haman"—*"Boooo!"*—"hated the Jews, and he especially hated Mordecai. He decided he would ask the king's permission to kill them all! But neither Haman"— *"Boooo!"*—"nor the king knew that I, Queen Esther, was also a Jew." She put her finger to her lips, as if telling the children to keep her secret. "Uncle Mordecai told me I must go to the king and beg for the lives of my people. 'Maybe this is the reason God let you become queen—for such a time as this,' he said. But I was afraid! Very afraid. No one was supposed to go into the king's court unless the king asked him to come—not even the queen. I could be killed! But it was either my life—or the lives of all my people."

Meanwhile, Ruth said, the king remembered that Mordecai had once saved the king's life but had never been rewarded. The king asked Haman *("Boooo!")* what he should do for a man he wished to honor. Stuck-up Haman *("Boooo!")* thought the king wanted to honor *him*. So he slyly suggested putting the king's own robe on this man, let him ride the king's own horse, and tell a nobleman to lead the horse all over the city, crying, *"This is how the king honors this man!"*

"Good idea!" said the king. "Go and honor Mordecai in this way."

The kids laughed and laughed as Ruth nodded solemnly. "Now Haman"—*"Boooo!"*—"was *really* mad."

As Ruth continued her story of brave Queen Esther, I suddenly remembered that telling Old Testament stories at the Cook County Jail was how Ruth had first met Yo-Yo. Yo-Yo, hardly more than a kid herself and trying to bring up two younger half brothers, had forged a check to put food on the table and clothes on their backs . . . and ended up serving an eighteen-month prison sentence.

All of us Yada Yadas knew the story. How Ruth and Ben had helped Yo-Yo get on her feet after her release, got her a job at the Bagel Bakery (where nobody seemed to mind the denim overalls she always wore), and became substitute "grandparents" to Pete and Jerry, her teenage brothers. Ruth had brought her protégé to the Chicago Women's Conference almost two years ago, even though Yo-Yo had been dubious about the "Jesus thing" back then. We all thought our smother-mother Ruth and Yo-Yo the ex-con had forged a bond tighter than family. Yet lately that bond seemed to be unraveling—

Sheesh. I hadn't called Florida yet about Saturday. But she was right. We needed to get to the bottom of this mess . . .

My class clapped and clapped when Ruth finished her story. They really whooped when she passed out the traditional Purim cookie called Hamantaschen, shaped like the three-cornered hat Haman supposedly wore as chief adviser to the king.

I gave her a hug as she gathered up her props. "Thank you so much for coming, Ruth. My students will never forget Queen Esther."

Chanda gave *me* a hug before she followed Ruth out the door. "Dat story hit me right 'ere." She tapped her fist over her heart. "God took dat girl out of de poor 'ouse an' put her in de palace. *Irie, mon!*"

"Just like you, Chanda," I whispered. "Maybe you won that lottery for a reason."

"Humph." She rolled her eyes. "'Cept it didna come wit no king."

I PICKED UP FLO Saturday morning at ten, and we drove into the parking lot of Yo-Yo's apartment building twenty minutes later. She must have been watching for us, because her door popped open, and she leaned over the railing of the walkway that ran the length of the second-story, like a two-story motel. "Be right there!" she hollered.

Two minutes later, she hopped into the minivan. "Where we goin'? Starbucks?"

"Thought we'd hit Kaffe Klatch on Lincoln Avenue. It's close. Okay with you?"

Yo-Yo shrugged. "Don' matter ta me. I don't really like coffee."

Florida guffawed. "Well, we do. They got other stuff. How's Pete and Jerry?"

We did catch-up on our kids as we headed for the coffee shop and parked along the street. Comfy couches and overstuffed chairs clustered around coffee tables invited customers to sink down and stay a while. "Cool," Yo-Yo said, flopping down on a couch by the front window. Flo and I ordered a white chocolate mocha and a cappuccino. Yo-Yo settled for soup and a sandwich.

"Thanks for invitin' me out," Yo-Yo said, blowing on her soup. "Haven't seen you guys for a while."

"Uh-huh. Whose fault is that?" Florida got right down to business. "Fact is, that's what me and Jodi wanna talk to you about. Whassup with you ditching Yada Yada lately?"

Yo-Yo shrugged. "Oh, you know. Stuff. Chasin' after Pete an' Jerry. My mom's in rehab, thinks she can get the boys back. Drivin' me nuts."

I took the bait. "All the more reason to come to Yada Yada, Yo-Yo. We've all got 'stuff.' That's why we pray for each other."

"Now hold on here," Florida said. "Let's not dance in the mud and cloudy up the water. What I wanna know is . . . whassup with you an' Ruth? You've been ducking out ever since the twins was born."

Yo-Yo squirmed and looked away. Finally she muttered, "Nothin'. Things change, is all."

"Got that right. Things changed big-time for Ruth an' Ben when the twins was born." Florida's voice softened. "But that don't mean they don't care about you any more."

"Oh, yeah?" Yo-Yo spit her words out like rotten teeth. "Do they ever call the boys any more? Take 'em places? How 'bout forgettin' ta pick me up for Yada Yada, huh?" She cussed right out loud. "They don' know I exist any more!"

I wanted to protest. Of *course* Ruth and Ben still cared about Yo-Yo and her brothers! But . . . it might be hard to prove. Had to admit the twins consumed their time and energy. But why couldn't Yo-Yo understand that? Having babies at their age was a big deal. I was sure it wasn't personal.

Half a minute—it felt longer—had gone by and we'd all been silent after her outburst. Then Yo-Yo pushed away her mug of soup, leaned back against the sofa cushions, and folded her arms across the bib of her overalls. "But it don' matter. The boys an' me, we all right. We don' need them two anymore."

Ouch. Yo-Yo had leaned hard on Ruth and Ben the past few years as she patched her life together again after getting out of prison. And, now, suddenly, her props weren't there and she was hurting, big-time.

"But maybe they need you." The words were out of my mouth before I had time to think about what I wanted to say.

Yo-Yo's eyes narrowed. "Whaddya mean?"

Florida leaned forward. "What she means is, Ruth and Ben have been there for you and your brothers a long time now, an' now they ain't. We'll grant you that. They off in the ozone some-where." She flittered her hand and rolled her eyes, then got serious again. "But maybe that's good."

Yo-Yo snorted. "What's good about it?"

"Hear us out, girl. I said good, 'cause sometimes God knocks the props out from under us when we get too used to leaning up on people for ever'thang. People-help is good, far as it goes. But people gonna let you down. They just human; we all are. Maybe it's time you start leanin' on God for a change."

Yo-Yo slouched even further down on the couch, hands jammed in her overall pockets, brow furrowed, as if mentally chewing on what Florida was saying. "Maybe."

"No maybe about it," Florida said. "You been spoon-fed on the Word up till now. An' that's okay, 'cause you just a baby Christian. But seems to me God is sayin' it's time for Yo-Yo Spencer ta grow up. Walk yo' own walk. Talk yo' own talk. Give back some o' what you been given."

Yo-Yo picked up her soup mug, stared into it for several long moments. Finally she muttered, "Guess I see what you sayin' 'bout needin' to lean on God more. Just"—her face suddenly got blotchy, and she wiped the back of her hand across her eyes—"kinda hurts, ya know? Ruth gettin' pregnant, Ma gettin' high . . . it's always somethin'. Somethin' more important than me and my brothers. Mom dumped me and my kid brothers ever' time she shot up, which was most of the time. Then Ruth and Ben showed up—now, *poof!* They gone too. What was I expectin'? That things would be different?"

Florida's eyes and mouth twitched, as Yo-Yo's words touched a wound not quite healed. "Yeah. Know what you mean, baby," she said softly. "But I'm here to tell you the truth. God don't abandon nobody. Ever."

We all sat in silence a long time. Finally Yo-Yo looked up, a frown etched between her eyes. "Flo said somethin' 'bout givin' back. But don' seem like Ruth an' Ben need nobody these days. It's all 'Havah this' and 'Isaac that,' actin' like them babies the only people in the world. What do they need me for?"

I grinned. "Well, I've got one idea. Ben's still driving Ruth everywhere 'cause she let her license expire, who knows when. But if Ben takes her to the driver's license facility, they have to take the twins with them, and you know *that's* not going to happen. What if we"—I pointed to Yo-Yo and myself—"offer to babysit the twins next weekend so she can get her license? Could be fun! Whaddya say?"

I PULLED UP IN FRONT of Florida's house after taking Yo-Yo home. "Thanks, Flo. Glad you asked me to go with you to talk to

Yo-Yo. She's really lonely, poor kid. But I think she . . . what?"

Florida hadn't heard a word I said. She was staring at the front of her house. "What are all them big boxes doin' on the front porch? Somebody just dump they trash on us?" She was out of the car, up the walk, and onto the porch in two seconds.

I followed. "What is it?"

The name *Wickes Furniture* was stamped all over the boxes. We looked closer. "Contents: One wicker loveseat, four cushions" . . . "Contents: One wicker chair, two cushions" . . . "Contents: one side table with shelf" . . .

Florida stared at me, mouth dropping. And then we both said it together:

"Chanda!"

28

I had just come out of the church kitchen the next morning, after popping my "No Fail Chicken-and-Rice Casserole" into the oven to slow-bake for the Second Sunday Potluck ("no fail" when I remembered to *turn on the oven*, as Stu likes to remind me), when I saw Chanda George parking her Lexus. The next moment, Rochelle and Conny climbed out of her car along with Chanda's three kids. I zipped over to the glass doors to greet them as they all came in, but Chanda held up her hand as she breezed past. "Mi know whatchu tinking, Sista Jodee: not enough seatbelts. But de girl only move in yesterday! Goin' to take mi at least a week to get a bigger car."

I closed my mouth and grinned. That wasn't what I was thinking, but it was a good point. I slipped over to Avis, who was getting a big hug from Conny. "I sleeped in a big-boy bunk bed, Grammy! On the top! An' I didn't fall out, 'cause it gots rails."

"Oh you did, did you?" Avis let him go and watched wistfully as the little boy skipped away.

"So. Rochelle accepted Chanda's invitation?"

She nodded. "Yesterday. Rochelle had a long talk with Chanda, looked at the house, realized Conny would have playmates, and she'd have her own bedroom . . . didn't take her long to say yes." Avis sighed. "I don't know how long we can keep it a secret from Dexter. Too many people know. Or they will." She tipped her chin toward Conny, who was excitedly telling Carla Hickman about sleeping in a big-boy bed.

"Well, we should at least tell the Yada Yada sisters not to be talking out of school—to anyone. But speaking of Dexter, does he know yet about . . .?" I deliberately didn't finish my sentence.

She shook her head. "No. A health professional has been trying to contact him and set up a meeting, but so far he hasn't returned any of her calls. But it needs to happen soon. Like *yesterday*. No telling how many other . . ." Her voice dropped off.

How many other women he's infected, I mentally finished. I doubted Dexter was going to quit fooling around, though, even if he did find out he had HIV and had infected his own wife.

The beckoning chords of the song "Here I Am to Worship" announced the beginning of the morning service. Avis squeezed my elbow and whispered, "Just pray, Jodi," before slipping into the empty chair beside Peter.

FLORIDA GRABBED MY HAND and cornered Chanda right after the service as the tables were being set up for our Second Sunday Potluck. "Okay, out with it. Did you order me up some wicker porch furniture this week?"

"Why you 'ave to know? So what if mi did—dat not sound like 'tank you' to mi."

Florida rolled her eyes. "Chanda! Of *course* I'm gonna say thank you—but you gotta stop raining down expensive gifts on your friends. It's . . . awkward. You know we can't do nothin' like that for you."

"Humph. Don't de Bible say it more blessed to give dan receive? Just wanted to bless you, Florida Hickman. Send dem back if you don't want dem." Chanda pushed past us and headed for Oscar Frost, who was putting away his saxophone.

Florida scowled as she watched her go. "Humph. Messed that up, didn't I? Now she thinks I'm an ungrateful jerk."

I was distracted by Chanda talking to the saxophonist, her smile big, waving her hands, then pointing out her kids scattered around the room. What was she *doing*? Oscar Frost had to be ten years her junior—at least! But the twenty-something musician was talking pleasantly with her, his face relaxed and smiling. Not flirting, just friendly. Guess the kid could handle himself. Except . . . he wasn't the one I was worried about. I didn't want Chanda to get hurt. Again.

I turned back to Florida. "So what are you going to do? Send the stuff back?"

"What?" She shook her head, setting her 'do of little twists bouncing. "I might be a jerk, but I'm not stupid." She lowered her voice and leaned in. "Next Sunday, Jodi Baxter, is the first day of spring. Week from today, you can find me sittin' on my porch in that new furniture—rain or shine!"

OR SNOW.

A sloppy mix of rain and snow started right in the middle of our church business meeting, while we still sat around the lunch tables. I watched shoppers outside dashing for their cars in the parking lot. Chanda and Rochelle, neither of whom were members of SouledOut, had already left right after the potluck with their kids.

". . . to kick off our youth outreach this spring," Pastor Cobbs was saying. "And I don't just mean the youth of families in this church." He swung an arm wide, indicating the streets all around the church. "We've got a mission field right here on our doorstep, half a mile in every direction. Gangs, drugs, dropouts, pregnant teens, STDs . . . you name it, kids out there are swimming in it. Brother Rick, you want to say something?"

Rick Reilly, who'd been the youth group leader at Uptown, stood up. "Oscar Frost . . . Oscar, stand up. That's right, this young man hides behind his saxophone, but he's coming out with his hands up!" Everyone laughed as Oscar stood, grinning sheepishly. "Anyway," Rick went on, "Oscar recently volunteered with Captives Free Jail and Prison Ministry, along with some of our other men—Denny Baxter, Peter Douglass, several others. That experience opened his eyes to the importance of getting to these kids *before* they end up at the JDC. But we need more volunteers and we need new ideas."

He picked up a clipboard and handed it to the nearest table. "We're devoting our March men's breakfast—next Saturday, brothers—to praying for God's wisdom and direction for our youth ministry. Right after the breakfast, at ten o'clock, we're having a youth ministry brainstorming meeting here at the church. If you're interested—sisters, this includes you—put your name and phone number on the sheet that's coming around. And if you don't put your name on the sheet but change your mind next Friday"— more laughter—"come anyway." Rick sat down.

I watched the clipboard as it made its way around the room. Josh had been so gung-ho about the potential for youth outreach when our churches merged. But Rick Reilly hadn't mentioned his name today, and frankly, Josh hadn't said anything about youth ministry since he and Edesa got up in church and asked for volunteers for the Manna House shelter in January. Well, that was understandable if he couldn't do both.

But now that Manna House is defunct . . .

Two tables over, I saw Josh take the clipboard and hold it in both hands for what seemed like a long time. Then he handed it on.

My insides mushed. What in the world was going on with our son?

As usual, the Hickman/Wallace household needed rides after the meeting, so we took Becky Wallace and Little Andy, though Andy begged to go home with us so he could play with "the nice brown doggie."

Becky sighed. "Not today, Andy. We only got a couple more hours till you hafta go back to your"—she practically gagged— "other house."

"Another time for sure, Andy," I said. "Willie Wonka doesn't play much anymore, but I know he'd love to see *you*."

As we dropped Becky and Little Andy off in front of the Hickman's, I noticed the large boxes were still on the porch. "What's that?" Amanda piped up from the third seat. "The Hickmans aren't moving *again*, are they?"

"Nope. Porch furniture, actually."

"Oh. Cool. Why don't we get a porch swing, Mom?"

I left that one unanswered, wondering whether to say something to Josh, sitting in the front passenger seat next to Denny. As Denny navigated the one-way streets between the Hickmans' and our house, I spoke my thoughts. "Josh, I noticed you didn't sign the sheet about youth outreach. I thought that possibility interested you most when our two churches merged." At the wheel, Denny glanced at me in the rearview mirror, but I couldn't read what it meant. Too late now.

Josh turned his head away and looked out the side window. Finally, he said, "Dunno, Mom. Need some time to think about it, I guess."

Another glance from the rearview mirror. *Okay. I got it. 'Don't push it.'*

STU CLATTERED DOWN THE BACK STAIRS, heading for work early Monday morning in semidarkness, just as I was trying to coax Willie Wonka out into the backyard. "Hey! Happy birthday!" I grabbed her on the porch and gave her a big hug. Good thing I'd already looked at the calendar this morning. "What is this? The big thirty-six?"

She made a face. "Sheesh, Jodi. Can't I get older without you announcing it to the whole world? Say, you want help getting Wonka down the stairs?"

"Sure." With me tugging gently on Wonka's collar and Stu half-pushing, half-lifting from his tail end, we managed to get the old dog down the four steps from our porch to the backyard.

"I get home at five-thirty if you want help getting him back up the steps," she deadpanned over her shoulder as she headed for the garage.

"Ha! They're predicting snow tonight. Make that an hour later." I watched her go. Even at thirty-six, Stu cut a youthful figure with her long, ash-blonde hair flying from beneath her red beret, belted jacket, and pants tucked inside lace-up boots.

I was still waiting on Willie Wonka, shivering inside my jacket under a heavy cloud cover, when I heard, *"Psst.* Jodi. Is she gone?"

I looked up. Estelle was leaning over the second-floor porch railing, dressed only in a large loose caftan. Another Estelle sewing project. "Yes, ma'am." I grinned.

"I'm fixin' a birthday dinner for Stu when she gets home. Can you Baxters come up at six o'clock? That would make it a party."

"We'd love to." Just knowing I wouldn't have to cook dinner tonight was a gift to *me.* "But get back inside, Estelle! Just looking at you blowing in the wind up there makes me feel like an ice cube."

She laughed and disappeared inside.

The day remained gloomy, with gusts up to fifteen miles per hour. *Sheesh. What a dreary day for a birthday,* I thought, glancing from time to time out my classroom windows. But if Estelle could cook as well as she could sew, we were in for a treat. Maybe that's what we all needed—some friend time together, candles, good food, laughter . . .

I picked up the mail on my way into the house after school and rifled through it as I headed for the kitchen. *Oh, great.* A letter addressed to Josh from the University of Illinois. *Humph.* Probably a form letter saying his acceptance a year ago is now out of date and it's too late to apply for this year, so too bad, forget it.

Disgusted, I tossed the letter on the dining room table—and that's when I saw it.

Doggy diarrhea all over the kitchen floor. I groaned.

But where was Willie Wonka? I called his name, even though I knew that didn't do any good, deaf as he was. But I found him soon enough, crouched under the dining room table, head on his paws, his worried eyes looking up at me as though I'd caught him red-handed with his paw in the cookie jar.

"Oh, Wonka. Poor baby. Come here, boy . . . come on. It's all right. You couldn't help it." The dog inched his way out from under the table on his belly, still cowering. "What's the matter, baby?" I stroked his head reassuringly. "You don't feel good?"

Then the smell hit me, and I realized that not only the floor needed cleaning up, but the dog too.

By the time Denny and Amanda came in the back door stomping off slushy snow from their shoes, holding a hot-pink hibiscus plant for Stu, I'd given Wonka a bucket bath, the kitchen and dining room floors smelled of disinfectant, and our old child safety-gate now barricaded the doorway between kitchen and dining room. "What happened?" they chorused, looking from the gate to the dog penned into the kitchen.

I made a face. "I'll spare you the gory details. But we better keep him in the kitchen until he feels better—and take him out more often."

Josh still wasn't home from work by six o'clock, so I left a note for him on the dining room table to come upstairs when he got home, and the three of us braved the half-hearted snow flurry to hustle up the outside back stairs to Stu and Estelle's apartment. Estelle had outdone herself: tablecloth, candles, Stu's china, and a savory meal of chicken and dumplings, Cajun red beans and rice, green beans swimming in butter, and steaming hot cornbread.

Stu shook her head at the spread, embarrassed and pleased at the same time. "You cooked. You found my china. My parents sent me a card and a package—first one in years. Somebody brought me flowers. It doesn't get better than this!"

"Well, put that overgrown bush in the middle of the table and let's get started," Estelle fussed. "Food's gettin' cold."

We were halfway through the meal when Josh came in the back door. "Sorry. Got a ride, but traffic was awful. Uh, happy birthday, Stu." He slid into the empty chair, tattooed arm peeking out of his cut-off sleeveless sweatshirt, hair pulled back into a ponytail. "Don't let me stop the conversation."

Stu waved her fork. "Uh . . . thanks. I was just about to give Estelle some good news. Found out that organizations providing in-home elder care often use Certified Nurse Assistants. And several colleges in the Chicago area have CNA programs."

Estelle frowned. "College? How many years do I hafta go to school?"

"Not years. Months. Maybe two or three."

Estelle brightened. "Really? I could do that."

"And *experience* doing elder care is a real plus, so your work with MaDear should be a good reference."

"Lord, Lord." Estelle rolled her eyes. "The Lord knows I got *experience*. Took care of my mother, God rest her soul, *and* my great-aunt . . . *humph*. MaDear was a kitten compared to my great-aunt. *Mm-mm*. Sure glad I don't believe in reincarnation."

We laughed and helped clear the table—except for Josh's plate—while Estelle brought in hot peach cobbler and set it in front of Stu. "Had to use canned peaches," she grumbled. "Just ain't the same, ain't the same a'tall."

Couldn't prove it by us. We cleaned up the peach cobbler and sat back with overstuffed sighs. "This was fun," Amanda said. "We oughta do this more often. I mean, we don't have to wait for a birthday, do we?"

"That's a great idea," I said. "In fact, I was thinking we should invite Precious and Sabrina to come for supper some weekend soon." Was it my imagination, or did Josh wince? He busied himself finishing up his peach cobbler and said nothing. I ignored His Sullenness. "Estelle, do you know if they're still at the Salvation Army shelter? You and Stu can come, and it'll be a party."

"Good idea," Stu said. "Except let Estelle and me help with the cooking. That'll be fun."

We said goodnight and drifted downstairs behind the kids. "Estelle seems to be a good housemate for Stu," I murmured to Denny as we came in the back door. The floor was still clean, thank God. "And looks like Wonka is holding his own."

We stepped over the safety gate into the dining room. I noticed that the envelope from the University of Illinois had been opened and the letter stuffed halfway back inside. I pulled it out, expecting a generic form letter. But my heart suddenly tripped a light fantastic.

"Dear Joshua Baxter," it said. *"Congratulations! You have been accepted into the undergraduate program for the 2004–2005 school year . . ."*

29

I handed the letter to Denny. He skimmed it, eyebrows going north. "Wait a minute. This isn't U of I. It's UIC... Josh? Come here at minute!"

What? I picked up the envelope. Denny was right. This wasn't from the University of Illinois in Champaign/Urbana. The letterhead said UIC—University of Illinois Chicago Circle campus.

A moment later, Josh appeared in the archway of the dining room. "Yeah?"

Denny waved the letter. "Were you going to tell us about this?"

Josh shrugged. "It only came today. Found it lying on the table."

"I mean, tell us that you'd applied to UIC. When did that happen?"

Another shrug. "Right after New Year's I guess. Deadline was January 15."

Denny and I looked at each other. "You'd already been accepted at U of I," I said. "Why did you decide to apply to the Chicago

263

campus? I mean, wouldn't it have been simpler just to submit your intent to enroll at U of I? What about the application fee?"

"I'm working, Mom. Figured it was up to me."

I nodded, still flummoxed. "Guess I, um, owe you an apology. I thought you'd just let the college deadlines pass—or decided not to go next year."

"Don't sweat it." He turned to go.

"Wait a minute, Son. Sit down for a minute, okay?" Denny pulled out a chair from the table. The three of us sat. "Does this mean you've decided to go to school this fall?"

Josh diddled with his fingers on the tabletop. "I don't know. Maybe."

"But . . . why did you apply if you're not sure?" I asked.

Another shrug. "Well, I was leaning that way. When I applied, I mean. But . . ."

"And now?" Denny prodded.

Josh sighed. "I dunno, Dad. Things change, that's all." He threw open his hands. "Look. I know you guys want me to cough up my five-year plan. But I don't know what I want to do next fall. I don't know what I want to do *now*. At least give me credit for sending in the application." He pushed away from the table. "Can we leave it now?"

Denny waved him off. "Yeah, okay." But I could see he was ticked off.

When we heard Josh's bedroom door close, Denny leaned forward. "I don't get it, Jodi. What's going on? What did he mean, 'things change'? What?"

I was tempted to smile. "You sound like me." But I was thinking. "Okay. He sent that application in early January. Back then,

Josh was upbeat, working his job at Software Symphony, volunteering at Manna House with Edesa, eager beaver about the church merger and Pastor Cobbs's vision for youth ministry. A few weeks later . . . the fire leveled Manna House. Since then, he's been like a cardboard cutout of himself. That's what, I think."

"Okay. You're right. I've been trying to allow for that. It was traumatic for a kid his age. Traumatic for a lot of people, frankly. Good grief, Jodi, when I got the call, I was so scared, thinking about what could have happened to my wife, my son . . ."

I stared at Denny. I didn't know he'd been scared.

"But life happens! The world doesn't stop while we mope around. We pick ourselves up and go on. Why can't he see that?" Denny slumped back in his chair.

I shook my head. All the things I'd been thinking the past few weeks were coming out of my husband's mouth. Laid back, easygoing Denny, spouting off like a Jodi-whale.

Then, to my astonishment, his voice got husky. "Now, someone like Mark Smith, he's got good reason to be spinning his wheels. After the beating those punks gave him, he's not sure he can teach again. Maybe he's afraid to try, afraid to find out he can't. But even with Mark, it tears me up to see him not even try. He has so much to offer—*still* has so much to offer."

"Wait a minute, Denny. Weren't we talking about Josh? We shouldn't—"

"I know, I know. I just mean, Josh is a kid who's got a lot going for him. But here he is, acting like he's hit a brick wall the first time he hits a bump in the road. Frankly, I don't care what he does—go to school, don't go to school, do this, do that. Just . . . set a goal and go for it!" He threw up his hands. "But what are we supposed to do?"

I felt a strong nudge in my spirit. There *was* something we could do. I laid a hand over my husband's. "I don't know either, Denny. But let's pray for Josh—you and me. Right now. Maybe in our bedroom. You know, 'where two or three are gathered together in My name'—that kind of praying. Asking God for wisdom. Asking God to move mountains. Trusting God . . . all that stuff it says in the Bible but is so hard to do."

A small smile cracked his tense features. "You're right. Again. Gee, twice in five minutes." He stood up, our fingers interlocked, and we headed toward our bedroom. "I kinda like this, Jodi."

IF NOTHING ELSE, our prayer time together set me free emotionally. Or spiritually. It was sometimes hard to separate the two. But agreeing with Denny Sunday night to put Josh in God's hands helped me loosen up the rest of the week. I didn't need to keep bugging Josh. I didn't need to keep bugging God. God was at work. God was in control.

And okay, had to admit I was proud of Josh for applying to UIC *without* us bugging him. *Sheesh.* That alone ought to give me hope that my firstborn was going to grow up.

Denny and I really should pray together more often, I thought several times that week. But in the helter-skelter of everyday life, it was harder than I thought. Thursday night rolled around, Denny was down at the JDC leading a Bible study for kids awaiting trial, and we still hadn't prayed together again. He'd mentioned one kid, who had to decide whether to take a plea bargain and serve two years, or fight his case and go to trial. And another, who rarely spoke up but came every Thursday . . . and another who seemed a natural-born leader. And then there was Chris Hickman.

We should pray for all these boys by name together! See what God would do! *Well, maybe Saturday morning would be a good time . . .*

I forgot that Saturday was the men's breakfast at SouledOut, and Denny had to leave the house early. Correction. *Earlier.* In order to hob-nob and pray with "the Bada-Boom Brothers" an hour before the breakfast, which meant picking up Ricardo Enriques down in the city, who "just happened" to be home for the weekend in spite of his long-distance trucking job. I felt a twinge of resentment at not having *any* mornings that week together—and then wanted to slap myself upside the head. *Hoo boy!* I should talk. Denny probably felt that way every time Yada Yada met on Sunday evenings.

Well, we just had to find a way where it wasn't either/or.

"I need the car when you get back," I told Denny, as he did an awkward hop over the child safety gate still penning Willie Wonka in the kitchen. "Yo-Yo and I are going to babysit the twins so Ben can take Ruth to get her driver's license."

"Ben? That's later, right? Because I think he's coming this morning to—" Just then Denny caught his pant leg on the gate and nearly did an end-zone tackle with the toaster. "Good grief, Jodi! Can't we get rid of this gate? Wonka hasn't had any more accidents this week, has he?"

I rolled my eyes at him. "Two. You just weren't here to clean them up."

"Well, put him outside then. It's supposed to get up to sixty today. Maybe we need to build a doghouse or something."

As if knowing we were talking about him, Willie Wonka slunk over to the air vent that heated the kitchen and sank down on top of it with a sigh.

THE OUTDOOR THERMOMETER WENT UP, but a drizzly rain came down. When Denny returned with the car, I left Wonka in the kitchen with the gate still in place. "Take him out a couple of times, will you?" I asked, grabbing my purse and the car keys. "Precious and Sabrina are coming tonight for supper, and I don't want the house smelling like disinfectant."

"Better than the alternative," Denny snorted, head inside the refrigerator. He came out with a carton of orange juice. "Have you seen Josh? He didn't show up for the youth ministry meeting at SouledOut—at least not by the time I left. I didn't stay; knew you needed the car."

I shook my head and jerked a thumb toward the bedrooms. "He came out once, looked at the rain, and went back into hibernation."

"Humph." Denny swigged straight from the orange juice carton, then wiped his mouth on his sleeve as he capped it. "Hey, guess what. Ben came to the men's breakfast this morning—actually, came to the prayer time beforehand with Peter, Mark, Carl, and Ricardo. I invited Oscar Frost too—that made seven. I think he'll fit in. Last Thursday night when we rode back from the JDC, I sensed he'd really like a mentoring relationship with some older guys."

I suppressed a smile. *The Bada-Boom Brothers . . . nope, nope. Gotta quit that, Jodi. It might stick.*

"Anyway," Denny said, replacing the orange juice back in the fridge, "Ben took us by surprise. Peter asked how we could pray for him, and he got all croaky, said he just wanted to thank God for his babies. Before the twins, life was kind of like the old black-and-white TVs. Now everything is in living color."

"*Ben* said that?" I edged toward the door.

"Yep. And . . . oh, right. You've gotta go. But remind me to tell you something else when you get back."

Oh, great. I did have to go, but now that "something else" would bug me for the next three hours.

I picked up Yo-Yo, and we arrived at the Garfields' house around eleven. Ruth's usually neat flower garden bordering the front of the brick bungalow was a tangle of last year's dead flowers and weeds. Being "huge with child" last fall, she didn't do her usual surgical fall cleanup. But I had no doubt she'd have the twins out here in a month or two, teaching them—at the tender age of five months—the fine points of gardening.

"Maybe she changed her mind," Yo-Yo said nervously as I punched the doorbell.

The door opened. *"Ay ay ay!* You come at last." Ruth gave Yo-Yo a mama bear hug, as if she hadn't been sure we'd show. Then, ignoring me entirely, she bustled off into the next room, tossing off a half-dozen instructions over her shoulder.

"Don't worry," Ben snorted, standing in the foyer holding her coat. "The *shtick* is all written down. You'd think we were taking off for a week in Honolulu." He rolled his eyes. "She's had the *shpilkes* all morning. *Oy vey.*"

I slipped Yo-Yo a tissue and hinted that she should use it on her cheek where Ruth had left a lipstick-red smudge. Yo-Yo rubbed furiously. It was the only time I'd seen anything close to makeup on her clear, boyish face.

Ben finally dragged Ruth out the door. Yo-Yo and I stood at the picture window, each holding a twin, and waving good-bye. Ruth hollered something at us, but Ben practically stuffed her into the big Buick and pulled away.

Yo-Yo and I looked at each other and burst out laughing. "*Sheesh.* The rest oughta be a piece of cake," I gasped.

Yo-Yo jiggled Isaac on her shoulder. "Hey there, big guy. You ready to go to sleep or somethin'? . . . Whoa. Jodi! What was that? My shoulder is all wet!"

Isaac had thrown up his last meal all over Yo-Yo's T-shirt and his own sleeper.

I laid Havah tummy-down on a blanket in the living room with a few toys and did my best to sponge off Yo-Yo's clothes with a washcloth from the bathroom. Found a clean sleeper for Isaac and changed his wet diaper while I was at it. He kicked and wiggled, but I sang a couple of rounds of "Six Little Ducks" and finally managed to get him clean and packaged once again.

"Hey." Yo-Yo stood in the doorway, hands stuffed in her overall pockets. "You're good at that. I never did babysit or nothin' when I was a kid."

I grinned. "I'll show you. It's not too bad one at a time."

"Yeah. But *two*? Glad we doin' this together."

According to Ruth's list, we were supposed to feed the twins baby food at noon, then put them down for a nap. The jars of peas and carrots ended up all over their faces, the high chairs, and us— sort of like vegetarian finger paint. The peaches went better, but the whole process meant another change of clothes for both babies this time. I changed Havah, then held her while I led Yo-Yo step by step through the process with Isaac . . .

Take off the soiled sleeper. Peel back the sticky tabs of the disposable diaper, throw it in the diaper pail, and wipe his bottom with a baby wipe. Dust on baby powder, while making sure he doesn't nosedive off the changing table. Now pick up his feet with one hand, slip the new disposable under his bottom, and press the tabs. Wrestle his arms and legs one at a time into the sleeper, snap the snappers . . .

"Whew!" Sweat beaded Yo-Yo's forehead. "I had no idea it was so much work!"

I nodded. Frankly, I'd almost forgotten.

We put the twins down in their cribs, darkened the room, and wound up their musical mobiles—but the babies immediately set up a wailing duet. "Ignore them. They'll get quiet," I said as we tip-toed away.

They didn't. The wailing got louder. Yo-Yo couldn't stand it. "Forget the list," she said. "Let's just hold them. What's wrong with that?"

We tiptoed back into the room and each picked up a baby. The wailing dwindled to hiccups by the time we got back to the living room. "Put on some of that high-falutin' music they got," Yo-Yo said, settling down into a rocking chair with Isaac. "Aw, look, he wants to suck my finger."

Cradling Havah with one arm, I found a Mozart clarinet concerto, stuck it in the CD player, then settled down in Ben's recliner. Nestled in the curve of my arm, Havah looked up at me with her large dark eyes. "You're a beauty, little one," I murmured . . . and watched as her eyelids flickered, dropped, and closed.

I glanced over at Yo-Yo. She was watching the baby in her arms, a look I'd never seen there before. Tenderness? Longing? Awe?

271

"He's asleep," she whispered, still staring at Isaac's face, gently rocking.

"Havah too," I whispered back. The music, turned low, blanketed the room. I almost drifted off myself.

The clarinet concerto finally ended. "Thanks, Jodi," I heard Yo-Yo say.

I opened my eyes. "Thanks? For what?"

"For what you an' Flo said, about how it's time to give back." She looked down at the baby sleeping in the nest she'd made with one ankle crossed over the other knee. "Didn't know givin' back was like gettin' too."

30

*H*ow'd it go?" Denny looked up from the computer when I got back.

"She's legal. Finally! Ben looked like he had a few more white hairs, though."

Denny laughed.

"But it was a big deal for Yo-Yo to help take care of the twins. I think she and Isaac bonded. A good thing." I opened the fridge and pulled out the two lasagnas I'd made that morning. *A very good thing—like sticking a finger in the dike of her crumbling relationship with Ruth and Ben.* I turned on the oven to preheat. *No, more like picking up a slipped stitch and knitting it back into a seamless whole.*

I glanced at the clock. Four-thirty already. Stu was supposed to pick up Precious and Sabrina and bring them about five-thirty. Estelle was baking homemade French bread and pie. Guess all I needed to do was set the table and add a tossed salad. Wine with Italian food? No, better not.

"Amanda!" I yelled. "Did you clean the bathroom? . . . Denny, would you vacuum the living room before they get here? And where's Josh? He needs to take Wonka for a walk around the block."

By the time we heard the garage door go up, I'd lit candles on the table and the lasagnas were bubbly. Estelle came in the front door with her bread and crumb apple pie ("Don't like them back stairs in rain or snow, uh-uh," she complained) just as Stu and our two former houseguests came in the back.

"Precious! Sabrina! I'm so tickled to see you guys again!" I gave Precious a hug, then held her at arm's length. Both had their hair braided into long extensions. "Girl, you are looking *good*. Gee, you two look more like sisters than mother and daughter."

Precious laughed and poked Sabrina. "Uh-huh. Hear that, 'Brina?"

Sabrina, dressed in tight jeans, skimpy tank top, and a body-hugging sweater, turned her eyes away, as shy as the day she first came to our house—and then she saw Willie Wonka. "Aw, there's my baby." The teenager squatted down and hugged the dog, who obligingly licked her face.

We took down the child gate until everybody got in and the food was on the table, then penned Wonka back in the kitchen. He whined at the gate.

"Can't we let him in?" Sabrina petted him over the gate. "He don' scare me anymore."

"It's not that, Sabrina." I tried to be delicate. "He's having some, um, bowel difficulties. We keep him in the kitchen lately, close to the door."

"*Eww.*" Sabrina made a face and found a chair on the far side of the table. Amanda looked disgusted. I wasn't sure if it was because I said the "B" word, or because Sabrina's loyalty to her dog was so shallow.

After holding hands around the table and singing "Thanks! Thanks! We give You thanks!"—though we didn't sound quite as good as when T. D. Jakes sang it—the lasagnas disappeared at an incredible rate. Good thing I'd made two! The conversation bounced from one person to another, as we caught up after almost two months.

"We've got a new name for our church," Stu offered. "SouledOut Community Church. The teenagers came up with it . . . Can I have some more garlic bread?"

Precious passed the breadbasket. "Now that's cool. I like that. Sabrina an' me, we worship now an' then with the Salvation Army. But I'd like to find us our own church. Whatchu doin', Estelle? You ever finish that vest you was crochetin' for your grandboy?"

Stu laughed aloud. "That, and two more, plus about ten outfits for herself."

"Humph. Gotta do somethin' to keep these hands busy. Won't be doin' much sewing for the next few months, though. I'm goin' back to school—at my age!" Estelle beamed. "I applied this week for the Certified Nurse Assistant program at Chicago Community College."

"That's where Edesa goes to school!" Amanda piped up.

"*Did* go to school," Josh murmured. "She transferred to UIC. Getting her degree in Public Health now, remember?"

"Oh. Well, aren't they connected or something? They're both in the Loop."

"Speakin' of school, Sabrina gettin' almost all Bs now," Precious bragged. "Some of them Salvation Army folks helping tutor her, praise Jesus."

"Ma, don't." Sabrina rolled her eyes.

"Well, baby, we got lots to be thankful for. Even that Manna House fire gonna reap good things, you wait an' see."

"Well, now, that's right," said Estelle. "Reverend Miz Handley called me up this week, said the board wants to set up an advisory board made up of former residents and volunteers, an' asked me who I thought would be good to ask." She pointed her fork at Josh. "I told her she should ask you, Josh. You one of the few mens who volunteered, and you always had good ideas."

This time I did not imagine it. The color drained right out of Josh's face.

"Uh . . . I don't think so." He laid down his fork.

"Now, why not?" Precious jumped in. "You an' that girl Edesa really livened up Manna House. The kids was always excited when you two showed up. That's what that advisory board needs—some youthful blood." She looked around the table. "Now wouldn't that be grand if Manna House rose from the ashes, like the Phoenix bird, bigger an' more beautiful each time? The old had to go so the new could come."

I gaped at her. "How'd you know about the Phoenix bird?" A homeless single mom from the streets of Chicago didn't seem the type to read mythology.

Precious simpered at me. "Girl, you could put me on that *Jeopardy* show with what I know."

"Uh, could I be excused?" Josh didn't wait for an answer but picked up his dishes, stepped over the gate in the doorway to the kitchen, came back empty-handed, and headed for his room.

"Josh? Wait a minute." Estelle, for all her bulk, was up from the table and heading off our son in the hallway in less than two seconds. A moment later, she crooked her finger at Precious and the three of them headed for the living room.

"Well, if we're done . . ." Amanda pushed back her chair. "Wanna listen to Audio Adrenaline in my room, Sabrina?" The two girls disappeared with only, "Call us when you serve the pie, Mom."

Denny, Stu, and I looked at each other. "Uh, what just happened here?" Stu said.

I folded and unfolded my napkin. "Estelle wants to talk to Josh, I guess."

Denny scratched the back of his head. "Hm. Hope she knows what she's doing. He's not been the talking type lately. Guess I'll make coffee."

For the next several minutes, the three of us puttered in the kitchen, loading the dishwasher, cutting Estelle's crumb apple pie, getting out dessert plates, pie forks, and coffee mugs. "Don't get out the ice cream yet," I said. "I'll go see if they're ready to come back for dessert."

I slipped off my shoes and padded silently down the hallway toward the living room, not sure if I should interrupt. I heard Josh's voice. Well, at least he was talking.

". . . should never have let the kids talk me into plugging in the tree again. I *knew* it was a fire hazard. My mom and I talked about it."

I stopped, realizing this was not the time to go in.

"But, oh yeah, I wanted to be Mr. Nice Guy to the kids. Everybody says, don't be hard on yourself. It wasn't your fault, Josh."

Josh's voice turned bitter. "Well, you know what? That doesn't help! I *feel* like it was my fault. If I'd taken out that tree, it never would have happened! What if . . . what if someone had gotten hurt that night? Or killed? It could've happened. Kids, women, who had nothing in the first place, ended up with *less* than nothing! Oh, God . . ."

The last words were muffled. I peeked around the corner of the archway into the living room. Josh's head was in his hands. Estelle and Precious sat on either side of him on our couch. Tears puddled in my eyes and spilled over. *Oh, my son, my son* . . . I wanted to rush into the room and gather him into my arms. *Don't keep blaming yourself!*

And then I heard Precious say, "Sounds like you need to be forgiven."

Josh lifted his head and looked at her. "Yes." His voice sounded strangled, but he nodded. "Yes . . . yes . . ."

"Well, now." Precious put her arm around my son. "*I forgive you.* I know what you done—or didn't do—wasn't on purpose, an' we all make mistakes. But you right, it coulda been a whole lot worse than it was, only by the grace of God. But He got that grace for you, too, baby. He knows you sorry, and He forgives you. An' so do I."

Josh's shoulders began to shake. Suddenly he was sobbing into his arms. I could hardly stand it, but I knew God was holding me back. *It's not for you to do, Jodi,* said the Voice in my spirit. *He needs their forgiveness, the residents of Manna House.*

"I forgive you, too," said Estelle, also putting an arm around Josh. "Now go on, let it all out. It been too long a-comin'."

As quietly as I could, I fled to my bedroom, shut the door behind me, and fell on my bed. *Oh, God, Oh, God!* my heart cried out. *Why couldn't I see it?* The brick wall that had been closing in on my son ever since the fire was his own sense of responsibility and guilt. He *could* have prevented what happened. He didn't. He didn't need to be told it wasn't his fault.

He needed to be *forgiven.*

31

*T*he weather turned windy and cold again on Sunday with snow flurries predicted—the first day of spring, ha!—but I didn't even care. The cold spell in Josh's heart had broken last night. I could feel it in the atmosphere.

Josh had excused himself from pie the night before, but when it was time for Precious and Sabrina to go home (well, if you can call a shelter "home"), he came out of his room and offered to drive them. He still wasn't back when we went to bed—we hadn't set any curfew since he'd graduated from high school—but he was up early the next morning and jogged the short mile to the Howard Street Shopping Center to set up the sound board. And when we got there, I saw him talking to Rick Reilly. *Interesting.* Josh had blown off the youth-ministry brainstorming meeting yesterday. What now?

"We celebratin' Stu's birthday tonight?" Florida asked me after church.

I blinked. We'd already celebrated Stu's birthday at our house—but that wasn't Yada Yada. "Um, sure. Got any suggestions?"

"Stu been a good friend to Little Andy an' me," Becky popped in. "I'd like ta make the cake. But not one o' them round things. Flat. *In* the pan."

I laughed and gave Becky a hug. "You got it. I'll pass the word. We meet at Chanda's tonight. You guys want a ride?"

But when I pulled up in front of the Hickman house later that afternoon, I had to laugh. Florida, bundled in her winter coat, was sitting like a snow queen in her new wicker furniture on the porch. "Tol' ya I was gonna sit on my porch the first day of spring, rain or shine!" she yelled. But when Becky came out with a cake pan, Flo ran for the minivan. "Turn that heater up, girl! My fingers is froze."

Avis was already at Chanda's house when we arrived, getting the VIP tour of Rochelle's new bedroom and "the boys' room," which Conny was sharing with Chanda's boy, Tom. Florida and I ran up the stairs to peek, too, while Becky took her cake to the kitchen.

We had a good turnout at Yada Yada that night, including Ruth, who drove herself and Yo-Yo, and didn't let us forget it. "What? You are surprised? If I can birth two babies at my age, what's a little ol' driver's license?"

Yo-Yo rolled her eyes behind Ruth's back. "Huh. The license was easy; it's the driving that needs a little work," she muttered.

Our other surprise was Hoshi, who arrived with Nonyameko. "Most of the Northwestern students have gone home for spring break." Hoshi grinned, returning our hugs. "ReJOYce Campus Club meeting was cancelled."

"What about dat Sara?" Chanda asked, as she and Rochelle brought in a tray of coffee mugs along with a pot of good Jamaican coffee. The aroma was heavenly. "Did you bring her? Don't she only live a couple burbs nort' of 'ere?"

Hoshi shook her head. "She says no every time I invite her. But I told her we pray for her and are grateful for what she did, turning in those men who hurt Dr. Smith." Hoshi's lip suddenly trembled, and she busied herself looking for a tissue in her pocket.

Nony put an arm around Hoshi. "It is all right, my sister. God is working out His purpose in spite of what happened. One day Sara will come so we can love on her."

"Mm-hm," I heard Adele murmur. "So I can get my hands on that hair too."

I gaped at Adele. "That's it! That's what we can do."

Adele frowned. "Do what?" Others were looking at me, too.

"Hoshi, do you know when Sara's birthday is? Something to celebrate. We could collect money as a gift to give her the works at Adele's Hair and Nails—haircut, color, set, manicure, pedicure . . . you know, the works! Hoshi can tell her it's from all of us, to let her know she doesn't have to be afraid."

"Dat's a good idea." Chanda reached for her purse. "'Ere's a twenty to start."

I felt like rolling my eyes. She didn't have to announce *how much*. But others nodded, liking the idea. I took Chanda's twenty. "Whatever people want to contribute. We can collect next time too."

Just then, Becky entered with her cake in an aluminum nine-by-thirteen pan, candles flaming. "Happy birthday to Stu . . ." she warbled, and we all joined in. Estelle had brought a card "From the Whole Gang," which we all signed. But Becky had the best idea of all.

"I just wanna say, Stu's somethin' else. I don't know many folks who woulda taken me into their house, just to give me an address so I could get out on parole. I know I ain't the easiest person ta live with—"

Stu put a hand over her mouth, hiding a grin.

"—but she took a chance on me anyhow. Now I'm in my own place, but she still workin' the system to help me get Andy back. So on her birthday I just wanna say, I love ya, Stu girl." Becky Wallace grabbed Stu in a bear hug while we all clapped.

Flo spoke up. "Yeah, well, Stu found Carla, when DCFS lost track of *my* baby. An' she treated my man like a *man*, asked him ta help her move, let him know she needed him, trusted him with the job. Men like Carl, they need ta be needed. So I thank ya, too, girl." Another big hug.

"I wasn't sure if I wanted Stu to move into the apartment above us," I admitted. "Even though I'm older than Stu, I always felt like a little kid around her, she's so . . . so good at everything."

A chorus of "Hear, hear!" went up, laughter and clapping.

"But I have to say, Stu is nothing if not a loyal friend. She might make me feel like a dork"—more laughter—"but, frankly . . ." I stopped, realizing that what I was about to say was actually true. "Frankly, she's more like the sister I never had growing up." I stepped over to Stu and gave her a tight hug, amid more clapping. "I love you, Stu," I whispered in her ear.

"I love you, too, Jodi," she whispered back. She looked around at all the Yada Yadas sitting all over Chanda's living room. "Frankly, *you all* have been the family I didn't have for so many years—and you still are, even though God's starting to give my natural family back to me. Now that God and I got honest." She took the tissue Hoshi handed her and blew her nose.

Avis smiled. "Looks like we have a lot to give thanks for

tonight. Why don't we continue with our thanksgivings?" Her glance fell on her daughter Rochelle, perched on the arm of Chanda's leather couch. *"I* want to praise God and thank Chanda for offering her home to my daughter and grandson." Now *she* got teary. More tissues. "In the midst of a tough time for Rochelle, God is also pouring out His blessings. Mm!" Avis raised a hand in the air. "Thank You, Jesus! You are so good! So *good!*"

Rochelle smiled shyly at her mother's spontaneous praise. "I'm thankful to Chanda too. But I also want to say I'm grateful to Nonyameko, who is helping me see that HIV isn't something to be ashamed of. Fear and silence will only keep me from getting the help I need. Many women and children are suffering from this disease through no fault of our own. Though *some* people . . ." A flash of anger burned in her eyes.

Whew. That's deep, I thought. I had never heard Rochelle speak so boldly.

The moment of anger passed. "One more thing I am thankful for. My *stepfather,* Peter Douglass"—Rochelle used the word deliberately, tossing a teasing smile at her mother—"is starting a Manna House Foundation to raise money to rebuild the shelter."

I heard a gasp from Edesa. "Oh! *Es verdad?* It is true?"

Avis smiled. "Yes. Peter came home from the men's breakfast at SouledOut yesterday with this great idea. The last few months, some of our husbands have been meeting before the monthly breakfast to pray for one another, that God would use them in new ways. For Peter, starting a foundation to rebuild the shelter that had taken in our own daughter seemed like a way to give back."

"Gloria al Dios!" Delores Enriques beamed. "Ricardo came home and told me about the foundation." She grimaced apologetically to

Edesa. "I knew you would be so happy, *mi hermana*. But I did not know if the news was mine yet to tell."

Excited comments flew. I wondered if that was the news Denny had wanted to tell me. Nony clapped her hands together, then burst out laughing, like a little girl dying to tell her secret. "Has a holy fire baptized our men, sending them into the market-place like on the day of Pentecost?"

"Hm. Don't know about *that*," Florida murmured. "Ain't heard Carl speak in no tongues and don't think I will."

We joined Nony's laughter, but Adele always could read between the lines. "You got more 'holy fire' to tell us about, Nony?"

Nony nodded, pressing her hands flat together in front of her smile. "Yes . . . yes. Mark *also* came home from the men's breakfast yesterday and asked me to go out for coffee so we could talk. Sisters . . ." She blinked back sudden tears, but her smile stayed fixed. "It has been many months since my husband did that. He said he had not planned to tell me yet, not wanting to disappoint me if he failed, but the brothers encouraged him to include me in his plans."

Adele rolled her eyes. "*What* plans? Girlfriend, you better tell us quick."

Nony's smile widened. "He decided—no, *we* decided—we should move forward with our plans that were so viciously aborted last summer, unless God shuts the door."

A universal gasp greeted this announcement. "Ya mean, like, you guys goin' to South Africa again?" Yo-Yo asked bluntly.

Nony nodded. "Mark has decided to apply once more to the University of KwaZulu-Natal as guest instructor. Yes, he is afraid—afraid they will reject him because of his recent medical history. But Carl and Peter and Denny told him—how do Americans say it?—to 'get off his duff" and live again." Now the tears spilled over, but Nony lifted her face in praise. "Oh, Lord God, thank You! You are making a way out of no way, a stream in the desert, a path over the mountain!"

For several minutes, the rest of us joined Nony's praise, which became prayers for God's favor on Mark Smith's application and the birth of the Manna House Foundation. But as we praised and prayed, I struggled inside. Mark Smith "getting off his duff" was a *huge* answer to our prayers. But if the Sisulu-Smiths *did* move to South Africa, we might be saying good-bye to them for . . . for who knew how long!

Oh God! How can it be good news and hurt so much at the same time?

The Voice in my spirit nudged me. *Your Yada Yada sisters are a gift, Jodi Baxter—not a possession. You know how Nony has longed to return to her homeland, how her heart aches for the suffering caused by HIV and AIDS. Would you keep her from My plans for her and Mark?*

Well, of course the answer was no—but that didn't help my feelings any.

Besides, the Voice within continued, *I have plans for you, too, Jodi— but you must keep your heart and your mind open. My plans are not your plans. Be alert; My Spirit is moving. Think of the possibilities . . .*

"Hey. Earth to Jodi. You collecting the money for Sara's makeover?" Becky Wallace stood in front of me, trying to give me a wadded-up bill.

With a start, I realized the prayers were over and people were starting to leave. "Oh, yeah, sure. Thanks, Becky." I stuffed the bill in my pocket along with Chanda's twenty and started to put on my jacket.

"Sister Jodi?" Edesa pulled me aside. "Does . . . do you think Josh knows about the Manna House Foundation?"

287

I thought a minute. "I don't know. He didn't go to the men's breakfast yesterday. Denny might have told him, but I don't think so. The first I heard about it was tonight." Her eyes seemed imploring. *What is she really asking me?* "Estelle did tell him about the advisory board. He . . . wasn't interested. But that was before . . ." I hesitated. What happened last night was probably not my news to tell.

But she nodded. "I know. He came to my house last night." She looked up at me, her dark eyes huge, black diamonds in her sweet mahogany face. "He asked me to forgive him for his part in the Manna House fire."

So. That was what Josh did after taking Precious and Sabrina home! "And?" I asked gently.

"I forgave him. I was glad! You see, I had been blaming him in my heart, holding it against him. We are very traditional in my country. To me, he is a man, even though he is young. And a true man always protects the women and children, but his carelessness put us all in danger. Those women had nothing but lost everything. But . . . I, too, asked him to forgive me, for holding blame in my heart. I was not honest with him; I only held him away."

She sniffled, and I found a clean tissue to give her. As she wiped her eyes and blew her nose, I felt a tenderness toward this young woman I'd never felt before. God's Spirit had told me to be alert, that His Spirit was moving. That His plans were not my plans. *To think of the possibilities . . .*

"He loves you, you know."

I don't know who was more startled by my murmured words—Edesa or me. She stared at me, eyes rounded. And then her chin quivered beneath a small smile. "I know," she whispered.

32

hew. So much had happened over the weekend, I felt like an amateur juggler, trying to keep all the prayers in the air but dropping half of them in the hurry-scurry of a muddy school week. I was a tad jealous of Hoshi's week off from classes between her winter and spring quarters. What I wouldn't give for even one day off, just to catch up with myself!—not to mention the weekend laundry that still needed folding. But Chicago schools still had three weeks to go before our spring break.

On the other hand, I told myself that Thursday, while navigating a chain of sidewalk puddles and trying to keep dry under our old black umbrella, it'd been raining most of the week, even though the temperatures had finally climbed into the sixties. Maybe having spring break after Easter would give us some warm, sunny days to enjoy, time to plant some flower boxes for the back porch . . .

Unfortunately, another puddle in the kitchen greeted me when I got home from school. My initial frustration evaporated when I saw poor Willie Wonka, curled up in a corner, looking at me miserably. "Aw, it's all right, Wonka," I murmured, getting out the bucket and disinfectant. I mopped up the mess with a rag and dried the floor, then lowered myself beside Wonka and pulled his head into my lap. The tip of his tail patted quietly as I stroked his head and scratched behind his ears. "Guess it's time for another trip to the vet, eh, old boy? Don't worry," I crooned. "The vet's our friend, remember? Maybe she can help us with this problem."

A thunderclap rattled the windows. I decided against trying to take the dog out, and just sat on the floor with my back against the wall, petting his once silky brown fur that had grown dull and thin, showing his ribs—until the phone rang. I scrambled to my feet and caught it on the third ring. "Mom?" Amanda sounded desperate. "Can you call Dad and ask him to pick me up at school on his way home?"

I looked at the clock. "You're still at school? I was expecting you any minute."

A loud crack of thunder drowned out her next few words. "—language lab, but I can't go outside now to wait for the bus. It's raining buckets!"

I squeezed my eyes shut. "Sorry, honey. Tonight's the night Dad goes to the JDC. He's probably on his way downtown already."

"But Mo-om! I'll get soaked standing at the bus stop!"

"Oh . . . ask the school office for a phone book and call a cab."

"Really?" She sounded interested. "A cab?"

Well, why not? What could it be—five dollars? Ten?

"FIFTEEN DOLLARS!"

Amanda, casting anxious looks out the front door at the blinking hazard lights of the Yellow Cab, rolled her eyes. "Mo-om. You *told* me to call a cab. The meter said eleven-something—almost twelve. And you're supposed to give a tip, you know."

Somehow, I scrounged up the money, thinking ruefully that fifteen dollars was half a night out for Denny and me—maybe a *whole* night out if we went to CrossRhodes Café where we could split a large Greek salad with gyros slices and a large order of lemony Greek fries and still have enough left over to rent a video. *On the other hand,* I thought, as Amanda grabbed an umbrella and ran out to pay the cab driver, *she's home safe and dry. That's worth a lot, thank You, Jesus.*

Josh called to say he was working late to get a big software shipment out before the weekend, and not to wait supper for him. So I served up two plates of Pad Thai from a box, saving a plate for Denny, while Amanda tried to coax Willie Wonka into the dining room for a half-hour reprieve from his kitchen jail cell. But the dog just wagged the tip of his tail, sighed, and laid his head down on his paws.

"Mo-om! What's the matter? He won't come!" The next moment, she took her plate and flopped on the floor beside the brown Lab. "I'm gonna eat in the kitchen with Wonka."

I shrugged. "Huh. Guess it's either eat by myself in the dining room or join the sit-in." I sank to the floor beside my daughter and the dog with my plate, making Amanda laugh. "Say, got any ideas for Dad's birthday next week?" April first, his birthday, was a week from today. "Oh, wait. That's a Thursday! He won't even be here for supper."

Amanda dug into her Pad Thai noodles. "Don't sweat it, Mom. Just celebrate on Friday. Dad won't care. He probably gets tired of April Fool's jokes on his birthday anyway."

DENNY WAS PUMPED when he got home from the JDC, as usual. He leaned against the counter, eating his plate of Pad Thai standing up, while he related the latest saga of the Bible study in Unit 3B. "Two of our regulars weren't there tonight. Found out one was found guilty of first-degree murder at his hearing and has been shipped out to the Joliet Youth Center. Makes me sick, Jodi. I don't think he was the shooter, but because he was present at the time of the shooting, they got him on the accountability law. He cooperated, told what he knew, but they used it against him. The *shooter*, on the other hand, had enough street smarts to keep quiet—and he was acquitted for lack of evidence." He shook his head and fell silent, eating his microwave-warm noodles.

Oh God! Is that what will happen to Chris Hickman? No, Lord, please . . . I swallowed. "How do you know this? I thought you weren't supposed to talk to the kids about their cases."

"Oscar Frost, mostly. He's been trying to follow the cases as they're reported in the newspaper, buried somewhere in the *Metro* pages, and online."

"What about Chris? Was he there tonight?"

Denny nodded. "Yeah. He looks good. Has lost that sullen look he'd been affecting, and from all I can tell, doing good in his schoolwork too . . . though, man!" He waved his fork. "The kids can't take any textbooks out of the school area. They're not even supposed to have pencils in their cells—anything that could double as a weapon. So much for homework and studying. But . . ." Denny chewed thoughtfully. "Don't think school is uppermost in his mind. His disposition is coming up at the end of the month. He asked me to pray."

Definitely. I really needed to check in with Florida and find out how she was doing. Funny how easy it was to forget that her mother-heart must be weeping every day Chris was in jail. She seemed so strong; "life goes on" and all that.

"Hey. Almost forgot." Denny pulled a sheet of paper from his briefcase. "Don't know if you'd be interested, but the school at the JDC is looking for a volunteer English teacher to help the boys produce a play for their parents. Their regular teacher got mono and won't be back for several weeks. I thought of you."

"Me?" Was my husband crazy? "I have a full-time job, Denny. And I teach *third graders*. What do I know about teenagers?"

He chuckled. "You've got two of your own. And half your friends have teenagers—Florida, Yo-Yo, Delores. These boys aren't that different. Well, yeah, true, they've come from some tough situations, made some bad choices. But under the skin, they're just kids. Just kids . . ." He squatted down and scratched Willie Wonka behind the ears. "Hey, old buddy. I hear you're going to see the vet this weekend." He ran his hand thoughtfully over the dog's thin body. "Anyway, think about it, Jodi. You're a teacher—a good teacher. This would be something different, a way to reach out. It could be a lot of fun. You might have to do it during spring break, though."

Give up my spring break?

Think of the possibilities, Jodi . . .

"Man, I don't know, Denny." I held out my hand for the sheet of paper. "Is that some information about what they want?"

He grinned up at me. "Uh, not exactly. It's a form from the Sheriff's Department for a background check."

THE RAIN WOKE ME up just minutes before the alarm. "Ohh," I groaned. *More rain!* Four days in a row! And it wasn't even April yet. That would make taking Willie Wonka outside miserable for me *and* the poor dog. But—I swung my legs out of bed—it had to be done, or we'd have another puddle in the kitchen *before* school.

I pulled Denny's bathrobe around me and stuck my feet into my slippers, shuffling toward the kitchen. I missed my "Wonka alarm clock," snuffling his nose into my face, letting me know he had to go out. But since he'd started to have bladder and bowel problems, we couldn't let him sleep in our bedroom anymore.

"Wake up, sleepyhead," I said, swinging one leg over the safety gate in the kitchen doorway, then the other, and turning on the light. I sleepily filled the coffeepot with cold water, scooped coffee into the basket, and punched the On button. The coffee might as well be dripping while Wonka and I had our big adventure into the wet-and-wild outdoors.

The dog hadn't moved, curled up on his doggy cushion near the door. "Hey, c'mon, Wonka," I said, shaking him gently. "Let's get this over with."

He still didn't move.

Suddenly, fear grabbed my throat. My heart started racing. "Wonka!" I yelled, this time shaking him roughly. No response. "Oh God, Oh God, oh nooooo . . . " I fell backward, as if I'd been shocked with an electric current. *"Denny!"* I screamed, scrambling to my feet. "Come here! Quick!"

Footsteps thudded from the bedroom. Doors opened, more footsteps. Within seconds, Denny, in sleep shorts and T-shirt, had yanked the safety gate from the doorway and was at my side. Josh and Amanda, their hair tousled, their eyes wide, were right behind him.

"Wonka . . ." My voice barely came out in a whisper. Denny immediately squatted down on one knee and held his fingers to the dog's neck.

"Oh, Mommy! . . . Oh no! He's not . . . he's not . . . is he?" Amanda started to cry. Josh reached out and put his arm around his sister, pulling her close.

Denny, still down on one knee, turned and looked up at us . . . and nodded slowly.

I burst into tears. Amanda threw herself down and covered Willie Wonka's body with her own. "Wonka! Don't leave me! Don't leave me!" Her whole body shook with sobs. "You're my only friend, Wonka! Please, *please*, don't go . . ."

And then our arms reached out for each other, all four of us surrounding our beloved dog, our friend, whose love was unconditional . . . and we cried.

33

I didn't go to work that day. I couldn't. We let Amanda stay home too. We called the high school and said we had a death in the family—which was true. But when I called Bethune Elementary, I simply told the office I had a family emergency and needed a substitute. "And could you leave a message for Mrs. Douglass to call me?"

The rain was still coming down hard. Denny stood on the porch, hands in the pockets of his jeans, watching the rain cascade off the garage roof, forming a wet trench on the ground. Finally, he motioned to me to join him outside and to close the door. "I suppose we could call Animal Control and they would—"

"No, Denny! They'll just . . . just 'dispose' of him in some garbage pit. A dead animal doesn't mean anything to them. We can't let Willie Wonka . . ." I choked up.

"I know. That's what I was going to say. Maybe we're supposed to call Animal Control, but I want to bury him ourselves. Only problem . . ." Denny tipped his chin at the soggy backyard. "We can't dig a grave in weather like this. Weather report says it's supposed to clear later this afternoon, though. Might be all right tomorrow." He shook his head. "But I don't know, Jodi. Think Amanda can deal with it? Wonka's body in the house all day, I mean. Especially if she's not going to school."

"Better than the alternative!" I snapped—and immediately repented. "I'm sorry, Denny. I just can't bear the thought of strangers taking Wonka away."

"I know." His voice was tender. He pulled me into his arms and we just held each other for a few minutes.

"Whoa! Look at the lovebirds." Stu came clattering down the back stairs, half hidden under her umbrella. "I'm late. See you later." She dashed for the garage.

Just as well. I wasn't ready to talk about Wonka yet. We'd tell her tonight.

When we came back into the kitchen, Amanda had wrapped her bright yellow comforter with the black geometric designs around the dog's body—way too much blanket for our small kitchen. But I quietly toasted some bagels for Denny and Josh, who decided to go on to work. "We'll bury him tomorrow, sweetie," Denny said, kissing the top of Amanda's head as he came back into the kitchen, dressed in slacks, shirt, and tie. "When the rain stops, okay?"

She nodded mutely.

He tipped up her chin. "You going to be okay?"

Amanda pulled away and didn't respond. He let her go, grabbed a bagel and a travel mug of coffee, and headed for the garage, Josh right behind him.

Suddenly the house felt cavernous. Yawning like an empty

mouth, and nothing to fill it. What was I going to do all day? I couldn't put on some loud gospel music to drown out my sorrow, as I usually did. It wouldn't feel right, not with Wonka's motionless body wrapped in his yellow-and-black shroud on the kitchen floor. Maybe not going to work was a bad idea. I could go in late . . . . no. I should stay with Amanda.

The phone rang. "Jodi?" It was Avis. "Ms. Ivy said you had a family emergency! What happened?"

I told her about Willie Wonka. "Amanda's a wreck. I need to stay with her. And to be honest, I'm pretty much a basket case myself. I'm sorry, Avis. Just today."

"Oh. Well . . ."

I could almost hear her struggling between the professional Mrs. Douglass (*"What? You want to stay home because your dog died? What about your third graders, who are very much alive? I'm putting you on professional probation!"*) and Avis, my friend.

Avis won. "All right, Jodi. Family emergency it is. And . . . I'm really sorry for your loss. Give Amanda a hug for me."

Her words wrapped themselves around me, and I had another cry after we hung up. *Get hold of yourself, Jodi Baxter. You didn't cry this much when MaDear died!* I blew my nose and stood looking at the garish yellow-and-black pile in the corner of the kitchen. Should I try to find another blanket? Something smaller and—

"Mom?" Amanda came into the kitchen, noiseless in her socks, and stood beside me. Our arms slid around each other's waist. "I don't wanna put Wonka into the wet ground just wrapped in a blanket. Can't Daddy and Josh make a box or something? We could line it with something soft, maybe cut up my comforter, and sew it to fit."

Cut up her comforter! Suddenly it didn't matter. Why not? What was one comforter anyway, compared to a decent burial for Amanda's lifelong friend?

THE RAIN STOPPED SHORTLY AFTER NOON. That evening, Josh and Denny built a box—basically, the deep bottom drawer from an old chest of drawers sitting unused in the basement, with a new lid that fit snugly over the top. Amanda and I cut up her comforter and sewed it together on two sides, vaguely resembling a dog-size sleeping bag. Amanda then sewed a pillowcase out of the same padded material, stuffing it with pieces of wadded-up comforter to make a pillow for Wonka's head to rest on.

It was time to let Wonka's friends know. I dialed upstairs when I heard Stu arrive home. "What?" she cried into my ear. "Why didn't you tell me this morning? I rushed right past you . . . Oh, Jodi, I feel so stupid."

"It's all right, Stu. We weren't ready to talk about it."

"I'm so sorry, Jodi. You want me to call anyone? The rest of Yada Yada?"

Relief sighed in my spirit. "Yes, please. We're going to bury him in the backyard tomorrow morning at ten—in case anyone wants to come. Like maybe Becky. She and Wonka were good buddies when she lived with you." *Becky . . .* I felt like bawling all over again. Little Andy had wanted to come play with "the doggy" a couple of Sundays ago, and it hadn't happened. Now it never would.

Josh and Denny lifted Willie Wonka's limp body into the soft bag, then laid him in the box, head on the pillow. "Don't put the lid on, not yet," Amanda begged. She bent down and kissed Wonka's still-silky ears—then fled to her bedroom.

I checked on her before going to bed. She lay curled up in her bed, her old faded comforter, once pink, now barely beige, in service once more. As I leaned over to kiss her, she grabbed my arm and pulled me onto the bed. "Mom? Why is God taking everything away from me?"

I could barely breathe.

"I mean, first José left me . . . and then MaDear died, and, and, she was practically a relative . . . and now Willie Wonka." The sobs started again. "I mean, *why*, Mom?"

I didn't have an answer. So I just held her and let her cry.

SOMETIME DURING THE NIGHT, the clouds disappeared and the early morning sun kissed rooftops, trees, and bushes, inviting the world to come outside. Josh and Denny dug a hole out by the garage, where Becky had worked so hard to make a flower garden last year. I stood and watched them, suddenly aware of the sparrows flittering through the still-bare tree limbs. A few landed on the bird feeder Denny had hung for me last year, pecked hopefully, then flew away, still hungry.

But I turned away. I couldn't think about the birds. Not yet.

At ten o'clock, Stu and Estelle came down the back stairs and joined us in the backyard. A huge white-and-silver SUV I didn't recognize pulled up in the alley behind our garage. A moment later, Florida, Cedric, and Carla tiptoed respectfully into the back yard, followed by Chanda's three kids and Becky Wallace— carrying Little Andy! "I get Andy two full weekends a month now, not just Sundays," she whispered to me, setting the curly-headed boy down. "Ain't God good?"

Andy made a beeline for Denny. "Hi, Big Guy!" he squealed,

throwing his arms around Denny's leg. And then he saw the open box. The little boy stared. "Why is the doggy in the box?"

Denny shot a quick glance at Becky, who mouthed above Little Andy's head, "*I didn't know how to tell him!*"

Denny nodded at Becky, gathered all the children around the box, and started talking to them in a calm voice. "When dogs get very old, one day their body just stops working, just like people. But that doesn't mean we forget about them . . ."

I leaned toward Becky. "How'd you get here? I mean, whose monster SUV?"

She snorted. "Chanda's. She leasin' it for a few weeks ta see if she wants somethin' that big. Came in handy today, fer sure."

Chanda joined us in the backyard ten minutes later, muttering, "De parking all *chacka-chacka* in dis neighborhood." But she hushed when she realized Denny was inviting the children to say something about their friend, Willie Wonka.

"He never bited me," Little Andy said solemnly.

"Sometimes he licked my face," Carla added.

"Whenever we came to see him, he wagged his tail." Dia wiggled her skinny rump. "I wish I had a tail to wag."

We laughed softly, then fell silent around the box holding our beloved Willie Wonka. "Amanda?" Denny prodded gently.

Amanda pulled something out of a paper bag. It was her old, favorite stuffed Snoopy dog, more grey than white now, one eye missing, one ear sagging. She laid it in the box with Wonka's body. Her lip trembled. "I . . . guess I have to grow up now."

Just then, footsteps came running on the walk alongside our house. José Enriques burst into the backyard, followed by a gasping Edesa. "Are we too late, *Señor* Baxter?" he cried. The teenager's dark eyes took in the circle of adults and children around the hole, the pile of dirt, the box still sitting on the winter-dead lawn. "Amanda, I—"

Amanda didn't let him finish. She threw herself into José's arms and burst into tears. "Oh, José! You came!"

THE BACKYARD WAS QUIET NOW. Chanda's vanload decided to go to the zoo and thank God for all the animals. The pile of dirt had been shoveled back into the hole and smoothed over the top. Becky promised she'd be back to plant some special flowers over the grave. "We'll call it Wonka's garden, right, Andy?"

I peeked out the kitchen window as I chopped vegetables for soup. José and Amanda sat cross-legged on the damp ground, shoulders hunched, picking at the brown grass, talking. On the porch, Josh and Edesa sat on the porch swing, soaking up spring's first rays, sometimes talking, sometimes just sitting quietly as the swing squeaked gently.

"God," I murmured, putting the lid on the pot and turning up the heat, "thank You for little graces, even in the middle of sad times like today . . . for José showing up, just when Amanda needed a friend . . . for Edesa and Josh able to sit comfortably together— though You might be the *only* One who knows what's going on with those two." I don't think prayers are supposed to end with rolling eyes, but I did it anyway.

When the pot was bubbling and the smell of garlic and basil filled the kitchen, I opened the back door. "Edesa! José! You want to stay for lunch? Got plenty of soup."

José jumped up. "Oh no, I can't, *Señora* Baxter. I have to

rehearse with the band at one o'clock. My father's on the road today, so I am filling in. What time is it?"

I glanced at the kitchen clock. "Fifteen minutes to twelve."

Amanda danced on her toes hopefully, but José shook his head. *"Gracias,* Señora Baxter. But we came by el and—"

"Chill, José." Josh pulled out his car keys and playfully tossed them in the air. "I'll take you guys home. We only need thirty minutes to get there—forty, tops. Stay for Mom's soup."

34

*D*enny said he didn't want a big hullabaloo for his birthday, not so soon after losing our dog. So even though Stu and Estelle offered to come downstairs to help us celebrate on April first, I said no thanks, we were putting off his birthday until the weekend, and then we were going out to dinner, "just family."

It had been a strange week. The tears had dried up, but the hollow feeling in our lives remained. No Willie Wonka to trip over when we came in the door. No *click-click-click* of his nails on the hardwood floors. No muzzle pushed into our laps as we watched TV or sprawled in the recliner. And especially no kissy-face ritual when Amanda came home from school.

But I couldn't let Denny's actual birthday go past unnoticed, even though we'd put off going out until Friday. So while he was at the JDC Thursday evening, I made a chocolate tunnel cake. It even came out of the bundt pan in one piece, shiny and firm, belying its gooey center. I lit candles in the living room, put the cake on our old oak coffee table that was "fashionably stressed" after years of snacks and feet—with and without shoes—and made a pot of decaf coffee.

"What's this?" he said, coming into the living room after his long day, dropping his briefcase and loosening his tie. He lifted an eyebrow suspiciously. "You promised no April Fool's jokes this year."

"No joke. Just cake. I promise."

The front door banged. "I smell chocolate," Josh said. He stopped at the living room door. "I thought we weren't celebrating Dad's birthday till tomorrow."

"Well, um, I cheated. Get your sister. We're having cake."

A funny peace settled over the living room as the four of us dug into the cake by candlelight. "Mm," Amanda said, ignoring her fork and breaking her slice into gooey pieces, licking her fingers after each bite. "You haven't made this for a long time, Mom—oh!" She looked at her father guiltily. "We didn't sing 'Happy Birthday.'"

He gave a dismissive wave. "That's okay. Just eat."

"But can we say *happy* birthday? Even if, you know, we're kinda sad?"

Denny chewed thoughtfully. "Sure. Because I am happy, you know."

"You are? But—"

"Well, I'm sad because we're missing Willie Wonka. But, I'm happy we got him when *you* were just a pup, snickerdoodle"—he reached over and pinched Amanda's nose—"because it was fun watching you two grow up together. And I'm happy because my wife, who's put up with me for twenty years—"

"Twenty-*one*," I corrected. "Twenty-four if you count dating."

"—and my two best kids—"

"You only *have* two kids," Josh pointed out.

Denny ignored the interruptions. "—are here with me right this moment, eating 'tunnel of fudge' cake. It doesn't get much better than that."

"Da-ad." Amanda rolled her eyes.

"I'm serious. Who knows if we'll all be together next year? Actually . . ." Denny put down his empty plate and leaned forward, forearms resting on his knees, looking around our small circle, ". . . Willie Wonka's death marks the end of an era for the Baxter family. I realized that was true, 'Manda, when you put your Snoopy dog in the box with Wonka's body and said, 'Guess I have to grow up now.'"

She made a face. "Yeah. But I was kinda mad. I didn't want any ol' stuffed dog if I couldn't have my real one."

Denny reached for our daughter and pulled her close to him on the couch, wrapping one arm around her shoulder. "But it's true, you know. You've had a rough time this winter. José broke up with you. MaDear died. Now Willie Wonka's gone. Familiar props have been knocked out from under you."

"But José came back! Well, not really. He said he's missed me, wants us to still be friends. Not like, you know, before—all tight and exclusive and stuff. But . . ." Amanda shrugged. "It's okay. I'm glad we can be friends."

Denny smiled at her. "Exactly. I think God knows you're strong enough to forge ahead even without the familiar props. In fact, tonight at the JDC, our study group came across this verse." He fished in his briefcase for the Bible he'd taken that night, and flipped pages. "Okay, here it is. First Corinthians, chapter thirteen:

307

'When I was a child, I talked like a child, I thought like a child, I reasoned like a child. But when I became a man'—you know, grown—'I put childish things behind me.'"

He looked up. "Oscar and I talked to the boys that part of growing up is learning to face up to the consequences of mistakes and bad decisions. But it's also learning to overcome disappointment, even the loss of friends or family. Life isn't always fair. Bad things happen. But life keeps rolling. We have to keep rolling, too. Roll with the punches, roll with God's help."

"Can I see that?" Amanda reached for her dad's Bible and studied the page. Then her eyes widened. "Look at the next verse! It says, 'Now I know in part; then I shall know fully, even as I am fully known.'" She looked up thoughtfully. "It's kinda saying we don't always know *why* things happen, but we will someday—because God knows everything about us."

I watched my husband and daughter, gratefulness squeezing my heart. Amanda had cried, *"Why, Mom? Why?"* I didn't feel badly that I didn't have any answers that night. That wasn't the night for answers. But tonight, she was listening. Listening to the Word.

Josh cleared his throat. "Uh, can I cut in? I know you guys have been waiting for me to grow up, leave the nest, whatever."

I hid a grin. *Well, yeah.*

"But what you said, Dad, about God sometimes knocks the props out from under us . . . guess that sums up what I've been feeling. When Dr. Smith was attacked by those racists, well, that knocked the rosy color off my world, that's for sure. But I kept doing this, doing that, thinking I wanted to save the world, college could wait, all that stuff, until . . . well, the fire, you know. Kinda burned up my self-confidence."

The candles were starting to drip wax on the coffee table. But I couldn't take my eyes off my son, sandy hair falling over his ears and curling down onto his neck, blue tattoo peeking out from under the sleeve of his T-shirt, both knees of his jeans ripped. Jesus was right. It was what was on the *inside* of a person that counted with God.

"But Edesa and I, we've been talking, and she kinda showed me God takes things away sometimes, so all we have left to lean on is God. Funny thing, though, those women and kids at the shelter—they lost a lot more in that fire than I did. But women like Estelle and Precious, they still had something I didn't . . . confidence in God. Ya know?"

My eyes blurred. Amanda was watching her brother with her mouth half open. Denny pulled out his handkerchief.

Josh threw out his hands. "But I think God's telling me He can guide a rolling stone better than a stick-in-the-mud. So I went ahead and enrolled at UIC for the fall semester, you know, the Chicago Circle campus. Maybe international studies, not sure yet. Relating across cultures, that kind of thing. But staying in Chicago means I can get involved with the youth outreach at SouledOut on the weekends—maybe even sit on that advisory board for the new Manna House shelter." He cast an impish look at me. "Don't worry, Mom. I'm gonna look for an apartment or somethin'."

"Sounds good, Josh. Real good." Denny lifted an eyebrow. "But you were going to tell us this . . . when?"

Josh grinned. "Hey. Happy birthday, Dad."

I CRAWLED INTO OUR QUEEN-SIZE BED, propped myself up with both pillows, and watched Denny pull off his tie, then his belt, then his shoes. He saw me watching him and grinned. "Best birthday I've ever had."

I nodded. It had been a magical night—the kind of magic created when God breaks into our everyday world with angels making announcements and stars bringing wise men. The kind of magical night when you're just grateful you were present to see God at work, even though you didn't have anything to do with it.

Well, maybe the chocolate cake helped. Got us together, anyway, unplanned and unrehearsed.

"I've been thinking," I said. "What you said about life keeps rolling. So when stuff happens, we have to roll with the punches and keep going with God's help."

He raised a quizzical eyebrow at me as he finished undressing and pulled on his sleep shorts and T-shirt.

"I mean, not *just* 'keep going,' but moving outward. You know, like Mark Smith applying again to that university in KwaZulu-Natal. Nony is so excited—not just about the possibility of going back to South Africa, but because Mark is 'rolling' again, moving forward, instead of telling himself he can't."

Denny crawled into bed beside me and stole his pillow back. "Yeah. God is good. *Real* good."

Which was true, though I could hardly imagine Yada Yada without Nony. She was the one who taught us about praying the Scriptures right back to God, claiming His promises, something I was still learning. But . . . I couldn't let myself think about losing Nony right now.

I propped myself up on one elbow and faced Denny. "But that's going to be a big change for Yada Yada. And it's not the only one! Hoshi graduates in June. What's *she* going to do? Especially if the

Sisulu-Smiths leave and sell their house. That's been her home for the past year. And our family is facing big changes too. Like you said, in a way Wonka's death marks the end of an era for our family. Our kids are growing up. Josh will be moving out, Amanda graduates next year . . . that whole empty-nest thing."

"Mm-hm." Denny breathed out a sleepy sigh. "And your point is?"

I hesitated. Was I really ready to take the plunge? But wasn't that what God had been saying to us tonight? Time to uncircle the wagons. Time to get rolling!

"The point is . . . I think I want to do that drama thing with the kids at the JDC. If the position is still open."

"YOU GONNA DO *WHAT*?" Florida said before worship started on Sunday morning. Daylight Savings had dragged us out of bed an hour earlier that day, but the fact that it was Palm Sunday and the beginning of Holy Week helped ensure that the majority of SouledOut members made it by the new time.

"I'm applying to the Nancy Jefferson School at the JDC as a drama coach volunteer." I grinned. "The English teacher got mono or something."

Florida stared at me. "Since when you a drama coach? I thought you taught third grade. An' one thing I *know*, they ain't got no third graders at the JDC. Huh. Not yet, anyway." She wagged her head. "But I tell ya, Jodi, they got some kids up in there young as ten. Breaks my heart."

Now it was my turn to stare. "*Ten!*" Ten was fifth grade.

"Yeah," she said glumly. "Those gangs are recruitin' shorties at a younger an' younger age—then these babies end up holdin' drugs for the big dudes, or smugglin' weapons, or even usin' 'em to make themselves feel big an' bad. Maybe it's good they get caught; keeps 'em off the street for a while anyway. But I dunno, the JDC ain't all it s'posed ta be—oh! Hey there, Nony. Hey, Mark."

We both got warm hugs from the Sisulu-Smith family, who had just come in. "Yada Yada tonight at my house, sisters?" Nony shrugged off her coat. "Help me pass the word that we are still collecting money for that gift certificate for Sara. Hoshi found out Sara just had a birthday in March—but thinks our idea would still work as a belated birthday gift."

Carla Hickman's age group was busily handing out palm fronds, and Avis set her big, falling-apart Bible on the small wooden stand that served as a pulpit, ready for the call to worship. "Talk to you later," I whispered to Flo, then took a palm frond and scurried to my seat beside Denny. But my mind was backpedaling. *What did Flo mean, the JDC isn't all it's supposed to be? What am I getting myself into? Have I leaped before I looked?*

But Avis's strong voice pulled me into the reason we had gathered that morning. "Blessed is He who comes in the name of the Lord!"

We all repeated her words: "Blessed is He who comes in the name of the Lord!"

Little Andy's voice piped up, "She *s'posed* to say, 'Good mornin', church.'" Becky Wallace's face turned a bright pink as the other children tittered.

Avis smiled. "Imagine for a moment that we are worshipers on our way to the temple in Jerusalem. And then the whispers start. 'Jesus of Nazareth is coming!' . . . 'You mean the Healer?' . . . 'Could He be the Messiah?' Excitement mounts. And then they see Him coming down the road, riding a humble donkey. 'He's coming! He's coming!' Suddenly people are breaking off palm branches to wave." Avis began to wave the palm frond she held in her hand. "Others take off their cloaks and lay them in the road. The children began to sing; soon the cry was heard all along the road into Jerusalem—"

As if on cue, the praise team and instruments launched into a song: *Hosanna! Hosanna! Blessed is He who comes in the name of the Lord!* Palm fronds waved all over the blue-and-coral-painted room. I hadn't heard this particular song before, but it was easy to pick up.

As we repeated the "Hosanna" lines at the end of the song, Oscar Frost put down his saxophone and picked up a pair of maracas. The drummer laid down his sticks and began a thudding beat with his hands on a set of congas. Suddenly the praise team was singing the song again—in Spanish:

Hosanna! Hosanna! Bendecido es Él que viene en el nombre del Señor!

I saw Amanda's face light up. *Hosanna! Hosanna! Bendecido es Él que viene en el nombre del Señor!* Children jumped up and down, waving their palms. In fact, it was impossible to stand still. People began moving away from their seats, forming a processional around the room. The waving palms, throbbing drums, and joyful words did seem as if we were welcoming the One we'd all been longing for—the Messiah, the Savior, the Son of God who came to live among us.

But even as we sang and waved our palms, we passed the plain wooden cross on the wall of our storefront sanctuary. And it hit me with renewed clarity: between two joyful Sundays—Palm Sunday and Easter—came the Cross.

35

hoa. That whole Cross thing stayed on my mind all afternoon. *Hope and joy. Suffering. Resurrection.* Jesus said, *"Take up your cross and follow Me."* That meant we went through that cycle too. *Hope and joy. Suffering. But never despair, because then came the promise of resurrection.*

But at least I remembered to bring the money we'd already collected for Sara's "belated birthday present" as Yada Yada gathered at Nony's house that evening. To my delight, Hoshi was still at the house since the ReJOYce campus meeting she and Sara attended started an hour later. Hoshi beamed as others added to the collection.

Ruth was the last one to arrive, lugging a baby carrier. "A cold her brother has," she announced, lifting a pink-cheeked Havah out of the swaddled blankets, leaving us to figure out whether that was the reason she didn't bring Isaac, too, or whether leaving one fussy baby with Ben was more than enough. Seeing what Hoshi was doing, Ruth dug in her purse, stuffed several bills into Havah's tight baby grip, and cooed, "See? Havah wants to help Sara too . . . okay, sweetie, let go now . . ."

Finally, Hoshi shyly handed the basket of bills to Adele. "Will this be enough for—how do you say—a 'makeover'?"

Adele pocketed the money without even counting it. "Just right." She handed a gift certificate to Hoshi in exchange. "Tell Sara to call that number for an appointment."

Nony, her sculpted braids freed from the African headwrap she'd worn that morning, poured tea and passed a plate of sugary lemon bars as the conversation drifted to Holy Week celebrations.

"Easter sure was the biggest day of the year when I was comin' up Baptist," Florida said. "Didn't matter how poor we was, my mama decked us out in lacey anklets, patent leather shoes shined with Vaseline, ruffled dresses—and new underwear in case we got run over. And an Easter hat! Mm-mm. I felt so grown-up wearin' a big ol' Easter hat like all the big mamas."

Adele fanned herself with a small paper plate. "You forgot hair. Mama pressed mine—first straightened it with Vaseline and a hot iron comb, then curled it with iron curlers heated on the stove. Ouch. I think that's when I decided I wanted my own salon, to save little girls from all that torture."

Florida was shaking with laughter now. "Same, same. But first, we had to make it through Good Friday. Always had seven different preachers, preachin' the Seven Last Words of Christ. Sometimes lasted till midnight!"

Stu grinned. "And I thought *our* Good Friday service was long. In the Lutheran church, we prayed the fourteen Stations of the Cross. We walked solemnly from station to station around the church, where somebody read the relevant scripture: Jesus condemned to death . . . Jesus carrying His cross . . . Jesus falling under the weight—all the way to His death and burial. After each station, everybody said, 'Lord have mercy, Christ have mercy, Lord have mercy,' and someone blew out the candles at that station, until the whole church was dark." She twisted a strand of long hair around one finger. "Easter, of course, was full of light and joy, lots of banners and big organ music."

Yo-Yo rolled her eyes. "Huh. Only time I ever remember goin' ta church with my mama was Easter. Oh, yeah. Couple of times we went at Christmas. Kinda got the idea if you showed up on Easter and Christmas, you could forget it the rest of the time."

"At least you went to church," Becky said. "I thought Easter was Easter eggs and Easter bunnies. My dad took me to an Easter egg hunt once when I was little. A couple of months later he split, an' I don't remember ever seein' him again."

Florida squeezed Becky's hand. "That's why Jesus came, girl, to heal all that."

"At least the Easter bunny has not made it across the border into Mexico!" Delores huffed. Then her eyes got wistful. "But the whole country celebrates from *Domingo de Ramos* to *Domingo de Gloria*—Palm Sunday to Easter. Every year on *Viernes Santo*, Holy Friday, there is a big procession through the streets in every town. A man wearing a bloody crown of thorns carries a cross, escorted by men dressed as Roman soldiers. Everyone ends up at the Catholic church to repent of our sins that sent Jesus to the cross."

Chanda shook her head. "In Jamaica, Easter just a big party, like a carnival. Mi remember mama looking so sad, down on she knees, praying for all dem heathens, not even know what dey do. But she not so sad she not make Easter buns and cheese!" Chanda closed her eyes and sighed. "Mm. Dem buns so sweet and spicy and *full* of raisins! Mm-mm."

"Sounds like hot cross buns," I said. "My mother used to make them—sweet rolls with a cross of white frosting. You can get them in the grocery stores, but they don't taste anything like home-made—not that *my* kids have ever had the homemade version." Everyone laughed. "But what I remember most is sunrise services. I always thought that was so exciting—getting up while it was still dark on Easter morning, going to a local football stadium, a bunch of churches all together usually, and watching the sun rise, then singing some glorious hymn, like 'Christ the Lord Is Risen Today!'"

Heads nodded. Several had been to at least one sunrise service.

Yo-Yo squinted thoughtfully. "At the Bagel Bakery, we're makin' a lot of foods for Passover. Funny that the Jewish folks have a holy day same time as the Christians."

Ruth, who was jiggling Havah over her shoulder, practically choked. "Same time as . . .!" She rolled her eyes. *"Oy vey."*

"What? What'd I say?" Yo-Yo threw out her hands.

"Here." Ruth handed the squirming baby to Adele. "What? You don't read your Bible?" She tapped her noggin with one fin-ger. "What feast was Jesus celebrating with His disciples the night Judas betrayed Him?"

"Huh. Passover, of course," Florida said. "But that's Old Testament stuff, Ruth—pardon me sayin' so. We ain't under the Law an' all that anymore, thank ya, *Jesus!*"

Yo-Yo snorted. "You said it. I have a hard enough time keepin' the Ten Big Ones, much less all them itty-bitty rules in the Old Testament."

Ruth *tsked-tsked* through her teeth. *"Oy, oy, oy.* It's time all you *New Testament* Christians celebrated a *Seder*, along with Jesus, who seemed to think it was important to show His disciples the hidden meanings in the ancient Passover meal."

Most of us looked blank. "Seder?"

"Seder—the Passover ritual celebrated in Jewish homes all over the world to remember God's deliverance from Egypt." Ruth's exaggerated patience sounded like she was talking to my third graders. "For Messianic Jews, the Seder takes on a deeper meaning, foretelling the coming of the Messiah." Ruth got up and paced around Nony's family room. "Hm. Hm. How could we do this? . . ."

Hoshi glanced at her watch and started to slip out of the room.

"Hoshi, wait one moment," Nony said quickly. "Let us pray with you before you go to meet Sara." Nony turned to Ruth. "Please forgive the interruption, my sister. But Hoshi must leave."

Ruth nodded, still deep in thought, murmuring to herself.

Nony stood with an arm around the slender Japanese student and prayed that Sara would receive our gift as an offering of our love. Adele, still holding Havah, who had fallen to sleep over her shoulder, added a prayer of blessing over Hoshi for "walking her talk" by loving Sara.

Hoshi whispered, "Thank you" and slipped out . . . but the prayers just kept coming. Florida asked God for mercy at Chris's final hearing later that month, when his fate would be decided by a judge in the juvenile court.

"Thank you, God, that he wasn't sent to adult court," Stu murmured.

"Yes! Thank ya, *Je*sus." Florida had to blow her nose.

"Nony?" I heard Avis ask quietly. "Has Mark heard from the university yet?"

Eyes opened. Nonyameko shook her head. "Not yet. We are trusting God to do what is best."

But Avis prayed that Mark would receive favor from the University of KwaZulu-Natal, and that we could send out this couple with gladness in our hearts.

Well, that last part might be a stretch, I thought with a pang.

"And bless de whole Baxter family," Chanda said suddenly, "feeling so sad wit' losing dey sweet dog."

She took me by such surprise, a lump grabbed me in the throat. I reached over and squeezed her hand. But it reminded me that I had something to share. "Um, sisters? I'd appreciate your prayers, because I volunteered to help the school at the JDC put on a play. The regular English teacher got mono and had to take a leave. Denny told me they were looking for a substitute, so . . ." I sucked in a big breath. "That's how I'll be spending my spring break. It's a big stretch for me, but with one of our own children at the JDC, seems like a responsibility I need to own too."

"Jesus, Jesus . . ." Florida grabbed the tissue box.

Adele chuckled. Couldn't blame her. It was pretty funny. Me, Jodi Marie Baxter, taking on a classroom of juvenile delinquents— well, guess they were "innocent until proven guilty"—even if it was for a short time. But, still chuckling, Adele prayed for me. "Lord, don't know who's gonna learn more, the boys and girls at the JDC, or Sister Jodi here. But it's so unlikely, it's gotta be one of Your ideas. And whatever comes out of this drama thing, Lord, wash it all over with Your love."

Avis wrapped up our prayers, and we started to break up the circle when Ruth said, "All right. Gonna be tight but we'll do it."

We all looked at her. What in the world was she talking about?

320

"Seder. At our house this Thursday, the night Jesus celebrated Passover with His disciples before Judas betrayed Him. Six o'clock. Bring your children. It is very important that the children understand—that is the Jewish way."

"At your house?" I blinked. "What about Ben? I mean, how is he going to feel about a bunch of Christians celebrating a traditional Jewish feast?"

"That," Ruth said, a puckish gleam in her eyes, "might be the whole point."

36

*R*uth had bustled out to her car with Havah snugly strapped into the carrier before what she'd said sunk in. *Thursday night? With kids?* That was a school night!

Except it wasn't—which I discovered when I got home and looked at the calendar. Spring vacation began next Friday—which "just happened" to be Good Friday. *Mm-hm.* The Chicago school system's way of accommodating a religious holiday without risking a lawsuit.

Okay. So how to sell my family? Denny was out; he'd be at the JDC Thursday night—*with* the car. Maybe Chanda could pick us up in her monster SUV. But getting a ride was the easy part. Convincing Amanda and Josh to come with me, when I didn't have a clue what to expect, was the bigger challenge. But I had one ace up my sleeve.

I called Delores. "Are you, um, coming to the Garfields' for that Seder thing on Thursday with the kids?"

"No, I am sorry, *mi amiga.* I work three to ten this week. But Edesa said she would bring the *niños.* José will help her."

Bingo! I hung up, smiling. That's what I wanted to know. My kids would come.

I tried to keep my students on task that week, but it was a losing battle. They could smell spring vacation in the air. But the idea of sharing holiday traditions, as we'd done at Yada Yada Sunday night, might keep their interest. Was I pushing the line between church and state too far? Shouldn't be, if I included other faiths. I did a search online but came up zero for any Muslim holy days during the month of April. But I asked Caleb Levy to come prepared to tell us about the Jewish Passover, and asked for other volunteers to describe how they celebrated the Christian "holy days" of Good Friday and Easter. That sparked a sea of waving of hands—the usual litany about yellow marshmallow chicks, Easter egg hunts, and the Easter bunny.

Mercedes LaLuz waved her hand. *"My* mama says there's no such thing as the Easter bunny. Easter is when *Jésus Christo* got raised from the dead."

Lamar Jones snorted. "Another fairy tale."

"Just a minute, Lamar." I chose my words carefully. "For some people, Easter is a way to celebrate that spring is coming. But Christians believe something very important happened many years ago at this time of year. Jesus Christ, whom Christians believe is the Son of God, was killed by His enemies, buried, and rose from the dead—and that's why *they* celebrate." *How am I doing, God?*

But before I got in too deep, I steered a corner. "The Jewish faith also celebrates Passover at this time of year. Caleb, can you tell us what 'Passover' means?"

Caleb walked to the front of the room, pushing his glasses up on the bridge of his nose. I tried to keep a straight face. This kid was destined to be a college professor. "Well. Thousands of years ago, the Jewish people were slaves in Egypt." The class got quiet. "God chose Moses to lead the people out of slavery. But King Pharaoh didn't want to let them go. So God sent all kinds of terrible plagues—frogs and lice and flies *and* the Nile River turned to blood."

"Blood! *Eww.*"

Caleb looked triumphant. "But Pharaoh *still* wouldn't let the slaves go free. So God got mad and sent the Angel of Death to kill the oldest son in every house. But Moses told the Jews that if they splashed the blood of a lamb on the door of *their* houses, the Angel of Death would *pass over* that house and nobody would die. That scared King Pharaoh so much he finally let the Israelite people go. That's why Jewish families celebrate Passover, to remember how God rescued them from slavery."

Caleb dipped his head like a little bow and sat down. For a moment, the class stared open-mouthed. Then they started to clap.

"Wow!" Bowie Garcia shouted. "They oughta make that into a video game!"

I KICKED MYSELF LATER. Why didn't I point out that there is a connection between the Christian celebration of Good Friday and the Jewish celebration of Passover? *Jesus was a Jew, and He and His disciples were celebrating the Passover meal in Jerusalem the same night He was captured and killed by His enemies.* Would have been educational, that's for sure.

Funny thing was, I never thought much about that connection. Most of the Christians I knew didn't either. After all, that last Passover meal had become "The Lord's Supper" or "Communion"— what we celebrated once a month in the church I grew up in by eating a broken cracker and a plastic thimble of grape juice or wine to represent the broken body and blood of Jesus. I certainly didn't connect it much with the Jewish Passover. But Ruth had said the connection was built in from the beginning . . .

I found myself looking forward to celebrating Seder with Yada Yada.

Of course, Ruth managed to rope all of us into the preparations. "Jodi," she'd barked into the phone early that week with no preamble. "You want you should make potato kugel or matzo ball soup? Never mind. Yo-Yo can pick up some kugel from the Bagel Bakery. Make the soup. Just follow the recipe on the back of the box of matzo meal. Cook a chicken first; you need chicken broth."

Two minutes later, the phone rang again. "Add carrots, celery, and some of the chicken. Just make sure you have plenty of broth to cook the matzo balls. And tell the other Yada Yada sisters to pray for Ben."

Pray what for Ben? Didn't he want us to come? And how many was I cooking for, anyway? I only had one large soup pot, so I decided one pot would have to do. So Wednesday night found me boiling a large stewing hen with carrots and celery. When I got home from school on Thursday, I mixed matzo meal with egg and a bit of broth and dropped the balls into the boiling broth. By the time Chanda tooted her horn out front, I had a pot of hot matzo ball soup—I hoped. What did I know?

Josh and Carl Hickman were catching a ride from work with

Peter Douglass and Avis, so Amanda and I and the soup pot climbed into the Yukon Denali along with Chanda's three kids, Rochelle and Conny, and Florida and her two youngest. Eleven passengers. Still two over the nine-passenger limit for this huge SUV.

"You need a bigger car," I *umphed*, squeezing in between Dia George and Carla Hickman, and setting the soup pot, wrapped in a heavy bath towel, on the floor.

Chanda, in the driver's seat, grinned into the rearview mirror. "Mi know dat. Driving dis baby is fun. Mi should be a city bus driver!"

When we pulled up in front of the Garfields' home, the house already looked jam-packed through the front window. Inside, a string of card tables and collapsible portable tables snaked from the dining room, through the front hallway, and into the living room, covered with white plastic tablecloths, and set with colorful paper plates, matching paper napkins, and clear plastic tumblers. Tall white candles, small bouquets of flowers, and bottles of wine and sparkling grape juice on each table added a festive touch. Laughter and curiosity filled the small, brick bungalow.

With a touch of guilt, I realized I hadn't called anybody to "pray for Ben," as Ruth had asked. But he seemed comfortable enough to me, teasing the kids and showing off the twins, each one sporting a new tooth and matching crawlers. Only Isaac's raspberry-colored facial birthmark told them apart.

"Sit! Sit!" Ruth beamed when everyone had arrived. She set a china plate displaying several food items on the table in front of two chairs in the middle of the long line of mismatched tables as Ben, wearing his traditional yarmulke, joined her.

We all found places to sit. Counting kids and adults, there must've been thirty of us! I glanced around. Josh was holding baby

Havah, a sight that unsettled me a little bit since he and Edesa were sitting together with the Enriques kids clustered around them. They looked like a family with a passel of kids. *Sheesh, Jodi! Don't go there.*

As parents shushed children, Ruth solemnly lit all the candles, murmuring a Jewish blessing. Then Ben Garfield cleared his throat. "Welcome to our Passover meal. It's not often we share this meal with Gentiles. In fact, in my case, never." That got a laugh. "This meal is called a Seder, which means 'order'—but hardly applies to the raucous Jewish family I grew up in." Another laugh. We were starting to relax.

Ben picked up a set of pages stapled together. "You can follow along the simple Seder service beside your plate. But you're getting off easy. Two nights ago, we celebrated the first night of Passover with my relatives, using the traditional Haggadah. Thirty-two pages it is—in Hebrew! Sixty-four when they include the English translation."

Now groans mixed with the giggles. Ruth poked him to get on with it.

"All right, all right." Ben cleared his throat again, reading from his Seder service. *"'We celebrate the Passover in obedience to God's command in the Torah'*—that's the Old Testament, to you *goyim*. *'In days to come, when your children ask you, What does this mean? say to them, With a mighty hand the Lord brought us out of Egypt, out of the land of slavery.'"*

"Hallelujah!" Florida said. "Guess that gives your people an' my people somethin' in common—'cept our people was freed less'n a hundred fifty years ago. We still tryin' to put it all behind us."

Ben scowled. Ruth smoothed over the interruption. "To remember is good, so we can thank God for His deliverance." She nudged her husband.

Ben cleared his throat again. To his credit, he did a neat summary of the story up to the point where the Egyptian Pharoah refused Moses' demand to let the Jewish slaves go. "For this next part," he said, "everybody needs to have a little wine or grape juice in their glass—but don't drink it."

Bottles were tipped, filling the plastic glasses half an inch. Now Ben told the story of the ten plagues. "When I call out one of the plagues, dip your finger in your wine, and flick it onto your plate while you repeat it. Ready?" He dipped his own finger. "Blood!"

Fingers dipped all around the table, flicking wine or grape juice onto the paper plates. "Blood!" we echoed.

"Frogs!" *Flick, flick.* "Lice!" . . . "Flies!" . . . The kids were really getting into it now. "Boils!" *Flick, flick* . . . "Hail!" . . . "Locusts!" The shouts were getting louder. "Darkness!" . . . "Death of the firstborn!"

The tables suddenly got quiet. It didn't seem fun anymore.

"Finally," Ben said solemnly, "Pharoah let the Jewish people go."

Ben continued leading us through the shortened Seder service. We all turned our pages. "Who's the youngest child here? Not counting Havah and Isaac. They can't read. Dia, sweetheart? You want to ask that question on the next page?"

Seven-year-old Dia squinted at the paper. "Too many hard words."

"I'll do it!" Ten-year-old Michael Smith, sitting beside Nony, waved his hand wildly. "Here? Okay. *Why is this night different from all other nights? On all other nights we eat all kinds of bread, but tonight we only eat matzo.*" He looked up. "What's matzo?" His mother pointed to the matzo crackers on the table. "Oh. Okay. *On all other nights we eat many kinds of vegetables and herbs, but tonight we only eat bitter herbs.'"* He made a face. *"'On all other nights, we don't dip one food into another, but tonight we dip the parsley in salt water, and we dip the bitter herbs in . . . in . . .'* What's that word?"

"Charoset," prompted Ruth. The "ch" was guttural. She beamed at Nonyameko. "A *boytshikl* he is, Nony. You should be proud."

Dia pouted. "I wanted to read. I just didn't know them big words."

Ben opened his mouth but Ruth took over. "Questions are asked at every Seder—it's tradition. So . . . feel free! But first we give answers to Michael's questions." She picked up the china plate in front of her and pointed to the three matzo crackers. "Matzo reminds us that when the Jews left Egypt, they had no time to bake bread with yeast."

"Tastes like cardboard . . . just my opinion," Ben cracked behind his hand.

Ruth ignored him, continuing to explain the items on the plate. The sprig of parsley dipped in salt water, "a reminder of tears shed during slavery." The *choroset,* a mixture of chopped apples, nuts, and wine, "a reminder of the clay used to make bricks for Pharoah's buildings, which was eaten with bitter herbs"—she pointed to a mound of ground horseradish—"because our days in Egypt were bitter."

"What's that bone for?" Yo-Yo pointed at the plate.

Ben picked it up. "A lamb bone—"

"I know *that* part!" Carla interrupted. "Caleb Levy told us at school. God was going to kill all the firstborn boys in every family, but He secretly told the slave people to kill a lamb and smear its blood all over the doors of their house. When the Angel of Death saw the blood, it was s'posed to *pass over* that house. *Pass over,* get it?"

Ben grinned. "Very good, *bubeleh*. Now, let's do the *afikomen*—"

"Wait, wait. Back up a minute," Becky said. "I've been reading my Bible, like ya tol' me to, Avis, and that John the Baptist guy called Jesus 'the Lamb of God.'" She turned to Ben. "So was that blood-of-the-lamb thing, ya know, some kind of prophecy about Jesus or something?"

Nods and murmurs went around the tables.

Ben colored. "Uh, well, now . . ." He glared at Ruth helplessly. And suddenly I realized why Ruth had wanted us to pray for Ben—that he would see the truth behind the Seder meal he had celebrated every year of his sixty-odd years of life.

Oh God! I'm sorry I didn't pray, sorry I forgot to ask others to pray. But I'm praying now . . .

Ruth whispered to Ben, and handed him the three matzo crackers from the plate. "All right," he growled. "Let's move on so we can eat. The middle matzo we break"—which he proceeded to do—"and wrap it in a special cloth, and hide it." He wrapped the broken piece of matzo in a cloth napkin. "This is called the *afikomen*. Now . . ." His voice took on its former bounce. "All the children close your eyes. Tight. No peeking!"

Laughing, all the adults sitting near children made sure they didn't peek, while Ben snuck around the two rooms pretending to hide the napkin here, then there. I never did see where he finally hid it.

"After the meal," Ruth said brightly, "the children may hunt for the *afikomen*. The one who finds it can hold it for ransom until Ben forks over some money."

Yo-Yo butted in. "Wait. We can ask questions, right? So, like, do the three matzos represent that Trinity thing—God the Father, God the Son, and God the Holy Spirit? Ben just broke the middle one—is that what Jesus was doing when He broke the bread at Passover and said, 'This is My body, broken for you'?"

José grinned. "Whoa. And then broken matzo gets buried . . ."

"I know, I know!" Cedric Hickman waved his hand. "An' when we find it, Mister Garfield has to pay a ransom, 'cause Jesus paid the ransom for our sins! 'Cept Mister Garfield ain't God, but I guess that's okay."

We couldn't help it; we broke up with laughter. Even shy Carl Hickman had to chuckle. Ruth beamed. "Are these children smart, or what?" But Ben looked flustered, as if he was losing control of the situation.

Ruth said, "Now eat! Eat!" as if it was an order. My matzo ball soup came out hot from the kitchen, along with sturdy paper bowls. Then roasted chicken, potato kugel, and cooked carrots swimming in butter and dill. We laughed, ate, made faces at the gefilte fish, and passed the babies from lap to lap.

All except Ben. Ben had turned quiet.

37

"Next year in Jerusalem'?" Denny raised a curious eyebrow as I told him how the Seder service had ended, with the traditional cry of displaced Jews all over the world. "And how many glasses of wine did you say you had? *Four?*" He was clearly enjoying goading me.

We were sitting at the dining room table, while Denny finished the plate of chicken and potato kugel I'd brought home and heated up for him. I rolled my eyes. "The wine was mostly symbolic. Little sips. Seriously, Denny. I wish you could've been there. It was . . . I can't explain it. It helped me understand Jesus the Messiah, the fulfillment of prophecy, in a new way. But Ben got pretty uncomfortable with some of the questions Becky and Yo-Yo asked. Hope he's not mad."

"Hm. Sorry I missed it." He got up and tossed the paper plate in the trash. "Sorry I missed your matzo ball soup too. Oh, before I forget. The principal at the JDC school would like to meet with you personally—tomorrow if possible. They're hoping to pull off this play in the next couple of weeks." He grinned at me. "You're on, Jodi."

I stared at him. It wasn't as if I was surprised. Avis said she'd gotten a call from the JDC, wanting a reference. My background check had checked out—second time this year. But hearing Denny say, *"You're on, Jodi,"* made my mouth go dry.

"Uh, sure, I could go tomorrow. It's Good Friday, no school—oh. You know that. Can I get there by el? Where am I supposed to go? What's the principal's name again? Do I need to take anything with me? Or . . . anything I *shouldn't* take with me? Do they want me to actually start tomor—"

Denny reached out and put his fingers on my mouth to stop my prattling. "Hey, hey. Tell you what. I'll go with you tomorrow, okay? We'll go by el to map out the way; maybe some days you can take the car. We'll figure it out. You're going to do great, Jodi." He pulled me out of my chair into an embrace. "I'm proud of you."

I let myself relax against Denny's chest as his arms held me close. I wasn't sure about "great." But if Denny went with me tomorrow and helped me figure out where to go, *that* was definitely great.

NO SCHOOL. The wonders of a Friday without the usual Baxter hurry-scurry made me feel delicious when I woke up. I no longer had to get up before everyone else to let Willie Wonka outside, either . . . though I'd give anything to feel his nose snuffling my hand once more, even if I *did* have to get up early, even on holidays. But today, I could go back to sleep . . .

Then I remembered. I was going to the juvenile detention center today. Today, of all days, I definitely needed some prayer time!

Coffee cup, Bible, and afghan in hand, I curled up in the recliner near the front windows. At times like these, I really did miss Wonka. His brand of loyalty meant I was never really alone in the house; he was always faithfully underfoot. Early mornings had been our special times—me in the recliner, Wonka splayed out on the floor under the footrest.

But today it was just me and God. Cuddled in the afghan, I found where I'd last stopped reading—Paul's letter to the Philippians. I needed an encouragement for today. Had to admit I was nervous. This whole thing wasn't my idea. But seemed as if God had dumped it in my lap and nudged me to say yes. Wasn't I learning that if God was in it, I didn't have to be afraid? All I had to do was be faithful, and God would take care of the rest . . . right?

I tried to focus on my reading. In chapter three, the apostle Paul said if anyone qualified for bragging rights about how "religious" he was, he was the man. But then he said none of that self-important religious stuff counted. Only knowing Jesus Christ and what He could do in our lives—that's what counted.

Kinda like me, when I let my "good Christian girl" pride get in God's way.

"But one thing I do," he wrote. "Forgetting what is behind and straining toward what is ahead, I press on toward the goal . . ."

Press on. Wasn't that what Denny was trying to tell our kids the night of his birthday, that sometimes we had to let go of what was behind us and press on? Well, he said, "get rolling," but same difference. My old King James Version used the phrase, "press toward . . . the high calling of God."

I closed my Bible and stared out the window. Suddenly I realized that the limbs of the trees along Lunt Street were no longer bare. I brought the recliner's footrest down with a bang—a move that used to send Willie Wonka scrambling—and pressed my nose to the window. Thousands of swollen buds created a shimmering green fuzz along each limb, ready to burst into life. The old leaves were dead; the new ones were waiting in the wings, eager to dance along every branch, catching the wind.

A funny joy bubbled up in my chest. *Today is full of possibilities. Press on, Jodi, press on. Do it for God and His children at the JDC.*

DENNY AND I GOT HOME from the JDC in time to eat a bowl of soup out of the Crock-Pot and make it to the Good Friday service at SouledOut that night. It was a simple service, not long, with various "readers" reading the story of Jesus eating the Passover meal with His disciples for the last time . . . the prayer of agony in the Garden of Gethsemane . . . Judas's betrayal . . . the desertion by the other disciples . . . the trial of Jesus . . . and His execution on a Roman cross. Throughout, the music group wove songs—mostly old hymns—about "the blood of Jesus."

I have to admit I had a hard time keeping my mind focused on the service. My mind was still so full of the Seder service the previous night, with all its prophetic symbolism, pointing to these very events we were singing about—the saving "blood of the lamb" splashed on the wooden doorposts . . . the broken matzo, hidden, and then "resurrected" . . .

And then there was my visit to the juvenile detention center just a few hours ago. I hadn't realized it was just a few blocks from the Cook County hospital where Delores worked. Denny and I had to take the Red Line el all the way past the Loop to the Roosevelt Road station, then catch the westbound Roosevelt Road bus. Took over an hour! It wasn't so bad doing it with

Denny, but I couldn't really imagine doing it by myself five days a week next week.

Glancing at Avis and several of my other Yada Yada sisters soaking up the Good Friday service, I thought of the Yada Yadas who did not have cars. *Oh God. Is that what it takes for Delores and Edesa to come to Yada Yada every time? Neither one has a car . . . and they're so faithful.* I squared my shoulders. *Suck it up, Jodi. Press on.* If they could do it, so could I.

As we sang, "What can wash away my sin? Nothing but the blood of Jesus . . ." my mind drifted to my interview with the school principal at the JDC that afternoon. After we'd gone through a metal detector and taken the elevator up to the second floor, we sat in a waiting room with molded plastic chairs until the principal came out to greet us. She gave us visitor tags, then we were buzzed through the glass-paneled security area—not one, but two doors, where security personnel could see all directions—into the main part of the second floor, which housed the school.

The principal had given us a short tour of the school, which wasn't in session, since it had the same holidays as any other Chicago public school. The windowless rooms had the regular stuff of classrooms—desks, marker boards, maps, textbooks. "Classrooms for boys and girls are separate. Each residential floor is color-coded," our host explained, "so your students will be wearing purple, green, or blue DOC uniforms. Our youngest residents and the girls occupy the top floor."

Our last stop had been the large, all-purpose room where "school events" were held. No stage. No lights. Not what I'd imagined when I volunteered to supervise a school play. "What about props? Costumes?" I ventured.

The principal shrugged. "You can ask. Not making any promises, though."

Then we sat in her office, while she explained basic rules ("Do not ask your students about their case") and my temporary responsibilities. I was bursting with questions about the children and teenagers within these walls, but did my best to listen to my volunteer assignment.

"We do two or three drama or musical presentations for parents and staff every year. This year, our English teacher was trying to introduce the kids to some classic literature through drama. Then she came down with mono! The other teachers are covering her classes, but no one had time to take on the drama too." The principal gave me an encouraging smile. "We're happy you've volunteered, Mrs. Baxter."

"Will I meet the students today who are doing the drama?" I'd asked.

She shook her head. "But I will give you a copy of the scripts she was going to introduce. There are a couple you can choose from. Next week is spring break, so the students who signed up to do the drama don't have classes next week. We can give you three hours, nine to twelve, each morning."

"And if we need more time?"

The principal shrugged. "You'd probably lose half your kids if they had to give up afternoons. They like to play softball or basketball outside, now that the weather's getting warmer."

I'd blinked at her. "Outside?"

Denny grinned. "Oh, yeah. Forgot to tell you. The top three floors are built like a square doughnut, with the residential units around the outer ring and an open recreation area in the middle."

He pointed to the ceiling of the second floor. "Right up there."

I'd tried to picture it in my mind—and got the picture. Open to the sky—but completely surrounded by the building. Whatever way one looked at it, this was a jail for juveniles, kids, waiting for their hearings, waiting to hear whether the state judged them guilty or not guilty, waiting to hear their "dispositions" or sentences.

Kids like Chris Hickman . . .

I'd been able to walk away today. But not Chris. Now, as I sat in the "sanctuary" of SouledOut Community Church singing the closing song, "At Calvary," I glanced over at the Hickman family, sitting together in the dimly lit room. Wet streaks glistened on Florida's face as Oscar Frost's saxophone rode under the words of the chorus . . .

Mercy there was great, and grace was free;
Pardon there was multiplied to me;
There my burdened soul found liberty,
At Calvary!

How would I hear those words if I were in Florida's and Carl's shoes? Would their son be "pardoned" for his sins? Would he be given liberty?

Oh Jesus! my heart cried. *Your mercy to me was great when I was accused of vehicular manslaughter in the death of Jamal Wilkins. Please have mercy on Chris. He says he had nothing to do with the holdup of that 7-Eleven, and . . . and I believe him. His only crime was bad judgment in the friends he chose. Oh God, please, let Your blood cover his transgression and bring him home to his family.*

WHEN THE GOOD FRIDAY SERVICE WAS OVER, the pastors encouraged us to leave quietly, reflecting on our Savior's death. But outside in the parking lot, I saw Hoshi getting into the Sisulu-Smith minivan. I ran over and poked my head inside. "Hoshi! Did you give our gift certificate to Sara? Did she accept it?"

A smile lit up Hoshi's long, thin face. "Oh yes, Jodi. She was much flustered, but we met at the student center for lunch yesterday, and she said she'd made an appointment at Adele's Hair and Nails for Saturday."

Saturday! That was tomorrow—and Adele's Hair and Nails wasn't that far from our house. Did I dare "just drop in"? I'd been praying for Sara so long, ever since that fateful day our eyes had met at the plaza on Northwestern's campus. I wanted to tell her how God had changed my heart when she went from "that girl in the sundress" to "Sara" . . .

Which gave me an idea.

38

The bell over Adele's shop door tinkled as I pushed the door open. Was I doing the right thing? Or was this another one of my "brilliant" ideas that could blow up in my face? I'd felt a little sneaky, calling the shop first thing this morning to find out what time Sara's appointment was, hoping Takeisha or Corey would answer the phone. But wouldn't you know it—Adele picked up.

"Jodi Baxter," she'd said suspiciously. "You want to know Sara's appointment time . . . why?"

I blew out a breath. With Adele, honesty was always the best policy. "Because I made something for her—a small gift. I want to give it to her."

Silence. Then, "Suit yourself. Ten o'clock." And she hung up.

I waited until ten-thirty to give plenty of time for Sara to get in the chair. I'd had too many *trauma-dramas* at Adele's Hair and Nails to want to precipitate another one. But the last time I'd seen Sara—when Hoshi had tried to bring her new friend to Yada Yada when we'd met at the Sisulu-Smith home near the NU campus—Sara had taken one look at the house, at Nony and Mark, and run the other way.

The bell tinkled again as the door wheezed shut. Adele glanced up and acknowledged me with a nod—a nod that seemed to say, *Just sit a while.* So I did. I sank onto the couch by the front window, picked up a copy of *Essence* magazine, and flipped through it, my eyes not on its pages but on the young woman in the chair.

Adele snipped and shaped. Sara watched the process in the mirror with sober eyes. *When should I talk to her?* I wondered. But I felt a check. *Not yet.* The not-quite-wedgie cut—shorter in the back, a little longer in the front, sweeping forward, bangs brushed to the side—already freshened her plain features. But she was so . . . colorless. A touch of lip gloss, some plum blush on her cheeks, and mascara to darken her pale lashes would—

Ha! Listen to yourself, Jodi. A lot you know about makeup.

Adele handed Sara a hair-color chart, which Sara studied while Adele swept up the dishwater-blonde hair on the floor. Finally, she pointed, and Adele mixed the color chemicals, shaking the rubber bulb while running her fingers thoughtfully through the girl's hair. Adele chatted with other customers and staff—though she ignored me—while she saturated the girl's hair with the color mixture, as though allowing Sara a reprieve from being the center of her attention.

Finally, Adele piled Sara's wet hair on her head, covered it with a breathable cap, and pointed to a plastic chair in the hair dryer section. "Sit there," she said. "No, not under the dryer. We need to leave that on for twenty minutes." As the young woman moved to a chair behind the partition, Adele gave me the eye and tipped her head.

I picked up the plastic bag I'd brought with me and peeked around the partition. "Sara?"

Her head jerked up at her name. "Do I know you?"

I pulled over an empty chair. "My name is Jodi Baxter. We have a mutual friend, Hoshi Takahashi."

She reddened. "Oh. Yes, I've seen you before. Your p-prayer group . . ." She touched the cap on her head. "You all g-gave me this gift certificate, Hoshi said."

I smiled and nodded. "Yes. It's our way of saying thanks."

Her color deepened. "Don't know what for." Her eyes found her lap.

I tried to keep my voice easy. "All of us are deeply grateful for your courage, for going to the police, and—"

"Don't want to t-talk about that." Her hands clenched, and her mouth pinched into a thin, straight line.

"No problem. Actually, that's not why I spoke to you. I wanted to give you this." I laid the plastic bag in her lap.

She stared at the bag. "What is it?"

"Before you open it, I want to tell you something. It's not my intention to drag up painful memories, but—"

"Then don't."

"All right. But after the, um, first time I saw you"—I didn't mention it was at the so-called freedom of speech rally on the NU campus where the leader of the White Pride group she'd been part of proceeded to insult "mud races" and everyone else who wasn't white—"God told me to pray for you. But I didn't know your name. So for a long time, I just prayed for 'that girl in the sundress.' Not very polite, I know, but I kept praying for you anyway."

She said nothing, but seemed to be listening.

"And then Hoshi told us about meeting a new friend named Sara. Of course, I didn't know it was *you*, not until, uh . . . later." Again, I deliberately didn't mention the day she came with Hoshi to the Sisulu-Smith home, which had ended in such disaster. "But God kept telling me to pray for you, so now I could pray for you by name. Sara."

I pointed to the package. "Now you can open it."

At first, I thought she wasn't going to. But after a moment's hesitation, she pulled the bag off and held the eight-by-ten-inch frame in her hands. I had used the computer to write her name, "Sara," in a beautiful script on some fancy vellum paper, and right beside it the meaning of her name. "Princess."

She snorted. "What is this, some k-kind of joke?"

"No, no. That's what the name Sara means—'Princess'! In our prayer group, we like to find the meaning of each person's name. Hoshi's name means 'Star.' Mine means 'God is gracious.'"

She frowned. "Well, somebody g-got it wrong somewhere, because I'm certainly no p-princess. Cinderella, maybe."

I almost laughed. Maybe she meant Cinderella sitting in the ashes while her nasty stepsisters went to the royal ball. But Cinderella became a *real* princess. Well, as real as it gets in a fairy tale. "No, I don't think the meaning of your name is wrong. Because that's how God sees you. His princess. His royal daughter."

To my surprise, tears suddenly dripped down her cheeks, and she fished in her pockets for a tissue. She blew her nose. Then, she peered closely at the smaller words within the frame. "What's this?"

Thought she'd never ask! "It's from the Bible." I reached out and turned the frame slightly so I could see the words. "I paraphrased it just a little, but you can read it yourself in the book of Isaiah, chapter forty-nine: *The Lord called me before my birth; from within the womb He called me by name. . . . [I said], 'The Lord has deserted me; the Lord has forgotten me!' [But God said,] 'Never! Can a mother forget her nursing child? Can she feel no love for a child she has borne? But even if that were possible, I would not forget you! See, I have engraved your name on the palm of my hand.'"*

As I read the words aloud, I momentarily forgot about Sara. That last phrase! When I chose those verses, I just wanted to let Sara know that God knew her personally, *by name*. But suddenly it seemed like another prophecy in the Old Testament about Jesus! God told Isaiah He'd written his name—and mine, and Sara's, and everybody's—*on the palms of His hands*. And just yesterday, Good Friday, we'd all been reminded that His Son, Jesus, stretched out those hands, the ones with our names on them, on the cross, taking the punishment for our sins—

"How d-did you know?" Sara's tight whisper broke into my thoughts.

"What? Know what?"

"About my mother. I never t-told Hoshi." She looked at me accusingly. "Have you been d-digging up stuff about me?"

I was stunned. "No! I don't know anything about you. Except . . . I know that God loves you. And I've been praying for you almost a whole year."

Adele's large form loomed above us. "Time's up. Need to rinse that color out 'fore it takes you someplace you don't wanna go."

Sara stood up and put the frame back in the plastic bag. I gave Adele a look, which, properly interpreted, told her to go jump in the lake. Didn't she realize something important was happening

345

here?! Adele gave me a look right back that said not even the end of the world was going to stop her from rinsing out her customer.

But Sara held the bag close to her chest as she followed Adele to the sinks. Halfway there, she turned back and mouthed silently: *"Thank you."*

I SAT IN THE CAR a full five minutes before I turned on the ignition. Half of me wanted to whoop and holler, *"Praise Jesus!"* that Sara whatever-her-last-name had received my gift. I was glad, *so glad*, that I'd obeyed the prompting of my heart to research the meaning of her name for her and to frame it, glad that God had given me those verses in Isaiah to include.

The other half of me was dying of curiosity. What in the world did she mean, did I know about her mother? What about her mother? Something in those verses, the part that said, even if a mother *did* forget her child, God never would . . . Had Sara been abandoned by her mother? Didn't she live up on the North Shore somewhere, in the hoity-toity suburbs north of Chicago?

And, I had to admit, I wanted to see the final transformation of Sara's makeover. All I'd seen so far was the haircut and color application—and even then, her hair had been wet. Hadn't been set, dried, or combed out. No makeup, no manicure or pedicure. Should I go back in? Offer her a ride home? I had no clue how she got here. Maybe she had her own car.

Just go home, Jodi. The Spirit Voice within seemed to put a quiet hand on my shoulder. *You gave your gift. Now give Me room to work.*

A knock on my window made me jump. A Chicago police parking enforcement uniform made a circular motion with her finger. I rolled down the window. "You plan to sit here all day, lady? Because your parking meter has run out, and if you don't move or feed the meter in the next thirty seconds, I've got to give you a parking ticket."

I nodded and rolled the window back up. "Okay, okay, Lord. I heard you the first time," I muttered as I stuck my key in the ignition. "You didn't have to send a cop too."

Five minutes later, I pulled the Caravan into a parking spot in front of our house and headed inside, picking up yesterday's mail, which was still in the box—*what's this?* A business envelope addressed to me from the Super Skatium. *Hoo boy.* Still standing on the porch, I ripped open the envelope. It'd been over four weeks since I'd written. Had our petition done any good?

I pulled out the single sheet of paper. "Dear Ms. Baxter," I read aloud. "Thank you for informing us of your concern. We are proud of our ten years in the Chicago community, serving a widely diverse clientele and providing quality entertainment for young and old alike." *Yeah, yeah, yeah.* I skimmed on. ". . . sorry for any inconvenience or disappointment you experienced. We hope you will come again and—" . . . *blah blah blah.*

I sighed and sank down on the top step of the front porch. Huh. So much for that. The Skatium manager had probably had a good snicker-fest with the DJ before shooting off his thinly veiled reply: *"Change our music? You gotta be kidding, lady!"*

Made me want to gag.

Now what? Organize a boycott? *Yeah, right.* It wasn't as if I knew a hundred people who went skating every week. The Skatium wouldn't even notice. Go out to the Skatium with a protest sign? *"The Skatium plays X-rated music!"* Not really my style. Maybe a letter-writing campaign. If they wouldn't pay attention to one letter, what about ten letters, or twenty, or thirty, or—

Whoa. Slow down, Jodi.

What? Oh, right. I was doing it again, Old Jodi response, jumping on my high horse and riding off in ten directions. *But, God, it makes me mad, thinking about the raunchy music they're feeding to all those young kids! Is it too much to ask for one, measly, family-friendly skate night? Do I just give up at the first resistance?*

The Voice in my spirit cut into my thoughts. *Not too much to ask. It's a good idea. But . . . is this your battle right now? Didn't you just agree to spend your spring break at the juvenile detention center, starting Monday?"*

Well, yeah. Good point. I felt pretty clear that saying yes to the JDC was something God wanted me to do. When would I do any of that other stuff?

I squeezed my eyes shut and crumpled the letter. *Okay, God. I think I get it. But God? This business of hearing the Holy Spirit— knowing what's from You and what is just distracting me from doing what You want me to do . . . it's hard, You know?*

I stood up and unlocked the front door. I had Easter dinner to plan and a couple of scripts I needed to read.

39

When we arrived at SouledOut the next morning, a row of Easter lilies graced the front of the low stage, a bevy of little girls in pastel dresses darted about in patent leather shoes, and people came in greeting each other happily: "The Lord is risen!" "He is risen indeed!"

I was trying to feel resurrection-ish, but after reading the scripts that had been handed to me two days ago—a short, modernized version of Shakespeare's *Much Ado About Nothing* and a dramatized version of Washington Irving's *Legend of Sleepy Hollow*—I felt more like someone who'd be facing a firing squad the next day. I'd *never* pull this off!

But I now had an inkling—just an inkling—of how Mary Magdalene must have felt when she ran into Jesus walking among the tombs that first Easter morning. Someone she never expected to see there. She couldn't believe it. But such a welcome sight!

Because when I came in the door, the girl named Sara stood by the hot drink table with Hoshi Takahashi, sipping coffee from a paper cup. Not the Sara I'd last seen at Adele's salon with gooey wet hair piled up on her head. No, *this* Sara had warm honey-blonde hair with sunny highlights and a fresh bounce, with just enough curl to tuck the ends under sweeping below her ears. Yes, and just enough makeup to highlight her pale eyes and give some color to her usually lifeless skin.

Lord, You sure are an Almighty God. What kind of miracle had brought crowd-shy Sara to *church*?

Hoshi was introducing her simply as "my friend from school." But when I slipped over to the coffee table, she beamed. "Sara, this is Jodi, one of my Yada Yada sisters."

Sara nodded shyly. "I know. We m-met yesterday." A small smile tipped the corners of her mouth.

"Oh?" Hoshi's eyebrows raised.

Let Sara tell Hoshi if she wanted to. I just grinned and said, "I'm so glad to see you again, Sara. Welcome to SouledOut. And you look great. Really great." I wanted to grab her in a big ol' hug, "that girl in the sundress" I'd prayed for so often the past year—but decided not to push it. I didn't know what God was doing with Sara, but the Holy Spirit had clearly told me to back off now and give Him some space to work.

Pastor Clark's voice called out over the general hubbub. "Church, find your seats!" Adults and children scurried to stand by their chairs. "The Lord is risen!"

"He is risen indeed!"

And with that cue, the praise team with keyboard, drums, electric bass, and saxophone launched into the wonderful Easter hymn: "Christ the Lord is risen today! Ah-ah-ah-ah-ah-le-eh-lu-u-ia!"

I opened my mouth and belted out the *alleluias*, grinning so big

I thought my earrings might pop off. *Lord, I know it's not a go-down-in-the-history-books miracle, but . . . thank You! Thank You!*

It wasn't until we'd welcomed visitors and sat down again on the comfortable, cushioned chairs from an "anonymous friend," that the firing-squad feeling loomed once more. *Oh Lord,* I moaned silently. *I'm going to need another miracle tomorrow.*

I HAD TO LEAVE THE HOUSE by seven-thirty the next morning in order to be at the juvenile detention center by nine o'clock. Denny, bless him, walked me to the Morse Avenue el station. The temperature was once again sagging in the low forties.

"You sure you feel okay taking the el?"

I nodded. But I lied.

"You got the cell phone?"

I nodded again. "Don't worry. I'll call if I need to, but I ought to be home by one-thirty or two." *That's right, Jodi, press on. Keep rolling.*

The ride was long, especially with no one to talk to. As we jostled from station to station, I read and reread the scripts the English teacher had wanted to introduce. Brave woman. Maybe in a fully equipped school with honor students. Kids who'd already read Shakespeare and Irving. But kids off the street, in trouble with the law, struggling to get their GED? Not to mention we were already weeks behind schedule. The production was supposedly on the calendar for April 24—barely two weeks away.

If I weren't so terrified, it'd be hilarious. Crack-up, take-me-away-in-a-straitjacket funny. *God, You got me into this. You've gotta get me out!*

But I guess God decided not to spirit me away in a fiery chariot like the prophet Elijah, because at nine o'clock I was standing in front of the rows of chairs in the all-purpose room on the second floor of the JDC, sweating in my armpits as a handful of boys shambled through the door, followed by two men I presumed were guards. The boys, ranging in age, I guessed, between thirteen and sixteen and dressed in various colored DOC uniforms, flopped into chairs and slouched on their tailbones.

"Sit up, gentlemen!" barked one of the guards, who proceeded to park himself on a chair at the back of the room along with the other guard, arms folded.

I looked at "my" students—and blinked. Chris Hickman sat among the boys, his eyes averted. I almost didn't recognize him with his almost shaved head. I wanted to shout. *Thank You, Jesus!* But if Chris didn't want to acknowledge our relationship, I'd respect that.

"Good morning."

A few of the boys mumbled, "Mornin'."

"My name is Mrs. Baxter, and I understand that we're here to produce a play." A few nods. "But tell you what. This isn't a lecture. We need to get acquainted, and we need to figure out how we're going to do this play. Each of you, grab a chair from the front row and pull it into a circle . . . that's it." I took a chair and started the circle. As the boys slowly complied, I counted noses. Ten.

"Let's start with names." I could remember ten names.

Ramón . . . Jeremy . . . Chris . . . Terrance . . . James . . . T-Ball—

"Not your street name!" yelled the guard at the back. "Real names, gentlemen!" Snickers from the boys.

. . . T.J. . . . Mike . . . Kevin . . . Rashad . . . David. Mostly African-American or Latino. Only James was obviously white. Rashad was probably black but had a Muslim name.

Given my restrictions on asking anything about their personal lives, I got down to business. "Your English teacher selected two possible plays to put on for your parents. It's your choice." I gave a brief summary of both plays, starting to relax. *Just stick to business, Jodi. Do what you can do. They're just kids . . .*

"*Legend of Sleepy Hollow?* Yeah, saw that on TV once." T.J. grinned. "I wanna be that headless dude who smoked the ol' scarecrow guy, what's-his-name."

"Ichabod Crane," I said, but T.J. was pretending to screw off his head and "throw" it like a fastball at Kevin. The boys laughed. "*Bam!* Busted, man!"

"Yeah. Forget that Shakespeare crap." Jeremy, who seemed to be the oldest—or at least the biggest—of the group, nailed that one into a coffin.

"All right." I dug into my tote bag and handed out photocopies of the *Sleepy Hollow* script ("No staples, nothing sharp," the principal had said). "Let's just read through it. Don't worry about who's who. We can assign parts later. Ramón? You want to start? Just go around the circle."

But we hadn't even made it to the bottom of the first page when I realized we were in trouble.

"Katrina? A *chica*? I ain't readin' no girly part."

I read the part of Katrina.

A couple of the boys read well. I was surprised and pleased. They were smart. Bright. But Mike stumbled over every other word. Chris read tonelessly. And by the time we got to the third page, Jeremy tossed the script to the floor. "Aw, this is dumb. Who cares about some ol' ghost story? What's this gotta do with us?" His outburst drew a chorus of "Yeah, man" and "Got that right" from the others.

Frankly, I had the same question. *Maybe*, if we had two months, these boys might catch a vision for classic literature. *Maybe*, if their English teacher wasn't down with mono, she could pull this off. But they had me, I had two weeks, and we didn't have a play.

Don't panic, Jodi. Think!

"All right." I laid down my script. That surprised them. "Talk to me. What do you want to do?"

The boys looked at each other. No one spoke for several seconds.

T.J. was the first with an opinion. "Action, man! We wanna do some action." He pulled out an imaginary pistol. "Ya know, *bam bam bam!* Blowing da cops—uh, da rivals' heads off."

"Hey! None of that!" snapped one of the guards.

Thank you, mister. I took a breath. "Okay. Action. What about the rest of you?"

"We could, ya know, do some rappin'. I got Snoop Dogg's latest *down*, man." Terrance stood up, affecting the hunched shoulders and distorted fingers of a rap artist, and letting go with a string of snappy words I could hardly understand, though I caught the S-word a few times.

"Uh, okay. Rapping. Though I bet you could write your own. What else?"

The group fell silent.

I had no idea where I was going with this, but I asked, "What do you want to do when you get out of here? What do you want to be when you grow up?"

Now eyes rolled and heads began to shake. "Huh. We ain't goin' ta grow up," Rashad muttered. "Ain't you heard? We destined for prison or da ice house. If da cops don't pop us, some rival will."

I stared at the young faces around me. No one contradicted

Rashad, a good-looking young man, seemingly bright. He should be going to college. But he'd already given up.

I made another stab. "You don't have to be a statistic. Who are your heroes? Somebody you look up to, who overcame diversity to do great things. Dr. Martin Luther King? He was a great man. He had a dream for young people like you—and it didn't include prison or the, um, 'ice house.'"

Jeremy shrugged. "So? They popped him too."

His words hit me like a fist in the mouth. I couldn't breathe. Had no words. I just stared at Jeremy until he broke our gaze and looked away.

Tears stung my eyes. Suddenly I was mad. Angry that these young men, one of whom was the son of my Yada Yada sister, thought they had no future. Maybe I'd believe it, too, if I was thirteen, fourteen, or fifteen and already in trouble, sitting here in the Juvenile Detention Center . . . except I *knew* Chris could have a future. He had *talent*. He was *smart*. He had parents—a whole lot of people, in fact—who *cared* about him. And if it was true for Chris, it could be true for the rest of them.

A vague idea started to spin a web in my brain. I found my voice. "Look. It might seem like we've wasted our first day, and we don't have that many days. But it's not wasted. You decided what you *don't* want to do. That's a start. And you gave me a lot to think about. I'm going to go home, and when I come back tomorrow, we're going to put together a play, a show—whatever—ourselves. Don't know what yet. But"—I cast a wry grin at T.J.—"it'll have some action. *Maybe* some rapping. Something that'll make your parents or guardians sit up and take notice. I just need one thing from you."

Ten pairs of eyes shifted from one to the other, then back at me. "What's that, Mrs. B?" Jeremy said.

"Promise me you'll come back tomorrow. All of you."

Shrugs, a few grins. "Yeah, why not." "Yeah, we'll be here." The boys filed out—all except for Chris Hickman, who lagged behind.

I wanted to hug him. But I just said, "Hey, Chris."

"Uh, thanks, Mrs. B, for not lettin' on our families are tight. But . . . I dunno about comin' back tomorrow. I heard it was you comin' ta do a play, I thought it might be fun. But I can't talk or act or any of that stuff."

The idea web in my head was catching more flies. "Don't worry about that. I have an idea for you—but can we talk about it tomorrow? Will you come?"

He thought it over. "Okay. Tomorrow. But that's all I promise."

I DON'T EVEN REMEMBER walking to the bus stop. Barely remembered the ride home on the el. My mind was buzzing. Jeremy was right. A lot of "heroes" had been shot and killed, even in my lifetime. Dr. King, President Kennedy, his brother Bobby. Civil rights workers like Medgar Evers. Earlier American heroes, too, like Abraham Lincoln, who was from Illinois. Just like the prophets of old.

That's what we do to prophets, Jesus said.

Pieces of ideas floated and collided in my head like meteor fragments. I needed a connection, something to piece all the pieces together. *Wasn't Dr. King killed in April? What else happened in April?*

I leaned my head against the window of the northbound el as it creaked and groaned around the Loop, then headed north toward Rogers Park. "God," I whispered, "You said if we lack wisdom, to ask for it. I need a whole lot of wisdom right now! I *know* I can't do this in my own strength. This whole situation is way over my head. But I have a crazy confidence that You put this in my lap, so I've gotta trust You're going to come through. I just . . . don't see how yet."

My breath was steaming up the window; a couple of passengers nearby looked at me strangely. So I shut my mouth but continued my talk with God. *Don't mean to tell You what to do, Lord, but . . . I've got less than twenty-four hours to get my act together.*

I felt better as I got off the el at Morse Avenue and headed home. God put this in my lap, but I'd just put it back in His.

When I got home, I found a note from Denny. *"Amanda and I went to a movie. How'd it go? Love, D."* They weren't home. Good. And Josh was at work. Good. Because I didn't want any distractions.

"Wouldn't mind if you were home, though, Wonka," I murmured to the silence as I turned on the computer and waited for it to boot up. Yeah, I missed Wonka lying on my feet when I had some serious praying and thinking to do.

40

I was genuinely glad to see all ten boys saunter into the JDC school all-purpose room the next morning. Even Chris. I motioned them to sit in the same circle of chairs. "Thanks. I know you didn't have to come. But I have an idea for a play—actually, the idea came from you." I grinned. "God helped a lot too. Here's the deal . . ."

I leaned forward. Curious, the boys all leaned in. I shared my idea, sneaking a peek now and then at the two guards who sat cross-armed at the back of the room. One glared at me, frowning, as I passed out the stuff I'd found online to provide background; the other chewed absently on his nails.

So far, so good.

"Okay," I said. "We need four volunteers to make these speeches. You can't read them; you have to memorize them. We can make them shorter, though—I've marked the main thoughts."

"Huh!" T.J. snorted. "James is the only one who can play a white dude."

"Hey! Don' matter to me," Ramón smirked. "Might be my only chance to be prez-i-dent." The others laughed.

"Exactly," I said. "These heroes belong to all of us—white, black, Latino. Don't think of it as giving a speech. Become your character. Speak as though these thoughts, these feelings, these ideas came from inside *you*." I looked around the circle at the ten boys, clothed in their purple, green, and blue uniforms. "But we need some action scenes too."

T.J. raised a fist. "Aiiiight!"

Once again, we huddled. Their laughter punctuated the process. By the end of the three hours, we'd selected our four main characters, selected the villains, and brainstormed the final act. When the guards looked at their watches impatiently, I released the boys, but asked for another minute with Chris.

"Yeah, I can do that gangbangin' stuff, Mrs. B., long as I don't hafta give one o' them long speeches."

"Sure. You'll do fine in the action scenes. But that's not the main part I have for you." I pulled out some drawings and photographs and gave them to him. "Think you could paint these characters?" My arm swept from one end of the wall behind me to the other. "Big as a wall?" I grinned. "I've actually seen your work on a wall before."

His eyes nearly popped. "They'd *never* let me do that here! Man! I'd be in so much troub—"

"Whoa, whoa!" I laughed. "I don't mean actually on the *wall*. I mean a backdrop for our play. You've heard the idea. Work with it. Include these characters somehow."

He looked at me sideways, frowning dubiously. "You could do that? Get me stuff to paint with, I mean? Stuff to paint *on*?"

Good question. I was going out on a limb here . . . way out. "To be honest, Chris, I don't know. But I'm going to try. But there's something you can do."

"Me! What?"

"Pray about it. Let's leave it to God to move the mountains."

A slow smile leaked over his features. He balled up his fist and held it out. I balled up mine and we touched, fist to fist. "I'll do that, Mrs. B."

I SPENT ALL AFTERNOON trying to get permission from the "powers that be" at the JDC to allow Chris Hickman to use spray paint and airbrushes under strict supervision. No dice. Chalk. That was their compromise. Colored chalk. Did they have a budget for this play? No budget. Okay . . . I wasn't going to let a little thing like money stop this production, even if my husband and kids had to eat rice for the next few weeks.

Once I arrived home, I got on the phone with Josh in the mailroom at Peter Douglass's business. Could he rustle up some very large cardboard boxes that could be flattened and taped together with duct tape to make a wall?

"Sure, Mom. Whatcha doin'? Putting me out in the doghouse?"

"Hm. Good idea. But, sorry. This doghouse isn't for you."

To my delight, a trip to Goods, the huge art store in Evanston, yielded big, fat colored chalk, and a whole palette of smaller poster chalks in intense colors. Who needed spray paint? Almost giddy, I drove our minivan on Wednesday to lug everything down to the JDC. Even got those two bored guards involved in flattening and taping.

Chris's eyes popped again when I handed the various chalk sets to him. "Really? Really? I can use these? I mean, legal-like?"

I couldn't help it. I gave him a hug. They could lock me up, for all I cared.

"WHAT? You're going to spend Saturday at the JDC too?" Denny asked me Friday evening. We were in the backyard grilling steaks to celebrate the last day of spring vacation, which had finally shaken off the doldrums and hit the eighties. "You fly out of here every morning like you're meeting a secret lover." He stuck out his lip. "I'm jealous. Spent all week by myself working on tax forms."

"Denny Baxter!" I swatted his backside with the barbecue tongs I held in my hand. "You're the one who took the kids to New York last year and left *me* home during spring break." Well, I'd had doctor's orders not to travel, but hey, I could use guilt too.

Denny stuck a fork in the sizzling steaks and turned them over. "So it's going good? You seem excited about the whole project."

I was bursting to tell Denny what we were doing. But on the off-chance he might be able to attend the performance along with other "staff," I wanted him to be surprised.

"I am! It's going great—I think. Not sure I know what I'm doing, but I'm having fun." I turned a big grin on Denny. "Best part, I think the boys are having fun too."

Denny sat down beside me on the steps. "So what now? School starts next week."

He wasn't going to like this part. "Uh, I'd like to go down to the JDC after school a few days, maybe Monday, Wednesday, and Friday, to make sure the performance holds together. The boys are putting it on for family and staff next Saturday. If I could, um, take the car, maybe I wouldn't get home too late."

He frowned. The silence was filled by a dozen sparrows happily flitting about the back yard. Finally, he said, "Guess so. You taking the car tomorrow? Can you wait till I pick up Ricardo for the men's breakfast? And what time are you getting back? I have some errands I need to do."

Irritation nibbled at the edges of my peace. *Don't feel guilty, Jodi. He's had all week to do his stupid errands!* But I bit back the smart remark. "Sure. I can wait. And I'll be back by two or three. Earlier if it's really important."

He shrugged. "No, that's okay. Just so I know—oh, heck!" He leaped for the grill. "The steaks!"

I WOULD'VE LET Denny drop me off at the JDC when he drove to Little Village to pick up Ricardo Enriques the next morning, and taken the train home, but I was sure the JDC didn't want me coming in at six-thirty. But I got there at ten, and we did a run-through of the whole performance. It was rough, but we still had a week to smooth it up.

What pleased me most, though, was Chris's backdrop. One hardly noticed that it was done on cardboard boxes that had been flattened and taped together. "It's beautiful, Chris," I said, watching him work on the four scenes that blended into each other.

Chris grinned. "Thanks, Mrs. B. But don't tell my folks about it, okay? They're comin', ain't they?"

"You bet." *They'd better.*

As I drove home via Lake Shore Drive and Sheridan Road,

windows open, enjoying the balmy weather in spite of the thunderstorm building up over the lake, I tried not to think about all the stuff I *didn't* do during spring vacation—like putting away winter clothes, doing spring housecleaning, filing all the bills and tax forms. But for some reason I didn't care. I doubted I would say fondly in my old age, "Oh yes, that was the spring I cleaned out the closets." But I didn't think I'd ever forget the spring break I spent putting together a drama at the JDC.

Pulling into the garage, I felt half-giddy with the warm weather, imagining how surprised the Hickmans would be next week, and—finally—realizing I *did* need to spend the rest of the weekend working on lesson plans for the next two months and grading papers. I was halfway up the walk to the house before I noticed my family clustered on the back porch watching me. Denny had a silly grin on his face.

"Oh! Hi guys. Uh, what's up?"

"Mo-om!" Amanda rolled her eyes. *"Look!"*

I looked. And then I saw. A row of solid wooden flower boxes, painted a deep forest green, ran the length of the back porch railings. Sprays of cheerful white daisies decorated each one. My mouth fell open. "What . . .? When . . .?"

"That's not all, Mom." Amanda ran down the back steps and pulled me around the side of the house to the front. More flower boxes ran the length of the front porch.

My men followed. "Dad figured if we were going to get any flowers this year, we better get you some flower boxes," Josh said. "After all, we don't have anybody on house arrest this year to tackle the flower beds."

"But . . . but . . ." I ran up onto the porch and examined the boxes closely. "These are handmade!"

Denny's grin widened. "You were kind enough to abandon us completely this week. We had plenty of time to make them. Amanda stenciled the daisies."

Amanda blushed. "The boxes needed something to look pretty till you can plant some flowers. Would've bought you some, but the greenhouses say it's still too early."

"We got potting soil, though." Josh jerked a thumb back toward the garage. "Bags and bags of it."

I was speechless. I'd barely thought of my family all week—and all week they'd been plotting and making something special for me. I threw my arms around Denny, then hugged my kids. "Thank you so much," I finally managed. "All of you. Really. It's the best gift you could've given me—and it's not even my birthday, or Mother's Day, or anything!"

"Sure, Mom." Amanda and Josh each gave me a quick peck and disappeared inside. But Denny walked me hand in hand around to the back again and sat us down in the porch swing.

"Not quite the best gift," he said.

"What do you mean?"

His side dimples deepened. "Well, thought you might like to know. This morning, Ben Garfield came to the prayer time we've been having *before* the men's breakfast, and asked about coming to church at SouledOut. I think his exact words were, 'Would they accept a crusty old Jew like me?'"

Now my mouth really did drop open.

"According to Ben, he was pretty upset by all of the 'Jesus

questions' at the Seder last week. But he started to read the New Testament to see if all that stuff was true—something he'd never done. Then he started in on the Old Testament. And a lot of things started to make sense, just like Yo-Yo and others were pointing out."

Oh, that was funny. Yo-Yo, of all people, teaching Ben Garfield a thing or two. "But doesn't he go with Ruth to Beth Yehudah sometimes? That's a Messianic congregation. Hasn't he heard that stuff before?"

Denny shrugged, still grinning. "All I know is, the brothers prayed with Ben Garfield this morning, who said he wanted to stop messing around the edges of faith and really believe that the Messiah has come."

41

The best gift, indeed! Ben Garfield had become a *Christian*?! I was so excited I wanted to call all the Yada Yada sisters and tell them. Then I realized Yada Yada was meeting this weekend . . . somewhere. I checked the list taped to a kitchen cupboard door. At my house, yikes! They'd find out tomorrow anyway. Let Ruth tell them.

If Ben told her. Communication between those two was weird at best.

But when we got to church the next morning, sure enough, Ben and Ruth's pearly green Buick was already in the shopping center parking lot. And there they were, taking up half a row with two baby carriers, two diaper bags, and the twins, dressed in— what else?—matching knitted sweaters and caps, though Havah's was yellow and Isaac's blue.

But what I noticed most was that Ben was wearing his yar-mulke. What was that about? By his own admission, Ben hadn't been a very religious Jew. But maybe his Jewishness made even more sense now that he saw the fulfillment of the Old Testament prophecies about a coming Messiah.

I was so moved that Ben and Ruth had come to church together, all I could do was give Ben a big, long hug. "Welcome," I whispered in his whiskery ear. And I didn't just mean welcome to our church. By the look he gave me, I think he understood.

Chanda and her kids showed up, too, along with Rochelle and little Conny, the cutie. What was going on? Chanda was a member of Paul and Silas Apostolic Baptist, like Adele. On the other hand, Rochelle's parents were members here. Maybe Chanda's household was taking turns at both churches, since Rochelle had moved in. Or—

Sheesh. I sure hoped Chanda wasn't chasing that *fine* Oscar Frost.

Avis led worship that morning. Peter must have told her about the "Bada-Boom Brothers" praying with Ben yesterday, because she couldn't stop smiling, couldn't stop praising. The call to worship was from Psalm 125: "Those who trust in the Lord are like Mount Zion, which cannot be shaken but endures forever!" she cried. "As the mountains surround Jerusalem, so the Lord surrounds his people both now and forevermore."

Beautiful, I thought. *Let Ben know our faith is rooted in his.*

The praise team followed with the spiritual, *"Tell me, how did you feel when you come out the wilderness? . . ."* The whole congregation leaned into the song, clapping and singing it again and again. I snuck a glance at Ben and Ruth, each bouncing a five-month-old on their hips in time to the rhythmic music. *"Did your soul feel happy when you come out the wilderness? . . ."* Neither one was singing the words, but both had the kind of wobbly smile that betrayed a well of happy tears.

Between clapping, singing, the sunshine streaming in through the wall of windows, and temperatures predicted in the high eighties—*hot* for April—a lot of handkerchiefs came out to mop sweaty faces, and a couple of men propped open the glass double doors. During the lengthy service, several of us walked and jiggled the babies in the back of the room when they got fussy, since we didn't have a nursery yet.

Afterward, the Garfields were mobbed by greeters, both friends and strangers. Ruth took me by surprise when she sought me out and pulled me aside. "You prayed; God answered, Jodi. *Toda raba* . . . thank you."

I flinched. "Um, to be honest, Ruth, I forgot to pray for Ben until the middle of the Seder. Worse, I forgot to tell the other Yada Yadas to pray like you asked."

She patted my arm. "Do not worry. God answered, *yo?* My prayers, your prayers, all the Yada Yada prayers that have gone up for my Ben. God is faithful."

I grabbed her in a hug. "Yes, God is so faithful," I murmured as Stu and Estelle joined us. "Uh . . . hi guys. See you all tonight? Yada Yada's at my house. Pass the word, will you? I've gotta zip home and clean house"—I groaned—"not to mention finish lesson plans and grade a zillion more homework papers."

Estelle wagged a finger in front of my face. "Slow down, Jodi Baxter. Stu and I will bring snacks tonight, won't we, Stu?" She elbowed Stu in the ribs. "An' I'll be down an hour early to run yo' vacuum cleaner or whatever else you think needs doin'." The finger wagged some more. "An' don't you be oh-no-ing *me*. You should know by now I'm a stubborn old woman. Now"—She eyed the room from side to side—"where are them babies? I'm not leavin' till I get me some sugar."

BY THE TIME the Yada Yadas started arriving at five o'clock, I had finished the stack of papers I had to grade, my lesson plans would at least get me through the next two weeks, and Estelle had swept through our house as if her hair were on fire. Stu brought down her homemade cranberry bread, still hot from the oven—though Josh and Amanda sweet-talked her out of two whole slices on their way out the door to the SouledOut youth group at the church. "Your cranberry bread is my favorite, Auntie Stu," Josh teased.

"Don't you 'Auntie Stu' me, you overgrown sheepdog," she grinned, flicking his shaggy hair out of his eyes.

I was surprised to see Hoshi come in with Nonyameko. I peered behind them. "Is Sara with you?"

Hoshi shook the silky black ponytail at the nape of her neck. "No. But she wants me to tell all of you thank you very much for the gift certificate."

"Mm-hm. That Adele sure did work wonders on that girl," Florida murmured, her mouth full of crumbly cranberry bread.

Hoshi laughed. "Yes. It has given her more self-confidence. So, today I tell her, 'Sara, you will have to go to ReJOYce tonight without me. I cannot come.' It will be—how do you say?—good for her." Hoshi winked impishly.

Nony slipped an arm around the girl's slender waist. "The truth is, sisters, Hoshi misses Yada Yada more than she lets on. And tonight she needs prayer for her future, after graduation. But we will share later, yes, my sister?" She gave Hoshi a tender kiss on her long, smooth cheek and sat down in our overstuffed chair.

Whoa. I kinda sorta remembered that Hoshi was scheduled to graduate from Northwestern University this year, but I hadn't given any thought to what came after. Would she return to Japan? Or . . . what?

Ruth bustled in *without* any babies, but we mobbed her anyway. Those of us from SouledOut knew the good news already, and everyone else found out soon enough that Ben had prayed with "the brothers" to receive Jesus as his Messiah. I waited until the hugs and hubbub died down to satisfy my curiosity. "Um, Ruth, why did Ben want to come to SouledOut? Don't get me wrong—I'd love to have my favorite grouch at our church." Ruth and I both laughed. "But, what about Beth Yehudah? I mean, that's Christian *and* Jewish. I've learned so much about my own faith from you two."

Ruth rolled her eyes. "Beth Yehudah yesterday, SouledOut today. A church marathon we did this weekend!" She thought a moment. "But for Ben, he considers Denny and the other Yada Yada husbands as true brothers, who accepted him, even valued him, for who he was. He wants to worship with them for a while . . . or 'hang,' as Yo-Yo would say. *Oy-oy-oy.*"

By now, most of the group had arrived, and Avis rounded us up, encouraging us to start our praise and worship time. Chanda slipped in scowling as we sang one of our old favorites: *"Hold to His hand, God's Almighty hand . . . !"*

"Are you okay?" I whispered to her.

She muttered something dark about the terrible parking.

I wanted to guffaw. *Well, yeah, Chanda, if you're going to insist on driving that monster SUV.* But I didn't. She'd bought the thing so she could haul kids and families around, bless her. So I just gave her a hug and brought in another chair from the dining room.

As I sat down again, Avis was opening her Bible. "I want to share a scripture from Hebrews, chapter twelve," she said. "'Therefore, since we are surrounded by such a huge crowd of witnesses to the life of faith, let us strip off every weight that slows us down, especially the sin that so easily hinders our progress. And let us run with endurance the race that God has set before us. We do this by keeping our eyes on Jesus, on whom our faith depends from start to finish.'"

My ears perked up. *Whoa.* More verses about running the race, moving forward, like the ones God had showed me in Philippians last week.

Avis closed her Bible. "It occurred to me as I read these verses that they speak both to the one running the race of faith, and to the 'crowd of witnesses' urging the runner on. Each one of us in this room finds herself in both roles—running the race of faith, and encouraging each other when we falter." A gentle smile bathed Avis's face as she looked around the circle. "I just want to say thank you, my sisters, for being there for my family this year. It has been so hard to see my precious daughter suffer abuse in her marriage, and now have to deal with HIV. Thank you especially, Chanda, for taking Rochelle into your home."

Chanda squirmed. "Aw, *irie, mon*! It's all good. For we too!"

Edesa, her nutmeg skin glowing in the warm evening, leaned forward with a wide smile. "I, too, want to say *gracias* to Chanda for her encouragement. She made a generous donation to the new

Manna House Foundation, and promised matching funds to anything else we can raise in the next two years. We can start building this summer!"

"Awright, Chanda!" Yo-Yo punched the air, spurring a general round of clapping and hooting and praise to God.

Chanda was genuinely embarrassed. "Mi tink dat was supposed to be *anonymous*, Edesa girl. But since you got such a big mout', mi say dat dis group help mi see dat lottery money belong to God anyway." She folded her arms across her bosom as if to say, *An dat's dat.*

I watched Chanda, realizing what a wonderful, funky sense of humor God had. He could use anyone and anything, no matter how ordinary or unlikely—in fact, He seemed to like "ordinary" and "unlikely" the best!—to work out His grace in this world.

Nony spoke. "That word is for me tonight, Avis. To press toward the goal. To set aside every weight. To run with endurance." She pulled a long envelope from her bag. "Mark got a reply from the University of KwaZulu-Natal—"

Eyes widened. "Did he . . .?" several started to say but did not finish.

Nony smiled and shook her head. "No, he has not yet been accepted. But they are interested, and would like to interview him in person, so we—"

We? I had expected her to say, *"So he is flying to South Africa for an interview."*

"—are leaving for South Africa as soon as the boys are out of school in June, as we had planned before."

A collective gasp seemed to suck the air out of the room for several moments. But Nony's heart was in her smile. "Mark says it does not matter if he is offered a job at the university or not. If God is calling us to South Africa as a family, we will better know what our options are if we are there in person. All of us. Northwestern has extended his sabbatical for two more years. Praise You, Jesus." Her eyes closed and her hand lifted in silent praise. Just as suddenly, her eyes opened, and she turned to Hoshi. "We have asked Hoshi to consider going with us when she graduates in June. She has become a much-loved member of our family, and there is quite an international community in KwaZulu-Natal, many Asians as well. But . . . it is up to her, of course."

Now my heart really started to flutter. *Nony and Mark leaving? Hoshi maybe leaving too?* What was going to happen to Yada Yada? I knew God wanted us to reach out beyond our little group. But did that have to mean *losing* each other?

Someone said, "Hoshi? What are you thinking?"

Hoshi seemed surprisingly calm at such a momentous crossroad. "That is why I wanted to come to Yada Yada tonight, to ask all of you to pray with me about my future. I had always planned to return to Japan, but"—her almond eyes saddened—"as you know, my family has turned against me. I am grateful for Nonyameko and Dr. Smith's invitation to accompany them. It is true; they are my family now. But . . ." She grew thoughtful. "Befriending Sara and getting acquainted with what ReJOYce is doing on campus has touched me deeply. There are so many lonely, empty souls on the Northwestern campus. I feel drawn to work with them, but . . ." She took a deep breath. "I don't know what God wants me to do. So I ask you, dear sisters, to pray."

"Exactly what we should do." Avis reached for the hands on either side of her. "What other prayer requests do we have tonight?"

"Oh, help me, Jesus!" Florida's cry made me jump. She'd been strangely silent all evening, but suddenly pent-up words burst out. "Pray with me, sisters. Chris's final hearing is a week from Wednesday, last week of the month. I can hardly sleep nights, worried about my baby." Her head wagged from side to side; she thumped her chest. "He didn't do nothin', I know it. I believe that with all my heart. Pray, sisters. Pray that the judge will see the truth." Her head wagged harder. "Don't know what I'll do if he—"

The tears started to flow.

I felt torn. I'd almost forgotten that Chris's hearing was coming up! He hadn't said anything to me during play practices; maybe he wasn't supposed to talk about it. I wanted Florida to be excited about coming to see the play, but Chris hadn't wanted me to tell her what he was doing. With Florida all torn up about the upcoming hearing, how could I share my excitement at what God was doing with this "homegrown" play—in my life, in the lives of the boys taking part? And I needed prayer. Oh boy, did I still need prayer! God would have to pull it together or it would fall flat.

But several sisters had surrounded Florida; others were laying hands on Hoshi and Nonyameko and starting to pray. I blinked back hot tears, joined others on their knees beside Florida, and laid a hand on her shaking shoulder as Yada Yada pelted heaven.

Lord, hear my prayer too. Please, don't forget this play . . .

AS WE BROKE UP OUR CIRCLE, Ruth asked, "So. We meet where next time?"

"I'm next on the list," Avis admitted. "But that's the weekend of Peter's and my first anniversary, and we might—"

"Your anniversary?!" Yo-Yo screeched. "Hey, guys, know what that means? It's Yada Yada's anniversary too! Two years—and we haven't killed each other yet." People started to laugh. Had it really been a year since Avis "jumped the broom" with Peter Douglass? *Two* years since God had thrown us together at the Chicago Women's Conference as Prayer Group 26?

"*Our* anniversary, too, Yo-Yo." Becky grinned. "We got baptized in Lake Michigan right after Avis's wedding last year—remember?"

"Yowza." Yo-Yo high-fived everyone within reach. "We gotta do somethin' special. *Really* party—hey! Delores. Your man doin' a gig at La Fiesta that weekend?"

Delores shrugged. "Not sure. I'll find out."

Florida shook her head. "I dunno . . . might not feel like partyin' if Chris's hearing don't go right."

I grabbed her and whispered in her ear. "Have faith, sister. Have faith!"

42

*I*knew putting in a full day at Bethune Elementary, and then driving downtown to the juvenile detention center would stretch me thin as razor wire. Before I collapsed into bed Monday night, I e-mailed a frantic SOS to Yada Yada for prayer support, then buried myself beneath the covers.

On Wednesday, I grabbed a few *Israel and New Breed* CDs to keep my praise going on the commute. But when I bumbled into the all-purpose room at the JDC with my bag of scripts and a box of props, nine sour faces waited for me—and the principal.

"What? Where's Jeremy?"

"That's what I came to tell you. He had his disposition yesterday. The judge gave him two years for dealing; second offense. They took him to the Illinois youth prison in Joliet this morning."

"But . . . he was doing the Dr. King speech!" My heart felt like it was flopping down around my ankles. "Couldn't they have waited till next week?" I sank into the nearest chair. "Sheesh. Way to take the guts right out of our play."

The principal gave a sympathetic shrug. "I'm really sorry, Mrs. Baxter. Do the best you can. I'm sure the parents will understand." She slipped out of the room.

I closed my eyes and pressed my fingertips against my temples. *Yeah, right.* What were we going to do now? Me get up there and read Jeremy's part? That'd be a comedy, for sure.

Wait a minute, Jodi. Jeremy was sent to prison for two years—and he's only sixteen. And you're worried about your play?

I sighed. *You're right, Lord. I'm sorry. But I really don't know what to—*

I felt someone tapping on my shoulder. I opened my eyes. "What is it, T.J.?"

The boy gave me a lopsided grin. "I'll do Dr. King."

"You?" I managed an appreciative smile. "I thought you just wanted to do the 'action' parts. Besides, the play's only three days away. How would you memorize—"

"I already done it."

I blinked. "You've *already* memorized the Dr. King speech?"

T.J. nodded, still grinning. "Yeah. Jeremy was in my unit, so he used ta make me listen to him say his part over and over, an'—" He shrugged. "I dunno. I jus' learned it."

I couldn't help it. I started to laugh. Then I stood up and clapped my hands once. "All right. Thank you, T.J. Let's do a run-through of the whole thing . . ."

ALL THE WAY HOME, I confessed my lack of faith and praised God for preparing T.J. ahead of time—our "ram in the bush," just like He did for Abraham and Isaac. T.J. had done a passable job with the Dr. King speech. Ramón, James, and Rashad had their parts memorized too. The action parts . . . well, I just hoped the audience wouldn't laugh. My actors got a little carried away sometimes. But Chris's backdrop was finished and helped pull the whole mishmash together. "Thank You, *Jesus!*" I yelled at the top of my lungs right in the middle of homegoing traffic on Lake Shore Drive.

I thought my next hurdle would be convincing Florida and Carl that showing up Saturday night for the "spring play" at the JDC was important to Chris—without actually telling them what it was about or what Chris was doing.

But that was before I arrived at the JDC Friday afternoon. This time the principal met me outside the all-purpose room. Our eyes locked. *Uh-oh.* I tried to steel myself. "Who's gone now?"

She shook her head. "No one's gone. They're all inside, but . . . we've had an incident. I just wanted to prepare you." She opened the door and I walked in, my heart flopping around my ankles again.

The two guards parted as I walked between them. The boys sat slumped in the chairs, shoulders hunched. Except Chris. Florida's son paced back and forth in front of the backdrop, fists clenched, muttering every cuss word he'd ever heard. When he saw me, he hurtled toward me in three angry strides. "See?" He flung a hand toward the backdrop. "See? It don't matter what I do, Mrs. B. I ain't gonna go *no*where."

I stared at the backdrop. Four long gashes snaked across the four beautiful figures he'd drawn on the cardboard "wall." Slashes with something sharp. Knife? Box cutter? Fingernail file? I whirled to face the principal. "How could this happen?!" I was one pitch short of shouting. "Isn't this door kept locked?!"

Get a grip, Jodi. Satan would really like you to lose it right now. Is God faithful, or not? I took a deep breath and lowered my voice. "I'm sorry. Never mind. I . . . just need some time with the boys. Yes, all of them. We need to decide what to do together."

I heard the door close as the principal left. The guards respectfully withdrew to the back of the room. But I walked slowly along the backdrop, tracing the slashes with my finger, like Thomas touching the wounds in Jesus' hands and feet and side. *Wounds . . . that's what these are . . . wounds . . .*

I turned to face the boys who were watching me. "Chris? I'm truly sorry this happened. I don't know why someone would do this. Maybe something ugly happened to them and they took out their anger on your artwork because it's beautiful. I don't know. But I do know this: what the devil intended for evil, God can turn into something good."

Chris snorted in disgust. The other boys rolled their eyes.

"Wait—hear me out." I sat down and motioned the boys to draw their chairs close. "Whoever did this thought he was going to ruin our play. But without knowing it, this backdrop perfectly fits what we've been trying to say all along. We're not going to fix it. We're going to use it just the way it is. And this is why . . ."

THE NEXT DAY Denny and I arrived at the JDC two hours early. The performance was scheduled for seven o'clock, but I wanted to be sure the room was set up, give the boys a pep talk, make sure we had no last minute "surprises" . . . and to pray.

"Go early and pray over the room," Avis had urged me on the phone. "Touch each chair, pray for each parent or staff who comes tonight. Pray for the boys. Pray *with* the boys if you can. Peter and I will be praying for you here at the house." I grinned as we pulled into the parking structure next to the JDC. Avis had done more than pray. She'd loaned her car to the Hickmans, who didn't want to ride with us and have to sit around for two hours.

I wished Amanda and Josh could've come, but Denny barely squeaked in, because he was the husband of the "play director" *and* a JDC volunteer. By now the security *schtik* was routine, and we hurried to the all-purpose room with the few props I'd managed to scrounge up from Bethune Elementary's costume box.

To my surprise, the room was already unlocked. I heard voices inside. *Oh no. What now?* With a sense of dread, I opened the door . . . and stopped dead in my tracks.

The two guards who had accompanied the boys for each play practice were mounting spotlights on tripods, adjusting them to fall on Chris's damaged backdrop and various spots in front of it. The one the boys called Mr. Wheeler turned his head. "Oh, hey, Mrs. Baxter. This your husband?" He came over and shook Denny's hand.

"What's this?" I raised my hands toward the lights on left and right.

"Oh, Gonzalez over there . . . he swiped 'em from his church. Thought you could use 'em tonight." Wheeler scratched his jaw. "We've been watching what you're doin' with the boys for this performance. We'd like to help. We'll be your light techies tonight, if it's all right with you."

"All right with—! It's wonderful! That's what we really needed to highlight the different parts! But, uh, we don't have time to practice with the lights, to work out—"

"Aw, don't worry about that, Mrs. B. We got it down. Don't forget, we've been watching you practice for days. Gonzalez over there—he does this all the time for big performances at his church."

Denny chuckled in my ear as we left them to their work. "Any other surprises, 'Mrs. B'?" I just shook my head, and got down to the praying business before my actors arrived at five-thirty. It was a little awkward with the guards-turned-light-techies there, but no way was I going to skip over this part. If it wasn't prayer holding this play together, I didn't know what was!

THE ROOM WAS PACKED by seven o'clock. I saved a couple of seats for Florida and Carl in the second row; good thing, because they slipped in at six-fifty-five. The principal welcomed the parents, administrators, staff, and visitors, including someone from the mayor's office. She introduced me briefly, but all I did was introduce each one of that night's cast by name. "The stage set for tonight's performance was designed by Chris Hickman, age fourteen," I added, and sat down.

The lights went out. Well, not completely, for security reasons, I guessed. But dim enough so that David slipped onto the "stage," and seemed to suddenly appear, illumined by one spotlight. David was articulate, and the boys had unanimously elected him to be narrator. "Welcome," he said. "Tonight we bring you 'Voices from the Past—Voices for Our Future.' Sit back, enjoy—but most of all, listen."

The spotlight died. When the lights came up again, two "gangs" came at each other from opposite sides of the room, three purple uniforms against three green uniforms, yelling insults, making dares, calling names. I could see parents squirming, glancing at each other. As they met in the middle, Kevin (purple) pushed T.J. (green). Suddenly T.J. drew a fluorescent green water gun (I'd been firmly told not to use anything that looked realistic), pointed it at Kevin and yelled, *"Bam! Bam!"*

Kevin fell in a heap to the floor. The other boys ran in two directions. Left lights died. Right lights followed the "shooter" and his homies. "Why'd you pop him, man?" Mike yelled at T.J. "You didn't hafta kill him!"

"He was dissin' me, man. Didn't ya hear? *Nobody* disses me, man."

The spotlight came up again on Kevin, still sprawled on the floor. David, who hadn't been one of the gangbangers, knelt down beside him, shaking his head, moaning. "He was goin' ta go to college. He wanted ta build bridges and skyscrapers. *Why* do we kill our brightest and best? Won't we ever learn?"

The audience was clearly uncomfortable. I heard murmurs and chairs squeaking as the spotlights dimmed. When the spot came up again, James—even paler under the bright light—stood in the middle of the stage with a "stovepipe hat" on his head and an Abe Lincoln beard anchored to his chin. I heard a few titters, but they quickly died when James spoke. "I, Abraham Lincoln, President of the United States, by virtue of the power in me . . . do order and declare that all persons held as slaves within these States and henceforward shall be free!" The room grew even quieter as he paraphrased the Emancipation Proclamation. ". . . And I hereby charge the people so declared to be free to abstain from all violence, unless in necessary self-defense . . ." James drew himself up, needing no mic as he boomed the last words. "Upon this act, sincerely believed to be an act of justice, warranted by the Constitution . . . I invoke the considered judgment of mankind and the gracious favor of Almighty God!"

People in the audience began to clap—but just then Terrance came out of the shadows and pointed the fluorescent green water gun at "Abe Lincoln." *"Bam! Bam!"* James dropped to the floor. I heard several gasps around me. The spot moved to Chris's chalk drawing of President Lincoln with the ugly slash across it, lingered . . . then died.

When the spotlight came up again, David stood with his head hanging. "Why do we kill our brightest and our best? Won't we ever learn?"

Lights out . . . lights on. Rashad was "on stage" wearing a shirt and tie. "My name is Medgar Evers. Thank you for giving me this opportunity to speak by radio. I speak as a native Mississippian, educated in Mississippi schools, serving overseas in our nation's armed forces against Hitlerism and fascism. I mention this because I believe I am typical of many loyal Mississippians of color, who are equally devoted to their State and want only to see it assume its rightful place in the democratic scheme of our country."

The room was completely silent as Rashad, quoting Medgar Evers's speech, painted a tough picture of the Jim Crow years. Finally "Medgar Evers" said, "What does the Negro want?" Rashad ticked off the end of segregation . . . to register and vote without handicap . . . more jobs at all levels . . . desegregated schools. "The Negro has been in America since 1619, a total of three hundred and forty-four years. He is not going anywhere else; this country is his home. He wants to do his part to help make his city, state, and nation a better place for everyone regardless of color and race."

Denny took my hand and squeezed as Rashad said, "Thank you," and started to walk off. I heard an "Oh no!" behind me as the shadowy figure appeared, pulled out the fluorescent green water gun and—*"Bam! Bam!"*—"shot" him in the back. "Medgar Evers" fell to the floor. The spotlight moved to Chris's drawing of the civil rights leader on the backdrop. In the strong light, the ugly gash across the drawing stood out even more glaringly.

David moved into the spotlight. This time he threw his hands up. *"Why* do we kill our brightest and our best? Won't we ever learn?"

The third scene featured Ramón wearing a white shirt and tie. No one would have guessed who he was supposed to be, except that he stood next to Chris's drawing of President John Kennedy for a moment before he moved to center stage. "My fellow Americans." He didn't quite make the stretch from Latino accent to Bostonian inflections, but he tried. "The oath I swore before you and Almighty God—as the thirty-fifth president of the United States—is the same solemn oath our forefathers prescribed nearly a century and three-quarters ago." People were leaning forward. "The world is very different now . . . yet we hold the same revolutionary belief—that the rights of man come not from the generosity of the state, but from the hand of God."

I was so proud of Ramón. Amazed that he had dropped all his S-words and F-words for the stirring words of this inaugural address. ". . . And so, my fellow Americans: ask not what your country can do for you—ask what you can do for your country."

But noone clapped. The audience tensed. Sure enough.

385

Out came the shadowy figure and the water gun. *"Bam! Bam!"* Ramón dropped to the floor. And David repeated his sorrowful line: "Why do we kill our brightest and our best? Won't we ever learn?"

By the time T.J. took the stage, even Denny's grip on my hand was tight. T.J., too, had on a shirt and tie. The spotlight followed him as he paused by the drawing of Abraham Lincoln, looked up into that craggy face, then moved to center stage. When he spoke, I was amazed how he deepened his voice, rolling his words, sounding very like Dr. Martin Luther King. "Five score years ago," he started, "a great American, in whose symbolic shadow we stand today, signed the Emancipation Proclamation. . . . But one hundred years later, the Negro still is not free."

I held my breath. But T.J. had spoken the truth; he knew this speech backward and forward. *"I have a dream* that one day this nation will rise up and live out the true meaning of its creed: 'We hold these truths to be self-evident: that *all* men are created equal.' *I have a dream . . ."* At the end of Dr. King's "I have a dream" litany, T. J. finally raised his arms proudly. "When this happens, when we allow freedom to ring from every state and every city, we will be able to speed up that day when all of God's children, black men and white men, Jews and Gentiles, Protestants and Catholics, will be able to join hands and sing in the words of the old Negro spiritual, 'Free at last! Free at last! Thank God Almighty, we are free at last!'"

The audience couldn't help it. They burst into applause. But once more, the shadowy figure appeared with that evil water gun. *"Bam! Bam!"* T.J. crumpled to the floor. The spotlight moved to Chris's drawing of the great man, with its ugly gash.

But this time the original "gangbangers" of the cast (minus T.J.) came slowly out of the shadows from both sides, once more in their purple and green uniforms, and stood sorrowfully on either side of the "body" of Dr. King. They looked at one another across T.J.'s crumpled form. The Purples said, "Why do we kill our brightest and our best? Won't we *ever* learn?"

The Greens replied, "Maybe it could start with us." Hands reached out. Purples and Greens touched fist on fist, up, down, then slapped open hands in the familiar street greeting, friend to friend.

The lights dimmed. The actors slipped to the back of the room. Now I expected the lights to come on, and the audience would clap for the wonderful job the boys had done. But the lights stayed dim; no one clapped. The audience sat silently, as if stunned. And then I heard a sound coming from the second row where Florida was sitting.

The sound of someone crying.

43

I got teary myself the next few days, every time I remembered how Florida and Carl had walked slowly along the backdrop after the performance, whispering together, as if seeing Chris's talent for the first time. I don't know what she said to him, but I saw her hug her boy a long time, and he had to brush the back of his arm across his eyes.

But the next day at church, she planted herself in front of me. "Hate to admit it, Jodi Baxter, but you was right about Chris. I didn't see no use for all that scrawlin' he was doin', but after seein' what he did for that play? Now I *know* God got His hand on my son, an' He gonna raise him up to *be* somebody. I'm thinkin' it's time I quit tellin' God what He's s'posed ta do, and just start askin' God to work out His own purpose for my boy, no matter what happens next Wednesday!"

Had to laugh, though, at the message she left on our answering machine on Monday. "I meant what I said yesterday, Jodi, 'bout trustin' God for Chris no matter what happens at the hearing

Wednesday. But that don't mean *you* ain't s'posed to keep prayin' that the judge do right by my boy an' send him home!"

I did pray—as I walked to school, every time I saw Carla, every time I saw Chris's name on the sticky note I'd stuck to the bathroom mirror. But I was also having withdrawal pangs after spending two weeks with "the boys" at the JDC, and now suddenly . . . nothing. It seemed like a dream. *God? What was it all about? Will I ever see those boys again? What's going to happen to T.J. and Ramón and David . . . and Chris?*

As Wednesday's hearing approached, my anxiety level heightened, as if Chris were my own son. What if he was sent away to Joliet, like Jeremy? *Oh God! . . .*

I tried to be a reassuring presence for Carla, offering once more to take her home with me after school if Florida and Carl were delayed for some reason. When the dismissal bell rang on Wednesday, she hung around my desk after the other kids piled out of the room while I packed up my things. "Can I erase the board, Miz Baxter?"

"Sure, honey. Just leave today's homework assignments."

"Hey, Carla," a male voice growled. "Ready to go home?"

Both of us jumped. I hadn't heard the door open. Nor did I expect to hear that voice in my classroom—

"Chris!!!" Carla screamed, scattering papers, books, and stumbling over chairs as she threw herself into her brother's arms. I was so astonished, I just watched in a daze as he swung her around and around, laughing so hard I thought both of them were going to fall over.

When Chris finally did put her down, Carla kept hopping up and down and hanging on him, so that finally he dragged her along like a ball-and-chain to where I stood, my mouth hanging like it'd been propped open with a toothpick. "Hey, Mrs. B." He laughed. "You glad to see me?"

"Glad?!" Now I laughed, grabbing him in a hug. All that fear and worry and prayer and hoping came blubbering out of me all at once. Then I held him at arm's length. "But . . . you're out? Home? Free? Just like that? No sentence?"

"Nope. Judge believed me, that I didn't know nothin' 'bout that robbery till after it happened. Dropped the armed robbery charges. But she tol' me I was headin' for big trouble if I hung out with them gangbangers anymore. Said if I got picked up again, she'd put me in the slammer so fast, my ears would be ringin'." He made a face. "Man, felt as if she'd blistered my behind by the time she got through."

Carla tugged on his arm. "C'mon, Chris! Let's go home!"

"Yeah. My folks are waitin' outside for us. Come on out, Mrs. B, say hi."

I walked down the hall with Chris and Carla and out the school's double doors, once again wondering why I was so sur-prised when God answered our prayers. I'd told Florida, *"Have faith, sister"* . . . but when it came to my own—

"Hey, Jodi!" Florida waved out the passenger-side window of a navy blue Toyota Corolla. "Ya like it? Tol' ya God was goin' ta put a car in that garage of ours. One of Carl's coworkers sold it ta him. Only ninety thousand miles—pretty good for a '97."

"Is it ours, Mama? Really, truly?" Carla pulled open the back-seat door and hopped in. Chris slid in after her.

Carl waved at me from behind the wheel and the car started to move. Florida just laughed. "God is good, Jodi!" she yelled back at me. "All the time, God is good!"

391

THE WEATHER FORGOT TO LOOK at the calendar that week-end. May Day—the first of May—fell on Saturday, but the warm temperatures of April had fallen once more into the forties, along with a chilly rain.

Who cared! We were going to La Fiesta Restaurant that evening with the rest of Yada Yada and our families to party our socks off.

"Where's Josh? Isn't he coming?" Stu asked as she and Estelle piled into our Caravan with Denny, me, and Amanda.

I rolled my eyes. "Yeah, I think so. He disappeared around noon today, said he'd meet us there."

"I hope they don't put us off in some party room an' make us listen to Mr. Enriquez's band piped in or somethin'," Amanda grumped.

"That's why we didn't *say* we were coming as a group. Ricardo told us to come early and just fill up the place!" I glanced at Denny. Sure hoped that worked. The whole point was to listen to Ricardo's mariachi band, dance, eat, laugh. Celebrate!

Because we sure had a lot to celebrate that night—not the least of which was that the whole Hickman family would be there. All five of them.

Most of us arrived around five-thirty, give or take fifteen min-utes. By the time Ricardo arrived with his band at six o'clock—an hour earlier than usual, his "gift" to the restaurant, but really to us—we had filled up half the main room of the restaurant with its festive magenta walls, orange stucco ceiling, and terra cotta tiled floor. The wait staff, attired in white shirts, black pants or skirts, and black string ties, rushed about getting menus, water glasses, and silverware for everyone. When a young server spilled water all over Delores's lap, Delores patted the air in a calming gesture. *"Ninguna prisa. Estamos muy bien."*

"What'd she say?" I murmured to Amanda.

Amanda shrugged. "'No hurry. We are fine' . . . something like that."

By the time most of us had our food—plates heaped with flautas, enchiladas, burritos, quesadillas, and more, along with the necessary rice and beans, tortilla chips, and salsa—the band was well into their first set, a string of mariachi favorites such as *"Tú Sólo Tú"* and *"Volver, Volver."* José was playing a mandolin in the band tonight, and brought the house down with a mandolin solo on *"Dos Arbolitos"*—"Two Little Trees." Amanda clapped so hard I thought she was going to break her chair.

Chanda and her kids arrived late, as usual—though parking her monster SUV couldn't be the excuse tonight, since the restaurant had a good-size parking lot in back. I was happy to see that Rochelle and Conny came too. I craned my neck and skimmed the tables nearby. Was everyone else here? The five Hickmans and Becky filled one table, with Little Andy climbing all over Chris . . . Delores and her four dark-eyed *niños* sat with Avis and Peter . . . Ruth and Ben *noshed* with Yo-Yo and her brothers, who each held a twin . . .

My eyes lingered on the Sisulu-Smith table, where Mark and Nonyameko and their boys laughed and talked with Hoshi and Adele. Would we ever gather like this again, all the Yada Yadas with our families, to celebrate what God had done for us? What would the next year look like for Yada Yada? Becky and Estelle had been added this last year—one saved from prison, the other from the fire. *Sheesh, Lord. If You have new sisters for Yada Yada, couldn't you send them in less dramatic fashion next time?*

I tackled my quesadillas. Well, at least we were all here right now. I should just be thankful for the moment—wait a minute! My head jerked up. Everyone was *not* here.

Josh and Edesa were missing.

I was so flummoxed that I almost missed Ricardo Enriques at the mic, wearing the elegant *charro* suit of the mariachi band, introducing the next song. ". . . for my wife, Delores, who had a birthday this month." He stepped off the small stage and stopped at Delores's table with his large *guitarrón*, making her blush and sending the Enriques children into giggles.

Stu poked me. "Good grief! Yada Yada forgot Delores's birthday!" Huh. Did she mean Yada Yada—or *me*? Whatever. We'd make it up to her.

Ricardo's serenade was beautiful. "What is he singing?" I whispered to Amanda.

"It's '*Las Mañanitas*'," she whispered back. "Something about 'the lovely psalms sung by King David . . . today we sing them to a loved one who happy will be.'"

Delores was beaming when Ricardo rejoined his band on the stage. But once again, Ricardo leaned into the mic. "We have another special occasion to celebrate tonight. A young couple who have an announcement to make, but I don't see them—oh, there they are. Ladies and gentlemen . . ." The entire band began strumming their guitars and violins like a stringed drum roll. ". . . may I present Joshua Baxter and Edesa Reyes."

I clutched Denny's arm. *Young couple? Announcement?* My heart nearly stopped as Josh and Edesa walked into the room hand in hand, as if they'd been waiting in the wings of a stage. Edesa, wearing a lovely white eyelet dress and fringed black-and-rose shawl, smiled radiantly beneath a halo of tiny black ringlets framing her mahogany skin. An audible gasp traveled around the tables. Amanda squealed.

Josh, looking manly and grown up in spite of the sandy hair curling down over the collar of his open-necked shirt, quickly took the mic and grinned our way. "Hey, pipe down, sis. Don't steal my show." They stood together in the spotlight, my tall Caucasian son and the beautiful young black woman from Honduras. Josh put his arm around Edesa. "I asked her to marry me—"

Edesa laughed and took the mic away from him. "And I said yes. In a year or two." She held up her left hand. A simple diamond on her third finger flashed in the light.

The entire room erupted in a volcano of cheers, clapping, squeals, and laughter. I was so stunned I could hardly breathe; Denny's tight grip around my waist didn't help.

The band began to play. Ricardo took the mic. "Josh and Edesa have requested '*Amar Es Para Siempre*'—'To Love Is Forever.' For you gringos, the song says: 'You're my reason, my peace, my faith, my light . . . your smile is the sun of every dawn.'"

The band began to play. Josh took Edesa in his arms and, grinning at each other, they danced. It looked like a combination of a waltz and a salsa, but what do I know? But in the midst of the sweet violins and the floating figures in the spotlight, I heard that still, small Voice in my spirit . . .

Trust Me, Jodi. Trust My Spirit within these young people. Time for you to let go. And—think of the possibilities!

Book Club Questions

1. Have you ever attended a Jewish holiday celebration or ceremony, such as Rosh Hashanah (Jewish New Year), Yom Kippur (Day of Atonement), Purim (Story of Esther, Festival of Lots), Sukkot (Feast of Booths), Pesach (Passover), or Hanukkah (Festival of Light)? Or maybe a ceremony such as a *brit mila* (ceremonial circumcision), *bar mitzvah* (a boy's coming of age), *bat mitzvah* (same for a girl), or a Jewish wedding? Share your experience. In what way might these celebrations enrich our own faith?

2. How do you respond to the "blending" of Uptown Community and New Morning Christian Church? What do you see as the strengths/weaknesses of being a "homogeneous" church? What do you see as the strengths/weaknesses of being a "heterogeneous" church? How important do you think it is to reflect some of the diversity that is the body of Christ within a local body?

3. What name for the blended church in this novel would you have voted for? Why? Have you ever been part of naming a church or group? Was it a good experience? How important is *naming* an organization? A new baby? Your own name?

4. In what way do you identify with Jodi's struggles with Old Jodi responses (worry, stewing, acting first and praying later) and New Jodi responses (praying first, waiting on God, listening for God's voice, seeking counsel from others)?

5. Now that you've read Book 6 in the Yada Yada series, what *growth* do you see in the other characters (e.g., Chanda's attitude toward money; Nony and how she handles her desire to return to South Africa; Yo-Yo and Becky, the "baby Christians"; Florida facing myriad challenges in her family; Avis's seeming "perfection" becoming more "real")? What character's growth do you identify with most—and why?

6. When the Holy Spirit speaks within Jodi, does that seem real to you? How is Jodi learning to hear the Holy Spirit? In what way does God's Spirit speak to you? How can you discern between "God's still, small voice" and your own thoughts and feelings?

7. Denny tells his almost-grown kids that sometimes we have to let go of the past in order to go forward. Are there events or people in your past you are hanging on to that are keeping you from "rolling" with God?

8. Two of the Yada Yada sisters are ex-cons. Both came to faith because someone visited them in prison. In *Gets Rolling*, both Denny and Jodi volunteer at the juvenile detention center

and are surprised at the eager responsiveness of these young "criminals." *Read Matthew 25:34–36 and Hebrews 13:1–3.* What priority do Jesus and Paul give "prison ministry"? Have you ever visited someone in prison? What do you think would happen if you did?

9. In *Gets Rolling*, the Yada Yada Prayer Group begins to reach beyond their group in new ways. Is God nudging *you* to "reach out" beyond your own circle of family and friends? In what ways? What are the challenges for you? How can you support one another?

10. Throughout this book, the Holy Spirit nudges Jodi, *"Think about the possibilities!"* What does that mean for her? What might that mean for you?

For more information about *The Yada Yada Prayer Group* novels or to contact author Neta Jackson, go to www.daveneta.com.

Starting a Yada Yada Prayer Group

*I*s God tugging at your heart to start a prayer group? You feel totally inadequate? God will give you wisdom, you betcha! (Read James 1:5 and ask!) There is no one-size-fits-all formula for putting together a prayer group, but here are a few things to consider:

Prepare yourself...
- First of all, bring your desire to God and pray about it! (Funny how often we skip this step.)
- Ask another sister to pray with you. "If two of you agree . . . about anything, it will be done for them" (Matthew 18:19).
- Read *The Power of Praying Together* by Stormie Omartian (Harvest House). This sister knows what she's talking about!

Then...
- **Share with your pastor** what you want to do. Choose a time for your prayer group that does not conflict with other church meetings or responsibilities.
- **Who needs it?** A prayer group for women in your church is perfectly legitimate. (Many "church" women are lonely or alone.) Or, maybe God is calling you to reach beyond your circle of friends—to neighbors, co-workers, another parent at your child's school, across cultural or racial boundaries. This takes prayer and intentionality.

- **Personally invite other sisters to join you.** (If two of you are in agreement about starting a prayer group, each of you could invite one more. That's four. Then those four each invite one. That's eight. A good beginning!)
- **Meet in your home**—or ask another sister to host. Or share hosting among all the members of the prayer group. Meeting in homes helps create a circle of intimacy. Also, women who are not members of your church may feel more comfortable coming to a home meeting. (But if God directs you to meet at the office, at the park, at a coffee shop, at the jail, or at the church—you do it!)
- **Size?** Don't let the group get too big. Twelve is usually maximum for a small group. Eight to ten is a good number. (If lots of women want to become a part, you may need to divide into two groups! What a wonderful "problem" to have.)
- **Leaders:** Be sure one or two of the sisters who are well grounded in the Word of God are willing to function as leaders/facilitators.

The meeting itself. . .
- **Fellowship.** Allow at least fifteen minutes for women to arrive, get snacks or drinks, and unwind.
- **Worship.** Begin with a scripture, a song, or prayers of praise to get your focus where it needs to be—on God alone.
- **Word/Prayer.** Your group may be a Bible-study-with-prayer, or just a share-and-prayer time. Either way, you will need someone to facilitate so you *do* leave time to pray.
- **Respect!** Agree together that personal things shared in the group are to remain in the group—not fodder for gossip.

(However, if things come up that are too big to handle in the group, the leaders may need to seek outside counsel.)

Last, but not least . . .
- **Pray during the week** for the women who attend the group. Call to check on anyone who is missing; pray for them over the phone if need be.
- **Expect God to do great things** in you and through you as you pray!

TOM CLANCY'S POWER PLAYS: ruthless.com

A Berkley Book / published by arrangement with
RSE Holdings, Inc.

PRINTING HISTORY
Berkley edition / November 1998

The Penguin Putnam Inc. World Wide Web site address is
http://www.penguinputnam.com

ISBN: 0-425-16570-1

BERKLEY®
Berkley Books are published by The Berkley Publishing Group,
a member of Penguin Putnam Inc.,
375 Hudson Street, New York, New York 10014.
BERKLEY and the "B" design are trademarks belonging to Berkley
Publishing Corporation.

PRINTED IN THE UNITED STATES OF AMERICA

10 9 8 7 6 5 4 3 2 1

Tom Clancy's
POWER PLAYS

ruthless.com

CREATED BY
TOM CLANCY
AND
MARTIN GREENBERG

B
BERKLEY BOOKS, NEW YORK

CLEAR AND PRESENT DANGER

The killing of three U.S. officials in Colombia ignites the American government's explosive, and top secret, response . . .

"A CRACKLING GOOD YARN!" —*Washington Post*

THE SUM OF ALL FEARS

The disappearance of an Israeli nuclear weapon threatens the balance of power in the Middle East—and around the world . . .

"CLANCY AT HIS BEST . . . NOT TO BE MISSED!"
—*Dallas Morning News*

WITHOUT REMORSE

The Clancy epic fans have been waiting for. His code name is Mr. Clark. And his work for the CIA is brilliant, cold-blooded, and efficient . . . but who is he really?

"HIGHLY ENTERTAINING!" —*Wall Street Journal*

RED STORM RISING

The ultimate scenario for World War III—the final battle for global control...

"THE ULTIMATE WAR GAME...BRILLIANT!"
—*Newsweek*

PATRIOT GAMES

CIA analyst Jack Ryan stops an assassination—and incurs the wrath of Irish terrorists...

"A HIGH PITCH OF EXCITEMENT!"
—*Wall Street Journal*

THE CARDINAL OF THE KREMLIN

The superpowers race for the ultimate Star Wars missile defense system...

"*CARDINAL* EXCITES, ILLUMINATES...A REAL PAGE-TURNER!" —*Los Angeles Daily News*

THE BESTSELLING NOVELS OF
TOM CLANCY

EXECUTIVE ORDERS

The most devastating terrorist act in history leaves Jack Ryan as President of the United States . . .

"UNDOUBTEDLY CLANCY'S BEST YET."
—*Atlanta Journal & Constitution*

DEBT OF HONOR

It begins with the murder of an American woman in the back streets of Tokyo. It ends in war . . .

"A SHOCKER CLIMAX SO PLAUSIBLE YOU'LL WONDER WHY IT HASN'T YET HAPPENED!"
—*Entertainment Weekly*

THE HUNT FOR RED OCTOBER

The smash bestseller that launched Clancy's career—the incredible search for a Soviet defector and the nuclear submarine he commands . . .

"BREATHLESSLY EXCITING!"   —*Washington Post*

continued . . .

SEVENTEEN

"THIS," NORIKO COUSINS SAID, "IS ONE *AMAZING* room."

Nimec reached for the little blue cube of chalk on the bridge of the pool table.

"So people tell me," he said, rubbing the chalk on the tip of his cue stick with a circular motion. "It's where I come to loosen up, get my thoughts right."

They were in the billiard parlor on the upper level of his San Jose triplex, a painstaking recreation of the smoky South Philadelphia halls where he'd spent his youth ducking truant officers, while pursuing an education of a sort that certainly wouldn't have moved them to reexamine his delinquent status. But in those days Nimec had only cared about one man's approbation, and in attempting to gain it had been a most attentive student . . . or, as he liked to put it, if SATs and grade-point averages could measure one's aptitude at bank shots, combinations, and draw English, he'd have been a shoe-in for a full college scholarship.

At any rate, he'd captured every detail of the old place—at least as filtered through the subjective lens of his recollection—from the cigarette burns on the green baize tabletops to the soda fountain, swimsuit calendars,

milky plastic light fixtures, and Wurlitzer juke stacked with vintage forty-fives circa 1968, a machine he'd picked up for a song at an antique auction and which, after some minor repairs, could still shake and rattle the room to its ceiling beams with three selections for a quarter.

Right now it was belting out Cream's cover of the old blues standard "Crossroads." Clapton's improvised guitar lead slipped around Jack Bruce's bass line like hot mercury, taking Nimec back, conjuring up a memory of his old pal Mick Cunningham, a few years his senior and newly back from a hitch in Nam, bopping between rows of regulation tables, raving about Clapton being *fucking huge* in Saigon.

Mick, who'd had a problem with junk, which had also been fucking huge in Saigon, had been shivved to death in a prison exercise yard in '75 while doing a nickel for attempted robbery, his first offense, a heavy sentence by anyone's standards.

"One ball, over there," Nimec called, waggling his stick at the left corner pocket in the foot rail. He had won the opening break.

Noriko nodded.

He leaned over the side of the table and set the cue ball down within the head string, just shy of the center spot. Then he placed his right hand flat on the table's surface and slid the cue into the groove between his thumb and forefinger. Sighting down the length of the stick, he stroked twice in practice, then drove for the cushions on the opposite rail, giving the cue some left English and follow. The ball banked off the cushion at a slightly wider angle than he'd intended and hit the one thin, but still pocketed it neatly and scattered the triangular rack, leaving him with a couple of easy setups.

"You know what you're doing," Noriko said. When he'd shot, she thought, his eyes had shown the steely concentration of a marksman.

"I ought to," he said. "My father was the sharpest hustler in Philly. Shooting pool is what he did. His dream was that I'd carry on the family trade after he was gone, and I worked hard at learning it."

"Your mother have anything to say about that?"

"She wasn't around, maybe wasn't even alive. Blew the nest when I was three or four. Guess she wasn't impressed that I could count all my toes and fingers." He took his stance again. "Three ball, center pocket."

He aimed and shot, kissing his ball off the eleven. It pocketed with a solid chunk-chunk-chunk.

Noriko looked at him with mild wonder, waiting, twirling her stick vertically between her palms, its butt end on the floor. Nimec had always seemed the epitome of the straight-arrow cop—or ex-cop as the case happened to be. The side of her chief she was seeing was a revelation.

"If you don't mind my asking," she said, "how'd you wind up wearing a badge?"

Nimec faced her and shrugged.

"There was no dramatic turning point, if that's what you're curious about," he said. "Besides playing pool, our other favorite sport in the old neighborhood was hanging out on street corners and getting drunk and starting fights. Everybody wailed on everybody else, seven days a week . . . grown men pushing teenagers through windshields, teenagers pounding on little kids with trash cans, kids smashing bricks down on alley cats. It was hierarchical like that." He shrugged again. "I got tired of it after a while, and suppose the structure and the pay

and the benefits of being a police officer appealed to me. One very typical day I took the exam and passed. A few months later I got my appointment, figured I'd see how it went at the Academy.''

"And it went well," Noriko said.

"Yes," he said. "It did. And sort of killed my budding career as a pool shark."

He turned back to the table, called his next shot, and put it down the chute. On the juke "Crossroads" ended and Vanilla Fudge's rendition of "Keep Me Hangin' On" keyed up. Noriko waited.

"You know Max Blackburn?" Nimec asked, his eyes moving over the table.

"Only by reputation," she said. "He's supposed to be the best at what he does. Ever since Politika, everybody's been talking about him like he's Superman."

Nimec saw a possible combination rail shot at the eleven ball, and lined up for it.

"Max is a good man, no question," he said. "Enjoys connecting the dots to solve a problem, which is why I often use him as a troubleshooter. The past six months he's been assigned to the Johor Bharu ground station, taking care of a range of things, some of which were, shall we say, not for the record. And dicey." He looked over his shoulder at Noriko. "Almost a week ago he dropped out of sight in Singapore, and nobody's heard anything from him since."

She watched him without saying anything.

"Max would never stay out of contact this long unless something were very wrong," Nimec went on. "He's too dependable a man."

He took his shot, but his wrist tensed at the last instant and he stroked the cue harder than he'd wanted. The ball

missed the hole and caromed off the cushion, too fast, its angle too narrow.

"The dicey stuff Blackburn was doing," Noriko said in a slow, considering voice. "Is it something we can talk about?"

"Later, certainly," he said. "First, though, I need to know if you'd be willing to head out to where he is. Or was. And help me track him down."

"I get a team?"

"Just me," Nimec said. "If we need support we can get it from the Johor crew."

She looked at him.

"I'd understand if you don't want to get involved," he said. "Your participation would be strictly voluntary."

"And off the record," she said.

"Right."

There was a pause.

"One question," she said. "Was I asked on this job because I won't stick out in a crowd of Asians, or because of my experience in the field?"

"You sensitive about your ethnicity?"

"Sensitivity has nothing to do with it. I'm half Japanese. It's a logical question. Was it my slanted eyes or my ability?"

Nimec gave her a small, tight smile.

"Both," he said. "Your background might open some doors a little quicker. It might make certain things easier for us in certain situations, and with certain people. It's a leg up. But I wouldn't want you without knowing absolutely that I could trust you with my life, no matter how thick it gets."

She looked closely at his face a while, then nodded.

"I'm in," she said. "What's our game plan?"

"Step one, we finish playing pool. Step two, I clear our trip with Gordian. Step three, we go get our suitcases."

"And if the boss doesn't give us the go signal?"

Nimec considered that a moment.

"Max is my friend," he said. Firmly. "Which means we'd have to skip right on ahead to step three."

Early on the day Roger Gordian was scheduled to depart for Washington, he was joined by Chuck Kirby and Vince Scull in the glass-enclosed veranda of his Palo Alto home. The three of them were seated at a large cane table talking seriously over their breakfast, drinks, papers, and open briefcases. The morning was bright and warm, and there was a flower-scented breeze wafting in through the louvered panels. On a freestanding easel near the table was a chart Gordian had prepared for their meeting. His daughter Julia had stopped by to wish him luck in D.C., and brought the greyhounds with her, and she and Ashley were running them outside on the grass.

Gordian had just finished summarizing his plan, and could already see the unhappiness on Chuck's face. He waited until the attorney wasn't looking and checked his watch, thinking he had a good half hour before his third visitor showed, time enough to deal with Kirby's inevitable objections. Not that it would be easy.

He glanced out at the yard, bracing himself. Whipping downhill in pursuit of a tossed plastic rabbit, the dogs were curves of graceful motion against the greenness of the sprawling lawn. As usual Jack, the brindle male, had outsprinted Jill, the teal-blue female. Though both had been bred for the dog track, and Jill was sleeker and younger, her skittish temperament had disqualified her

from competition, while Jack had run a great many races before he'd been retired.

Julia had gotten the dogs from a greyhound adoption program out of Orange County about six months ago. Had they not been rescued and placed, they would have been euthanized, which was the common practice of racetrack owners when their dogs were no longer competitive, whether for reasons of age, disposition, or any physical deficit that hampered their coursing performance. Gordian had been originally amazed to learn from his daughter that, on average, unadopted track dogs were retired and put down when they were five years old, having barely reached a third of their natural life expectancy . . . and always when he watched their spirited and energetic play, the amazement returned in its fullness.

After all the acts of inhumanity he'd seen people carry out on other people, all the personal losses he'd accumulated as a result of war and terrorism, Gordian didn't know why such waste—lesser by far in the grand scheme of things—ought to surprise him anymore. But it did, and somehow he felt that was better than if it hadn't.

He took a sip of his coffee, and listened to Kirby begin arguing that he was about to commit the worst blunder of his life.

"Gord, I've heard every word you've spoken and tried my damnedest to keep an open mind," Chuck said. "But to do what you've proposed before considering a less extreme strategy—"

"Sometimes you have to lose a limb to preserve the health of the body," Gordian said. "Sometimes survival itself depends on it."

Kirby shook his head. "You're talking about wholesale dismemberment," he said. "Not the same."

Gordian's clear blue eyes were so calm it was almost unsettling. *Like Moses after receiving the Ten Commandments,* Kirby thought.

"Chuck, I haven't said this would be painless. And because you're my friend, I believe that pain is the thing you're trying to spare me," he said. "But I've already accepted it, you see. Mentally and emotionally, I've already let go."

"*Let go?* Of everything you built up over a decade? Everything you've worked your ass off to—"

"If you stop for a second you'll realize you're overreacting," Gordian said with unassailable forbearance.

Chuck turned to Scull. "Vince? Is that what you think? I know your analysis is that Gord's plan is doable, but my question is really whether it *ought* to be done. Whether you're endorsing it."

Scull nodded affirmatively.

"All we're asking is that you give us a chance here," he said. "Listen to what the coach has to say."

"And look at my graphic while you're at it," Gordian said. "Please."

Kirby pressed his lips together, breathed deeply through his nose, and looked. It was an organizational chart of UpLink broken down according to the market areas served by its corporate divisions and subsidiaries.

"As you pointed out yourself, Chuck, we've grown tremendously since the early nineties," Gordian said after letting him study the diagram. "When we secured the contract to provide our GAPSFREE missile-targeting system to the military, I knew the company's future was assured, and realized I was in the position I'd been hoping to reach all my life. I was successful and financially se-

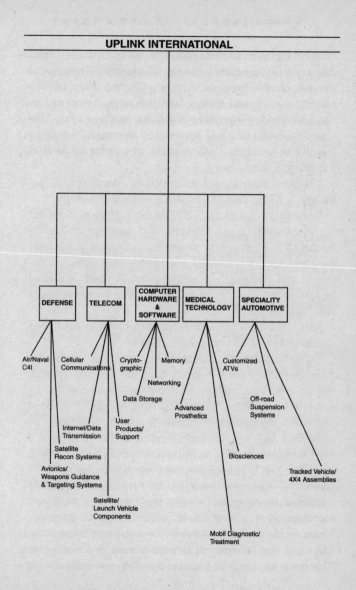

cure . . . my individual needs were taken care of . . . and that opened up a whole range of choices. Choices I'd never been able to consider before. Choices about how to put my money and energy into things that mattered to me, into making a positive difference in this world.'' He rose from the table and approached the easel, gesturing broadly at his chart. ''My mistake was trying to do it in too many different ways.''

''Heaven help us, you're sounding like Reynold Armitage,'' Kirby said. ''And that gives me the chills.''

Gordian smiled wanly. ''We'd be foolish to discount his assessment of our strengths and weaknesses merely because the language in which he's couched it troubles us,'' he said. ''It's always possible to learn from our enemies, and Armitage's essential point is valid. We need to look at the areas where we're bleeding away resources and liquidate them.''

Kirby searched for a response, but Gordian continued speaking before he could think of one.

''Chuck, I'd be confident of our expertise in the defense business even if I didn't have the earnings to back me up,'' he said, placing his hand on the box at the diagram's upper left. ''We're the best because I've been guided by my past experience as a combat pilot, and can remember the sort of technological improvements I'd have wanted when I was in the cockpit flying air strikes over Khe San.'' His hand moved one box to the right. ''I also know our communications unit represents UpLink's tomorrow, irrespective of early-stage profits or losses on our investment . . . and that its potential has yet to be unlocked.'' He paused. ''Those two are our core operations. The ones that are integral to what I want to accomplish. The ones we have to protect. But ask yourself, do we

really belong in computers? Medical tech? Or how about specialty automotive? We only got into *that* because I wanted to make improvements to the factory-standard dune-hoppers we were using in our more rugged gateway locations.''

''Which you did.''

''And now that we've assembled a large fleet of vehicles, and our competition has incorporated our modifications into their own product—and in some cases outclassed us, if you want my frank opinion—why not release the company to management who can give it proper guidance? After all, its profitability as an UpLink company has been been marginal from the very beginning.''

Kirby rubbed the back of his neck.

''I don't know,'' he said. ''Putting aside the automotive unit for a minute, you've done well in the other supposedly nonessential areas. Just as a for-instance, the prosthetics subsidiary meets both of your fundamental criteria for an UpLink company. It helps people and makes money. The artificial limbs it produces are first-rate and have captured a respectable share of the global market—''

''And I'm very proud of that,'' Gordian said. ''But my passion and knowledge don't lay in medicine. I've short-changed the division in terms of personal attention, and have never quite gotten my market bearings. And the R&D budget for our biotech firm eats up something like forty million a year.''

''Which is not at all excessive,'' Kirby said. ''Your people are working on new drug therapies for everything from male impotence to cancer. Cutting-edge research costs money, but the financial and humanitarian payoff

from a single major pharmaceutical advance certainly justifies the initial expenses.''

''I'd agree with you if this were a normal, as opposed to a predatory, business environment,'' Gordian said. ''The fact, however, is that we are under attack and need to focus. Because the medical division is in the red, it is lowering the valuation of UpLink's shares. As it stands, if I want the medical operation to continue, my choices are to either slash its budget or sustain it with the profits we earn from, say, our avionics branch. Money that could otherwise go toward higher-performance transmitters and receivers for our cellular network, or reducing the debts we incurred after the Russian debacle . . . and face it, Chuck, those are just two of many obvious examples I could offer.''

Kirby drank his Bloody Mary and was quiet a while. On the lawn one of the greyhounds had caught the plastic rabbit and flashed behind an alderberry bush, where it was throttling the toy between its jaws. The sound of its squeaker had apparently gotten the other dog envious, and it was jumping antic circles around the hedge. Standing nearby, Ashley Gordian and her daughter looked like they were having fun.

He wished he could have said the same for himself.

''Gord, listen to me,'' Kirby said at length. ''If I read you correctly, your strategy for averting a takeover is based on the assumption that the value of UpLink stock, and thus shareholder confidence, will be boosted once you've gotten back to basics and released capital to your most profitable ventures. Ordinarily I'd agree that it's a sound defensive approach, since a higher corporate valuation will curb sell-offs, force up a hostile acquirer's bid, and make him wonder if his move is worth the trouble

and drain on his checkbook. Except this is *no* ordinary situation. Marcus Caine has already obtained a large chunk of UpLink stock. He's committed. Furthermore, UpLink's market decline has less to do with any real or perceived overdiversification than with investor fears that your stance on crypto will put you way behind rivals who are eager to sell overseas. And since you're obviously not going to sell off your cryptography firm—''

''Who says?'' Gordian interrupted, the patient, forbearing expression back on his face.

. Kirby looked at him a moment, then turned briefly toward Vince Scull.

''Both of you *are* shitting me here, right?'' he said.

Scull shook his head.

Taken aback, Kirby waited a minute before saying anything more.

''Gord, I don't understand,'' he said disbelievingly. ''You've fought so hard to maintain control of your cryptographic technology . . . to turn it over to someone else . . . to chance that it will be distributed abroad . . .'' He spread his hands. ''You've never quit a fight before. I can't believe you'd do it under any circumstances.''

''Not *just* any,'' Gordian said. ''Chuck, I—''

Gordian broke off, his eyes going to the sliding doors that opened from the house to the veranda. Andrew, his domestic, had appeared with Richard Sobel, the third guest he'd been expecting for breakfast.

''Sir, I've shown Mr. Sobel in as you asked,'' Andrew said.

''Morning,'' Sobel said, tipping the other men a wave.

Gordian motioned him to an empty chair at the table. ''You're right on schedule, Rich,'' he said. ''Join the party.''

Kirby gave Gordian a level glance, saw his spreading grin, and suddenly understood everything.

"You can relax now, Chuck," Gordian said, his smile growing even larger. "Our White Knight has arrived to save the day."

EIGHTEEN

THE FAX WAS ON SIAN PO'S DESK WHEN HE CAME INTO work that morning—a dispatch out of Central HQ advising of a nationwide police search for an American named Max Blackburn, and accompanied by a passport photograph and some sketchy details about the circumstances of his disappearance. All personnel were to be on alert for information regarding his whereabouts, and immediately relay it to CID. The same notice, Sian Po knew, would have been forwarded to the divisional headquarters at Clementi, Tanglin, Ang Mo Kio, Bedock, and Jurong, as well as to hundreds of command center and vehicular computer stations over the Incident Based Information System.

Wishing to remain undisturbed, the commander immediately buzzed his receptionist, instructed her to hold his calls for the next half hour, and read the dispatch over a cup of green tea. It contained only a few brief paragraphs about last week's mysterious scene outside the Hyatt, and they conveyed little that was new to him. However, the material about the parties involved was most intriguing. There were fuller descriptions of the men who had accosted the American . . . and most importantly, there was the profile of Blackburn himself. Printed beside

his photo, it included data about his age, general physical chacteristics, and employer, a satcom outfit called UpLink International operating in the Johor area.

Sian Po drank his tea and reflected back on his stroll in the park with Fat B. What in the world was the club owner into? His nose told him it was something big.

He set down his cup, thinking. The report was as interesting for what it didn't reveal as what it did, and had put several questions into his mind. There was nothing to indicate where the facts about Max Blackburn and the other men had come from. And no mention of the woman Sian Po had heard was involved. Why? Could it be that she was the source of the information? That she'd been located and was perhaps being kept under wraps? CID investigators were customarily tight-lipped, quick to mark their turf, and loath to accept assistance from other departments in the Force. It was conceivable those bastards knew where she was or had her in custody—or under police protection, whichever. If they did, they would not share that secret with anyone at ground level. Not as long as they could help it.

Still, Sian Po had his useful contacts, including a supervisor in intelligence who would be glad to talk to him for a cut of his own payoff from Fat B. And Fat B had strongly hinted the sum would be considerable. He had to be careful, though. Ask what he needed to ask without divulging too much in exchange. The main thing was to find out about the woman, find out where she was. For now that would be a sufficiently juicy morsel to pass along. He would see what else might develop afterward.

Placing the report on his desk beside his teacup, he reached for the phone and made his call.

• • •

Nimec managed to catch Gordian in his office at a quarter past eleven in the morning. The boss was rushed, and expectedly so; he'd arrived late after a business parley at his home, and only planned to stay long enough to take care of some odds and ends before leaving for the airport. Vince Scull, Chuck Kirby, Richard Sobel, and Megan Breen—the four of whom were flying to D.C. as passengers in Gordian's Learjet—had already driven on ahead in a company car, and the hurried atmosphere had made it all the more difficult for Nimec to tell him about Blackburn . . . and then persuade him to green-light a trip overseas so he could look into what was going on with Max.

Harder than either, however, was disclosing that he'd let Max undertake a hidden probe into Monolith-Singapore's books without first seeking Gordian's consent . . . the unstated but clearly understood reason being that had it been a sure thing the idea would have been scotched out of hand.

Gordian's reaction to the news about Max—and Nimec's admission—was a predictable mix of anger, dismay, and concern.

"It's beyond me how you could have been part of something this reckless, Pete," he said. He was leaning forward with his right elbow on his desk blotter, his head tilted slightly downward, rubbing the corner of his eye with his index finger. "Completely beyond me."

Nimec looked at him from across the desk.

"I'm sorry," he said. "I won't try to justify it. But consider the big picture. Marcus Caine had been using the crypto bill to impale you in the press. And Blackburn believed Monolith was engaged in a series of illegal business practices and hiding evidence of it in Singapore. It was reasonable to suspect some of those activities might

have been aimed at causing damage to UpLink—''

"So instead of coming to me with those suspicions, the two of you launched a caper that could have easily sunk us in quicksand. And likely has, from what you're saying.''

Nimec was quiet for a minute, then nodded.

"Yes, we should've notified you, and we didn't,'' he said. "It was a stupid mistake. And I'm afraid to think about how dearly Max may be paying for it.''

Silence.

Gordian was still leaning against the edge of his desk, massaging the corner of his eye with his fingertip.

"Let's back up a second,'' he said. "You're convinced Blackburn's in some kind of trouble?''

Nimec gave him another nod.

"And you want to go extricate him from it.''

"If I can,'' Nimec said. "With some help.''

Gordian shook his head. "It's tough for me to believe Caine's people would go so far as to harm Max. Regardless of what he might have gotten wind of.''

Nimec moved his shoulders. "We can't make assumptions about how much Caine might or might not know. Or who his people are. Or what sort of people *they're* involved with.''

Gordian placed both hands on his desk and studied them, his lips pressed together.

"It's a hell of a time for me to make this sort of decision,'' he said, looking up at Nimec. "I'm flying to Washington in a little while. And I've got my mind on other matters beside that.''

"Caine's hostile bid,'' Nimec said.

"Yes.''

There was another period of silence. It fell over them with a weight that was almost palpable.

"All right," Gordian said finally. "See what you can do. But if something comes up, you'd damned well better consult with me. I lost too many good men and women in Russia to tolerate anyone in this organization taking unnecessary chances."

Nimec breathed.

"Thanks," he said, rising from his chair. "I only regret not being able to join you in D.C. You'll have a crack security detail, but it's going to be a madhouse."

Remaining seated, Gordian looked at him and shrugged dismissively.

"Just be careful to watch your own back," he said. "My guess is I won't be facing anything deadlier than potshots from reporters."

Nimec offered a thin smile.

"Probably right," he said. "But somebody's got to worry."

"Marcus, what's wrong?"

"Nothing."

"Obviously *something's* wrong."

"Give it time. I need to relax."

Lying in bed with Caine amid the restored deco furnishings of their room at the Hotel De Anza, her face beside his on the pillow, her naked body pressed against him, Arcadia Foxworth licked her fingertip and slid her hand under the sheets, tracing a slow line of moisture down his stomach.

He lay there, tense and unresponsive.

"Tell me," she said, raising her head off the pillow. "Is there somebody else?"

"Only you," he said distractedly.

"Well . . ."

"Well, what?"

"There's your wife," she said. "She's one I know of, anyway."

He broke off his thoughts and looked at her.

"What's that supposed to mean?" he said. "Must you be jealous of Odeille?"

"Hardly," she said. "It isn't important what you do with her when we're not together. But when we are, I want you here. Thinking about me."

"Arcadia," he said, "let's not argue."

"I'm not arguing."

"Then let's not continue with whatever sort of conversation we're having. I've been under a great deal of pressure lately. That's all there is to it."

She looked at him, easing closer over the mattress, the bare white flesh of her breasts against his shoulder.

"Okay," she said, taking him into her hand, tightening her fingers around him beneath the sheet. "Usually, though, it's pressure that gets you going."

He lay there on his back, very still, staring past her face at the ceiling. What was he supposed to say? That his dealings with Nga had taken him over a line he'd never expected to cross? That he'd been coerced into ordering the *murder* of Roger Gordian—and Lord knew who else would be on that plane—and would soon have blood on his hands? Would *that* help her understand why he wasn't feeling especially aroused?

"Stop," he said abruptly. "It isn't happening."

"I've come two thousand miles from New York to be with you," she said.

''Nobody twisted your arm.''

Her eyes widened. She pushed away from him, her hand retreating from where she'd had it, grabbing the sheet, tugging it up over her chest.

''You son of a bitch,'' she said.

Caine threw his legs over the side of the bed and strode naked across the room to the chair on which he'd put his clothing. He kept his back to her as he silently got dressed.

''Aren't you going to say anything?'' Arcadia said. She had sat up against the headboard.

He waited until he was fully clothed before turning to answer.

''Yes,'' he said. ''I'm thinking that you're right. I should be honest about what's bothering me. You *deserve* honesty.''

She looked at him.

He didn't know why he said what next came out of his mouth, other than that it made him feel better, released some of his pent-up anxiety and frustration.

''You're lovely, Arcadia. First-class. But you've walked a long road from the streets of Argentina, and I like my women younger,'' he said. ''The simple fact is that you don't excite me anymore.''

Her mouth actually dropped open. She looked as if she'd been slapped.

It occurred to Caine that he might have gone further than he'd intended, that there was little chance she would ever want to see him again after this ugly scene.

Once more over the line, he thought. Yet strangely, it didn't seem to matter . . . although *why* it didn't was a question he'd have to consider later on.

"Don't bother yourself about the hotel tab, I'll take care of it," he said.

And turned from her shocked face, opened the door, and left the room.

NINETEEN

"LOCAL TRAFFIC, LEARJET TWO ZERO NINE TANGO
Charlie, ready to go off Runway Two at the east end,"
Gordian was saying into his mike, informing any nearby
multicom users of his departure. The small private airfield
UpLink shared with a handful of other Silicon Valley
firms had no ground radio facilities, but the nationwide
advisory frequency of 122.9 was often monitored by pilots, and his practice was to broadcast his takeoff and
landing intentions as a courtesy to them and a hedge
against unwanted—and potentially disastrous—midair
encounters.

Not that it looked as if there would be anything but
smooth flying today. With a clear blue sky, high ceiling,
and gentle winds, Gordian was anticipating a takeoff into
ideal weather conditions. His only fillip of concern, and
very slight concern at that, had come when he'd lowered
his flaps while taxiing and noticed the hydraulic-pressure
gauge drop off a hair more readily than normal.

This was something a less cautious pilot probably
wouldn't have detected, nor found of much interest if he
had, and quite understandably so. Gordian himself
couldn't see any reason to worry. Though the aircraft's
flaps, speed brakes, and landing gear all operated on the

same hydraulic line, they would continue to respond properly, if perhaps a bit slowly, with the fluid level on the low side. Further increasing his confidence was the knowledge that his engine instrument-and-crew-alerting system—or EICAS—annunciators would flash a warning to indicate a problem with the circuit, serious or otherwise. And they had remained dark.

Still, he couldn't help but feel disappointed in Eddie, who'd inspected the plane the day before, and was usually an even bigger stickler for safety than he was . . . too thorough to let even a minor abnormality slip past his attention.

But later for that, he thought. As always in the moments before going airborne, Gordian could feel the sky exerting an almost physical pull. Moving the throttles forward, he concentrated on the EFIS panel in front of him, his eyes shifting between its flat-screen primary flight displays—arranged in the same "standard T" of old-fashioned analog instruments—and the bars of his ITT gauge, which measured the internal temperature of the turbofans. A hot start could lead to engine failure within seconds, making the ITT readout one to watch carefully.

Nothing to trouble him on that score; the turbos were operating well within standard limitations.

Its compressors whining and sucking in air, its wheels rumbling over the tarmac, the Learjet rolled up the centerline straight as an arrow. Gordian felt the shove of acceleration, and then the excitement that had accompanied each of the hundreds of takeoffs he'd flown over the past thirty years. He snapped his eyes to the window and quickly observed the distance markers along the runway—a feature as rare to civilian fields as it was common to military ones, and emplaced at Gordian's direction as a nod to his fighter-jock days.

Returning his attention to the EFIS, Gordian saw his virtual airspeed bug indicate that he had reached 104 knots, go-or-no-go speed. He conducted a last-minute check of the crucial displays. Everything was running smoothly, the bank of caution lights still out, his system readings A-okay. *Go.*

He released the stick, gripped the yoke with both hands, and rotated the jet to a seven-point-five-degree nose-up angle for liftoff. There was a slight jolt and another familiar tingle of excitement as his wheels left the pavement. His hands on the control column, Gordian increased his pitch to ten degrees and continued his ascent.

After several seconds he again looked outside to confirm what the altimeter and his own physical sensations had already told him. He had reached a positive rate of climb, the ground rapidly dwindling beneath him, the undivided blue of the sky pouring into his windshield.

His gear and flaps up, Gordian accelerated to two hundred KIAS, or over three hundred miles per hour. At a thousand feet he would very gradually trim airspeed until he attained cruising altitude.

Right now, though, it was time for an announcement to his passengers.

He switched on the cabin intercom.

"Vince, Megan, Rich, we're on our way," he said. "ETA in D.C. is nine o'clock. So make yourselves comfortable and try not to discuss business. There'll be plenty of time for that later." He reached for the "off" switch, thought about the chattery teeth Scull inevitably got when he flew, and added a few words for his benefit. "There's a bottle of Glenturret in the wet bar for anyone who wants it. Courtesy of your captain. Later, folks."

Smiling a little, feeling easier with himself than he had in weeks, Gordian cut the intercom and settled back into his pilot's chair for the trip.

In a drawing room at the Leominster country club in Southampton, Reynold Armitage was gazing out the window at the ocean. It was a drab, chill day in eastern Long Island, and the threat of rain had driven the gulls close to shore. They wheeled in erratic circles, their wings tearing ragged holes in the stationary film of mist that had settled over the beach and jetties. Distantly across the water, Armitage could see a lighted buoy twinkling bright and red.

Ensconced in the armchair opposite him, William Halpern released a long, heaving sigh. Wearing dark flannel pants and a herringbone blazer, he was a spare, white-haired man in his mid-fifties with an undershot chin and virtually neutral complexion.

"Awful outside, isn't it?" he said in a haughty Connecticut Yankee accent. "The forecast was for sunny and warm, you know."

Using his wheelchair's joystick control, Armitage swiveled around to face his host. He was feeling winded from the dampness, which exacerbated the respiratory problems associated with his condition. The mere act of breathing was a reminder of the limitations of his failing body. Yet from the way the president and chief executive of MetroBank seemed to take the bad weather as a personal affront, one would think *he* was the man in poor health.

"It's difficult to make predictions for the shore," Armitage said. "Don't bother yourself about it, William. I'm hardly up to a stroll on the beach, and found the ride in your corporate helicopter to be quite entertaining."

"I'm glad," Halpern said, although he still had the look of someone who had booked reservations at an exclusive restaurant and found his meal to be a cold disappointment. He glanced out the window again and then settled back, appearing resigned and vaguely disgusted, as if realizing there were no one in charge of the climate to whom he might complain. "I wanted a discreet and quiet spot for our meeting, you see."

Armitage said nothing. There were, he thought, any number of quiet places in Manhattan where they could have met with greater convenience. But even in their elevated circles a Leominster membership was a glowing symbol of status, and Halpern obviously liked to showcase it. He was also well aware of the attention being paid to Marcus Caine's grab for UpLink voting stock, and with MetroBank retaining a significant percentage of the company, wouldn't want to start rumors flying by being seen with Roger Gordian's most noted media critic.

No, there was nothing mysterious about Halpern's desire to meet where they were. The real question for Armitage was why he'd wanted to get together in the first place. And with their mannerly preliminaries out of the way, he wasn't about to kill time waiting for an answer.

"So," he said. "What gossip about the financial community can we exchange? Let's think of something blisteringly hot and in the news. Something that gets flashbulbs popping. Shall we?"

Halpern looked at him.

"There's Monolith and UpLink," Armitage said with an arid little smile. "Not to mention UpLink and Monolith."

Halpern seemed perplexed by his sarcasm. "I've sat down with some of the men on MetroBank's executive

board to discuss liquidating our UpLink shares," he said. "Prior to a formal meeting, you understand."

"And?"

"The consensus to go ahead with the sell-off hasn't materialized as I'd expected."

"Interesting," Armitage said.

"It gets more interesting," Halpern said. "As you know, I have no allegiance to Roger Gordian, and think his mission to save the world by planting a wireless telephone booth in every garden is nothing but horse crap."

"You're mixing metaphors," Armitage said. "And being a tad reductionist about his goals, wouldn't you say?"

Halpern shrugged. "Call it what you will, I am concerned with MetroBank's stake in his corporation only insofar as its profitability, or lack of same. But there are directors on the board who feel a personal loyalty to the man, and have been reluctant to part ways with UpLink despite the diminishing returns on our investment. Before yesterday, though, I'd convinced most of them that hanging tight would be an abdication of their fiduciary responsibilties."

"And what's changed that?"

"Not 'what,' but 'who,'" Halpern said. "Gordian himself phoned three senior executives. He requested they hold off on considering any offer from Marcus Caine until he's had a chance to meet with them."

Armitage wondered if he was expected to be surprised.

"A sensible preemptive move," he said. "And one with nothing behind it. As long as UpLink's value continues to deteriorate, your board is obliged to take a serious look at Marcus's bid. Money, not loyalty or misplaced faith in Roger Gordian, is what will count in the final tally."

"And Gordian has promised to address shareholder doubts about UpLink's future at his press conference tomorrow," Halpern said. "He assured the directors he would be making a major, positive announcement. And that they would, at the very least, want to reassess their options after hearing what he has to say."

This time Armitage raised his eyebrows.

"I thought his reason for going to Washington was to protest the Morrison-Fiore legislation," he said.

"So did I," Halpern said. "And I'll tell you something else. His top securities attorney caught a red-eye out to San Jose last night. Canceled all his other appointments at the last minute."

"How do you know?"

Halpern stared at him.

"I have my contacts," he said, shrugging again. "You . . . and Marcus . . . can take my word for it. Something's in the air."

Armitage inhaled. His chest felt tight. If the feeling persisted, he would have to page his nurse into the room and be administeed a respiratory dilator. He felt a sudden bolt of hatred, and wasn't sure why. Nor was he even certain toward whom it was directed.

Outside the window a seabird emitted a shrill, ribboning cry as it plunged through the low veil of fog.

He looked at Halpern.

"I appreciate the tip, William," he said. "But the one thing you haven't told me is where you come down in this."

Halpern crossed his legs and was silent a moment.

"We've known each other for years, and you've always given me sound financial advice," he said finally. "But as you said yourself, this business is about money,

not loyalty or faith . . . and like all bankers, I'm an agnostic."

"Meaning you'll be listening to Roger Gordian's statement before deciding whether to stay behind the bid."

Halpern nodded, brushing a speck of lint off his trousers.

"Yes," he said without hesitation. "And very closely."

On a stubby finger of rock jutting off his island base's ocean side, Kersik stared out across the benighted water at the lights of Sandakan Harbor. Restless, he had left camp alone, thinking the freshness of the breeze would somehow dispel his somber mood, but instead it had made him feel worse. He supposed it was his knowledge of the violence that soon would be launched from his pristine shoreline, the deaths that were inevitably to come. There would be dozens, perhaps hundreds . . . if not many, many more. For a just cause, yes, or anyway a cause in which he squarely believed. But wasn't that the same ancient, self-righteous madness which drove every act of war?

Men fought. They had always fought, whether armed with stones, arrows, guns, or nuclear torpedoes. And they found their reasons. Indeed, Kersik sometimes felt that belief in a cause was nothing but a dark funnel into which both heroes and villains leaped with equal certitude, all tumbling together like clown players in a circus. Like the man who presently ruled Indonesia as if he were a Javanese king, parsing the nation's wealth out to his courtesans . . . like his predecessor, and Suharto, and those who had come before them, Kersik saw himself as being on the right side of history. Zhiu Sheng, Nga, Luan, they too were *right* from their individual perspectives—and

yet the forces that had moved them into alignment were far too complex to be defined by absolutes.

Kersik's brow creased above his bushy eyebrows. Wasn't the judgment of right or wrong only a matter of who survived to render the verdict when the smoke cleared and the spilled blood of the dead was washed away? He had renounced his allegiance to his country's government and was about to place himself in defiance of ASEAN, Japan, and the United States. The entire world, really. Before all was said and done, he would be called a rogue, an international pariah. And what would he think of *himself* in the end? Might a division ultimately form in his own mind . . . half of him feeling validated, half condemned?

Kersik gazed out at the lights of a city that in the last 150 years had been governed once by the Germans, twice by the British, and exploited by traders, gunrunners, and timber lords from diverse corners of the globe. That during World War II was invaded by the Japanese and leveled by American bombs . . . and that now literally and ironically held the keys to the fate of both those nations.

Kersik stood and thought and looked out across the ocean swells . . . and after a while became dimly aware of a scurrying in the mangrove thicket behind him.

He turned, snapping on his flashlight, his right hand falling to the holstered Makarov at his waist. The sound had not really alarmed him; the only men on the island were the Thai's seawolves and his own commando units, and both groups had lookouts posted along the shore. Still, he was beyond all else a soldier . . . and good soldiers had cautious habits.

He trained the beam of his flash at eye level, saw nothing but smooth, gangling mangrove trunks and prop roots,

and lifted it higher. Just below the leaf cover, a flying lemur clung to the bark and watched him with huge orb-like eyes.

For a moment Kersik experienced a queer, almost dizzying transference, imagining how he might appear to the strange little creature—clumsily threatening, out of place, himself the real alien. He withdrew his hand from his pistol grip as if it were red-hot, feeling an intense and incomprehensible guilt.

The creature studied him for another second or two with its perfectly round eyes, and then spread its flight membranes and kited off into the forest blackness.

Shaken and hardly knowing why, Kersik stepped into the brush and walked back toward camp.

As one of the test pilots of the original Learjet had told Gordian about its maiden run, the flight had gone better than expected and he'd expected it to go well.

That about said it for the trip to Washington.

Now, approaching Dulles International Airport at 8,500 feet and 350 knots downwind, autopilot off, the night sky clear and moonlit, Gordian cross-checked the Global Positioning System and VOR windows on his horizontal-situation indicator for a course fix, then radioed ahead to request airspace clearance.

"Washington, Learjet Two Zero Nine Tango Charlie, over Alexandria VOR at eight thousand, landing Dulles. Squawking one two zero zero," he said, finishing his initial communique with the standard numeric identification code for civilian aircraft.

A moment later the traffic controller responded, providing the computer code by which his radar-beacon system would differentiate Gordian's plane from other

aircraft in the vicinity as it was guided down.

"Good evening Nine Tango, Washington Approach. Squawk five zero eight one and ident. Radar contact established, cleared into Washington Class B airspace. Descend and maintain four thousand."

"Roger. Learjet Nine Tango, squawking five zero eight one. Understand cleared into the TCA. Out of eight for four."

The buildings and illuminated landing strips of Dulles in sight below, Gordian trimmed power and entered a steady sink, carefully monitoring the instrument panel, making small heading corrections as he descended. Less than ten minutes later he again contacted the man on the ground floor.

"Approach, Learjet Nine Tango, level at four."

"Learjet Nine Tango, roger. Am familiar and would like Runway One Four Left."

"Cleared for approach One Four Left," the Approach controller began after a brief pause, then vectored and sequenced him into the lineup of arriving aircraft.

Not at all to Gordian's surprise, Approach concluded the transmission by informing him he would have to hold and circle at four thousand feet. In D.C. and other major cities, the terminal environment was often stacked with inbound traffic, in which instances one could look forward to a tedious wait.

He re-engaged the auto and informed his passengers they would have time for at least a couple of Scull's equally tedious jokes.

It was twenty-five minutes before the controller assigned a further descent altitude and then handed Gordian over to the tower—not as long as it might have taken, although he was still glad to be out of the pattern. The

repetitive banking maneuver had been tiresome, and gobbled up more fuel than he would have preferred.

He switched to the tower frequency and identified himself.

"Learjet Two Zero Nine Tango Charlie cleared to land Runway One Four Left," the ATC acknowledged.

Gordian took the wind headings from him, rogered, and then read down the items on his computerized final checklist, mentally ticking them off to the line above Gear and Flaps. Although it sometimes seemed he had memorized the various checklist tasks when he was still in diapers, Gordian conscientiously ran through it before, during, and immediately after each flight. To do otherwise would be to deny his own fallibility, and that was not a mistake he ever intended to make—most especially not at the risk of people's lives.

Gordian returned his attention to the HSI, saw that he was coming in range of his final landing fix, and prepared to resume his checklist procedures. At just below six hundred feet and about a mile west of the runway, he was set to enter the base leg, and could see the brightly lit sprawl of the airfield in easy detail.

He pulled down the lever to deploy his wheels, expecting to feel the mild thump of the gear mechanisms lowering through the doors.

Instead the red master warning light suddenly illuminated.

The landing gear alerts on his EICAS began to flash.

An electronic alarm tone sounded from an overhead speaker.

Gordian's eyes widened. The breath catching in his throat, he pulled the landing gear handle up, then down again.

The red lights kept blinking.

The horn kept blatting into the silence of the cockpit with deadly insistence.

Gordian felt his heart clench as the ground rushed closer and closer up on him, the runway spooling toward his windshield.

The wheels, he thought.

With less than two minutes to go until he hit the ground, the landing gear hadn't lowered.

TWENTY

WHETHER JAMMED TIGHTLY INTO THE COACH SEC-
tion of some ready-for-the-scrapyard commercial jetliner,
or, as was presently the case, hugged gently by a leather
club seat in Gordian's state-of-the-art executive Learjet,
Vince Scull was a white-knuckle flier all the way, no
matter that he had logged hundreds of hours in the air
fulfilling his professional responsibilities at UpLink.

A lot of risk-assessment people, especially those whose
job it was to research international markets, relied on
second- or third-hand source material—news reports, so-
ciological studies, statistical reviews, and so on. Scull,
however, thought that was for slackers who might as well
have spent their time picking their underwear out of their
cracks as writing up analyses. In his opinion, if you
wanted to learn about a place, you went there, breathed
the air, ate the food, and if you were lucky, kissed a few
of the local *frauleins* or *signoras*. And, unfortunately, if
you wanted to get to the foreign country you wanted to
learn about, you had to fly.

So he flew. Which didn't mean he had to like it, or
pretend to anyone else that zipping around the world the
way he did merited flight wings, unless maybe they were
the ones that belonged to that Greek kid Zorro or Aesop

or whoever it was that went too close to the sun and got his tail feathers fried.

It was during the takeoffs and landings that Scull always had his worst anxiety attacks, mainly because somebody had once told him they were the times at which the airfoils were under the most stress from physical forces . . . not that he knew shit about physics or flying, except that it seemed there *were* more accidents at those critical stages than when the planes were under way, so maybe there was something to what he'd heard.

Be that as it may, the reason Scull was now gripping the armrest of his seat like a convict in the electric chair waiting for somebody to turn on the juice was that Gordian was making his final approach into Washington, one of those very stages of air travel that scared the living crap out of him, never mind the boss was an Air Force-certified Flying Ace. It was also why he was crooning a jumbled medley of Sinatra hits under his breath—*the summer wind came blowin' in across New York, New York, ring-a-ding and doobie-doo*—serenading himself with old standards being another tried-and-true Scullian method of coping with tension and blocking the unwanted from his mind.

He did not care if he would have to endure ribbing about his nervousness from Megan Breen, who was sitting just across the narrow aisle to his right. Nor did he care if he heard about it from Nat Sobel or Chuck Kirby, who were immediately behind him, bullshitting with Meg like a couple of makeout artists at a cocktail party instead of helpless prisoners of a tin can that just happened to be capable of shooting through the troposphere at close to Mach One, the fucking speed of sound.

All he really *did* care about was reaching *terra firma*

in one piece, and the rest of them could keep the Glen-turret, which had admittedly gone down nicely, although his personal favorite malt was this brand from far western Scotland called Bunahabhain, an unpronounceable name that always left his mouth sounding like something Ralph Kramden might have said when Alice caught him red-handed in a lie. . . .

Clutching his seat, singing quietly off-key with his eyes shut, Scull was trying his best to remain oblivious to the plane's descent when a sound from the cockpit—the sliding door to which was partially open because Gord had been talking to Chuck about something earlier in the fight—bored into his awareness like a drill bit.

He snapped open his eyes and peered into the cockpit. From the position at which he was sitting, he could see about half of Gordian's back, and about the same amount of the pilot's console. The boss didn't seem to be in any kind of panic, but that didn't mean anything. This was the guy with the cool head and bombardier eyes, the guy who had been released from a five-year getaway at the Hanoi Hilton, their special all-the-torture-you-can-take package, with his head high and his back straight and his lips sealed as tightly as the day of his involuntary check-in. This was definitely the guy you wanted beside you in the proverbial foxhole, and if something was wrong, you would never be able to tell from looking at him.

But the noise coming from the cockpit, the noise was like an electronic version of an automobile horn, a grat-ingly repetitive *blaat-blaat-blaat* that damned well sounded to Scull like a warning alarm.

He looked at Megan, glanced around at Richard and Chuck. All three of them were also trying to see into the cabin, and their faces said they were, if not quite as

worried as he was, then still pulling high Nielsen distress ratings.

Blaat-blaat-blaat-blaat . . .

"Anybody know what the hell's going on?" he asked in a loud voice. "Christ in a barrel, what's that *noise?*"

The others were silent.

Scull swallowed. His palms felt suddenly moist. And no goddamned wonder.

Coming from a plane full of talkers, that mute silence had frightened him more than just about anything he could have imagined.

Gordian breathed, filling his lungs with oxygen, his mind working rapidly. He was belting toward the runway at over a hundred feet a second without wheels, a situation that would have the gravest consequences unless he took action to change it. Which left no room for indecision.

Think logically, he told himself. *The problem's evident, now isolate its cause.*

He recalled the unusually quick drop in hydro pressure when he'd extended the flaps on takeoff. Yet if the pump motor had failed, the crew-alerting system would have detected it. Ditto if the sensors had gotten readings that indicated a low fluid level in the reservoir. Furthermore, the compressed nitrogen inside the fluid accumulator was supposed to provide supplemental pressure to system components in the event of leakage . . . within a certain threshold. When the fluid loss from a specific component became too great, or there was too much air in the line, it would be unable to keep up with demand and bring the pressure back to where it should be.

Meaning what? Gordian gnawed his bottom lip. Meaning he was looking at a drastically reduced fluid level—and therefore a sudden and unmanageable demand—in a

particular area of the system, possibly the landing gear actuator cylinder. The gear had a mechanical uplock that wouldn't release without hydro power, even with the lever in the down position . . . and there was no manual override.

Okay, next. Options.

He could Mayday the ground facility, wait for them to foam the runway and bring fire and medical crews to the scene should he need to make a gear-up landing. But having to circle the field had depleted his fuel reserve, and foaming took time. While he had enough Jet A in his nacelles to safely abort and execute a go-round, he didn't believe he could stay in the air long enough for the process to be completed. In which case he would have to belly onto the pavement, something that would very likely spark an explosive engine fire and leave little but ashes for the ground crews to clean up.

Come on, come on. You want to avoid a messy outcome, get to the essence of all this.

He had compromised hydraulics. Gear assemblies stuck in the up position. And an urgent need to bring them down.

No, wait. Not down. Off.

He had to be precise in his thinking. What the hydraulic pressure really did was keep the gear assemblies in the retracted position by making them rest on the uplocks. If he could only get the assemblies *off* the uplock brackets, their own weight load would finish the task, causing them to drop through the well doors. In other words, they would bring *themselves* down.

Gravity.

Gravity was the problem, and it was also the solution. Gordian reached for a selector button under his multi-

function display and punched up the G-meter screen. The bar was level at one-G—which meant the gravitational force on the aircraft was "normal," or equivalent to that of an object at rest on the ground.

Shooting a glance at the display, Gordian reduced flaps, gripped the control column with both fists, and pulled back on it abruptly, tilting up the nose of the plane, hauling it into a sharp climb. An instant later he shoved *forward* on the column, dropping the plane toward the runway again.

Gordian's stomach lurched. The airframe shimmied around him. The roller-coaster bump in altitude thrust him back and down into his seat, then up and out so violently he would have smashed into the windshield had he not been strapped in.

So far, so good.

He reached for the landing gear lever, not bothering to check the MFD. With his bottom floating off his seat as if he were being hauled up by an invisible hand, Gordian already knew he was at zero-G. And if he'd reckoned correctly, he would not be the only thing floating.

The gear would be too.

Right off the uplock.

Praying that God, Sir Isaac Newton, and his own common sense were at oneness, he pulled the lever down for the third and last time.

The wide band of his seat belt cutting into his flabby middle, his eyeglasses first clamping down on the bridge of his nose and then flying off his face, his thin fringe of hair flattening out and then sticking straight up, Scull felt like the ball in some maniacal game of ping-pong.

Buffeted by wildly shifting Gs, the cabin pitched and

shook. Magazines swept past him in a tumultuous flap. His eyes large with fear and confusion, he saw Megan's briefcase shoot up the carpeted aisle like a stone skipping over water, followed by a file folder Chuck Kirby had been perusing behind her, paper spewing from inside it. A banana somebody had been eating was next, then a pen that fired past like a small missile. He heard bottles of liquor, soda, and spring water clank and rattle in the wet bar, heard Richard Sobel uncharacteristically shouting out invective. Carry bags whumped against the interior of overhead storage bays.

"*Shit!*" he screamed, attaching his own contribution to Sobel's sting of epithets.

Suddenly he heard a thump under his feet.

Several thumps.

Pure, unalloyed terror leaped into his throat, jetted icily up his spine.

He stopped yelling.

Certain he was going to perish, Scull suddenly remembered that he wasn't alone, remembered there were four other people in the plane with him and—call him a dinosaur chauvinist, what was the fucking difference now anyway?—realized one of them was a woman who might need comforting.

Thinking he would do what he could, he turned toward Megan, reaching out to grip her hand—

And was stunned to see relief beaming from her face.

"It's okay, Vince, calm down," she said, leaning toward him, *her* hand falling gently over *his* wrist. "Listen, the cockpit alarm's stopped."

"Huh?"

"The alarm," she repeated slowly. "It's stopped. We're landing."

He perked his ears. It had indeed stopped. And so had the rocking. But what had those thumping noises been about?

Suddenly the intercom crackled to life.

"Everyone, I'm sorry for the jostling. There was a little problem releasing the landing gear, but our wheels are down now and we're fine," he heard Gordian say, as if in answer to his unvoiced question.

"Landing gear," he muttered.

"What?" Megan said. "Couldn't hear you."

He looked down at where she was still holding his arm, and smiled.

"Just saying I love you, too, babycakes," he said.

TWENTY-ONE

FROM AN ASSOCIATED PRESS WIRE REPORT:

Washington, D.C.—UpLink International Chairman Roger Gordian and a group of core supporters have arrived for a news conference at the Washington Press Club scheduled to coincide with tomorrow's White House enactment of the Morrison-Fiore cryptographic deregulatory bill. It is thought Gordian will restate his well-known opposition to the bill, a stance which has drawn criticism from many quarters of the government and high-tech industry.

The stakes are high for Mr. Gordian amid reports of mounting and widespread stockholder discontent, and Monolith Technologies' recent bid for a large voting share of his corporation. Questioned by reporters soon after his self-piloted Learjet touched down at Dulles International Airport, the besieged defense and communications titan gave no comment on rumors that his press conference will include a sur-

prise announcement of his resignation as CEO of UpLink.

President Ballard and his media aides, meanwhile, have chosen to downplay the crypto bill's significance, wishing instead to emphasize the President's visit to Asia later this week for the signing of the SEAPAC maritime defense treaty, an event to be held aboard an advanced nuclear submarine in Singapore's coastal waters. . . .

FROM THE *STRAITS TIMES*:

Body Found by Coastal Villagers

Banda Aceh, Indonesia—Local police authorities have reported the discovery of human remains by fishermen operating off Lampu'uk, a remote village at the nation's northernmost point, near a frequently traveled sea lane where the Straits of Melaka open into the Indian Ocean.

There has been no official word about the body's condition, nor any indication whether its identity has been established. However, eyewitnesses present when the corpse was found describe it as belonging to a male who had apparently been afloat at sea for some days.

A forensic examination to determine the cause of death is said to be pending.

While little else about the case is known, the International Maritime Bu-

reau and other regional investigatory
agencies are said to have been contacted. It is routine procedure for the
IMB and ASEAN law-enforcement
groups, who maintain close cooperative links and shared databases of persons reported missing or lost at sea, to
consult when handling incidents of this
type.

Gordian remained at the field after the others had gone
ahead to their hotel rooms and, accompanied by a couple
of Pete Nimec's security aces, met with the airframe and
power-plant mechanic at UpLink's leased hangar.

Minutes after being told what had happened to the gear,
the shocked A&P man was under the Learjet's wing on
a wooden creeper.

"No sign of exterior leakage, and the fittings seem to
be intact," he said now. "Wait, hold it a second, I want
to take a closer peek at something."

The mechanic ran the tips of his index and middle fingers over a spot at the bottom of the fuselage, closely
holding a flashlight on it with his other hand. Then he
rubbed the fingers against his thumb and sniffed them.

"Got a whiff of Skydol, and there's some on my finger
from outside the actuating cylinder." He pulled his head
out from beneath the plane to look up at Gordian. "Can't
tell anything from that alone, though, since you're always
going to have some minor fluid loss. I'm going to need
to get in and check the whole circuit. From the sequence
valves to the main system line."

Gordian squatted down beside him.

"I want to know what went wrong, Mike," he said.
Then, thinking about Max Blackburn, he decided to fol-

low a hunch. "Do me a favor and check for any signs of tampering, will you? Four people almost lost their lives today because of me. Four of my dearest friends."

Mike turned off the flash, rolled out from beneath the plane, and stood, wiping the fluid residue from his hand with a rag.

"Maybe this is only a groundhog's way of seeing it," he said, "but from what you told me a couple minutes ago, I'd say it was you who *saved* their lives, sir."

Gordian shook his head.

"It isn't a matter of perspective," he said tersely. "Federal aviation regulations state the pilot in command has ultimate accountability for the aircraft. And for the safety of its passengers. Makes no difference whether they were jeopardized because of a sloppy preflight in San Jose, a mechanical failure in the air, my own judgment, or a combination of factors. I am responsible for everything that happens in the air."

Mike looked at him without speaking.

"I got lucky, Mike," Gordian said, his face tight. "You understand? I just got lucky."

Mike swallowed and gave him a slow nod. "I won't leave this hangar till I've combed over the bird from top to bottom," he said.

Gordian briefly patted his arm. "Thanks. It's appreciated."

He turned to the pair of Sword ops.

"I'd like you to stick around here with Mike. Give him any help he needs."

The two security men exchanged glances.

Gordian could see they were unhappy with his order, which was understandable. Lean and serious and zoned-

in, they were professionals whose effectiveness hinged on rigorous discipline. Their assignment was to protect him, and it went against everything in their training and mental conditioning to ease up.

"It's okay, I'll be fine," he assured them. "I'm heading straight to my hotel room and plan to stay there all evening."

"Sir, we received direct orders from Mr. Nimec to stay with you," one of them said.

Gordian nodded. "I know, Tom," he said. "But if you don't tell him you left my side for a few hours, I won't either."

The bodyguard looked pensive.

"It would be best, sir, if we could check in with you over the phone this evening," he said.

"Certainly, but please try not to reach any premature conclusions if I don't answer," he said. "It's been a rough day, and I need a long shower and some sleep."

The bodyguard hesitated a moment, and Gordian resisted a smile. He'd suddenly remembered his paternal angst when Julia was a teenager going out on dates, and found himself amused despite his tension and lowering fatigue.

"Gentlemen, my car's waiting, and the driver must be getting impatient," he said. "I'll see you later."

Tom was quiet another moment, and then nodded, his expression a mixture of chagrin, worry, and vague disapproval.

"Have a good rest, sir," he said.

"I'll try," Gordian said.

And still wrestling back a smile, turned, flapped his arm up over his shoulder in a loose, weary wave, and strode out of the hangar.

•   •   •

"So, Alex, what I'm saying is that it looks like I can get you to dine with the POTUS and the other heads of state in the officers' wardroom."

"Is that what you're saying?" Nordstrum said.

"That is exactly what I'm saying," Stu Encardi said. "Right there in the belly of the beast we call Seawolf."

They were talking over a lunch of quesadillas, cactus salad, and chili at the Red Sage on Northwest Fourteenth, roughly midway between the Kennedy Center and the White House.

"And who's setting this up?"

"Terskoff."

"The Press Secretary."

"The Press Secretary *himself*," Encardi emphasized.

Nordstrum ate some of his quesadilla. "What's the catch?" he said.

"Excuse me?"

"The catch, the snare, the hook," Nordstrum said. "Whatever it is that's going to sink into my flesh if I take the bait."

Encardi combed back a wave of his lush black hair with his fingers.

"Oh," he said. "You mean President Ballard's request."

Nordstrum looked at him. "Stu, I think you're a decent fellow," he said. "But if you don't stop playing dumb, and get to the point, I'm going to leave this table, stroll into the kitchen, find one of the cactus plants they use for the salads *before* its spines have been removed, then come right back here and shove it up your ass."

Encardi frowned. "Ouch," he said.

"Yes," Nordstrum said, and speared another wedge of quesadilla with his fork. "Very definitely *ouch*."

Encardi leaned forward confidentially. "Okay," he said. "All the President requests is that you absent yourself from Roger Gordian's press conference tomorrow. That is, assuming you've considered attending."

"Ah-hah," Nordstrum said, chewing.

"Now don't think the White House is trying to restrict your ability to express your opinions," Encardi went on. "Ballard merely feels SEAPAC is a far more vital part of his agenda—and his legacy—than approving the crypto legislation. And that it's slipped out of the spotlight because Gordian versus Caine makes snappier news copy."

"Ah-hah," Nordstrum said.

Encardi spread his hands.

"Think about it," he said. "You're the one heavy hitter in the press who's reported on SEAPAC from its earliest stages of negotiation to the present. Who's consistently stressed its importance to our regional interests in Southeast Asia. Don't you think it'll further sidetrack the public if they see you with Gordian at the podium? There are already enough things distracting their attention."

"Ah-hah," Nordstrum said, chewing placidly.

Encardi frowned with exasperation. "God damn it, Alec, *now* who's being incommunicative? You asked me to be right-on with you and I'm doing it. So, please, let's have some feedback."

"Sure," Nordstrum said.

He carefully set his knife and fork down on his plate and straightened.

"I had planned on standing beside Roger Gordian tomorrow and will do that come hell, high water, or sugar-coated coercion from the highest levels of government," he said.

Encardi brushed back his dense swirl of hair again.

"Alec, you could be interviewing Prime Minister Yamamoto over caviar and champagne instead of chowing down in the goat locker with the enlisted personnel. Don't pass up the opportunity of a lifetime."

Nordstrum crossed his arms. "You're annoying me," he said.

"Alec—"

"Don't whine, it makes you look like a schoolboy."

Encardi frowned, wiped his mouth furiously with his napkin, and tossed it down on the table.

"Okay, I quit," he said.

"Good," Nordstrum said. "Anything else you want to ask while I finish eating?"

Encardi looked at him and sighed.

"Yeah," he said after a brief interval. "You ever hear of Diver Dan and Baron Barracuda?"

Nordstrum shook his head disinterestedly.

"Some help you are," Encardi said.

The transcontinental haul from San Francisco to Johor Bahru had been a grueling and seemingly endless affair for Nimec and Noriko Cousins, with a late-night change-over from their 747 to a prop-driven rattletrap in Kuala Lumpur, and, following their jump to JB, a treacherous forty-minute drive over dark, winding, poorly mapped roads in the rental car Nimec had reserved at the airport.

Though Nimec had been at the Johor ground station on only one prior occasion, and though it had occurred to

him before departing the States that it might be wise to have somebody from the local Sword contingent come out to the airfield and meet them, he had finally decided to drive to their end destination himself. He supposed that part of it was a natural predisposition toward seeking camouflage, a trait that made him lean toward maintaining a low profile until he was clearer about where Max's probe had been taking him . . . and what might have gone wrong. But there was also a part of him that simply liked cowboying it, and while he would have admitted it to no one—including, to some extent, himself—the truth was that being lifted from his ordinary milieu had aroused that long-dormant facet of his personality.

At any rate, it was just shy of five in the morning when Nimec found UpLink's corporate emblem on a sign marking a dirt service road and, looking off beyond the tree line to his right, glimpsed the concrete and aluminum buildings of the ground station in the near distance.

He swung up over the hard-pack toward the station's perimeter gate and braked about twenty feet before reaching the guard booth. There was an ATM-sized biometric reader on a concrete island to his left—one of the recent improvements Max had made to the security net. Whereas most UpLink facilities used either iris or fingerprint scanning at various levels of access, Blackburn had wanted to tighten the identification requirements at restricted entry points by using multiple biometric passkeys, and had the scanner platforms designed to his specifications.

Nimec lowered his window now and swept his thumb over the platform's thermal-imaging strip while simultaneously waiting for the iris scanner to digitally photograph his eyes—two cameras matching them to a computerized facial template, the third taking a high-res

snapshot of his iris. All three images were then checked for a variety of characteristics and compared with information previously enrolled in the security mainframe's database.

Seconds after he'd pulled up to the multiscanner, the "toll light" above the motorized gate in front of him shifted from red to green and a computer-synthesized female voice issued from a speaker in the platform.

"Identification complete, Peter Nimec," it said in English. "Please proceed."

Nimec drove on through the gate toward the complex, nodding to the uniformed man in the guard booth as he passed him.

"This isn't quite the sort of place I expected," Nori said from the backseat, looking out the window in the dawnlight. "It's so . . . I don't know . . . colorless."

Nimec shrugged with his hands on the wheel.

"Utilitarian's the word I'd use," he said. "Didn't realize you hadn't been to any of our ground stations. They all come out of the same cookie cutter. After a while you get used to the no-frills decor."

"I suppose." She sat back and yawned.

Nimec glanced into the rearview.

"Tired from our journey to the East?" he asked.

"And wired," she said.

"Not a good mix if you plan to get any sleep." He lifted a folded newspaper from the passenger seat and held it out to her over his shoulder. "Here, take this copy of the *Straits Times* I grabbed at the KL airport. Maybe it'll help you relax."

"I don't remember seeing you read it."

"That's because I haven't yet," he said. "And I doubt I'll manage to keep my eyes open long enough to do so."

Nori took the paper from his hand, set it down beside her, and yawned again.

"Thanks," she said. "I'll be sure to fill you in on the local news over breakfast."

He nodded.

"Just don't forget my horoscope," he said in a tone that might or might not have been serious.

Sian Po had no sooner gotten to bed after returning home from his night shift at the precinct than he closed his eyes and dreamed he was in a gambling parlor managed by Fat B. There were women and flashing lights and he had somehow won an astronomical sum of money, hillocks of which surrounded him on every side.

The knock at his door awakened him just as, in his dream, he had begun to dance with a magnificent blonde who'd slid down off a pole and then told him she'd come all the way from Denmark to make his acquaintance.

Sian Po opened his eyes, jolted from the sparkle and glitz of his fantasy to the bland, curtained dimness of his studio apartment. Where had the sexy dancer gone?

He frowned with the realization that she didn't exist, and glanced at his alarm clock. It was five A.M. Had he thought he'd heard something?

There was another rap on the door.

Still a little disoriented, he got out of bed and went over to it in his pajamas.

"Who is it?" he grunted, rubbing his eyes.

"I've something for you from Gaffoor," a hushed male voice said from out in the corridor.

Sian Po's bleariness instantly dissipated at the mention of his insider with CID. He unbolted his lock and pulled open the door.

The man was about thirty and dressed in civilian clothes, a light cotton shirt and sport jacket. Another investigator, or so Sian Po believed.

"You in Gaffoor's unit?" Sian Po asked.

The man shrugged noncommittally, extracted a white legal envelope from his jacket's inner pocket, and held it out to Sian Po.

"Take it, *ke yi bu ke yi,*" he said.

Sian Po snatched it from his hand.

The man stood there giving him a blank look. "I'll tell Gaffoor you received his message," he said, and turned down the hall.

The door shut behind him, Sian Po eagerly tore open the envelope. Inside was a folded sheet of paper. He slipped it out and read the note that had been written across its face.

Excitement flooded his squashed features.

Unbelievable, he thought. Just unbelievable.

Heedless of the hour, Sian Po hurried over to his bedside stand, located Fat B's phone number in his datebook, and rang him up.

As though the dream had been a true and marvelous premonition, his jackpot had arrived.

TWENTY-TWO

IN THE CORRIDOR OUTSIDE THE EAST ROOM OF THE
White House, a room throbbing with reporters, prominent
members of Congress, and other official guests invited to
the Morrison-Fiore bill-signing ceremony, the President
was both aggravated and anxious to put pen to paper.

He was aggravated because he had wanted to sign the
bill while sitting behind the staunch and sturdy solidity
of the Resolute Desk in the sound and secure comfort of
the Executive Office, wanted to sign it at midnight when
the folks around him were home in bed, or elsewhere in
bed, or in some cases skulking between beds, zipping up,
unzipping, getting tangled up *inside* their zippers, whatever the hell they chose to do with themselves when the
sun went down and the lights were out here in the golden
city on the Hill.

He was anxious because now that he'd been induced to
make a huge ceremonial affair of the signing—C-SPAN
cameras dollying about, kliegs in his face, the whole nine
yards—he wanted it over and done with so that public
attention could be turned to something of real significance
to him, namely SEAPAC, a child he had guided from
infancy, watching it take on polish, refinement, and sophistication under his savvy political eye. A treaty that he

viewed as the most important policy effort of his tenure in the White House. That he believed was the blueprint for a new strategic and logistic collaboration in the Pacific Rim. That he was certain would reinforce America's ties with its Asian partners, and decide the future of its own security interests in the region. What was Morrison-Fiore in comparison, besides a piece of moot legislation, easing commercial restrictions that had already been bypassed with countless loopholes?

Impatient to get to his desk now—no Resolute by any means, no strong, lasting article of furniture made from the timbers of a bold expeditionary vessel, but rather a comparatively lightweight and characterless hunk of wood rolled out under the portrait of George Washington especially for this morning's swinging Big House hullabaloo—the President glanced into the room, where the function's primary mastermind, Press Secretary Brian Terskoff, stood to the right of the entryway schmoozing with a young woman Ballard recognized as an executive from the news department of one of the major television networks. A place where Terskoff might very well be seeking employment once the sorry, obstinate bastard got the ass-kicking he'd long deserved.

And what better time than the present to do that? Ballard suddenly thought.

He caught Terskoff's eye and crooked a finger at him, then waited as he pushed his way through the sea of invitees and into the corridor.

"Yes, Mr. President?" he said, stepping close.

"What's the delay?"

"They're working a bug or two out of the satellite feeds, technical stuff," Terskoff said. "We'll be on in five."

The President looked at him.

"On in five," he echoed.

Terskoff nodded. "Maybe less."

The President kept looking at him.

"You sound like the stage manager of a talk show."

Terskoff seemed flattered.

"In a sense, that's my role here today," he said.

The President leaned in close. "Brian, if I'd had it my way, the signing would have been handled as a routine piece of business, something that passed quietly in the night," he said. "Instead, thanks to you, we've got ourselves a spectacle."

"Yes, sir, I believe we do," Terskoff said proudly, glancing into the room. "A *stately* spectacle. That is my preferred approach to these events."

"Your preferred approach."

"Very much so, Mr. President."

Ballard frowned, nibbling the inside of his cheek. "You know," he said, "it occurs to me this approach might have been utilized to promote another of my little endeavors. One I feel hasn't been quite the attention-grabber I'd anticipated it might be."

Terskoff scratched behind his ear, all at once unsure of himself.

"You're referring to SEAPAC," he said.

"Yes," the President said, snapping his index finger at Terskoff's chest. "You guessed it. And what I'm thinking, Brian, is that it's still not too late to change things. For example, we could have football cheerleaders accompany me to Air Force One as I leave for Singapore tomorrow. Or better yet, *Playboy* models *dressed* as cheerleaders. They could be spelling out the name of the treaty while they do their pom-pom waving on the field.

'Give me an S, give me an E,' and so forth. And they could have the word SEAPAC written out across their bikini tops in sequined letters, one letter to each model. How's *that* for a stately spectacle, as you phrased it?''

Terskoff grimaced. ''Mr. President, I know you feel the treaty has been neglected in favor of Morrison-Fiore. But please understand, the press feeds on the sensational. The best one can do is give them what they want, and I choose to do it in whopping portions—''

''I've heard that song a hundred times before, which is more than enough,'' he said. ''Let me tell you something, Brian. You fucked up. You and the pack of propeller-heads you call a staff. And as a result, an initiative to which I've dedicated tremendous effort has been sidelined.''

''Sir—''

Ballard raised his hand like a traffic cop.

''I'm not finished,'' he said. ''Crypto isn't my fight. It never has been. I've never wanted to go to blows with Roger Gordian over it, not publicly, and yet that's exactly what's happening today. At this very instant, he's across town putting on his big Everlast gloves. And that does not make me happy.''

A pause.

''Mr. President, if there's anything you feel I can do . . .''

''Actually, there is,'' Ballard said. ''For starters, you can notify those television people that I'm entering the room in thirty seconds, whether they're ready or not. And then you can take that pretty news executive you were chatting up out to lunch—the Fourth Estate might be an appropriate restaurant—and see whether she can find a

place for you in her department. Because I'll be expecting your letter of resignation on my desk when I return from Asia next week. You got me?''

Terskoff had paled. "Sir . . .''

The President pointed to his wristwatch.

"Twenty seconds," he said.

His lower lip quivering, Terskoff hesitated for another two of those seconds, then whipped around and plunged into the East Room.

Precisely eighteen seconds later, the President heard his name announced and made his entrance.

The Murrow Room at the NPC Building was packed with newsies. Like some huge, self-replicating organism, the Washington press corps had divided between two fronts of a battle that it hoped was about to reach a roaring public climax, with the President and Roger Gordian hurling verbal thunderbolts across Pennsylvania Avenue. They wanted banner headlines, they wanted dramatic sound and video bites, they wanted to keep the legion of attorneys and ex-politicos who had been reborn as television commentators regularly bickering through the next ratings sweeps period. They wanted bombs bursting in air, and Gordian was a little intimidated by their expectation— probably because he knew there wasn't much chance of reaching the level to which the bar had been elevated. A lifetime of conducting one's affairs with businesslike restraint scarcely prepared a man to generate oratorical hellfire.

In the end, though, it didn't matter to him whether they were disappointed. Nor would it have been devastating had none of them showed up, leaving his electronically amplified words to float unheard above a roomful of

empty chairs. He had come to make his stand, and win or lose, that was ultimately the best anyone could do.

Mounting the podium, he waited for a long moment, Chuck Kirby, Megan Breen, Vince Scull, and Alex Nordstrum behind him on the right, Dan Parker, Richard Sobel, and FBI Director Robert Lang on his left.

"Ladies and gentleman of the press, thank you for coming today," he finally said. "Right now, only a few short blocks away from here, the Morrison-Fiore cryptographic deregulation bill is being signed into law. I don't know what personal feelings any of you may have about it, but for the past several months I have tried to make mine clear. My opposition to the decontrol of cryptographic hardware and software remains firm and uncompromising. Still, there seems to be some confusion about my views, and that is at least fifty percent of the reason I am addressing you today."

Gordian paused, adjusted his microphone.

"I know a little about technology and its importance as a binding and unifying global force," he continued. "I believe that knowledge is freedom, and information the core and cornerstone of knowledge. I have tried with my communications network to break down the barriers that keep people around the world in darkness and tyranny. And I am extremely proud of my successes.

"But the reality is that America has its enemies. We would be mistaken to confuse the globalization of advanced technology with the abdication of our rights and imperatives as a sovereign nation, and I believe Morrison-Fiore is a disturbing step along that road. My critics, on the other hand, argue that I am vainly trying to put the genie back in the bottle by advocating we control encryption technology as we might any other powerful tool.

They argue that because cryptographic software may be smuggled across the transparent borders of cyberspace with relative ease, we ought to pretend those borders do not exist, rather than better define and regulate them. That because we acknowledge the inadequacies and inconsistencies of current laws, and the real and great obstacles to applying them across *territorial* borders, we should abandon them altogether rather than work toward bringing them into greater harmony.

"This sort of thinking admittedly baffles me. Are we to cease attempting to check electronic piracy only because it may be difficult to do so? Refuse to engage a problem only because it may be daunting? If that's to be the case, where do we draw the line? Should we next allow arms and narcotics to flow unchecked between nations? This is no strained comparison. International criminals and practitioners of violence already know encryption technology can afford them a formidable advantage over law enforcement, a new and sophisticated layer of secrecy by which their activities can be concealed. They know it, and they are fast learning how to capitalize on that knowledge.

"I assure you, when we concede an advantage to crime and criminals, we do worse than allow the disintegration of legal boundaries. We risk the disintegration of our will as a civilization. And that, ladies and gentlemen, frightens me more than anything as an individual. . . ."

Nordstrum skimmed his eyes over the crowd of reporters. He thought Gord was doing superbly, and although his notoriously jaded colleagues were a tough bunch to read, and there were very few nodding heads, they at least seemed inclined to listen . . . which was really the critical

thing today. Gordian needed their agreement much less than their interest. That translated into coverage, whereas boredom meant obscurity in the back pages.

Nordstrum was only disappointed that he'd forgotten to convey Craig Weston's message to Gordian. *It's not the locks, it's the keys,* he'd said, obviously alluding to the proprietary codes which were used to access, or rather, non-technically speaking, "descramble," data that had been encrypted. The problem of their safe storage was an aspect of the issue that certainly might have borne a touch more emphasis in Gordian's statement, and Nordstrum had fully intended to suggest that to him. But somewhere in the process of meeting Gord and the others at their hotel, and hearing about the near-calamity that had occurred when they'd been landing at Dulles, it had slipped his mind.

Well, perhaps he'd be able to prompt Gord to address the subject during the journalistic grilling—politely known as a Q and A session—that would follow his prepared comments. In fact, that might be the best time for him to do so, since Gordian would likely need a respite from the inevitable bombardment of questions about the Monolith bid, and the surprise announcement he was going to make on that track.

Reminding himself all over again of the hell he would catch at the gym if he failed to keep his promise to the admiral, Nordstrum turned his full attention back to the press conference.

Sitting aboard the monorail as it ran a smooth, circular course around the high-tech theme parks, man-made beaches, and other bustling tourist attractions of Sentosa Island, Omori peered through his binoculars and watched

the boosted fleet of naval patrol boats maneuvering in the waters off Singapore's coastline. Their presence had become increasingly noticeable over the past few days, entire squadrons assembling in advance of the Seawolf's run. Security in the city itself was likewise tighter than Omori had ever seen it; walking from the train station to the ferry terminal, he often had been forced to detour around police barricades along the motorcade routes to be taken by arriving dignitaries. Indeed, the Malaysian Prime Minister was already in town, having come a day ahead of his counterparts from Indonesia and America to visit with the governor of Pulau Ubin, with whom he shared close personal ties.

The mission that had brought Omori from Tokyo also reflected long-standing ties . . . to the Inagawa-kai syndicate of which he was a high-placed *kuromaku,* or power broker; to Nga Canbera; to the politicians within the Diet whose opposition to SEAPAC had brought them into alliance with a broad group of foreign and domestic interests, all of which had pledged to make the treaty come undone, and bring about the humiliation and downfall of its internationalist sponsors.

Omori felt a jostling against his right arm now, lowered his glasses, and looked over at the little boy in the seat beside him. He was shifting restlessly about, repeatedly asking his mother when they would reach the Entertainment Mall. Omori frowned, and patted the child's shoulder to gain his attention.

"You should be patient and behave for your mommy," he said. " She is very good to bring you here and cannot make us go any faster."

The boy fell still, looked at him in the wide-eyed, anx-

ious way children did when scolded by strangers, and then looked up at his mother.

Omori glanced at her and smiled in commiseration. The boy was a cute and precocious one, like his own son of about the same age. Omori prayed he would live to see his wife and family again. Children were his truest joy.

He turned back to the window, raised the goggles to his eyes, and continued looking out at the harbor. The number of vessels in the patrols had no meaning to him. Let them bring in the entire Navy if they wished. A small team of men, properly equipped and striking with accuracy, could penetrate any massive line of defense.

Tonight, after he'd finished reconaissance and freshened up a bit, he would meet with the members of the insertion party and review their final preparations. Then there would be nothing to do but await word to proceed, and check his E-mail for a critical file from Nga.

For the moment, however, Omori would relax and enjoy his ride. He hoped the world leaders aboard the Seawolf would enjoy theirs as well.

"In conclusion, I'd like to return for a moment to the example of the genie. Would I like it put back in the magic lamp, the lamp itself sealed away from the eyes, the very *awareness,* of man? My life's work is evidence to the contrary. As I interpret the story, it wasn't the genie's power to work wonders that heaped so much pain and trouble upon poor Aladdin. The cause, I think, was Aladdin's lack of judgment about how to use his gift, a failure to understand the exceeding degree of caution and restraint with which it needed to be managed. Power itself is never to be feared. Its uses are determined by the hands

into which it falls. With passion and intelligence anything is truly possible.

"But as evolving technologies create new possibilities for us, as in a sense we use science to work magic, our eternal responsibility is to choose those uses which will build rather than destroy, liberate rather than imprison, bring gain rather than loss upon us as a species. It's a responsibility that hasn't changed in essence since the discovery of fire or the wheel, although as the tools become more complex, so do our choices. Mistakes are inevitable, but I hope and believe we will learn from them, and be wise enough to correct those we can. If so, then you can take my word for it . . . the genie belongs among us. And he's in the very best of hands."

Gordian pushed aside his written notes, and sipped from the glass of water on the lectern. *Not too shoddy,* he thought. It didn't bother him that the applause was merely polite. Rushed, even. The main thing was that he believed his delivery had been okay, and that his comments had a pretty good chance of penetrating the sieve of the media and getting out to the public.

He took a deep breath, drank some more water, and leaned toward the mike again.

"At this point, I'd be glad to take some questions," he said.

A clattering commotion as three quarters of the room sprang off their chairs.

Gordian pointed to the guy in the first row with the famous Website.

"Mr. Gordian, we were informed you would be making a significant announcement on the corporate front," he said. "And though you did not address the issue in your speech to us, I'm wondering if there's anything you

can reveal about your future as chairman of UpLink International.''

Gordian looked at him with genuine surprise.

Damned if he hadn't nearly forgotten in all the excitement.

''Oh, yes,'' he said. ''Now that you remind me, there certainly is.''

The East Room erupted into noisy, enthusiastic applause the instant the President hastily and perfunctorily put his signature on the last page of Morrison-Fiore, no longer a bill now, but law of the land. Congratulations flew. The Senate whips clasped hands. The Speaker of the House and his rival from the minority party embraced in bipartison triumph. The Veep posed for photographs, basking in his Commander in Chief's reflected light, hoping it would enhance his own glimmer when his turn to seek his party's nod for the Presidency came about in two years or so.

Disgusted, President Ballard wanted to get to sleep.

He had a long flight to Singapore ahead of him in the morning, and then a historic ride on a submarine that it looked like nobody on the planet was going to notice.

''. . . and Mr. Sobel will acquire the firms comprising UpLink's entire computer products division, including Stronghold Security Systems, our cryptographic hardware and software subsidiary. As someone who has known and worked with Richard for over a decade, I have confidence my corporate children will attain impressive and unprecedented levels of success.''

Gordian pointed to one of the upraised hands in front of him.

"The young lady from the *Wall Street Journal,* " he said. "Ms. Sheffield, is it?"

She nodded and stood. "Sir, with all due respect, how will that growth be possible as long as Mr. Sobel preserves your restrictions on crypto export? Many industry analysts disagree with your contention that a cryptographic firm can focus primarily on the domestic market and remain profitable. Or will those policies be relaxed after the sale?"

Richard suddenly stepped up to share the podium.

"With our host's permission, I'm going to answer that myself," Sobel said. "I can unequivocally state that I support Roger Gordian on the encryption issue and will carry on his present policies to the letter. Success is all in how you approach the marketplace, and my electronics firm is existing proof that the analysts you mention are wrong. Our net profits have increased every year for the past five years. We have grown slowly by intention and built a solid reputation designing latchkey systems for corporate clients . . . using many of Roger Gordian's cryptographic products. As a service-and-support-oriented company, we believe Roger Gordian's superior data-encoding systems will both attract new clients, and present limitless advantages to our existing ones."

Sheffield asked Richard a brief follow-up about his specific last-quarter earnings, and then it was Gordian's turn again. Before taking the mike, though, he tapped Richard on the elbow, leaned close, and whispered for him to stay put, figuring they were certain to have the chance to drop their final bombshell before too long.

"What sort of reaction has the breakup proposal generated from your board?" a reporter asked.

"I've spoken over the telephone with everyone on it,

and can tell you my plan has been welcomed with almost complete unanimity," Gordian said. "I foresee no problem obtaining the board's endorsement when we convene sometime next week."

Another reporter. "Your computer division aside, there are a number of subsidiaries in UpLink's medical and automotive branches which you've said will also be up for sale . . . and which have yet to find buyers. How do you expect your shareholders react to these, ah, forced separations?"

"Very positively, I hope," Gordian said. "The spun-off entities remain under skilled and imaginative management, people who will be able to implement their ideas with greater freedom than ever outside the pressure of a large corporate bureaucracy. And while it would be unrealistic for me to expect full confidence from our shareholders at the onset, I think most will be initially reassured by the package of financial bonuses we're preparing, and eventually become true believers. We're dedicated to our investors and guarantee their concerns will be addressed."

A half-dozen more wearisome questions, most regarding the technical aspects of the breakup. What sort of financial bonuses? Will you be retaining any stock in the divested companies? If so, what percentage is to be floated to shareholders?

Question Number Seven was the charm, fired at him courtesy of someone from *Business Week*:

"Mr. Gordian, how will your plans be effected should the Spartus Consortium finalize the sale of their stake in UpLink, which amounts to fully one fifth of the company—an *enormous* minority holding—to Marcus Caine,

who we all know hasn't been over to your home for dinner lately?''

It was a setup Richard couldn't resist.

''As part of our overall deal, UpLink will be placing an equal portion of its stock in my hands,'' he said, stepping in seamlessly. ''If Marcus Caine wants to make himself an uninvited guest at the table, he'll have to sit across from Roger Gordian and myself from now on, look us both squarely in the eye, and learn it isn't an all-you-can-eat. And let me tell you, people, if Caine tries grabbing anything from *my* plate, he'd damned well better watch out for my fork.''

A beat of surprised silence from the audience, and then laughter over Richard's quip.

A great, rising swell of laughter.

Gordian looked out at the room, and was embarrassed by the realization that he was grinning himself.

But not *too* embarrassed.

Boom, he thought. *Bombshell delivered.*

And dead-on in the crosshairs, no less.

In his office watching C-SPAN, Caine lowered the croissant he'd been eating to his desk, then glanced circumspectly over at his secretary. When Deborah had come in with his coffee and pastries, he'd asked her to stay and take notes regarding the press conference, and she was now sitting on the sofa with her laptop, typing, her gaze fixed on the screen. Perhaps too intently. She'd passed a hand across her mouth a moment ago, briefly shielding it from sight. Had she found Sobel's remarks amusing? he wondered. He would have liked to tear out her throat just on the suspicion. If his belief ever hardened into surety, she could look forward to her walking papers. He would

see that she never set foot in an office again, not as an employee.

Caine felt his stomach burning savagely. It was as if he were on fire inside.

Those bastards, he thought incredulously. Those bastards. They should have been dead. Killed when Gordian tried to land that plane. The people he'd sent to work on it had *assured* him they would be. But somehow . . . somehow nothing had happened to them. And instead—

Instead . . .

He had to credit Gordian's resourcefulness. By segmenting off entire divisions of UpLink, he would almost certainly gain the capital to dispose of his outstanding debts. By parting with the cryptographic operation, he had eliminated the greatest cause of his shareholders' dissatisfaction, and no doubt raised the price of UpLink stock to its highest level in years. And by handing Sobel a chunk of the core outfit—making him White Knight and Squire all in one—he had forged an alliance that would decisively give him control of the company just when it had been within Caine's grasp. In order to overthrow that alliance, or even mitigate its control, Caine—or any buyer of voting stock—would now need to acquire an improbable and newly expensive number of shares.

A terrible, nauseous crashing sensation added itself to the pain tearing at Caine's gut, and he was suddenly afraid he might be sick. Even knowing what he'd set in motion at Gordian's data-storage facility tonight didn't help. Nga and his confederates would get what they wanted . . . but he . . .

Think it, an inner voice insisted. *At least have the courage to think it.*

No. No. No.

His hand shaking, he lifted the plate of croissants off his desk, slipped it into his wastebasket, and stared at the television screen in an agony of his own hatred.

No.

He would not, could not concede that he was beaten.

TWENTY-THREE

SOUTHEAST ASIA
SEPTEMBER 29/30, 2000

"—ELLO, MAX? MAX, IT'S KIRSTEN. CALL ME ON MY mobile soon as you can."

"Max, this is Kirsten again. Still waiting to hear from you."

"Hello, Max? Same message as before."

"Max, where are you? It's been four days and I'm getting really concerned. My sister and her husband are telling me to call the police, and maybe they're right. This is all so confusing for me. So please, if you hear this, get in touch."

"Max, I've decided to do what Anna wants and contact the authorities—"

Nimec clicked off the answering machine and looked at Nori in silence.

Though it was still not yet full morning in Johor, and both were running on empty, they were in Blackburn's spare, single-room living quarters at the ground station, having decided to check it out for clues to his whereabouts before heading off to bed. There had been nothing to help them on that score, but Kirsten Chu's frequent and increasingly worried messages—the most recent of which had been left two days earlier according to the machine's time/date stamp—at least revealed that *she*

had not completely vanished from the face of the earth as well. And while the messages also seemed to confirm Nimec's feeling that Max had gotten into some kind of serious fix, they ultimately engendered more questions than they answered.

"Sounds like she's staying with her sister," Nori said after a while.

"Hiding out's more like it," Nimec said. "You catch the sister's name or do I have to run through the tape again?"

"Anna," Nori said. "No second name, though. And Kirsten mentioned there being a husband, so it'd be a different surname from her own. Makes it harder to track her down."

"A lot of married women keep their family names these days."

Nori shook her head.

"You're thinking like an American," she said. "Asian societies aren't quite so liberated."

Nimec sighed.

"Why the hell would she ask Max to call on her cell phone?" he said. "Wouldn't it have been simpler to just leave *Anna's* number for him?"

Nori thought about that a moment.

"Simpler for us, absolutely, but her situation's another matter," she said. "Put yourself in Kirsten's shoes. Whatever she's been into with Blackburn, it's something her family's probably better off not being enlightened about."

"For their own safety, you mean."

"Right," Nori said. "The less they know the better. Also, it sounds to me like Max would have been against Kirsten calling the authorities to report whatever happened—"

"Or at least *she* feels that way," Nimec said. "We can figure out why later, but go on, I didn't mean to interrupt."

"My point is that she seemed to be under pressure from her family to make the call, and would've been torn in two different directions about actually doing it. Could be the sister and her husband had misgivings about Blackburn . . . why wouldn't they, when you consider the whole situation? If you're Kirsten, you're going to feel uncomfortable about having him get in touch with you on their home phone, maybe kicking off a round of difficult questions from Sis. The other way's a lot more private."

"Except, as you've already indicated, it stinks as far as we're concerned," Nimec said. "Joyce has numbers for Kirsten's home and business phones, but not the cellular."

"No address?"

"Besides her office at Monolith, no."

"What about Max's notes on his investigation? The ones he gave to Joyce?"

"I didn't even know they existed until yesterday, when I called to tell her I'd be coming to Johor. They're encoded on his PIM, and it'll take some time to decrypt and go through them."

She nodded, thinking. "I assume we want to steer clear of the badges."

"For the time being, yes. Not that we even can be sure she's phoned them. Or, if she has, that she's told them where she's staying."

"It's even an open question *which* police force she'd call," Nori added. "Her sister could live on either side of the causeway. Or elsewhere. National borders are close in this neck of the woods."

"True enough, but we do we know *Kirsten* lives in Singapore. If we're lucky, she'll be listed in the public telephone directory. And that might give us the info we need."

"Maybe, maybe not," Nori said. "Most young, single women leave their addresses out of the listings. It's standard protection against sickos."

"Now *you're* the one thinking like an American . . . and a New Yorker at that," Nimec said with a wan smile. "Singapore isn't the kind of place where there's going to be a problem with obscene phone callers. If she's in the book, we'll likely find out where she lives. . . ."

"And the next step would be to get in there and look around for something with Sis's address written on it," Nori said, completing his thought.

Nimec nodded agreement.

"I hate to risk breaking and entering," he said. "But if we have no better alternative . . ."

Nori wobbled her hand in the air to interrupt him, then gestured to the key he was holding, a spare they had obtained from Station Security to gain access to Blackburn's room.

"Leave that part to me," she said.

It was a little past four in the afternoon when the two men in the Olds Cutlass drove up to the entry gate of the UpLink Cryptographics facility in Sacramento, slowing to a halt as they reached the guard station.

"Detective Steve Lombardi," the driver told the guard through his open window. He tilted his head toward the man in the passenger seat. "My partner here's Detective Craig Sanford."

The guard regarded them through his mirrored sunglasses.

"How can I help you?" he said.

"We need to speak to the supervisor in charge," Lombardi said. "We've got a subpoena for crypto keys, you know the deal."

The guard nodded. It was SOP for law enforcement to deliver court orders whenever there was an investigation or legal action involving the release of data-recovery keys used by UpLink software. With everybody from banks to supermarkets to Mafia hoods using crypto in their daily business operations nowadays, and thousands of keys stored in the data-recovery vaults, and all kinds of civil and criminal cases in which computerized files were requested as evidence, it wasn't unusual to get as many as four or five visits a week from police officers delivering subpoenas.

"Just need to see your ID and papers," he said.

The driver took the requested items out of his sport jacket and gave them to the guard. A moment later the passenger reached over and passed the leather case holding his own badge and identification through the window.

The guard angled his mirrored lenses down at what he'd been handed, glancing over the police tins, unfolding the court papers.

"Everything kosher?" the driver asked.

The guard studied the ID and paperwork another second, then nodded and returned them through the window of his booth.

"Go right on ahead, fellas," he said.

The doorman at the luxury condo near Holland Road, on the eastern part of Singapore Island, had scarcely arrived

for his morning shift when he saw the pale blue taxi pull up near the entrance and discharge its passenger, a slight, nicely dressed young woman carrying a couple of over-stuffed travel bags. The luggage aside, she *looked* as though she'd been traveling, her hair slightly messed, a somewhat frayed expression on her face.

As she struggled toward the building with the bags, he set down his tea and rose from his desk to get the door.

"Can help?" he asked in typical Singlish fashion, blending English words with Chinese sentence structure.

She set the bags down on the carpeted floor of the vestibule and fussed her hair into place.

"Yes. Or I hope so, anyway," she said. "I'm here for Kirsten Chu."

The doorman regarded her a moment. Her American accent explained why he had not recognized her as an occupant of the high-rise. But he was familiar with the woman whose name she'd mentioned.

"Apartment Fifteen, I can call up, *lah*." He reached for the intercom's handpiece. "Your name, please?"

"No, you don't understand," she said. "Kirsten won't be home until tonight, and I was supposed to let myself in. But now I can't. . . ."

She let the sentence trail off.

"Yes?" he said.

"Maybe I'd better start over." She looked upset. "I'm her sister Charlene, and I'm here visiting from the States. Did she mention my name to you, by any chance?"

He shook his head.

"Well, I suppose there wouldn't have been any need. . . ." she muttered to herself, rubbing her forehead.

"Yes?" the doorman said again. He was becoming increasingly baffled.

When she looked up at him, her large brown eyes were moist.

"You see, I have a key to her door . . . well I *had* a key to her door . . . but I think I may have lost it at the airport. . . ."

"Yes?" he said for the third time, suddenly afraid she might burst into tears.

"Listen," she said agitatedly. "I don't quite know how to ask you this . . . it makes me feel so *foolish* . . . but could you let me into her apartment? I haven't any idea where else to wait for her . . . she went to pick up our other sister, Anna . . . and isn't supposed to be home until very *late,* you see . . . and I've got these *bags* . . ."

He gave her an uncomfortable look. "That against rules, miss. Okay if you want leave bags with me, but I not can—"

"Please, I'll show my passport if you need identification," she said at once, her voice trembling. She crouched over the bags she'd deposited on the vestibule's carpet, unzipped one of them, and began fumbling around inside it.

"Miss—"

The doorman cut himself short. Just as he'd feared, she had begun to sob. Tears spilling down her face, she bent there in front of him, pulling items out of the bag, dropping some of them in her distress, stuffing them hastily back into the bag and fishing out others. . . .

"Wait, wait, my papers are in here *somewhere* . . . I'm so sorry . . . I just have to find them. . . ."

The doorman looked at her, feeling sorry for her, thinking he couldn't just stand there and watch her cry.

"It okay, miss. It okay," he said finally, reaching for

the intercom button. "I call superintendent, tell him let you in, no problem."

Noriko stood and wiped a hand across her eyes.

"Thanks, that's so kind," she said, sniffling. "Really, I don't know what I'd've done without you."

The driveway leading up to the encryption facility terminated in a parking area outside the main entrance, the left side of which was reserved for staff, the right for visitors. The men in the Cutlass swung into the visitors' section, found an empty slot, strode across the lot toward the flat cinder-block building, and approached the armed guard posted at the door.

"Detectives Lombardi and Samford?" he said, smiling pleasantly.

They both nodded.

"I was informed you gentlemen were on your way from the gate," he said, and gestured toward the walk-through weapons-detector beside his station. "If you'd please leave your service weapons with me, and place any other metal articles you may have in the tray to your right, you can step through the scanners and come in."

"We're cops, and cops carry guns," the man who'd announced himself as Lombardi said. "It's in our regulations."

"Yes, and I apologize for the inconvenience. But a facility of this nature has to take added precautions, and most departments cooperate with them," the security man said. "If you'd prefer, I can call ahead to Mr. Turner . . . he's the supervisor you're going to see anyway . . . and request that he waive the requirement. I'm sure it wouldn't be much of a problem."

Lombardi shrugged.

"No need," he said. "Policy's policy."

The two men unholstered their firearms—both were carrying standard Glock nines—and turned them over to the guard, then deposited their coins and key chains in the tray and passed through the archway.

"Thanks for your cooperation," the guard said. He looked at his LCD display, gave the items in the tray a cursory glance, then held it out for the detectives to retrieve their property. "Follow the entry hall straight back, turn right, then cut another right at the end of that corridor. Supervisor's office will be the fourth door down. I'll have your weapons right here when you leave."

Lombardi stuffed his key chain into his pocket.

"Just hope we don't have to chase any armed robbers while we're here," he said, smiling a little.

The guard laughed. "Have no fear," he said. "This place is as safe as they come."

Nori slipped into the rear of the white company Land Rover parked in a shopping mall off Holland Road, three blocks up from Kirsten Chu's residence.

"Found what we wanted," she said. "And more."

"Any problems getting in and out?" Nimec asked from the front passenger seat.

"Nope. The doorman has a crush on me. He talked the super into giving me a key," she said. "Anyway, I've got a personal phone book with a number and address for a Lin and Anna Lung in Petaling Jaya."

"Where the hell's that?"

"Back over the causeway, *lah.* Outside KL." This from the driver, a Malay named Osmar Ali who was with the Sword detail at the ground station.

Nimec nodded.

"You sure you have the right party?" he asked Noriko.

"Pretty much," she said. "I also dug up an open mailing envelope with a return address that matches the one in the book. There were some photos of a couple and two kids inside it. And a letter starts with a 'Dear Sis.' "

"Okay." Nimec turned to look at Osmar. "Petaling Jaya . . . is it within driving distance?"

Osmar shrugged. "Can go, yes, but it a few hundred kilometers," he said in rough English. "Be faster we drive back to ground station, take helicopter."

Nimec thought in silence a moment. Then he reached for the cell phone resting in the molded-plastic cup-holder beside him.

"Better let me have that number, Nori," he said. "I want to see if anybody's home before we come knocking on their door."

The pair of men strode through the corridor after leaving their guns at the checkpoint, their eyes noting the button-sized lenses of surveillance cameras near the ceiling. Unlike commercially produced cameras, these miniature units were recessed behind the walls rather than mounted on visible brackets, and would have gone unnoticed by the average person.

They reached the T-juncture at the end of the hall, but instead of immediately turning right as instructed, paused to scan the doorways in both directions.

Midway down the corridor branching to their left was an office door marked SECURITY. The one who called himself Lombardi gave the other an almost imperceptible glance and they went over to it, walking side-by-side at an easy pace, nodding amiably to a woman who passed them going the opposite way.

Two plainclothes security men were sitting at a bank of closed-circuit monitors when the office door opened inward from the corridor. They were not surprised, having seen the approaching detectives on their screens, and assumed they wanted information.

"Can we help you gentlemen?" one of them said, swiveling to face the door.

The man called Lombardi entered, followed by his partner. They let the door close behind them.

"We're looking for the supervisor's office." He smiled, his hand casually tucked in his pants pocket. "Thought it was supposed to be right around here somewhere."

"Took a wrong turn," the security man said. "When you leave this office, hang a right and—"

Lombardi's hand came out of his pocket holding his key ring. Before the security guards could register what was happening, he brought up its rectangular fob and quickly tugged back the attached chain with his free hand. This cocked the firing mechanism of the weapon, which was only three inches long and contained two .32-caliber bullets. He pointed it at the man facing him and pushed a button on its side.

The slug that coughed from the tiny gun's bore would have been lethal at twenty yards, and the shooter was a mere fraction of that distance from his target. It struck the guard in the middle of the forehead and killed him instantly, slamming him back into the panel of monitors.

The shooter pivoted toward the other guard. His face white with shock, he was reaching for the holstered weapon under his jacket. The shooter pushed the button and fired his second shot, striking the guard in the center of his face. And then the face was gone. The body

sprawled backward, blood, bone fragments, and tissue spraying the screens and walls behind him.

The shooter looked at his partner, gesturing toward the dead men.

"Close," he said. "I only expected there to be one of them."

The man near the door nodded.

"Let's take their guns and get on with it," the shooter said.

When she heard the phone ring at nine-thirty, she wondered if perhaps Anna had forgotten something in her rush to leave the house. The kids had acted up and been late getting ready for school, and Anna, who dropped them off every morning on her way to work, had made her exit amid quite a hustle and bustle.

"Hello?" she said, picking up.

A strange male voice. "Kirsten Chu, please."

She hesitated, her heart suddenly banging in her chest. She'd been expecting a call from the police, which was the reason she hadn't volunteered to help out her sister and deliver Miri and Brian to their classrooms herself. The police, this had to be the police. Anna and Lin . . . and Max, of course . . . were the only other people who'd know to find her here. And the person at the other end wasn't any of the latter.

"Who's calling?" she asked in a cautious tone. Purposely offering no acknowledgment of her identity.

"My name is Pete Nimec, and I'm—"

She didn't even hear him finish the sentence, so completely overwhelming was the recognition that swept over her. Her heart beat harder, faster. She inhaled, feeling as if the breath had been knocked out of her.

"Dear God, that's the *name*," she said, the words springing from her mouth on their own. "You're Max's friend, aren't you? The one he wanted me to call?"

A beat of silence. "Yes, I am. I—"

"How is he?" she interrupted. Worry had swept chillingly through Kirsten's initial excitement. If Max were all right, why wouldn't *he* be calling?

"Kirsten, we need to meet. I have to speak with you in person, find out what's happened to him. To both of you."

"You mean you don't know. . . ."

"No, Kirsten. I don't. No one's heard from him."

She clutched the phone, her hand shaking around it. Her entire *arm* shaking.

"Then how . . . how did you get this number?"

"I'll explain all that later. I promise. Right now it's just urgent that we get together. I'll come to you there. It's probably best if you stay put."

Kirsten breathed.

What reason was there to trust this man? This name Max had mentioned once in a moment of urgency? This *voice?* The truth was that she hardly even knew whether *Max* was the person he'd seemed to be. . . .

Except that wasn't true. She *did* know. Maybe not everything about him. Maybe not as much as she should have known. But as she'd told Anna just days ago, she loved him. . . .

Had loved him long before he'd put his own life at risk to save her . . .

And what was love, always, always, but a leap of faith?

"All right," she said. "I'll be waiting."

• • •

301

The supervisor at the encryption facility—the name plaque on his office door read Charles Turner—was shaking his head as he pored over the court papers he'd been issued.

"I must tell you, this is rather atypical," he said, glancing up at the two detectives standing before his desk.

"How so, sir? I checked the subpoenas myself to make sure they crossed all the t's."

"No, please, don't misunderstand me," Turner said. "The papers are fine. But normally I get advance notification from the officers coming for the codes. They're stored on compact disc in our vaults, you understand, and there's a rather stringent checkout process. Going through it at the last minute, well, I'll have to drop everything, Detective Lombardi. . . ."

"We're really sorry for the inconvenience," the man standing in front of him said. "But this is our first time dealing with a matter of this type as officers."

Turner sighed and rose from his desk, looking annoyed and somewhat flustered.

"You may accompany me to the data-storage wing, though only authorized personnel are allowed in the vaults. You'll have to stay out in one of the waiting areas while I track the disk you want."

"Will it take very long?"

"It shouldn't," Turner said. "The corporation whose key-codes are being requested isn't one I recognize offhand, but the disks are catalogued on our electronic database. I can rush everything through in half an hour, maybe a little faster."

"That'd be fine with us."

Turner *harrumphed,* and came around the desk toward the door.

"Lead the way, sir," the detective said, falling in behind him.

The men had left Penang State, southeast of the Malaysia-Thailand border, shortly after they'd received the call from Luan. That had been some hours ago, at dawn, and they'd been driving their van down the main coastal highways to Selangor ever since. The trip would have been lengthy under the best of traffic conditions, but there were herds of beachgoing tourists jamming the roads near the bridge and ferry terminals to Georgetown, and the delays had stretched miserably in the hot, beating sun. The men in the van had, furthermore, wanted to keep a moderate speed so as not to risk being pulled over by police. The kris tattoos on their hands would bring about an instant search, and once that happened their problems only would be starting. If the police found their weapons, they could look forward to many hours of painful interrogation, followed by many years of being locked away in prison holes. And that would be a far cry from the reward they were expecting for the successful completion of their task.

The Thai had promised them a fortune.

A fortune in greenbacks for capturing a woman and delivering her to him in Kalimantan.

They had joked crudely about her physical attributes when they received the call. And in spite of their grindingly slow progress, it would not be long before they saw the object of Luan's desire for themselves. They were already better than halfway down through Perak, and would be crossing into Selangor within a couple of hours.

303

With luck, Kirsten Chu would be at the address they had been given. And if not, they would gladly wait there for her to arrive.

She was, after all, one woman who was very much worth it.

TWENTY-FOUR

"IS THERE SOME KIND OF PROBLEM, MR. TURNER?"
the man calling himself Lombardi asked from where he
sat in the waiting area.

Holding the court papers, a puzzled expression on his
face, Turner glanced at him as he returned through a doorway he'd entered just moments ago.

"The name of the corporation simply doesn't show on
our database," he said, approaching his chair. "I don't
know what to make of it."

Lombardi rose and sidled up to him, studying the papers over his shoulder.

"I'm no expert at this high-tech stuff, but could be it's
just misspelled," he said.

Turner shook his head. "The computers will essentially
correct for that sort of error by searching for approximate
matches. In this case, nothing came up."

Lombardi grinned.

"Then I guess those papers are fake and the company
doesn't exist," he said.

Turner looked at him. "I don't understand. . . ."

Lombardi reached under his jacket and drew the Beretta he'd taken from one of the murdered security guards.

"Oh, I think you do," he said, and rammed the handle

of the weapon upward into Turner's nose, shattering his septum and sending tiny slivers of bone into his brain. Turner dropped instantly to the floor, his eyes rolling up in their sockets, dark blood spouting from his nostrils. He spasmed twice, emitted a labored gurgling sound, and died.

Lombardi gestured to the other man as he got up off his seat. Then both went around the body and passed through the entry to the vault area.

A short while before the ringing of the doorbell startled her into alertness, Kirsten had slipped into a doze on the sofa, a kind of syrupy exhaustion having settled over her in the late morning, and stayed with her as she'd done some routine chores—washing the breakfast dishes, straightening up the living room, and gathering the kids' toys from around the apartment and garden and hauling them back into their bedroom closet.

Afterward, sitting down to listen to some light jazz on the stereo, hoping it would calm her mind, she had been surprised at how fast her eyelids had started getting heavy, and thought it quite incredible that she could be simultaneously clipping along full-steam on nervous energy and feeling so mentally fatigued that her brain almost seemed immersed in a pool of thick, lukewarm glue. It was a little like the way she'd felt as a university student studying for final exams, living for days and nights on coffee and chocolate . . . only many times more intense.

And now the sound of the buzzer had practically sent her bouncing off the couch, still half out of it, yet conscious of her nerves revving up to speed again.

She glanced at the clock on the wall opposite her. Could Nimec have arrived already? Under average cir-

cumstances it would have been highly unlikely he could have made it in so short a time . . . but he'd explained that he would be returning to the UpLink ground station in Johor, and would probably travel from there into KL by helicopter. Which had also told her a couple of things about him beyond the obvious fact that he was in a hurry. One, he was at least as concerned about Max as she was. And two, he had the sort of clout with Max's boss to pull some major strings, maybe even worked for UpLink himself—

Bzzzzzzzzz!

She crossed the room to the door, straightening her blouse, smoothing her skirt down with her hands. Whoever was out there was really leaning on the bell.

"Yes?" she said, reaching for the doorknob. "Who is it?"

"Johor police," a man said from outside. He was speaking Bahasa. "We want to see Kirsten Chu."

"Excuse me?" she replied in the same language. The blunt, gruff quality of his voice had surprised her as much as his response.

"It's about her call," he said. "We need to ask her some questions."

Kirsten didn't move, hardly even breathed. She was still holding the knob, her fingers suddenly sweating around it.

The Singapore cop with whom she'd spoken had said the Johor authorities would be in touch . . . but she hadn't expected them to just show up at the door. Wouldn't they want to phone and make an appointment, if for no other reason than to spare themselves a needless trip in case she wasn't home?

And does he really sound like a police officer? she thought.

Her pulse fluttering in her temples, she raised the spyhole cover, peered outside. . . .

And felt her stomach turn to ice.

Never mind how he'd sounded, none of the men standing in the walk outside—she could see four or five of them through the little two-way mirror—looked anything *like* police investigators. Their hair was long, their clothes sloppy, and their eyes . . .

Even had they been wearing bright silver badges and starched blue uniforms, their eyes would have given them away.

"Come on," the one nearest the door said. "Open up."

She pulled away from the spyhole and inhaled shakily.

"Just a minute," she said. "I need to put something on."

The man slammed the door with his forearm.

"Forget the games," he said. "Open it."

Her fingers harrowing her cheeks, Kirsten took a step backward across the living room.

"Open up!" the man said, beating the door again, hitting it so hard she was afraid it might fly off its hinges.

Terrified, her breaths coming in sharp little bursts, Kirsten whirled and plunged through the apartment.

An instant later the door crashed open behind her.

The entryway through which the intruders had left the waiting room led to a short passage, which itself gave into another small, boxy room that was bare except for a computer workstation on the right, and a wall-mounted biometric scanner across from it beside a reinforced steel door.

"Lombardi" went straight over to the scanner. This was the part of the job that made him uptight. He'd been telling Turner the truth when he remarked that he was no technical wizard, and felt it would have been easy enough to steer the supervisor back into the room at gunpoint, force him to let the system take his readings, and in that way gain access to the vault. But the concern was that Turner might have triggered some discreet alarm had that been done. Caine's instructions had been explicit, and they'd been warned not to deviate from them under any circumstances.

Standing before the scanning unit, Lombardi raised his left hand to the level of the cameras designed to image his facial and iris characteristics, turning it so the artificial star-sapphire ring on his fourth finger would be visible to their lenses. Then, keeping that hand perfectly motionless, he placed his right hand flat on the machine's glass optoelectrical pad. Ordinarily this would both activate the unit and take readings of his fingerprint and palm geometry, which would then be converted to algorithms and matched to stored employee-identification data. But by an arcane process he did not quite understand, the specific star pattern on his ring would key a match with a simple data-string buried in the system mainframe's hard drive, which caused—or, according to Caine, was supposed to cause—the normal image-recognition sequence to be bypassed.

Lombardi held his breath and waited, one hand up, the other on the unit's clear glass interface, staring at its eye-level VDU. A red light had begun to glow beneath the glass, indicating the scanner had been activated by his touch . . . but if all was going as planned, the readings of its thermal sensors would be ignored by the computers.

Five seconds went by.

Ten.

He waited.

And then the words CLEARED TO ENTER appeared in the middle of the screen.

He exhaled, heard the faint click of the vault's lock mechanism retracting, and turned to his partner, who was already working open the heavy steel door.

They were in.

Kirsten ran toward the back of the apartment, hearing the door burst open behind her, hearing the men who'd been outside come pounding through the living room at her heels. She had only a vague notion of what to do, but it was *all* she had, and there was no choice except to go with it. If she could make it to the back door before they caught up, get into the building's central parking court, then maybe—

Suddenly a hand reached out from behind and snatched the sleeve of her blouse, pulling at her, yanking her backward. She stumbled, and almost lost her balance, but somehow managed to keep her legs underneath her, keep *moving,* carried by her own forward momentum. She twisted sharply as her pursuer tried to get his other hand around her, heard a loud ripping sound, and then was free of his grasp, racing across the room again, scrambling toward the door, a ragged streamer of cotton dangling from her arm.

"Hey!" he shouted. *"Stop, you bitch!"*

Kirsten was within several feet of the back door now, the kitchen on her immediate right, the hallway leading to the bedrooms on her left. She lunged ahead, shooting her hand out in front of her, reaching for the doorknob,

thinking she might make it, thinking she really might, when the man whose grip she'd managed to escape a moment earlier sprang at her in a flying tackle, the full weight of his body whumping into her, his arms clamping around her waist.

He spun Kirsten around and swept her in toward his chest, trying to get a firmer hold on her. Frantic, she snatched a glance past his shoulder, saw his companions rushing up through the living room, and thrust her hands out at his face, clawing at him, digging her fingers into his eyes.

That bought her a momentary reprieve. Emitting an animal yelp of pain, her attacker shoved fiercely away from her and covered his face with his hands, spinning in a blind semicircle, bowling wildly into the men behind him. At the same time, Kirsten flung herself at the door, clutched the knob, and tore it open.

Gasping for breath, a gale wind of terror and desperation roaring through her brain, she dashed out into the automobile court.

When the white-smocked techie first opened the door to the security office, the coffee she brought the guys every day at the same time balanced on a cafeteria tray in one hand, she simply couldn't credit her eyes. She stood there in the doorway, looking at the bodies and the blood streaming from the unrecognizable remains of their heads, the blood spattered everywhere in the room, the blood and strings of gristle covering the monitors on which closed-circuit images of the halls were still flashing through their preset sequences as if nothing eventful had occurred to disrupt the daily routine, and then suddenly the world went into a crazy tilt and the two coffee cups

spilled from the tray and hit the floor where there was all that blood and gore and she opened her mouth wide and screamed, screamed at the top of her lungs. . . .

Screamed until long after half the people in the building had come running toward the office to see what in the name of God and his blessed angels was the matter.

Kirsten squatted on her haunches between two parked cars, trembling with fright, trying not to move, afraid the slightest sound would give her position away to her pursuers. She could hear their feet crunching on the asphalt as they moved up and down the aisles, searching for her amid the rows of slotted vehicles. There weren't as many cars in the lot as there would have been at night, when many more residents of the apartment complex would be home from work, but she would take what small blessings she could . . . and for the first time in her life feel grateful for the large government-sponsored housing developments that had virtually wiped out the city's traditional architecture.

More footsteps. Closer. She hugged herself, trying to think clearly through her fear. If she could manage to hide until someone came along either to leave or fetch his car . . . or perhaps inch her way around toward the driveway leading to the street, then maybe she'd have a chance to get some help. . . .

Kirsten heard the crunch of another footfall, this one no more than two aisles down to the left of her, then an entirely different set a little further off to the right.

They were boxing her in on either side.

She stiffened, biting down on the fleshy part of her hand, stifling a mutinous scream. While part of her kept insisting that she give in to the urge, there was a more

rational part that understood it would be the worst mistake she could possible make. If she screamed, they'd know exactly where she was, would be on her in an instant, well before anyone could come to her aid.

No, she dared not do it. Dared not make a sound. Dared not move a muscle.

The moment she did, Kirsten was sure she would be theirs.

The optical mini-CDs were stored in specially designed, alphanumerically-tabbed electronic "stacks" lining the walls of the vault. Once inside, the pair of intruders had been able to locate the object of their search within seconds. At the touch of a button, the disc was scanned, identified by a bar code imprinted on its surface, and then ejected from the repository in a gleaming stainless-steel tray.

Slipping the disk into a protective plastic sleeve he took from a wall dispenser, Lombardi dropped it into the breast pocket of his jacket and gave his partner the ready signal.

The two men strode from the vault less than three minutes after entering it, passed through the waiting area without a glance at the dead supervisor, and reentered the outer corridor as if they had nothing to hide.

They were swinging back into the main entry hall when the lab tech's screams pierced the air and all hell broke loose around them.

Kirsten knew she wouldn't be able to hide from her pursuers much longer.

The man she'd heard on her left had reached the end of the aisle he'd been searching, swung into the aisle immediately beside the one where she was crouched, and

then turned back up in her direction, pausing every couple of steps to poke his head back and forth between the cars. He was now standing directly across from her, separated from her by a single row of vehicles. And the others were closing in from elsewhere around the court.

The man on the left took a step up the aisle, then another. Kirsten's breath came to a stop. She could see his boots and the bottoms of his jeans under the chassis of the car she was leaning against. Her heart was booming in her ears like a timpani, and in the panicky, half-crazed moment before she got a handle on herself, Kirsten was afraid he'd be able to hear it as well.

In a minute or so he would turn up her aisle, and it would be over.

She had never in her life felt so terribly helpless and alone.

God, God, what am I going to do?

No opening had presented itself. Nobody had driven in or out of the lot, and she had no reason to think anybody would before it was too late to make any difference.

She suddenly realized the only thing she could do was run for it, break for the driveway, and hope that by some miracle she could reach the street before they did. She knew even that wouldn't necessarily mean she was safe— the men who'd come after her and Max had been willing to strike on a thoroughfare as busy as Scotts Road, strike with hundreds of pedestrians around, for godsakes. If this group was just a fraction as bold, they might not have the slightest concern about who saw them.

But she hadn't any choice. It was either leave the pot or be cooked.

She waited another second, took a deep gulp of air, and then forced herself to spring to her feet.

The man on the left spotted her instantly. Their eyes made the briefest contact, hers full of hunted terror, his absent of any hint of sympathy or compassion.

Then he rasped an order to his companions and came hurtling across the aisle at her.

Kirsten turned and fled.

The first indication that something was wrong came the moment they pulled their rental car up to the curb, and was the only one they needed. If there were a way to think things were normal after arriving at a person's home and finding the door kicked in, Nimec didn't know it.

He glanced out the windshield at the street, at the outside stairs, at the walkways spanning the rows of doors on the building's upper stories. All were empty.

"Have your weapons ready," he said to Noriko and Osmar. He withdrew his own Beretta 8040 from its concealment holster, ejected its standard ten-round clip, and chocked in the twelve-round magazine/grip extension. "Don't seem to be any eyes around, but if somebody does call the local gendarmes, we'll get it straight with them later."

Following his lead, the others jogged out of the car and across the ground level unit's front yard to the partially open door.

Nimec instinctively moved to the right of the door frame, gesturing the others to the left, making sure there was some wall between them and whatever potential threat might be inside.

"Kirsten, this is Pete Nimec!" he called through the opening, leaning his head around the splintered jamb. "Are you okay in there?"

No reply.

He pulled back against the wall, cocked his pistol, and looked across the doorway at his teammates.

"Go!" he said.

They rushed into the apartment and fanned out in a practiced crossover maneuver, Nimec moving to the left of the entrance, gun held ready, Noriko and Osmar following him and buttonhooking to the right. The three of them rapidly pivoted to cover the center of the room with their weapons, legs apart, making broad sweeps of their sectors of fire.

They seemed to be alone in the place.

"Kirsten, you here?" Nimec called again.

Still no answer.

Noriko tapped his arm. "Look," she said, pointing straight across the living room.

The back door was wide open.

Nimec's eyes flicked between her and Osmar.

"Come on," he said, and rushed toward the door.

The two intruders paused in the hall and exchanged glances. Confused, frightened staffers poured from doorways on either side of them. Not a word was spoken. They could see that the greatest commotion was down the left bend of the corridor, and knew the bodies of the guards had been discovered. Their original intention had been to walk out the main entrance, and they would have to gamble on still being able to leave that way in the disturbance. It would be dangerous, but any attempt to leave the building through emergency exits would trip sensors that would likely pinpoint the specific door being opened. And they had no illusions about having eliminated the threat from security. The men at the surveillance monitors would not have been the sole members of the

plainclothes team on premises. And there was the uniformed guard at the door.

The intruders could only keep their fingers crossed that he'd be sufficiently distracted for them to slip past. Otherwise, they'd have to kill him, too.

They moved forward through the scared, noisy people in the corridor, and were nearly at the checkpoint where they'd had to leave their guns when an alarm sounded, a loud on-and-off noise that grated on the eardrums. The guard at the door seemed to be tracking them with his eyes as they approached.

"We're going out to radio for assistance," the one who'd called himself Lombardi said. His hand was in his jacket pocket.

The guard looked at him.

"I'm sorry," he said. "The building's been sealed."

"Don't insult me," Lomardi said. "We have a job to do."

He started to move forward, Samford walking beside him. The alarm grated on and on.

The guard clamped a hand around Lombardi's arm.

"You need to call somebody, we have phones in here," he said. "But nobody's leaving."

Lombardi smiled. His hand was still in his jacket.

"Don't bet on it," he said, and squeezed the trigger of the pistol he'd taken from the guards in the monitor room.

Hit at point-blank range, the security guard catapulted backward off his feet, a cloud of blood exploding from his chest. Lombardi pumped two more bullets into him as he dropped to the ground, finishing him.

He turned to his companion and waved him along. He was aware of screams, pale faces, racing feet behind them on the concrete floor.

They hastened toward the door, and got as far as the archway of the weapons detector when someone behind them shouted out an order to halt. They kept walking.

"I said freeze!" the voice repeated. *"This is your final warning!"*

Without turning, they quickened their pace.

A gunshot fired out from behind them. Lombardi whirled and saw a plainclothes guard in the center of the corridor, both hands around a gun, his knees bent in a shooter's stance. Lombardi returned fire, missed, heard a *thud-thud-thud* from the suited guard's gun, and then was slapped across the middle by something he didn't see. He looked down at himself, his eyes wide with shock, and had just enough time to glimpse the bloody amalgam of flesh and shredded clothing that had replaced his stomach before he crumpled in a dying heap.

The other intruder reached for his own gun, but before he'd gotten it out of his pocket saw two more plainclothesmen emerge from the branching corridors at his rear. They all had their weapons drawn, and had triangulated their aim to put him in a perfect crossfire.

"Hold it!" he said. Dropping the gun to the floor, kicking it away from him, and slowly raising his hands above his head. "Don't shoot, okay? *Okay?*"

Their guns extended, the Sword ops moved in and took him.

Swinging around the grille of a car, Kirsten tore into the aisle and ran like hell, making for the driveway in a wild headlong dash.

She heard overlapping footsteps behind her, close, close, and pushed herself to move even faster, her legs pumping, arms working at her sides like pistons—

And then, suddenly, one of her pursuers sprang from behind a parked car several yards in front of her.

Between her and the driveway.

His right eye was bloodshot and swollen, and there was a thin line of blood trickling down his cheek from its lower lid.

It was the man she'd grappled with in the apartment. He had some kind of gun in his hand—a submachine gun, she thought, though she was hardly an expert—and was holding it out at her.

"No more shit from you," he said in Bahasa.

She halted, glanced over her shoulder.

Two more of the men who'd come for her were walking quickly up the aisle in her direction, their firearms held downward, flat against their legs. The fourth stalker had emerged near the spot where she'd been hiding.

"Just come on over here, I won't hurt you," said the one blocking her path to the driveway. He motioned with his gun. "Let's go."

Kirsten didn't budge, and was amazed to realize she was shaking her head in the negative.

He shrugged, holding his weapon steady. She could hear the other three coming close behind her.

"You want to wrestle some more, we wrestle," he said, and took a step forward.

"Hold it right there! *Bayaso reya!*"

The voice echoing through the court stopped all four of the men in their tracks. An expression of stunned surprise on his features, the one in front of Kirsten abruptly looked around for its source.

"*Drop the gun!*" the voice said in Bahasa.

Still looking from side to side, the man blocking the

driveway moved the gun off of Kirsten, but didn't lower it.

Kirsten heard a crack like the sound of a detonating firecracker. And then a blossom of crimson appeared in the middle of the man's rib cage and he pitched facedown to the asphalt, his submachine gun clattering from his grasp.

"I hope the rest of you are smarter," the voice said. "It's finished."

Kirsten turned her head, saw one of the gunmen behind her start to raise his weapon, instantly heard two more sharp cracks—only now coming from a different part of the court. The man screamed and fell over clutching his knees, blood spraying out from between his fingers.

The remaining pair of men tossed down their weapons and started to run, scrambling out of the aisle, and then bolting wildly toward the driveway exit. No one tried to stop them.

Her eyes wide and staring, Kirsten looked uncomprehendingly around the court, and all at once saw a brown-skinned Malay spring to his feet behind the tail of a car, several aisles down and directly across from where the first stalker had fallen dead. An instant later two more people appeared near the one who'd been shot in the knees—a white man with close-cropped hair and an Oriental woman.

The man with the short hair holstered his gun beneath his jacket and approached her.

"Kirsten, it's okay, you're safe," he said in a calm, level voice. "I'm Pete Nimec."

She started to say something in response, but her throat had closed up, and her teeth were chattering too violently.

Instead, she strode over to him, put her face against his shoulder, put her arms around him, and started crying.

Noriko had gone to wait in the apartment with Kirsten while Nimec and Osmar took care of business in the parking court.

"Mr. Nimec," Osmar said. "There is something I must show you."

"Right."

Nimec finished flex-cuffing the wounded man, folded a blanket he'd gotten from the apartment under his head, then went over to Osmar.

Kneeling over the body of the one he'd dropped, the Malay lifted his motionless hand off the asphalt.

"You see kris tattoo?" he said, glancing up at Nimec.

Nimec nodded. "Guy I cuffed has exactly the same marking on him. What the hell is it, some kind of cult sign?"

Osmar shook his head.

"Is more like what you Americans call . . ." He made a low sound of concentration in his throat, as if groping hard for words. Then he snapped his fingers. "Ah," he said. *"Colors."*

"Gang colors, you mean," Nimec said. "As in the Crips and Bloods."

Osmar nodded, and placed his finger on the tattooed skin. "The kris, many pirate gangs have such marks. But you see designs on blade?"

Nimec squatted beside him for a closer look. He did indeed see them—grotesque anthropomorphic figures that reminded him a little of the paintings on Egyptian tombs.

"They are *rakasa,*" Osmar said. "Demons. Different for each brotherhood."

Sudden understanding spread across Nimec's features.

"These two punks . . . someone familiar with regional gang crime would be able tell their affiliation from the markings," he said

Osmar nodded again. "And this one, I know well from when I was with police," he said. "The men work for Khao Luan. He is Kuomintang."

The word rang a vague bell. Nimec searched his memory a few seconds.

"A heroin trader?" he said finally.

Another nod. "None are more powerful. The Thai army, they make him to flee during pacification program. Ten years ago, maybe more. Since then, he is in Indonesia."

Nimec gave him an imperative look. "Where? Does anybody know *where*?"

"Everyone knows, and everyone fears to touch him," Osmar said. "In parts of Banjarmasin, the Thai has longer arms than the government."

Nimec was quiet, letting it all sink in. What connection could a man like that have to Monolith? What on *earth* had Max stumbled onto?

After a moment he clapped a hand on Osmar's arm and nodded firmly.

"My friend, we're about to do some more island-hopping," he said. "And I promise you, if this guy's involved in Blackburn's disappearance, I'll cut his fucking arms off myself."

TWENTY-FIVE

THE SURVIVING MEMBER OF THE PAIR THAT GOT INTO the Sacramento vault hadn't talked—not to the Sword detail that apprehended him, not to the Feds after he'd been given into their custody. And it was anybody's guess whether he was *going* to talk.

Gordian, however, wasn't sure that was essential to determining who had been behind the act.

The main question for him, then, was of motive.

Back in San Jose now—he had booked reservations aboard a commuter flight while the A&P mechs continued their inspection of the Learjet in Washington—Gordian sat at his desk opposite Chuck Kirby, trying to put the pieces of a complex and profoundly troubling puzzle into place. They had already run through the whole thing a couple of times, but neither man felt it would hurt to bounce it around once more.

"Let's try it back to front," Gordian said. "Starting with the break-in at the Sacramento facility."

"Sure, why not," Kirby said. "Doing it the other way hasn't nailed it."

"I don't know whether it *can* be nailed, not with the fragmentary information we have," Gordian said. "But

we can get closer, make some more important connections.''

Kirby nodded. ''The disc they took off the dead man, then,'' he said.

''The disc,'' Gordian repeated, sighing. ''The keycodes are used in communications systems UpLink has designed for a wide range of naval vessels. Obviously they would be of enormous value to any number of interests, both foreign and domestic.''

''Allies and enemies, for that matter,'' Kirby said. ''Everybody spies on everybody else. It's wide open until you look at how the thieves penetrated the vault.''

''Exactly.'' Gordian's face was sober. ''And if not for the surveillance videos capturing what happened after they killed poor Turner, the techies might've taken weeks, even months to find out. The wicked beauty of it is that the system defeated itself.''

''And that's still the part I can't quite grasp,'' Kirby said.

''It probably isn't vital that you do . . . although the concept isn't really that difficult,'' Gordian said. ''It involves basic computer file architecture, the way hard drives are set up. There's a minimum amount of space allocated for every file on a hard drive . . . the larger the drive, the larger the allocation. Regardless of how much data you have in a file, the computer reserves that minimum space.'' He thought a moment. ''Imagine a department store that only has gift boxes of a single size for their merchandise, no matter whether you're buying a tengallon hat or a gold forget-me-not for your wife's necklace. Since the box needs to be pretty big to contain the hat, that tiny charm's not going to be too visible when it's placed inside. In fact, it may even get lost.''

Kirby nodded. "The data-strings that let the thieves through the system's backdoor . . . you're saying they were too small to be noticed. Like the charm. And they slipped past your whiz kids when the software employed by the biometric scanner system was examined for back-doors prior to installation."

"And the techs can't even be held at fault," Gordian said, nodding. "Do a careful diagnostic of *any* hard drive, and you'll find the percentage of file-space being utilized out of whack with the actual number of stored bytes. You store one word-processing file with a couple of words on it, another with several pages of text, and it's probable both are grabbing the same amount of space. When the technicians are looking for Trojan horses, they typically sniff around for long, complex algorithms such as the type needed to match fingerprint or voice characteristics. In this case, the backdoor key was short and sweet . . . a ba-sic geometric pattern . . . a small item in a big box."

"The star on the sapphire," Kirby said. "Incredible."

"To me, what's more incredible is that our security system's primary biometric software was produced by— and acquired from—Monolith Technologies, of all god-damn outfits under the sun," Gordian said. He shook his head. "Talk about an incomprehensible oversight . . ."

"Don't beat yourself over the head with it, Gord," Kirby said. "Their stuff's the best being made. And the system was implemented a while before the problems be-tween you and Caine started brewing. Viewed as an iso-lated incident, the break-in wouldn't even necessarily place Caine under suspicion. There could be rogue hack-ers within his company—"

Gordian's face tightened.

"It isn't hackers who tried to steal UpLink out from

under me. Nor was it hackers who used Reynold Armitage as a point man in advance of the raid, or had my plane's landing-gear system sabotaged, or made Max Blackburn vanish into thin air.''

Kirby released a breath. ''We can't prove Caine's direct involvement with any of that. . . .''

''It's just the two of us here, Chuck. This isn't about what I can prove, but what I know,'' Gordian said. ''Over the past seventy-two hours, the A&P team in D.C. has traced the plane's entire hydraulic circuit for leaks a half-dozen times. And found nothing. Also, the mechs here at home have paper checklists verifying they conducted the full preflight a day before we left, including eyeball inspections of the system's gauges and connections.'' He paused. ''Somebody tampered with that plane after it was prepped. And the guard at the airport, a man named Jack McRea, fessed up to having left his post for several hours a couple nights ago.''

''And has since been released from your employ, I hope,'' Kirby said.

Gordian nodded. ''Far as he's been willing to admit, he was lured off to a motel by long legs and a miniskirt. Suckered into leaving the hangars wide open.''

The room was silent a few moments.

''The logical jump still bothers me,'' Kirby said. ''Tying Caine to an attempted murder without evidence, for godsakes.''

''Mur*ders,* plural,'' Gordian said. ''You were on that plane too, Chuck. As was Megan and Scull.''

''Gord, my point is—''

''I know what it is. And again, I'm not talking about specific evidence, but getting a handle on the totality of events that have been wheeling around my head. Max is

investigating Caine's business operations in Asia, Max drops out of sight. I take on the Morrison-Fiore Bill, Caine jumps into the ring as a challenger, then as a person who wants to devour my corporation. Somebody breaks into my encryption facility, they do it using a backdoor in Caine-designed software. And so on and so forth. There's too much coincidence. And now the whole thing seems to have taken on a sense of acceleration . . . almost desperation. . . .''

"Or urgency," Kirby said. "If we're going to walk the road you're inclined to lead us down, the keys on that disc they tried to snatch are at the heart of this."

Gordian nodded, his hands steepled under his chin.

The two men sat there quietly a while, thinking everything through.

Five minutes passed, then several more.

More thought, more silence.

Suddenly Gordian sat forward, his eyes widening.

Chuck looked at him. "Something the matter?"

"That word you used," he said. "*Urgency.* It's just that . . .''

He let the sentence trail off, moistened his lips.

Chuck kept looking at him.

"Oh, my God, how could I not have seen? That's why it's come to a head now. *My God,* the ceremony . . . the maiden run is today!"

"Gord, what the hell's *wrong*?"

Gordian shot his hand across the desk and gripped Kirby's wrist.

"The Seawolf," he said, speaking rapidly. "Its command and control systems . . . the systems that run the sub . . . they use UpLink encryption software. And the spare keys, the keys are on that disc."

Kirby was staring at him incredulously. "Gord, I'm not sure I'm reading you, or *want* to be reading you. But even if I am, the thing to remember is nobody got hold of them—"

Gordian sliced his right hand through the air to silence him, still digging the fingers of his left into Kirby's wrist.

"They aren't the only keys, Chuck," he said abruptly, his face white as a sheet. "You understand? We're talking about a nuclear submarine, a boat the President's going to be aboard. *And they aren't the only keys.*"

Watching his team ready themselves on the transportable dock, Omori was convinced he had done well, both in selecting his divers and finding a suitable launching area for the insertion. Notched into the coast of Pulau Ringitt— a small island less than five kilometers south of Sentosa— the saltwater inlet was protected by a zone of mud and marsh that made it the sort of place few people wanted to go sloshing around in.

Omori checked his watch. Not much longer now. Not much longer before his men climbed into the underwater delivery vehicle and the time for preparation was over at last.

He was eagerly looking forward to that moment.

Invisible beneath its camouflage netting, the delivery craft rested on a floating dock amid the thick rushes near the bank. Its bullet-shaped, fiberglass hull was windowless, and though this aided in reducing its detection signature, it also meant Omori's team would be navigating solely on their instruments once they lowered the canopy.

He regarded them from the stern of the speedboat which had towed the dock into position twenty-four hours earlier, and with which he would soon guide it back into

deeper water. The four divers had already slipped into their wetsuits and Oxy-57 breathing apparatus. While these had not been designed for the depths at which they would be operating, Omori had been assured the closed-circuit gear would provide breathable air for the limited time their use would be required.

He glanced at his watch again, his frequent reading of its face the only outward sign of the pressure he was feeling. The act to which he had wholeheartedly committed himself would boost the *Inagawa-kai* to unchallenged dominance over competing Yakuza syndicates, and would guarantee him a personal status to surpass that of Oyabuns and Emperors. But even that did not begin to describe what it would mean. Nothing like it had ever been done. Nothing. It would be remembered forever.

The prospect of future glories pushing any thought of failure from his mind, Omori switched on his minicomputer and waited for Kersik's electronic message to appear.

The show was not turning out to be quite what Alec Nordstrum had expected.

No, scratch that, he thought. As a writer, it was his job to use language precisely. And as a member of the press, he had an ethical obligation to be fair.

The show was fine. A tour of the Keppel Harbor area, much fraternal camaraderie between President Ballard and his fellow heads of state, a beautifully organized and executed military parade composed of American, ASEAN, and JMSDF forces, and now the speechifying phase of the ceremony, held on the dock against the sleek, dark shape of the Seawolf. Soon Alex would be invited aboard the sub

with the small party of invited journalists, and off they would slip into the octopus's garden for the signing of SEAPAC . . . at which point he'd probably be forced to sit in with the bilgewater.

And that, he supposed, got to the crux of his complaint.

The show was fine, but his seats were lousy. Whereas he'd thought he'd be getting a backstage pass, and had planned to watch the action from the wings, thus far he'd gotten the equivalent of general admission at a rock concert.

He stood in the crowded press area on the waterfront, listening to the Japanese Prime Minister's remarks, getting bumped, jostled, and elbowed by scores of his rude and disorderly international colleagues, thinking this was surely just the first foul taste of Encardi's revenge, and that pretty soon he would be made to drink long and deep of its bitter waters. Already the President had snubbed him. The President's coterie of advisors had blown him off. Perhaps he was being oversensitive, but once or twice he'd even thought that some members of the President's Secret Service detail—men Nordstrum knew by name, and in some cases worked out with at the gym—were shooting dirty looks his way.

He had dared to go with his conscience, to stand with Roger Gordian, and for that had become a marked man, banished from grace, cast among the rabble.

Politics, he mused. *Always politics.*

Nordstrum sighed, trying his best to follow Yamamoto's speech . . . which was not easy with some reporter from an Italian news organization shouting and blowing kisses across his face to a female news anchor from a French television show. *Questa sera, mi bella.*

Dear God, the price one paid for holding to convictions in this world.

He glanced disconsolately at his watch. Another forty minutes or so before he'd be able to make his path to the ramp with the others getting into the nuclear-attack submarine. Even if he *was* restricted to the waste-processing facilities, he'd be grateful to be aboard. Damned grateful.

As far as he could see, his situation couldn't get any worse than it already was.

The Chinese hovercraft had arrived at the atoll under cover of darkness, transported in the well decks of two civilian tankers that had been refitted for military usage. Nearly ninety feet long and half as wide, each amphibious landing craft was powered by four sixteen-thousand-horsepower turbines—two of which fed the shrouded air-screws that would thrust it along at better than fifty knots, the others driving the centrifugal fans that provided vertical lift, allowing the craft to float above sea and strand on a smooth cushion of air. Their decks bristled with pintle-mounted 12.7mm Type 77 machine guns and 40mm grenade launchers.

Standing on the beach of the lagoon, General Kersik Imman watched his men board their vessels in preparation for the Sandakan raid, most of them filing up the ramps onto the four lozenge-shaped flotation craft assembled at the tide line, the rest climbing into a swarm of slender aluminum-hulled cigarette boats. All were suited as he was, in woodland fatigues, their faces veiled by cammo netting, their rucksacks and load-bearing harnesses laden with combat equipment. In strict adherence to Kersik's specifications, the light-assault rifles slung over their

shoulders were factory-new, and would make effective personal weapons. Zhiu Sheng had delivered as promised, and for that—as for many other qualities—Kersik deeply respected him.

Perhaps one day they would meet again in some civilized place, a place far from this wretched island where the mosquitos were as fat as grapes from the blood on which they endlessly gorged, a place where they could sit at tables and chairs instead of hard straw mats that cramped their buttocks, a place where they could comfortably reminisce about all they had seen and done since they'd first met as younger men, one an Indonesian general full of pride and aspiration, the other a spirited Communist builder seeking to give shape to Utopia. Both holding dreams of Asian unity and greatness.

Yes, Kersik thought, perhaps they would indeed meet at some future time, and discuss how their greatest dreams had been attained at stages of their lives when most men were snugly wrapped in soft blankets of contentment. And together they would recollect the monumental day the Japanese and Americans who sought to dominate the region—and the ASEAN *wayang kulit* puppets with whom they worked their intricate shadow plays—were swallowed by an underwater behemoth of their own creation.

For now, though, there was only the certain prospect of the attack about to be launched, and the soul-heaviness of an old warrior who knew in his weary heart that the basic equation of war was always out of balance, the accretion of violence always beyond control, the smallest of gains always bought and paid for with the blood of far too many irreplaceable human beings.

Adjusting his pack on his shoulders, Kersik strode

across the sand and boarded the vessel that would carry him to battle.

Khao Luan strode along the boardwalk toward his dwelling on the canal, popping fried, sugared pieces of *tempe goreng* into his mouth, thinking he'd been foolish not to have the canoe vender fill an extra container for him. At the rate he was going, there would be nothing left of the soybean cakes by the time he sat down at his table.

Stress always made him hungry, and he had awakened famished today. With good reason, too. This business he'd gotten into . . . Sandakan . . . the hijack of a nuclear submarine . . . the *hostage taking* of the President of the United States. . . .

For him, it had all been about keeping the sea routes open for his trade. SEAPAC represented a threat to that trade, a solidifying of cooperation between regional governments in matters relating to the patrol of their waters, a substantial impediment to the flow of contraband from Thailand and elsewhere. Disrupting the treaty signing, perhaps even suspending its implementation indefinitely, had seemed a reasonable and pragmatic aim, a sound business strategy for one intent on staying at the top of his game.

Ah, though, how it had evolved.

He walked on, tossing another bit of food into his mouth. Until this morning, he'd been able to concentrate on the particulars rather than the broad contours of the plan, doing his part, taking it a step at a time. Which was how he generally approached things. But with its realization at hand—less than an hour away, unbelievably—the full weight of what he and his allies had undertaken had begun pressing down on him. And while he'd decided that the best way to deal with that pressure was to pretend

this was any other day . . . well, it was difficult, that was all.

Luan reached the ladder that climbed to his door, paused at its foot, and looked into his box of *tempe*. Two pieces left. Really, really, he would have to send the men out for more.

He shook both remaining cakes into his mouth, absently tossed the container over his shoulder into the water to his right, and gripped the ladder frame to hoist himself upward.

Inches from where the cardboard box had joined the other refuse floating along the canal, a young female vendor in a loose-fitting sarong hunched forward in her canoe, her head lowering behind mounds of fruit, her hand slipping under a natty hank of cloth.

When that hand reappeared a moment later, it was holding a flat, palm-sized radio.

"Empire State to South Philly, do you read?" the vendor said in a quiet voice, transmitting over a trunked digital channel.

"Loud and clear, Empire State. The rooster back in the barn?"

"Just strutted in, big and nasty in life as in pictures," she said.

A brief pause.

She bent lower, waiting, holding the radio out of sight.

"Sit tight, Empire State," the voice replied after a second. "We're on our way to pluck his feathers."

Jointly sponsored by the ASEAN republics from its original blueprints to its funding and final construction, the Sandakan cryptographic key-storage bank was the largest in Asia, and the second largest in the world, ranking only

behind a subsequently built facility of its type in Europe. In terms of proportion, it was to most of the world's other key-recovery banks what Citibank was to a small-town S&L. Sprawling across many acres of shoreline, the concrete-and-steel structure gave a fortresslike impression, and was protected by a sophisticated array of alarm systems and guard units of chiefly Malaysian and Indonesian composition. All this security was in place for a simple reason: The spare key-codes stored within its vaults were those of the region's largest governmental, military, and financial institutions.

It had been regarded as a logical, convenient, and secure place for the Japanese and American governments to store the spare keys to many of Seawolf's encrypted operational systems, including those which controlled its Advanced SEAL Delivery System—or ASDS—docking hatches. These would allow a fully pressurized mini-sub containing from eight to twelve special-op divers to launch and recover its personnel during insertions requiring long-distance, deep-submergence transport. As planned, when the SEALS returned from a mission aboard the sixty-five-foot ASDS vehicle, the computers aboard their vessel would signal the Seawolf's control systems to open the ASDS hatch so that the crew and passengers—and their equipment—could reenter the submarine via its docking chamber, and move from there onto its main decks.

Nga Canbera did not know, and would never know, precisely which Japanese government official had passed this information on to the Inagawa-kai, which had in turn relayed it to him through Omori.

And what difference does it make? he thought, sitting in his den now, watching the SEAPAC ribbon-cutting cer-

emony on television. He had remained home from the office to watch it undistracted, putting on his finest silk robe for the occasion. So far—given his knowledge of what would happen once the dignitaries were under way—it was proving to be quite a source of amusement.

For him the challenge of the game was the important thing, and though Nga had experienced his moments of apprehension lately, he felt the play would have been meaningless without an edge of danger. Today he would put aside his worries and *enjoy* himself. Could the Seawolf be tricked into swallowing a poison pill? After all, it was in theory only a matter of putting the right keys in the wrong hands—wrong from the American and Japanese standpoint, that is. And while Marcus Caine's failure to deliver the command-and-control keys had been a setback, it had in a sense only added to the excitement. Once Kersik got his hands on the Sandakan keys, Omori's divers would still be able to open the ASDS hatch. After that, they would simply have to put greater reliance on force than finesse, and use guns and bullets rather than keystrokes and passwords to take the submarine.

And maybe, if he were very fortunate, there even would be a little bloodshed to make things more interesting.

His eyes wide with disbelief, U.S. Secretary of Defense Conrad Holden looked at the telephone receiver in his hand as if it had been invaded by an evil poltergeist . . . albeit one that possessed the voice and speech mannerisms of Roger Gordian, someone he'd known for many long years.

"Roger, are you certain?"

"I'm telling you it's going to be Sandakan, Conrad.

And it will roughly coincide with the sub's embarkation. They won't want to give us time to disable the key-codes."

"But the sub's launching in a half an *hour*—"

"Then get off the phone with me and call somebody who can stop this from happening!"

Hotter and sweatier than he was accustomed to feeling, Luan was about to change his shirt when he heard it: the regular *thup-thup-thup* of rotors beating the air, rapidly getting louder and closer.

He looked across the room to where Xiang and his bodyguards had been throwing a pair of dice.

"What's that sound?" he said, already knowing the answer. The army helicopters had been ubiquitous when he was driven from the hills of northern Thailand.

The pirate tossed down the dice and turned abruptly to his fellows.

"Get your weapons," he grunted. "We're being attacked."

Leaning out the door of the Bell Jet Ranger chopper, Nimec extracted shells from his utility webbing, slapped them into his 12-gauge and pumped the forestock to chamber the first round. Like Osmar and the other three Sword ops in his team, he had on a pullover cowl, gas mask, and black Nomex Stealthsuit. The Zylon body armor underneath his shirt was both lighter and stronger than Kevlar.

Nimec gestured for the pilot to lower the chopper to a stabilized hover, and peered at the wooden structure below. There were a number of windows on all sides. He

chose one of them as his target and pulled the trigger of his pump gun.

The finned CS bomblet disgorged from its muzzle in a train of propellent vapor, punched through the window, and burst open to release a cloud of tear gas.

Nimec chambered another round, fired, and loosed a third at the Thai's hideout. Billows of white smoke erupted from the windows.

He slung the weapon over his shoulder—he also had an MP5K against his side—donned his gloves, and signaled his companions to the door.

A moment later the rope line was dropped from its hoist bracket. One after another in quick succession, the men gripped the line and fast-roped to the boardwalk like firefighters sliding down a pole.

Submachine-gun volleys erupted on the ground almost the instant they alighted—stuttering from inside the house, from the dwellings around it, and from the wooden walkway that ran the length of the canal.

His head ducked low as his teammates laid down a lane of covering fire, Nimec raced around to the front of the hideout.

A man surged into his path from the gushing smoke of the building, bringing an FN P90 up in his direction. But he was half-blinded from the CS, and Nimec was quick to react. He jogged out of the way as the pirate released a stream of 9mm rounds. Nimec raked him across the middle with a burst from his MP5K, then kept dashing for the entrance without a backward glance.

He paused in front of the heavy plank door, sprayed the lock with bullets, and kicked it in with the flat of his foot. With his peripheral vision he could see Osmar running up on the left.

He looked over at him, signaled a crossover entry, and ticked off a three-count with his fingers.

Together they rushed forward into the house.

Minutes after the ribbon-cutting fanfare concluded, the delegation of world leaders was ushered across the gang, over the black anechoic tiles covering Seawolf's hull-like rubber flagstones, and then down into the sub by its executive officer. President Ballard dropped through the hatch first, followed by Prime Minister Yamamoto and the Malaysian and Indonesian heads-of-state.

The press contingent came next, Alex Norstrum at the back of the line, straining to see past a tall, broad-shouldered Canadian reporter who had been directed to board ahead of him.

As the group filed through a passageway toward the control room, Ballard felt as if he were about to step into the set of a Hollywood space opera, something about starships and wormholes in the space-time continuum. And in a sense he *was* entering a time machine, one which was capable of hurling him back through the accumulation of years and distance that had brought him to middle age, stripping the overlay of political cynicism and calculation from his face, and briefly revealing the excited countenance of a ten-year-old orphan from the Mississippi boondocks whose dreams had fueled a long, difficult journey from poverty to the Presidency. He goggled at the equipment and status boards filling up every corner of the brightly lit space with open wonder, his wide eyes no sooner landing on one piece of gadgetry than getting snagged by another of equal or greater fascination.

The sub's commanding officer, Commander Malcolm R. Frickes, USN, was saluting his guests from the control room entryway.

"It is my honor and privilege to welcome you all aboard," he said, stepping aside to let them enter.

Ballard enthusiastically returned the salute, swallowed, and gestured toward the periscopes on a raised platform in the center of the room.

"Do I get to look through one of *those*?" he asked.

Frickes smiled.

"Sir, you're the Commander-in-Chief," he said. "And that means you get to do anything you wish."

General Yussef Tabor, commanding officer of the Malaysian Army's 10th Parachute Brigade, could scarcely believe the orders that had just come down the line. He was to deploy his three airborne battalions—almost three thousand men—to Sandakan at once and assist the regular key-bank guard units in defending the beachhead.

Against *who* or *what* it was to be defended was unclear—but he at last saw an opportunity to be a true soldier. As the closest element of Malaysia's Rapid Deployment Force, stationed in Sabah less than thirty miles from the city, his would be the first of the support units to arrive. And that sat just fine with him.

After a decade of hunting illegal immigrants like a dogcatcher chasing down helpless puppies, it was high time for a mission he could be proud of.

Overcome with tear gas, his face tomato-red, Khao Luan was uncontrollably retching and coughing as Xiang tried to drag him into the barn. Gripping him under both arms from behind, the pirate opened the door and started to back his way through, but was still trying to maneuver his boss's weight when Nimec and Osmar burst into the house.

Osmar thrust his weapon out.

"Hold it!" he shouted in Bahasa. "Both of you!"

Breathing hard, Xiang stared at him a moment through thick braids of CS gas. Then, still partially supporting the Thai with one hand, he whipped the other behind his back and brought a donut-shaped P90 around on its strap.

The burst went wide, peppering a roof support, chewing out splinters of wood, Osmar got down into a crouch and fired back, intentionally aiming low. With Luan between him and the big man, he wanted to avoid shooting to kill, knowing the Thai might hold the answer to Blackburn's disappearance.

Luan sagged, clutching his meaty thigh, blood spraying from his femoral artery. Xiang tried to keep him erect, but was unable to manage it, and he went down with a crash. Retreating into the barn, the pirate triggered his weapon, sweeping it in an arc between Osmar and Nimec. Glass shattered somewhere in the house.

This time it was Nimec who fired back, squeezing off two crisp trigger pulls, *brrrat-brrrat.* He could hear sporadic exchanges of fire out on the walkway, and now and then a groan from one of the incapacitated pirates on the floor.

"*Cuff Luan and the rest of these bastards!*" he shouted to Osmar through his gas mask. "*I'm going after him!*"

Sea spray roiling up behind them, the four hovercraft scudded over the waves on pillows of air, flanked by dagger-shaped speedboats. They had covered nearly two thirds of the distance to the beach, and would be making landfall within a matter of minutes.

In the forward deckhouse of his vehicle, Kersik lifted his binoculars to his eyes to scan the LZ. He had mustered

a force of close to three hundred men, outnumbering the key-bank guard by a third, and with the further advantage of surprise—

Kirsik blinked once, twice.

His eyes widened and widened against the lenses of the binoculars.

At first the dots he had seen against the fleecy backdrop of the cloud looked like insects. A sweeping, descending swarm of locusts.

But he knew all too well what they were.

Paratroopers.

Hundreds of them. *Thousands*. Alighting on the beachhead.

Had his ears not been filled with the deafening roar of the airscrews he might have heard the transports arriving sooner, heard them as he could now, *buzzing,* the buzz becoming a whine, the whine becoming a drone. . . .

He let the glasses drop from his trembling fingers and ran to the deckhouse radio, but by the time he'd transmitted his warning to the other vessels the incoming fire had begun, and the world was exploding all around him.

Omori had hardly seen the small email notice appear on his LCD before he realized the message was not from Kersik at all, but his contact in the Japanese Diet . . . a member of the Nationalist minority whose leaking of top-secret intelligence about the Seawolf had been at the core of the hijack plan since its initiation.

He opened the message and felt his stomach turn on itself.

Though there was only one word on his screen, it was sufficient to make him realize his plans had just come to an abrupt and crashing end:

YAMERU.

ABORT.

Omori dug his knuckles into his forehead and released a high mewl of anguish that instantly drew the attention of all four divers on the floating dock.

He did not look at them, or say anything to them. They would know what had happened just from looking at him.

Kersik, he thought, his fist pressing deeper into his brow.

Kersik had failed.

If he'd been holding a knife in his hand, Omori would have plunged it into his heart and brought the pain to an end then and there.

A blow to the rib cage almost dropped Nimec the instant he plunged through the door.

Stunned, scintillae whirling across his vision, he reeled against the wall of the barn, his MP5K sailing from his fingers.

He clamped his jaws around the pain in his chest. Whatever hit him had felt like an iron mallet, and if he'd been running straight rather than angling through the door, would have probably caught him below the diaphragm and made him lose consciousness. But the muscles of his chest had absorbed enough of its impact to keep him on his feet.

He gulped down a mouthful of air, struggling to get hold of himself—

And saw the giant's fist coming at him barely in the nick of time. He rolled sideways, twisting his head to avoid its pile-driver force, then slipped another blow as the pirate came charging in at him, his arms raised to get

him in a squeeze hold, meaning to crush him against the wall with his bulk.

Nimec wasn't going to give him the chance. He could feel the strength flowing back into his legs and knew he had to move, stay out of the giant's reach, avoid going toe-to-toe with him at any cost. It had been his hand, his bare *hand,* that caught Nimec the first time. He'd have to make sure he didn't let it happen again.

Waiting until Xiang was almost on top of him, Nimec cocked his front leg and kicked it speedily up and out at his solar plexus. He heard the slam of his foot against the giant's flesh, saw him lurch backward, and followed through with a second snap kick to the same area.

Xiang staggered back another step and Nimec used the moment to scramble away from the wall, dancing on the balls of his feet like a boxer, getting a rhythm under him, working up some steam.

But the pirate was quicker on his feet than his size would have indicated. Rounding on Nimec, he lunged forward, rushing him head-on.

Nimec tried feinting sideways, but was a hair too late. A sinewy forearm smashed across his lips and his head rocked back on his neck. He tasted blood, felt his knees weaken a little. Xiang hit him again, this time in the throat with his elbow. Nimec gagged, his eyes blurring.

And then, suddenly, Xiang's massive palms clapped down on either side of Nimec's head, his fingers forming a cage around his jaw and cheekbones. Nimec raised his own hands, wedged them up inside Xiang's forearms, gripped his wrists, and tried with all his strength to pry them apart. But the giant only held on and began steam-rolling forward, carrying Nimec along with him, backing Nimec across the floor of the barn then ramming him up

against the wall opposite the door with an impact that jarred him to the bone.

He brought his face in close to Nimec, his features a quivering mask of rage, his breath gusting into his nostrils.

"You want to fight, I'll break your fucking neck right here!" he bellowed, shaking Nimec, battering his head against the wall. "Right here like I did to that other American!"

Nimec's eyes widened. His heart pounded and swelled within him until its beating seemed to fill the universe.

Like I did to that other American.

Groaning from exertion, he pushed against the pirate's wrists, pushed, pushed—

Right here.

That other American.

Pushed—

For an instant he thought the pirate's grip would never relent . . . and then, miraculously, it did.

Shoving off the wall, Nimec brought his knee up fast, driving it into his crotch. Xiang's hands fell away from his head. Nimec hit him again, hard to the face with his fist, kept pressing. Threw another jab, another, another.

The giant started to sag, but Nimec didn't let up. He just kept thinking that Max was dead, and this was the man who'd killed him.

Two, three, four more powerful jabs, and then Xiang surprised him. He fell forward heavily, lumbering into Nimec and knocking him backward.

In that moment, as the two men separated, Xiang lifted his bloody face, his lips twisted into a sneer, and pulled his kris from its sheath.

Nimec froze, staring at that long, wavy blade, but Xi-

ang didn't give him time to react. The giant lunged forward, the knife flickering toward Nimec's throat.

Nimec moved back a half step, pivoting on the ball of his left foot, and reached out. His right hand caught the back of Xiang's knife hand. His left hand slapped the inside of the giant's elbow, then turned and lifted the elbow up and out. Without pausing, Nimec stepped forward, pulling the giant toward him, and buried the knife deep into Xiang's chest, directly below the rib cage and angling up toward the heart.

Xiang remained on his feet another few seconds, looked down at the knife jutting from the center of his rib cage with an expression of utter astonishment, and dropped onto his face.

Nimec stepped back, breathing hard, the pain of his wounds rising up within him, and looked down at the fallen giant.

It was, at last, over.

EPILOGUE

"JUST DAYS AGO, I SAT HERE AND EXPLAINED TO someone how I knew about Marcus Caine's crimes without being able to prove them," Gordian was saying. He placed his hand on the wallet-sized digital recorder on his desk. "Now I've got proof, thanks to you."

"And Max," Kirsten said from the seat opposite him. "If not for him, I'd never have gotten it. And to be honest about it, might have kidded myself into thinking nothing strange was going on at Monolith."

Gordian looked at her, his frank blue eyes meeting her brown ones.

"For a while, maybe," he said. "But sooner or later you'd have stopped kidding yourself. And you'd have done exactly what you did."

She shrugged. They were silent a moment, just the two of them in the office. Outside the window behind Gordian, Mount Hamilton rose through the late afternoon smog, massive and somehow benign in its fixed solidity.

"Maybe you're right," she said at last. "But I'd noticed a lot of unexplained payments to American lobbyists crossing my desk. Sums that went far beyond what they should have been receiving for their services. And as I

started paying closer attention to them, I realized they always followed visits to my department head from someone who was with the Canbera bank in Indonesia.'' She shrugged again. ''Anyone with open eyes could have seen the money was graft to American politicians. The lobbying group to whom it was going was specifically hired to promote deregulation of cryptographic technology in Washington. But it wasn't until I mentioned it to Max that I allowed myself to see the truth.''

''And it was Max who convinced you to snoop around in the computer databases for financial discrepancies.''

''And plant the voice recorder in the Corporate Communications director's office.'' She shook her head. ''It's hard for me to believe how indiscreet they were. I mean, I walked right in there every day before my boss arrived, tucked it behind the sofa, and picked it up every evening between the time he left work and when the maintenance woman came to do her cleanup. Then I'd walk back to my own office and upload everything onto a computer disk before heading home. It went on like that for two months.''

''People get away with murder long enough, they get arrogant. They get arrogant, they start to think nothing can touch them. And as a result we've got half a dozen conversations about the payoffs between the director and Nga Canbera . . . and a couple with Marcus Caine's voice added to the mix. Coming over your former boss's speakerphone loud and clear.''

''The CEO of Monolith himself imparting his wisdom about which government officials to target for bribes,'' Kirsten said. ''Incredible, really.''

They were quiet again for a while. Then Gordian

leaned forward, meshed his fingers on the desk, and looked steadily at her face.

"Kirsten, I didn't ask you here to the States because I needed to have the voice recorder and disks hand-delivered," he said. "I wanted to tell you in person how deeply I appreciate what you've done. And also let you know that I'd be honored to have you working for UpLink—wherever in our organization you'd prefer—should you want a job with us."

She smiled a little. "That's a very generous offer . . . but I hope you won't be offended if I decline to accept it, at least for now. I'd like some time to myself. Time to . . . re-group. You understand?"

His eyes were still holding steady on her.

"Yes, yes, I do," he said. "As long as you understand that the offer stands if you ever change your mind. And that I never forget my friends."

She nodded, her smile growing larger. It was very gen-uine and very beautiful, and Gordian thought he knew what Blackburn must have seen in it.

"Is it back to Singapore for you, then?" he said.

She was quiet a moment, then nodded again.

"For a time, anyway. But there's one more thing I have to do here in America before I go."

Armitage sat by the answering machine in his office, his eyes staring out of his wasted features with a cold vitality which seemed to demand and consume all that was left of his life force—like small, mean creatures arising from detritus, feeding on decay.

There had been a number of messages from Marcus Caine waiting for him this morning, each more panicked and desperate than the one preceding it.

No more of that, he thought.

Bound to a failing body and his wheelchair, he was determined to cast off unnecessary ballast. It was hard enough to manage without the dead weight.

"Erase messages," he said, activating the device with a voice chip produced in one of Monolith's San Jose factories. He paused a moment, then set it to screen and disconnect any calls originating from Caine's home or office, verbally inputting the numbers to be blocked.

He did not want to be dragged down with Marcus as his role in the SEAPAC affair, the campaign finance scandal, and numerous other damning episodes became known. Indeed, any association with him at all would be a severe liability.

How quickly things changed. He had believed Caine a likely candidate to win Uplink International and forge a media/technology monopoly that would extend around the globe as no single entity of its type had done before . . . and as a plum for being instrumental in bringing that about, Armitage was to have been handed Uplink's biosciences division on a silver platter. Who could say what new treatments for his condition might have emerged with the company's resources at his disposal? Who could truly say?

But Marcus had disappointed him, *failed* him, and none of that was to be.

He pulled air through his throat and released it in a watery sigh. Perhaps the ALS would get him in the end. Almost certainly it would. But he would live long enough to see Marcus go down first. . . .

And no doubt write many interesting and widely read columns about his fall.

• • •

"There it is. You can check everything out if you'd like."

Marcus Caine sat on the leather-cushioned sofa in his study, a square of mahogany wall paneling pulled back on his right to reveal an open wall safe.

The man he'd spoken to stepped across the room and peered into the safe. He reached a hand inside, extracted a banded pack of bills, rifled their edges, then put them back and looked into the safe another minute.

"It contains over a million dollars in cash. And some trinkets . . . diamonds, my dear wife has always loved her diamonds . . . worth a great deal more."

The man shifted his gaze toward Caine. He was smallish with a pencil mustache and gray eyes that matched the color of his sport jacket.

"You sure you want me to do this?" he said.

Caine spread his arms over the top of the backrest, tilted his chin up, and laughed—a sound that reminded the man a little of crows.

"What's the problem? Are you afraid you'll screw up, the way your friends did at the airport? Or how about Sacramento—shall we discuss that merry fucking romp?"

"There's no reason to talk to me that way," the man said. "Those were tough assignments."

Caine laughed his harsh, cawing laugh again.

"Then let's see you tackle an easy one," he said. "Earn your money this time. And spare me the humiliation of becoming the poster boy for Court TV for a year or so, to be followed by a lifetime of prison interviews."

Silence.

The man walked across the room, stopped in front of Caine, and reached under his jacket. The weapon he brought out from underneath it was a Heckler & Koch .45 P9S.

A moment passed. Still standing there, he took a sound suppressor from his inside pocket and screwed it onto the barrel.

"You worried about how your wife finds you?" he asked.

Caine straightened, and brought his arms down off the backrest. The pained humor was gone from his face and his eyes were watery.

His mouth suddenly tightened.

"Earn your money," he snapped. "Make a fucking mess for her."

The man nodded, cocked the gun, and angled its bore up at Caine's head. There was the sound of Caine sucking in air, and then the muted thud of bullets leaving the gun as he pulled the trigger ten times, emptying the magazine.

When his job was finished, the man holstered the gun, walked back around the couch to the safe, and quickly emptied it, transferring everything that had been inside to his briefcase.

He paused briefly at the door on his way out. Looked at the body and the blood on the sofa and walls. And nodded to himself with satisfaction.

Got what you paid for, he thought.

The inscription on the gravestone was elegant, a quote from Wordsworth:

> *O joy! That in our embers*
> *Is something that doth live,*
> *That Nature yet remembers,*
> *What was so fugitive.*

Reading it, Kirsten wiped a hand across her eyes.

"I remember, too, Max," she said. "I remember."

Behind her, Pete Nimec waited quietly, standing in the shade of the Japanese maples that grew where Blackburn had been laid to rest, his body flown back from Malaysia soon after his identity was confirmed.

Kirsten knelt over the soil that filled the grave, still loose under her fingers.

"Atman and Brahman," she said. "Sometimes, Max, we need illusion to show us the truth in ways we can manage . . . and though I can't be sure, I sometimes think you didn't understand that, and sold yourself short because you didn't. That you felt guilty about asking me to make difficult choices, and let that guilt get in the way of your opening up to me." She felt moisture on her cheeks. "The thing is, Max, I believe Roger Gordian is right. That you were really showing me the way to my own conscience. To my own heart."

She tasted salt, touched her fingers to her lips, touched the place where Max's name was carved on the gravestone.

"You . . . what we had . . . it was *Brahman,* my sweet love," she whispered. "It was truth."

Kirsten lingered there a moment, her eyes closed as if in prayer or repose.

Then she rose, turned from the grave, and strode slowly to where Pete Nimec was waiting.

"You okay?" he asked softly.

She looked at him, smiled a little.

"I will be," she said.

Red Storm Entertainment, Inc., was founded in November 1996 by best-selling author Tom Clancy and Virtus Corporation, the leader in 3-D multimedia authoring tools, to create and market multiple-media entertainment products. Red Storm Entertainment is privately held: Principal owners are Tom Clancy, Virtus Corporation, and Pearson plc, one of the world's largest and most respected media groups.

Red Storm Entertainment's objective is to lead the market in the development of entertainment products in multiple forms-interactive computer and console games, board games and related merchandise. To that end, the company is developing products that will satisfy hard-core gamers' appetites as well as appealing to a new, broader user community who is attracted to realistic and intelligent games.

Red Storm Entertainment released its first game, **Tom Clancy's Politika**, in November 1997, and will release five new products in 1998.

Tom Clancy's
ruthless.com

How Ruthless Can You Be?

Now you've seen how ruthless a modern CEO can be when pursuing an enemy. But that experience doesn't have to end when the novel does. The latest computer game from Red Storm En-

tertainment will challenge you to find the corporate raider lurking inside you.

Tom Clancy's ruthless.com is a bitter contest of economic growth and conquest set in the high-stakes world of modern corporate raiding. It combines the crushing grip of business expansion with the rapier strikes of deceit, dirty tricks, and outright crime. Each of the 1 to 6 players ruthlessly expands their empire, overrunning the others and grinding them into yesterday's dust until only one corporation alone wields true dominance. Special Activities are the spice of the game; players may invest time and money into Legal assaults, Dirty Tricks, and Hacking runs. Finally, Executive Orders involve the growth of the players' CEOs as well as subordinate Executives; these characters gain experience, skills, and personality traits throughout the game.

Tom Clancy's ruthless.com is a strategy game whose resource management and competition techniques carry the trappings of the business world, whose players are not concerned with spreadsheets and depreciation, but instead with the no-holds-barred actions their company takes in a global marketplace where greed is not good—it's great.

Features:
—Strong multiplayer component, including full chat, over a LAN, hot seat or the Internet
—Simultaneous turn-based strategy game
—Flexibility due to three modes of gameplay: Campaign, Scenario, Multiplayer
—Unprecedented dark graphic novel art
—Low system requirements: works on older computers

System Requirements:
OS: Windows 95 or later
CPU: 120 MHz Pentium or better
Network Play: Properly configured TCP/IP connection at 14.4 kbps or faster
RAM: 16 MB minimum, 32 MB preferred
Hard Disk: No specific requirements
CD-ROM: 4x speed or faster
Display: 800 x 600 Hi Color
3-D Acceleration: not required
Audio: DirectSound playback preferred

Tom Clancy's ruthless.com is available from the software retailers near you.

The Internet.

Parental discretion

included.

It's all within your reach.

AT&T WorldNet® Service

Your Internet is ready.

The Internet you've been waiting for, with Cyber Patrol® to protect your kids.

With AT&T WorldNet® Service, you and your kids enjoy fast, one-click access direct to the Internet. But because a free, one-year subscription to Cyber Patrol is included, your kids don't have access to inappropriate Web sites. Now your whole family can e-mail, chat, create personal Web pages and surf to their hearts' content. Because with AT&T WorldNet Service, there's always a lifeguard on

To sign up for AT&T WorldNet Service, visit us at www.att.net/wns or call

I 800 WORLDNET

Internet

Tom Clancy

Rainbow Six

Putnam

RED STORM RISING

The ultimate scenario for World War III—the final battle for global control . . .

"THE ULTIMATE WAR GAME . . . BRILLIANT!"
—*Newsweek*

PATRIOT GAMES

CIA analyst Jack Ryan stops an assassination—and incurs the wrath of Irish terrorists . . .

"A HIGH PITCH OF EXCITEMENT!"
—*Wall Street Journal*

THE CARDINAL OF THE KREMLIN

The superpowers race for the ultimate Star Wars missile defense system . . .

"*CARDINAL* EXCITES, ILLUMINATES . . . A REAL PAGE-TURNER!" —*Los Angeles Daily News*

THE BESTSELLING NOVELS OF
TOM CLANCY

EXECUTIVE ORDERS

The most devastating terrorist act in history leaves Jack Ryan as President of the United States . . .

"UNDOUBTEDLY CLANCY'S BEST YET."
—*Atlanta Journal & Constitution*

DEBT OF HONOR

It begins with the murder of an American woman in the back streets of Tokyo. It ends in war . . .

"A SHOCKER CLIMAX SO PLAUSIBLE YOU'LL WONDER WHY IT HASN'T YET HAPPENED!"
—*Entertainment Weekly*

THE HUNT FOR RED OCTOBER

The smash bestseller that launched Clancy's career—the incredible search for a Soviet defector and the nuclear submarine he commands . . .

"BREATHLESSLY EXCITING!"   —*Washington Post*

continued . . .

A group of multi-cultural friends and their families
prepare for the event of the season. Novel will include
recipes for celebrating the season.

the
yada yada
Prayer Group
GETS DECKED OUT

a Novel

neta jackson

Includes a guide to forming your own
Yada Yada Prayer Group.

Acknowledgments

I would like to thank Jerome Preisler for his creative ideas and his invaluable contributions to the preparation of the manuscript. I would also like to acknowledge the assistance of Marc Cerasini, Larry Segriff, Denise Little, John Helfers, Robert Youdelman, Esq., Tom Mallon, Esq., the wonderful people at The Putnam Berkley Group, including Phyllis Grann, David Shanks, and Tom Colgan, and Doug Littlejohns, Kevin Perry, the rest of the *ruthless.com* team, and the other fine folks at Red Storm Entertainment, as well as Hank Beard for his help sabotaging a Cessna. As always, I would like to thank Robert Gottlieb of the William Morris Agency, my agent and friend. But most important, it is for you, my readers, to determine how successful our collective endeavor has been.

Tom Clancy's
POWER PLAYS

ruthless.com

ONE

THE FREIGHTER HAD BEEN CHRISTENED THE *KUAN YIN,*
after the Chinese goddess of mercy, but what doubt can
there be that its crew felt abandoned by their guardian
spirit at the end?

They had set out from the city of Kuching in Eastern
Malaysia at eight P.M., the cargo deck of their fifty-foot-
long, half-century-old steamship loaded with palm oil and
spices tagged for distribution in the wholesale markets of
Singapore. Despite intermittent rain, gusting winds, and
reduced visibility, the chop was moderate and the pilot
had maintained a steady speed of fifteen knots almost
from the time he got under way. He expected an un-
eventful run followed by a night of drinking in a dockside
bar; even now in the wet season, the main sea lane was
short and direct, taking just less than four hours to cross
the strait and then swing up the coast to Sembawang
Wharf, on the north side of the island.

With little to do until they reached port, the four members of the loading crew were playing cards in the vessel's
boxy hold by nine o'clock, leaving the upper deck to the
pilot and boatswain. The former, of course, had no choice
but to remain at the helm, although any sympathy his
shipmates might have felt for him was blunted by their

resentment of his superior attitude, higher salary, and relatively spacious bridge, with its soft leather chair and posters of nude women tacked up among the charts.

On the other hand, the boatswain was extremely well regarded by his fellows, and had been invited to join in the gambling. A man named Chien Lo, he ordinarily would have accepted with enthusiasm, but tonight had chosen instead to remain on deck with the freight. Given the bad weather conditions and his conscientious nature, he was understandably concerned that the lashings might come loose in the strong ocean winds.

Around ten o'clock the tropical downpour eased off a little. It was in all likelihood only a brief lull, and Chien resisted the urge to go below with the others. Trouble waited with the greatest of patience, his wife was fond of saying. Still, he decided it would be a good time to break for a smoke.

As his dear, loving spouse had also told him—she was quite *full* of advice—it was best to enjoy life's small pleasures while one could.

Even as Chien Lo put his match to the tip of his cigarette, two Zodiac inflatable watercraft had glided from the rushes and mangrove roots rimming a tiny islet some forty degrees east of the freighter's bow. Fitted with stabilizing fin rails and powered by sound-baffled ninety-horsepower outboards, they planed across the water at close to fifty knots, fast enough to eat up the *Kuan Yin*'s lead in minutes, cutting parallel wakes that roiled out behind them like the contrails of jet fighters. Soon the blot of land from which they had launched was swallowed up in darkness and distance.

There were twelve men in the pirate gang, its leader an

Iban tribesman of huge proportions, the rest natives of the southern islands, their number divided evenly between the fast-moving inflatables. The designated thrower in each group wore leather gloves and had a coiled nylon rope ladder snaplinked to his belt like a mountain climber. All had concealed their features, some with plain canvas sacks that had holes cut out for the eyes, nose, and mouth, others with old rags and T-shirts they had simply tied over the lower halves of their faces. They had identical kris knife tattoos on the backs of their hands as symbols of their criminal brotherhood. They wore swim vests over their dingy, tattered clothes. They were equipped with assault rifles and carried daggers in scabbards at their waists. And they were ready to put their weapons to lethal use without compunction, as the expressions of cold malignity under their face masks might have shown.

While the seizure of a freighter was an act they had committed scores of times, their present job was unusual in that it would not involve theft of the ship's cargo, nor robbing the crew of personal valuables that could be fenced on the black market—except perhaps as fringe benefits. Yes, the bars, whorehouses, and cockfight parlors of Sibu would have to do without their patronage for a while. Tonight they would be taking the ship into Singapore, and once there would have other things to keep them busy.

As the silent-running Zodiacs approached the stern of the *Kuan Yin,* they veered off in separate directions, the headman's craft swinging toward its port side, the other angling to starboard, both of them slowing to match the larger vessel's speed.

For perhaps two minutes after pulling abreast of it, the pirate boss stared measuringly at his objective, sweeping his gaze over its rust-scabbed metal hull. He wore a denim jacket, a scarf around his forehead to keep his long, rain-drenched black hair from whipping into his eyes, and a bandanna over his mouth and chin. Reaching into his breast pocket for a small flask of *tuak,* he tugged the bandanna down below his lips and swigged back some of the potent alcoholic drink. He took a second deep pull and swished it around his mouth, his face tilted skyward, drizzle sprinkling his exposed, windburned cheeks. Then he swallowed again, slipped his mask back in place, jerked his head toward the short, wiry man with the rope ladder on his belt. "Amir," he said, and sliced his hand through the air, signaling him to proceed with the raid.

The thrower nodded, reached down between his knees, and snapped open the lid of a stowage compartment between the bottom of his seat and the Zodiac's aluminum floorboard. From this compartment he extracted a second rope, this one a twenty-foot single rope with a "bear-claw" grappling hook at its end. He let out a measure of slack, and then began laying up half the coils in his left hand, taking the half attached to the metal hook into his right. Finally he stood and moved to the side of the craft that had edged up to the freighter, his feet planted wide against the undulant rocking and swaying of the current.

Stepping down on the rope's bitter end, Amir turned toward the cargo ship and heaved the grappling hook up at it, letting the weight of the hook carry the line on, the rest of the line paying out of his left hand.

The iron hook clamped onto its gunwale with a solid thump.

An instant later the thrower heard a similar noise from the opposite side of the freighter, and exchanged an anticipatory look with his four companions. All of them knew that sound meant the other raiding party had also been successful in mooring their Zodiac to the *Kuan Yin*.

Chien was standing with his elbows on the starboard rail and the cigarette dangling from his lips when he heard a thumping sound off the quarter. Then, moments later, a second thump from the same general area.

He frowned, thinking the peace and quiet had been too perfect to last. The *Kuan Yin* was now twenty nautical miles southeast of its destination, chugging along amid the scattered outcroppings of rock, soil, and lush tropical vegetation that were some of the Raiu chain's smallest islands. Spread in clusters across a vast expanse of the South China sea, they were mostly nameless and undeveloped, and Chien always found the passage between them to be a welcome interlude before reaching the congested harbor of Singapore.

He stared out at the water and considered ignoring the noise until he'd finished his cigarette, but could not stop fretting. What if there were drums of unfastened cargo rolling and crashing about the deck?

Chien shrugged and flicked his still-burning cigarette stub into the water.

Responsibility had its burdens, he thought, and then turned to walk aft and check things out, unaware of the murderous presence about to slip aboard the vessel.

A moment after hooking on to the gunwale, Amir secured his end of the rope to a mounting ring on the Zodiac's floor. Smoothing his gloves over his fingers, he turned to face the cargo vessel. Then he straddled the line, grasped it firmly in both hands, and jumped off toward the freighter, his legs spread, the line pressed against his body for maximum tension.

His cleated boots braced against the freighter's hull, he climbed with a kind of rhythmic shimmy, and was on deck in less than a minute. Once aboard, he unfastened the rope ladder from his belt, tightly fixed the upper part of it to the handrail, and pitched the remainder of its length over the side of the ship to the inflatable craft below.

The man who caught it quickly began his ascent, placing his foot on the nylon sling ropes that served as spreaders between the vertical mainlines. He knew the others would follow one at a time to avoid putting too much strain on the ladder.

Scrambling to the top of the ladder, he reached up toward the first man's waiting hand so he could be helped over the gunwale.

His upper body and elbows were already on the freighter's deck when Chien Lo, coming aft to investigate the mysterious thumps he had heard moments earlier, discovered to his horror that his ship was under siege.

Crouched on deck, the first pirate heard the boatswain's footsteps a split second before he actually pivoted on his haunches to see him approaching. By then he'd decided what to do. He didn't know how many other crewmen would be on deck, but would not wait for them to be alerted. The man had to be taken out right away.

Chien Lo had halted several yards toward the fore of the deck, staring at the invaders in shock and dismay, his legs turned to brittle shafts of ice. He had perceived the intention of the man already on board even without being able to see his face. The dark, narrow eyes peering through slits in his hood told him everything he needed to know. There was murder in them, pure and simple.

Chien Lo broke suddenly from his paralysis, spun around, and ran for the vessel's bow, where he knew the pilot would be manning the bridge. But the smallish pirate's swiftness and agility were good for more than just climbing. He sprang to his feet and streaked after Chien, whipping his knife from its scabbard, moving almost silently despite the thick-soled boots he had worn to provide traction while boarding the freighter.

He overtook the boatswain in a flash, lunging at him, grabbing him from behind, locking his arms around his chest, the force of his tackle throwing him belly-down onto the deck.

Chien produced a little bleat of pain and fear as a hand twisted itself into his hair and yanked his head up and back. Then the hard, cold edge of the pirate's knife met the soft, warm flesh of his throat and sliced it open from ear to ear.

Chien felt no real pain, only something that shook through his nerves like raw voltage. Then the pirate released him and his face hit the deck again and he died with a long, spasmodic shudder, his nose, mouth, and eyes in a pool of his own blood.

The pirate rose to his feet, dragged Chien's body to the edge of the deck, and kicked it overboard. In the vastness of the open sea it seemed there was hardly a splash as it hit the water and was swallowed up.

When the pirate returned to where he'd tied the ladder to the handrail, he found that the second pirate had managed to haul himself aboard. The rest of their team and five of the men in the other raiding party were also on deck, waiting for the last pirate to complete his climb.

A moment later he was up and they were all racing toward the forward part of the ship.

The pilot sank beneath the wheel in a lifeless heap, his blood pattering from his maps and *Playboy* pin-ups like falling rain. His killer had made fast work of him after entering the bridge, stealing up from behind, and slicing open his throat just as the first man aboard had done to Chien Lo. Caught completely by surprise, he hadn't even known what hit him, let alone gotten a chance to hail for assistance.

Now a second pirate came in, sidestepped the corpse, and took the wheel. His eyes roaming over the instrument panel in front of him, he nodded to the first man, who clapped him on the back, sheathed his dripping blade, and then rushed outside to give the others the good news.

They had taken full control of the vessel. Next they would deal with its remaining crew.

"Get on you knees, hands behind you heads!" the Iban shouted from the stairwell. Although every one of the ship's hands looked like Malays, he'd barked his orders through his bandanna in a serviceable if unpolished English. The national language had many variations in dialect, and he wanted to avoid confusion.

The crewmen gaped up at him from the card table, faces stunned, playing cards spilling from their fingers in a fluttery welter. Footsteps clattered behind the pirate leader as the rest of his band followed him down the metal risers from the deck.

"Do it now or I kill you all!" the Iban grunted, noting the crew's frozen hesitation and motioning them away from the table with the snout of his Beretta 70/90.

The four men complied, making no attempt at resistance, getting up in such a rush they clumsily knocked over several chairs.

They knelt in the middle of the cramped little hold and looked at the raiders in silence.

The Iban noticed that one of the captives had slipped off his wristwatch and was holding it out in his hand, offering up the timepiece as if to get done with the affair as quickly as possible. He knew what the man was thinking, and almost pitied him. None of the recent anti-piracy operations by Malaysia, Indonesia, the Phillippines, and China had done anything to decrease the high incidence of attacks in local waters. With thousands of jungled islands and vast stretches of ocean to patrol, the naval authorities could not hope to keep pace with their quarry, let alone ferret out their hidden land bases. Regional shipping companies were well aware of this, and simply figured losses to theft and hijacking into the overall cost of their operations.

The pirate chief's eyes moved over the faces of the sailors. While they looked tense and anxious in the cast of an overhead light fixture, none of those faces seemed especially fearful. And why should they be? The men were seasoned hands. They would have been through hijacks before, and expected to be robbed and sent off safely in dinghies and lifeboats. That was how it usually went.

The poor, stupid bastards hadn't any idea what had happened to their mates up above.

The Iban waved over one of the pirates who had come rushing down the stairs at his heels. The man stepped up to him and leaned in close for his orders.

"I don't want their papers messed up, Juara," the Iban

warned in a coarse whisper, this time speaking his native tongue, Behasa Malayu. "That happens, all this is for shit, you understand?"

Juara's affirmative grunt was muffled by the dirty white towel shrouding his mouth and chin. A blockish, thick-necked man with a shaved head and lot of surplus weight around the middle, he gestured briskly to a couple of the other hijackers, who moved toward the kneeling seamen and ordered them to toss everything in their pockets onto the floor.

The ship's hands again did as they were told without challenge. Juara covered them with his rifle while his two companions went and gathered up their surrendered possessions, depositing them in a small heap on the table. When the hands had finished emptying their pockets, the pirates frisked them down to make sure they hadn't withheld anything.

Satisfied they'd gotten what they wanted, they nodded to Juara.

Juara motioned the pair back to his side, then turned to look at the Iban headman.

"Get it over with," the Iban said.

He tried to keep his voice hushed, but it was deep enough to seem almost booming in the constricted silence of the hold. A terrible understanding dawned on the crewmen's features as their captors swung up their rifle barrels.

Now they finally know, the pirate thought. *And they fear.*

One of the ship's hands opened his mouth to scream and started to his feet, but then the raiders triggered their weapons and he fell backwards, his clothes riddled with bullet holes, most of his head blown away. Swept by the hail of gunfire, the rest of the *Kuan Yin*'s crew also went down in a cloud of blood, bone, and tissue, their arms and legs sprawling out wildly in their final throes.

The big Iban waited for the guns to stop their racket, then stepped over to the card table and randomly lifted a wallet from the pile of items that had been taken from the crewmen. He was eager to finish this last bit of business and return to the open deck; his ears rang from the shooting, and the air down here stank of burnt primer, blood, and the voided bowels of the dead.

He opened the wallet and found a driver's license in a transparent plastic sleeve. There was more identification in the other compartments. The slain crewman to whom the wallet had belonged was named Sang Ye.

The Iban made a low, pleased sound in his throat. He hoped the sailor had lived his life fully and spent his money well. At any rate, his wallet and identity now belonged to someone who would make good use of them.

There were big things in the works, very big, and the Iban was eager to reach Singapore and get cracking.

He thought of the sheet of paper folded in his breast pocket, thought of the instructions that were written on it, thought of everything they were worth to him. Surely more than he'd made in any dozen hijacks.

The American, Max Blackburn, didn't stand a chance. No more than the crew of the ship had stood one. . . .

Not the slightest chance in the world.

TWO

WHEN ROGER GORDIAN WAS THIRTEEN YEARS OLD, he built a tree house in a scrub lot where he'd often gone to play with his friends. As originally conceived, it was to have been a lookout against adults who came within homing range, and a refuge from older children who were potential troublemakers. He'd sketched out the blueprint for it himself, and realized those plans with the help of his two best pals: Steve Padaetz, his next-door neighbor, and Johnny Cowans, a fidgety little kid who'd been nick-named "Clip" for no reason anybody could remember. At one point, Roger had considered fortifying their tree house against marauders with a ring of elaborate booby traps, but none of the dozen or so he devised ever got beyond the planning stage. Truth be known, the boys hadn't really expected a raid of any kind—that had just been a fanciful notion, something to enhance their frolics with a tingly edge of secrecy and adventure. There were very few kids in the neighborhood whom they considered enemies, and even fewer who were interested enough in their whereabouts or activities to hassle them.

Or so the boys thought, anyway.

The ladder and tools they'd used to construct the tree house had come from Roger's parents' garage. Steve had gotten the actual building materials from the hardware store/lumberyard owned by his dad, although Roger never really got around to asking whether they were obtained with Mr. Padaetz's knowledge or consent. Somehow it didn't seem important at the time; the boys had needed little to complete their hideaway besides some two-by-fours, a few sheets of wood siding, and a box of nails, the unexplained absence of which would hardly have been enough to put Padaetz Home Improvements, the biggest family-owned business in Waterford, Wisconsin, on the financial skids.

The Sentry Box, as the tree house came to be called, had been at the center of the three boys' lives for an entire summer, beginning shortly after they got their final-quarter sixth-grade report cards, and ending a couple of weeks before the opening bells of junior high rang out. During the two hot, dreamy months that stretched between, they had idled away the daylight hours in and around it, swapping baseball cards and comic books and bad dirty jokes, poking around the woods, and conducting fruitless searches for the Indian arrowheads that, at least as schoolyard mythology had it, littered the undeveloped fields of Racine County.

Sometime in late August, the boys had started fashioning what was to have been an outdoor gymnasium in the patch of grass directly below the tree house, using some additional lumber they'd managed to scavenge together over the long season. There were still two weeks to go before classes resumed, and they figured they had over a month beyond that until the weather got too cold for them to mess around outdoors after completing their homework and chores. They had built horizontal and parallel bars, and begun work on an exercise horse . . . but their expansion was abruptly aborted when the raid they'd once half-worried about became a devastating reality.

The kids—teenagers, really—responsible for marring that idyllic period were Ed Kozinski, Kenny Whitman, and Anthony Platt, who was Kenny's third cousin and bore an attitude of perpetual, surly belligerence that marked him as someone to avoid at all costs. Perhaps two years older than Roger and his friends, this ghastly trio had never before taken the slightest notice of them, concentrating instead on acts of petty vandalism, finding ways to filch beer and cigarettes from local groceries, and making crude advances to girls who, by and large, pretended they didn't exist. Somehow Anthony had learned about the tree house, and had gotten the idea that those girls might be more accepting of him and his cohorts if they had a nice, private, tucked-away spot where they could all go to get drunk and make out.

The moment that thought reared itself from the bottom sludge of Anthony's mind, the Sentry Box was effectively lost to the younger boys; they had wandered out to the tree house one morning and found Kenny and company occupying it like counterparts from some science-fictional negative universe. Their outdoor gym-in-the-making had been ruined, the pieces of wood they'd used to build their apparatus scattered about the field. The words "Jive Palase" were spray-painted across two sides of the tree house in huge, bright red letters, the second half of its new name unintentionally misspelled in what would have been a comical twist had the circumstances surrounding it not been so painful. To Roger Gordian, it felt almost like a desecration.

Watching Roger and his companions from the entrance, Anthony sat with his legs swung out over the side of the box, a Parliament in his hand and a contemptuous grin on his face. The comics, trading cards, and everything else Roger's group had hoarded inside it had been unceremoniously dumped, and lay among the welter of beer bottles, empty potato chip bags, candy wrappers, and crumpled cigarette packs on the ground beneath it.

Roger and company barely had time to register what had happened before they were pelted with a fusillade of stones from their own lookout post. They had briefly considered taking a desperate stand against the invaders, but then one of those whizzing rocks had struck Clip dead center in his forehead and he'd dropped into the dirt, howling at the top of his lungs, blood streaming into his eyes from a wound that would later require four stitches and a tetanus shot. Roger had known then that he'd been beaten; worse, he had known it was no contest, and felt crushingly ashamed of his defenselessness. The other boys were bigger, meaner, and tougher than anybody in his little group. And they had been ready and waiting for a fight.

As Kenny's gang had begun climbing down the tree after them, Roger and Johnny had helped Clip to his feet and fled the scene.

It had been Gordian's first experience with a hostile takeover, and four decades and change later, the memory still stung.

That the sting seemed especially acute tonight was quite understandable, given the distressing little bulletin his visitor had just delivered from the Wall Street front.

"We went back there maybe two, three months later," he said now, finishing his story. "By then Kenny and his parents had moved out of town, and his cousin was, I don't know, just sort of neutralized without him. Anyway, we returned and found the tree house destroyed, same way the gym had been. Boards sticking out of the snow, nothing intact. I don't know if it had been deliberately trashed, or if the numbskulls that moved in on us brought it down out of carelessness and stupidity. Doesn't matter, I suppose. What *does* matter, and what still bugs me whenever I remember this sorry little episode, is that I surrendered the tree house to those punks in the first place. Let them take something that was mine, something I'd built from scratch, without a fight.''

Charles Kirby looked at Gordian a while, and then drank some of his scotch and soda. It was nine o'clock at night and he was exhausted and jet-lagged after a long flight from New York. Still, he had joined Roger in the book-lined study of his Palo Alto home because he'd felt the news he was carrying was too important to wait until morning.

Gord not only paid the law firm of Fisk, Kirby, and Towland a handsome retainer for their advice and representation in corporate affairs, he was also a close personal friend. When Kirby had learned that the Spartus consortium, UpLink International's largest shareholder, intended to sell off its twenty-percent interest in the company, he'd immediately known what it augured, and had decided to fly out and tell Gordian about it face-to-face.

Studying Gordian's troubled features, he knew he'd made the right decision. A lean, graying man of forty-five with intelligent blue eyes, jutting cheekbones, and lips so thin that even his broadest smiles seemed wan, Kirby was wearing a dark-blue worsted suit over a white dress shirt that had lost its necktie, and been unbuttoned at the collar, somewhere around cruising altitude . . . a sartorial anomaly Gord had remarked upon the moment

Kirby arrived at his house. *Chuck, you're the most fastidious dresser I've ever met. The guy who sent me illustrated instructions on making a Windsor knot, and taught me that it was traditional for the bottom of a sport jacket to line up with the knuckle when your hands are straight down against your legs. The tieless look gives me an idea something's wrong. Big-time.*

Accurate enough, Kirby thought, sipping his scotch.

"Well, at least the creeps didn't get to enjoy the place for long," he said from the plump leather chair opposite Roger. "Bet you ten to one they never got any girls up there with them either."

"Nice try, Chuck. But let's not skirt the issue," Gordian said. "I'm a grown man, for godsakes. You'd think I could do better than to make the same mistakes that I did when I was still looking ahead to peach fuzz and my first kiss."

"Gord, listen to me—"

"I want to know how I could have been blindsided. How I could leave myself open to having somebody try and grab UpLink right out from under my nose."

Kirby drained his scotch, lowered the glass, and rattled the melting ice cubes inside it.

"You want me to sit here watching you bash away at yourself?" he said. "I wasn't aware that was part of our professional arrangement, though I can check with my partners to be absolutely certain."

"Could you really?"

Kirby frowned at his sarcasm.

"Look," Gordian said. "I've established my organization in dozens of countries, placed my employees at extreme risk in some of them, lost good people in others. If I can't learn my lessons, can't compete when the stakes are high, I shouldn't be fooling around in the big leagues.''

Kirby sighed. Granted, they were looking at a very serious problem, but Gordian ordinarily wasn't the sort of man to let self-pity and defeatism through the door no matter how hard they tried shoving their way in. What the hell was wrong with him? Could this be a kind of delayed reaction to the encryption-tech controversy . . . a case of the psychological bends after finally coming up from leagues underneath it?

Kirby thought about it a moment, and supposed that might be the case, considering how long it had dragged on and the flak Gordian had taken because of his public stance against the new government export policies. Maybe the operative factor here was exhaustion, and Gord was simply tapped out from waging too many battles on too many fronts at once. Maybe. And yet he couldn't help but feel that something else was eating away at him, as well.

''I won't deny you were vulnerable, but why blame it on recklessness?'' he said. ''You've had a lot of strains on your financial resources lately, ranging from some outlays that were merely unavoidable, to others that you couldn't have anticipated without a crystal ball.''

Gordian's peremptory look told Kirby he didn't need to be further reminded. In that way the two men were alike: They made their points with a minimum of words. And besides, both of them had done the arithmetic many times over. There had been the huge price tag of manufacturing, launching, and insuring the constellation of low-earth-orbit, Ka-band satellites needed for UpLink's orbital telecommunications network, the multimillion dollar cost of rebuilding the Russian ground station after it was nearly leveled by a terrorist attack the previous January, and the simultaneous expenses of getting the ground stations in Africa and Malaysia fully operational.

An ambitious program of corporate initiatives, to be sure. But Gordian's diversification from the defense technology that had earned him his fortune, while to some extent spurred by military downsizing, was not essentially profit-motivated—and that had always impressed the hell out of Kirby. Gord was not an ego-driven person. Nor was he an acquisitive one. Having made enough money to last him ten lifetimes, he could have done what a lot of fabulously rich men did and rested on his laurels, gone on long cruises to warm places, turned to breaking Guinness world records, whatever.

More than anything, though, Gordian had a heartfelt desire to help create a better world, and believed to his core that the problem of eliminating global tyranny and oppression required communication-based solutions. Having grown up in an era of Berlin Walls and Iron Curtains, he was convinced that nothing—neither military buildups, nor leadership summits, nor treaties—had done as much to bring those Cold War barriers down as information seeping through their cracks. Information, he believed, was the ultimate key to personal and political freedom. His goal, his *vision,* was to provide that key to the broadest number of people he could imagine . . . which, Kirby supposed, made him a pragmatic idealist. Or was that oxymoronic?

Now Gordian began to speak again, leaning forward, his elbows on his knees, his hands clasped together.

"Make no mistake, Chuck, I'm not second-guessing my business decisions with regard to the company's expansion," he said. "But I do fault myself for not preparing a defensive strategy against a shark attack. And it isn't as if I haven't had good counsel. You've advised me time and again to implement staggered terms of office on the board of directors. My friend Dan Parker, the congressman, tried to persuade me to lobby more forcefully for specific anti-takeover legislation in this state. I did neither.''

"Gord—"

Gordian raised a hand to silence him.

"Hear me out, please. As I said, this isn't just a *mea culpa*," he went on. "A minute ago, you said something about my needing a crystal ball to predict what's happened. Well, in a way, I had one. I don't think Spartus putting its stake on the market comes as a total shock to either of us. Look at the articles in the *Wall Street Journal*. The endless commentaries on those CNN and CNBC financial programs. Every aspect of my company's operations has been subjected to criticism and ridicule, a great deal of it originating from a single source. Is it any wonder the value of our stock has gone into the sewer?''

"For the record, my comment related to your expenses, not the devaluation of UpLink shares," Kirby said. "But I agree that the great and exalted financial prophet Reynold Armitage has done a trash-and-burn number on you in the media. If he's the source you're talking about, that is.''

"None other." Gordian folded his hands on his knees again. "Spartus panicked, and though I figured I'd be able to settle their fears when I called them, they can't really be blamed for not buying my reassurances. Tell me the truth, Chuck. Have you ever seen anything like Armitage microanalyzing our 10-K information on the air? And then putting such an incredibly negative spin on it? Because I find it damned curious.''

Kirby didn't say anything, just shook his head. Yes, Armitage was an expert securities analyst, able to sniff the wind for market indicators better than almost any of his peers. What did it matter to the general financial community that he was also a pompous, mean-spirited son of a bitch? Some sons of bitches got listened to without being liked very much—and when Armitage spoke, investors large and small perked their ears.

Which was understandable, Kirby thought. Since becoming a constant presence on the money shows, Armitage had helped many, many stockholders to better understand the market and choose successful ventures. But he had also occasionally hurt struggling firms with imprudent calls, skewing figures to suit his predictions, baiting corporate leaders, seeming to relish making them look foolish. As Gordian had pointed out, you had to be ready to take your knocks when you were playing in the big leagues. And despite his sudden attack of self-doubt, he *was* a player ... one of the best. However, what had raised Armitage's campaign against UpLink—and campaign seemed the only appropriate word for it—to an inexplicable level of viciousness was the timing of his disclosures.

The very day UpLink had released its yearly report to stockholders, Armitage had gone on *Moneyline* with the firm's 10-K and charged that there were critical discrepancies between the two statements. That had been untrue. Certainly, the reports presented their data in different lights, but annual reports were traditionally intended to emphasize a company's strengths and future goals, while the 10-K form was a dry listing of financial statistics prepared for the Securities and Exchange Commission as a matter of law. By presenting those stats out of context—failing to weigh temporary debts and liabilities against projected venture profits, for instance—one could easily give the impression that a business had gotten into much worse shape than was actually the case. And Armitage had gone a giant step beyond that, exaggerating the significance of every expense, minimizing every gain, and analyzing profit-loss ratios in the worst possible light to depict a company on the verge of ruin.

Damned curious indeed.

Still without speaking, Kirby rose, went over to the wet bar in the opposite corner of the room, and refilled his glass with scotch, leaving out the soda this time. As usual, Gordian's mind was hitting on all its well-oiled cylinders. Why the constant attacks from Armitage? As far as he knew, Gordian had never stepped on his toes, never even met the man. *Why,* then? The question had been buzzing around Kirby's own head for weeks like a nettlesome wasp, and the only answer that came to him amounted to nothing more than a suspicion. It was one he'd hesitated to share with Gordian, feeling it would be rash to do so without any substantiation.

"Hope you don't mind me helping myself to more of the expensive stuff," he said, turning to Gordian.

"Get it while it lasts," Gordian said with a grim smile, downing what was left of his own drink, then holding it out toward Kirby.

Kirby stepped over with Gordian's own favorite Beefeater—and splashed a healthy measure into Gordian's glass.

Their eyes met then, the look that passed between them lasting only a brief moment. Yet it was significant enough to give Kirby all the confirmation he needed that Gordian was thinking the exact same thing he was.

It was, he guessed, time they aired what was on their minds.

"Gord, do you believe this takeover bid was orchestrated?" he asked, the words leaping out of his mouth before caution could prevail. "That Armitage has been going at you with the intention of destroying shareholder confidence and—"

"And provoking a sell-off," Gordian said, nodding. "This whole thing reeks of behind-the-scenes manipulation."

Kirby inhaled, exhaled. He could feel the silence of the room pressing down on him with a weight that was almost tangible.

"If that's true," he said, "it would at least suggest that Armitage is in somebody's pocket."

"Yes." Gordian's tone was flat. "It would."

The two men faced each other soberly, their eyes holding.

"You have any idea who that somebody might be?" Kirby asked.

Gordian sat there quietly while the antique clock across the room ticked off a full minute.

"No," he replied at last, hoping his sincerity would be accepted without challenge.

He was, after all, lying through his teeth.

THREE

"TAKE MY WORD FOR IT, THIS HERE COUNTRY WOULD be the perfect retirement spot for Barney the Dinosaur," an American expatriate in Singapore once told a visitor from New York City. Or so he was quoted in the press, at any rate.

The comment—which was made in response to an inquiry about where some risque entertainment might be found, and would later become famous throughout the island—was overheard by a magazine writer amid the cacophonous chirping, tweeting, and trilling of innumerable performing birds. It was a Sunday morning, and Singaporean bird fanciers, mostly ethnic Chinese, had brought their thrushes, *mata putehs,* and *sharmas* out for the weekly avian singing competition at the intersection of Tiong Bahru and Seng Poh Roads, hanging their bamboo cages from specially built trellises above the public benches and outdoor cafe tables lining the street.

"You want cheap thrills, you got literally two options: dream X-rated tonight, or head on over to Fat B's, at the east end," the expat had continued to the utter mystification of his visiting friend . . . and the gleeful amusement of the eavesdropping writer, who, realizing she'd stumbled upon a perfect opener for her regular Lifestyles column, listened carefully while the birds peeped and cheeped their bright, vacant melodies into the sunshiny air.

Indeed, Fat B's, a decadent hole-in-the-wall tucked away behind a rotted shop-house facade in a narrow Geylang District *larong,* was unquestionably the seediest bar on the island republic. It was also a very busy place, drawing patrons night after night despite the stringent national morals laws, clinging to its grubby existence like some resistant bacilli on an otherwise scrubbed and sanitized operating room surface. Exactly *why* authorities tolerated it was anyone's guess, although there were rumors of ongoing bribes to police officials, and compromising photographs that had been waved over the head of a high-placed government minister as insurance against a shutdown.

With its crumbling walls and ceiling covered with purple foil, bathed in black light, and decorated with giant crepe-paper rafflesias, painted wooden folk masks, blowpipes, bead strings, dragon banners, and century-old human skulls that had once hung in the longhouses of Borneo headhunters, the interior of the bar was outdone in crassness only by its owner, Fat B . . . who, contrary to what his name suggested, was not fat at all, but physically slight, and had gained a reputation for being a bold exclamation point of a man through a mixture of conspicuously non-Singaporean aggressiveness and flamboyance, characteristics he was supposed to have inherited from his wealthy Straits Chinese ancestors. Those who had business dealings with him also knew of a certain hard, forbidding look that became evident in his eyes when his anger or suspicion was aroused, giving him, at such times, the appearance of a wary crocodile.

Tonight Fat B was wearing a collarless yellow silk shirt printed with colorful explosions of peonies, black shark-skin slacks, a diamond stud in his right earlobe, and jade-encrusted rings on eight of his fingers. His jet-black hair was slicked straight back over his head and had an almost buffed appearance. He sat at his usual table in the rear of the bar, his back to the wall, keeping a watchful eye on every coming and going at the door.

"Here's what you came for, Xiang," he said, sliding a brown manilla envelope to the big, long-haired man seated opposite him. "Odd how so much effort goes into providing such a slim package. But it's just that way when you're trading in information. It weighs nothing and everything at the same time, *lah*."

Xiang just looked at him, then silently reached out for the envelope and lifted it off the table. Fat B tried not to show that he'd noticed the kris tattoo on the back of his hand, thinking his interest wouldn't be at all appreciated . . . not by this retrograde brute. Still, he continued to regard him with hooded fascination. In the old days, his people had run around the Malaysian jungles stark naked—or just about—their skin covered with dragons, scorpions, and the like, flaunting those tattoos as symbols of courage and manhood.

His eyelids half lowered, Fat B wondered if the muscular Iban's entire body was adorned with such markings, and considered what an impressive sight that would be. Impressive and, no doubt, very painfully achieved.

Seemingly oblivious to the barkeeper's scrutiny, Xiang unclasped the envelope, folded back its flap, and looked inside.

Fat B watched and waited. Pop music squalled from stereo speakers at the four corners of the room, Eastern lutes, harps, and cymbals looping discordantly over Western-style synthesizers and electric guitars. Strobes splashed the foil-draped walls with violet light. Bar girls in short skirts and tight, swoop-necked blouses, and with too much makeup on their faces, laughed showily with the men who were paying for their drinks. Most of the women carried small purses that opened only after they led their companions into the staircase behind the barroom, or up to the small, private rooms on the building's second floor. Then they would make their illicit transactions, willing flesh for cold cash, fifty percent of which went into Fat B's pocket.

For no particular reason, Fat B thought suddenly of an ancient Chinese expression: *Everything can be eaten.*

His lips puckered thoughtfully, he stared across the room at the pair of men who had arrived with Xiang. They hovered near the entrance in their shabby clothes, one dragging on a cigarette and looking directly back at him, the other gazing upward at the wall, apparently studying the painted folk masks. Both also would have the dagger tattoo on their hands, of course.

Glancing cautiously over each shoulder to make sure he wasn't being watched, Xiang unclipped the envelope and looked inside. It contained a stack of nine or ten photographs. Reaching in with one hand, he pulled them out just far enough to expose their upper borders, and then gave them a quick scan, riffling their edges with his thumb, ignoring the sheet of paper clipped to the last snapshot. Then he returned them to the envelope, closed the flap, and looked back up at Fat B.

"Who's the girl?" he said in English.

"It's all in the little fact sheet I enclosed. Her name is Kirsten Chu and she is employed by a company called

Monolith Technologies. Very attractive, don't you think?'' Fat B offered the pirate a relaxed smile. "It's unfortunate her parents stuck her with a Western name, but I believe she was born and educated in Britain. So it goes.''

Xiang stared at him, his eyes flat. "You know what I mean. I didn't expect there to be two of them.''

Fat B tried to look as if there was nothing about the envelope's contents that should have required explanation.

"Listen,'' he said. "She's just a beautiful lure dangling at the end of a very short line, you understand? Her movements are easy to track. Stay on her and she'll lead you to the American.''

"What's their connection?''

"I don't ask, our employers don't tell.''

"She a national?''

Fat B waited a moment before he replied, listening to shrieky Chinese vocals pierce a loud disco rhythm thudding from the sound system. Ordinarily he enjoyed the ratcheted-up volume and uneasy merging of musical traditions, but now it was all starting to grate on him, the sweeps of electronic sound jangling his nerves, the female rap singer's falsetto highs tearing into his eardrums like steel spikes.

He'd been optimistic things would go more smoothly.

He took a deep breath, exhaled, then finally nodded, his smile tightening at the corners.

"Don't make more out of this than there is,'' he said. "It isn't that big a deal.''

"Bullshit. You think I'm stupid? An American with no business being in this country disappears, it's one thing to clean it up afterward. But a citizen? A *woman*? You've got to be joking. Something goes wrong and we're caught, I can look forward to a lot worse than six strokes of the *rotan*."

Fab B chuckled. "In Singapore, a fellow with my habits and appetites is liable to receive that sort of punishment just for getting out of bed in the morning. It might be said that our system of justice stems directly from Christian notions of original sin."

Xiang looked at him with his dark, empty eyes but said nothing.

Apparently, Fat B thought, his little stab at humor had gone over the *ah beng*'s head. In fact, he himself was no longer smiling, his mood having taken a sharp and rather abrupt downturn in the past few seconds. It wasn't as if the money was coming out of his own pocket, but he didn't like being interposed between this thug and their mutual employers. Negotiation wasn't his favorite activity, and he'd hoped—perhaps foolishly—that the pirate would simply take the envelope and leave.

"Really, what's the problem?" he said. "If you can grab both of them alive, fine. But it's this Blackburn who's truly valuable to our employers. Your main concern with the woman should be making certain she isn't left behind as a witness."

"If this is so easy, why couldn't your people take care of it? They followed her. They took the pictures. They could have gone ahead with the next step."

"We each have different ways of making ourselves useful. This country is where I live, you understand? I'm here for the long term. You're in and out, *lah*." Fat B shrugged again. "Let's not waste any more breath discussing it. We're both already committed, after all."

Xiang was silent. Fat B stared past him at the door,

waiting for him to make up his mind, anxious for their transaction to be concluded. How had he wound up haggling with the brutish creature? The whole distasteful episode had given him a headache.

He waited some more, watching a couple of grimy men step in from the alley and then head over to the bar.

"All right," the pirate said at last. "But I better get the rest of my money soon as it's done. You better make *sure* of it."

Fat B looked at him with quiet malice.

"Of course," he said, nodding. "It will be my pleasure."

The two men regarded each other a moment without exchanging another word. Then Xiang stuffed the envelope containing the photos under his denim jacket, pushed his chair back from the table with his feet, got up, strode to the entrance, and departed, his two companions falling in at his rear.

A small hiss slipping through his front teeth, Fat B sat very still and watched the door swing shut behind them.

Blackburn had picked up the puppet at an open-air bazaar—this was a while back, during Dipvali, the Hindu Festival of Lights. Needing a break from his responsibilities at the ground station, he had taken a few days off and gone to the coast to enjoy the frenetic celebration, taking in the sidewalk dancers, musicians, and magicians, sampling the delicious curries and *satays,* browsing the crafts stalls, and just strolling at his leisure amid the exuberant banners, floral decorations, sprays of colored rice, and endless strings of candles, lamps, and lightbulbs brightening every door and window.

Wearing an elaborate turban with a peacock feather jutting straight up out of its bottom wind, a maroon shirt with glittery gold threads woven through its fabric in vertical stripes, and steel bangles on one skinny wrist, the vendor who'd sold Blackburn the puppet had looked like a street-corner sultan in his holiday finery. His open, spirited smile had revealed the black-stained teeth and reddened gums that were telltale signs of habitual *betel* chewing—an addictive concoction with mildly intoxicating properties, the betel probably made him look ten years older than his natural age.

Blackburn remembered the strong scent of exotic spice on his breath as he had stepped up close to make his pitch, a pair of two-dimensional leather puppets in each hand, waving them aloft on slender rods. He remembered their painted colors looking gaudy and brilliant in the midday sunshine, remembered the exquisite detail of their hand-tooled features, and most especially remembered admiring the workmanship of the one in the vendor's left hand. The one that had, in fact, first caught his eye, and was now hanging above him on the wall of his office—some sort of animistic figure, part elephant, part man.

"Fifty *ringgits,* twenty-five American dollars!" the man had been shouting as he manipulated the puppet over his head. Out of curiosity, Blackburn had stopped to ask the vendor which Hindu diety the puppet represented, speaking English because he had not yet become proficient in Bahasa, having been in Malaysia less than a month at the time.

Smiling his big, resin-stained smile, wagging his head up and down as if he'd understood Blackburn, the vendor had thrust the puppet into his face and enthusiastically hollered, "Yes, yes! Fifty *ringgits,* twenty-five American dollars!"

"It's Ganesha, son of Shiva. . . ."

The voice was female and carried a musical British accent. Blackburn had turned in its direction to see an Oriental woman of perhaps thirty or thirty-five, a strikingly *beautiful* woman with a sweep of angle-cut black hair, slanted brown eyes, and skin that had been tanned the color of almonds and cream in the perpetual August of the tropics. Wearing summer khakis, a loose cotton blouse, and sandals, she was carrying a Coach handbag over her shoulder, a bag he'd known must have cost more than the combined yearly income of everyone living in that village.

Blackburn remembered immediately noticing that she had a magnificent body. Even through her baggy clothes, he'd been able to tell. It was the way she carried herself, he supposed. But he'd always had an eye for that sort of thing.

One of your best assets in the field, he thought now, three months later, his face troubled, his inner voice edged with self-contempt. Sitting by the phone in his office, he couldn't remember whether the desire to go to bed with her, and the idea of convincing her to become a fly on Marcus Caine's wall, had been linked from the very beginning. Oh, he'd felt a superficial attraction right away, but when had he ever met a good-looking women he *hadn't* thought would be fun in the sack?

Actually wanting her was another story, though. Wanting her, and then deciding he could *use* her. . . .

He thought suddenly and unexpectedly about Megan Breen and how different it had been when they were together. Not better, but easier, without guilt. They had liked each other and felt lonely and isolated in the bleak Russian winter. Neither had held expectations of their affair going beyond what it was. There had been no secret agendas between them, nothing to hide. It had been up front and without manipulation, the lines and limits clearly defined.

Of course, he hadn't known who she worked for until at least five minutes into their conversation, which had begun with them chatting about the puppet.

"... a god representing man's animal nature," she had said.

He'd looked at her and smiled. "Thanks. Sounds like the perfect mascot for my office."

"You'll see his image on a lot of pendants and charms," she said, returning his smile. "They're worn as protection against evil and bad fortune."

"*Better* than perfect," he said. "Think I'll hang him right over my phone. For when the boss calls to check up on me."

Her amused grin broadened.

"I can tell you the asking price is very fair," she said. "A lot of time goes into making these *wayang kulit* puppets, at least the quality ones. This man's even have bison horn rods."

"Is that also supposed to be good luck?"

"Not if you're a bison, I suppose. But it shows quality workmanship. Most of the puppets they sell to tourists have wooden rods."

Blackburn looked into her dark brown eyes, and realized she was studying his own. "That phrase you used . . . *wayang.* . . ."

"*Kulit,*" she said. "Roughly translated, it means 'shadow play.' An enactment of the Hindu epics using maybe a hundred puppets, and a full orchestra. It's an ancient form of entertainment in this part of the world, and a way of keeping certain traditions alive. These days, though, Nintendo beats it hands down for popularity.''

"Same old, same old, I guess," he said.

"Maybe so, but it's an awful shame. The puppet masters—they're called *dayangs*—spend years and years learning their craft. They make their puppets by hand, and provide the voices and movements of all the characters. During a show the puppets are manipulated behind a white cotton screen, with oil lamps throwing their shadows onto it—when the lighting's done right, the shadows are colored, you know. The audience is split into two groups, so that one group sees the shadow play in front of the screen, and the other sees the puppet show and musicians behind it.''

"Representing the separation between the material and the sublime, the self and the godhead," he said. "Worldly illusion and ultimate truth—"

"Atman and Brahman," she said, giving him a look that was comprised of equal parts surprise and curiosity. "I see you're familiar with Hindu philosophy."

"The Beatles school, anyway," he said. "I must have worn out five copies of George Harrison's *All Things Must Pass* when I was in college."

They stood there silently a moment, facing each other, their eyes still in contact. The crowd jostling around them, the pungent smell of cooking smoke thick in the sultry air.

"Fifty *ringgits,* twenty-five American dollars!" the vendor yelled at the top of his lungs, pushing up closer to them, obviously worried that he'd been forgotten.

Blackburn reached into his pocket for his wallet, got out two bills—a twenty and a five, U.S. currency—and payed for the puppet. The vendor gave him a little bow of thanks and briskly moved off into the crowd, leaving Blackburn holding his new acquisition with a faint look of bemusement on his face, like someone who has won a stuffed animal at a country fair shooting gallery and abruptly realizes he hasn't the slightest idea what he's going to do with it.

"Well," the woman said. "I'm sure the puppet will make an interesting conversation piece when you bring it to work with you. Don't see many like it in the States, I'll bet."

Blackburn gave her a quizzical glance, not quite sure what she meant. Only a moment later did it dawn on him that she was assuming his office was in America. A natural enough mistake, considering that he was obviously American, and that he'd payed for the puppet with American money.

"Actually, my pal Ganesha here won't be leaving the peninsula in the foreseeable future," he said. "Guess I should properly introduce myself. My name's Max Blackburn. I work security for a company called UpLink International, and right now I'm based at our regional headquarters in—"

"Johor, isn't it?" She suddenly burst out laughing as they shook hands, putting him at a loss as to what he could have said that was so funny. She recovered briefly, but then saw that the bemused expression he'd been wearing on and off over the last several minutes was very much back in evidence, and broke up again.

Still, he noticed she hadn't let go of his hand. Which was something on the plus side, anyway.

"I'm sorry, you must think I'm awfully rude," she said, getting control of herself at last. "I'm Kirsten Chu, and it happens that I work for Monolith Technologies, Singapore. The Corporate Communications Division. I'm here on holiday, visiting my sister and nieces.''

Understanding spread across Blackburn's features.

''Ah-ha,'' he said. ''So *that* explains why you're in conniptions.''

''It does indeed,'' she said. ''Our employers are very much archrivals, aren't they? For the past six months I've done nothing but huddle with our lobbyists and publicists about the encryption flap, brainstorming ways to counter Roger Gordian's opposition.''

Though Blackburn would not realize it until several months later, that was the moment he had decided to use Kirsten. The exact moment. It had been a calculating, unemotional decision, entirely separate from the genuine attraction he felt toward her. And all the time they had spent together since, all the nights their bodies had been locked in passion, using her had been very much a part of it.

''Well, judging by how badly things are going for us, you're doing a helluva job.'' He'd flashed an engaging smile, letting a hint of flirtatiousness slip into his voice. Calibrating both for maximum effect. ''But does being on opposite sides of a professional dispute mean we can't make friendly overtures?''

''Overtures,'' she repeated.

''Right. A personal truce.''

Their eyes met.

''I suppose,'' she said, ''it could be possible.''

''Then let's seal it over dinner tonight.''

''Well . . .''

''Please,'' he said, not giving her time to answer. ''I guarantee a mutually agreeable resolution.''

She looked at him a moment longer. Smiled.

"Yes," she said. "I'd love to have dinner with you."

And that was that. The beginning of an affair that had turned out to be enormously satisfying for him. Great sex, great inside information.

What more could a man desire?

Now Blackburn sat in the silence of his office, his face troubled, looking out his window at the sprawl of low, prefabricated buildings that constituted the Johor ground station, hating to think of the danger he'd put her in, *refusing* to let himself think about it, instead turning his mind back to the part that was real for both of them, imagining her body moving against him, joined to him, their cries of pleasure mingling in the darkness of her bedroom, going on and on into the night.

Yes, that part of it was real.

Real.

He reached for his phone, dialed her office number, waited for her secretary to connect them.

"Max?" she said, picking up a moment later. "Did you get my messages?"

"Yeah," he said. "Sorry I couldn't get back to you till now. They're adding components to the alarm system, and I had to oversee the whole thing. Took me most of the morning to get the glitches smoothed out."

Her voice became hushed. "Guess I got a little anxious. Something's turned up, and I think it could be important. Perhaps the very thing you've been looking for."

"You'd better not say any more right now."

"Agreed. Even if I wasn't at the office, it would be much too sensitive to discuss over the phone."

"Got you. We'll talk about it in person, then."

"Will you be coming this weekend?"

"Yes," he said.

"Such enthusiasm," she said.

He told himself to put away the guilt.

"Just tired," he said. "Barring any unforseen developments, I'll be taking a lorry over the causeway tomorrow morning."

"Bringing along your overnight bag?"

"It's been packed since yesterday," he said.

"Not too full, I hope. Clothes won't be necessary for the weekend agenda I've planned."

"Toothbrush and deodorant?"

"Now *they're* absolute requirements." She laughed. "I have to run, Max. Love you."

Blackburn's eyes moved from the window to the spot where he'd hung the puppet on the wall.

Atman and Brahman, he thought. *Illusion and truth.*

"I love you, too," he heard himself say.

Wondering if the words sounded as empty and mechanical over the phone as they did to his own ears.

FOUR

"CONGRATULATIONS, ALEX. I'LL BET EVERY POLITI-cal columnist in the country's writhing in the light of your greater glory."

Alex Nordstrum smiled a little uncomfortably as he walked into the conference room, hoping Gordian's comments, coupled with his late arrival, wouldn't give rise to certain impressions about him. That they might be accurate impressions was beside the point. Why be blatant? Conceit was a quality Nordstrum preferred to bear with discretion; he had an old Harvard classmate who'd been wearing his Phi Beta Kappa fraternity key on a gold fob for the past twenty years, and it was never a pretty sight.

"So you've heard about my upcoming submarine ride," he said, taking his place at the table. And how was that for understatement? Or had he struck a false note right there? Maybe it was a mistake trying to appear blasé about being handpicked for the small group of reporters who would accompany the President and several other world leaders—all of whom were intent on milking a treaty-signing event for every bit of public attention it was worth—on a "ride" aboard a Seawolf nuclear sub.

Yes, maybe he ought to let the others in the room be freely awed.

"May I ask who gave you the news?" he said, knowing Gordian could have gotten it from any number of political and business contacts, including at least a couple of the individuals present at the meeting. Although the list of invited reporters had been released only hours earlier, this was a plugged-in bunch if there'd ever been one.

"My source insisted on anonymity," Gordian said. "Anyway, Alex, you'd better pour yourself some coffee. We've got a lot to talk about this morning, and you just might feel like you're already underwater before we're finished."

A workable segue to more relevant matters of discussion, Alex thought.

He looked around the room, nodding his acknowledgment to the parties who'd arrived ahead of him. Most of the faces he saw were very familiar, belonging to Gordian's core group of friends and advisors. There were two UpLink employees at the table besides Nordstrum himself, who, as Foreign Affairs Consultant, was technically a freelancer: Vice President of Special Projects Megan Breen, seated to Gordian's immediate right, and Risk Assessment Manager Vince Scull at his left. Directly across from Nordstrum was Dan Parker, the congressman from California's Fourteenth District and Gordian's closest confidant since the days when they'd flown bombing sorties with the 355th Tactical Fighter Wing in Vietnam. In a chair alongside Parker sat another government official, Robert Lang, chief of the FBI's Washington, D.C., bureau.

The man poring over a document at the far end of the table was Richard Sobel, founder and CEO of Secure Solutions, a young Massachusetts-based encryption tech outfit. He both rounded out the small group and, by mere virtue of his presence, symbolized all the reasons it had come together this morning. Nordstrum couldn't have said whether it was more significant that a competitor in the field of cryptographic technology was here to offer Gordian his support and alliance, or that Sobel was the only one of fifty leaders in the software business to accept Gord's invitation.

"Okay, let's get rolling," Gordian said now, the intense gravity of his manner hardly lifted by a cordial smile. "First, I want to thank all of you for coming. Second, I want to be clear about how much I appreciate *why* you've come. It obviously would have been easy to remain silent and invisible. Our unified stance on the encryption issue has already caused most of us considerable problems, and it's a fair bet they're going to increase exponentially in the next couple of days." He paused and glanced over at Megan Breen. "The credit for putting together the statement I'll be reading at our press conference goes entirely to Ms. Breen. Assuming everyone received a copy by fax and has gotten a chance to review it, I believe you'll agree she's done a magnificent job of boiling our concerns down to media-friendly sound bites."

"Absolutely," Sobel said, looking up at her from the sheet of paper he'd been scanning. "Megan, if I thought I had any chance of poaching you from Roger, I'd make an offer right now and be off, never mind the order of the day."

Megan smiled at the compliment. A tall, slender woman of thirty-six, with huge sapphire eyes and shoulder-length auburn hair currently worn in a French braid, she looked crisp and able in a violet blouse and a gray designer blazer-and-slacks combination. Being that he was a heterosexual male with what he regarded as a good eye for attractive women, Nordstrum had long ago observed that she was a knockout. Being that she was a professional colleague, Nordstrum recognized it wasn't politically correct to give that observation any air time, and had wisely kept it to himself . . . although he reasonably suspected that many of her other male business associates, a couple of whom were in the room at that very moment, shared his atavistic view. Or hadn't there been a jag of envy in Scull's voice when he'd conveyed the rumors about Meg and Max Blackburn heating up the Russian winter last year?

"While Roger may have put it a bit too flatteringly, I *did* want to make our comments brief and straightforward," Megan was saying. "Still, I hope none of you will hesitate to let me know if there's anything that should be added, removed, or clarified. We have forty-eight hours before President Ballard signs the Morrison-Fiore Bill, which gives me ample opportunity to fine-tune any part of the statement that needs it. I think, though, that our message really is a simple one."

"Looks that way from where I sit, too," Vince Scull growled. His fringe of hair in a careless uproar around a shiny expanse of scalp, a frown creasing his bulldog face, Vince appeared to be on the verge of an angry eruption. This was nothing unusual to people who had been exposed to him for any length of time, since his total range of emotions ordinarily seemed as narrow as it was volatile, with splintery annoyance being the lowest gradient on the scale, blistering fury the highest, and radical fluctuations between these extremes occurring once every hour or so. "We put the crypto out overseas without restrictions, and presto, every bad guy with a computer link can buy himself electronic communications that law enforcement can't crack. If Ballard's got the high-wattage brain they say he does, he ought to be able to understand that without any problem. I mean, it's pretty damn obvious, isn't it, Bob?''

The FBI man shrugged. ''In all fairness, there are gray areas. A valid argument says the bad guys have *already* gotten their hands on the technology through Internet dissemination, not to mention American companies who've circumvented the law by selling crypto abroad through their international subsidiaries. Follow that line of reasoning, and you have to ask whether it pays to restrict our software manufacturers from competing on the foreign market.''

''Can't put the genie back in the bottle, so put him to work instead. That's the same crap I've been hearing for *years* from people who want to legalize dope. And let me tell you, it doesn't make any sense. Back when I was wearing a cop's badge, I saw—''

''Listen, you asked me something, I answered,'' Lang interrupted. ''If I needed to be persuaded, I wouldn't be here today, putting my career and reputation on the line. As Dan can attest, I've argued vehemently against deregulation before a dozen congressional committees.''

''I agree,'' Gordian said. ''There's no need to rehash the whole policy debate at this table. Our purpose should be to make sure we haven't overlooked any means of stopping Morrison-Fiore, or effectively presenting our case—and our solidarity—to the public, the government, and the rest of the industry.''

Nordstrum had been thinking precisely the same thing, and was relieved Gordian had gotten the static out of the air before sparks started flying.

"Regarding your last few points, I'd say reading our little declaration to the National Press Club on the day of the signing is perfect strategy," he offered. "It will stir up controversy, grab media attention, take a story that would otherwise appear on page nine of the dailies and put it right on page one, above the fold." Nordstrum paused thoughtfully, adjusting his wire glasses on the bridge of his nose. "As to throwing some last-minute hurdle in front of the bill . . . short of locking the President out of his office the day after tomorrow, or conspiring to break his writing hand, I honestly don't see how it would be possible."

"Any ideas, Dan?" Gordian asked.

"I opt for breaking his hand," Parker said, but Gordian could only manage a feeble approximation of a smile in response.

Parker studied his face, and for perhaps the fourth time that morning observed that he was not looking well at all. His cheeks were ashen, and there were deep lines under his eyes that gave him the appearance of someone who hadn't had a decent night's sleep in weeks. Gordian wasn't the sort of man who was quick to share his problems, but he generally got around to it with Parker long before they swamped him. He had opened up to him about his difficulties readjusting to freedom after five years in a Hanoi POW camp, confided in him when his marriage hit a rocky patch a while back.

Lately, though, he'd been sealed tight, leaving Parker to play guessing games with himself about what was wrong. His instincts told him it was something personal . . . but a hunch was a hunch, and with Gord keeping quiet, and the shit flying in every direction because of the crypto debate, he hadn't had a chance to pursue it very far.

Parker suddenly became aware of the silence around him, realized Gordian was still waiting for his answer.

"From a political standpoint, I think we ought to be looking ahead to the next session of Congress," he said, shoving his concerns about Gord to the back of his mind. "Take a hard line now to gain a public-relations edge, advocate a return to the previous Administration's policy of setting firm limits on the level of encryption software that's authorized for foreign sale . . ."

"And perhaps ease toward some compromise as things pick up again in the Hill," Gordian said, completing Dan's thought. "I like it."

"So do I," Lang said. "As it reads, I believe Morrison-Fiore will be calamitous to our national security. But certain changes could be incorporated that would mitigate its damage."

"Such as . . . ?"

"Off the top of my head, a clear-cut provision banning export of plug-in encryption cards, and critical components for multiplex encoding units, like the type used by our armed forces—the same type you and Mr. Sobel are refusing to market abroad."

"Another thing would be a tough set of international laws and standards managing the operation of key recovery centers," Parker said. "These places are essentially private banks where governments deposit the digital keycodes to their data-scrambling software. Right now, police and intelligence agencies can subpoena the banks to turn over the codes . . . although the civil libertarians are challenging that power in various courts."

He looked at Lang. "Correct me if I'm wrong, but my

understanding is that there are no effective international treaties which would compel a key recovery center in one country to turn its keys over to another, even if the nation requesting them can prove they're needed to counter a threat to its security.''

Lang nodded. ''You're dead-on. A terrorist with sophisticated electronic equipment could theoretically cripple our economy, even disable our military computers, while the ambassadors are wrestling over what legitimately can and can't be done under existing cooperation agreements.''

For a moment Gordian sat staring out the office's floor-to-ceiling window at the San Jose skyline, and the vague humps of the mountains off to the southeast. Then he shifted his attention back to Dan.

''What about the Foreign Trade Commission?'' he said. ''Setting our sights on the future, I'm wondering if anybody there eventually could be nudged toward at least some of our positions.''

''Never happen,'' Parker said. ''Olivera, the head of the organization, is a militant free-trader. More important, he's a Ballard appointee who's been brown-nosing the President since they were poli-sci majors at the University of Wisconsin. Not for all the Chapstick in the world would he tear his lips away from the President's backside. Nor would he allow his underlings to stray.''

''Somebody in Congress, then. Preferably the NSC.''

Parker shook his head. ''I know of several men on the panel who are privately sympathetic, and one who actually views Morrison-Fiore as a poison seed in our national defense system. But all come from states where the software industry has tremendous clout, and where people are afraid of losing jobs because of an inability to enter foreign markets." He smiled ruefully. "Do you have any idea what my opposition to the bill has cost me in votes? Being the representative from Silicon Valley? I'd probably have alienated fewer constituents if I got bagged for armed robbery . . . with an Uzi and the stolen goods in hand."

Gordian looked outside again, past the broad stretch of Rosita Avenue, to where the Diablos went marching up to Mount Hamilton, its distant flank barely visible through a thin veil of smog. Closer by, one could still see a few of the aging food-processing plants and plastic factories that had once formed the industrial base of the city . . . but they were really nothing more than relics. Technological research and development had been San Jose's lifeblood for over twenty years; its economic survival was dependent on the hardware and software outfits that gave a huge chunk of the population their employment. Dan Parker was deliberately understating the price he would have to pay for standing by his principles . . . and by his friend. In doing so, he had quite possibly committed political suicide.

Gordian turned from the window and ran his eyes around the table, letting them settle briefly on each face, each member of the coalition that had gathered around him. Parker was immediately—almost *physically*—struck by the realization that some of the old steel had returned to his gaze.

"We should discuss our travel arrangements for the trip to Washington," Gordian said. "I think we're ready for the next round."

FIVE

FROM THE *STRAITS TIMES*:

Investigation of "Phantom" Freighter Continues

Authorities Increasingly Look Toward Piracy As Explanation for Crew's Disappearance

Singapore—Nearly 48 hours after the freighter *Kuan Yin* was mysteriously abandoned by its crew in Sembawang Harbor, its undelivered cargo remains in the possession of local customs officials, who have revealed that they are consulting with their Malaysian counterparts and the Piracy Center in Kuala Lumpur regarding the possibility of a hijacking at sea.

According to Tai Al-Furan, a spokesman for the Customs Ministry, the vessel is licensed to Tamu Exports, a commercial shipper based in East Malaysia. Mr. Al-Furan confirmed that it left Kuching Harbor sometime on the evening of Sept. 15 with a manifest of general wholesale goods designated to arrive in Singapore that same evening. No other stops were scheduled in transit. It was also revealed that the ship was fully laden when found at anchorage early on the morning of the 16th, adding questions about the motive for a pirate raid to deepening concerns about the present whereabouts of its crew, which is said have consisted of almost a dozen seamen.

''The shipowner is being very cooperative and has provided our investigators with a complete list of those who were legitimately aboard the *Kuan Yin* when it set sail,'' Mr. Al-Furan told reporters.

While Mr. Al-Furan acknowledged fears that the crew members may have been forced to evacuate at sea by a hostile boarding party—giving rise to speculation that the vessel was commandeered as a means of gaining the perpetrators false documents and illegal entry into Singapore—he expressed optimism that a more routine explanation might be found for their disappearance.

''We are keeping open minds about what may have happened to them, and see no reason to jump to any conclusions at this point,'' he stated.

Mr. Al-Furan would neither confirm nor deny rumors that signs of armed violence, including apparent bullet holes, have been discovered by police in the vessel's lower deck.

Despite joint efforts by the Association of Southeast Asian Nations (ASEAN) to combat maritime crime, the frequency of pirate attacks in China and throughout the region— many of them sponsored by underworld syndicates—has increased by more than 50% over the past decade, with their level of violence also escalating. Last year alone over 400 seamen were either assaulted or killed by pirates, an alarming figure in light of recent improvements in the equipment and interdiction methods used by counter-piracy patrols. . . .

They had been following the woman for two days. According to their information, the American would likely appear tonight. And it would be tonight that they struck. Otherwise, it might be another week before they had their chance, a week during which the investigation of the *Kuan Yin* hijacking would broaden and escalate into a manhunt, and the assumed identities of the ship's crew would become increasingly useless to Xiang and his men. They wanted to be long gone from Singapore by then.

The guest house they had been staying in was a shuttered, run-down building crammed between two other dilapidated structures in a twisty *larong* not far from Fat B's. They had booked three rooms at a cheap rate, and though the accommodations in each were limited to a few sagging cots, a shaky corner table ringed by some equally lopsided chairs, and a washbasin with a dripping faucet, the out-of-the-way location and sordid atmosphere discouraged tourists and other meddling transients from seeking the place out, which was Xiang's only real requirement.

In fact, comfort was the last thing on his mind this evening.

His tattooed chest bare, he sat with both arms on the table, having wedged a small piece of cardboard under one of its legs to steady its irritating wobble. On its surface before him was a photograph of Max Blackburn. To his right was a candle he had set to burning in a flat metal ashtray. Beside the candle was a long, thin needle with a round ceramic handle. Across the room from Xiang, two of his men, Sang and Kamal, had pushed their cots to one side and given themselves space for the supple, tiger-style martial arts exercises of *karena matjang.* The shades were drawn and the electric fixtures in the room were off, and the candlelight projected their weaving shadows onto the walls and ceiling.

Thrown loosely across one of the cots were the clothes they would be wearing when they took Blackburn and the woman later on that night. Nondescript khakis, denims, and long-sleeved cotton shirts. The clothes of soft, weak people who lived safe and easy lives.

I suggest you get something to wear that will let you blend in, the peacock at the bar had said. His advice had been well taken, though he'd thought Xiang too witless to detect the mockery behind his neutral expression. Perhaps assuming size and stupidity went hand in hand. It was a mistake people often made in dealing with the Iban. And it only played to his advantage.

Now Xiang reached out with his large right hand, lifted the needle off the table, and held its carefully sharpened end into the flame. Let the others practice their *kata.* He had his own special method of preparation, of steeling himself for what lay ahead of them.

He waited silently, holding the needle out by its handle,

watching it heat up. When it was red-hot he pulled it out of the flame, then raised his left hand in front of his face, his fingers straight up and close together. He stared at it for several moments, his eyes slitted with concentration, almost as if he were reading his own palm. The glowing needle was still in his opposite hand.

Now he brought the needle horizontally toward his left hand, aligning its tip with his little finger just below the upper joint. His lips pressed tightly together, he slid the needle into the finger, piercing the soft flesh behind its pad, pushing it through until the tip came out the other side with a little squirt of blood.

Perspiration filming the wide expanse of his brow, he drove the needle further into his hand. It penetrated the fourth finger below the knuckle, cauterizing his flesh as it lanced on through and then exited again, its point emerging to prick his middle finger.

Xiang continued pushing in the needle until it had skewered all of his fingers except his thumb, rotating it once or twice to avoid nicking bone. There was an almost trancelike absorption on his face.

Slowly, then, he curled the hand into a fist around the needle. A minute went by, two, three. His fist tightened. He felt the needle's heat and pressure blaze across the inner joints of his fingers. Blood greased his wrist and went splashing down onto the photograph of Max Blackburn. The more excruciating his pain became, the harder he squeezed down on the invasive metal, causing the skin of his fingers to stretch and bulge around its length. The dribble of blood quickened and intensified, slicking his forearm, covering the image on the photo. His fist tightened some more. The pain was a wave to be ridden and crested by sheer force of will, and he did not want it to stop.

He sat there with glazed and unblinking eyes, oblivious to the other two men as they continued their ritual exertions, their shadows slipping back and forth across the room, integrating and drawing apart in the liquid patterns of their millennium-old fighting techniques.

"It will be done," he hissed under his breath. "It will be done."

His fist tightened, tightened, tightened.

A half hour later, Xiang pulled the dripping needle from his flesh.

He was ready.

The second time they'd been together—the first was that crazily exciting weekend in Selangor, when Max Blackburn swept into her life like a whirlwind, swept her into *bed* before she had a chance to think about what she was doing, or even ask herself whether anybody was at the wheel in her swoony little head—the subject of Marcus Caine's business ethics had come up in their conversation. Actually, Max had *brought* it up. Over dinner at a Thai restaurant on Scotts Road, she recalled.

They had finished their meal, and were on their second bottle of claret, and a half hour later would be grappling breathlessly in Max's suite at the Hyatt, the clothes they had shed leaving a scattered trail to the door. In between, though, they had drunk their wine and discussed her employer. Briefly, it was true. Very briefly, because they'd both been looking forward to more delightful activities than talking shop. But long enough to touch off a sequence of events that would eventually turn her world inside out.

The workday over, alone except for the cleaning woman out in the corridor, Kirsten Chu sat in the quiet of her office knowing that she was about to blow her career, and perhaps her entire life, to smithereens. Maybe sometime in the future, just so it would make clear and easy sense, she would convince herself that it was done out of conscience, moral indignation, and her refusal to become a passive accessory to acts that went far beyond the boundaries of international law. *A woman of principle.* Yes, that assessment by way of fuzzy hindsight had a nice ring, and would make her feel good about her decision in the reflective moments of her dotage. But right now, running an internal truth check, she could find only one overarching motive for what she was doing.

Of all the damn reasons in the world, it was out of love and longing for a man she barely knew anything about.

How bloody romantic.

Kirsten glanced at her wristwatch and saw that it was five-thirty, almost time to be off; Max was meeting her outside the Hyatt in half an hour. She popped the disk that would be the instrument of her professional demise out of her computer's CD-R drive, and for several moments afterward just sat there shaking her head, staring at the lethal circle of plastic, remembering that conversation at the restaurant as clearly as if it had occurred only yesterday.

Ah, Max, Max, Max. The question he'd posed to her was fairly indelicate, and probably would have been off-putting if it had come from anyone else. But that was the essential Blackburn, wasn't it? He had a way of saying things to her that other people couldn't, not without instantly and appropriately causing her defenses to harden. Indeed, she had felt vulnerable to him from the beginning.

He somehow turned tactlessness into a disarming quality, perhaps because he knew it worked for him, and took such confident pleasure in his knowing.

What he had asked, seemingly out of the blue, was whether she had any strong feelings about her employer's "underhanded corporate tactics." As if it were an obvious *given* that there was something wrong with the manner in which Marcus Caine did business. The sky is blue, the sea is wide, Marcus Caine is an unscrupulous crook. Elementary, my dear Kirsten.

At first she hadn't known what to say, had just looked at him over the rim of her wine glass, wondering if he really expected her to say anything. And he had just waited, letting her know that he did.

"I think," she'd replied finally, still hoping to avoid the subject, "your question is in violation of our declared truce."

"Nope, I've checked the rules, and they're very clear that it's acceptable," he said, that self-assured, damnably engaging look in his eyes. "Feel free to answer without risk."

She had not understood why his question made her so uncomfortable. Not then, and not for a while afterward. She had not yet been willing to admit, either to Max or herself, that he'd touched upon an already raw nerve. That the financial irregularities she had been noticing at Monolith—*irregularities,* ah, yes, she'd always thought of them like that at the time, always trivialized the significance of anything suspicious that crossed her desk—could be routinely explained away.

"Well, I'm sure that's his reputation among sour-grapes competitors, and his adversaries in protracted political battles," Kirsten said, more sharply than she'd intended. Charming as he was, Max's cockiness had irritated her. "Otherwise . . ."

"Actually, I was thinking of the class-action lawsuit against him a couple of years back," Max said. "You remember it?"

As one among an army of publicists who'd worked to stem the tide of bad press arising from that affair, Kirsten had remembered it all too well. Because Caine's new operating system was second only to Microsoft Windows in popularity—and catching up fast—it was common practice for software manufacturers to provide Monolith with pre-release versions of their products for compatibility trials. This was a mutually beneficial, even crucial, arrangement, since an operating system was useless without programs that could run within its graphic environment, and a program was dead on the shelf unless supported by one of the three standard operating systems.

The problems occurred when Monolith began patenting and marketing software that the developers claimed was nearly identical to the beta programs they'd sent out for evaluation. Their charge was that Caine's techies had lifted their intellectual properties, made minor changes to their graphic interfaces and proprietary architecture, and then stamped a Monolith logo on the retail packaging. In essence, that Monolith had rapaciously stolen their products and sold them as its own.

Sitting across from Max in the restaurant, Kirsten had put down her glass and leaned forward, her arms folded on the table.

"You certainly must know the matter was resolved out of court," she said.

"With a huge cash settlement from Caine."

"That isn't the same thing as an admission of guilt.

When you're a public figure, it's sometimes worth a great deal to get an issue out of the spotlight. Especially when the alternative is to let it drag on and become an impossible distraction.''

Max had spread his hands. ''There are other bones to pick with Caine. His flagrant disregard of the OECD anti-bribery convention, for instance.''

''You just said it yourself, Max,'' she said. ''It's an international convention, not a formal treaty. Meaning that it has no teeth. It's hardly a crime or a sin for Marcus Caine to exploit the gutlessness of its signatories . . . especially the French and Germans, who until last year were giving *tax deductions* to companies that exchanged cash payoffs for foreign contracts.''

She paused, took a breath. ''For God's sake, I'm not going to sit here and defend everything my boss does professionally. Nor can I vouch for what he's like personally. But he's the first man to own a truly interactive cable television network with affiliates on four continents, which makes him an entrepreneurial genius from my standpoint. If his competitive methods are occasionally ruthless, than so be it. What counts to me is that they're legal—''

''Or at least have never been conclusively proven to be *illegal*.''

''—and that he pays his employees very, very well,'' she'd gone on, speaking right through his interruption.

''I'd point out that there's real merit to the old cliché about money not being everything, but that would be kind of a cliché in itself,'' Max said. He gave her a tight smile. ''Wouldn't it?''

She looked at him with an odd mixture of consternation and amusement.

"Tell me, Max," she said. "Do you extend your services to UpLink for free? Troubleshooting around the world like a knight errant in Roger Gordian's holy crusade to link all of humanity with cellular phones and wireless faxes?"

If not for Max's frank, earnest look, what he'd said next might have caught her altogether by surprise. As it was, it instantly made her regret her sarcasm.

"Roger Gordian is a great man, and I would lay down my life to protect him," he'd said simply.

Whammo.

Now, looking back at that night, she recalled nearly being blown off her seat by those words. Somehow, their incredible strength and conviction bulldozed through her remaining emotional barriers, and caused her feelings for him—feelings she'd believed, or wanted to believe, consisted overwhelmingly of physical desire—of *lust,* leaving aside the delicate frills and flowers—to soar toward honest-to-God romantic love at warp speed. That had been a new and startling emotion for her, and she hadn't quite known how to handle—

A voice from the doorway suddenly intruded on her thoughts. "*Wah!* Excuse me, Miss Chu. Thought everybody go home. Come back later or not?"

Kirsten had identified the cleaning woman by her Singlish even before she looked up to see her head poking through the door. When she'd first returned to Singapore after completing her education at Oxford, Kirsten's ears had been forced to undergo a crash readjustment to the local patois, an idiosyncratic hodgepodge of English, Hokiien Chinese, and Indian phrases that jangled unharmoniously in the air wherever she went, and seemed especially favored by working-class immigrants from neighboring islands and the Phillippines.

Perhaps, she thought wryly, this was because they enjoyed watching upscale *kiasu* suffer migraine attacks while deciphering the latest term that had been added to the mix.

"No, Lin, that's okay." She clicked her computer into its preset shutdown routine and turned it off. "I was just wrapping up here."

The door opened wider and Lin clattered in with her cart.

"Why you work so late, *lah*? Is Friday night, should go out, get away from office." She winked. "Where your handsome American?"

Kirsten smiled, reached for her briefcase, and put the CD-R into an interior pocket—right beside the digital audio recorder on which Max would find a little something extra that was bound to make him ecstatic.

"Actually, the handsome American and I are planning to meet at his hotel and then dance away the night at Harry's," she said. And, as far as she was concerned, drink it away too. After turning the information she'd uncovered over to Max, information that might bring down a company that had been more than generous to her with its professional advancements, and that the group-centered Eastern traditionalist in her insisted was deserving of her loyalty, come hell or high water, she would need a whole lot of something potent to wash away the bad taste in her mouth.

"You have nice time," Lin said, a grin breaking across her broad face. "Promise tell me about it Monday, *lah*?"

Kirsten snapped her briefcase shut.

"As much as I can without shaming myself," she said.

• • •

Blackburn hastened up Scotts Road toward the Hyatt, his shoes slapping the pavement, navigating his way through thick city traffic, hordes of department store shoppers, and countless tired and slightly buzzed office workers making their post-cocktail-hour migrations home. It was seven o'clock in the evening, but the sun was only beginning to lose some of its solid-feeling intensity. Perspiring heavily, his shirt already wet as a sponge, he felt in desperate need of a shower . . . ah, yes, great way to start the weekend. Worse, he had arranged to meet Kirsten at six, and while he had called her on his cell phone to let her know he'd be late, it bothered him that he was running even later than anticipated. That she would be alone with the hottest of hot potatoes in her possession, waiting for him to show and take it from her hands.

She deserved better from him.

Most frustrating for Blackburn was the fact that he had started out with ample time to spare, having caught a lift to the bus terminal in Johor Bahru with a member of his security team, and then hopped the JB–Singapore express heading across the causeway. In the past, he'd found this to be a fast and hassle-free means of transportation from the mainland—far better than driving one of the company Land Rovers—since the buses had their own designated lanes and normally bypassed the customs posts where trucks and automobiles would get bottlenecked for lengthy stretches of time. However, tonight everything on the bridge, including public and private buses, had been subjected to exhaustive checkpoint procedures, causing delays in both directions. And though no one conducting the inspections had bothered to explain the reason they were taking place, many of his fellow passengers were convinced they were tied to the *Kuan Yin* affair that had been monopolizing the news broadcasts all week. With nothing to do but wait out the extended stops, they had noisily formed a consensus that officials were searching for the cargo ship's hijackers, or for confederates who might try slipping across the border from Malaysia to assist in their getaway.

Max didn't know about that; he had been too preoccupied with a security analysis at the ground station to follow the story's every sensational development. Still, he had noticed men in the epauleted uniforms of the Singapore Police reinforcing the usual contingent of customs bureaucrats, and assumed something very much out of the ordinary was in the air.

Of course, he'd had other things pressing on his mind as the bus continued fitfully over the Johor Strait and then onto the Bukit Timah Expressway, skirting a lush, carefully managed flourishing of parkland as it bore south to Ban San terminal. If Kirsten had finally dug up the evidence he'd been hoping to obtain from Monolith's computer databases, then the shadow play he'd initiated the day they met was about to reach its conclusion. But at what cost to her? She would be finished at Monolith. And the hard, cold truth was that he would be nearly finished with Kirsten.

Yes, she deserved better, much better, than she was bound to get from him in the end.

Blackburn had discharged the matter from his thoughts for the remainder of the trip in. Upon reaching the station on Arab Street, he had switched to a city bus and ridden it into the center of town, where traffic had once again slowed to a crawl, this time due to typical rush-hour congestion. Convinced he could make better progress on foot, he'd gotten off on Orchard Road and strode hurriedly west past the sleek, glass-fronted shopping centers lining the street like modern crystal palaces, their facades reflecting hard-pointed sun-darts that stung his eyes in spite of his dark glasses.

Now he swung right onto Scotts, squinting into the glare toward yet another exclusive shopping strip and the high tower of the Regency beyond.

Kirsten was waiting at her usual spot beside the main entrance, her hair pouring loosely over the shoulders of an eggshell-colored dress, looking out into the busy one-way thoroughfare, probably expecting him to arrive with the steady stream of cabs and buses moving past the hotel. As he approached her, Max instantly felt the mingled guilt and desire that always swelled up in him when they met. She had given herself to him without inhibition, and in its own way his craving for her was equally fierce, but Max did not love her as she had come to love him, and he had told her that he did only because it forwarded his selfish objectives. And though his lies and manipulations had profaned even their moments of greatest intimacy, he knew that he would keep leading her down the garden path until he got what he wanted . . . and that it wouldn't even be that hard.

No, God help me, not hard at all, he thought, stepping quickly toward where she was standing.

Xiang sat behind the dashboard of a panel truck outside the Hyatt's service entrance on the uphill side of Scotts Road. Less than half an hour earlier, the truck's original driver had been delivering fresh linens to the hotel. Now his naked corpse was in back, wrapped in a red-stained tablecloth from the very pile of linens he had been unloading when the Iban stole up behind him. Blood trickled from the ear through which Xiang had inserted his six-inch *kanata* needle, rupturing the man's eardrum, driving the needle up into the soft meat of his brain via the auditory canal, killing him instantly and silently.

The white uniform blouse that had been stripped from his body had smears of blood on the collar and was almost impossibly snug on Xiang, but he felt confident no one would notice it while he remained in the truck. Still, he was growing anxious. Where was the American? He could not stay parked at the loading ramp indefinitely without arousing suspicions.

Wrestling down his impatience, Xiang dipped his head slightly to look as if he might be resting behind the wheel. And waited. With luck, the murdered driver would soon have company.

Back on the street, the rest of the strike team had assumed various positions around the hotel, two covering its doors, a pair in front of the Royal Holiday Inn complex across the street, another four dispersed between the north and south corners of Scotts Road.

The men were similar in general appearance. Black-haired and stony-eyed, with angular features, skin the color of sunbaked clay, and compact builds over which the muscles were strung like taut leather cords. Each had concealed a weapon of one kind or another in the loose-fitting, casual clothes that allowed them to troll unnoticed among the hurrying crowd.

The swarm of people posed no hindrance to them. Nor did the remaining daylight. It would have been riskier to strike in darkness, when the street was emptier and activity along its sidewalks would be less frenetic. At night their movements would draw the eye like sudden ripples in a still pond; now the noise and confusion of pedestrian traffic would camouflage them in plain sight.

The woman had been standing at the Hyatt entrance for some time, looking out at the street as if she expected someone to join her at any moment. And, of course, that was exactly the case. They had been stalking her for days like wolves on the hunt. Tonight she would draw their real quarry into their circle, and they would do the job they had been paid to do.

Now the woman chanced to look in the direction of Orchard Road and her eyes widened.

The watchers took note. She smiled, waved, her expression pleased and a little excited.

The watchers observed this as well.

They turned in the direction she was facing, their eyes keenly anticipant, tracking the path of her gaze. *Finally,* they thought as one. Though the man walking toward her wore aviator sunglasses, he was easily recognizable as the individual in their photographs. He raised his hand in an answering wave and stepped up his pace.

''Max!'' she called, descending the hotel steps.

The watchers moved in to take them.

SIX

"**GET IT STRAIGHT, ALEX. IT ISN'T THE LOCKS, BUT**
the *keys* your friend Gordian should be training his sights
on . . . ah, stuff it up this contraption's wire-clogged ass-
hole, I'm falling behind the pacer!"

In his career heyday, Rear Admiral Craig Weston, Ret.,
had been among the biggest of the U.S. Navy's big fish
in his position as chief officer of SUBGRU 2, the command organization for all attack submarines on the Atlan-
tic coast, based, along with the primary student training
facility of America's submarine force, in Groton, Connecticut. This included the three nuclear submarine squadrons docked along the deceptively tranquil New England
shoreline, as well as two squadrons split between home
bases in Charleston, South Carolina, and Norwalk, Vir-
ginia—a total of forty-eight SSNs, one research submarine, and numerous support vessels. Considering that the
payload of conventional and nuclear munitions aboard a
single SSN was sufficient to erase a major coastal city
from the map, the magnitude of the destructive force that
had been under Weston's control was, in a word, remark-
able.

For Alex Nordstrum, the best part of observing Weston
on the rowing machine at the Northwest Health and Fit-

ness club was seeing how much of that force he seemed
to have taken with him into retirement. A tall, lean man
in his late sixties with a silver flattop crew cut,
stormcloud-gray eyes, and a jaw like a lofty mountain
ledge, Weston approached his morning workouts with utmost seriousness and concentration . . . and a biting fe-
rocity that was often manifested as a rather prolonged
salvo of expletives, characterized by creative anatomical
references, and uttered at a volume just quiet enough to
avoid violating the gym's rules of acceptable conduct.

"Son of a bitch! I'm on you now, you hungry fucking
crotch louse!'' he growled, accelerating the rhythm of his
strokes. He was wearing gym shorts and an athletic shirt
to showcase—quite intentionally, Nordstrum believed—a
physique that would have been impressive on someone
thirty years his junior, and been considered truly phenom-
enal on a man his age in the best of health. Having recently undergone a program of intensive chemotherapy to
combat prostate cancer that had metastacized to his lymph
nodes, Weston had almost achieved superhuman status in
Alex's estimate. Lateral muscles bulged in his thighs as
he began his drive. Abdominals and pectorals that looked
two inches thick flexed under his tank top midway
through his extension. Biceps swelled on his arms as he
pulled the handles to complete his stroke, then leaned
back in toward the flywheel for his recovery, his hips
swinging slightly, the tension cord vibrating like a bow-
string.

On the exercise bicycle beside him, Nordstrum glanced
down at his own softening middle, felt a twinge of embarrassment, and fingered the touchpad to increase his
level.

"I thought you'd be giving me background on the Seawolf today,'' he said, struggling not to sound winded. ''So how come we're talking about Roger Gordian?''

''Don't be a wise guy,'' Weston said. ''I'm not always this generous with my advice.''

Alex frowned. ''Okay, have it your way. But I really do need that information.''

''And you'll get all you can handle in a minute.''

Weston rowed, his sinews working, inhaling and exhaling softly through his nose. His eyes were centered on the rowing machine's video screen, where tiny red and blue boats were racing over green water past a strand of white beach in a computer-simulated regatta. Nordstrum waited for him to resume speaking, peripherally aware of the smooth-operating silence of the modern equipment filling the gym. There was the occasional pneumatic hum of inclines being raised on the treadmills, and now and then the metallic clank of weight adjustments on the presses, but what he mostly heard were the sounds of controlled human exertion in uncluttered acoustical space: measured expulsions of breath, the rhythmic pounding of feet on rubber.

''Let me ask you something,'' Weston said at length. ''Which would be of more concern to you—a bunch of thieves moving next door with a home security system identical to yours, or those same crooks moving in without *any* security of their own, but having the tools and wherewithal to disable your system? To open your front door, switch off your alarms, and walk into your bedroom any time you're sleeping or gone?''

''Rhetorical as posed,'' Nordstrum said. ''I'd prefer they have neither.''

''So would anybody, but that wasn't one of my choices. Indulge me, will you?''

Nordstrum shrugged and pedaled, his upper body bent forward over the handlebars, the towel around his neck damp with perspiration.

"Suppose I wouldn't want them getting into my house," he said.

Weston looked at him briefly. "There it is. My whole point. Gordian wants to make his case about crypto tech to the public, it ought to be *his* point too."

"That as far as you're going to spell it out?"

"Yes," Weston said, and then turned toward the screen again. "What do you want me to tell you about the sub?"

Nordstrum wondered if he'd missed a segue. "Everything you can. I should probably know what sort of boat I'll be riding in."

"And writing about."

"As a conscientious member of the press, and someone who doesn't like looking foolish," Nordstrum said.

Weston eyed the screen, produced another stream of epithets, and pulled more forcefully at the cable.

"You ever see that old TV program *Voyage to the Bottom of the Sea*?" he said. "My boys used to watch it religiously when they were young. Sunday nights at seven. When I was on tour I'd have to call in and listen to their episode summaries."

Nordstrum shook his head. "We didn't receive American programming in Prague at the time. Blame my ignorance on the Commies."

"Sure, forgot where you grew up," Weston said. He drove, recovered. "On the show there was a futuristic sub called the *Nautilus,* named after the one in the Jules Verne story. The Seawolf's its real-life equivalent, loaded with capabilities that the designers of Los Angeles-class vessels could only imagine. Goddamn thing's a testbed for advanced naval warfare technologies. It's got a modular construction for limitless upgrades. New low-signature hydrodynamics, and integrated detection, telemetry, and communications systems. Carries the usual array of anti-ship Harpoons, Mark 48 torpedoes, mines, you name it, plus the new Block 5-series Tomahawk. A land-attack missile that can hang in the air for up to two hours and has more warhead options than I can rattle off, including Hard Target Smart Fuze munitions able to penetrate to twenty feet underground before detonation.''

He winked and lowered his voice confidentially. ''While the Navy doesn't *officially* have nuclear-armed Tomahawks aboard its subs, the capability naturally exists.''

''Naturally,'' Alex said.

''I should add that the Seawolf's able to operate in the littorals.''

''Near ports, cities, enemy strongpoints, other land-based targets.''

''Exactly.'' Weston examined his reflection in the floor-to-ceiling mirrors, swore disgustedly under his breath, and straightened his posture. ''Before I get into more detail, you ought to know why the Seawolf's deployment under SEAPAC isn't just one of the President's typical mental farts, but his worst stinking room-clearer yet.''

''Let me take a wild stab at it,'' Nordstrum said. ''You're troubled by the prospect of having Japanese, South Korean, and other regional crew components aboard, even in exclusively non-combat roles . . . medical, research, and the like.''

''You know me well, Alex. It's the treaty's dumbest provision.''

Nordstrum pedaled. Though Weston hadn't yet broken a sweat, *he* was already starting to feel bushed.

"I don't know, Craig," he said. "Maybe you used the wrong television show for your analogy. The better comparison might be thinking of the Seawolf as a kind of USS *Enterprise*. Representatives of the world's peace-loving peoples consolidating their resources to guard against the Klingons."

"Never understood how that sappy shit got so popular," Weston said.

Nordstrum smiled. "Be that as it may, you know our Asian Pacific allies have been moving toward greater participation in regional military operations for some time. The Japanese alone spend millions on joint ballistic missile defense research with us every year. And there *are* Klingons in their part of space. North Korea's got Nodong-2's capable of dropping chemical and biological weapons into the heart of Tokyo." He paused, feeling a little out of breath. "This isn't anything that was pulled out of a hat, but a logical evolution of existing strategic policies."

"So you've stated ad infinitum in the editorial pages," Weston said. "And here I thought you were only doing it for a free thrill-ride on a submarine."

Nordstrum gave him a look. "Should I be offended by that comment?"

"It was a joke," Weston said without a trace of humor in his expression. "Look, cooperation is one thing. But how did we go from that to letting foreign seamen live and work aboard a nuclear sub, a fucking leviathan of the deep? What were our defense and intelligence communities *thinking* when they allowed it? I've never been phobic about the Japanese, but they will do what's in their own best national interest. For the past few years that's included joint military exercises with China and Russia. They're reaching out in directions besides just *ours.*"

"I've never suggested SEAPAC doesn't have its risks. Obviously there have to be tough security procedures—"

"You mentioned medical personnel. As you'll see for yourself in a couple of weeks, even the biggest sub feels like a claustrophobic tin can once you've been aboard a while. It's a short hop from the infirmary to the torpedo room. Or the control room. Ghosts have a way of floating between decks, Alex. Of going wherever the fuck they want without being noticed. Because they can make their damned selves invisible."

Weston rowed silently, seemingly with nothing more to add, and having shed very little light on the technical workings of the submarine. How had they gotten side-tracked onto policy matters?

Alex swung his leg off the bike and wiped his forehead with his towel.

"That's it for me," he said. "Feel like breakfast?"

"I owe this cocksucking torture machine another fifteen minutes of my life," Weston said. "Next time, though. We'll have some pancakes."

"Sure," Nordstrum said, starting toward the locker room.

"Alex—"

He paused and looked over his shoulder.

"It's the key, not the lock. Tell that to Roger Gordian. Before the press conference. Okay?"

Alex regarded Weston a moment, then nodded.

"Okay," he said.

SEVEN

THE SUBTLEST OF VISUAL CUES JACKED BLACKBURN to heightened alertness. He could not have expressed the feeling in words; it was instinctive, programmed into his neural circuits by long years of battle experience with the Special Air Service. And he trusted it no less than his eyes and ears.

The man who had triggered his reaction had been poring through a magazine as he waited at the bus stop—so why had his eyes flicked over the upper edge of the magazine as Blackburn walked by? And why the sharp look of recognition on his features, the abrupt stiffening of his posture?

Why, all at once, had Blackburn gotten the powerful sense of being *watched*?

Perhaps twenty yards ahead of him, Kirsten was starting down the stairs in front of the Hyatt's entrance. Max slowed his pace and pulled back his gaze. He ranged it from right to left across an area several feet away and parallel to him, then reversed direction, scanning a larger, farther sector until it once again encompassed Kirsten. His attention had divided itself, automatically and simultaneously keying into separate frames of reference: the particular and the general, the narrow and the wide, points and lines.

Blackburn marked the bodies of the people within eyeshot as stationary and moving objects, drawing correlations between their positions and the broader patterns of foot traffic. Scouting for any peculiarities in their interrelationships.

Several were readily apparent.

There was a man launching off the curb directly across the street to his left, beyond the pedestrian crossing, then weaving through traffic toward his side of the street—a rare sight in a country that punished jaywalking with steep fines. Another was advancing from a short distance up the sidewalk, shoving through the crowd. Two more were rapidly converging on the hotel from opposite sides of the entrance.

Blackburn snapped a glance behind him, felt the skin on the back of his neck prickle. The man he had passed at the bus stop was pushing toward him, the magazine he'd been holding no longer in evidence.

All four of the men were around the same age, Asian, and wearing the same basic style of clothing.

The entire surveillance took under eight seconds and left him with little to consider. He had learned to be aware of everything that happened around him and quickly digest what he observed. It was clear now that he had walked into a trap. A *closing* trap. He did not know for certain who his enemies were, how they were deployed, or even their total number . . . but he did know the positions of five of them.

He walked on, trying to control his nerves, making a tremendous effort to conceal the fact that he'd spotted his attackers. Kirsten was halfway down the steps now, the men nearest the hotel closing in on her. Which could only mean they—or whoever had sent them—knew something about the Monolith files. He had to to get her away from them. But *how*?

Scanning the area near the hotel, he came up with an idea.

Without wasting an instant, he reached into his sport jacket for his palm phone, flipped it open, thumbed the power button, keyed up one of the speed-dial numbers stored in its memory, and hit "Send." Hoping to God that *Kirsten's* cell phone was on, and that she would answer his call if it was.

Kirsten had almost reached the sidewalk when her cellular trilled in her purse. She paused, looked toward Max, and smiled. He had lifted his own phone to his ear. Was he going to mutter sweet nothings to her as he came up the street?

Moving against the handrail, she set her briefcase down on a step and got out the phone.

"Hi-ho," she said into the mouthpiece. "I see you're finally—"

"Don't talk. There isn't time."

Confused, she looked across the short distance between them and saw that his face was as serious as his tone.

"Max, what's wrong?"

"I said to be quiet and *listen*."

Her stomach clenched with tension. She swallowed, nodded, her hand squeezing the phone.

"There's a taxi stand up the block to your right. Walk over to it as fast as you can without running."

She nodded again, looking at him with wide, questioning eyes. The stand was in the opposite direction from Max. What was going on?

Suddenly the emotion gripping her middle was no longer anxiety but fear.

The disk. God, this had to be connected to the—

''I want you to jump into a cab and get the hell away from here. I'll contact you soon. Understand?''

She gave him a third nod.

''Go!'' he said.

Her heart knocking, she replaced the phone in her bag, snatched up her briefcase, and hastened down the remaining stairs to the street.

The two members of the strike team nearest the woman saw her stop and pull out her cell phone, then looked down the street at Blackburn, saw him talking into *his* phone, and immediately knew they'd been discovered.

One of them raised a hand to signal this to the others.

Bare seconds later he saw her resume walking, reach the bottom of the steps, and swing away from Blackburn toward the cab stand.

He and his companion increased their pace, pushing through the crowd, confident they were close enough to intercept her before she reached it.

Blackburn was still a few steps away from Kirsten when he saw the man turn his head toward her, turn his head toward him, and then give what was clearly a signal to his companions.

Not good, Blackburn thought. If the man had seen both of them on their phones, he wouldn't have to be a genius to conclude they were talking to each other, and that his group's little ambush was no longer any kind of secret.

The gesture would have warned his friends to hurry up and make their move.

Kirsten had reached the pavement, turned away from him, and started hastily toward the taxi stand, where a line of robin's-egg-blue Comfort cabs were waiting to pick up fares. The pair of men who'd been covering the door had veered off after her, right on her tail, blocking her from Blackburn's sight.

His teeth clenched, Max bumped quickly past a group of women with shopping bags hung on their arms, shuffled past some dark-suited businessmen, and then moved up behind the pair at a fast walk, using every available ounce of self-restraint to keep from actually breaking into a run. If he did that, it was a safe bet his attackers would do the same, and he had no way of telling whether he'd made all of them, or whether there might be someone he *hadn't* identified even nearer to Kirsten than the two men in front of him—and in an easy position to outrace him.

He gained on the men, gained some more, and when he was almost on top of them suddenly swung around to their left, quickstepping off the curb, then stepping back onto it, passing them, putting himself between them and Kirsten. He was three feet behind her now, maybe less.

Almost close enough to touch her.

Almost. . . .

He heard hurried footsteps coming up behind him, and lunged ahead with a burst of speed, no longer checking himself, knowing there wasn't any room left for hesitation. Reaching her at last, he hooked his right arm around her shoulder and swept her along toward the idling cabs, bracing her so she wouldn't trip head over heels onto the asphalt, using his body to shield her from their pursuers.

Rigid with shock, Kirsten stumbled along uncomprehendingly for several feet, trying to resist—then all at once realized it was Max and loosened up, letting him steer her forward.

She glanced over at his face as they approached the cab stand, her eyes bright with distress, their cheeks almost touching. "Max, dear Heaven, *Max,* I thought you were one of them. I—"

"Shhh!"

Kirsten fell silent, her body trembling against him. She had no sooner registered that he was looking past her toward one of the standing cabs, than he reached out and tore open the taxi's door so violently she had the wild idea that its handle would come off in his grasp.

What followed would always be a blur in Kirsten's recollection. One instant they were together, she under his arm, Max practically carrying her along, and the next he'd shoved her into the backseat of the cab, and was standing on the street, standing there alone, leaning through the door from outside.

"Selangor!" he shouted at the driver.

The man behind the wheel jerked around to look at him through the safety partition, his shoulder rattling the clutch of religious trinkets dangling from his rearview mirror.

"Sorry, no long distance, *lah,*" he said, shaking his head.

Blackburn jammed a hand into his pants pocket, hurriedly yanked out his billfold, and tossed it into the front seat.

"There's more than two hundred American dollars in it," he said. "Take her and it's all yours."

Kirsten was gaping up at him with a kind of helpless desperation. The driver, meanwhile, had already lifted the billfold off the seat and was peering into it with astonishment.

"Max, I don't understand," she cried shrilly. "What's happening? Why aren't you *coming*?"

"Stay with your sister," he said. "If you don't hear from me in a few days, I want you to get in touch with a man named Pete Ni—"

Max felt a hand seize on his left elbow from behind. He tensed, trying to keep himself planted between the two attackers and the cab.

"Get moving!" he screamed into its interior, then pulled his head out of the door, slamming it shut with his right hand. He could see the reflections of the two attackers in the window—one still holding onto him, the other trying to scramble past him to the car.

For a seemingly endless moment the cab remained stationary, and Max was sure the driver wasn't going to bite at his offer. Then he saw him push down the lever of the meter to start it running, and expelled a sigh of relief.

Her face bewildered and terrified, Kirsten shifted around in her seat as the taxi angled from the curb, staring at him through the rear window.

Their eyes met briefly, his narrow and resolute, hers moist with tears . . . and then the taxi joined the heavy flow of northbound traffic, and was gone.

It was the last they ever saw of each other.

Max heard a short, frustrated breath escape the man that had taken hold of his right forearm.

"You come with me, *kambing*," he hissed, and tightened his grip. His lips were against Max's ear, his body pressing up behind him.

Max didn't budge. The man's partner had jogged after

the cab for several yards, then been forced to get out of the way of speeding traffic, scrambled back onto the sidewalk, and turned around—but he hadn't yet returned to where they were standing.

Which left Max with a small but workable opening.

Moving with reflexive swiftness, he brought his left arm around in front of him, reaching across his middle, shifting his weight onto his right leg to pull his captor sharply toward him. As the man staggered forward with one hand still clamped over Max's forearm, Max put his free hand over it, gripped three of its fingers, and bent them back hard.

The man released him with a gasp of pain and surprise, struggling to regain his balance.

Max moved away from him and wheeled in a full circle, glancing up and down the street. A few nearby pedestrians had paused to gawk at the scuffle, but most were hustling past as if they hadn't noticed anything unusual. Maybe they really had not, or maybe they were just mindful that, however prosperous, Singapore was still a dictatorship where it was best to mind one's own business.

Either way, he had more urgent concerns. The magazine reader was coming at him from the left, and now he had the jaywalker for company. A third member of the strike team was hustling toward him from the right. Counting the man he'd just shaken off, and the man who had been chasing the cab—both of whom were behind Max—the odds against him were at least five to one.

The only direction left open was straight ahead, toward the hotel.

He ran across the sidewalk and bounded up the stairs to its entrance.

●　　●　　●

Max cut a line through the lobby without a backward glance. He was acquainted with its layout from his regular stays in UpLink's long-term guest suites, and he knew what he was looking for. To the rear of the desk and main lounge area was a bank of elevators and, on their right, a short, straight corridor leading to a service entrance. Beyond that, a stairwell that would presumably take him down to the basement and loading doors. No hotel security guards on duty, or at least none in sight . . . and he'd been hoping their presence might turn aside his pursuers. Still, if he could reach the service entrance before his pursuers caught up to him—a big "if" since they'd been following right on his heels—he'd be able to shake them by ducking out the side of the hotel.

Max saw a clot of new arrivals making a commotion at the check-in desk, German tourists from the sound of them. Hoping for momentary cover, he plunged into the noisy, milling group, then moved on past the entrances to the hotel dance club and bar, past the elevators, and over toward the service entrance, still not looking back over his shoulder—no time for that, no time at all.

The gray metal door was slightly recessed from the wall and had a pane of wired glass set into it at eye level. No one was anywhere near it. Max turned the knob with his left hand, pushed the door open with the flat of his right, went through, and stepped from carpeting to bare concrete.

Blackburn took a hurried look around—narrow flights of stairs ran up and down from where he stood on a wide landing. He started toward the descending stairs, but got no further than the end of the landing before the door crashed open behind him, a hand clamped onto his shoulder, and he was pulled backward with tremendous wrenching force.

Max caught hold of the rail an instant before he would have gone stumbling off his feet. He whirled on whoever had grabbed him, found himself standing with a butterfly knife pressed against his throat.

"Come with me." It was Jaywalker. Facing him from inches away, his fist clenched around the weapon's double handle. "Now."

Blackburn met his gaze and saw no hint of human emotion in it, only a sort of cold, vortical emptiness. Then he heard muffled footsteps and broke eye contact, switching his attention to the door pane. Magazine Man and two others were approaching from the outer hall. They would burst through onto the landing within seconds. And there was still nobody else around.

Blackburn stood motionless. His hands at his sides. The blade against the right side of his throat, less than an inch below the ear, where it could easily slice into his carotid artery. Blood trickled down from where its razor edge had broken his skin.

His mind raced. He was carrying a Heckler & Koch MK23 in a concealment holster against his waist, but his assailant wasn't going to give him the chance to draw it. He was in the most vulnerable position he could imagine, and the close quarters left precious little room to maneuver.

So what, then?

He didn't have a split second to waste debating it with himself. Sweeping his left arm up from his side, he slammed the outer part of his forearm against the back of Jaywalker's knife hand, knocking the blade away from his throat, then grabbing his wrist to keep him from bringing it back up. Caught by surprise, Jaywalker tried to tear free, but Blackburn held fast to him, bringing his knee up into his groin. Jaywalker doubled over, gasping for air, his knife clattering to the floor. Max moved in closer and followed with a rapid combination of punches to the head—left cross, right jab, left hook. Gasping for breath, his nose and lips bleeding, Jaywalker staggered back against the rail. Max didn't relent for a heartbeat. His chin tucked low in a boxer's stance, he hit his opponent with another smashing blow to the side of his face, putting all his weight into it, wanting to take him out before he could recover . . . and before his friends came to his assistance.

But he only got half of what he wanted. As Jaywalker dropped to the floor in an unconscious heap, the fire door winged open and the others bolted through onto the landing. The one in the lead was small and wire-thin, wearing a baggy tan shirt, chinos, and Oakley sunglasses. Running up behind him, Magazine Man was perhaps a head taller and a good deal bulkier.

It was Oakley that proved to be trouble of a sort Max never could have seen coming.

He was reaching for his gun when Oakley dropped into a low squat, and, spinning on one leg, snapped the other leg out parallel to the floor, the side of his foot striking Max's ankle with shocking impact as the kick reached the end of its arc. Caught completely off guard by the move, firebolts jagging up to his knee, Max went staggering, fumbled for the rail, was unable to grab it this time, and tumbled down the stairs.

He rolled twice, somehow keeping his right hand fastened around the butt of his semi-auto, his other arm twisting underneath him as he threw it out to brace his fall. He hit the lower landing with an audible crash, winced, a huge flare of pain suffusing his entire left side.

There was little doubt he'd seriously injured his shoulder blade, perhaps even fractured it.

He still had his gun, though. Still had the blessed thing cocked and ready in his fist.

Rocking onto his back, he saw Oakley hurtling down toward the landing, toward *him,* coming on like a goddamned homing missile. The funneling, empty look hadn't left his eyes. Aware he'd be finished if his shot went awry, Max brought up the pistol, aimed dead center at his attacker's rib cage, and squeezed the trigger.

The report was oddly flat and unechoing in the concrete stairwell, but its effect was nonetheless dramatic. Blood and shreds of material blew from the front of Oakley's shirt as the heavy .45 ACP slug tore into him. His sunglasses whirled off his head and smacked against the wall. He sailed backward as if suddenly having been switched into reverse, his arms flailing, his eyes wide and unbelieving. Then he sprawled limply onto the stairs.

Max glanced past his body at the upper landing, saw that Magazine Man had slipped a hand under his baggy shirt, and fired again before he could pull whatever the hell he was reaching for.

There was another flat thud from his gun muzzle, another explosion of crimson, and Magazine Man went down clutching his chest.

Blackburn knew he'd only gained a brief reprieve, and struggled to a sitting position. The three men he'd overcome couldn't have been too far ahead of the rest of his attackers. If they'd stayed in contact with them—which was likely—the others would be coming through the door at any moment.

His situation was going to get worse, much worse, once they did.

He needed to move fast.

Max got to his feet, grasping the rail with one hand to support his weight. His ankle and shoulder wailed from their injuries. He looked up and down the basement corridor into which he'd fallen, saw large double doors perhaps ten or fifteen feet over to his right, and made a snap decision to see where they led.

He boosted himself off the rail with a small gasp of exertion, reached his goal with a few limping steps.

Suddenly there was a loud crash—the stairwell door flying open behind him.

Then footsteps.

Banging down the stairs.

Max felt a thrill of renewed urgency. It wasn't hard to visualize the newcomers' reactions when they saw what he'd done to their friends. They would not be pleased, to say the least.

He pushed the whole length of his body against the metal lock bar, and the doors opened out. Weak daylight flooded over him. Ahead was a loading ramp that rose to a short alley lined with Dumpsters. A delivery truck was parked at the curb at the mouth of the alley. The word ''New Bridge Linens'' painted across its flank in English, a delivery man on the driver's side of the cab.

Max paused. Saw that the delivery man's head was craned so he could peer out the passenger window. Saw the expression of menacing scrutiny on his features. And realized he'd been about to go running straight toward his opponents' getaway vehicle.

The delivery man turned toward his door, threw it

open, and emerged from the truck, hurrying around its front grille toward the alley. Max could tell at a glance that he was enormous, and did not feel like having to take him on. In the best of conditions it would be a tough fight, and he was far from at his best right now. His gun upraised in his right hand, he withdrew into the doorway, grabbed the lock bar with his left hand, and hauled back on it, praying he could find another way out before his pursuers overtook him—

Exquisite pain sliced through his right arm all at once. It jerked into the air as if snagged on a fishing line, jerked out of his control, the semi-auto flying from his fingers. A harsh breath escaped Max's lips as he glanced incredulously down at himself and saw that something *had* caught onto him below the elbow, tearing through his jacket sleeve, actually sinking into his flesh—a kind of metal grappling hook at the end of a thin chain, what he believed was a goddamned martial arts weapon the Chinese called a flying claw. The man grasping its handle ring, his stare devoid of mercy, could have been Oakley's twin.

The double doors flung wide open behind Max. With his peripheral vision he saw the bulking figure of the man move up on his left.

He desperately gripped the tautened chain with his good hand and struggled to tear it loose, but the claw wasn't coming out, the claw had gouged too deeply into his arm, the claw was buried inside him.

My God, who are *these guys?* he thought, his blood streaming thickly from his wound, dripping over the chain to the floor. The man at the other end of the weapon holding onto it like someone engaged in a deadly tug of war. *Who—?*

Before he could finish asking himself the question, the driver's massive hand swung out at his temple and the world exploded into blinding whiteness and then went black.

EIGHT

FROM *THE WALL STREET JOURNAL*:

Industry Focus: Roger Gordian's Growing, Failing Monstrosity
BY REYNOLD ARMITAGE

There is drama in the numbers: by its own accounting estimates UpLink's earnings have fallen 18% in the past year, the largest slide in its third consecutive quarter of decline. Its stock prices continue to drop at an even more precipitous rate, having closed the week by falling $15.4656 to $45.7854 a share on Big Board composite volume of 100 million shares, a decline of 25%. As a result of these losses the corporation's market value has plunged by about $9 billion, considerably below even the gloomiest of analysts' predictions and raising new questions about whether the high-tech giant can support its heavy investment in a global "personal communications satellite" network—one requiring the launch of about 50 LEOs and 40 gateway stations around the world, for a total investment of over $3 billion over the next five years.

There is drama in the numbers, but the entire story is more complicated than they reveal upon first examination. Certainly the defense and communications operations at the heart of Roger Gordian's past success desperately need to have the causes of their ill health diagnosed and remedied. But to completely understand the forces bringing down his parent company, one must look at the poor track records of its spawn. To offer but a few examples: the lackluster performance of UpLink's specialty automotive subsidiary, the chronic profit drain of its medical devices and power generation divisions, and the recent Dow losses suffered by its computer hardware and software offshoots due almost entirely to Gordian's imperious and unreasonable decree against the sale of cryptographic technology to emerging overseas markets. Indeed, the catalog of failures and borderline failures for what had been one of America's leading companies seems endless.

Unease runs deep among investors, who fear that Roger Gordian has created a patchwork monster, a multilimbed aberration whose lifeblood is being diverted away from its corporate center to sustain its unwieldy reach. To be blunt, as UpLink's once highly valued stock continues to lose ground, it becomes less critical to ask whether its problems are due to hubris, inattention, or simple bad judgment on the part of its executives, and fitting to state the obvious bottom line—its board has failed to uphold its basic fiduciary responsibility to shareholders, namely guaranteeing a premium return on their investments.

Let us pause here to consider an image of cojoined or "Siamese" twins—better yet, make them triplets—their bodies connected by an implacable tube of flesh, nerves, and intertwined blood vessels. In the cradle, they coo and embrace. As young adolescents they plan for a future that seems a bright, infinite frontier.

But adulthood brings change and discord. One of them grows to enjoy composing gentle romantic poetry. Another's great pleasures are drinking and arm-wrestling in rowdy taverns. The third simply likes to fish in the sun. Miscreated, mismatched, and miserable, they try to reach some lifestyle accommodation, equally dividing their time between preferred pursuits, but their basic incompatibility of nature causes all three to fail.

The poet cannot write because the long nights in hard bars make soft, lyrical thoughts impossible, and because he suffers hangovers from the alcohol flowing through their common bloodstream. The prodigal grows depressed and contrary while his versifying brother struggles to focus on the intricacies of rhyme and meter. Their constant arguing exhausts the fisherman, so that he merely sleeps away his mornings by the stream, and his rod frequently drops from his fingers to be dragged off into the water by a darting bass or trout, gone with a splash.

Eventually the three brothers wane and perish. The cause stated on their death certificates? One does not know the medical term, but perhaps it might rightly be called overdiversification.

What can be done to spare UpLink from a similar demise? For answers we might contrast the untenable generalism of its expansion to the cautious, focused growth of Monolith Technologies. . . .

Although it wasn't yet time for the reception to conclude, Marcus Caine was feeling bored and stuffy-headed in the packed United Nations chamber. From his place at the dais, he sat staring past exotic floral arrangements at a profusion of television cameras, cables, floodlights, and microphone booms, all manipulated by a crew of scurrying technicians. Behind him was a large collapsible backdrop showing the U.N. symbol, a globe viewed from the North Pole and surrounded by olive branches. Because this was a UNICEF event, there was the added touch of a woman holding a young child in the center of the globe. Caine's wife, Odielle, sat quietly at his right, her face thin and clamped. On either side of them were officers of the organization's Executive Board and high-ranking members of its parent body, the Economic and Social Council. Below him, rows of interpreters in headsets were translating their insipid, windy speeches into six languages.

As the current speaker droned away about Caine's philanthropic largesse, he absently glanced down the length of the table at Arcadia Foxcroft, *Lady* Arcadia, his connection to the Secretariat, and the woman who had arranged the ongoing event. Wanting to stop his mind from drifting off entirely, he stared at her, made her his fixed point of concentration. It wasn't hard. She had the sort of face one would expect to see on a fashion model's headshot—exciting, glamorous, provocative. Her peach-colored dress accented a spectacular figure. Lively blue eyes flashing, delicate lips parting over perfect white teeth, she was having a conversation with the fellow next to her, laughing at something he'd said. Though he couldn't hear the laughter from his seat, Caine was very familiar with the sound of it.

Somehow it always made him think of sharpened glass.

Caine watched her. A man-killer, Arcadia. And aware of it, as were all women of her type. She brushed back a wisp of auburn hair, revealing one of the diamond earrings that he'd bought for a small fortune at Harry Winston's and given her while they were in bed the previous night. He had dropped them between her thighs after they made love, and she had found that tremendously arousing. As she'd put them on, and then slid on top of him, groaning breathlessly, awakening him to delight again, he'd wondered how many other sexual dalliances she was having even while they conducted their affair, how many other partners were lavishing her with expensive gifts. Doubtless quite a few. Which was all right. Bad girl, Arcadia. He had his fair share of her, and thought it was only sporting to let the rest of the boys have theirs.

Besides, he liked to imagine her engaging in hidden, illicit acts out of his presence . . . just as he thrived on the tension of having his wife and mistress seated in the same room, rubbing elbows, making small talk, secrets running between them like unseen trip wires.

Caine was dimly aware that another speaker had taken the microphone. A famous Hollywood actress who had married a New York congressional leader, semi-retired from the big screen, moved out to East Hampton, damped her incandescent beauty behind scholarly wire glasses, and become a dedicated spokeswoman for children's causes. Caine wished he'd dated her when the chance had presented itself some years back. Now she was expressing her admiration of his professional standards, his accomplishments in wedding the mass media to computer technology, his inroads into new Asian cable television markets. She raised a chuckle from the crowd with a line that used the word ''gizmo,'' shifted her tone to one of sober concern, and last but not least, praised his unflinching commitment to the Children, capital C. Thanks to Marcus Caine, she concluded wryly, it was truly becoming a small world after all.

Throughout the speech Caine kept his eyes on Arcadia, watching her flirtatious interaction with the dignitary beside her. He understood her quite well; indeed he and she were alike in a great many ways. Born in Argentina, the illegitimate daughter of a wealthy German expatriate and his one-time maid, she had been raised by her mother without paternal involvement or financial assistance, and was turning tricks in the streets of Buenos Aires before she was twelve. A decade and several wealthy clients later, having taught herself the manners and forms of sophistication, she slept her way into England's green and pleasant bowers, married a sputtering old lord who was ripe for the grave, secured his inheritance, and thus guaranteed her place in elegant High Society—make that capital H, capital S, please. She was a poseur, plain and simple. An urchin who had snuck into the ball and charmed her way into favor with the invited guests. No wonder her every gesture seemed an exaggeration. As if she constantly needed to prove herself *to* herself.

Yes, Caine understood her. As he sat among U.N. appointees chosen for their social status and connections, graduates of elite schools, men and women whose bloodlines and fortunes could be traced back centuries, pampered exquisites who were little more than walking family crests, how could he not? They were to the manor born. His father had been a sales executive who retired with a moderate pension after an undistinguished and psychologically anesthetizing career. His mother had taught third grade until she became pregnant with him and settled into being a housewife. Caine himself had been a good student throughout his youth, and attended Harvard for two years on a merit scholarship—but it had been withdrawn in his fourth semester when he'd gotten into some difficulties, and he'd never obtained his degree. Had he not fostered several important friendships before his expulsion he'd have been finished even before entering the race.

The fine ladies and gents in his company would have been astonished, completely astonished, if they knew what he thought of them, how *contemptuous* he was of them. . . .

A flurry of movement to Caine's immediate right, near the podium, suddenly intruded on his thoughts. He straightened in his chair, breaking his attention away from Lady Arcadia. The speaker presently delivering an encomium to his humanitarianism was Amnon Jafari, Executive Secretary ECOSOC, and he seemed about to wrap things up. A group of dark-suited men had appeared from behind the collapsible wall with a six-foot-long blow-up of Caine's endowment check to UNICEF—three million dollars, which he'd promised to double once it was matched by donations from other wealthy individuals. The mock check was backed with plywood, and there were two members of the group holding it at each end.

The Secretary's voice was a deep tenor, and its volume grew as he ended his speech, expressing his gratitude to Caine with a final burst of enthusiasm. Caine heard his name boom from Jafari's lips to the acoustical drop ceiling, and then carry across the chamber to the VIP floor and public galleries. Applause crashed through the room like thunder.

It was time for him to accept the accolades. He would enjoy standing before the cameras while trying to outdo the pompous verbosity of his hosts.

He rose, went to the podium, and clasped Jafari's right hand in both his own. Then the Secretary stepped aside and Caine turned to face the crowd, the oversized reproduction of his check making a splendid prop behind him. He began his comments by thanking the roster of U.N. officials responsible for the event, speaking without reference to notes or the Teleprompter—Caine's eidetic memory was one of his strongest assets.

"Yes, I am honored to be here," he said when he was through rattling off names. Flashbulbs popped, cameras dollied in for close-ups. "But more than anything, I am grateful for the opportunity to stand before you today with a challenge. As many of you know, I have long been committed to extending the global reach of interactive electronic media, and especially Internet technology—for it is my belief that they are the modern magic that can unite the inhabitants and governments of Planet Earth and truly make us one, the tools that will bring about our next evolution as a species. Cyberspace allows us all, young and old, rich and poor, the great and the humble, to meet on a level field. A field with ever-expanding horizons and limitless potential.''

He paused for some scattered handclaps, glanced over his wife's head at Lady Arcadia. She met his gaze and smiled at him, her lower lip tucked alluringly between her front teeth.

''Yet as we take our first steps into the infant twenty-first century, we must proceed boldly rather than tentatively to assure that none are denied access to this dynamic realm of information and knowledge. Those of us who have been blessed with lives of material comfort are obliged to share the rewards we have enjoyed. Listen up and listen well: It is time to dedicate ourselves to guiding and educating the children, so that they too may grow without limitation, and attain new and fulfilling horizons. Time for each of us extend a hand, and pledge a portion of our wealth to bringing them technology that will immeasurably improve their lives. It is a hard fact that advancement requires money. Schoolroom computers, high-speed DSL modems, Internet connections—none of these come free. From Bahrain to Barbados, from Afghanistan to Antigua, from the industrial capitals of Europe to the emerging nations of West Africa, the youngest and least fortunate of us must be guaranteed access. . . .''

Caine went on in that vein for perhaps ten more minutes, and then decided to quit before he talked himself hoarse. His standing ovation was punctuated with cheers and bravos. He noticed that Odielle's clapping was rather feeble and halfhearted, and that her pinched expression seemed even tighter than it had been all morning—could it be she'd seen him exchange intimate glances with Arcadia, even knew something about his trysts with her? The thought made him tingle with a kind of giddy excitement.

But later for that. The show wasn't over yet, not until his Southeast Asian business associates—his *benefactors,* as they would have preferred to be considered—saw him run through his greatest hits. Doubtless, they would be watching and listening for them in front of their television screens.

Caine stood quietly until the crowd subsided, then announced that he would be taking a few questions from the press corps.

Predictably, the first one shouted at him had nothing whatsoever to do with his gift to UNICEF, or his challenge to the rich, or his crusade to put the deprived youngsters of the world on-line.

"Mr. Caine, as you know, the Morrison-Fiore bill will be signed into law the day after tomorrow." Caine recognized the reporter from the network newscasts; he had a scoop of dyed brown hair and an alliterative name. "Could you please give us your thoughts about that, and also about the fact that Roger Gordian is expected to simultaneously hold a press conference in Washington to declare his continuing opposition to the President's relaxed encryption policies."

Caine looked thoughtful. "I respect Mr. Gordian for his tremendous past accomplishments. But he has already expressed his views on the subject, and the people have voiced their grassroots opposition through their elected representatives. This is about our children and our grandchildren. About the *future*. Regrettably, Mr. Gordian has turned his eyes in the opposite direction.''

''If I may follow up, sir . . . as the bill's most vigorous proponent in the public sector, will you be going to Washington for the signing ceremony?''

''I haven't yet decided.'' Caine manufactured a smile. ''The President has been gracious enough to extend an invitation, but one day a week in the spotlight seems like plenty to me. Quite candidly, I've had enough of hotel rooms and am itching to get back to work.''

The reporter sat down and a second man sprang to his feet.

''Do you believe there's any link between Roger Gordian's stance on the encryption issue and UpLink's diminishing stock values?''

Beautiful, Caine thought.

''That's a question better asked of an investment banker than a software developer,'' he said. ''I'm really not here to speculate on my colleague's business difficulties. But if I may argue the obvious, the fortunes of *any* technology firm rise or fall on the willingness and ability of its leaders to look ahead rather than behind them.'' He paused. ''Now, if we may get back to the children's initiative I've proposed today. . . .''

But of course they didn't, which was exactly what Caine had wanted and anticipated. In the remaining minutes of the Q and A, Roger Gordian's name was mentioned half a dozen times, mentioned until he almost became an unseen presence at the press conference.

But not a participant to it, Caine thought. Today the floor was his, and his voice alone was being heard.

Engrossed in his own performance, he called on another reporter.

The future indeed.

That was very much what it was all about.

"Roger—"

Putting his hand over the phone, Gordian looked up at his wife as she appeared in the doorway of his study, wedged the receiver between his neck and shoulder, and held his pointer finger aloft.

"Just a minute, hon."

"You said that *twenty* minutes ago. Before you called Chuck Kirby."

"I know, sorry, we tend to get long-winded," he said distractedly. "Right now, though, I'm just buzzing the airport. I intend to fly the plane into Washington for the press conference, and want the mechanics to check it out. . . ."

Ashley gave him a look that meant business. "Gord, what do you see in front of you?"

He cradled the receiver. "A wonderful but increasingly impatient spouse?"

She still wasn't smiling.

"Gorgeous, too," he said, knowing he was in for it.

"It's been three hours since I came home from the salon with shorter hair and blonder highlights than I've ever had in my life, and you've been holed up in here the entire time, too busy to notice," she said. "This is Saturday. I thought you were going to take the evening off."

He didn't say anything for a moment. Three hours since Ashley came home? Yes, he guessed it was. The afternoon seemed to have raced past before he'd managed to get a handle on it. As had the six months since his continual absorption with his work, his *calling* as she referred to it, had brought them to the brink of divorce. Always, he seemed to be trying to catch up. It was only after the murders of his dear friends Elaine and Arthur Steiner in Russia—a hail of terrorist gunfire having ended their lives and thirty-year marriage without reason or warning—that Gordian had awakened to what a gift he had in Ashley, and realized with terrible clarity how close he was to losing her. A half year of intensive counseling and earnest commitment had helped bridge many of the rifts between them . . . but every now and then there were marital ground tremors that reminded him the bridges weren't all that steady. Not yet, anyway.

"You're right, that's what I promised." He stretched his neck to work out a kink of tension. "I apologize. Do you suppose we can start over from here?"

Ashley stood there in front of his desk, a trim, elegant woman whose youthful good looks had made no discernible concessions to early middle age, her sea-green eyes very still as they met his gaze.

"Gord, listen to me," she said. "I'm not a pilot. I don't even like to sit near the window in a passenger plane and be reminded there are clouds underneath me, rather than over my head where they *belong*. But you've always told me how being in the cockpit of a jet frees up your mind, gives you a feeling of perspective and . . . what's that term you use? Ambient space?"

"Either that or altitude sickness," he said, smiling wanly. "You're a good listener, Ash."

"It's my best quality." She slowly crossed the room to his desk. "That space you talk about . . . it's a kind of luxury that you afford yourself, and I'm glad you're able to do it. But sometimes I'm also a little jealous of it. Do you understand?"

He looked at her.

"Yes," he said. "Yes, I do."

She expelled a long sigh. "I'm not blind to what's going on. I read Reynold Armitage's latest bunk in the *Wall Street Journal*. I hear you and Chuck talking about stock sell-offs. I saw your face when the evening news carried Marcus Caine's remarks about you at the U.N. And I can imagine how it must sting."

Gordian started to answer, then hesitated, his brow furrowed, his lips pressed tightly together. Ashley waited. It was his nature to hold his thoughts in close, and she knew he often had difficulty raising the lid on them.

"I once met a snake-oil advertising man who would've called Caine's tactics a pseudo advocacy campaign," he said at length. "Or pseudo *adversary* campaign, it depends. He's been running both at once, you see. The basic idea is to use a public issue to gain attention for your firm, while promoting certain corporate agendas without being overt about it. You get the target audience to notice you by creating or stepping into a controversy, and then slip in the message you really want to convey between the lines. It's the marketing equivalent of a stage magician's top hat and cloak."

"And Marcus's so-called Children's Challenge obviously would be an example of the first type of campaign."

"A perfect example. Gives him an aura of take-charge philanthropism, a moral platform that's virtually attack-proof. You know anybody who's against kids?"

She gave him a faint smile.

"I can think of a few times when our own bugaboos were young that *we* almost qualified, but you've made your point," she said. "The pseudo adversary campaign . . .

that would be his dispute with you over the crypto bill, wouldn't it?''

He nodded. ''If you're going to play this sort of game, the potential rewards should always outweigh the risks, and Marcus is well aware that the issues surrounding encryption really don't excite much public reaction. The average person doesn't see how relaxing export controls is going to make any difference in his daily life. Nobody cares except special-interest groups within the high-tech industry on one side, and the law-enforcement and intelligence communities on the other.''

Ashley paused to digest it all.

''The strategy behind the UNICEF crusade isn't too down-deep,'' she said finally. ''Let's give the kids computers and sell more Monolith software and have everybody feel good and pat themselves on the back. But what's he trying to achieve by taking you on over encryption? I don't see the . . . the *subtext*.''

Gordian shrugged a little.

''You've asked the million-dollar question,'' he said in a vague tone. ''And I'm not sure I can answer it.''

Silence filled the room. Ashley realized he was sinking beneath it again, and leaned forward, lightly touching the fingertips of both hands to the edge of his desk.

''I understand how you feel, Gord,'' she said. ''Do you accept that as a given?''

The question caught him by surprise.

''More than just accept,'' he said in a quiet voice. ''Knowing that you understand . . . it's like a prize I've won without quite being sure how I did it, or whether it's even deserved. It makes me stronger than I'd be if I didn't know.''

She smiled thoughtfully, looking straight at him. ''I'd

never, never want to minimize your difficulties, or suggest there's anything in the world I wouldn't do to help you with them. But what I was starting to say before . . .''

He studied her face in the brief pause. ''Yes?''

''I was going to say that if you'd put those problems away for a few hours, if we could share some of the space you get up at thirty thousand feet right here on the ground, *together,* I'd trade UpLink, this house, our cars, every cent we have, everything we own. Or do you always have be to alone in the pilot's seat to let go?''

There was more silence. Ashley thought she could see the detached, inward-looking expression gradually lift from his features, but wasn't sure. Perhaps it was only wishful thinking.

She came close to exhaling with relief when he slowly reached out, covered her hand with his own, and let it rest where he'd put it.

''Let's go out to dinner, you name the restaurant,'' he said. ''Your enchanting new haircut deserves to be viewed by one and all.''

She smiled gently.

''You may have noticed,'' she said, ''that my membership at Adrian's spa and beauty salon wasn't among the things I indicated a willingness to surrender.''

He looked into the oceanic greenness of Ashley's eyes and smiled back at her.

''I very well may have,'' he said.

NINE

WHEN MAX BLACKBURN FIRST TOLD PETE NIMEC
that he'd gotten a line deep into the working guts of Monolith, and that he was using it to trace what he'd described
as "improper business practices and financial arrangements," Nimec had listened with close interest—and by
not ordering him to abandon his investigation posthaste,
had tacitly okayed its continuance. Still, as Chief of Security at UpLink, he had cautioned that UpLink would
under no circumstances be dragged into a situation that
might be perceived as corporate spying; the potential liabilities were far too great. Nimec had also pointed out
that it would be inadvisable for Max to provide any further details about the probe should he decide to move
ahead with it on his own string . . . unless or until he
turned up something of concrete significance.

Max had gotten the gist without anything more having
to be explained. Deniability had been established with a
nod and a wink—as it always was. If his activities came
to light, no one else at UpLink would be dragged into the
consequent chocolate mess. Nimec wanted clean hands
and fingernails from the level of clerk to upper management.

Officially, that had been the end of his involvement in

the fishing expedition. Unofficially, he had been eager to see what developed. And was becoming increasingly so as Marcus Caine's public attacks on Gordian intensified.

Their understanding kept very much in mind, Max had been exceedingly circumspect with his references to the matter in the three months since their initial phone conversation about it . . . when he mentioned it at all, that was. Nimec had gleaned that Blackburn's conduit into Monolith was a female employee with whom he'd originally formed a—quote, unquote—social relationship and only later enrolled as an informant. That she held a high-level position in the office of Corporate Communications, Singapore. Beyond these two pieces of information, he knew little else.

Of course there were other legitimate reasons for the men to stay in touch. Max had been sent to Malaysia for the purpose of emplacing security procedures at the Johor ground station, and many of his plans required Nimec's input and advance approval. Which was why he'd tried phoning Blackburn from his home office at four o'clock Sunday afternoon, making it the first thing Monday morning Johor time. After reviewing an expensive upgrade Max had proposed to the bionetric scanners last week, he'd decided to give him the green light to begin installation—only to learn that he hadn't yet arrived at the office.

"Mr. Blackburn was in Singapore for the weekend, and it's quite possible he's run into delays getting back across the causeway," his receptionist had said. "The causeway crossing has been awful lately . . . some sort of ship hijacking has Customs bollixed. Still, I'm certain he'll be in soon. Would you like me to try contacting him on his mobile?"

"No, it isn't anything urgent, just tell him I called when he gets in," Nimec said.

That had been eight hours ago, and Max still hadn't been in touch. Nor had *he* had a chance to give Max another ring; the child-custody arrangement Nimec had worked out with his ex-wife allowed him weekends with their son Jake, and he'd just returned from dropping the twelve-year-old off at home after taking him to a baseball game.

Still, Nimec wondered if his message had somehow gotten lost or slipped Max's mind, and wanted to try him one more time before turning in for the night. Blackburn's greatest weakness was a tendency to let curiosity lead him in too many directions at once, and he needed to be reminded that the ground station was his primary responsibility.

Nimec went over to his desk, picked up his phone, and keyed in Max's number.

"UpLink International, Max Blackburn's office."

"Joyce, it's Pete Nimec again."

"Oh, hello, sir," she said. Then hesitated a beat. "Mr. Blackburn hasn't shown up yet."

Nimec raised his eyebrows. "Not all *day*?"

"No, I'm sorry. Nor has he phoned in."

"Have you tried calling him?"

"Well, yes. On his cell phone. I think I suggested it to you earlier—"

"And?"

"There was no answer, sir."

Nimec was silent a moment. There had been something odd about Joyce's tone from the moment he'd identified himself, and now he suddenly realized what it was. She was covering. And had been right off the bat.

"Joyce," he said at last, "maybe its my imagination, but you're sounding very protective."

She cleared her throat. "Sir, Mr. Blackburn was rather vague about his plans before he left. But . . ."

"Yes?" he prompted

"Well, to be truthful . . . I think they were of a personal nature."

"You think he's cozied up somewhere with his girl-friend? Is that it?"

"Um, perhaps . . . I mean, not that he specifically told me—"

"Your loyalty to Max is admirable. But besides your suspicion that he's gone off on an amorous toot, are you sure you're not keeping anything from me?"

"No, sir. Absolutely nothing."

"Then let me know soon as he materializes," Nimec said, and hung up the phone.

Seconds later he rose from behind his desk, switched off the light, and headed for the shower. If Max was deliberately trying to stay incommunicado, he was either having much too good a time accommodating his Mon-olith executive, or—to be fair—becoming overly preoc-cupied with the more substantial aspects of his investigation. Both possibilities left Nimec feeling an-noyed and a little uneasy.

When he finally got Blackburn on the horn, he intended to find out what he'd been doing, and if necessary remind him where he ought to be focusing his attention.

Independence was acceptable within limits, but no in-formation was worth the problems Max could cause by taking things too far.

• • •

Its diesels purring quietly in the late-night fog and darkness, the twenty-six-foot pleasure boat was within fifteen kilometers of the northern Sumatran coastline when Xiang, gripping the foredeck rail, sighted the bright glow of a floodlight almost directly abeam.

He remained still and calm at the foredeck rail, checking his wristwatch.

The yacht was traveling with its cabin and running lights off, but there was a chance it had been picked up by the radar or thermal-imaging sweeps of a fast patrol boat. Only a very small and random chance, though. He was confident the vessel's theft would not yet have been detected; his men had taken it out of its slip after midnight, stealing aboard when the landing had been nearly deserted, disconnecting its uncomplicated security alarms with a few clips of a wire cutter.

Restrained and tranquilized, the American had been driven to the head of the landing in the panel truck his captors had used during his abduction, then been brought onto the ship while its motors were warming up.

No one had been there to challenge the pirates. Investigators searching for the *Kuan Yin*'s hijackers had established tight controls at the airports, causeway, and commercial shipping docks—the obvious corridors of departure—but there hadn't been any strengthening of surveillance and inspection efforts at the marinas where the wealthy berthed their yachts and sailboats.

Xiang had counted on the improvised cordons being spotty, and planned from the beginning to exploit their inevitable holes. Singaporean authorities were used to chasing common smugglers, and tracking down illegal workers from Thailand and Malaysia whom they would herd into detention camps, flog with a cane, and send back to their native countries with their heads shaved in disgrace. They had no experience dealing with a manhunt of any scope, and even with the computerized IBIS command-and-control system they'd purchased from the Brits making it easier for field units to coordinate their efforts, they were far out of their league. Unlike the boat people washing up on their shoreline as if they were beached fish after a storm, Xiang and his outlaws were neither desperate nor docile.

Now Xiang peered into the conical beam of light shining at a right angle to him and waited, his jacket flapping in the warm south breeze. He could hear the grunt of a small outboard above the slapping of wavelets against his keel. Good, he thought. The boats manned by naval task forces were sped along by turbocharged engines and water-jet drives. This was nothing so modern or formidable.

As Xiang stood leaning over the rail, the floodlight suddenly went out and the heavy-hanging sea mist knitted water and sky into a screen of undivided blackness. He dropped his eyes to his wristwatch again, waited exactly five seconds, then looked back out at the water.

The light blinked rapidly on, then off, then on.

He glanced over his shoulder. Through the cabin windshield, he could see several of his men in the cockpit. Behind the wheel, Juara looked out at the searchlight, then lowered his head to study a compass and chart in the faint glow of the binnacle. After a moment Juara straightened up and nodded to Xiang, confirming that they were at the proper coordinates for their rendezvous.

Pleased, Xiang unclipped the high-intensity flashlight from his belt, held it out in front of him, and returned the hailing signal with his response. On, off, on, off. Then on and off again after a fifteen-second interval.

He hung on the rail until he could see the outline of the pickup launch, then went quickly into the cabin and down the gangway to the lower deck, wanting to assure himself that the prisoner was ready to be brought ashore.

TEN

"SERIOUSLY, JASON, THIS OUGHT TO BE CALLED 'Cholesterol Corner' or 'Arterial Sclerosis Way' or something," Charles Kirby said, looking down at his Rudy Guiliani hero sandwich, which contained a precarious mountain of corned beef, pastrami, Muenster cheese, and Swiss cheese, with a dripping mantle of Russian dressing and coleslaw at its lofty summit. Altough he had been tempted by the Barbra Streisand, with its multiple strata of turkey and roast beef, he'd found himself incapable of reading its name off the menu, thinking it had a rather unmanly ring.

"Why's that?" Jason Weinstein said, and stretched his mouth to encompass a pastrami, corned beef, and liver-heaped Joe DiMaggio, which he'd chosen over a Tom Cruise only because he'd never been a big fan of the latter's movies.

Kirby pushed his chin at the window. "Well, with that Lindy's Famous cheesecake place on the corner, and the Famous Ray's pizza joint across the street, somebody could build a famously successful practice opening a walk-in cardiac center on the block, don't you think?"

Jason shrugged indifferently, bit into his food, and reached across the table to grab a half-sour dill off the pickle dish, visibly chagrined over its nearer proximity to Kirby. Why Jason hadn't simply asked him to *pass* the pickles across the table rather than opting for the boardinghouse reach, as his grandmother would have called it, was something that Kirby couldn't for the life of him understand. He was a Wall Street lawyer, for God's sake. Where the hell were his dining manners?

He reached for his knife and fork, cut a wedge off his sandwich, and ate it in silence, having decided that any attempt to raise it to his mouth would result in an unstoppable landslide of sliced meat and cheese—Jason's ability to perform that gravity-defying task notwithstanding.

Suppose you need to have grown up in Brooklyn, he thought.

Jason chewed and swallowed with unfettered relish. "Better than sex, isn't it?"

"Maybe not for me," Kirby said. "But pretty good, I admit."

Jason gave him a look that said there was no accounting for taste.

"Okay, talk. Why'd you spring for lunch?"

Kirby sat for a moment.

"You represent the Spartus consortium. Or at least your firm does," he said. "I want to know who's buying its stake in UpLink."

"Whom *you* happen to represent."

"There isn't any conflict of interest," Kirby said. "The sale's a matter of public record—"

"Or will be once the i's are dotted and the t's are crossed," Jason said. "To be accurate."

Kirby shrugged. "All I'm asking is that you save me some legwork."

Jason lowered his Joe DiMaggio to his plate and regarded it with a kind of lusting admiration.

"You suppose they cure the meat themselves?" he said.

"Come on, Jase," Kirby said.

Jason looked him. "Sure, why not, but you never got it from me," he said. "The high bidder's a firm in Michigan called Midwest Gelatin. I don't guess I need to tell you its specialty."

Kirby scowled. "Some local jelly producer has the capital to buy up thousands of shares of UpLink? You're shitting me."

"I speak the truth," Jason said. "And that was *gelatin,* not jelly. It's used in everything from home insulation to sneaker insoles to ballistic testing. There's also a pharmaceutical variation which goes into the headache pills you gulp by the bottle. For your information, Midwest happens to be the largest chemical manufacturer of its type in the country."

"It public or private?"

"Number one," Jason said. "It's a subsidiary of a canning company which is wholly owned by a public corporation that manufactures plexiglass sheeting. Or chinaware, I frankly forget which."

Kirby considered that while Jason dove into his sandwich.

"Are you aware if there's anyone, um, of *note,* in Midwest Gelatin's upper management? Or that of its parent companies?"

Jason was looking at him again.

"You want to follow the paper trail, find out who's behind the move on UpLink, I suggest you talk to Ed Burke when we get to the park," he said.

"Our Ed?" Kirby pointed to the front of his uniform shirt, on which the word STEALERS was printed in gold capital letters. "The first baseman?"

"The canner's one of his biggest clients," Jason said, nodding. "Just *please* promise that my name won't enter the conversation."

"Thought I already had."

Jason shook his head. "No, no, you didn't."

Kirby made the scout's honor sign with his index and middle fingers.

"Promise," he said.

Satisfied, Jason turned to watch a thin, elderly-looking waiter scoot past the table with a tall stack of dishes expertly balanced on his arm.

"He's been working here since I was a kid," he said. "Three decades hustling on his feet, can't imagine how he does it."

"Could be he loves it here as much as you do," Kirby said.

Jason's gaze continued following the waiter's energetic trajectory down the aisle.

"Bet that's it," he said very seriously, and took another huge bite of his improbable sandwich.

Reynold Armitage's twenty-two-room duplex was in a palacial landmark building with balustrades and cornices and an ornate iron-and-glass marquee shading its Fifth Avenue entry opposite Central Park. The trappings of status and wealth were as evident—some would say *egregiously* evident—within his apartment as they were without; passing through the front door, one entered a long, wainscoted reception hall leading into an octagonal salon and then a living room with a parquet floor, massive fireplace, and haughty oil portraits under a vaulted ceiling. Continental silver gleamed on antique tables, Venetian glass goblets and decanters winked diamond points of light from breakfront cabinets, and dynastic Chinese vases perched like fragile blooms atop finely wrought marble gueridons.

Marcus Caine found it all very impressive, though not nearly so much as the scrupulous attention Armitage had payed to concealing the matrix of integrated electronic systems designed to compensate for his physical disabilities—most of which relied upon Monolith's leading-edge voice-recognition technology.

Ordinary men fit their homes with handicap access ramps, priviliged ones with lifts and elevators, he'd once told Caine. *I want you to give me something better than either.*

Caine sat sipping his vermouth as the parlor doors opened seemingly of their own volition, and the master of the house made his entrance . . . the grandiosity of which was unaffected by his wheelchair-bound condition. In a certain way, rather, it lifted him from the merely pretentious and gave him an air of solitary dauntlessness. Don Quixote stalking windmills, Ahab versus the white whale, persistance against any odds. It was the warp and woof of highest drama.

"Close," Armitage said in a barely audible undertone, his power wheelchair carrying him forward with the faintest mechanical hum. Behind him the double doors swung quietly shut. "No interruptions, take messages."

He came up to his guest and halted the chair with a joystick on its left armrest. Once it had been on his right side, but over the past several years that hand had become too seriously atrophied to be of any use.

"Marcus," he said, raising his voice to a normal level. "Sorry to have kept you waiting, but I was on a call. Fortunately you look quite settled. Absorbed in meditation, even."

"Admiration," Caine corrected. He indicated his surroundings with a slight flick of his hand. "This is a fascinating room."

An intense man of fifty with a narrow face, dark, watchful eyes, and a widow's peak of straight black hair, Armitage appeared surprised.

"And here I've always seen you as all business," he said. "It seems you're *growing,* Marcus. In fact, my estimate of you soared to new heights after your appearance at the U.N. I really want to compliment you on that one."

Caine gave him a cool glance. "Do you, now?"

"Absolutely. You came across as very likeable, which is everything from a public relations standpoint. There are pollsters who measure that sort of thing, as you're surely aware. How else would we know which celebrities to hire for product endorsements and situation comedies?" A sardonic grin crept across his lips. "I'd give you a clap on the back if I could."

Caine tried not to look uncomfortable.

"Have you considered," he said, "that I may have learned a few tricks from watching *you* on television?"

Armitage shook his head. "I occupy a unique niche. My readers and viewers don't have to like me, just listen to me. And they will as long as my financial advice is solid . . . and I'm able to communicate it." He paused and swallowed, the muscles of his throat straining to perform the basic function. "Would you like Carl to refill your glass, or should we get right down to what you wanted to discuss?"

"I'll pass on the drink, thanks." Caine wondered if Armitage's brittle references to his disease were shading his own impressions of how quickly it was advancing, or whether his speech in fact seemed thicker than when they'd last sat face-to-face. It was entirely possible, he supposed. That had been well over a month ago, and the progression of ALS could be rapid even with experimental drug therapies. "Tell me how things went with the president of MetroBank."

Armitage looked at him. "Don't hold me to this, but I think I've convinced Halpern to accept your bid."

Caine felt a stir of excitement. "Are you serious?"

"What's important is that *he* seemed to be," Armitage said. "Of course, he's going to need his board of directors to rubber-stamp the sale, so it might be prudent to hold off celebrating until after he meets with them next week."

Caine ignored the caveat. His face was suddenly hot. "Their stock comes to, what, nine percent of UpLink?"

"Closer to ten, actually," Armitage said.

Caine made a fist and jabbed it stiffly in the air.

"Son of a bitch, this is fantastic," he said. "Fantastic."

They were quiet. Reynold's crippled right hand twitched a little as a dying nerve cell in his brain misfired, his padded wrist brace rapping the armrest of his chair. Caine looked away. Nine percent, he thought. Added to the stock purchase already in the works, it would give him a *hugely* dominant share of UpLink. He'd have what he wanted, and so would the goddamned Chink who had him by the balls.

Several minutes passed before Armitage broke the silence.

"I hesitate to do this," he said, "but there's something I'd like to ask you on another subject."

Caine shrugged absently. "Sure, go ahead."

"It concerns the problem in Singapore . . . that Blackburn fellow who was poking around over there."

"Forget it," Caine said. "It's finished."

Armitage cocked an eyebrow.

"How was it taken care of?" he asked.

Caine shook his head like a dog shaking water off its fur. The subject troubled him and he didn't like it impinging on his thoughts. What was it with Armitage's seeming compulsion to make him uneasy?

"I neither know nor have any interest in knowing," he said.

"Has anyone conclusively determined why the man was spying on you?" Armitage persisted.

"I told you, I stick to running my business. It isn't my direct concern."

"Not yet, anyway," Armitage said flatly.

Caine shot him a glance. "What the hell's that supposed to mean?"

"Don't be irritated," Armitage said. "I'm only pointing out that you'd do well to stay on top of even the more disagreeable aspects of your endeavors. If my health problems have taught me anything, it's that control can slip away in a blink."

Caine set his glass down on the table beside his chair.

"Well, thank you for the advice," he said, and rose to his feet. "I'll put it under my belt."

The thin, vaguely scornful grin had returned to Armitage's face.

"Leaving already?" he asked.

Caine nodded.

"I have a flight home to catch tonight," he said. "As

you suggest, I need to keep a close eye on things, which includes making sure the Left Coast hasn't fallen into the Pacific while I've been away.''

Armitage regarded him steadily,

''Marcus, my friend,'' he said. ''You're finally learning.''

''This is all a bad dream,'' Ed Burke said. ''Right?''

''I wish,'' Charles Kirby said.

It was the bottom of the eighth in the Stealers-Slammers contest with the Slammers leading 6–0, the Stealers at bat, one man languishing on second, and the third up, Dale Lanning of the law firm of Lanning, Thomas, and Farley, a strike away from going down to obliteration.

Huddled with his teammates in the dirt patch behind home plate, Kirby watched the Slammers' outfielders move in so close they could see the flop sweat glistening above Lanning's upper lip. While no one would have challenged his reputation for getting legal adversaries to back away from his clients, his display of batting skills had prompted a very different reaction on the diamond.

''Maybe he'll pull it out under pressure,'' Burke said.

''I'm not optimistic.''

Kirby snatched at a cluster of dandelion pods floating past him in the diffuse early autumn light. There had been a time when you wouldn't have seen dandelions in the city any later than mid-August, he thought. But over the past decade New York summers had gotten longer and warmer, so that fall seemed more a calender event than a true seasonal shift. The previous year, in fact, the trees had remained in lush foliage until a January freeze finally snapped the deep-green leaves off the branches. They had hit the sidewalk and scattered like bits of glazed ceramic.

Deciding he'd postoned the inevitable long enough, Kirby turned to Burke and gave him a confidential little nod, motioning him aside from the rest of the team.

"Ed," he said, "I need to ask a favor."

"Let me guess," Burke said. "You want me to kill our batting ace before he causes us further humiliation."

Kirby opened his hand and released the dandelion seeds into the air.

"Actually, I'd like you to tell me who's behind the raid on UpLink," he said. "I'm talking about the person moving the chess pieces."

Burke looked at him. "What makes you think I've got that information?"

Kirby just shrugged. Burke pushed some dirt around with the toe of his sneaker. At the plate Lanning let a low pitch go by, and adjusted his grip on the bat.

"I give it to you, I'm putting in a great big whopping chit," Burke said.

Kirby nodded. And waited.

"There's a firm called Safetech in Danvers, Massachusetts, that designs and manufactures polymer glass replacement products," Burke said. "Security panels, hurricane-resistant windows, antiballistic laminates, and so on. Its clients range from real-estators to department-store chains to the State Department and DEA. Safetech is the corporate entity making the acquisition . . . through various offshoots."

"The person," Kirby said. "I want to know the *person*."

"I was just getting to that," Burke said. He looked down at his foot, still scuffing out tracks in the dirt. "Safetech's front men are a pair of MIT grads who were rich with technical know-how and nothing else. When they came up with their business concept, they took it to someone who offered them an interest-free startup loan in exchange for a silent partnership in the operation. A fifty-one percent share.''

''Not an unusual deal if you need to raise finance capital,'' Kirby said. ''Nor is it the worst.''

Burke shrugged. ''What counts is the two underfunded brainstormers found the lending terms acceptable.''

''And the identity of the generous third party is . . . ?''

Burke looked at him again.

''Marcus 'Moneybags' Caine,'' he said. ''Your boy Gordian's number-one detractor.''

Kirby took a deep breath, released it, and gazed out at the plate in time to see Dale Lanning swing his bat a mile high of the ball.

Burke bent to pick their gloves up of the ground, and handed one to Kirby.

''That's *allll,* folks,'' he said, frowning. ''Time for us to let the prosecutors score more points. I'm telling you, this has *got* to be a goddamn nightmare.''

Kirby appeared to be looking out across the field at something Burke couldn't see.

''It is,'' he said, slipping on his glove. ''It very definitely is.''

ELEVEN

ALTHOUGH IT WAS ONLY A LITTLE PAST EIGHT IN THE morning, Zhiu Sheng had noticed a dramatic reduction of trade at the floating market as the motor canoe brought him to where the waterway narrowed and the wooden stilt houses of impoverished locals came crowding up on either bank. Most of the peddlers and buyers had appeared at daybreak, preferring to get their business out of the way before the heat and humidity became too oppressive—the former with their goods displayed on the decks of small boats or log rafts, the latter poling along in shallow dugouts, or arriving via *klotoks* like the one he had hired, forming long lines of slow-moving watercraft in the canals twisting through outer Banjarmasin like the tentacles of some languorous octopus.

Zhiu saw small boats loaded with bananas, star fruits, lichees, melons, and salaks; with green vegetables; with fish, eel, cray, and frog; with selections of precooked foods. Conspicuously, he did not see a single vender selling chicken meat, once the largest source of animal protein for Indonesia's citizens, now an imported delicacy served mainly to foreigners in Jakarta's expensive restaurants. Rising feed prices coupled with the devaluation of the *rupiah* had devastated the poultry industry when the so-called "Asian miracle" lost its glow, resulting in most of the native breeding stock being liquidated. The American chicken farmers had moved in to exploit the livestock shortage and essentially captured the market . . . their success ironically assured by the greed of Chinese and Malaysian feed producers, who had refused to lower their prices or extend credit to the Indonesians.

Zhiu understood supply and demand, but it vexed him nonetheless.

He rode in silence, looking with steady fascination at the other vessels winding along the canal. In addition to the market craft, there were postal boats, water buses, and tublike rice barges with sailcloth tops wobbling toward docks at the city center. It was a scene that brought back memories of his last visit to this district nearly three decades ago, when Sukarno's PKI was at its height of power and had sought to establish a united Communist front with the government in Beijing. He had come, then, as an official envoy of Zhou Enlai to help organize state construction projects . . . a straightforward assignment for a man whose revolutionary passion was still in full blush.

Like many things in life as one became older, the circumstances of his present trip were laced with greater complexity, Zhiu thought.

He accepted the differences and rarely looked back on his beginnings, but supposed returning to this place after so long a duration of years had made him reflective. How hard Sukarno had struggled to eradicate the stain of Western cultural influence, and how painfully he would have viewed its indelibility. Even here it could not be ignored. A few moments earlier, a group of white tourists had darted past in rented speedboats, reminding him of noisy macaques with their round eyes, sunburned red cheeks, and loud excited voices. But he'd clamped down on his annoyance, preferring, as always, to look on the bright side. At least the water spouted by their outboards dispelled the mosquitos, and added a relieving coolness to the semblance of a breeze coming off the Barito River.

"Pelan-pelan saya," Zhiu told his canoe guide in Mandarin-accented Bahasa. He pointed toward a woman selling rice cakes from a boat that had been cobbled out of warped old boards.

"Ya."

The canoe man cut his motor, paddled up to the rickety boat, and reached down beside him for a bamboo pole with a nail fastened to one end. Extending the pole across his bow, he speared a rice cake for Zhiu Sheng and held it out for him to sample.

Zhiu took a bite, swallowed, and tossed a bronze-colored coin onto the vender's deck.

"Terima kasi banyak," she said, smiling with gratitude.

Zhiu instructed the guide to restart the outboard, and settled back for his light breakfast.

A short while later, the canoe man turned a bend in the canal, swung toward a house and rice barn overhanging the near bank, and informed his passenger they had reached their destination. Zhiu did not bother saying that he'd already guessed it for himself. The further they had progressed beyond the market, the more he'd sensed eyes watching from behind shuttered windows, and noticed hard young men tracing his progress with quick, covert glances from the walkways connecting the ramshackle structures.

Khao Luan was like a feudal warlord to the people of this area, giving them just enough to keep them loyal, but not so much that they might become independent of him.

Now the canoe man again silenced his engine, and rowed up to a ladder running into the muddy water from the dwelling's front door. Three teenagers sat on separate rungs—two boys in faded denim shorts and T-shirts, and a girl wearing similar shorts and a halter of some sheer, revealing material that had been tied below her breasts to expose her midriff. There was a kind of affected sexuality about her that at once saddened and disgusted Zhiu Sheng. The boys also seemed to be playacting at roles they did not quite grasp, sitting with their shoulders hunched and smoking unfiltered cigarettes as they listened to an enormous radio blasting out American rock music.

They slouched under the hot sun, staring into the water as if they might find something other than aimless drifts of reeds and sediment beneath its torpid surface.

The Asian miracle, Zhiu Sheng thought dryly.

He saw them raise their eyes from the crawling water as his guide brought the canoe up beside the ladder. All of them had bad complexions. All looked dirty and undernourished. Their expressions were bored and impassive and uniformly sullen.

He waited until the canoe had been lashed into a berth composed of four vertical bamboo poles, then paid the guide, lifted his carryall onto his shoulder, and rose to step ashore.

The teenagers watched him a moment longer. Then the taller of the boys stood up to block his approach, crossing his arms over his puffed-out chest, doing what he thought was expected of him under some artificial standard of toughness.

It would probably kill him in a streetfight before he was twenty.

Zhiu Sheng finished his rice cake, then rubbed his fingertips together to wipe off its pasty residue.

"Saya mahu laki bilik," he said from the prow of the boat. "I'm here to see the men inside."

The tall boy stared down at him, letting his cigarette dangle from his lips the way they did in American gangster movies. The smoke curling from its tip carried the pungently sweet odor of cloves.

"What is your name?" he asked.

Zhiu was in no mood. "Go on. Let the men know their friend from up north has arrived."

"I asked you—"

"Berhenti!" Zhiu checked him with a motion of his hand. "Stop wasting my time and do it."

The boy stared at him for a second, then turned and went up the ladder to the door, taking longer than he should have, wanting to save whatever face he could with his companions.

Let him have that, at least, Zhiu thought. *He may never have anything else.*

The boy knocked on the door—two slow raps, a pause, followed by three rapid ones—and waited a moment before pushing it open. Then he leaned his head through the entry and said something and waited some more. After a brief interval Zhiu heard a male voice answer from inside the house. Though the words were unclear to him, their tone was unmistakeably harsh and reprimanding.

The boy turned from the door and shooed away his friends, who climbed down to the landing and went hurrying off somewhere along the bank.

"Ma'af saya," he said nervously, offering Zhiu Sheng a contrite bow. "I did not mean to offend—"

"Never mind."

His patience exhausted, Zhiu brushed past him and ascended the shaky ladder, half expecting it to buckle under his feet.

He was met at the entrance by a pair of lank, brown-skinned islanders with undulant kris tattoos on their hands. Was it not said that such a dagger could claim a victim merely by being driven into one's shadow? Perhaps so, Zhiu thought. But ancient myths aside, he believed the semi-automatic rifles slung over the men's shoulders would prove much more lethal.

"*Selamat datang,*" one of them said. He bowed his head deferentially. "Welcome."

Zhiu nodded and went inside.

The interior of the dwelling was a large rectangle, its floor and walls made up of bare plywood boards, the high peaked roof supported by tiers of slanting beams. Midway down the length of the right-hand wall was a closed door with a third islander standing guard in front of it. Towering and rigid, he had coarse features, long black hair, and was bare-chested under an open denim jacket with cut-off sleeves. The blockish muscles on his torso and upper arms were heavily covered with tattoos. In addition to his rifle, he carried a knife—a kris, no doubt—in an elaborately tooled leather sheath on his belt.

Zhiu ran his eyes over to the middle of the room, where the men he had come to meet—General Kersik Imman, Nga Canbera, and the drug trafficker, Khao Luan—were waiting at a long plank table.

Glancing up from a conversation with the others, Kersik was the first to acknowledge his presence.

"Zhiu Sheng, you look well," he said, dipping his head. "How was your trip?"

"Hot, tedious, and hopefully worthwhile," Zhiu said.

A smile touched Kersik's thin, lined face. While the eyes below his shaggy brows were as strong and sharp as ever, he had aged a great deal over the past several months and, in civilian clothes now, possessed an almost grandfatherly mien that hid his true severity of nature.

By contrast, Zhiu thought, Canbera looked scarcely older than the children outside, and like them seemed to be working at a role that was beyond him. Political subversive, champion of the poor. His soft features and vain demeanor put the lie to it, though. As did his social position. The eldest son of a diamond baron, Nga had been born into immeasurable wealth, and handed control of Banjarmasin's largest bank only to serve as a place marker on his family's sprawling financial game board. He understood nothing of human struggle, and less of material hardship. Nor did the spoiled upper-class activists with whom he secretly consorted . . . and whose national reform movement he was helping to fund.

He was a narcissistic dabbler, interested in gratifying his own conceits, and would leap for the safety net of privilege if the consequences of his actions overtook him.

"*Sawasdee*. My place isn't nearly as well appointed as Kersik's residence, but, as a humble exile and outsider, it's the best I can do."

This from Khao Luan himself. Seated at the head of the table, he raised his hands in the traditional Thai greeting, palms together as if in prayer, his fingertips just below his nose to indicate familiarity. On their previous meetings, Zhiu noted, he had steepled his hands lower and closer to his chest—the stranger's *wai*.

The significance of the gesture was not lost on Zhiu, and it admittedly distressed him . . . for was a man not measured in large part by his associations? Still, he returned it without hesitation. The time for misgivings was long past. And corrupt as his occupation might be, the Thai was without pretense and worthy of respect.

"Please," Luan said, indicating an empty chair on his right. "Make yourself comfortable."

Zhiu went over to the table and regarded him carefully. Round and balding, Luan had a smooth wide forehead, bow-shaped lips, and a light mustache and chin beard. His cheekbones were perfectly flat and covered with soft, shiny pads of flesh. He sat with his chair pushed back from the table, his short-sleeved batik shirt hanging out over his waist sash, straining at the seams around his big stomach, and unbuttoned at the collar to reveal a thick ring of Hmong silver. There were dark blotches of perspiration on his chest and under his arms.

"The American," Zhiu said, lowering himself into his chair. "Where is he?"

Luan nodded toward the door in the right wall.

"My friend Xiang and his sea wolves are keeping a close eye on him."

"Has he told you anything?"

Luan was silent a moment before replying.

"He's been, ah, unable to communicate this morning, but I expect he'll be coming around shortly," he said. "Maybe then we'll all learn what we want to know."

Zhiu darted a surprised glance across the table at General Kersik. "He was captured, what, four days ago?"

Kersik brought his head up and down, a slow nod.

"He's a tough one," he said.

"No need to be concerned, we'll get what we want out of him soon enough," Luan said. He smiled thinly. "The White Lady has her ways."

Zhiu raised his eyebrows. "Heroin?"

"They've scarcely been apart since we introduced him to her yesterday," Luan said. "She'll charm him into talking."

"It is barbaric."

"It is necessary," Kersik said. "And preferable to some alternatives."

"As our prisoner should conclude for himself before too long," Luan said.

They were quiet. Zhiu found himself staring at the enormous pirate. He seemed somehow to exist in his own space, immovable and dangerous, his calm unfeeling eyes those of a Mesozoic creature poised to strike.

"What I think ought to worry us is the woman," Nga said.

Zhiu shifted his attention to him. "Chu, is that her name?"

"Kirsten Chu. She's dropped out of sight. And there's no telling what she's discovered about our involvement with Monolith, or what sort of proof she's taken with her. A tremendous amount of information could have been routed through her division of the company."

"I assume we have people looking for her in Singapore?"

"And elsewhere," Luan said.

"Still," Nga said. "It could hurt us badly if the Americans learn of—"

"I've been trying to reassure Nga that he's jumping ahead of things," Kersik interrupted. "Let's stay with what we know. This could have been a case of industrial espionage, having nothing to do with us."

"She's repeatedly accessed Monolith's most sensitive financial databases from her office computer terminal. Made dozens of telephone calls to the UpLink groundstation in Johor . . . and probably many more that can't be traced because they went to a secure line,'' Nga said. ''Are you suggesting that we simply forget about her?''

''You really must try to become a more receptive listener,'' Kersik said. ''Without the American to guide her, it's likely she won't know where to turn, or what to do with any documentation she might have. Probably she'll surface on her own. If not, we'll eventually find her.'' He motioned toward Zhiu Sheng with a slow, gliding wave of his hand. ''Let us put speculation aside, and get to the point of why our comrade has traveled here.''

Zhiu nodded slightly. Despite his equable manner, Kersik was looking hard at him.

''I've brought positive news,'' he said. ''Those I represent are prepared to supply whatever munitions you require. The high-speed boats will be more difficult to obtain, but should also be forthcoming.''

''And the landing craft?''

''You'll have to settle for fewer than requested.''

''How many?''

''Three, perhaps four.''

Kersik pinched the bridge of his nose. ''The assault rifles, they've never been fired?''

Zhiu knew he was thinking about their integrated silencers, which quickly became ineffective with use.

''They are factory-new Type 85's.''

Kersik continued to look thoughtful. ''We must be guaranteed prompt delivery. As you know, our window of opportunity is quite small.''

''Any date we agree upon will be firm,'' Zhiu said. ''You have my word.''

Kersik drew a long breath.

''I'm concerned about how the reduced number of watercraft will effect our invasion capabilities," he said. "It means revising the entire operational plan."

"Perhaps not as drastically as you might think. The attack boats are heavily armed. And the amphibious craft can be refitted to hold larger complements. Insofar as available manpower, there would likely be no difference at all. If you want me to go over the specific modifications—"

"Later," Kersik said. He hadn't taken his eyes off Zhiu's face. "Your government. What is its position toward our venture?"

"Officially, nothing is known of it."

"And speaking practically?"

"I can tell you there will be no opposition at any level," Zhiu said, selecting his words with utmost care.

Kersik nodded with satisfaction.

"Yes," he said. "That much *is* good news."

Zhiu let his eyes roam around the table.

"I hope, then," he said, "that none of you will object to the terms of payment."

Luan pursed his lips, reacting with predictable wariness.

"Which are?" he said.

"I'm obliged to require the full sum in advance."

"What?" Nga said, his eyes flashing incredulously. "You can't be serious."

Zhiu remained very still.

"We are asking for a great deal on short notice," he said. "The suppliers have expenditures of their own. It is reasonable for them to expect hard currency in return for the risks they are taking."

"And what of *our* risks?" Nga said in a tight voice. "I've done much for you and the Zhongnanhai you represent. My bank's international position could be irreparably damaged if things go wrong.''

"That is very much appreciated. But, regrettably, this isn't a situation in which my superiors can barter off a portion of the cost, or make any other concessions.''

Nga bridled. "Forgive me, Zhiu, but it sounds to me as if you're offering up excuses for PLA profiteers. How can you expect us to—?''

"Enough,'' Kersik interjected. "I understand your frustration, Nga. But we are compelled by certain exigencies, and must acknowledge that our needs are rather special.'' He glanced at Luan. "What do you say?''

The Thai hesitated a moment, then shrugged his chunky shoulders.

"Attached as I am to my money, I nevertheless consider my portion of the expenses already spent, and suppose it makes little difference when I physically part company with it,'' he said. "Let's not bicker over what can't be changed, and instead move on to important matters of planning. We've been so focused on Sandakan and what comes after, that none of us are talking about the data-storage vaults in the United States. They are essential to our success and at least as highly guarded as—''

The door to the rice barn opened, surprising them. They fixed their attention upon Xiang as one of his pirates leaned through from the other side, addressed him in a low whisper, then withdrew into the barn, leaving the door ajar.

Xiang turned back around, looking straight at the Thai.

"The American's opened his eyes,'' he said.

The room went silent.

Luan smiled slightly and cast an eager glance around the table.

''Excuse me, brothers,'' he said, heaving his bulk off the chair. ''I have to go to work.''

He followed Xiang into the barn, pushing the door heavily shut behind him.

TWELVE

BLACKBURN CAME TO WITH A START, DISORIENTED, bathed in sweat, clusters of black motes floating across his vision. His eyes were battered and swollen, his body throbbing with pain in a dozen places. Where was he? Why couldn't he move his arms?

He realized he was in a chair . . . slumped forward in a hard, straight-backed chair . . . and jerked to an upright position. Too quickly. Dizziness washed over him and his stomach contracted. He fought to push back the nausea, the taste of vomit rising in his throat. For several seconds it was touch-and-go, but then the sickness began to recede.

He squeezed his pulsing eyes shut and sucked in breath after labored breath.

Okay. All right. Let's try it again. But slower.

He rolled his head to relax the aching tendons of his neck, lifted it an inch or two—slow, slow—and opened his eyes again.

Better.

Blinking, he looked himself over.

His shirt was bloody and torn. Had he been shot? No, no, he didn't think so. There had been a bad tumble in the hotel stairway. Then that iron claw, or whatever it was, sinking into his arm. He'd been trying to get it out, and then somebody or something had hit him. And afterward . . . ?

What had happened afterward?

Max gulped down another mouthful of air. *Come on, come on, what happened?* He got little besides brief, elusive flashes, and wondered if he'd sustained a concussion from the blow to his head, or maybe the fall down the stairs. There had been long periods of oblivion alternating with moments when he half awakened and took in confused snatches of reality.

At one point he'd been in a truck . . . the delivery truck outside the hotel. That was where he'd first been handcuffed, in the vehicle's rear compartment. There had been a body back there next to him. A dead man, probably the original driver. He had been stripped of his clothing, and a mixture of blood and some other, viscous fluid was oozing from his ear. Max remembered lying there beside the naked corpse on sheets wet with gore . . . and that was all. He didn't know how long he'd been kept in the truck or where he'd been taken afterward. Just had a vague sense of time slipping away. Then being lifted, carried a short distance, and dropped flat on his back.

More time passed. He'd been in a close space, registered monotonous rolling, pitching movements. It had been like that for a while. Then a strong, freshening wind gusted over him. There had been a salt breeze. An abrupt realization that he was on a boat, they were transporting him somewhere on a *boat* . . .

He'd slipped back into unconsciousness, awakened once somewhere else. Another truck? Another boat? It was no good, that part was almost entirely a blank. He could recall nothing about it except for having been moved yet again to what he supposed was his present location, a barn of some sort. It was wide and dim and stewingly hot with a thatch roof and steps rising to a loft. Both his wrists had been cuffed to the arms of the chair. The restraints were standard police-issue metal bracelets.

His watchdogs were anything *but* cops, though. He'd recognized a few from the bunch that had pursued him at the hotel, including the big one, the one he'd first seen waiting in the truck, and who had come at him through the service door. . . .

Blackburn felt his head clearing. With each interval of consciousness more of what had happened came back to him, his scattered bits and pieces of memory weaving into a coherent thread and drawing him toward a full recognition of his predicament.

Here in the barn he'd been asked questions, mostly by the one who seemed to be in charge—Luan, that was his name. Asked questions and beaten hard when he refused to answer. But that hadn't been the worst of it. Not by far. He had been through brutal ordeals before, and believed he could have withstood their interrogation for quite some time.

Oh, shit. These goddamned bastards came to the same conclusion, didn't they?

The hairs at the back of his neck prickling, he remembered the needle. How could he have forgotten it even for a *second*?

Maybe, though, that was why his mind had switched itself off for a while. To provide a cessation from what was otherwise unavoidable. To spare him from thinking about the needle.

The first time had been the roughest. They'd held him down, torn off his shirt sleeve, and jabbed the needle into the bend of his arm. Because he'd been struggling, the one with the syringe had botched several attempts at piercing a blood vessel. But eventually he'd succeeded, pressing the needle flat against his skin, inserting it down the length of the vein, drawing a little blood to make sure he'd gotten a good hit. And then depressing the plunger.

Blackburn had made a small sound, a kind of moan, and slid back in the chair, his head nodding, his eyes rolling back under their lids. Wildcat tingles had rushed up his arm in what seemed to be a direct line to his brain, then widened out into ripples of numbing warmth that spread through his flesh and bones and viscera until he went slack. And the horror, the really overpowering horror of it, was that a part of him had *welcomed* the nullity it brought. He'd trained his mind and body to endure the severest punishments, but to have his pain drawn out of him in a great merciful *whoosh* like heaven taking a deep breath. . . .

Baifen, Luan called it.

Chinese slang for heroin.

She was a seductive bitch, and that was what they were counting on.

His memories rushing back on him now, Max glanced at the inside of his left arm and saw the black and blue where he'd been injected . . . how many times? Five, maybe six. There were blisters under his elbow where the spike had slipped and some of the drug was inadvertently pumped between his skin and muscle. The first couple of times they'd shot him up, a ferocious rash had spread from his elbows to his shoulders and neck, but his system had adjusted, and the redness and terrible itch were slowly fading.

Blackburn was still taking stock when he heard movement to his right. He looked up and saw one of his guards—he'd counted four of them in the dimness—step over to a door on the opposite wall, open it, then lean out to speak with somebody on the other side . . . the big guy from the delivery truck, who was also apparently his superior. When he came striding into the barn a moment later, Luan was right behind him.

Here we go again, Max thought, steeling himself.

He watched in silence as Luan moved to a table about six feet away, where his captors kept the heroin and works, as well as a water pitcher and small gas burner for cooking the drug. He saw orange flame spurt from the burner, saw Luan drop a chunk of the heroin into a spoon, then saw him mix it with some water and then hold the spoon over the heat.

After perhaps a minute of boiling he dropped a cotton swab into the spoon, let it swell up with liquid, pushed the needle into it, and raised the plunger to filter the narcotic solution up through the cotton.

"My friend, you have kept your secrets against much persuasion, but sooner or later you must tell me what I need to know," Luan said, approaching with the hypo. He spoke English well enough, though his tongue kept bumping against the wrong syllables.

Max sat there without response.

"You will not compromise your honor by breaking your silence," Luan said. Coming closer. "Your employers would be pleased with you. A man cannot be expected to tolerate more than you already have on their behalf."

Max said nothing.

Luan shook his head. It had become something of a perverse, repetitive drill—the unanswered questions, the beating, and, once that failed, the junk. They were simply exploring their options, Max thought. Reasoning that sooner or later he'd either succumb to the pain or the desire for release. *Insidious cocksuckers*. Given intravenously, heroin rushed into the brain's pleasure centers within seconds. Addiction would take a while, but the craving for it . . .

That was the worst part, wasn't it? The part his mind had cringed away from acknowledging, and the reason it had shut itself down.

The craving had already wormed its fine but perceptible roots into him.

Luan came another step forward.

"I already know who you are, and who you work for, leaving only one thing unknown," he said. "What were you after, Max Blackburn?"

Silence.

"One last thing," Luan said. "Tell me."

It occurred to Max that he would have been interested in hearing Luan answer that very same question . . . and that his ignorance on that score was a good indication Kirsten had managed to stay outside his tracking range. You dealt with the uglies of the world long enough, you came to understand they could rationalize the vilest actions imaginable . . . his present circumstances unfortunately being a clear case in point. Had they gotten her in their talons, they would have used any means available to squeeze her for what they wanted.

No, they didn't have her. Or at least it helped a little to think so.

He kept staring at Luan in silence.

The Thai's face had grown sorrowful. "It shouldn't matter to me, but I want to give you fair warning. While you may not remember how to use your tongue at the moment, it is certain that you will before I leave here. You understand?''

Max swallowed dryly. No, maybe he didn't understand, not altogether. But he had an awful feeling that he soon would. He'd kept an eye on the big guard, watched him sidle over to the table, reach for a knife sheathed against his leg, then stand there near the burner with the weapon in his hand. It was a kris, its blade about six inches long and shaped like a sine wave. . . .

Something new and different, he thought

Luan was standing right in front of him now, regarding him with careful appraisal, his false sympathy only serving to counterpoint the menace in his gaze.

Finally he pursed his lips and discharged a sighing breath.

''No,'' he said resignedly. ''I don't think you're going to take my advice after all.''

He turned partially toward the big watchdog.

Nodded.

Max glanced over at the table and felt his stomach tighten.

The watchdog had raised his knife to the flame, was holding it over the flame, its blade rapidly heating up, becoming radiant in the dimness of the barn.

''Xiang,'' the Thai said.

The big man turned and advanced on Max, the knife flashing red-hot, almost seeming to pulse in his grip. Out of the corners of his eyes, Max saw two other guards suddenly appear from the shadows, one on either side of him. Each clasped a shoulder and pressed it hard to the chair, pinning him against the backrest. He strained against them, but their hands were as unyielding as the steel cuffs on his wrists.

He tensed throughout his body, his heart striking mallet blows in his chest.

In no hurry, Xiang hung over him a moment like a living, breathing mountain. Then he lowered the kris to his arm and sliced into his skin about an inch above the wrist, making a shallow, razor-thin incision that almost instantly withered around its edges from the heat of the blade. Max was seized with pain as Xiang carved into him, gliding the knife upward beneath his skin, stripping it away little by little, pushing the blade higher . . . higher . . . higher. . . .

Squeezing the chair's armrests, Max fought not to scream, clenched his teeth so he wouldn't scream, a raspy, wounded-animal sound tearing out of him instead. Veins bulged in his temples. His head whipped back and forth. He smelled the sickly-sweet odor of his own cauterized flesh and nerve tissue as it peeled away from the rising blade. He thrashed convulsively, heard the legs of the chair pounding the floor, banging on the floor, the loud thump of wood against wood matching the jerky violence of his spasms. He could see nothing beyond the insane, brilliant pain, think of nothing but the scream locked away in his throat, trying to tear free of his throat like a trapped thing with claws and teeth flinging itself against the sides of its cage.

Max only realized the cutting had stopped some thirty seconds after the Thai ordered it done. He thought it must have taken longer than that for Xiang to actually slide the knife out of his arm, flicking a long . . . *six inches* long, at least . . . shaving of skin to the floor.

Finally, the guards who had been holding him down backed off and he sagged into the chair, gulping down huge lungfuls of air, the muscles of his ravaged arm twitching and jumping.

He felt his consciousness draining and willed himself back to clarity.

Luan's face hovered in front of him.

"Your employer, Roger Gordian," he said. "Tell me what he wants."

Max sat there, motionless. Rivulets of sweat poured down his brow and stung his eyes. His arm felt coated with scalding oil.

Luan showed him the syringe.

"Tell me," he said. "I can make things better for you."

Blackburn met his gaze. Inhaled. Exhaled. And then gave him a slow nod.

Luan grinned and leaned in expectantly.

"My boss is . . . P. T. Barnum . . . and I'm looking for freaks for his tent show," Blackburn said in a weak voice. "Got them all here," he said. "A fat man"—he nodded toward the Thai—"a giant"—he nodded toward Xiang—"and more geeks . . . than you can count," he said, and rotated his head to indicate the guards standing to either side of him.

Luan's grin turned downward and mutated into something horrible and forbidding. He straightened, allowed the full weight of his gaze to press on Blackburn for a moment, then slowly shook his head.

"Stupid," he said, and then gave Xiang a command in Bahasa, pointing at Max.

Pointing at his face.

Blackburn saw the giant take a step toward him with the kris, the two watchdogs who'd restrained him once more appearing at the fringes of his vision.

He thought about how to prevent them from carving him up alive, decided there was probably nothing he could do, and figured he would try anyway.

Summoning what strength he had left, Max threw his weight forward as hard as he could, and managed to rock to his feet while still cuffed to the chair—his wrists chained to the armrests, the back of the chair a rigid plank against his spine, forcing him to bend at the waist so he was almost doubled over.

The two guards' surprise at his sudden move made them hesitate for only an instant, but that was all the time Blackburn needed to launch himself at the Thai, slamming him backwards into the table where he kept the works. As the heroin packets and still-flaming burner crashed to the floor in a welter, the fire hurling a wavery mesh of shadows about the room, he saw the watchdog on his left come charging straight at him, waited for him to get close enough, and wheeled in a semicircle, catching him across his middle with the upturned chair legs. The watchdog yelped in pain and dropped to his knees.

Max took a breath and steadied himself. Heard footsteps now, from his opposite side. The shadow pushing toward him might have been startling in its immensity had he not been braced for Xiang's attack. Still, his limitations of movement and balance made it impossible to avoid.

Gonna get hurt no matter what I do, he thought. *Might as well dish some hurt of my own.*

Whirling toward the giant, he lunged forward in a bullish rush, Xiang's torso looming up like a marble pillar as he drove in and butted him with his head.

Xiang snorted in anger and surprise, the kris dropping from his fingers. Max kept his head lowered and again slammed himself into his columnar chest. The gigantic islander staggered back but did not fall. His knife forgotten in his rage, he lurched forward like a wounded bear, his colossal arms spread wide, biceps expanding and rippling under his flesh. Snarling, he clamped his hands over Blackburn's shoulders and hefted upward.

Max felt a wrenching pain as his feet left the floor. Though he weighed a solid hundred-eighty pounds, Xiang lifted him seemingly without effort.

Blackburn saw an atavistic savagery in his features that instantly made him cold inside. The giant wasn't thinking about the information they were trying to get out of him. Wasn't thinking about what his boss wanted him to do. Wasn't thinking, period. His fury was a cyclone that had pulled him into its maw as it gained destructive energy and momentum. He was just along for the ride.

In a sense, they both were.

Xiang shook Max furiously, holding him suspended above the floor so they were almost eye-to-eye. He rattled out a groan, the strength he'd mustered through sheer willpower draining away, his body too hammered from abuse to comply with the demands he was making of it. Suddenly he knew what was coming, knew with such a sure sense of inevitability that he could almost hear a door shutting in his head. There would be no last-minute escape of the sort that might occur in a novel or film, no orchestral swells as the larger-than-life hero fought his way to safety. It stank, yes, but *real* life was like that sometimes, you never knew when the smell would come wafting up out of the kitty litter, and the best he figured he could do was express his feelings about it in a manner that would translate across any language barrier.

Filling his mouth with moisture, he spat in Xiang's face.

Xiang growled, actually *growled,* his cheek glistening with bloody saliva. He took a broad step forward, another, pushing Max up against the wall. Then, with a tremendous heave that bulged the muscles of his upper back and shoulders into a corded mass, he slammed Max backward with stunning force, pulled him in toward his chest again, slammed, pulled, slammed. Max tugged unavailingly at his cuffs, his upper body writhing, a mire of blood flooding his mouth, the chair splintering between his back and the wall, cracking into jagged pieces of wood that spilled to the floor underneath him as Xiang slammed and pulled and slammed. . . .

Lost in a roseate haze, Blackburn felt a snap somewhere in his neck, followed by a bright sparkle of pain. The haze darkened and solidified. From what seemed a great distance, he heard the Thai shout something in an agitated voice and a language he didn't understand. He had a sensation of disconnected free fall, as if he were a small stone plummeting into a bottomless chasm.

Then he ceased to feel anything at all.

"Stop!" The Thai clambered across the barn toward Xiang and grabbed his arm. "That's enough *lunacy!*"

The giant glanced over at him. An instant later, his face changed—the furious, wildly unreasoning look clearing from it. He turned toward the limp form he was pressing to the wall, stared at it a moment as if seeing it for the first time, and let it drop.

Luan knelt over Blackburn and hurried to check his

pulse. He didn't like the way his head was leaning, the rubbery tilt of his neck.

When his eyes jumped up to Xiang, they were glacial. ''He's dead,'' he said.

THIRTEEN

EVERY WEEKDAY MORNING AT 5:30 ROGER GORDIAN left his home outside San Jose, got into his raven-black 1984 Mercedes SE, then headed east along El Camino Real to the San Carlos Street exit and through the downtown area to UpLink's corporate headquarters on Bonita Avenue. Like Gordian, the Benz was in generally fine condition despite showing a few signs of age: a cranky starter here, a clogged line and worn part there, nothing that, in his estimate, couldn't be remedied with regular maintenance and an occasional highway workout.

Still, those around him fretted. Concerned about its reliability, Ashley had been pressing him to drive one of their newer vehicles to the office, but the Land Rover seemed too damn big and the '01 BMW too damn small, lacking substance and character, and resembling an electric shaver or a soap bar. Concerned about his personal safety, Pete Nimec had tried convincing him to hire a driver or bodyguard, but Gordian liked having the solitary time for thought as overflowing rural greenery became neatly fenced suburban yards and then a crowded metropolis, the transition seeming to mirror the thrust of human advancement itself.

And he liked driving along with his hands on the wheel

as the big V-8 engine ran with a low satisfying sound that reminded him of a perfect, sustained note coming from deep in the belly of an operatic tenor.

And he liked how there were just enough motorists on the freeway to give him a sense of forward progress, of linkage to other people pursuing their daily objectives, each of them slightly ahead of the pack, moving toward their destinations in lanes that would jam tight only a few hours later.

On his way to work now, he was undeniably pleased that he'd resisted Pete and Ashley's urgings. There were a number of things on his mind, things he needed to sort through without interruption, and the driver's seat of his car was the ideal place to do precisely that.

It always comes down to will, timing, and maneuverability, he reflected. *You have to avoid getting stuck on any one battle, and make sure you're ready to exploit any possible chance to take the opposition by surprise.*

That was modern combat doctrine in a nutshell, although in this instance Gordian was thinking neither about armed conflict, nor even the martial art of highway driving, but business, which he had long ago learned was its own species of warfare—coldly opportunistic, full of hidden traps, and capable of heaping loss and carnage upon the unprepared, the indecisive, and the inflexible.

The night before, Gordian had gotten his call to war from Chuck Kirby, who had phoned to confirm what he'd already known in his gut, and what legal disclosure requirements would reveal to the public within days: The tender offer for the Spartus holdings had been made by Marcus Caine through a rather thinly disguised corporate surrogate . . . specifically, a Midwestern concern called Safetech.

Okay, next item, he thought. Having established *what* Caine wanted, the issue of *why* he wanted it still remained to be tackled. A takeover seemed the obvious objective, but things were not necessarily that clear. The Williams Act and a whole slew of California securities and anti-takeover statutes compelled Safetech to state the reasons for its stock acquisition in a Schedule 13D filing to the Securities and Exchange Commission, and in other documents it was required to exhibit to shareholders. Even playing strictly by the rules, however, Caine had plenty of wiggle room in which to obscure his intent.

His offer-by-proxy left no doubt that he at the very least wished to remain discreet—and one thing Gordian knew about Caine was that he never stayed in the background unless there were some very compelling reasons to do so. While Marcus was often unsubtle, he was not unsophisticated. If he was preparing to mount a raid, he would bide his time until he was in the best tactical position to execute it. Hands down, he would represent himself in the schedule as seeking *not* to wrest control of UpLink from Gordian and its board of directors, but rather to obtain a substantial minority interest that would give him a say in managing its assets, and allow him to protect his investment. Whether that position would bear up under scrutiny was immaterial, because all the courts were likely to do in the event of false or incomplete disclosures was order that they be revised.

Meanwhile, Caine would be getting exactly what he needed: time to woo other large shareholders to his side, time to sidestep the Williams Act's disclosure provisions by purchasing smaller blocks of UpLink stock on the open market, time to develop and refine any number of additional takeover strategies . . . assuming, of course, that a complete acquisition was his goal.

How, then, to anticipate it? Kirby and his trustbusters were already formulating a civil action on the grounds that there were several sectors of the communications and technology industries where Marcus Caine's various interests in direct competition with UpLink. The lawsuit was a showstopper in that it would keep the lawyers and judges wading through a sea of complicated litigation, but unless the feds climbed aboard with a criminal antitrust suit of their own to bolster UpLink's challenge—something they were typically slow to do—it would result in a long battle of attrition with unpredictable results, and hunkering in had never been Gordian's style. As Sun Tzu once said, the possibility of victory lay in the attack. With all the resources at his disposal, there surely had to be a—

Gordian eased into the left lane to pass a lumbering trailer truck in front of him, a look of deep concentration on his features. Quite unexpectedly, his mind had turned back to the piece he'd read by Reynold Armitage in the *Wall Street Journal* the other day. What was it *he'd* had to say about Gordian's resources? The leadoff essentially had been a rant about his corporate diversification having led to wrongheaded management decisions, after which Armitage had drawn his grotesque Siamese twins metaphor, something about mismatched limbs and unsustainable growth. The article had prickled—but could it be Armitage had a *point*?

Gordian hesitantly had to admit that he might, and supposed part of his irritation over what he'd read stemmed from his having realized it from the beginning, if only on a semiconscious level. He could not afford to let his disdain for Armitage—or suspicions about his motives—

prevent him from intelligently evaluating his assertions. Emotionalism in a fight was blinding and corrosive. Regardless of its ultimate merit, his enemy had unwittingly given him a tip worth exploring.

And if it turns out he's right, what path does that take me down? Gordian thought, knowing full well that wasn't the question he needed to ask himself. The path was there before him, its direction clearly marked, and what he really had to learn was whether he'd have the strength and will to walk it . . . and accept the painful sacrifices to which it would inevitably lead.

Inhaling deeply, he glanced out the driver's window to see the sun perched fat and lazy above the mountains, as if it had found a comfortable nest where it might linger for all eternity, describing a constant, knowable horizon against which he could steer a warmly lighted path through the world.

Pity indeed life was never that simple.

It would have been a harried and difficult twenty-four hours for Pete Nimec under the best of circumstances. With only a couple of days to go until Roger Gordian and his closest advisors flew to D.C. for their press conference, a million and one security arrangements—everything from personnel selection to the job's involved Beltway logistics—needed to be finalized. In addition, there had been a series of unexplained lapses in the alarm net at the Nevada data-storage facility. And two of his Sword administrators at the Botswana satellite station had let a squabble over authority escalate into a bar fight that left one with cracked ribs, the other in a local jail, and Nimec with the problem of whether both deserved to be canned.

These were all matters requiring prompt attention, but it was Max Blackburn's unaccountable disappearance that had been occupying most of his thoughts . . . and the phone conversation he'd just had with Max's secretary had done a lot to exacerbate his worried mood.

On his previous call, which he'd placed from the UpLink building at six o'clock Tuesday night—eleven A.M. Wednesday, in Malaysia—Joyce had told him Max still hadn't returned to the ground station or contacted her with any explanation for his absence, making it almost four days since anyone had seen or heard from him. The protectiveness Nimec had detected in Joyce's voice when they'd had their initial talk had been replaced with a disconcerted, anxious tone.

"Joyce, I need you to be straight with me," he'd said. "Has he ever pulled a vanishing act before? Done anything like this at all?"

"No, sir," she answered without hesitation. "That's why I'm so confused. I honestly thought he'd be in touch at some point yesterday."

Nimec paused, thinking.

"The woman he's been dating in Singapore," he said after a moment. "Do you know how to contact her?"

"Well, yes, I'm pretty sure I have Kirsten's home and office numbers on file," Joyce said. "Max left both with me in case I—"

"I need you to do some checking," Nimec broke in. "Call this . . . Kirsten, is that what you said her name is?"

"Yes, Kirsten Chu—"

"Buzz her at work first, see if she can tell you what's happening. If you don't reach her, try her where she lives. And keep trying till you catch her. Let me know soon as you speak to her, okay? Doesn't matter how late it is here in the States, I'm a night owl anyway. You can take my home number.''

"Yes, certainly . . ."

In the six hours following that conversation, Nimec had attended to countless items of business, gone home, pushed himself through a strenuous *shukokai* karate workout in his dojo, showered, had a bite to eat, and then settled down in his den to read his E-mail—acutely conscious the entire while that hadn't heard from Joyce. She'd finally called back ten minutes ago, midnight PST, four in the afternoon Johor time.

"Any luck?" he'd said, recognizing her voice the second he picked up.

"I'm sorry, no," Joyce replied. "After we spoke I left several messages for her at Monolith . . . that's where she's employed, you know—"

Yeah, I know, all too goddamned well, he'd thought.

"—but she didn't return them. It was the same story when I tried her residence."

Nimec waited. He could tell there was more, and didn't think it would be good.

"Sir, I noticed a long pause between Kirsten's outgoing announcement and the tone on her home machine," she'd said at last. "It was the sort you'd get when there are already quite a few messages waiting. . . ."

"As if she hadn't been there to retrieve them for some time," he said, completing the sentence for her.

Another pause. He imagined Joyce nodding at her end of the line.

"Just before calling you, I took the liberty of phoning Kirsten's departmental receptionist," she went on. "I said that I was a personal friend, and had been trying to get in touch with her, and was wondering if it was possible that she wasn't checking her voice mail.''

''Yes? Go on.''

She breathed. ''Kirsten wasn't there. She's been gone since Friday and nothing's been heard from her. Everyone at her office is becoming very concerned. They say this is completely unlike her.''

Unlike her, unlike Max, unlike both of them. So where are they?

His head starting to ache, he'd thanked Joyce for her trouble, assuring her he'd be in touch, listening to *her* nervous assurances that she'd do the same the instant she had any news, and signing off.

Now, ten minutes later, Nimec's headache had exponentially worsened, becoming the type nothing but a good night's sleep would relieve. Except he was too wired to sleep, and therefore would have to suffer. Max was one of his most trusted and responsible men, and it was no use telling himself he was merely extending a weekend barn dance with his girlfriend. All signs were that he'd bitten off more than he could chew investigating Monolith . . . and God only knew what had gone wrong.

Nimec frowned as he stared at the wall opposite his desk, regretting his willingness to let Max go ahead with this thing in the first place. Yes, it had gone bad, he was becoming more convinced of it by the second. Exactly what to do about it would take a little thinking, but do something he would. . . .

And every one of his instincts told him it would have to be soon.

''I'm going to ask you a favor on a rather sticky affair,'' Nga was saying. ''Understand I would not trouble you if there were any other way.''

"It is ever my pleasure to be of help to you," Kinzo lied, though his true pleasure would have been to stay as far from Nga Canbera as possible. But face and money compelled one to do much that was disagreeable.

They were regarding each other across Nga's desk in his office at the Bank of Kalimantan, a sleek, bright space on the building's thirty-third floor that had a breathtaking ocean view, and was decorated in a modernist Oriental style: sparse furnishings, neutral woods, its walls unadorned except for a 17th-century Chinese screen depicting an idealized winter landscape.

"Perhaps you'll want to hold your decision until you hear what needs to be done," Nga said.

Kinzo waited in silence. Thin and small-eyed, with a face like a tight fist, he was vice president of Omitsu Industrial, an electronic components manufacturer in Banjarmasin that had originated as an equal Japanese-Indonesian partnership during the years of the tiger economy, and fallen under majority Japanese control after the tiger leaped too far for its own good and went crashing into a ditch.

This had been the typical story for Southeast Asian businesses in need of financial rescue at the end of the previous decade. While many Western analysts had been gleefully forecasting economic Ragnarok for the Japanese, they had done what they had excelled at doing throughout history—learning from their mistakes, adapting to changed circumstances, and ultimately turning misfortune into advantage. Their rebound strategy had been twofold. First, they had propped up joint ventures with companies in Thailand, Malaysia, Indonesia, and the Phillipines by offering infusions of operating capital in exchange for bigger pieces of the action: i.e., controlling shares. Second, they had reprioritized, shifting away from a dwindling Asian market and focusing on export to cash-rich American buyers.

Japan's shrewd exploitation of opportunity had not only yielded heaping economic dividends to legitimate businessmen, but also kept the sake flasks of *yakuza* criminal syndicates overflowing, bringing particular rewards to the influential Inagawa-kai, which was entrenched in the Asian banking community, which had itself capitalized a large percentage of the corporate buyouts. Indeed, a graphic analysis of these financial interrelationships might aptly portray a long line of smiling, satisfied men, each with his hand deep in the pocket of the fellow in front of him.

In the case of the Omitsu Industrial resuscitation, the Canbera family had both brokered the deal and provided lending capital to the Japanese investors under exceptionally generous terms of repayment. That the Canberas had myriad ties to the *yakuza* was something the borrowers knew and accepted from the outset. That they might be called upon to provide a host of illicit favors to their "black mist" creditors was likewise considered a distasteful but acceptable part of their payback agreement.

As the old saying went, Kinzo thought, it was necessary to cross many fjords in passing through the world.

"Let me tell you my predicament," Nga said, cursing Khao Luan and his barbarians for the onerous position in which they had placed him. "There was an accident yesterday involving a foreigner. A white man." He gave Kinzo a meaningful glance. "It was fatal, you see."

Kinzo sat there looking at him.

"I want to make it clear that I had nothing to do with what happened, and would personally choose to report his

death to the police," Nga said. "But the circumstances—
and the parties involved—are such that I would have a
difficult time proving it was unintentional."

Kinzo remailed silent.

Nga folded his hands on his desk, considering his next
words. This was the delicate part.

"There's a problem with the body," he said. And met
Kinzo's gaze with his own. "With disposal of the body."

Kinzo took a breath, released it, waited another moment. Then he slowly nodded, wondering what sort of
infernal madness Nga was flirting with . . . and dragging
him into as a reluctant participant.

"I have a shipload of cargo leaving Pontianak tomorrow afternoon," he said. "It will be crossing the Straits
of Melaka en route to points west."

Nga looked at him.

"Ah," he said. "The open sea . . . is a lonely place."

Kinzo nodded.

"Were a man to fall overboard on such a voyage,"
Nga said, "I would imagine he might never be found."

Kinzo moved his shoulders. "Even should the currents
wash him ashore, the ravages of the sea and fish upon his
body would make it hard for anyone to identify him. Or
conclusively establish the cause of his death."

Nga smiled a little.

"As always, my friend, you make perfect sense," he
said. "Give me the ship's name and exact place of departure, and I can arrange for the luckless one we have
discussed to be brought aboard tonight."

Kinzo saw the uneasiness at the edges of Nga's smile,
and decided to reinforce it with a cautionary word. He
disliked the banker and resented his outrageous imposi-
tion . . . and apart from that wanted to be sure Nga real-

ized this was no minor impropriety of the sort his father had been covering up his entire life.

"Since you seem to value my thoughts, I feel obliged to share some with you," he said. "If a man with no friends were to disappear without explanation, his loss would be a blank space that goes unnoticed and unfilled. But things rarely occur in a void, especially when it comes to human affairs." He paused, then leaned forward. "If there are people left behind to miss him, an investigation is a foregone certainty. Should it turn out to be persistent, even the total absence of physical remains might not be enough to keep the circumstances of his 'accident' from being unearthed. Attention must therefore be given to all possible eventualities. Do you understand?"

Nga stared at him. The smile had fled his lips.

"Don't worry," he said. "I'm taking care of everything."

Unconvinced, Kinzo didn't answer.

Kirsten stood looking at her sister in the kitchen of Anna's home in Petaling Jaya, neither woman speaking, their faces gravely serious. On the butcher block between them were neat piles of chiles, water spinach, bok choy, white radish, and other ingredients for the stir-fry they had been preparing for dinner. A bamboo steamer filled with bean sprouts sat on the stove top, the burner beneath it still unlit. Behind Kirsten, an electric rice cooker worked quietly.

Her face pale, Anna was trembling with distress, the knife she had been using to chop her vegetables forgotten in her hand.

"Maybe you ought to put that down before you cut

yourself,'' Kirsten said, nodding her chin slightly toward the knife. She gave Anna a strained smile. "Or me."

Anna stared at her as if she hadn't heard a word she'd said. The faint hiss of the rice cooker was all that broke the stillness in the room.

Kirsten opened her mouth to say something else, thinking even another tortured attempt at humor would be preferable to the silence . . . but then she decided to leave it alone. What had she expected anyway? Surely not sympathy. She had been staying with Anna and her family for several days now, having arrived with a concocted tale about needing to get away from things because of a romantic breakup, an emotional situation that had pushed her to the edge, all of it complete drivel.

It wasn't that she had meant to keep the truth from Anna and her husband, certainly not for this long, but whenever she'd started to share it with them, the words had refused to come. And so she had continued the deception until it had gotten out of hand—like everything else in her life recently.

At times, Kirsten had thought her guilty conscience and dreadful worries about Max really *would* drive her out of her skull, and by this morning had realized she couldn't bear her freight of secrets anymore. Her resolve firmed, she had planned to wait until her brother-in-law got home from work, sit him and Anna down in their living room, and tell them the truth, the whole truth, and nothing but the truth, so help her God.

But as a surgeon at a government hospital in KL, Lin was often detained with some emergency or other, and when he'd phoned to say that might be the case this evening—well, she had feared her determination might crumble before he arrived, and decided it might be best to make her confession to Anna alone rather than chance putting it off again.

Still, Kirsten hadn't been looking forward to it, and choosing the right moment had been difficult. Oddly enough, however, her mind had been on something else entirely as they'd started their dinner preparations a half hour ago, just before she came out with her story . . . or rather, before it had *leaped* from her mouth all on its own.

The incident she'd been remembering had occurred the previous day, when she was babysitting Anna's two kids, Miri and Brian. They'd been out in the condominium's small backyard playing, and Miri, who was five, had caught a grasshopper while poking around a flower bed, then started shouting for her older brother to find a jar to put it in. He'd run into the house in search of one, leaving her to stand there with her small hands cupped around the insect . . . but when he'd taken longer than Miri expected, her initial excitement over capturing it had turned into a sort of jittery dismay.

"It's getting away," she'd yelled, her eyes wide and frantic. "It's too *big!*"

In fact, it *had* been very big—that the local bugs were always of the king-sized variety was one of the harder things to which Kirsten had needed to get reaccustomed upon her return from England—even harder than the bloody Singlish—and what had presumably gotten her niece so upset was feeling the creature ricochet wildly around in her hands, beating its hard carapace against her palms as it strove to free itself, something that seemed much too large and alive to be contained for very long without inflicting a painful bite or sting.

Becoming aware of Miri's agitation, Kirsten had dashed over from where she'd been clipping a hedge across the yard, and had reached the poor kid just as she'd thrown her hands wide open to release the grasshopper, which had shot into the air like a rifle shell, escaping with a sort of ticking, clicking, fluttering sound that caused had Miri to jump with a shrill cry of startlement. It had taken Kirsten a while to get her settled down, and she'd only accomplished that after repeatedly assuring her the bug had gone away, *far* away, and would not be returning to exact some hideous insectile revenge upon her.

In a sense, Kirsten guessed that her own struggle to keep the truth locked up inside her had been akin to what happened to her niece—she had found herself scared and helpless, dealing with something that had proven much, much more of a handful than she'd bargained for.

And what in the world had she feared from Anna and Lin, anyway? How could any reaction be worse than letting them remain ignorant of the confusing, dangerous mess into which she'd gotten herself?

"Anna, please, listen to me," she said now, fumbling for words. "I'm so sorry . . ."

"Sorry?" Anna emitted a burst of harsh, pained laughter. "What am I supposed to say to that? What am I supposed to *do*?"

Kirsten was shaking her head.

"I don't know," she said. "All I can tell you is that I never intended to bring any of this into your home. And that coming here was a terrible mistake. I'll be out by tonight if it's what you—"

"Shit, will you stop making things worse?" Anna said sharply. "Bad enough you've been lying to us the entire time you've been here, letting us believe you're nursing a broken heart. Then I hear it's all about you being involved with spying on your employer, and this craziness about men *ambushing* you on one of the busiest streets in Singapore like something out of James Bond. And now, to make matters worse, you're saying *dzai-jyan,* good-bye, as if you think we'd be eager to see you walk out the door and get kidnapped, even killed, God only knows. I'm not sure whether to be angry, frightened, or insulted."

Kirsten felt her throat getting thick with moisture, and swallowed.

"May I request," she said, "that 'forgiving' be added to your multiple choice?"

Anna held her gaze for a long, silent moment.

The silence grew.

"Yes," she said finally, nodding. "You may."

Kirsten expelled a ragged sigh. "I'm so mixed up, Anna," she said, her voice barely above a whisper. "Max . . . he knows my cell-phone number, and promised to be in touch within days. When I got into the cab, he was starting to give me someone's name, a person to call if I didn't hear from him, but I didn't catch it. . . ."

"Kirsten, if you want my opinion, the people you *ought* to be calling are the police," Anna said. "This Max is the one who got you into trouble in the first place. I understand that you have feelings for him, but how do you know for a fact that *he* isn't a criminal? That the men who were waiting outside the hotel weren't the authorities?"

Kirsten shook her head vehemently.

"No," she said. "It isn't possible."

"But you've only known the man a few months. Why are you so positive?"

"Because, while I may be five years younger than you, I'm not some little schoolgirl who's got her head screwed on backwards,'' Kirsten said, her throat filling again. ''Look, I won't deny I'm in love with Max. Nor will I deny having had doubts about whether he shares that feeling, or even wondering on occasion whether my position at Monolith made me . . . useful to him. But I know . . . I *know* . . . he cares for me.'' Kirsten wiped her hand across her eyes, and it came away wet. ''You can go on arguing about whether he respected me in the morning, but he's not some kind of manipulative crook, or con man, or whatever. He risked his life to lead those men away from me. I can't just turn my back on him now.''

Anna sighed. ''That isn't what I was suggesting, and if you'd stop being defensive for a second you'd realize it,'' she said. ''All I'm saying is that you—*we*—are in a very serious situation, and need to get help. What's so terribly wrong with the idea of calling the police? With at least considering it before some harm comes to you, me, Lin, or the children?''

Kirsten opened her mouth to speak, and realized she didn't have a clue what she wanted to say . . . but no, that wasn't right. That was being dishonest with herself, and she was supposed to be coming clean here. She had more than a clue. She knew, absolutely *knew* what needed to be said, and she could not allow pride and stubbornness to get in its way.

Suddenly she found herself overtaken by emotion, hitching out uncontrollable sobs.

Anna set her knife down on the counter, then came around to Kirsten's side and took one of her hands.

''Kirst, I didn't mean—''

''No, don't,'' Kirsten said, furiously swiping tears from her eyes with her free hand, *hating* the tears as they poured down her cheeks in an unbottled stream. ''You did mean it, every *word*, and you're absolutely right. You let me stay here unconditionally, and in return I've put your entire family at risk. And that can't continue.''

Anna stood beside her in silence, looking at her, still holding her hand.

Meeting her sister's gaze, Kirsten leaned forward and kissed her gently on the cheek.

''It's time for me to take some advice besides my own,'' she said. ''I'm calling the police.''

FOURTEEN

"YOU WANT TO *WHAT?*" CHARLES KIRBY SAID, GRIP-ping the telephone in his Broadway office. "I can't believe you're serious."

"Believe it," Gordian replied from clear across the United States. "I've given some hard thought to the idea."

Not easily jolted, Kirby felt like hanging onto his chair.

"We spoke less than two days ago, and you didn't mention—"

"That's because it hadn't occurred to me yet," Gordian said. "I said I thought hard about the whole thing. Not hard and *long*." He paused. "Sometimes it's a matter of recognizing when you've gotten a genuine inspiration."

Still trying to recover his equilibrium, Kirby held the phone away from his mouth, inhaled, then slowly counted to ten. He glanced out the window, where many stories below and across the street people were hoisting placards in protest of something or other near the steps of City Hall, a more or less daily occurrence for as long as he'd had his office here. What was it that had brought them out today? He squinted to read the signs, realized he couldn't make out a word they said, and promptly forgot about them as he exhaled.

"Our paperwork for the antitrust suit's already three inches thick," he said. "We're almost ready to file it."

"Then go ahead and do so," Gordian said. "We both know its real purpose is to buy time, and we can use all we can get."

Kirby frowned. "Gord, my job is to give you legal counsel and representation. I can't make decisions for you. But I hope you're aware of the risk you'd be taking by going ahead with this."

"I can accept it," Gordian said. "Talk to somebody with a cold and you might get sick. Stroll past a construction site and a brick might fall down on your head. You can't crawl into a burrow."

Kirby was silent. *Breathe. Count to ten. Let it out.*

"You know, it's always a little scary when you get philosophical," he said after a while. "Just tell me you won't lock yourself on this plan until after you're back from Washington."

"I'd rather get things in motion sooner," Gordian said. "As a matter of fact, I was going ask that you head out here to meet with me and Richard Sobel the morning before we fly."

"But that's Thursday. The day after *tomorrow,*" Kirby said, flipping through his appointment book.

"I'll obviously understand if you can't make it, Chuck. Just as long as *you* understand that if you have any compelling reasons to dissuade me, it'll be your last chance to offer them."

Reaching for his pen, Kirby crossed a Thursday lunch date with a very attractive female colleague out of the book, and substituted the words "To San Jose."

"So quick bright things come to confusion," he muttered.

"What was that?" Gordian said.

"I said I'll be at your meeting," Kirby replied.

Just as Alexander the Great severed the Gordian knot with a swift and decisive whack of his sword—thereby gaining the favorable auspices of Zeus—so had Megan Breen and Peter Nimec concluded early on in UpLink's worldwide expansion that it needed a similar rapid-response capability, a security team that could cope with crisis situations where both regional stability and the company's interests were threatened, sharing intelligence with host governments, using scenario-planning techniques to defuse most problems before they hatched, and prepared to counter violence with forceful action of its own should that option be unavoidable.

Since their employer had been cooperative enough to have a surname (and bold disposition) that invited comparison with the legendary Macedonian, they had dubbed this arm of their far-flung organization Sword. And because of Nimec's access to the generally *inaccessible* society of law-enforcement professionals—he'd started out a beat cop in South Philly, moved to Boston in mid-career to garner an illustrious and still-unmatched record of closed cases for the BPD's elite Major Crimes Unit, and after yet a second geographical move wound up Chief of Special Operations in Chicago, all in less than two decades—they were able to lure the cream of the crop away from police and intelligence agencies around the world, staffing their pet project with men and women who were equal to any job.

One of the impressive Young Turks with Sword's New York branch, Noriko Cousins, had been a handpicked member of Nimec's team during the Code Name: Politika

177

investigation of about a year back, and was credited with being a major reason for its speedy progress and successful resolution. After her section chief, Tony Barnhardt, took early retirement due to injuries sustained during that probe, she had been a natural to fill his post, which, in keeping with Pete Nimec's loose-reigned executive approach, allowed her to run her show with very little topside interference. She rarely heard from Nimec unless it was important.

And so, when she got back from lunch this cool autumn afternoon to find three phone memos from him on her desk spindle, every one of them received during the hour she'd been out of the office, it struck her as safe to interpret the repeated calls as a sign that a matter of some urgency had cropped up.

Hustling over to the phone, she punched in his direct number without pausing to unzip her jacket.

He answered at once. "Nori, I've been anxious to hear from you."

No kidding, she thought.

"Is everything all right, sir?"

"I haven't decided yet," he said. "Look, I'm not going to twist your arm, but I'd like you to come out to San Jose, and would rather not explain why until you get here."

Surprised as Noriko was, she only needed a moment to decide. The personal and professional allegiance she felt toward her boss made it easy.

"When?" she said.

"Soon as possible. Tonight, tomorrow, if you haven't got anything else that's pressing."

"Nothing that my assistant can't handle," she said. "It's been quiet in these parts lately, knock wood."

"Good." He paused for several seconds, the prolonged silence somehow conveying the gravity of his mood even more than his tone of voice. "I know this is asking a lot, and apologize for being mysterious. But we really ought to talk in person."

"It's no problem," she assured him. "Let me get off the phone and start making arrangements. I'll get back to you soon as they're set."

"Later, then." Another pause. "And Nori?"

"Yes?"

"I suggest you pack plenty of lightweight clothes. We might be doing some traveling."

She rubbed the back of her neck, thinking that one over. *Curiouser and curiouser.*

"Will do, sir," she said.

It was what might have been called a perfect equatorial night at Pontianak Harbor, the air warm and clean, countless stars filling the sky, the water stretching off from the rim of the shore lustrous with their reflected light. At the docks, a flotilla of commercial vessels sat anchored amid a silent thicket of cranes and hoists, the off-loaded ships resting buoyantly beside others stacked from stem to sternpost with freight containers, their prows pushed deep into the water under the weight of their transport.

Most nights there was something of a dozing serenity in the quiet before daylight, when the roar and yell of dockworkers, and the constant, rhythmic swinging of booms, would forcibly overpower the soft lap of the current.

Most nights.

Tonight the loud rumble of a cargo truck had shaken the stillness, a muddy tarpaulin flapping over its rear as it rolled up to the transit sheds at the north end of the dock, swung onto the ramp outside their loading doors, and came heavily to a stop.

Moments later a pair of waiting men emerged from one of the darkened sheds and turned toward the big hauler. Looking out from behind its steering wheel, Xiang saw them enter the wide yellow fan of the headlights, their short, slicked-back hair and cherry-blossom arm tattoos marking them as *yakuza,* barely out of adolescence, yet old enough to have been recruited from the *bosozoku* motorcycle gangs that were the equivalent of training schools for the Japanese underworld.

Xiang nodded to Juara, who was riding shotgun. Then, leaving the headlights on, he cut the engine, stepped out of the cab, and rounded the front grille to approach the pair of *yakuza.*

Punks, he thought, regarding them with stony eyes. The smuggling and drug-trafficking alliances Japanese crime families had formed with the Southeast Asian syndicates had not only yielded lucrative results, but had put strutting small-timers like these to good use. The cleanup job they were doing was the sort nobody else would touch.

"You're fucking late," one of the toughs said in Bahasa. "We expected you here an hour ago."

Xiang tipped his head backward slightly, saying nothing. The cargo truck's passenger door flew open and Juara sprang out, an FN P-90 assault weapon in his hands, the tiny lens of a laser aiming system under its silenced barrel. Expressionless, he stood beside the hauler and pointed it in the general direction of the *yakuza.*

"Never mind that," Xiang said. "I want you to tell me who sent you to meet us."

The *yakuza* seemed momentarily confused. "Why? We look like IMB to you?"

"You look like sewer rats who are too stupid to know they're about to get their heads blown out their asses," he said, and motioned to Juara.

Juara angled the small, molded-plastic gun sharply upward to center a red dot of laser light upon the *yakuza*'s forehead.

"Tell me who sent you." Xiang repeated. His eyes locked on the tough's. "*Now.*"

The *yakuza* blinked, shrugged.

"We're doing this for a man named Kinzo," he said.

"Doing what?"

"Taking a dead *gaijin* for a trip out to sea," he said. "You satisfied?"

Xiang continued to stare at him without moving for perhaps another half minute, then finally pushed his hand out at Juara. The second pirate lowered his gun.

"The body's in back of the truck, wrapped in a tarp," he said. "Get it out of there and onto whatever ship's taking it away. And don't ask any more questions, you little shitbag."

Trying to conceal his relief, the *yakuza* shrugged and said something to his partner in Japanese. Then both of them went around the back of the truck to do their work.

As he watched them lift the American's body from the covered flatbed and carry it off into the shed, Xiang suddenly remembered something that gave him a foolish but nevertheless powerful desire to hasten on his way. He turned back toward the truck, briefly pausing to gaze out over the black water licking at the quay—the water that would soon swallow Max Blackburn into its depths—and found himself unable to dismiss the unsetting thought that had occurred to him a moment ago.

Pontianak was named after the Malay word for vengeful spirits.

An involuntary shiver running through his frame, he ordered Juara to return to the truck, then climbed inside himself and drove off into the night.

As with any deadly combustion, the Jakarta massacre was inevitable once its explosive ingredients made contact under flashpoint conditions.

The protest organizers, mainly university students belonging to various political elements loosely gathered under the "pro-democracy" umbrella—and, in fact, representing everything from mendicant Communists to militant ultra-Nationalists—had been planning the demonstration at the Cultural Center for a great many weeks, distributing jargonistic leaflets, fliers, posters, and placards; slogan-emblazoned T-shirts and baseball caps; even compact discs filled with fiery speeches and protest anthems meant to be ratcheted from boom boxes during the rally. On and around Indonesia's largest campuses, movement leaders had sought out converts with the zeal of religious proselytizers, gaining thousands of student supporters and managing to stir up a large percentage of the usually apathetic working class, which had endured four years of grinding deprivation after the Asian economic bubble suddenly burst.

Although the cohesive force binding the groups together was fragile, they possessed unanimity in their weariness with skyrocketing inflation, discontent with a government that had stubbornly resisted economic reforms, and anger with their President, in part because of his see-no-evil attitude toward bureaucratic corruption and waste, and in part due to his refusal to dismantle the state monopoly of key national businesses, all of which were controlled by his seemingless endless multitude of brothers, half-brothers, sons, son-in-laws, and nephews.

Together the dissidents constituted a populist force to be reckoned with.

The government, however, had also prepared itself for a coordinated display of muscle.

Concerned that the unrest spreading through the nation's campuses, villages, and cities would eventually open the door to outright rebellion, many ruling party officials had concluded that strong action was needed to counter a perception of government weakness. All knew that quashing the protest in the manner of the Chinese in Tiananmen Square might provoke international condemnation, and potentially damage relations with their Western and Japanese allies. Yet after weighing that risk against the real or imagined likelihood of a full-scale people's uprising, certain influential aides to the President decided it was worth taking, and gained his approval of a scheme that would show their tolerance with dissidents had finally reached its limit.

According to reliable estimates, the throng of protesters was nearly five thousand strong at the height of the rally, and their complaints ranged from the dead serious to the frivolous. There were men with signs denouncing repressive social policies, demanding industrial privatization, and decrying the lack of variety offered by their cable television servers. There were women campaigning for better educational opportunities, new laws to prohibit workplace discrimination, and the scarcity of cosmetics due to import bans. There were journalists of both sexes crying out for freedom of the press, urbanites lamenting the absence of reliable public transportation, suburbanites complaining about their neglected roads and highways, and environmentalists calling out for the emplacement of stricter pollution controls. There was was even a small but vocal group of gourmands expressing outrage over the recent closings of several four-star restaurants.

While fewer in number than the demonstrators, the military troops deployed to manage and contain them were clothed in body armor, and equipped with a wide range of weapons and crowd-suppression gear that gave them a considerable defensive and aggressive edge.

They also had a dirty little secret up their collective sleeve: plainclothes security agents pretending to be demonstrators and dispersed throughout the crowd. The infiltrators' job was to incite a confrontation with the troops, who of course knew of the plan, and would respond with a swift and violent show of force against the real protestors. It would not matter whether their reaction was criticized as excessive by those with a human rights agenda; quite the opposite, its clear and desired message was that the government was finished with civil disobedience, and would begin to punish agitators in the severest manner regardless of anything its critics might say.

To make things look good, the first staged incidents were kept at the level of pushing and shoving matches, the "protesters" getting increasingly out of control, the soldiers showing restraint and discipline in driving them back. The clashes gained in frequency, following a realistic pattern of escalation, and soon the troops were being pelted with rocks and bottles. Tear-gas grenades, pepper spray, water cannons, and riot batons were used to subdue the rock-throwers, who were dragged from the scene in hand- and leg-cuffs.

Next, several of the government plants at the skirmish line began hurling gasoline bombs, covering the area with orange splashes of flame and dark clouds of acrid smoke. That no more than twenty people were engaged in this conduct went unnoticed in the milling confusion. That every one of the bombs were either intercepted by the soldiers' ballistic shields, or tossed intentionally wide of where they could do true harm to their supposed targets, also escaped detection. The image of the troops being physically assaulted, firebombs rupturing around them, was the excuse they needed to move into full offensive mode.

Shotguns and automatic rifles were brought out of mobile arsenals and chambered with lethal ammunition. Armored personnel carriers rolled into the mob, provoking exponentially greater anger and hysteria. A young man rushed in front of the lead APC, and was run over before its driver could halt or swerve, the vehicle's treads flattening him horribly, leaving him a mangled and bloody corpse. A young woman who had been near his side leaped upon a trooper in hysterical retaliation, cut open his cheek with a shard of broken glass, and was beaten to the ground with nightsticks and brass knuckles. A couple of men who tried coming to her aid were clubbed unconscious. Somebody triggered an automatic pistol, and by that point it hardly mattered whether the person was a uniformed trooper, an undercover provocateur, or an actual protestor who had been driven to a frenzy by the violence.

The troops smashed into the crowd from all directions, letting loose with their heaviest firepower. Live parabellum rounds poured from their guns. People trying to flee were trapped in the press of bodies and fell screaming and crying, swept with gunfire, slipping on their own blood, crawling through pools of blood.

The television crews already on the scene were speedily joined by satellite crews that could provide live coverage of the melee.

Watching the event closely on television, Nga Canbera couldn't decide how to feel about it. He had poured a fortune in *rupiahs* into financing the demonstrators, caring nothing about most of their issues, but liking to play political games with the administration, largely because he resented the competitive advantage held by the President's businessman relatives—and in particular by one of his sons, a former college classmate who owned a bank that was propped up by government loans and investments, and consistently outperformed his own as a result.

Still, Nga found the rabble crude and undeserving of sympathy. Would the crackdown play to the ruling party's advantage, or further inflame its domestic opposition? And what if the International Monetary Fund withheld the balance of its economic recovery package, or even aborted it entirely in a knee-jerk spasm of humanitarianism? What effect would such a turn have on the Canbera family's holdings . . . and most perplexingly, *why hadn't he asked himself that before?*

It was all very confusing and intimidating, especially when he stopped to consider that his involvement with the students would only be the beginning, the very tip of what would surface if someone started digging around in his affairs . . . and that his complicity, however indirect, in the killing of the American spy could be the very thing that led to where his secrets were hidden. Kinzo's thinly veiled warning was well taken—there was so much, so much that could bring catastrophe upon him. And what would Kinzo have said if he'd known about his role in what General Kersik and the others were plotting? Nga didn't understand how the game could have gotten so complicated and dangerous, how it could have gotten so *big*. He felt in over his head.

He stared at the television. At the armored cars, the troopers, the pathetically frightened demonstrators being cut down in their tracks as they tried to scramble to safety. The President and his advisors deserved credit, at least, for having the courage to strike decisively, to chance the repercussions of bold action rather than wait until the wolves were at their door . . . and perhaps, Nga thought, there was something invaluable to be learned from that, a clue to what *his* course ought to be.

Again, it all came back to the words of advice Kinzo had offered. If Max Blackburn's employers began tracing the circumstances of his death, it would inevitably lead to Nga's own door. How, then, to preempt such an investigation? Yes, Marcus Caine eventually would be feeding on UpLink, *devouring* UpLink—Nga was no less confident of that than before. But as he had tried pointing out at the Thai's dismal hiding place, the process of consumption would take time. Too much time.

Nga continued staring at the TV, but his eyes were no longer focused on the chaotic images flashing across its screen. He was wondering if the problem was not that the game itself had gotten beyond him, but rather that his strategy needed to be broadened. That he had reached the stage where studied and incremental moves would no longer work . . . and where one swift move could win it all.

Nodding to himself like a man who has suddenly

realized the solution to a complex puzzle, he picked up the telephone and called Marcus Caine.

"Hello?"

"Marcus, hello. I'm actually surprised I was able to catch you at home. According to what I've been reading, you're the toast of the town these days."

Caine raised an eyebrow at the sound of Nga's voice. He'd been in front of his television for over an hour watching raw CNN satellite feeds of the Jakarta bloodbath. By the time the footage made it to the regular broadcasts, it would be edited for mass consumption, sparing viewers the more grisly scenes of atrocity—but he preferred his glimpses of the world's ugliness straight up. Diluted reality afforded little in the way of insight.

"Libertine that I am, I occasionally give my follies a rest and try catching up with the news," he said, wondering if the timing of Nga's call was any coincidence. "Speaking of which, what's this madness going on in your country?"

"Our beloved head of state is clamping down on his opposition, it seems."

"Does that distress you?"

Caine heard Nga sigh. "I suppose it depends on how these events come to bear upon my own fortunes."

Caine's eyebrow arched a little higher. He'd expected an earful of Nga's phoney rhetoric . . . sympathy for the common man, and all that nonsense. The apparently honest answer Nga had given him instead was almost startling.

"As long as your bank continues doing well, I imagine you'd be in a good position regardless of who comes out on top," he said, uncertain whether that was true considering Nga's habit of fucking around in Indonesian politics, and hardly giving a damn in any case. He was just filling the silence, really.

"Marcus, listen to me," Nga said after a moment. "We have to talk about Roger Gordian. Something's arisen that could have damaging implications for us unless it is addressed right away."

Caine stroked his chin, thinking. He had no idea what to make of Nga's cryptic statement, other than that it presumably concerned the takeover.

"I'll be formally announcing my intention to acquire UpLink in today's *Wall Street Journal*," he said. "The company's lawyers are certain to stall things in court, but I think it will all be smoke. Give me a few weeks and—"

"I said *Roger Gordian*. Not UpLink."

Suddenly disquieted, Caine thought some more, wishing Nga would just spit it out. "Does this have any connection to the son of a bitch who was nosing around my Singapore branch? I thought you took care of him."

A pause.

"Marcus, are we secure?"

"I can only vouch for my end of the line."

"Then we should be able to speak freely," Nga said. "The one you speak of is dead. And that's where the complications begin."

Caine suddenly realized his heart was beating fast. "I—I don't understand. I mean, what went wrong? And what does it have to do with me?"

"How it happened is a long story, but be assured it wasn't intentional," Nga said. "Really, though, abducting him was a mistake, and I objected to it from the beginning. Had he been released, he would have been able to share information about his captors with the authorities and his employer. His death, meanwhile, is surely going to bring about an investigation. In the end, what is the difference? People are going to want answers, and all roads lead in our direction.''

"Wait a second," Caine said. "You're speaking as though I had a hand in this. And I didn't. I didn't even want to know about it. Your friends came up with the brainstorm of taking him, when there had to be an easier way to find out what he was looking for. A *sane* way."

"Calm down. We can't reverse what's past. The important thing now is that we have the courage to deal with the rest of it."

"Don't give me that bullshit. You fucking deal with the rest, whatever it may be. I've repaid your loans ten times over. I've done everything you asked, like a fucking indentured servant. But this . . . I want no part of it."

Another pause, this one of longer duration than the first.

"Marcus, I needn't remind you that you've already participated in activities that would be considered treasonous offenses by your government. If your actions come to light you'll be imprisoned for life, if not executed. Why do you think Blackburn had to be stopped? There was no choice—"

"Don't say his name. And don't you dare call me a *traitor*," Caine protested. His voice had become shrill. "My God, I'm not used to this. Those sons of bitches you consort with, those thugs, it's their problem. What do you expect *me* to do about it, anyway?"

"Nothing directly. But there are men in the States who've performed certain kinds of tasks for us before. Who can get into and out of places without anyone witnessing anything. You know who they are, Marcus."

Caine was incredulous.

"No," he said. "I won't hear any more—"

"Yes, you will," Nga said. "I will tell you what has to be done about Gordian because there is no other choice. And for that same reason you will listen."

"No, no, no—"

"I will tell you, Marcus," Nga repeated.

And before Caine could interrupt again, he did.

FIFTEEN

SITTING IN HIS PICKUP OUTSIDE THE BAYVIEW MOTOR Inn, Jack McRea resisted the impulse to check his watch for the third time in ten minutes. He was torn between contradictory desires, part of him eager to see the woman he was supposed to be meeting arrive in her car, part of him hoping she wouldn't show. He had been unfaithful to his wife only once in over a decade of marriage, and that had been when his drinking had gotten out of control and Alice had moved out for a while. Furthermore, he had never before breached his trust as a county sheriff's deputy or screwed up any of the jobs on which he'd moonlighted to pay the bills. Not even when his alcoholic binging was at its worst had he done that.

Yet here he was in a motel parking lot when he should have been on duty at the private airfield where he worked as a night watchman. Here he was waiting for a woman he had met in a bar where he still occasionally had a couple of beers between the end of his shift at the sheriff's office and the beginning of his shift at the airport. He knew nothing about her except that her name was Cindi with two *I*'s, and that she was blond and had pretty eyes and looked fantastic in short skirts and high-heeled shoes. Also, she wore this glossy stuff on her lips that made them look very moist, and had an incredible, sexy smile, the kind of sexy that made your stomach tight.

When they had met at the bar last night, she'd told him she was waiting for a friend who'd stood her up, and he had bought her a drink because she'd seemed kind of down, and somehow or other they'd gotten kind of flirty, and she'd edged a little close on her stool, and when he'd given her a look to show he'd noticed, she just smiled, and sat there a while with her skirt way up high and her thigh touching his leg.

Well, one thing had led to another, and they'd gotten very touchy, and because it was obvious where they were heading, and just so she knew where they stood, he'd decided to come clean and tell her he was married. She'd giggled a little at his confession, and when he'd asked what was so funny, had put her finger on his wedding band and said she'd sort of figured it was either that or he was trying to look hard to get, and he'd realized how lame he must have sounded and started laughing, too. And then she'd told him she had a regular boyfriend, which made them even, or *almost* even, and for some reason that had gotten both of them laughing harder, and they were still laughing as they leaned in close to each other and deep-kissed, then began necking at the bar, saying how much they wanted to be alone, forget the wife, forget the boyfried, alone, damn near getting it on right there at the bar.

Jack had known of the Bayview from passing it on the way to work every night—work being the airfield, which was owned by a group of local businessmen who had partnered up to keep their corporate jets there, and was just a hop-skip-and-jump from the bar—and also because a couple of his married buddies had been there with women they were seeing on the sly, and told him the owners went out of their way to keep things nice and discreet.

He'd mentioned it to Cindi while they were practically climbing aboard each other's laps, and said he had a couple of hours before work, and would she like to go there with him and finish what they'd started? And that was when she had explained about the guy she was kind of dating, saying he was a long-haul trucker who would see her whenever he was in town, and was stopping by that night midway through a long run, and that even though she didn't expect him until much later, she figured he'd want a little something from her like he always did, which made her feel funny about, you know, being with Jack that same night.

Jack hadn't known what to think of her story, except that it left him feeling like he needed a cold shower, and he'd asked her outright if she was having second thoughts about getting into something with him, and she'd said, no, no, you've got it all wrong, and had put her hand between his legs, and told him her boyfriend would be gone the next morning, and that it'd just be better if they could get together when she could be free to give everything she had to Jack . . . that was exactly how she'd worded it, keeping her hand on him the whole time, rubbing him where it counted right in front of everybody in the place. And that smile of hers, that smile, it was—how did the song go?—sweet as cherry pie and wild as Friday night, something like that.

Everything I have.

Ah, God, how could he resist?

And so they'd wound up making their plans for tonight. His original idea had been to meet her at the bar around six o'clock, and then for them to drive over to the Bay-view, where they could be together for a couple of hours before he had to take over for the day guard at the airfield. But she'd said she had some important errands to run that evening, how about they made it a little later, maybe seven, seven-thirty, just to be on the safe side. And he'd told her that was no good for him because he really had to be at his night job by eight, which would leave them with, what, half an hour tops, and that he didn't think either of them wanted the first time they were alone to be a wham-bam-thank-you-ma'am kind of situation.

It had gone back and forth a while, the two of them trying to get at a way to make it happen, neither wanting to delay it again, but Cindi insisting she couldn't put off whatever she had to do, until at last she'd asked if he couldn't maybe be a little late for work, or find somebody to cover for him, or even sneak away from his post for an hour or so, which she thought would make it that much more exciting for them, kind of *dangerous* in a fun way, didn't *he*?

Crazy as it sounded when she brought it up, he'd im-mediately realized Cindi had hit on something. He *could* leave the gate unattended for a short time without any-body noticing; in fact, he'd done exactly that on occasions when he'd gone to buy a coffee or a pack of smokes for himself, and once or twice had even stopped for a brew before heading back to the airport. It wasn't as though he worked at Frisco International. There were rarely any comings and goings during his watch. He could clock in at his usual time, slip away for a couple of hours with Cindi, and be back without anybody being the wiser. And, yeah, she was right, it *did* somehow make things more interesting.

They had finally arranged to meet in the parking area of the Bayview—he'd given her directions, and she'd told him that she sort of knew where it was, anyway—at eight-thirty, which had given him long enough to punch the time clock at the guard booth, make sure the day man was gone, and head on over.

And here he was the very next night, looking at his watch yet again, waiting for her to arrive, wondering if she was going to let him down after àll their planning . . . *negotiations,* you could even call them. Which, he thought again, might be for the best. Alice was a good woman and had gone through a lot with him, and he knew it would kill him to lose her. But it hadn't been happening in bed for them since Tricia was born, and he was a healthy guy who had his needs. What he was doing tonight was only sexual, and had nothing to do with how he felt about his wife. Still and all, though, once these things got rolling you could never be a hundred percent sure you wouldn't get caught with your pants down, and he guessed that was why there was a small part of him that would be glad if—

The sound of an approaching car suddenly interrupted the flow of Jack's thoughts. He glanced into his side-view, saw a red Civic enter the parking lot behind a splash of headlights, watched it pull into a slot in the row of cars behind him . . . and then felt his pulse start to race as her long legs slid out the driver's side and she came walking toward him, sweet as cherry pie, wild as Friday night, wearing clothes that might have come right out of his hottest fantasies, clothes that made it impossible for him to think about anything besides what she would look like once he peeled them *off*.

He hit the button on his armrest to roll down his window, and waited.

"Waiting for anyone special?" she said, smiling as she leaned into his car, her great big eyes and the scent of her perfume making his heart race.

"Not anymore," he said, and reached for his door handle, knowing very well that he would not be heading back to the airport anytime soon, that he couldn't have claimed to care if he *never* showed up at work, and that, like goddamned Samson in the old Bible story, he was wonderfully, deliciously doomed.

Its location chosen with privacy in mind, the airfield edged on a narrow inlet of the lower bay just northeast of the border between Almeda and Santa Clara Counties. Each of the four cinder-block maintenance hangars had a distinctive corporate logo painted large on its rooftop and at least one outer wall, making visual identification easy for approaching pilots. There were some small prefab outbuildings and two runways, one just over two thousand feet long, and a 3,400-foot high-speed stretch for the larger propeller and jet aircraft. Tonight only a handful of birds sat on the ramps beneath the calm and quiet sky: a single-prop Pilatus, a larger King Air C90B twin-turboprop, Cessna and Swearingen bizjets, and three or four kit-built sport planes. A fleet of passenger copters rested with their wheels on the numbers on a helipad at the north end of the airport.

A small oval of blacktop with space for perhaps two dozen motor vehicles, the airport's parking area was vacant as the unmarked commercial van swung in from the tree-lined access road at half past eight, and then nosed against the fence running behind the hangars and apron.

The pair of men inside had encountered no one at the guard booth, which had been their certain expectation. The guard had been lured to a motel by a woman whose expert distractions would make it impossible for him to remember his own name, let alone his responsibilities at the airport.

Moments after its headlights and engine cut out, its driver and passenger exited the van and passed swiftly through the entrance to the hangar areas. Both wore green utility coveralls. The driver carried a wallet with forged identification, two small adjustable wrenches in a patch pocket on his chest, and an empty pint jar in one hand. The passenger was also holding counterfeit ID, but had nothing else on him except a silenced Beretta in a concealed holster.

The service road ran in a loop around the airport, and had a concrete sidewalk leading past the hangars. Reaching the walk, they spotted the UpLink hangar about thirty yards to their right, and turned quickly and silently in that direction.

If they came across someone who questioned their presence, they would explain that they'd been hired to perform last-minute preflight maintenance on Roger Gordian's Learjet and arrived late because of difficulty finding the airfield. They had brought the Beretta as a fallback should that answer fail to quell any suspicions.

As it was, they reached the hangar without encountering anyone and found the hangar door open to the cool night air. They entered, located the overhead light switch, and turned on the fluorescents. The hangar's interior smelled of fuel, lubricant, and metal.

Stabalized by wheel chocks under the high, flat ceiling, Roger Gordian's Learjet 45 was a sleek eight-passenger plane with upturned wingtips and powerful turbofans. The driver stood admiring it for a moment. It was a beautiful work of engineering, but like all things had its Achilles heel.

Now the driver of the van turned to the other man, gestured toward the front of the hangar with his chin, and waited as he went to stand lookout. Once in the doorway, the man with the gun stretched his head outside, glanced left, right, and then over his shoulder at his partner, nodding to indicate there was still nobody in sight.

The driver returned his nod, and then went and slid down under the plane. Turning on his back, he produced the wrenches from his pockets and got to work. He unscrewed the lid of the pint jar and set the open jar on his stomach. Then he clamped one of the tools to the line running from the landing gear cylinder and, holding it steady by the handle, loosened the cylinder's hydraulic fitting with the other wrench. He held the jar underneath the fitting as the fluid bled out, and kept it there until it was full. Then he twisted the lid back onto the jar, put the tools back in his pocket, and wriggled out from beneath the aircraft.

Less than fifteen minutes after they had entered the hangar, the two men were back in the van. The driver placed the jar of drained-off hydraulic fluid in the glove compartment, and then turned on the ignition and pulled out onto the access road.

When they rode by the guard station it was dark and empty.

The watchman was still out enjoying himself, and would no doubt remember his hours of stolen pleasure with a smile, never realizing they had all but guaranteed Roger Gordian's fiery death.

SIXTEEN

"I'M TELLING YOU, IF THOSE PEOPLE IN THE PRESS Office don't start doing their jobs, I'm going to give every one of them the boot myself, and Terskoff is the first guy whose ass gets to meet my foot," said President Richard Ballard, referring in his momentary pique to White House Press Secretary Brian Terskoff.

"Quite frankly, I don't think they're to blame," said Stu Encardi, whose official job title was Special Aide to the President, and who was now just waiting for the breeze to stir. "You know how it is with reporters. They cover what they want to cover."

Ballard pulled a disgusted face. "Oh, come on. We're about to enter into a genuinely world-changing treaty with Japan and other Far Eastern countries, we've got three regional leaders *and* yours truly participating in a signing ceremony aboard a nuclear sub, and you're trying to say the crypto issue is *sexier*? That's absurd."

"You think so?" Encardi said. "Granted, the numbers tell us people were hardly paying attention to crypto until this week, and they still don't get what the whole damn thing's about. But from my perspective, it's this escalating Gordian-Caine spat that's the hook for reporters. The treaty represents cooperation and harmony, and, well, conflict being the essence of drama—''

''Spare me,'' Ballard said. ''What the hell should we do as an attention grabber, get Diver Dan and Baron Barracuda down there underwater with us?''

''Excuse me, sir?''

''Never mind, you're twenty years too young,'' Ballard said, cocking an ear skyward. ''By the way, doesn't the breeze sound pretty moving through those leaves?''

''Yes, sir, it does.''

They were standing under a willow oak that a former First Lady had planted on the South Lawn as an everlasting reminder of her tenure at the White House, much as Encardi himself had been planted among the President's circle of confidants by *his* lovely missus, who had taken a shine to the thirty-year-old Yale man when he'd been one of the coordinators of Ballard's re-election campaign, sensing in him a kindred soul of similar outlook and attitude, and later finagling her husband into making him a member of his post-election advisory staff, feeling he would be the ideal surrogate to carry her approximate viewpoint to Ballard—be it on matters political or personal—whenever she wasn't physically present to do so herself.

Generally speaking, Ballard considered Encardi an insightful, practical, and dedicated pup, and liked having him around as the personification of his wife's *weltanshauung*. Still, he was occasionally bothered by the fact that the aide boasted a profusion of hair to rival a Hungarian puli, while only a miracle of artful combing concealed his own advancing, Rogaine-resistant baldness.

He also became annoyed when Encardi borrowed his wife's verbal tics, such as following every Presidential statement with a "You think so?" and beginning his replies with a pedagogic "Quite frankly," or "From my standpoint," both hearkening back to Mrs. Ballard's decades-long career as a college teacher. These were the sort of things that would make borderline days turn bad, and bad days a little worse, except when the gorgeous weather and the sound of the breeze rustling through Ballard's favorite tree made everything under God's blue sky appreciably better.

"Stu, let me give you some instant perspective," Ballard said. "Two days from now I'll be signing the crypto legislation while Roger Gordian makes a fuss down the Hill. Two months from now everyone will have forgotten all about it, and think Morrison-Fiore is the name of some Vegas animal-training act. But in the interim I'll have closed a deal that establishes the guidelines for America's security role in Asia over the next *twenty years,* and probably much longer. There's my posterity, or a decent chunk of it. We just have to make sure people notice."

Encardi regarded him in the light shade of the tree as the wind brushed through the drooping canopy overhead. There were gnats or something swirling around them. In fact, there were *always* bugs under this tree. For some reason he didn't quite get, they seemed particularly attracted to the vicinity of the goddamned willow.

He swished a squadron of tiny winged harriers away from his face, convinced he would be a much happier man if just once the POTUS would elect to stroll under a dogwood, elm, or alder while seeking to restore his inner calm.

"I'm thinking we need to make sure Nordstrum from the *New York Times* is given the red-carpet treatment," he said.

"And *I* thought we were already doing that," the President said.

"Well, we are, but we can always roll out more rug," Encardi said. "Nordstrum's the biggest proponent of our Asia-Pacific policy in the national media. Why not assist him in gaining interviews with the Japanese Prime Minister, as well as the Malaysian and Indonesian heads of state? Invite him to the dinner you'll be having aboard the Seawolf? Anything to give him a steady stream of material to write about."

Ballard stretched broadly and inhaled the fragrant air of the White House grounds, sunlight striping his face as it filtered through the long bushy willow leaves.

"*Ahhhhh,* I'm feeling almost relaxed," he said. "Isn't it a spectacular morning?"

"Spectacular," Encardi said listlessly, swatting away an insect.

Ballard looked at him.

"Your idea about Nordstrum sounds fine to me, but only for starters," he said, his brow creasing in thought. "You know, now that you mention him, it's kind of odd Roger Gordian hasn't convinced Nordstrum to write more about the encryption issue in his columns. He's a paid consultant for UpLink International, did you know?"

Encardi considered that a moment and shrugged.

"Could be he disagrees with Gordian on that one," he said.

"Or just finds the crypto stuff as dull and relatively inconsequential as anybody else," the President added.

Swathed in virgin wilderness, the atoll was one of hundreds speckling the Celebes Sea west of the Sabah coast and bordering on the Philippines' territorial waters. A circular reef formed a breakwater around its shoreline, where a dense band of mangroves buttressed it against tropical storms and enclosed the rain forest that lay further inland, itself a protective horseshoe surrounding the lagoon at the island's center on three sides.

The same terrain characteristics that sheltered the atoll from the ravages of sea and weather had made it an undetected—and virtually undetectable—site for the pirate enclave. Few outside their brotherhood had ever located it, fewer still had penetrated its natural lines of defense, and none who did so without invitation had left it alive.

Zhiu Sheng had been there but once before, and then only for a quick pass around the island's rim at the request of General Kersik, who'd wanted him to have a firsthand acquaintance with the logistics of the planned Sandakan invasion. Today, however, he was headed for the interior. An hour ago, the Chinese fishing trawler that had brought him from the port city of Xiamen in Fujian province had steered slowly through the narrow inlet to the lagoon, and then dropped anchor near the sand belt. The timing of its arrival had been propitious; minutes afterward, the stacked, charcoal-gray clouds of an anvil thunderhead had burst open with a flash of lightning that illuminated the sky for several seconds, ushering in a fierce tropical downpour. Had the boat still been in open waters, the rough surf and buffeting winds might have capsized it.

When the rain eased off, the vessel's crew, a dozen trusted, handpicked soldiers from commando units in the Guangzhou Military Region, had gotten to work offloading its cargo of unmarked crates into the dinghies that bore them ashore. Per their orders, they had on civilian khakis. For their part, Xiang and the handful of pirates who'd met them on the beach wore army camouflage fatigues, something that had not slipped past Zhiu's keen sense of irony. Far too often in the world, he thought, the roles of men became confused and indefinable.

Now, the large crates balanced on their shoulders, their shirts soaked with perspiration, the soldiers were tramping through the knee-high water of a stream that bent and twisted between narrow lanes of cycads, their pirate guides leading them ever more deeply into the jungle. At first they had needed to hack their way through the epiphytic vines and creepers with machetes, but the undergrowth had thinned in the half-light below the treetops, allowing for better progress.

A lifelong city dweller, Zhiu nevertheless felt pressed, hemmed in, and that feeling was becoming more intense as he went along. It was as if he'd been bumped backward millions of years to some prehistoric epoch, a setting to which men like Xiang seemed as plainly suited as he himself was to the streets of modern Beijing. Trailing behind the giant as they crossed the stream, he recalled the moment he'd first seen him in the Thai's hiding place, guarding the door to where the prisoner was being held—his eyes staring with an impassive watchfulness that seemed to take in everything around them, yet let nothing escape their surface. Though that look had chilled him, Zhiu had not fully understood it, not then, not even after what Xiang had done to Max Blackburn. But here, in this old and alien forest, he did. Here, he had come to recognize it as a look with origins beyond human memory, a look of primordial jungle and swamp, a look which belonged entirely and exclusively to the cold-blooded, pitiless hunter.

Zhiu waded on. Though his shoulder pack contained

only rations, water, and a first-aid kit, the passage through moving water had tired him, and he could see his men approaching exhaustion under the heavier weight of their burdens.

He was glad when Xiang finally mounted the stream bank and led the party back onto the forest floor.

It took another twenty minutes before they reached the camp, a cleared area with a group of temporary thatch shelters in front of a spoon-shaped limestone outcropping. Zhiu peered through the foliage screening the perimeter, and saw Kersik and five or six others near one of the hooches, all except the general carrying ported combat rifles—battered Russian AKMs from the looks of them. Like Xiang's pirates, the men wore jungle camo fatigues, but that was the extent of the comparison. Their training and discipline were evident at a glance, making them far more similar to his own team.

These were experienced soldiers, no doubt chosen from the KOSTRAD Special Forces divisions Kersik had commanded before his retirement.

Zhiu raised his eyes to the arched ceiling of leaves without tilting back his head. He could not see the snipers guarding the perimeter, but knew they must be hidden somewhere up above him, ready to pick off unwanted intruders from their firing positions.

''Ah, Zhiu, you've arrived,'' Kersik said, spotting him. He came forward and parted the brush. ''Our cause brings us to meet in unusual spots, don't you think?''

''Yes,'' Zhiu said, stepping past Xiang to take Kersik's offered hand. ''This one, I confess, breathes down my neck with its heat and humidity.''

Kersik smiled a little. ''I suppose being a native of the islands makes me impervious to their effects.'' He gave

Zhiu's men an estimating glance, then nodded in apparent approval, as if impressed by what he saw. "Come, you all must be tired. I'll show you where to put the shipment."

Motioning for them to follow, he turned back toward the camp and strode to the rock formation behind the hooches. A matting of palm fronds, sun-dried and bound together with rope, covered a large section of the stone face. Kersick called over a pair of his soldiers, gave them a mild order in Bahasa, and waited as they lifted aside the matting to reveal a pocket cave, its mouth about five feet high and equally wide.

Curious, Zhiu approached the cave, bent over slightly, and leaned his head in for a closer look. The opening seemed to give into a space of some depth—in fact, he could not see to the back of the tunnel. Beetles and other insects crawled in the thick layer of guano covering the rocks beyond the cave mouth. He listened a moment, and heard the faint flutter of roosting bats.

Unusual spots indeed, he thought.

He straightened and faced his men.

"We'll bring the arms in there," he said, gesturing at the cave entrance. He paused, thought of the slippery bug-ridden coat of guano they would have to walk over. "And be careful where you step," he added.

Anna was sitting on the living room sofa, her legs tucked under her, when Kirsten came in from the guest room after having gotten off the phone.

"I've just spoken with the police in Singapore," she said. "I gave them my name, told them about the men that went after me and Max, told them where I'm staying.

They already seemed aware of what happened outside the hotel.''

Anna gave her a look that said she'd expected as much.

"In a country where chewing gum's contraband and spitting on the street is a crime, a scuffle of that sort wouldn't go unnoticed,'' she said. "What did they want you to do?''

"They tried persuading me to return to the island and meet with an investigator, but I said I wouldn't. That I felt it was too dangerous to go back unescorted. When they realized I wouldn't budge, they said they'd have to arrange something with the police in Johor and would get back to me.''

Anna nodded sympathetically. "How do you feel?''

Kirsten wondered how to reply. She hadn't been to her own home for almost a week, was hiding from men who had been trying to abduct her or worse, and was still waiting to hear from Max after having left several unreturned messages on his answering machine. All of which left her very frightened and confused.

Furthermore, she felt vaguely as if she'd betrayed him by calling the authorities after he had specifically told her to wait for him to contact her, and had tried giving her the name of someone else to reach if he didn't. But he'd never finished getting it out of his mouth—either that or she hadn't heard him clearly from inside the cab—and though she was guessing the person might be someone at UpLink, her sister and brother-in-law had advised her not to call there, insisting it wouldn't do until she had a clearer idea of what Max had been into. For all she knew, they'd repeated endlessly, the Americans had dragged her into some kind of dishonest business. And without evidence to the contrary, it had been impossible for her to dismiss that possibility without seeming unreasonable.

Which left her with Anna's question. How, then, *would* she describe her psychic and emotional state? How to express the incommunicable?

She looked at her sister from the entryway, thinking.

"I feel," she said at last, groping for words, "as if the sky is upside down and world is in the wrong place. The *wrong place,* you understand?"

Overwhelmed, Anna started raising her hand to her lips in a gesture of mute distress, but caught herself at the last moment and let it drop back onto her lap.

"I'm trying, Kirst," she said in a dry, scared voice. "Please believe, I'm trying my very best."

"Truly, I consider the orchid to be the embodiment of our Asian heritage," Fat B was saying. "Lasting yet delicate, its success, its *flowering,* dependant upon an exacting set of conditions."

"Is that so?" Commander Sian Po of the Singapore Police Force said.

"Truly, truly," Fat B said. "Nurtured in the rich soil of their evolution, orchids thrive in abundance, generation upon generation draping our hills, blanketing our heaths and gardens. Change what is essential to their natural state . . . go too far trying to cross cultures . . . spoil the purity of their time-honored lineage . . . and they wane like homesick souls. And while you may call me eccentric, I have always held to the belief that their colorful blossoms are inhabited by the spirits of our ancestors."

"There is a widespread fancy that certain varieties may actually *steal* one's spirit, you know. That their sublime beauty, drawing its energy from the feminine principle, may entrance a man and capture his essence, drain his very *yin*.''

''No, no, I think that is ridiculous.''

''Well, I do, too. For that matter, I think this is all a pile of shit, so let's drop it. You arranged this meeting. If you have something to say, say it.''

Fat B glanced at him and nodded.

They were looking out over the rail of a walking bridge that spanned a koi pond in the orchid gardens on Mandai Road in the north of Singapore Island, admiring the darting fish and the silver-tinged purple brightness of the bamboo orchids planted near the pond.

''Do the names Max Blackburn or Kirsten Chu mean anything to you?'' Fat B asked.

The commander shook his head. ''Should they?''

Fat B hesitated. ''There was a disturbance on Scotts Road last Friday evening. Surely you're aware of it.''

The commander did not shift his gaze from the orchids. A short, heavy man with rather mashed-looking features, he had arrived here for their clandestine appointment sans badge and uniform, not wishing to be identified as a police officer, let alone one of high rank. It would, he knew, be very bad indeed if he were seen consorting with a disreputable character like Fat B.

''Scotts is Central . . . 'A' Division,'' he said. ''Not my jurisdication.''

Fat B found his brevity curious. He leaned forward with his elbows on the rail and gazed past the pond to where the flowers were quivering in a light breath of breeze, their glow in the copious sunshine surpassing even that of the hand-painted butterflies on his shirt.

''Your Geylang command encompasses thirteen neighborhood police posts and over three hundred officers,'' he said. "The incident to which I am referring involved a scuffle on the street in front of a large hotel. A very busy location. My information is that there were witnesses. Do you mean to tell me there were no reports? No departmental bulletins?"

The commander turned his head toward Fat B and gave him a phlegmatic look.

"Assuming there were," he said, "what connection do you have to the occurrence?"

"None, I assure you." Fat B shrugged. "Like yourself, I try not to stray beyond my own purview. But on occasion people ask me things, and I do my best to give them answers."

"And how generous are these people in their gratitude?"

"Very."

The commander inhaled, then let the air rush out his lips.

"Something odd *did* happen outside the Hyatt, and maybe inside as well," he said. "Exactly what, I'm not sure. But CID's involved."

"Criminal Investigation?"

"Yes. And more than one line element. Rumor has it that both the Special Investigation Section and Secret Societies Branch have their noses in this."

"Tell me everything that is known about the incident."

"There isn't much. Or if there is, the CID hotshots are keeping it to themselves." Sian Po shrugged. "I've heard a bystander gave us an anonymous call, and it was corroborated by another report. There was a confrontation at a taxi stand involving a *quai lo,* a woman, and some others. The woman rode off in a cab, and the white man stayed behind and is supposed to have been followed into the hotel lobby. We don't know what happened afterward, but it was all over by the time a patrol car arrived. Everyone involved seems to have vanished, and few bystanders admit to having seen anything. But that's the way it is.''

"Nobody wants trouble, *lah*.''

The commander nodded, and released another sigh.

"Even so," he said, "trouble comes."

They were silent a while. Fat B's eye caught a compressed medley of color flitting under the surface of the pond—a large rainbow koi. It darted into the shade of a water lily and stopped abruptly, its long body hovering in perfect stillness.

"Should Missing Persons reports be filed on either the *quai lo* or the Chu woman, I would very much appreciate being apprised of their sources,'' he said. "Also, my inquisitive friends would find any clues I could pass along about the woman's present whereabouts to be of special value.''

Their eyes met.

"Your friends," the commander said. "What will they do if they locate her?''

"I don't ask.''

The commander looked at him for a full minute without saying anything, then slowly nodded.

"I'll see what I can do," he said.

Fat B grinned with satisfaction. "And I'll make it worth your while.''

The commander lingered on the rail another moment, then turned to leave. Fat B didn't move. He did not think Sian Po would be inclined to stroll from the garden in his presence.

The commander took two steps up the bridge and paused, motioning toward Fat B's shirt with his chin.

"Those butterflies are quite splendid," he said. "They are of the Graphium species, are they not?"

Fat B nodded.

"I've heard they survive by sucking the piss of higher animals from the ground," the commander said.

Fat B controlled his reaction.

"Thank you for sharing that with me," he said. "Outwardly we are very different types of men, you and I, but love and knowledge of nature is our bond."

The commander looked at him and grinned unpleasantly.

"The money helps," he said, and strode away.

SEVENTEEN

"THIS," NORIKO COUSINS SAID, "IS ONE *AMAZING* room."

Nimec reached for the little blue cube of chalk on the bridge of the pool table.

"So people tell me," he said, rubbing the chalk on the tip of his cue stick with a circular motion. "It's where I come to loosen up, get my thoughts right."

They were in the billiard parlor on the upper level of his San Jose triplex, a painstaking recreation of the smoky South Philadelphia halls where he'd spent his youth ducking truant officers, while pursuing an education of a sort that certainly wouldn't have moved them to reexamine his delinquent status. But in those days Nimec had only cared about one man's approbation, and in attempting to gain it had been a most attentive student . . . or, as he liked to put it, if SATs and grade-point averages could measure one's aptitude at bank shots, combinations, and draw English, he'd have been a shoe-in for a full college scholarship.

At any rate, he'd captured every detail of the old place—at least as filtered through the subjective lens of his recollection—from the cigarette burns on the green baize tabletops to the soda fountain, swimsuit calendars, milky plastic light fixtures, and Wurlitzer juke stacked with vintage forty-fives circa 1968, a machine he'd picked up for a song at an antique auction and which, after some minor repairs, could still shake and rattle the room to its ceiling beams with three selections for a quarter.

Right now it was belting out Cream's cover of the old blues standard "Crossroads." Clapton's improvised guitar lead slipped around Jack Bruce's bass line like hot mercury, taking Nimec back, conjuring up a memory of his old pal Mick Cunningham, a few years his senior and newly back from a hitch in Nam, bopping between rows of regulation tables, raving about Clapton being *fucking huge* in Saigon.

Mick, who'd had a problem with junk, which had also been fucking huge in Saigon, had been shivved to death in a prison exercise yard in '75 while doing a nickel for attempted robbery, his first offense, a heavy sentence by anyone's standards.

"One ball, over there," Nimec called, waggling his stick at the left corner pocket in the foot rail. He had won the opening break.

Noriko nodded.

He leaned over the side of the table and set the cue ball down within the head string, just shy of the center spot. Then he placed his right hand flat on the table's surface and slid the cue into the groove between his thumb and forefinger. Sighting down the length of the stick, he stroked twice in practice, then drove for the cushions on the opposite rail, giving the cue some left English and follow. The ball banked off the cushion at a slightly wider angle than he'd intended and hit the one thin, but still pocketed it neatly and scattered the triangular rack, leaving him with a couple of easy setups.

"You know what you're doing," Noriko said. When he'd shot, she thought, his eyes had shown the steely concentration of a marksman.

"I ought to," he said. "My father was the sharpest hustler in Philly. Shooting pool is what he did. His dream was that I'd carry on the family trade after he was gone, and I worked hard at learning it."

"Your mother have anything to say about that?"

"She wasn't around, maybe wasn't even alive. Blew the nest when I was three or four. Guess she wasn't impressed that I could count all my toes and fingers." He took his stance again. "Three ball, center pocket."

He aimed and shot, kissing his ball off the eleven. It pocketed with a solid chunk-chunk-chunk.

Noriko looked at him with mild wonder, waiting, twirling her stick vertically between her palms, its butt end on the floor. Nimec had always seemed the epitome of the straight-arrow cop—or ex-cop as the case happened to be. The side of her chief she was seeing was a revelation.

"If you don't mind my asking," she said, "how'd you wind up wearing a badge?"

Nimec faced her and shrugged.

"There was no dramatic turning point, if that's what you're curious about," he said. "Besides playing pool, our other favorite sport in the old neighborhood was hanging out on street corners and getting drunk and starting fights. Everybody wailed on everybody else, seven days a week . . . grown men pushing teenagers through windshields, teenagers pounding on little kids with trash cans, kids smashing bricks down on alley cats. It was hierarchical like that." He shrugged again. "I got tired of it after a while, and suppose the structure and the pay and the benefits of being a police officer appealed to me. One very typical day I took the exam and passed. A few months later I got my appointment, figured I'd see how it went at the Academy.''

"And it went well," Noriko said.

"Yes," he said. "It did. And sort of killed my budding career as a pool shark."

He turned back to the table, called his next shot, and put it down the chute. On the juke "Crossroads" ended and Vanilla Fudge's rendition of "Keep Me Hangin' On" keyed up. Noriko waited.

"You know Max Blackburn?" Nimec asked, his eyes moving over the table.

"Only by reputation," she said. "He's supposed to be the best at what he does. Ever since Politika, everybody's been talking about him like he's Superman."

Nimec saw a possible combination rail shot at the eleven ball, and lined up for it.

"Max is a good man, no question," he said. "Enjoys connecting the dots to solve a problem, which is why I often use him as a troubleshooter. The past six months he's been assigned to the Johor Bharu ground station, taking care of a range of things, some of which were, shall we say, not for the record. And dicey." He looked over his shoulder at Noriko. "Almost a week ago he dropped out of sight in Singapore, and nobody's heard anything from him since."

She watched him without saying anything.

"Max would never stay out of contact this long unless something were very wrong," Nimec went on. "He's too dependable a man."

He took his shot, but his wrist tensed at the last instant and he stroked the cue harder than he'd wanted. The ball missed the hole and caromed off the cushion, too fast, its angle too narrow.

"The dicey stuff Blackburn was doing," Noriko said in a slow, considering voice. "Is it something we can talk about?"

"Later, certainly," he said. "First, though, I need to know if you'd be willing to head out to where he is. Or was. And help me track him down."

"I get a team?"

"Just me," Nimec said. "If we need support we can get it from the Johor crew."

She looked at him.

"I'd understand if you don't want to get involved," he said. "Your participation would be strictly voluntary."

"And off the record," she said.

"Right."

There was a pause.

"One question," she said. "Was I asked on this job because I won't stick out in a crowd of Asians, or because of my experience in the field?"

"You sensitive about your ethnicity?"

"Sensitivity has nothing to do with it. I'm half Japanese. It's a logical question. Was it my slanted eyes or my ability?"

Nimec gave her a small, tight smile.

"Both," he said. "Your background might open some doors a little quicker. It might make certain things easier for us in certain situations, and with certain people. It's a leg up. But I wouldn't want you without knowing absolutely that I could trust you with my life, no matter how thick it gets."

She looked closely at his face a while, then nodded.

"I'm in," she said. "What's our game plan?"

"Step one, we finish playing pool. Step two, I clear our trip with Gordian. Step three, we go get our suit-cases."

"And if the boss doesn't give us the go signal?"

Nimec considered that a moment.

"Max is my friend," he said. Firmly. "Which means we'd have to skip right on ahead to step three."

Early on the day Roger Gordian was scheduled to depart for Washington, he was joined by Chuck Kirby and Vince Scull in the glass-enclosed veranda of his Palo Alto home. The three of them were seated at a large cane table talking seriously over their breakfast, drinks, papers, and open briefcases. The morning was bright and warm, and there was a flower-scented breeze wafting in through the lou-vered panels. On a freestanding easel near the table was a chart Gordian had prepared for their meeting. His daughter Julia had stopped by to wish him luck in D.C., and brought the greyhounds with her, and she and Ashley were running them outside on the grass.

Gordian had just finished summarizing his plan, and could already see the unhappiness on Chuck's face. He waited until the attorney wasn't looking and checked his watch, thinking he had a good half hour before his third visitor showed, time enough to deal with Kirby's inevi-table objections. Not that it would be easy.

He glanced out at the yard, bracing himself. Whipping downhill in pursuit of a tossed plastic rabbit, the dogs were curves of graceful motion against the greenness of the sprawling lawn. As usual Jack, the brindle male, had outsprinted Jill, the teal-blue female. Though both had been bred for the dog track, and Jill was sleeker and younger, her skittish temperament had disqualified her from competition, while Jack had run a great many races before he'd been retired.

Julia had gotten the dogs from a greyhound adoption program out of Orange County about six months ago. Had they not been rescued and placed, they would have been euthanized, which was the common practice of racetrack owners when their dogs were no longer competitive, whether for reasons of age, disposition, or any physical deficit that hampered their coursing performance. Gordian had been originally amazed to learn from his daughter that, on average, unadopted track dogs were retired and put down when they were five years old, having barely reached a third of their natural life expectancy . . . and always when he watched their spirited and energetic play, the amazement returned in its fullness.

After all the acts of inhumanity he'd seen people carry out on other people, all the personal losses he'd accumulated as a result of war and terrorism, Gordian didn't know why such waste—lesser by far in the grand scheme of things—ought to surprise him anymore. But it did, and somehow he felt that was better than if it hadn't.

He took a sip of his coffee, and listened to Kirby begin arguing that he was about to commit the worst blunder of his life.

"Gord, I've heard every word you've spoken and tried my damnedest to keep an open mind," Chuck said. "But to do what you've proposed before considering a less extreme strategy—"

"Sometimes you have to lose a limb to preserve the health of the body," Gordian said. "Sometimes survival itself depends on it."

Kirby shook his head. "You're talking about wholesale dismemberment," he said. "Not the same."

Gordian's clear blue eyes were so calm it was almost unsettling. *Like Moses after receiving the Ten Commandments,* Kirby thought.

"Chuck, I haven't said this would be painless. And because you're my friend, I believe that pain is the thing you're trying to spare me," he said. "But I've already accepted it, you see. Mentally and emotionally, I've already let go."

"*Let go?* Of everything you built up over a decade? Everything you've worked your ass off to—"

"If you stop for a second you'll realize you're over-reacting," Gordian said with unassailable forbearance.

Chuck turned to Scull. "Vince? Is that what you think? I know your analysis is that Gord's plan is doable, but my question is really whether it *ought* to be done. Whether you're endorsing it."

Scull nodded affirmatively.

"All we're asking is that you give us a chance here," he said. "Listen to what the coach has to say."

"And look at my graphic while you're at it," Gordian said. "Please."

Kirby pressed his lips together, breathed deeply through his nose, and looked. It was an organizational chart of UpLink broken down according to the market areas served by its corporate divisions and subsidiaries.

"As you pointed out yourself, Chuck, we've grown tremendously since the early nineties," Gordian said after letting him study the diagram. "When we secured the contract to provide our GAPSFREE missile-targeting system to the military, I knew the company's future was assured, and realized I was in the position I'd been hoping to reach all my life. I was successful and financially se-

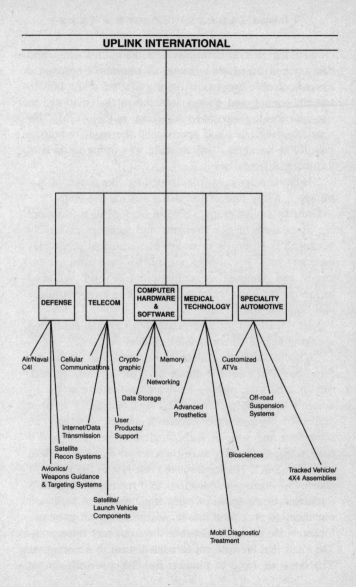

cure . . . my individual needs were taken care of . . . and that opened up a whole range of choices. Choices I'd never been able to consider before. Choices about how to put my money and energy into things that mattered to me, into making a positive difference in this world.'' He rose from the table and approached the easel, gesturing broadly at his chart. ''My mistake was trying to do it in too many different ways.''

''Heaven help us, you're sounding like Reynold Armitage,'' Kirby said. ''And that gives me the chills.''

Gordian smiled wanly. ''We'd be foolish to discount his assessment of our strengths and weaknesses merely because the language in which he's couched it troubles us,'' he said. ''It's always possible to learn from our enemies, and Armitage's essential point is valid. We need to look at the areas where we're bleeding away resources and liquidate them.''

Kirby searched for a response, but Gordian continued speaking before he could think of one.

''Chuck, I'd be confident of our expertise in the defense business even if I didn't have the earnings to back me up,'' he said, placing his hand on the box at the diagram's upper left. ''We're the best because I've been guided by my past experience as a combat pilot, and can remember the sort of technological improvements I'd have wanted when I was in the cockpit flying air strikes over Khe San.'' His hand moved one box to the right. ''I also know our communications unit represents UpLink's tomorrow, irrespective of early-stage profits or losses on our investment . . . and that its potential has yet to be unlocked.'' He paused. ''Those two are our core operations. The ones that are integral to what I want to accomplish. The ones we have to protect. But ask yourself, do we really belong in computers? Medical tech? Or how about specialty automotive? We only got into *that* because I wanted to make improvements to the factory-standard dune-hoppers we were using in our more rugged gateway locations.''

"Which you did."

"And now that we've assembled a large fleet of vehicles, and our competition has incorporated our modifications into their own product—and in some cases outclassed us, if you want my frank opinion—why not release the company to management who can give it proper guidance? After all, its profitability as an UpLink company has been been marginal from the very beginning.''

Kirby rubbed the back of his neck.

"I don't know," he said. "Putting aside the automotive unit for a minute, you've done well in the other supposedly nonessential areas. Just as a for-instance, the prosthetics subsidiary meets both of your fundamental criteria for an UpLink company. It helps people and makes money. The artificial limbs it produces are first-rate and have captured a respectable share of the global market—''

"And I'm very proud of that," Gordian said. "But my passion and knowledge don't lay in medicine. I've short-changed the division in terms of personal attention, and have never quite gotten my market bearings. And the R&D budget for our biotech firm eats up something like forty million a year.''

"Which is not at all excessive," Kirby said. "Your people are working on new drug therapies for everything from male impotence to cancer. Cutting-edge research costs money, but the financial and humanitarian payoff from a single major pharmaceutical advance certainly justifies the initial expenses.''

''I'd agree with you if this were a normal, as opposed to a predatory, business environment,'' Gordian said. ''The fact, however, is that we are under attack and need to focus. Because the medical division is in the red, it is lowering the valuation of UpLink's shares. As it stands, if I want the medical operation to continue, my choices are to either slash its budget or sustain it with the profits we earn from, say, our avionics branch. Money that could otherwise go toward higher-performance transmitters and receivers for our cellular network, or reducing the debts we incurred after the Russian debacle . . . and face it, Chuck, those are just two of many obvious examples I could offer.''

Kirby drank his Bloody Mary and was quiet a while. On the lawn one of the greyhounds had caught the plastic rabbit and flashed behind an alderberry bush, where it was throttling the toy between its jaws. The sound of its squeaker had apparently gotten the other dog envious, and it was jumping antic circles around the hedge. Standing nearby, Ashley Gordian and her daughter looked like they were having fun.

He wished he could have said the same for himself.

''Gord, listen to me,'' Kirby said at length. ''If I read you correctly, your strategy for averting a takeover is based on the assumption that the value of UpLink stock, and thus shareholder confidence, will be boosted once you've gotten back to basics and released capital to your most profitable ventures. Ordinarily I'd agree that it's a sound defensive approach, since a higher corporate valuation will curb sell-offs, force up a hostile acquirer's bid, and make him wonder if his move is worth the trouble and drain on his checkbook. Except this is *no* ordinary situation. Marcus Caine has already obtained a large chunk of UpLink stock. He's committed. Furthermore, UpLink's market decline has less to do with any real or perceived overdiversification than with investor fears that your stance on crypto will put you way behind rivals who are eager to sell overseas. And since you're obviously not going to sell off your cryptography firm—''

"Who says?" Gordian interrupted, the patient, forbearing expression back on his face.

Kirby looked at him a moment, then turned briefly toward Vince Scull.

"Both of you *are* shitting me here, right?" he said.

Scull shook his head.

Taken aback, Kirby waited a minute before saying anything more.

"Gord, I don't understand," he said disbelievingly. "You've fought so hard to maintain control of your cryptographic technology . . . to turn it over to someone else . . . to chance that it will be distributed abroad . . .'' He spread his hands. "You've never quit a fight before. I can't believe you'd do it under any circumstances.''

"Not *just* any," Gordian said. "Chuck, I—''

Gordian broke off, his eyes going to the sliding doors that opened from the house to the veranda. Andrew, his domestic, had appeared with Richard Sobel, the third guest he'd been expecting for breakfast.

"Sir, I've shown Mr. Sobel in as you asked," Andrew said.

"Morning," Sobel said, tipping the other men a wave.

Gordian motioned him to an empty chair at the table. "You're right on schedule, Rich," he said. "Join the party.''

Kirby gave Gordian a level glance, saw his spreading grin, and suddenly understood everything.

"You can relax now, Chuck," Gordian said, his smile growing even larger. "Our White Knight has arrived to save the day."

EIGHTEEN

THE FAX WAS ON SIAN PO'S DESK WHEN HE CAME INTO
work that morning—a dispatch out of Central HQ advising of a nationwide police search for an American named
Max Blackburn, and accompanied by a passport photograph and some sketchy details about the circumstances
of his disappearance. All personnel were to be on alert
for information regarding his whereabouts, and immediately relay it to CID. The same notice, Sian Po knew,
would have been forwarded to the divisional headquarters
at Clementi, Tanglin, Ang Mo Kio, Bedock, and Jurong,
as well as to hundreds of command center and vehicular
computer stations over the Incident Based Information
System.

Wishing to remain undisturbed, the commander immediately buzzed his receptionist, instructed her to hold
his calls for the next half hour, and read the dispatch over
a cup of green tea. It contained only a few brief paragraphs about last week's mysterious scene outside the Hyatt, and they conveyed little that was new to him.
However, the material about the parties involved was
most intriguing. There were fuller descriptions of the men
who had accosted the American . . . and most importantly,
there was the profile of Blackburn himself. Printed beside

his photo, it included data about his age, general physical chacteristics, and employer, a satcom outfit called UpLink International operating in the Johor area.

Sian Po drank his tea and reflected back on his stroll in the park with Fat B. What in the world was the club owner into? His nose told him it was something big.

He set down his cup, thinking. The report was as interesting for what it didn't reveal as what it did, and had put several questions into his mind. There was nothing to indicate where the facts about Max Blackburn and the other men had come from. And no mention of the woman Sian Po had heard was involved. Why? Could it be that she was the source of the information? That she'd been located and was perhaps being kept under wraps? CID investigators were customarily tight-lipped, quick to mark their turf, and loath to accept assistance from other departments in the Force. It was conceivable those bastards knew where she was or had her in custody—or under police protection, whichever. If they did, they would not share that secret with anyone at ground level. Not as long as they could help it.

Still, Sian Po had his useful contacts, including a supervisor in intelligence who would be glad to talk to him for a cut of his own payoff from Fat B. And Fat B had strongly hinted the sum would be considerable. He had to be careful, though. Ask what he needed to ask without divulging too much in exchange. The main thing was to find out about the woman, find out where she was. For now that would be a sufficiently juicy morsel to pass along. He would see what else might develop afterward.

Placing the report on his desk beside his teacup, he reached for the phone and made his call.

* * *

Nimec managed to catch Gordian in his office at a quarter past eleven in the morning. The boss was rushed, and expectedly so; he'd arrived late after a business parley at his home, and only planned to stay long enough to take care of some odds and ends before leaving for the airport. Vince Scull, Chuck Kirby, Richard Sobel, and Megan Breen—the four of whom were flying to D.C. as passengers in Gordian's Learjet—had already driven on ahead in a company car, and the hurried atmosphere had made it all the more difficult for Nimec to tell him about Blackburn . . . and then persuade him to green-light a trip overseas so he could look into what was going on with Max.

Harder than either, however, was disclosing that he'd let Max undertake a hidden probe into Monolith-Singapore's books without first seeking Gordian's consent . . . the unstated but clearly understood reason being that had it been a sure thing the idea would have been scotched out of hand.

Gordian's reaction to the news about Max—and Nimec's admission—was a predictable mix of anger, dismay, and concern.

"It's beyond me how you could have been part of something this reckless, Pete," he said. He was leaning forward with his right elbow on his desk blotter, his head tilted slightly downward, rubbing the corner of his eye with his index finger. "Completely beyond me."

Nimec looked at him from across the desk.

"I'm sorry," he said. "I won't try to justify it. But consider the big picture. Marcus Caine had been using the crypto bill to impale you in the press. And Blackburn believed Monolith was engaged in a series of illegal business practices and hiding evidence of it in Singapore. It was reasonable to suspect some of those activities might have been aimed at causing damage to UpLink—''

''So instead of coming to me with those suspicions, the two of you launched a caper that could have easily sunk us in quicksand. And likely has, from what you're saying.''

Nimec was quiet for a minute, then nodded.

''Yes, we should've notified you, and we didn't,'' he said. ''It was a stupid mistake. And I'm afraid to think about how dearly Max may be paying for it.''

Silence.

Gordian was still leaning against the edge of his desk, massaging the corner of his eye with his fingertip.

''Let's back up a second,'' he said. ''You're convinced Blackburn's in some kind of trouble?''

Nimec gave him another nod.

''And you want to go extricate him from it.''

''If I can,'' Nimec said. ''With some help.''

Gordian shook his head. ''It's tough for me to believe Caine's people would go so far as to harm Max. Regardless of what he might have gotten wind of.''

Nimec moved his shoulders. ''We can't make assumptions about how much Caine might or might not know. Or who his people are. Or what sort of people *they're* involved with.''

Gordian placed both hands on his desk and studied them, his lips pressed together.

''It's a hell of a time for me to make this sort of decision,'' he said, looking up at Nimec. ''I'm flying to Washington in a little while. And I've got my mind on other matters beside that.''

''Caine's hostile bid,'' Nimec said.

''Yes.''

There was another period of silence. It fell over them with a weight that was almost palpable.

"All right," Gordian said finally. "See what you can do. But if something comes up, you'd damned well better consult with me. I lost too many good men and women in Russia to tolerate anyone in this organization taking unnecessary chances."

Nimec breathed.

"Thanks," he said, rising from his chair. "I only regret not being able to join you in D.C. You'll have a crack security detail, but it's going to be a madhouse."

Remaining seated, Gordian looked at him and shrugged dismissively.

"Just be careful to watch your own back," he said. "My guess is I won't be facing anything deadlier than potshots from reporters."

Nimec offered a thin smile.

"Probably right," he said. "But somebody's got to worry."

"Marcus, what's wrong?"

"Nothing."

"Obviously *something's* wrong."

"Give it time. I need to relax."

Lying in bed with Caine amid the restored deco furnishings of their room at the Hotel De Anza, her face beside his on the pillow, her naked body pressed against him, Arcadia Foxworth licked her fingertip and slid her hand under the sheets, tracing a slow line of moisture down his stomach.

He lay there, tense and unresponsive.

"Tell me," she said, raising her head off the pillow. "Is there somebody else?"

"Only you," he said distractedly.

"Well . . ."

"Well, what?"

"There's your wife," she said. "She's one I know of, anyway."

He broke off his thoughts and looked at her.

"What's that supposed to mean?" he said. "Must you be jealous of Odeille?"

"Hardly," she said. "It isn't important what you do with her when we're not together. But when we are, I want you here. Thinking about me."

"Arcadia," he said, "let's not argue."

"I'm not arguing."

"Then let's not continue with whatever sort of conversation we're having. I've been under a great deal of pressure lately. That's all there is to it."

She looked at him, easing closer over the mattress, the bare white flesh of her breasts against his shoulder.

"Okay," she said, taking him into her hand, tightening her fingers around him beneath the sheet. "Usually, though, it's pressure that gets you going."

He lay there on his back, very still, staring past her face at the ceiling. What was he supposed to say? That his dealings with Nga had taken him over a line he'd never expected to cross? That he'd been coerced into ordering the *murder* of Roger Gordian—and Lord knew who else would be on that plane—and would soon have blood on his hands? Would *that* help her understand why he wasn't feeling especially aroused?

"Stop," he said abruptly. "It isn't happening."

"I've come two thousand miles from New York to be with you," she said.

"Nobody twisted your arm."

Her eyes widened. She pushed away from him, her hand retreating from where she'd had it, grabbing the sheet, tugging it up over her chest.

"You son of a bitch," she said.

Caine threw his legs over the side of the bed and strode naked across the room to the chair on which he'd put his clothing. He kept his back to her as he silently got dressed.

"Aren't you going to say anything?" Arcadia said. She had sat up against the headboard.

He waited until he was fully clothed before turning to answer.

"Yes," he said. "I'm thinking that you're right. I should be honest about what's bothering me. You *deserve* honesty."

She looked at him.

He didn't know why he said what next came out of his mouth, other than that it made him feel better, released some of his pent-up anxiety and frustration.

"You're lovely, Arcadia. First-class. But you've walked a long road from the streets of Argentina, and I like my women younger," he said. "The simple fact is that you don't excite me anymore."

Her mouth actually dropped open. She looked as if she'd been slapped.

It occurred to Caine that he might have gone further than he'd intended, that there was little chance she would ever want to see him again after this ugly scene.

Once more over the line, he thought. Yet strangely, it didn't seem to matter . . . although *why* it didn't was a question he'd have to consider later on.

"Don't bother yourself about the hotel tab, I'll take care of it," he said.

And turned from her shocked face, opened the door, and left the room.

NINETEEN

"**Local Traffic, Learjet Two Zero Nine Tango** Charlie, ready to go off Runway Two at the east end," Gordian was saying into his mike, informing any nearby multicom users of his departure. The small private airfield UpLink shared with a handful of other Silicon Valley firms had no ground radio facilities, but the nationwide advisory frequency of 122.9 was often monitored by pilots, and his practice was to broadcast his takeoff and landing intentions as a courtesy to them and a hedge against unwanted—and potentially disastrous—midair encounters.

Not that it looked as if there would be anything but smooth flying today. With a clear blue sky, high ceiling, and gentle winds, Gordian was anticipating a takeoff into ideal weather conditions. His only fillip of concern, and very slight concern at that, had come when he'd lowered his flaps while taxiing and noticed the hydraulic-pressure gauge drop off a hair more readily than normal.

This was something a less cautious pilot probably wouldn't have detected, nor found of much interest if he had, and quite understandably so. Gordian himself couldn't see any reason to worry. Though the aircraft's flaps, speed brakes, and landing gear all operated on the same hydraulic line, they would continue to respond properly, if perhaps a bit slowly, with the fluid level on the low side. Further increasing his confidence was the knowledge that his engine instrument-and-crew-alerting system—or EICAS—annunciators would flash a warning to indicate a problem with the circuit, serious or otherwise. And they had remained dark.

Still, he couldn't help but feel disappointed in Eddie, who'd inspected the plane the day before, and was usually an even bigger stickler for safety than he was . . . too thorough to let even a minor abnormality slip past his attention.

But later for that, he thought. As always in the moments before going airborne, Gordian could feel the sky exerting an almost physical pull. Moving the throttles forward, he concentrated on the EFIS panel in front of him, his eyes shifting between its flat-screen primary flight displays—arranged in the same ''standard T'' of old-fashioned analog instruments—and the bars of his ITT gauge, which measured the internal temperature of the turbofans. A hot start could lead to engine failure within seconds, making the ITT readout one to watch carefully.

Nothing to trouble him on that score; the turbos were operating well within standard limitations.

Its compressors whining and sucking in air, its wheels rumbling over the tarmac, the Learjet rolled up the centerline straight as an arrow. Gordian felt the shove of acceleration, and then the excitement that had accompanied each of the hundreds of takeoffs he'd flown over the past thirty years. He snapped his eyes to the window and quickly observed the distance markers along the runway— a feature as rare to civilian fields as it was common to military ones, and emplaced at Gordian's direction as a nod to his fighter-jock days.

Returning his attention to the EFIS, Gordian saw his virtual airspeed bug indicate that he had reached 104 knots, go-or-no-go speed. He conducted a last-minute check of the crucial displays. Everything was running smoothly, the bank of caution lights still out, his system readings A-okay. *Go.*

He released the stick, gripped the yoke with both hands, and rotated the jet to a seven-point-five-degree nose-up angle for liftoff. There was a slight jolt and another familiar tingle of excitement as his wheels left the pavement. His hands on the control column, Gordian increased his pitch to ten degrees and continued his ascent.

After several seconds he again looked outside to confirm what the altimeter and his own physical sensations had already told him. He had reached a positive rate of climb, the ground rapidly dwindling beneath him, the undivided blue of the sky pouring into his windshield.

His gear and flaps up, Gordian accelerated to two hundred KIAS, or over three hundred miles per hour. At a thousand feet he would very gradually trim airspeed until he attained cruising altitude.

Right now, though, it was time for an announcement to his passengers.

He switched on the cabin intercom.

''Vince, Megan, Rich, we're on our way,'' he said. ''ETA in D.C. is nine o'clock. So make yourselves comfortable and try not to discuss business. There'll be plenty of time for that later.'' He reached for the ''off'' switch, thought about the chattery teeth Scull inevitably got when he flew, and added a few words for his benefit. ''There's a bottle of Glenturret in the wet bar for anyone who wants it. Courtesy of your captain. Later, folks.''

Smiling a little, feeling easier with himself than he had in weeks, Gordian cut the intercom and settled back into his pilot's chair for the trip.

In a drawing room at the Leominster country club in Southampton, Reynold Armitage was gazing out the window at the ocean. It was a drab, chill day in eastern Long Island, and the threat of rain had driven the gulls close to shore. They wheeled in erratic circles, their wings tearing ragged holes in the stationary film of mist that had settled over the beach and jetties. Distantly across the water, Armitage could see a lighted buoy twinkling bright and red.

Ensconced in the armchair opposite him, William Halpern released a long, heaving sigh. Wearing dark flannel pants and a herringbone blazer, he was a spare, white-haired man in his mid-fifties with an undershot chin and virtually neutral complexion.

"Awful outside, isn't it?" he said in a haughty Connecticut Yankee accent. "The forecast was for sunny and warm, you know."

Using his wheelchair's joystick control, Armitage swiveled around to face his host. He was feeling winded from the dampness, which exacerbated the respiratory problems associated with his condition. The mere act of breathing was a reminder of the limitations of his failing body. Yet from the way the president and chief executive of MetroBank seemed to take the bad weather as a personal affront, one would think *he* was the man in poor health.

"It's difficult to make predictions for the shore," Armitage said. "Don't bother yourself about it, William. I'm hardly up to a stroll on the beach, and found the ride in your corporate helicopter to be quite entertaining."

"I'm glad," Halpern said, although he still had the look of someone who had booked reservations at an exclusive restaurant and found his meal to be a cold disappointment. He glanced out the window again and then settled back, appearing resigned and vaguely disgusted, as if realizing there were no one in charge of the climate to whom he might complain. "I wanted a discreet and quiet spot for our meeting, you see."

Armitage said nothing. There were, he thought, any number of quiet places in Manhattan where they could have met with greater convenience. But even in their elevated circles a Leominster membership was a glowing symbol of status, and Halpern obviously liked to showcase it. He was also well aware of the attention being paid to Marcus Caine's grab for UpLink voting stock, and with MetroBank retaining a significant percentage of the company, wouldn't want to start rumors flying by being seen with Roger Gordian's most noted media critic.

No, there was nothing mysterious about Halpern's desire to meet where they were. The real question for Armitage was why he'd wanted to get together in the first place. And with their mannerly preliminaries out of the way, he wasn't about to kill time waiting for an answer.

"So," he said. "What gossip about the financial community can we exchange? Let's think of something blisteringly hot and in the news. Something that gets flashbulbs popping. Shall we?"

Halpern looked at him.

"There's Monolith and UpLink," Armitage said with an arid little smile. "Not to mention UpLink and Monolith."

Halpern seemed perplexed by his sarcasm. "I've sat down with some of the men on MetroBank's executive board to discuss liquidating our UpLink shares,'' he said. ''Prior to a formal meeting, you understand.''

''And?''

''The consensus to go ahead with the sell-off hasn't materialized as I'd expected.''

''Interesting,'' Armitage said.

''It gets more interesting,'' Halpern said. ''As you know, I have no allegiance to Roger Gordian, and think his mission to save the world by planting a wireless telephone booth in every garden is nothing but horse crap.''

''You're mixing metaphors,'' Armitage said. ''And being a tad reductionist about his goals, wouldn't you say?''

Halpern shrugged. ''Call it what you will, I am concerned with MetroBank's stake in his corporation only insofar as its profitability, or lack of same. But there are directors on the board who feel a personal loyalty to the man, and have been reluctant to part ways with UpLink despite the diminishing returns on our investment. Before yesterday, though, I'd convinced most of them that hanging tight would be an abdication of their fiduciary responsibilties.''

''And what's changed that?''

''Not 'what,' but 'who,' '' Halpern said. ''Gordian himself phoned three senior executives. He requested they hold off on considering any offer from Marcus Caine until he's had a chance to meet with them.''

Armitage wondered if he was expected to be surprised.

''A sensible preemptive move,'' he said. ''And one with nothing behind it. As long as UpLink's value continues to deteriorate, your board is obliged to take a serious look at Marcus's bid. Money, not loyalty or misplaced faith in Roger Gordian, is what will count in the final tally.''

"And Gordian has promised to address shareholder doubts about UpLink's future at his press conference tomorrow," Halpern said. "He assured the directors he would be making a major, positive announcement. And that they would, at the very least, want to reassess their options after hearing what he has to say."

This time Armitage raised his eyebrows.

"I thought his reason for going to Washington was to protest the Morrison-Fiore legislation," he said.

"So did I," Halpern said. "And I'll tell you something else. His top securities attorney caught a red-eye out to San Jose last night. Canceled all his other appointments at the last minute."

"How do you know?"

Halpern stared at him.

"I have my contacts," he said, shrugging again. "You . . . and Marcus . . . can take my word for it. Something's in the air."

Armitage inhaled. His chest felt tight. If the feeling persisted, he would have to page his nurse into the room and be administeed a respiratory dilator. He felt a sudden bolt of hatred, and wasn't sure why. Nor was he even certain toward whom it was directed.

Outside the window a seabird emitted a shrill, ribboning cry as it plunged through the low veil of fog.

He looked at Halpern.

"I appreciate the tip, William," he said. "But the one thing you haven't told me is where you come down in this."

Halpern crossed his legs and was silent a moment.

"We've known each other for years, and you've always given me sound financial advice," he said finally. "But as you said yourself, this business is about money, not loyalty or faith . . . and like all bankers, I'm an agnostic.''

"Meaning you'll be listening to Roger Gordian's statement before deciding whether to stay behind the bid."

Halpern nodded, brushing a speck of lint off his trousers.

"Yes," he said without hesitation. "And very closely."

On a stubby finger of rock jutting off his island base's ocean side, Kersik stared out across the benighted water at the lights of Sandakan Harbor. Restless, he had left camp alone, thinking the freshness of the breeze would somehow dispel his somber mood, but instead it had made him feel worse. He supposed it was his knowledge of the violence that soon would be launched from his pristine shoreline, the deaths that were inevitably to come. There would be dozens, perhaps hundreds . . . if not many, many more. For a just cause, yes, or anyway a cause in which he squarely believed. But wasn't that the same ancient, self-righteous madness which drove every act of war?

Men fought. They had always fought, whether armed with stones, arrows, guns, or nuclear torpedoes. And they found their reasons. Indeed, Kersik sometimes felt that belief in a cause was nothing but a dark funnel into which both heroes and villains leaped with equal certitude, all tumbling together like clown players in a circus. Like the man who presently ruled Indonesia as if he were a Javanese king, parsing the nation's wealth out to his courtesans . . . like his predecessor, and Suharto, and those who had come before them, Kersik saw himself as being on the right side of history. Zhiu Sheng, Nga, Luan, they too were *right* from their individual perspectives—and yet the forces that had moved them into alignment were far too complex to be defined by absolutes.

Kersik's brow creased above his bushy eyebrows. Wasn't the judgment of right or wrong only a matter of who survived to render the verdict when the smoke cleared and the spilled blood of the dead was washed away? He had renounced his allegiance to his country's government and was about to place himself in defiance of ASEAN, Japan, and the United States. The entire world, really. Before all was said and done, he would be called a rogue, an international pariah. And what would he think of *himself* in the end? Might a division ultimately form in his own mind . . . half of him feeling validated, half condemned?

Kersik gazed out at the lights of a city that in the last 150 years had been governed once by the Germans, twice by the British, and exploited by traders, gunrunners, and timber lords from diverse corners of the globe. That during World War II was invaded by the Japanese and leveled by American bombs . . . and that now literally and ironically held the keys to the fate of both those nations.

Kersik stood and thought and looked out across the ocean swells . . . and after a while became dimly aware of a scurrying in the mangrove thicket behind him.

He turned, snapping on his flashlight, his right hand falling to the holstered Makarov at his waist. The sound had not really alarmed him; the only men on the island were the Thai's seawolves and his own commando units, and both groups had lookouts posted along the shore. Still, he was beyond all else a soldier . . . and good soldiers had cautious habits.

He trained the beam of his flash at eye level, saw nothing but smooth, gangling mangrove trunks and prop roots, and lifted it higher. Just below the leaf cover, a flying lemur clung to the bark and watched him with huge orb-like eyes.

For a moment Kersik experienced a queer, almost dizzying transference, imagining how he might appear to the strange little creature—clumsily threatening, out of place, himself the real alien. He withdrew his hand from his pistol grip as if it were red-hot, feeling an intense and incomprehensible guilt.

The creature studied him for another second or two with its perfectly round eyes, and then spread its flight membranes and kited off into the forest blackness.

Shaken and hardly knowing why, Kersik stepped into the brush and walked back toward camp.

As one of the test pilots of the original Learjet had told Gordian about its maiden run, the flight had gone better than expected and he'd expected it to go well.

That about said it for the trip to Washington.

Now, approaching Dulles International Airport at 8,500 feet and 350 knots downwind, autopilot off, the night sky clear and moonlit, Gordian cross-checked the Global Positioning System and VOR windows on his horizontal-situation indicator for a course fix, then radioed ahead to request airspace clearance.

"Washington, Learjet Two Zero Nine Tango Charlie, over Alexandria VOR at eight thousand, landing Dulles. Squawking one two zero zero," he said, finishing his initial communique with the standard numeric identification code for civilian aircraft.

A moment later the traffic controller responded, providing the computer code by which his radar-beacon system would differentiate Gordian's plane from other aircraft in the vicinity as it was guided down.

"Good evening Nine Tango, Washington Approach. Squawk five zero eight one and ident. Radar contact established, cleared into Washington Class B airspace. Descend and maintain four thousand."

"Roger. Learjet Nine Tango, squawking five zero eight one. Understand cleared into the TCA. Out of eight for four."

The buildings and illuminated landing strips of Dulles in sight below, Gordian trimmed power and entered a steady sink, carefully monitoring the instrument panel, making small heading corrections as he descended. Less than ten minutes later he again contacted the man on the ground floor.

"Approach, Learjet Nine Tango, level at four."

"Learjet Nine Tango, roger. Am familiar and would like Runway One Four Left."

"Cleared for approach One Four Left," the Approach controller began after a brief pause, then vectored and sequenced him into the lineup of arriving aircraft.

Not at all to Gordian's surprise, Approach concluded the transmission by informing him he would have to hold and circle at four thousand feet. In D.C. and other major cities, the terminal environment was often stacked with inbound traffic, in which instances one could look forward to a tedious wait.

He re-engaged the auto and informed his passengers they would have time for at least a couple of Scull's equally tedious jokes.

It was twenty-five minutes before the controller assigned a further descent altitude and then handed Gordian over to the tower—not as long as it might have taken, although he was still glad to be out of the pattern. The repetitive banking maneuver had been tiresome, and gobbled up more fuel than he would have preferred.

He switched to the tower frequency and identified himself.

"Learjet Two Zero Nine Tango Charlie cleared to land Runway One Four Left," the ATC acknowledged.

Gordian took the wind headings from him, rogered, and then read down the items on his computerized final checklist, mentally ticking them off to the line above Gear and Flaps. Although it sometimes seemed he had memorized the various checklist tasks when he was still in diapers, Gordian conscientiously ran through it before, during, and immediately after each flight. To do otherwise would be to deny his own fallibility, and that was not a mistake he ever intended to make—most especially not at the risk of people's lives.

Gordian returned his attention to the HSI, saw that he was coming in range of his final landing fix, and prepared to resume his checklist procedures. At just below six hundred feet and about a mile west of the runway, he was set to enter the base leg, and could see the brightly lit sprawl of the airfield in easy detail.

He pulled down the lever to deploy his wheels, expecting to feel the mild thump of the gear mechanisms lowering through the doors.

Instead the red master warning light suddenly illuminated.

The landing gear alerts on his EICAS began to flash.

An electronic alarm tone sounded from an overhead speaker.

Gordian's eyes widened. The breath catching in his throat, he pulled the landing gear handle up, then down again.

The red lights kept blinking.

The horn kept blatting into the silence of the cockpit with deadly insistence.

Gordian felt his heart clench as the ground rushed closer and closer up on him, the runway spooling toward his windshield.

The wheels, he thought.

With less than two minutes to go until he hit the ground, the landing gear hadn't lowered.

TWENTY

WHETHER JAMMED TIGHTLY INTO THE COACH SEC-
tion of some ready-for-the-scrapyard commercial jetliner,
or, as was presently the case, hugged gently by a leather
club seat in Gordian's state-of-the-art executive Learjet,
Vince Scull was a white-knuckle flier all the way, no
matter that he had logged hundreds of hours in the air
fulfilling his professional responsibilities at UpLink.

A lot of risk-assessment people, especially those whose
job it was to research international markets, relied on
second- or third-hand source material—news reports, so-
ciological studies, statistical reviews, and so on. Scull,
however, thought that was for slackers who might as well
have spent their time picking their underwear out of their
cracks as writing up analyses. In his opinion, if you
wanted to learn about a place, you went there, breathed
the air, ate the food, and if you were lucky, kissed a few
of the local *frauleins* or *signoras*. And, unfortunately, if
you wanted to get to the foreign country you wanted to
learn about, you had to fly.

So he flew. Which didn't mean he had to like it, or
pretend to anyone else that zipping around the world the
way he did merited flight wings, unless maybe they were
the ones that belonged to that Greek kid Zorro or Aesop

or whoever it was that went too close to the sun and got his tail feathers fried.

It was during the takeoffs and landings that Scull always had his worst anxiety attacks, mainly because somebody had once told him they were the times at which the airfoils were under the most stress from physical forces . . . not that he knew shit about physics or flying, except that it seemed there *were* more accidents at those critical stages than when the planes were under way, so maybe there was something to what he'd heard.

Be that as it may, the reason Scull was now gripping the armrest of his seat like a convict in the electric chair waiting for somebody to turn on the juice was that Gordian was making his final approach into Washington, one of those very stages of air travel that scared the living crap out of him, never mind the boss was an Air Force-certified Flying Ace. It was also why he was crooning a jumbled medley of Sinatra hits under his breath—*the summer wind came blowin' in across New York, New York, ring-a-ding and doobie-doo*—serenading himself with old standards being another tried-and-true Scullian method of coping with tension and blocking the unwanted from his mind.

He did not care if he would have to endure ribbing about his nervousness from Megan Breen, who was sitting just across the narrow aisle to his right. Nor did he care if he heard about it from Nat Sobel or Chuck Kirby, who were immediately behind him, bullshitting with Meg like a couple of makeout artists at a cocktail party instead of helpless prisoners of a tin can that just happened to be capable of shooting through the troposphere at close to Mach One, the fucking speed of sound.

All he really *did* care about was reaching *terra firma*

in one piece, and the rest of them could keep the Glenturret, which had admittedly gone down nicely, although his personal favorite malt was this brand from far western Scotland called Bunahabhain, an unpronounceable name that always left his mouth sounding like something Ralph Kramden might have said when Alice caught him redhanded in a lie. . . .

Clutching his seat, singing quietly off-key with his eyes shut, Scull was trying his best to remain oblivious to the plane's descent when a sound from the cockpit—the sliding door to which was partially open because Gord had been talking to Chuck about something earlier in the fight—bored into his awareness like a drill bit.

He snapped open his eyes and peered into the cockpit. From the position at which he was sitting, he could see about half of Gordian's back, and about the same amount of the pilot's console. The boss didn't seem to be in any kind of panic, but that didn't mean anything. This was the guy with the cool head and bombardier eyes, the guy who had been released from a five-year getaway at the Hanoi Hilton, their special all-the-torture-you-can-take package, with his head high and his back straight and his lips sealed as tightly as the day of his involuntary check-in. This was definitely the guy you wanted beside you in the proverbial foxhole, and if something was wrong, you would never be able to tell from looking at him.

But the noise coming from the cockpit, the noise was like an electronic version of an automobile horn, a gratingly repetitive *blaat-blaat-blaat* that damned well sounded to Scull like a warning alarm.

He looked at Megan, glanced around at Richard and Chuck. All three of them were also trying to see into the cabin, and their faces said they were, if not quite as worried as he was, then still pulling high Nielsen distress ratings.

Blaat-blaat-blaat-blaat . . .

"Anybody know what the hell's going on?" he asked in a loud voice. "Christ in a barrel, what's that *noise?*"

The others were silent.

Scull swallowed. His palms felt suddenly moist. And no goddamned wonder.

Coming from a plane full of talkers, that mute silence had frightened him more than just about anything he could have imagined.

Gordian breathed, filling his lungs with oxygen, his mind working rapidly. He was belting toward the runway at over a hundred feet a second without wheels, a situation that would have the gravest consequences unless he took action to change it. Which left no room for indecision.

Think logically, he told himself. *The problem's evident, now isolate its cause.*

He recalled the unusually quick drop in hydro pressure when he'd extended the flaps on takeoff. Yet if the pump motor had failed, the crew-alerting system would have detected it. Ditto if the sensors had gotten readings that indicated a low fluid level in the reservoir. Furthermore, the compressed nitrogen inside the fluid accumulator was supposed to provide supplemental pressure to system components in the event of leakage . . . within a certain threshold. When the fluid loss from a specific component became too great, or there was too much air in the line, it would be unable to keep up with demand and bring the pressure back to where it should be.

Meaning what? Gordian gnawed his bottom lip. Meaning he was looking at a drastically reduced fluid level— and therefore a sudden and unmanageable demand—in a particular area of the system, possibly the landing gear actuator cylinder. The gear had a mechanical uplock that wouldn't release without hydro power, even with the lever in the down position . . . and there was no manual override.

Okay, next. Options.

He could Mayday the ground facility, wait for them to foam the runway and bring fire and medical crews to the scene should he need to make a gear-up landing. But having to circle the field had depleted his fuel reserve, and foaming took time. While he had enough Jet A in his nacelles to safely abort and execute a go-round, he didn't believe he could stay in the air long enough for the process to be completed. In which case he would have to belly onto the pavement, something that would very likely spark an explosive engine fire and leave little but ashes for the ground crews to clean up.

Come on, come on. You want to avoid a messy outcome, get to the essence of all this.

He had compromised hydraulics. Gear assemblies stuck in the up position. And an urgent need to bring them down.

No, wait. Not down. Off.

He had to be precise in his thinking. What the hydraulic pressure really did was keep the gear assemblies in the retracted position by making them rest on the uplocks. If he could only get the assemblies *off* the uplock brackets, their own weight load would finish the task, causing them to drop through the well doors. In other words, they would bring *themselves* down.

Gravity.

Gravity was the problem, and it was also the solution. Gordian reached for a selector button under his multifunction display and punched up the G-meter screen. The bar was level at one-G—which meant the gravitational force on the aircraft was "normal," or equivalent to that of an object at rest on the ground.

Shooting a glance at the display, Gordian reduced flaps, gripped the control column with both fists, and pulled back on it abruptly, tilting up the nose of the plane, hauling it into a sharp climb. An instant later he shoved *forward* on the column, dropping the plane toward the runway again.

Gordian's stomach lurched. The airframe shimmied around him. The roller-coaster bump in altitude thrust him back and down into his seat, then up and out so violently he would have smashed into the windshield had he not been strapped in.

So far, so good.

He reached for the landing gear lever, not bothering to check the MFD. With his bottom floating off his seat as if he were being hauled up by an invisible hand, Gordian already knew he was at zero-G. And if he'd reckoned correctly, he would not be the only thing floating.

The gear would be too.

Right off the uplock.

Praying that God, Sir Isaac Newton, and his own common sense were at oneness, he pulled the lever down for the third and last time.

The wide band of his seat belt cutting into his flabby middle, his eyeglasses first clamping down on the bridge of his nose and then flying off his face, his thin fringe of hair flattening out and then sticking straight up, Scull felt like the ball in some maniacal game of ping-pong.

Buffeted by wildly shifting Gs, the cabin pitched and

shook. Magazines swept past him in a tumultuous flap. His eyes large with fear and confusion, he saw Megan's briefcase shoot up the carpeted aisle like a stone skipping over water, followed by a file folder Chuck Kirby had been perusing behind her, paper spewing from inside it. A banana somebody had been eating was next, then a pen that fired past like a small missile. He heard bottles of liquor, soda, and spring water clank and rattle in the wet bar, heard Richard Sobel uncharacteristically shouting out invective. Carry bags whumped against the interior of overhead storage bays.

"Shit!" he screamed, attaching his own contribution to Sobel's sting of epithets.

Suddenly he heard a thump under his feet.

Several thumps.

Pure, unalloyed terror leaped into his throat, jetted icily up his spine.

He stopped yelling.

Certain he was going to perish, Scull suddenly remembered that he wasn't alone, remembered there were four other people in the plane with him and—call him a dinosaur chauvinist, what was the fucking difference now anyway?—realized one of them was a woman who might need comforting.

Thinking he would do what he could, he turned toward Megan, reaching out to grip her hand—

And was stunned to see relief beaming from her face.

"It's okay, Vince, calm down," she said, leaning toward him, *her* hand falling gently over *his* wrist. "Listen, the cockpit alarm's stopped."

"Huh?"

"The alarm," she repeated slowly. "It's stopped. We're landing."

He perked his ears. It had indeed stopped. And so had the rocking. But what had those thumping noises been about?

Suddenly the intercom crackled to life.

"Everyone, I'm sorry for the jostling. There was a little problem releasing the landing gear, but our wheels are down now and we're fine," he heard Gordian say, as if in answer to his unvoiced question.

"Landing gear," he muttered.

"What?" Megan said. "Couldn't hear you."

He looked down at where she was still holding his arm, and smiled.

"Just saying I love you, too, babycakes," he said.

TWENTY-ONE

FROM AN ASSOCIATED PRESS WIRE REPORT:

Washington, D.C.—UpLink International Chairman Roger Gordian and a group of core supporters have arrived for a news conference at the Washington Press Club scheduled to coincide with tomorrow's White House enactment of the Morrison-Fiore cryptographic deregulatory bill. It is thought Gordian will restate his well-known opposition to the bill, a stance which has drawn criticism from many quarters of the government and high-tech industry.

The stakes are high for Mr. Gordian amid reports of mounting and widespread stockholder discontent, and Monolith Technologies' recent bid for a large voting share of his corporation. Questioned by reporters soon after his self-piloted Learjet touched down at Dulles International Airport, the besieged defense and communications titan gave no comment on rumors that his press conference will include a surprise announcement of his resignation as CEO of UpLink.

President Ballard and his media aides, meanwhile, have chosen to downplay the crypto bill's significance, wishing instead to emphasize the President's visit to Asia later this week for the signing of the SEAPAC maritime defense treaty, an event to be held aboard an advanced nuclear submarine in Singapore's coastal waters. . . .

FROM THE *STRAITS TIMES*:

Body Found by Coastal Villagers

Banda Aceh, Indonesia—Local police authorities have reported the discovery of human remains by fishermen operating off Lampu'uk, a remote village at the nation's northernmost point, near a frequently traveled sea lane where the Straits of Melaka open into the Indian Ocean.

There has been no official word about the body's condition, nor any indication whether its identity has been established. However, eyewitnesses present when the corpse was found describe it as belonging to a male who had apparently been afloat at sea for some days.

A forensic examination to determine the cause of death is said to be pending.

While little else about the case is known, the International Maritime Bu-

reau and other regional investigatory
agencies are said to have been contacted. It is routine procedure for the
IMB and ASEAN law-enforcement
groups, who maintain close cooperative links and shared databases of persons reported missing or lost at sea, to
consult when handling incidents of this
type.

Gordian remained at the field after the others had gone
ahead to their hotel rooms and, accompanied by a couple
of Pete Nimec's security aces, met with the airframe and
power-plant mechanic at UpLink's leased hangar.

Minutes after being told what had happened to the gear,
the shocked A&P man was under the Learjet's wing on
a wooden creeper.

"No sign of exterior leakage, and the fittings seem to
be intact," he said now. "Wait, hold it a second, I want
to take a closer peek at something."

The mechanic ran the tips of his index and middle fingers over a spot at the bottom of the fuselage, closely
holding a flashlight on it with his other hand. Then he
rubbed the fingers against his thumb and sniffed them.

"Got a whiff of Skydol, and there's some on my finger
from outside the actuating cylinder." He pulled his head
out from beneath the plane to look up at Gordian. "Can't
tell anything from that alone, though, since you're always
going to have some minor fluid loss. I'm going to need
to get in and check the whole circuit. From the sequence
valves to the main system line."

Gordian squatted down beside him.

"I want to know what went wrong, Mike," he said.
Then, thinking about Max Blackburn, he decided to fol-

low a hunch. "Do me a favor and check for any signs of tampering, will you? Four people almost lost their lives today because of me. Four of my dearest friends."

Mike turned off the flash, rolled out from beneath the plane, and stood, wiping the fluid residue from his hand with a rag.

"Maybe this is only a groundhog's way of seeing it," he said, "but from what you told me a couple minutes ago, I'd say it was you who *saved* their lives, sir."

Gordian shook his head.

"It isn't a matter of perspective," he said tersely. "Federal aviation regulations state the pilot in command has ultimate accountability for the aircraft. And for the safety of its passengers. Makes no difference whether they were jeopardized because of a sloppy preflight in San Jose, a mechanical failure in the air, my own judgment, or a combination of factors. I am responsible for everything that happens in the air."

Mike looked at him without speaking.

"I got lucky, Mike," Gordian said, his face tight. "You understand? I just got lucky."

Mike swallowed and gave him a slow nod. "I won't leave this hangar till I've combed over the bird from top to bottom," he said.

Gordian briefly patted his arm. "Thanks. It's appreciated."

He turned to the pair of Sword ops.

"I'd like you to stick around here with Mike. Give him any help he needs."

The two security men exchanged glances.

Gordian could see they were unhappy with his order, which was understandable. Lean and serious and zoned-in, they were professionals whose effectiveness hinged on rigorous discipline. Their assignment was to protect him, and it went against everything in their training and mental conditioning to ease up.

"It's okay, I'll be fine," he assured them. "I'm heading straight to my hotel room and plan to stay there all evening."

"Sir, we received direct orders from Mr. Nimec to stay with you," one of them said.

Gordian nodded. "I know, Tom," he said. "But if you don't tell him you left my side for a few hours, I won't either."

The bodyguard looked pensive.

"It would be best, sir, if we could check in with you over the phone this evening," he said.

"Certainly, but please try not to reach any premature conclusions if I don't answer," he said. "It's been a rough day, and I need a long shower and some sleep."

The bodyguard hesitated a moment, and Gordian resisted a smile. He'd suddenly remembered his paternal angst when Julia was a teenager going out on dates, and found himself amused despite his tension and lowering fatigue.

"Gentlemen, my car's waiting, and the driver must be getting impatient," he said. "I'll see you later."

Tom was quiet another moment, and then nodded, his expression a mixture of chagrin, worry, and vague disapproval.

"Have a good rest, sir," he said.

"I'll try," Gordian said.

And still wrestling back a smile, turned, flapped his arm up over his shoulder in a loose, weary wave, and strode out of the hangar.

• • •

"So, Alex, what I'm saying is that it looks like I can get you to dine with the POTUS and the other heads of state in the officers' wardroom."

"Is that what you're saying?" Nordstrum said.

"That is exactly what I'm saying," Stu Encardi said. "Right there in the belly of the beast we call Seawolf."

They were talking over a lunch of quesadillas, cactus salad, and chili at the Red Sage on Northwest Fourteenth, roughly midway between the Kennedy Center and the White House.

"And who's setting this up?"

"Terskoff."

"The Press Secretary."

"The Press Secretary *himself*," Encardi emphasized.

Nordstrum ate some of his quesadilla. "What's the catch?" he said.

"Excuse me?"

"The catch, the snare, the hook," Nordstrum said. "Whatever it is that's going to sink into my flesh if I take the bait."

Encardi combed back a wave of his lush black hair with his fingers.

"Oh," he said. "You mean President Ballard's request."

Nordstrum looked at him. "Stu, I think you're a decent fellow," he said. "But if you don't stop playing dumb, and get to the point, I'm going to leave this table, stroll into the kitchen, find one of the cactus plants they use for the salads *before* its spines have been removed, then come right back here and shove it up your ass."

Encardi frowned. "Ouch," he said.

"Yes," Nordstrum said, and speared another wedge of quesadilla with his fork. "Very definitely *ouch.*"

Encardi leaned forward confidentially. "Okay," he said. "All the President requests is that you absent your-self from Roger Gordian's press conference tomorrow. That is, assuming you've considered attending."

"Ah-hah," Nordstrum said, chewing.

"Now don't think the White House is trying to restrict your ability to express your opinions," Encardi went on. "Ballard merely feels SEAPAC is a far more vital part of his agenda—and his legacy—than approving the crypto legislation. And that it's slipped out of the spot-light because Gordian versus Caine makes snappier news copy."

"Ah-hah," Nordstrum said.

Encardi spread his hands.

"Think about it," he said. "You're the one heavy hit-ter in the press who's reported on SEAPAC from its ear-liest stages of negotiation to the present. Who's consistently stressed its importance to our regional inter-ests in Southeast Asia. Don't you think it'll further side-track the public if they see you with Gordian at the podium? There are already enough things distracting their attention."

"Ah-hah," Nordstrum said, chewing placidly.

Encardi frowned with exasperation. "God damn it, Alec, *now* who's being incommunicative? You asked me to be right-on with you and I'm doing it. So, please, let's have some feedback."

"Sure," Nordstrum said.

He carefully set his knife and fork down on his plate and straightened.

"I had planned on standing beside Roger Gordian tomorrow and will do that come hell, high water, or sugar-coated coercion from the highest levels of government," he said.

Encardi brushed back his dense swirl of hair again.

"Alec, you could be interviewing Prime Minister Yamamoto over caviar and champagne instead of chowing down in the goat locker with the enlisted personnel. Don't pass up the opportunity of a lifetime."

Nordstrum crossed his arms. "You're annoying me," he said.

"Alec—"

"Don't whine, it makes you look like a schoolboy."

Encardi frowned, wiped his mouth furiously with his napkin, and tossed it down on the table.

"Okay, I quit," he said.

"Good," Nordstrum said. "Anything else you want to ask while I finish eating?"

Encardi looked at him and sighed.

"Yeah," he said after a brief interval. "You ever hear of Diver Dan and Baron Barracuda?"

Nordstrum shook his head disinterestedly.

"Some help you are," Encardi said.

The transcontinental haul from San Francisco to Johor Bahru had been a grueling and seemingly endless affair for Nimec and Noriko Cousins, with a late-night changeover from their 747 to a prop-driven rattletrap in Kuala Lumpur, and, following their jump to JB, a treacherous forty-minute drive over dark, winding, poorly mapped roads in the rental car Nimec had reserved at the airport.

Though Nimec had been at the Johor ground station on only one prior occasion, and though it had occurred to him before departing the States that it might be wise to have somebody from the local Sword contingent come out to the airfield and meet them, he had finally decided to drive to their end destination himself. He supposed that part of it was a natural predisposition toward seeking camouflage, a trait that made him lean toward maintaining a low profile until he was clearer about where Max's probe had been taking him . . . and what might have gone wrong. But there was also a part of him that simply liked cowboying it, and while he would have admitted it to no one—including, to some extent, himself—the truth was that being lifted from his ordinary milieu had aroused that long-dormant facet of his personality.

At any rate, it was just shy of five in the morning when Nimec found UpLink's corporate emblem on a sign marking a dirt service road and, looking off beyond the tree line to his right, glimpsed the concrete and aluminum buildings of the ground station in the near distance.

He swung up over the hard-pack toward the station's perimeter gate and braked about twenty feet before reaching the guard booth. There was an ATM-sized biometric reader on a concrete island to his left—one of the recent improvements Max had made to the security net. Whereas most UpLink facilities used either iris or fingerprint scanning at various levels of access, Blackburn had wanted to tighten the identification requirements at restricted entry points by using multiple biometric passkeys, and had the scanner platforms designed to his specifications.

Nimec lowered his window now and swept his thumb over the platform's thermal-imaging strip while simultaneously waiting for the iris scanner to digitally photograph his eyes—two cameras matching them to a computerized facial template, the third taking a high-res snapshot of his iris. All three images were then checked for a variety of characteristics and compared with information previously enrolled in the security mainframe's database.

Seconds after he'd pulled up to the multiscanner, the "toll light" above the motorized gate in front of him shifted from red to green and a computer-synthesized female voice issued from a speaker in the platform.

"Identification complete, Peter Nimec," it said in English. "Please proceed."

Nimec drove on through the gate toward the complex, nodding to the uniformed man in the guard booth as he passed him.

"This isn't quite the sort of place I expected," Nori said from the backseat, looking out the window in the dawnlight. "It's so . . . I don't know . . . colorless."

Nimec shrugged with his hands on the wheel.

"Utilitarian's the word I'd use," he said. "Didn't realize you hadn't been to any of our ground stations. They all come out of the same cookie cutter. After a while you get used to the no-frills decor."

"I suppose." She sat back and yawned.

Nimec glanced into the rearview.

"Tired from our journey to the East?" he asked.

"And wired," she said.

"Not a good mix if you plan to get any sleep." He lifted a folded newspaper from the passenger seat and held it out to her over his shoulder. "Here, take this copy of the *Straits Times* I grabbed at the KL airport. Maybe it'll help you relax."

"I don't remember seeing you read it."

"That's because I haven't yet," he said. "And I doubt I'll manage to keep my eyes open long enough to do so."

Nori took the paper from his hand, set it down beside her, and yawned again.

"Thanks," she said. "I'll be sure to fill you in on the local news over breakfast."

He nodded.

"Just don't forget my horoscope," he said in a tone that might or might not have been serious.

Sian Po had no sooner gotten to bed after returning home from his night shift at the precinct than he closed his eyes and dreamed he was in a gambling parlor managed by Fat B. There were women and flashing lights and he had somehow won an astronomical sum of money, hillocks of which surrounded him on every side.

The knock at his door awakened him just as, in his dream, he had begun to dance with a magnificent blonde who'd slid down off a pole and then told him she'd come all the way from Denmark to make his acquaintance.

Sian Po opened his eyes, jolted from the sparkle and glitz of his fantasy to the bland, curtained dimness of his studio apartment. Where had the sexy dancer gone?

He frowned with the realization that she didn't exist, and glanced at his alarm clock. It was five A.M. Had he thought he'd heard something?

There was another rap on the door.

Still a little disoriented, he got out of bed and went over to it in his pajamas.

"Who is it?" he grunted, rubbing his eyes.

"I've something for you from Gaffoor," a hushed male voice said from out in the corridor.

Sian Po's bleariness instantly dissipated at the mention of his insider with CID. He unbolted his lock and pulled open the door.

The man was about thirty and dressed in civilian clothes, a light cotton shirt and sport jacket. Another investigator, or so Sian Po believed.

"You in Gaffoor's unit?" Sian Po asked.

The man shrugged noncommittally, extracted a white legal envelope from his jacket's inner pocket, and held it out to Sian Po.

"Take it, *ke yi bu ke yi,*" he said.

Sian Po snatched it from his hand.

The man stood there giving him a blank look. "I'll tell Gaffoor you received his message," he said, and turned down the hall.

The door shut behind him, Sian Po eagerly tore open the envelope. Inside was a folded sheet of paper. He slipped it out and read the note that had been written across its face.

Excitement flooded his squashed features.

Unbelievable, he thought. Just unbelievable.

Heedless of the hour, Sian Po hurried over to his bedside stand, located Fat B's phone number in his datebook, and rang him up.

As though the dream had been a true and marvelous premonition, his jackpot had arrived.

TWENTY-TWO

IN THE CORRIDOR OUTSIDE THE EAST ROOM OF THE White House, a room throbbing with reporters, prominent members of Congress, and other official guests invited to the Morrison-Fiore bill-signing ceremony, the President was both aggravated and anxious to put pen to paper.

He was aggravated because he had wanted to sign the bill while sitting behind the staunch and sturdy solidity of the Resolute Desk in the sound and secure comfort of the Executive Office, wanted to sign it at midnight when the folks around him were home in bed, or elsewhere in bed, or in some cases skulking between beds, zipping up, unzipping, getting tangled up *inside* their zippers, whatever the hell they chose to do with themselves when the sun went down and the lights were out here in the golden city on the Hill.

He was anxious because now that he'd been induced to make a huge ceremonial affair of the signing—C-SPAN cameras dollying about, kliegs in his face, the whole nine yards—he wanted it over and done with so that public attention could be turned to something of real significance to him, namely SEAPAC, a child he had guided from infancy, watching it take on polish, refinement, and sophistication under his savvy political eye. A treaty that he viewed as the most important policy effort of his tenure in the White House. That he believed was the blueprint for a new strategic and logistic collaboration in the Pacific Rim. That he was certain would reinforce America's ties with its Asian partners, and decide the future of its own security interests in the region. What was Morrison-Fiore in comparison, besides a piece of moot legislation, easing commercial restrictions that had already been bypassed with countless loopholes?

Impatient to get to his desk now—no Resolute by any means, no strong, lasting article of furniture made from the timbers of a bold expeditionary vessel, but rather a comparatively lightweight and characterless hunk of wood rolled out under the portrait of George Washington especially for this morning's swinging Big House hullabaloo—the President glanced into the room, where the function's primary mastermind, Press Secretary Brian Terskoff, stood to the right of the entryway schmoozing with a young woman Ballard recognized as an executive from the news department of one of the major television networks. A place where Terskoff might very well be seeking employment once the sorry, obstinate bastard got the ass-kicking he'd long deserved.

And what better time than the present to do that? Ballard suddenly thought.

He caught Terskoff's eye and crooked a finger at him, then waited as he pushed his way through the sea of invitees and into the corridor.

''Yes, Mr. President?'' he said, stepping close.

''What's the delay?''

''They're working a bug or two out of the satellite feeds, technical stuff,'' Terskoff said. ''We'll be on in five.''

The President looked at him.

"On in five," he echoed.

Terskoff nodded. "Maybe less."

The President kept looking at him.

"You sound like the stage manager of a talk show."

Terskoff seemed flattered.

"In a sense, that's my role here today," he said.

The President leaned in close. "Brian, if I'd had it my way, the signing would have been handled as a routine piece of business, something that passed quietly in the night," he said. "Instead, thanks to you, we've got ourselves a spectacle."

"Yes, sir, I believe we do," Terskoff said proudly, glancing into the room. "A *stately* spectacle. That is my preferred approach to these events."

"Your preferred approach."

"Very much so, Mr. President."

Ballard frowned, nibbling the inside of his cheek. "You know," he said, "it occurs to me this approach might have been utilized to promote another of my little endeavors. One I feel hasn't been quite the attention-grabber I'd anticipated it might be."

Terskoff scratched behind his ear, all at once unsure of himself.

"You're referring to SEAPAC," he said.

"Yes," the President said, snapping his index finger at Terskoff's chest. "You guessed it. And what I'm thinking, Brian, is that it's still not too late to change things. For example, we could have football cheerleaders accompany me to Air Force One as I leave for Singapore tomorrow. Or better yet, *Playboy* models *dressed* as cheerleaders. They could be spelling out the name of the treaty while they do their pom-pom waving on the field.

'Give me an S, give me an E,' and so forth. And they could have the word SEAPAC written out across their bikini tops in sequined letters, one letter to each model. How's *that* for a stately spectacle, as you phrased it?''

Terskoff grimaced. ''Mr. President, I know you feel the treaty has been neglected in favor of Morrison-Fiore. But please understand, the press feeds on the sensational. The best one can do is give them what they want, and I choose to do it in whopping portions—''

''I've heard that song a hundred times before, which is more than enough,'' he said. ''Let me tell you something, Brian. You fucked up. You and the pack of propeller-heads you call a staff. And as a result, an initiative to which I've dedicated tremendous effort has been side-lined.''

''Sir—''

Ballard raised his hand like a traffic cop.

''I'm not finished,'' he said. ''Crypto isn't my fight. It never has been. I've never wanted to go to blows with Roger Gordian over it, not publicly, and yet that's exactly what's happening today. At this very instant, he's across town putting on his big Everlast gloves. And that does not make me happy.''

A pause.

''Mr. President, if there's anything you feel I can do . . .''

''Actually, there is,'' Ballard said. ''For starters, you can notify those television people that I'm entering the room in thirty seconds, whether they're ready or not. And then you can take that pretty news executive you were chatting up out to lunch—the Fourth Estate might be an appropriate restaurant—and see whether she can find a place for you in her department. Because I'll be expecting your letter of resignation on my desk when I return from Asia next week. You got me?''

Terskoff had paled. "Sir . . .''

The President pointed to his wristwatch.

"Twenty seconds," he said.

His lower lip quivering, Terskoff hesitated for another two of those seconds, then whipped around and plunged into the East Room.

Precisely eighteen seconds later, the President heard his name announced and made his entrance.

The Murrow Room at the NPC Building was packed with newsies. Like some huge, self-replicating organism, the Washington press corps had divided between two fronts of a battle that it hoped was about to reach a roaring public climax, with the President and Roger Gordian hurling verbal thunderbolts across Pennsylvania Avenue. They wanted banner headlines, they wanted dramatic sound and video bites, they wanted to keep the legion of attorneys and ex-politicos who had been reborn as television commentators regularly bickering through the next ratings sweeps period. They wanted bombs bursting in air, and Gordian was a little intimidated by their expectation— probably because he knew there wasn't much chance of reaching the level to which the bar had been elevated. A lifetime of conducting one's affairs with businesslike restraint scarcely prepared a man to generate oratorical hellfire.

In the end, though, it didn't matter to him whether they were disappointed. Nor would it have been devastating had none of them showed up, leaving his electronically amplified words to float unheard above a roomful of empty chairs. He had come to make his stand, and win or lose, that was ultimately the best anyone could do.

Mounting the podium, he waited for a long moment, Chuck Kirby, Megan Breen, Vince Scull, and Alex Nordstrum behind him on the right, Dan Parker, Richard Sobel, and FBI Director Robert Lang on his left.

"Ladies and gentleman of the press, thank you for coming today," he finally said. "Right now, only a few short blocks away from here, the Morrison-Fiore cryptographic deregulation bill is being signed into law. I don't know what personal feelings any of you may have about it, but for the past several months I have tried to make mine clear. My opposition to the decontrol of cryptographic hardware and software remains firm and uncompromising. Still, there seems to be some confusion about my views, and that is at least fifty percent of the reason I am addressing you today."

Gordian paused, adjusted his microphone.

"I know a little about technology and its importance as a binding and unifying global force," he continued. "I believe that knowledge is freedom, and information the core and cornerstone of knowledge. I have tried with my communications network to break down the barriers that keep people around the world in darkness and tyranny. And I am extremely proud of my successes.

"But the reality is that America has its enemies. We would be mistaken to confuse the globalization of advanced technology with the abdication of our rights and imperatives as a sovereign nation, and I believe Morrison-Fiore is a disturbing step along that road. My critics, on the other hand, argue that I am vainly trying to put the genie back in the bottle by advocating we control encryption technology as we might any other powerful tool.

They argue that because cryptographic software may be smuggled across the transparent borders of cyberspace with relative ease, we ought to pretend those borders do not exist, rather than better define and regulate them. That because we acknowledge the inadequacies and inconsistencies of current laws, and the real and great obstacles to applying them across *territorial* borders, we should abandon them altogether rather than work toward bringing them into greater harmony.

"This sort of thinking admittedly baffles me. Are we to cease attempting to check electronic piracy only because it may be difficult to do so? Refuse to engage a problem only because it may be daunting? If that's to be the case, where do we draw the line? Should we next allow arms and narcotics to flow unchecked between nations? This is no strained comparison. International criminals and practitioners of violence already know encryption technology can afford them a formidable advantage over law enforcement, a new and sophisticated layer of secrecy by which their activities can be concealed. They know it, and they are fast learning how to capitalize on that knowledge.

"I assure you, when we concede an advantage to crime and criminals, we do worse than allow the disintegration of legal boundaries. We risk the disintegration of our will as a civilization. And that, ladies and gentlemen, frightens me more than anything as an individual. . . ."

Nordstrum skimmed his eyes over the crowd of reporters. He thought Gord was doing superbly, and although his notoriously jaded colleagues were a tough bunch to read, and there were very few nodding heads, they at least seemed inclined to listen . . . which was really the critical thing today. Gordian needed their agreement much less than their interest. That translated into coverage, whereas boredom meant obscurity in the back pages.

Nordstrum was only disappointed that he'd forgotten to convey Craig Weston's message to Gordian. *It's not the locks, it's the keys,* he'd said, obviously alluding to the proprietary codes which were used to access, or rather, non-technically speaking, "descramble," data that had been encrypted. The problem of their safe storage was an aspect of the issue that certainly might have borne a touch more emphasis in Gordian's statement, and Nordstrum had fully intended to suggest that to him. But somewhere in the process of meeting Gord and the others at their hotel, and hearing about the near-calamity that had occurred when they'd been landing at Dulles, it had slipped his mind.

Well, perhaps he'd be able to prompt Gord to address the subject during the journalistic grilling—politely known as a Q and A session—that would follow his prepared comments. In fact, that might be the best time for him to do so, since Gordian would likely need a respite from the inevitable bombardment of questions about the Monolith bid, and the surprise announcement he was going to make on that track.

Reminding himself all over again of the hell he would catch at the gym if he failed to keep his promise to the admiral, Nordstrum turned his full attention back to the press conference.

Sitting aboard the monorail as it ran a smooth, circular course around the high-tech theme parks, man-made beaches, and other bustling tourist attractions of Sentosa Island, Omori peered through his binoculars and watched the boosted fleet of naval patrol boats maneuvering in the waters off Singapore's coastline. Their presence had become increasingly noticeable over the past few days, entire squadrons assembling in advance of the Seawolf's run. Security in the city itself was likewise tighter than Omori had ever seen it; walking from the train station to the ferry terminal, he often had been forced to detour around police barricades along the motorcade routes to be taken by arriving dignitaries. Indeed, the Malaysian Prime Minister was already in town, having come a day ahead of his counterparts from Indonesia and America to visit with the governor of Pulau Ubin, with whom he shared close personal ties.

The mission that had brought Omori from Tokyo also reflected long-standing ties . . . to the Inagawa-kai syndicate of which he was a high-placed *kuromaku,* or power broker; to Nga Canbera; to the politicians within the Diet whose opposition to SEAPAC had brought them into alliance with a broad group of foreign and domestic interests, all of which had pledged to make the treaty come undone, and bring about the humiliation and downfall of its internationalist sponsors.

Omori felt a jostling against his right arm now, lowered his glasses, and looked over at the little boy in the seat beside him. He was shifting restlessly about, repeatedly asking his mother when they would reach the Entertainment Mall. Omori frowned, and patted the child's shoulder to gain his attention.

"You should be patient and behave for your mommy," he said. " She is very good to bring you here and cannot make us go any faster."

The boy fell still, looked at him in the wide-eyed, anxious way children did when scolded by strangers, and then looked up at his mother.

Omori glanced at her and smiled in commiseration. The boy was a cute and precocious one, like his own son of about the same age. Omori prayed he would live to see his wife and family again. Children were his truest joy.

He turned back to the window, raised the goggles to his eyes, and continued looking out at the harbor. The number of vessels in the patrols had no meaning to him. Let them bring in the entire Navy if they wished. A small team of men, properly equipped and striking with accuracy, could penetrate any massive line of defense.

Tonight, after he'd finished reconaissance and freshened up a bit, he would meet with the members of the insertion party and review their final preparations. Then there would be nothing to do but await word to proceed, and check his E-mail for a critical file from Nga.

For the moment, however, Omori would relax and enjoy his ride. He hoped the world leaders aboard the Seawolf would enjoy theirs as well.

"In conclusion, I'd like to return for a moment to the example of the genie. Would I like it put back in the magic lamp, the lamp itself sealed away from the eyes, the very *awareness,* of man? My life's work is evidence to the contrary. As I interpret the story, it wasn't the genie's power to work wonders that heaped so much pain and trouble upon poor Aladdin. The cause, I think, was Aladdin's lack of judgment about how to use his gift, a failure to understand the exceeding degree of caution and restraint with which it needed to be managed. Power itself is never to be feared. Its uses are determined by the hands into which it falls. With passion and intelligence anything is truly possible.

"But as evolving technologies create new possibilities for us, as in a sense we use science to work magic, our eternal responsibility is to choose those uses which will build rather than destroy, liberate rather than imprison, bring gain rather than loss upon us as a species. It's a responsibility that hasn't changed in essence since the discovery of fire or the wheel, although as the tools become more complex, so do our choices. Mistakes are inevitable, but I hope and believe we will learn from them, and be wise enough to correct those we can. If so, then you can take my word for it . . . the genie belongs among us. And he's in the very best of hands."

Gordian pushed aside his written notes, and sipped from the glass of water on the lectern. *Not too shoddy,* he thought. It didn't bother him that the applause was merely polite. Rushed, even. The main thing was that he believed his delivery had been okay, and that his comments had a pretty good chance of penetrating the sieve of the media and getting out to the public.

He took a deep breath, drank some more water, and leaned toward the mike again.

"At this point, I'd be glad to take some questions," he said.

A clattering commotion as three quarters of the room sprang off their chairs.

Gordian pointed to the guy in the first row with the famous Website.

"Mr. Gordian, we were informed you would be making a significant announcement on the corporate front," he said. "And though you did not address the issue in your speech to us, I'm wondering if there's anything you can reveal about your future as chairman of UpLink International.''

Gordian looked at him with genuine surprise.

Damned if he hadn't nearly forgotten in all the excitement.

''Oh, yes,'' he said. ''Now that you remind me, there certainly is.''

The East Room erupted into noisy, enthusiastic applause the instant the President hastily and perfunctorily put his signature on the last page of Morrison-Fiore, no longer a bill now, but law of the land. Congratulations flew. The Senate whips clasped hands. The Speaker of the House and his rival from the minority party embraced in bipartison triumph. The Veep posed for photographs, basking in his Commander in Chief's reflected light, hoping it would enhance his own glimmer when his turn to seek his party's nod for the Presidency came about in two years or so.

Disgusted, President Ballard wanted to get to sleep.

He had a long flight to Singapore ahead of him in the morning, and then a historic ride on a submarine that it looked like nobody on the planet was going to notice.

''. . . and Mr. Sobel will acquire the firms comprising UpLink's entire computer products division, including Stronghold Security Systems, our cryptographic hardware and software subsidiary. As someone who has known and worked with Richard for over a decade, I have confidence my corporate children will attain impressive and unprecedented levels of success.''

Gordian pointed to one of the upraised hands in front of him.

"The young lady from the *Wall Street Journal,*" he said. "Ms. Sheffield, is it?"

She nodded and stood. "Sir, with all due respect, how will that growth be possible as long as Mr. Sobel preserves your restrictions on crypto export? Many industry analysts disagree with your contention that a cryptographic firm can focus primarily on the domestic market and remain profitable. Or will those policies be relaxed after the sale?"

Richard suddenly stepped up to share the podium.

"With our host's permission, I'm going to answer that myself," Sobel said. "I can unequivocally state that I support Roger Gordian on the encryption issue and will carry on his present policies to the letter. Success is all in how you approach the marketplace, and my electronics firm is existing proof that the analysts you mention are wrong. Our net profits have increased every year for the past five years. We have grown slowly by intention and built a solid reputation designing latchkey systems for corporate clients . . . using many of Roger Gordian's cryptographic products. As a service-and-support-oriented company, we believe Roger Gordian's superior data-encoding systems will both attract new clients, and present limitless advantages to our existing ones."

Sheffield asked Richard a brief follow-up about his specific last-quarter earnings, and then it was Gordian's turn again. Before taking the mike, though, he tapped Richard on the elbow, leaned close, and whispered for him to stay put, figuring they were certain to have the chance to drop their final bombshell before too long.

"What sort of reaction has the breakup proposal generated from your board?" a reporter asked.

"I've spoken over the telephone with everyone on it,

and can tell you my plan has been welcomed with almost complete unanimity,'' Gordian said. ''I foresee no problem obtaining the board's endorsement when we convene sometime next week.''

Another reporter. ''Your computer division aside, there are a number of subsidiaries in UpLink's medical and automotive branches which you've said will also be up for sale . . . and which have yet to find buyers. How do you expect your shareholders react to these, ah, forced separations?''

''Very positively, I hope,'' Gordian said. ''The spun-off entities remain under skilled and imaginative management, people who will be able to implement their ideas with greater freedom than ever outside the pressure of a large corporate bureaucracy. And while it would be unrealistic for me to expect full confidence from our shareholders at the onset, I think most will be initially reassured by the package of financial bonuses we're preparing, and eventually become true believers. We're dedicated to our investors and guarantee their concerns will be addressed.''

A half-dozen more wearisome questions, most regarding the technical aspects of the breakup. What sort of financial bonuses? Will you be retaining any stock in the divested companies? If so, what percentage is to be floated to shareholders?

Question Number Seven was the charm, fired at him courtesy of someone from *Business Week*:

''Mr. Gordian, how will your plans be effected should the Spartus Consortium finalize the sale of their stake in UpLink, which amounts to fully one fifth of the company—an *enormous* minority holding—to Marcus Caine, who we all know hasn't been over to your home for dinner lately?''

It was a setup Richard couldn't resist.

"As part of our overall deal, UpLink will be placing an equal portion of its stock in my hands," he said, stepping in seamlessly. "If Marcus Caine wants to make himself an uninvited guest at the table, he'll have to sit across from Roger Gordian and myself from now on, look us both squarely in the eye, and learn it isn't an all-you-can-eat. And let me tell you, people, if Caine tries grabbing anything from *my* plate, he'd damned well better watch out for my fork."

A beat of surprised silence from the audience, and then laughter over Richard's quip.

A great, rising swell of laughter.

Gordian looked out at the room, and was embarrassed by the realization that he was grinning himself.

But not *too* embarrassed.

Boom, he thought. *Bombshell delivered.*

And dead-on in the crosshairs, no less.

In his office watching C-SPAN, Caine lowered the croissant he'd been eating to his desk, then glanced circumspectly over at his secretary. When Deborah had come in with his coffee and pastries, he'd asked her to stay and take notes regarding the press conference, and she was now sitting on the sofa with her laptop, typing, her gaze fixed on the screen. Perhaps too intently. She'd passed a hand across her mouth a moment ago, briefly shielding it from sight. Had she found Sobel's remarks amusing? he wondered. He would have liked to tear out her throat just on the suspicion. If his belief ever hardened into surety, she could look forward to her walking papers. He would see that she never set foot in an office again, not as an employee.

Caine felt his stomach burning savagely. It was as if he were on fire inside.

Those bastards, he thought incredulously. Those bastards. They should have been dead. Killed when Gordian tried to land that plane. The people he'd sent to work on it had *assured* him they would be. But somehow . . . somehow nothing had happened to them. And instead—

Instead . . .

He had to credit Gordian's resourcefulness. By segmenting off entire divisions of UpLink, he would almost certainly gain the capital to dispose of his outstanding debts. By parting with the cryptographic operation, he had eliminated the greatest cause of his shareholders' dissatisfaction, and no doubt raised the price of UpLink stock to its highest level in years. And by handing Sobel a chunk of the core outfit—making him White Knight and Squire all in one—he had forged an alliance that would decisively give him control of the company just when it had been within Caine's grasp. In order to overthrow that alliance, or even mitigate its control, Caine—or any buyer of voting stock—would now need to acquire an improbable and newly expensive number of shares.

A terrible, nauseous crashing sensation added itself to the pain tearing at Caine's gut, and he was suddenly afraid he might be sick. Even knowing what he'd set in motion at Gordian's data-storage facility tonight didn't help. Nga and his confederates would get what they wanted . . . but he . . .

Think it, an inner voice insisted. *At least have the courage to think it.*

No. No. No.

His hand shaking, he lifted the plate of croissants off his desk, slipped it into his wastebasket, and stared at the television screen in an agony of his own hatred.

No.

He would not, could not concede that he was beaten.

TWENTY-THREE

"—ELLO, MAX? MAX, IT'S KIRSTEN. CALL ME ON MY mobile soon as you can."

"Max, this is Kirsten again. Still waiting to hear from you."

"Hello, Max? Same message as before."

"Max, where are you? It's been four days and I'm getting really concerned. My sister and her husband are telling me to call the police, and maybe they're right. This is all so confusing for me. So please, if you hear this, get in touch."

"Max, I've decided to do what Anna wants and contact the authorities—"

Nimec clicked off the answering machine and looked at Nori in silence.

Though it was still not yet full morning in Johor, and both were running on empty, they were in Blackburn's spare, single-room living quarters at the ground station, having decided to check it out for clues to his whereabouts before heading off to bed. There had been nothing to help them on that score, but Kirsten Chu's frequent and increasingly worried messages—the most recent of which had been left two days earlier according to the machine's time/date stamp—at least revealed that *she* had not completely vanished from the face of the earth as well. And while the messages also seemed to confirm Nimec's feeling that Max had gotten into some kind of serious fix, they ultimately engendered more questions than they answered.

"Sounds like she's staying with her sister," Nori said after a while.

"Hiding out's more like it," Nimec said. "You catch the sister's name or do I have to run through the tape again?"

"Anna," Nori said. "No second name, though. And Kirsten mentioned there being a husband, so it'd be a different surname from her own. Makes it harder to track her down."

"A lot of married women keep their family names these days."

Nori shook her head.

"You're thinking like an American," she said. "Asian societies aren't quite so liberated."

Nimec sighed.

"Why the hell would she ask Max to call on her cell phone?" he said. "Wouldn't it have been simpler to just leave *Anna's* number for him?"

Nori thought about that a moment.

"Simpler for us, absolutely, but her situation's another matter," she said. "Put yourself in Kirsten's shoes. Whatever she's been into with Blackburn, it's something her family's probably better off not being enlightened about."

"For their own safety, you mean."

"Right," Nori said. "The less they know the better. Also, it sounds to me like Max would have been against Kirsten calling the authorities to report whatever happened—"

"Or at least *she* feels that way," Nimec said. "We can figure out why later, but go on, I didn't mean to interrupt."

"My point is that she seemed to be under pressure from her family to make the call, and would've been torn in two different directions about actually doing it. Could be the sister and her husband had misgivings about Blackburn . . . why wouldn't they, when you consider the whole situation? If you're Kirsten, you're going to feel uncomfortable about having him get in touch with you on their home phone, maybe kicking off a round of difficult questions from Sis. The other way's a lot more private."

"Except, as you've already indicated, it stinks as far as we're concerned," Nimec said. "Joyce has numbers for Kirsten's home and business phones, but not the cellular."

"No address?"

"Besides her office at Monolith, no."

"What about Max's notes on his investigation? The ones he gave to Joyce?"

"I didn't even know they existed until yesterday, when I called to tell her I'd be coming to Johor. They're encoded on his PIM, and it'll take some time to decrypt and go through them."

She nodded, thinking. "I assume we want to steer clear of the badges."

"For the time being, yes. Not that we even can be sure she's phoned them. Or, if she has, that she's told them where she's staying."

"It's even an open question *which* police force she'd call," Nori added. "Her sister could live on either side of the causeway. Or elsewhere. National borders are close in this neck of the woods."

"True enough, but we do we know *Kirsten* lives in Singapore. If we're lucky, she'll be listed in the public telephone directory. And that might give us the info we need."

"Maybe, maybe not," Nori said. "Most young, single women leave their addresses out of the listings. It's standard protection against sickos."

"Now *you're* the one thinking like an American . . . and a New Yorker at that," Nimec said with a wan smile. "Singapore isn't the kind of place where there's going to be a problem with obscene phone callers. If she's in the book, we'll likely find out where she lives. . . ."

"And the next step would be to get in there and look around for something with Sis's address written on it," Nori said, completing his thought.

Nimec nodded agreement.

"I hate to risk breaking and entering," he said. "But if we have no better alternative . . ."

Nori wobbled her hand in the air to interrupt him, then gestured to the key he was holding, a spare they had obtained from Station Security to gain access to Blackburn's room.

"Leave that part to me," she said.

It was a little past four in the afternoon when the two men in the Olds Cutlass drove up to the entry gate of the UpLink Cryptographics facility in Sacramento, slowing to a halt as they reached the guard station.

"Detective Steve Lombardi," the driver told the guard through his open window. He tilted his head toward the man in the passenger seat. "My partner here's Detective Craig Sanford."

The guard regarded them through his mirrored sunglasses.

"How can I help you?" he said.

"We need to speak to the supervisor in charge," Lombardi said. "We've got a subpoena for crypto keys, you know the deal."

The guard nodded. It was SOP for law enforcement to deliver court orders whenever there was an investigation or legal action involving the release of data-recovery keys used by UpLink software. With everybody from banks to supermarkets to Mafia hoods using crypto in their daily business operations nowadays, and thousands of keys stored in the data-recovery vaults, and all kinds of civil and criminal cases in which computerized files were requested as evidence, it wasn't unusual to get as many as four or five visits a week from police officers delivering subpoenas.

"Just need to see your ID and papers," he said.

The driver took the requested items out of his sport jacket and gave them to the guard. A moment later the passenger reached over and passed the leather case holding his own badge and identification through the window.

The guard angled his mirrored lenses down at what he'd been handed, glancing over the police tins, unfolding the court papers.

"Everything kosher?" the driver asked.

The guard studied the ID and paperwork another second, then nodded and returned them through the window of his booth.

"Go right on ahead, fellas," he said.

The doorman at the luxury condo near Holland Road, on the eastern part of Singapore Island, had scarcely arrived for his morning shift when he saw the pale blue taxi pull up near the entrance and discharge its passenger, a slight, nicely dressed young woman carrying a couple of over-stuffed travel bags. The luggage aside, she *looked* as though she'd been traveling, her hair slightly messed, a somewhat frayed expression on her face.

As she struggled toward the building with the bags, he set down his tea and rose from his desk to get the door.

"Can help?" he asked in typical Singlish fashion, blending English words with Chinese sentence structure.

She set the bags down on the carpeted floor of the vestibule and fussed her hair into place.

"Yes. Or I hope so, anyway," she said. "I'm here for Kirsten Chu."

The doorman regarded her a moment. Her American accent explained why he had not recognized her as an occupant of the high-rise. But he was familiar with the woman whose name she'd mentioned.

"Apartment Fifteen, I can call up, *lah*." He reached for the intercom's handpiece. "Your name, please?"

"No, you don't understand," she said. "Kirsten won't be home until tonight, and I was supposed to let myself in. But now I can't. . . ."

She let the sentence trail off.

"Yes?" he said.

"Maybe I'd better start over." She looked upset. "I'm her sister Charlene, and I'm here visiting from the States. Did she mention my name to you, by any chance?"

He shook his head.

"Well, I suppose there wouldn't have been any need. . . ." she muttered to herself, rubbing her forehead.

"Yes?" the doorman said again. He was becoming increasingly baffled.

When she looked up at him, her large brown eyes were moist.

"You see, I have a key to her door . . . well I *had* a key to her door . . . but I think I may have lost it at the airport. . . ."

"Yes?" he said for the third time, suddenly afraid she might burst into tears.

"Listen," she said agitatedly. "I don't quite know how to ask you this . . . it makes me feel so *foolish* . . . but could you let me into her apartment? I haven't any idea where else to wait for her . . . she went to pick up our other sister, Anna . . . and isn't supposed to be home until very *late,* you see . . . and I've got these *bags* . . ."

He gave her an uncomfortable look. "That against rules, miss. Okay if you want leave bags with me, but I not can—"

"Please, I'll show my passport if you need identification," she said at once, her voice trembling. She crouched over the bags she'd deposited on the vestibule's carpet, unzipped one of them, and began fumbling around inside it.

"Miss—"

The doorman cut himself short. Just as he'd feared, she had begun to sob. Tears spilling down her face, she bent there in front of him, pulling items out of the bag, dropping some of them in her distress, stuffing them hastily back into the bag and fishing out others. . . .

"Wait, wait, my papers are in here *somewhere* . . . I'm so sorry . . . I just have to find them. . . ."

The doorman looked at her, feeling sorry for her, thinking he couldn't just stand there and watch her cry.

"It okay, miss. It okay," he said finally, reaching for

the intercom button. "I call superintendent, tell him let you in, no problem."

Noriko stood and wiped a hand across her eyes.

"Thanks, that's so kind," she said, sniffling. "Really, I don't know what I'd've done without you."

The driveway leading up to the encryption facility terminated in a parking area outside the main entrance, the left side of which was reserved for staff, the right for visitors. The men in the Cutlass swung into the visitors' section, found an empty slot, strode across the lot toward the flat cinder-block building, and approached the armed guard posted at the door.

"Detectives Lombardi and Samford?" he said, smiling pleasantly.

They both nodded.

"I was informed you gentlemen were on your way from the gate," he said, and gestured toward the walk-through weapons-detector beside his station. "If you'd please leave your service weapons with me, and place any other metal articles you may have in the tray to your right, you can step through the scanners and come in."

"We're cops, and cops carry guns," the man who'd announced himself as Lombardi said. "It's in our regulations."

"Yes, and I apologize for the inconvenience. But a facility of this nature has to take added precautions, and most departments cooperate with them," the security man said. "If you'd prefer, I can call ahead to Mr. Turner . . . he's the supervisor you're going to see anyway . . . and request that he waive the requirement. I'm sure it wouldn't be much of a problem."

Lombardi shrugged.

"No need," he said. "Policy's policy."

The two men unholstered their firearms—both were carrying standard Glock nines—and turned them over to the guard, then deposited their coins and key chains in the tray and passed through the archway.

"Thanks for your cooperation," the guard said. He looked at his LCD display, gave the items in the tray a cursory glance, then held it out for the detectives to retrieve their property. "Follow the entry hall straight back, turn right, then cut another right at the end of that corridor. Supervisor's office will be the fourth door down. I'll have your weapons right here when you leave."

Lombardi stuffed his key chain into his pocket.

"Just hope we don't have to chase any armed robbers while we're here," he said, smiling a little.

The guard laughed. "Have no fear," he said. "This place is as safe as they come."

Nori slipped into the rear of the white company Land Rover parked in a shopping mall off Holland Road, three blocks up from Kirsten Chu's residence.

"Found what we wanted," she said. "And more."

"Any problems getting in and out?" Nimec asked from the front passenger seat.

"Nope. The doorman has a crush on me. He talked the super into giving me a key," she said. "Anyway, I've got a personal phone book with a number and address for a Lin and Anna Lung in Petaling Jaya."

"Where the hell's that?"

"Back over the causeway, *lah*. Outside KL." This from the driver, a Malay named Osmar Ali who was with the Sword detail at the ground station.

Nimec nodded.

"You sure you have the right party?" he asked Noriko.

"Pretty much," she said. "I also dug up an open mailing envelope with a return address that matches the one in the book. There were some photos of a couple and two kids inside it. And a letter starts with a 'Dear Sis.' "

"Okay." Nimec turned to look at Osmar. "Petaling Jaya . . . is it within driving distance?"

Osmar shrugged. "Can go, yes, but it a few hundred kilometers," he said in rough English. "Be faster we drive back to ground station, take helicopter."

Nimec thought in silence a moment. Then he reached for the cell phone resting in the molded-plastic cup-holder beside him.

"Better let me have that number, Nori," he said. "I want to see if anybody's home before we come knocking on their door."

The pair of men strode through the corridor after leaving their guns at the checkpoint, their eyes noting the button-sized lenses of surveillance cameras near the ceiling. Unlike commercially produced cameras, these miniature units were recessed behind the walls rather than mounted on visible brackets, and would have gone unnoticed by the average person.

They reached the T-juncture at the end of the hall, but instead of immediately turning right as instructed, paused to scan the doorways in both directions.

Midway down the corridor branching to their left was an office door marked SECURITY. The one who called himself Lombardi gave the other an almost imperceptible glance and they went over to it, walking side-by-side at an easy pace, nodding amiably to a woman who passed them going the opposite way.

Two plainclothes security men were sitting at a bank of closed-circuit monitors when the office door opened inward from the corridor. They were not surprised, having seen the approaching detectives on their screens, and assumed they wanted information.

"Can we help you gentlemen?" one of them said, swiveling to face the door.

The man called Lombardi entered, followed by his partner. They let the door close behind them.

"We're looking for the supervisor's office." He smiled, his hand casually tucked in his pants pocket. "Thought it was supposed to be right around here somewhere."

"Took a wrong turn," the security man said. "When you leave this office, hang a right and—"

Lombardi's hand came out of his pocket holding his key ring. Before the security guards could register what was happening, he brought up its rectangular fob and quickly tugged back the attached chain with his free hand. This cocked the firing mechanism of the weapon, which was only three inches long and contained two .32-caliber bullets. He pointed it at the man facing him and pushed a button on its side.

The slug that coughed from the tiny gun's bore would have been lethal at twenty yards, and the shooter was a mere fraction of that distance from his target. It struck the guard in the middle of the forehead and killed him instantly, slamming him back into the panel of monitors.

The shooter pivoted toward the other guard. His face white with shock, he was reaching for the holstered weapon under his jacket. The shooter pushed the button and fired his second shot, striking the guard in the center of his face. And then the face was gone. The body sprawled backward, blood, bone fragments, and tissue spraying the screens and walls behind him.

The shooter looked at his partner, gesturing toward the dead men.

"Close," he said. "I only expected there to be one of them."

The man near the door nodded.

"Let's take their guns and get on with it," the shooter said.

When she heard the phone ring at nine-thirty, she wondered if perhaps Anna had forgotten something in her rush to leave the house. The kids had acted up and been late getting ready for school, and Anna, who dropped them off every morning on her way to work, had made her exit amid quite a hustle and bustle.

"Hello?" she said, picking up.

A strange male voice. "Kirsten Chu, please."

She hesitated, her heart suddenly banging in her chest. She'd been expecting a call from the police, which was the reason she hadn't volunteered to help out her sister and deliver Miri and Brian to their classrooms herself. The police, this had to be the police. Anna and Lin . . . and Max, of course . . . were the only other people who'd know to find her here. And the person at the other end wasn't any of the latter.

"Who's calling?" she asked in a cautious tone. Purposely offering no acknowledgment of her identity.

"My name is Pete Nimec, and I'm—"

She didn't even hear him finish the sentence, so completely overwhelming was the recognition that swept over her. Her heart beat harder, faster. She inhaled, feeling as if the breath had been knocked out of her.

"Dear God, that's the *name*," she said, the words springing from her mouth on their own. "You're Max's friend, aren't you? The one he wanted me to call?"

A beat of silence. "Yes, I am. I—"

"How is he?" she interrupted. Worry had swept chillingly through Kirsten's initial excitement. If Max were all right, why wouldn't *he* be calling?

"Kirsten, we need to meet. I have to speak with you in person, find out what's happened to him. To both of you."

"You mean you don't know. . . ."

"No, Kirsten. I don't. No one's heard from him."

She clutched the phone, her hand shaking around it. Her entire *arm* shaking.

"Then how . . . how did you get this number?"

"I'll explain all that later. I promise. Right now it's just urgent that we get together. I'll come to you there. It's probably best if you stay put."

Kirsten breathed.

What reason was there to trust this man? This name Max had mentioned once in a moment of urgency? This *voice?* The truth was that she hardly even knew whether *Max* was the person he'd seemed to be. . . .

Except that wasn't true. She *did* know. Maybe not everything about him. Maybe not as much as she should have known. But as she'd told Anna just days ago, she loved him. . . .

Had loved him long before he'd put his own life at risk to save her . . .

And what was love, always, always, but a leap of faith?

"All right," she said. "I'll be waiting."

• • •

The supervisor at the encryption facility—the name plaque on his office door read Charles Turner—was shaking his head as he pored over the court papers he'd been issued.

"I must tell you, this is rather atypical," he said, glancing up at the two detectives standing before his desk.

"How so, sir? I checked the subpoenas myself to make sure they crossed all the t's."

"No, please, don't misunderstand me," Turner said. "The papers are fine. But normally I get advance notification from the officers coming for the codes. They're stored on compact disc in our vaults, you understand, and there's a rather stringent checkout process. Going through it at the last minute, well, I'll have to drop everything, Detective Lombardi. . . ."

"We're really sorry for the inconvenience," the man standing in front of him said. "But this is our first time dealing with a matter of this type as officers."

Turner sighed and rose from his desk, looking annoyed and somewhat flustered.

"You may accompany me to the data-storage wing, though only authorized personnel are allowed in the vaults. You'll have to stay out in one of the waiting areas while I track the disk you want."

"Will it take very long?"

"It shouldn't," Turner said. "The corporation whose key-codes are being requested isn't one I recognize offhand, but the disks are catalogued on our electronic database. I can rush everything through in half an hour, maybe a little faster."

"That'd be fine with us."

Turner *harrumphed,* and came around the desk toward the door.

"Lead the way, sir," the detective said, falling in behind him.

The men had left Penang State, southeast of the Malaysia-Thailand border, shortly after they'd received the call from Luan. That had been some hours ago, at dawn, and they'd been driving their van down the main coastal highways to Selangor ever since. The trip would have been lengthy under the best of traffic conditions, but there were herds of beachgoing tourists jamming the roads near the bridge and ferry terminals to Georgetown, and the delays had stretched miserably in the hot, beating sun. The men in the van had, furthermore, wanted to keep a moderate speed so as not to risk being pulled over by police. The kris tattoos on their hands would bring about an instant search, and once that happened their problems only would be starting. If the police found their weapons, they could look forward to many hours of painful interrogation, followed by many years of being locked away in prison holes. And that would be a far cry from the reward they were expecting for the successful completion of their task.

The Thai had promised them a fortune.

A fortune in greenbacks for capturing a woman and delivering her to him in Kalimantan.

They had joked crudely about her physical attributes when they received the call. And in spite of their grindingly slow progress, it would not be long before they saw the object of Luan's desire for themselves. They were already better than halfway down through Perak, and would be crossing into Selangor within a couple of hours.

With luck, Kirsten Chu would be at the address they had been given. And if not, they would gladly wait there for her to arrive.

She was, after all, one woman who was very much worth it.

TWENTY-FOUR

"Is there some kind of problem, Mr. Turner?" the man calling himself Lombardi asked from where he sat in the waiting area.

Holding the court papers, a puzzled expression on his face, Turner glanced at him as he returned through a doorway he'd entered just moments ago.

"The name of the corporation simply doesn't show on our database," he said, approaching his chair. "I don't know what to make of it."

Lombardi rose and sidled up to him, studying the papers over his shoulder.

"I'm no expert at this high-tech stuff, but could be it's just misspelled," he said.

Turner shook his head. "The computers will essentially correct for that sort of error by searching for approximate matches. In this case, nothing came up."

Lombardi grinned.

"Then I guess those papers are fake and the company doesn't exist," he said.

Turner looked at him. "I don't understand. . . ."

Lombardi reached under his jacket and drew the Beretta he'd taken from one of the murdered security guards.

"Oh, I think you do," he said, and rammed the handle

of the weapon upward into Turner's nose, shattering his septum and sending tiny slivers of bone into his brain. Turner dropped instantly to the floor, his eyes rolling up in their sockets, dark blood spouting from his nostrils. He spasmed twice, emitted a labored gurgling sound, and died.

Lombardi gestured to the other man as he got up off his seat. Then both went around the body and passed through the entry to the vault area.

A short while before the ringing of the doorbell startled her into alertness, Kirsten had slipped into a doze on the sofa, a kind of syrupy exhaustion having settled over her in the late morning, and stayed with her as she'd done some routine chores—washing the breakfast dishes, straightening up the living room, and gathering the kids' toys from around the apartment and garden and hauling them back into their bedroom closet.

Afterward, sitting down to listen to some light jazz on the stereo, hoping it would calm her mind, she had been surprised at how fast her eyelids had started getting heavy, and thought it quite incredible that she could be simultaneously clipping along full-steam on nervous energy and feeling so mentally fatigued that her brain almost seemed immersed in a pool of thick, lukewarm glue. It was a little like the way she'd felt as a university student studying for final exams, living for days and nights on coffee and chocolate . . . only many times more intense.

And now the sound of the buzzer had practically sent her bouncing off the couch, still half out of it, yet conscious of her nerves revving up to speed again.

She glanced at the clock on the wall opposite her. Could Nimec have arrived already? Under average circumstances it would have been highly unlikely he could have made it in so short a time . . . but he'd explained that he would be returning to the UpLink ground station in Johor, and would probably travel from there into KL by helicopter. Which had also told her a couple of things about him beyond the obvious fact that he was in a hurry. One, he was at least as concerned about Max as she was. And two, he had the sort of clout with Max's boss to pull some major strings, maybe even worked for UpLink himself—

Bzzzzzzzzz!

She crossed the room to the door, straightening her blouse, smoothing her skirt down with her hands. Whoever was out there was really leaning on the bell.

"Yes?" she said, reaching for the doorknob. "Who is it?"

"Johor police," a man said from outside. He was speaking Bahasa. "We want to see Kirsten Chu."

"Excuse me?" she replied in the same language. The blunt, gruff quality of his voice had surprised her as much as his response.

"It's about her call," he said. "We need to ask her some questions."

Kirsten didn't move, hardly even breathed. She was still holding the knob, her fingers suddenly sweating around it.

The Singapore cop with whom she'd spoken had said the Johor authorities would be in touch . . . but she hadn't expected them to just show up at the door. Wouldn't they want to phone and make an appointment, if for no other reason than to spare themselves a needless trip in case she wasn't home?

And does he really sound like a police officer? she thought.

Her pulse fluttering in her temples, she raised the spyhole cover, peered outside. . . .

And felt her stomach turn to ice.

Never mind how he'd sounded, none of the men standing in the walk outside—she could see four or five of them through the little two-way mirror—looked anything *like* police investigators. Their hair was long, their clothes sloppy, and their eyes . . .

Even had they been wearing bright silver badges and starched blue uniforms, their eyes would have given them away.

"Come on," the one nearest the door said. "Open up."

She pulled away from the spyhole and inhaled shakily.

"Just a minute," she said. "I need to put something on."

The man slammed the door with his forearm.

"Forget the games," he said. "Open it."

Her fingers harrowing her cheeks, Kirsten took a step backward across the living room.

"Open up!" the man said, beating the door again, hitting it so hard she was afraid it might fly off its hinges.

Terrified, her breaths coming in sharp little bursts, Kirsten whirled and plunged through the apartment.

An instant later the door crashed open behind her.

The entryway through which the intruders had left the waiting room led to a short passage, which itself gave into another small, boxy room that was bare except for a computer workstation on the right, and a wall-mounted biometric scanner across from it beside a reinforced steel door.

"Lombardi" went straight over to the scanner. This was the part of the job that made him uptight. He'd been telling Turner the truth when he remarked that he was no technical wizard, and felt it would have been easy enough to steer the supervisor back into the room at gunpoint, force him to let the system take his readings, and in that way gain access to the vault. But the concern was that Turner might have triggered some discreet alarm had that been done. Caine's instructions had been explicit, and they'd been warned not to deviate from them under any circumstances.

Standing before the scanning unit, Lombardi raised his left hand to the level of the cameras designed to image his facial and iris characteristics, turning it so the artificial star-sapphire ring on his fourth finger would be visible to their lenses. Then, keeping that hand perfectly motionless, he placed his right hand flat on the machine's glass op-toelectrical pad. Ordinarily this would both activate the unit and take readings of his fingerprint and palm geometry, which would then be converted to algorithms and matched to stored employee-identification data. But by an arcane process he did not quite understand, the specific star pattern on his ring would key a match with a simple data-string buried in the system mainframe's hard drive, which caused—or, according to Caine, was supposed to cause—the normal image-recognition sequence to be bypassed.

Lombardi held his breath and waited, one hand up, the other on the unit's clear glass interface, staring at its eye-level VDU. A red light had begun to glow beneath the glass, indicating the scanner had been activated by his touch . . . but if all was going as planned, the readings of its thermal sensors would be ignored by the computers.

Five seconds went by.

Ten.

He waited.

And then the words CLEARED TO ENTER appeared in the middle of the screen.

He exhaled, heard the faint click of the vault's lock mechanism retracting, and turned to his partner, who was already working open the heavy steel door.

They were in.

Kirsten ran toward the back of the apartment, hearing the door burst open behind her, hearing the men who'd been outside come pounding through the living room at her heels. She had only a vague notion of what to do, but it was *all* she had, and there was no choice except to go with it. If she could make it to the back door before they caught up, get into the building's central parking court, then maybe—

Suddenly a hand reached out from behind and snatched the sleeve of her blouse, pulling at her, yanking her backward. She stumbled, and almost lost her balance, but somehow managed to keep her legs underneath her, keep *moving,* carried by her own forward momentum. She twisted sharply as her pursuer tried to get his other hand around her, heard a loud ripping sound, and then was free of his grasp, racing across the room again, scrambling toward the door, a ragged streamer of cotton dangling from her arm.

"Hey!" he shouted. *"Stop, you bitch!"*

Kirsten was within several feet of the back door now, the kitchen on her immediate right, the hallway leading to the bedrooms on her left. She lunged ahead, shooting her hand out in front of her, reaching for the doorknob, thinking she might make it, thinking she really might, when the man whose grip she'd managed to escape a moment earlier sprang at her in a flying tackle, the full weight of his body whumping into her, his arms clamping around her waist.

He spun Kirsten around and swept her in toward his chest, trying to get a firmer hold on her. Frantic, she snatched a glance past his shoulder, saw his companions rushing up through the living room, and thrust her hands out at his face, clawing at him, digging her fingers into his eyes.

That bought her a momentary reprieve. Emitting an animal yelp of pain, her attacker shoved fiercely away from her and covered his face with his hands, spinning in a blind semicircle, bowling wildly into the men behind him. At the same time, Kirsten flung herself at the door, clutched the knob, and tore it open.

Gasping for breath, a gale wind of terror and desperation roaring through her brain, she dashed out into the automobile court.

When the white-smocked techie first opened the door to the security office, the coffee she brought the guys every day at the same time balanced on a cafeteria tray in one hand, she simply couldn't credit her eyes. She stood there in the doorway, looking at the bodies and the blood streaming from the unrecognizable remains of their heads, the blood spattered everywhere in the room, the blood and strings of gristle covering the monitors on which closed-circuit images of the halls were still flashing through their preset sequences as if nothing eventful had occurred to disrupt the daily routine, and then suddenly the world went into a crazy tilt and the two coffee cups spilled from the tray and hit the floor where there was all that blood and gore and she opened her mouth wide and screamed, screamed at the top of her lungs. . . .

Screamed until long after half the people in the building had come running toward the office to see what in the name of God and his blessed angels was the matter.

Kirsten squatted on her haunches between two parked cars, trembling with fright, trying not to move, afraid the slightest sound would give her position away to her pursuers. She could hear their feet crunching on the asphalt as they moved up and down the aisles, searching for her amid the rows of slotted vehicles. There weren't as many cars in the lot as there would have been at night, when many more residents of the apartment complex would be home from work, but she would take what small blessings she could . . . and for the first time in her life feel grateful for the large government-sponsored housing developments that had virtually wiped out the city's traditional architecture.

More footsteps. Closer. She hugged herself, trying to think clearly through her fear. If she could manage to hide until someone came along either to leave or fetch his car . . . or perhaps inch her way around toward the driveway leading to the street, then maybe she'd have a chance to get some help. . . .

Kirsten heard the crunch of another footfall, this one no more than two aisles down to the left of her, then an entirely different set a little further off to the right.

They were boxing her in on either side.

She stiffened, biting down on the fleshy part of her hand, stifling a mutinous scream. While part of her kept insisting that she give in to the urge, there was a more rational part that understood it would be the worst mistake she could possible make. If she screamed, they'd know exactly where she was, would be on her in an instant, well before anyone could come to her aid.

No, she dared not do it. Dared not make a sound. Dared not move a muscle.

The moment she did, Kirsten was sure she would be theirs.

The optical mini-CDs were stored in specially designed, alphanumerically-tabbed electronic "stacks" lining the walls of the vault. Once inside, the pair of intruders had been able to locate the object of their search within seconds. At the touch of a button, the disc was scanned, identified by a bar code imprinted on its surface, and then ejected from the repository in a gleaming stainless-steel tray.

Slipping the disk into a protective plastic sleeve he took from a wall dispenser, Lombardi dropped it into the breast pocket of his jacket and gave his partner the ready signal.

The two men strode from the vault less than three minutes after entering it, passed through the waiting area without a glance at the dead supervisor, and reentered the outer corridor as if they had nothing to hide.

They were swinging back into the main entry hall when the lab tech's screams pierced the air and all hell broke loose around them.

Kirsten knew she wouldn't be able to hide from her pursuers much longer.

The man she'd heard on her left had reached the end of the aisle he'd been searching, swung into the aisle immediately beside the one where she was crouched, and then turned back up in her direction, pausing every couple of steps to poke his head back and forth between the cars. He was now standing directly across from her, separated from her by a single row of vehicles. And the others were closing in from elsewhere around the court.

The man on the left took a step up the aisle, then another. Kirsten's breath came to a stop. She could see his boots and the bottoms of his jeans under the chassis of the car she was leaning against. Her heart was booming in her ears like a timpani, and in the panicky, half-crazed moment before she got a handle on herself, Kirsten was afraid he'd be able to hear it as well.

In a minute or so he would turn up her aisle, and it would be over.

She had never in her life felt so terribly helpless and alone.

God, God, what am I going to do?

No opening had presented itself. Nobody had driven in or out of the lot, and she had no reason to think anybody would before it was too late to make any difference.

She suddenly realized the only thing she could do was run for it, break for the driveway, and hope that by some miracle she could reach the street before they did. She knew even that wouldn't necessarily mean she was safe— the men who'd come after her and Max had been willing to strike on a thoroughfare as busy as Scotts Road, strike with hundreds of pedestrians around, for godsakes. If this group was just a fraction as bold, they might not have the slightest concern about who saw them.

But she hadn't any choice. It was either leave the pot or be cooked.

She waited another second, took a deep gulp of air, and then forced herself to spring to her feet.

The man on the left spotted her instantly. Their eyes made the briefest contact, hers full of hunted terror, his absent of any hint of sympathy or compassion.

Then he rasped an order to his companions and came hurtling across the aisle at her.

Kirsten turned and fled.

The first indication that something was wrong came the moment they pulled their rental car up to the curb, and was the only one they needed. If there were a way to think things were normal after arriving at a person's home and finding the door kicked in, Nimec didn't know it.

He glanced out the windshield at the street, at the outside stairs, at the walkways spanning the rows of doors on the building's upper stories. All were empty.

"Have your weapons ready," he said to Noriko and Osmar. He withdrew his own Beretta 8040 from its concealment holster, ejected its standard ten-round clip, and chocked in the twelve-round magazine/grip extension. "Don't seem to be any eyes around, but if somebody does call the local gendarmes, we'll get it straight with them later."

Following his lead, the others jogged out of the car and across the ground level unit's front yard to the partially open door.

Nimec instinctively moved to the right of the door frame, gesturing the others to the left, making sure there was some wall between them and whatever potential threat might be inside.

"Kirsten, this is Pete Nimec!" he called through the opening, leaning his head around the splintered jamb. "Are you okay in there?"

No reply.

He pulled back against the wall, cocked his pistol, and looked across the doorway at his teammates.

"Go!" he said.

They rushed into the apartment and fanned out in a practiced crossover maneuver, Nimec moving to the left of the entrance, gun held ready, Noriko and Osmar following him and buttonhooking to the right. The three of them rapidly pivoted to cover the center of the room with their weapons, legs apart, making broad sweeps of their sectors of fire.

They seemed to be alone in the place.

"Kirsten, you here?" Nimec called again.

Still no answer.

Noriko tapped his arm. "Look," she said, pointing straight across the living room.

The back door was wide open.

Nimec's eyes flicked between her and Osmar.

"Come on," he said, and rushed toward the door.

The two intruders paused in the hall and exchanged glances. Confused, frightened staffers poured from doorways on either side of them. Not a word was spoken. They could see that the greatest commotion was down the left bend of the corridor, and knew the bodies of the guards had been discovered. Their original intention had been to walk out the main entrance, and they would have to gamble on still being able to leave that way in the disturbance. It would be dangerous, but any attempt to leave the building through emergency exits would trip sensors that would likely pinpoint the specific door being opened. And they had no illusions about having eliminated the threat from security. The men at the surveillance monitors would not have been the sole members of the plainclothes team on premises. And there was the uniformed guard at the door.

The intruders could only keep their fingers crossed that he'd be sufficiently distracted for them to slip past. Otherwise, they'd have to kill him, too.

They moved forward through the scared, noisy people in the corridor, and were nearly at the checkpoint where they'd had to leave their guns when an alarm sounded, a loud on-and-off noise that grated on the eardrums. The guard at the door seemed to be tracking them with his eyes as they approached.

"We're going out to radio for assistance," the one who'd called himself Lombardi said. His hand was in his jacket pocket.

The guard looked at him.

"I'm sorry," he said. "The building's been sealed."

"Don't insult me," Lomardi said. "We have a job to do."

He started to move forward, Samford walking beside him. The alarm grated on and on.

The guard clamped a hand around Lombardi's arm.

"You need to call somebody, we have phones in here," he said. "But nobody's leaving."

Lombardi smiled. His hand was still in his jacket.

"Don't bet on it," he said, and squeezed the trigger of the pistol he'd taken from the guards in the monitor room.

Hit at point-blank range, the security guard catapulted backward off his feet, a cloud of blood exploding from his chest. Lombardi pumped two more bullets into him as he dropped to the ground, finishing him.

He turned to his companion and waved him along. He was aware of screams, pale faces, racing feet behind them on the concrete floor.

They hastened toward the door, and got as far as the archway of the weapons detector when someone behind them shouted out an order to halt. They kept walking.

"I said freeze!" the voice repeated. *"This is your final warning!"*

Without turning, they quickened their pace.

A gunshot fired out from behind them. Lombardi whirled and saw a plainclothes guard in the center of the corridor, both hands around a gun, his knees bent in a shooter's stance. Lombardi returned fire, missed, heard a *thud-thud-thud* from the suited guard's gun, and then was slapped across the middle by something he didn't see. He looked down at himself, his eyes wide with shock, and had just enough time to glimpse the bloody amalgam of flesh and shredded clothing that had replaced his stomach before he crumpled in a dying heap.

The other intruder reached for his own gun, but before he'd gotten it out of his pocket saw two more plainclothesmen emerge from the branching corridors at his rear. They all had their weapons drawn, and had triangulated their aim to put him in a perfect crossfire.

"Hold it!" he said. Dropping the gun to the floor, kicking it away from him, and slowly raising his hands above his head. "Don't shoot, okay? *Okay?*"

Their guns extended, the Sword ops moved in and took him.

Swinging around the grille of a car, Kirsten tore into the aisle and ran like hell, making for the driveway in a wild headlong dash.

She heard overlapping footsteps behind her, close, close, and pushed herself to move even faster, her legs pumping, arms working at her sides like pistons—

And then, suddenly, one of her pursuers sprang from behind a parked car several yards in front of her.

Between her and the driveway.

His right eye was bloodshot and swollen, and there was a thin line of blood trickling down his cheek from its lower lid.

It was the man she'd grappled with in the apartment. He had some kind of gun in his hand—a submachine gun, she thought, though she was hardly an expert—and was holding it out at her.

"No more shit from you," he said in Bahasa.

She halted, glanced over her shoulder.

Two more of the men who'd come for her were walking quickly up the aisle in her direction, their firearms held downward, flat against their legs. The fourth stalker had emerged near the spot where she'd been hiding.

"Just come on over here, I won't hurt you," said the one blocking her path to the driveway. He motioned with his gun. "Let's go."

Kirsten didn't budge, and was amazed to realize she was shaking her head in the negative.

He shrugged, holding his weapon steady. She could hear the other three coming close behind her.

"You want to wrestle some more, we wrestle," he said, and took a step forward.

"Hold it right there! *Bayaso reya!*"

The voice echoing through the court stopped all four of the men in their tracks. An expression of stunned surprise on his features, the one in front of Kirsten abruptly looked around for its source.

"*Drop the gun!*" the voice said in Bahasa.

Still looking from side to side, the man blocking the

driveway moved the gun off of Kirsten, but didn't lower it.

Kirsten heard a crack like the sound of a detonating firecracker. And then a blossom of crimson appeared in the middle of the man's rib cage and he pitched facedown to the asphalt, his submachine gun clattering from his grasp.

"I hope the rest of you are smarter," the voice said. "It's finished."

Kirsten turned her head, saw one of the gunmen behind her start to raise his weapon, instantly heard two more sharp cracks—only now coming from a different part of the court. The man screamed and fell over clutching his knees, blood spraying out from between his fingers.

The remaining pair of men tossed down their weapons and started to run, scrambling out of the aisle, and then bolting wildly toward the driveway exit. No one tried to stop them.

Her eyes wide and staring, Kirsten looked uncomprehendingly around the court, and all at once saw a brown-skinned Malay spring to his feet behind the tail of a car, several aisles down and directly across from where the first stalker had fallen dead. An instant later two more people appeared near the one who'd been shot in the knees—a white man with close-cropped hair and an Oriental woman.

The man with the short hair holstered his gun beneath his jacket and approached her.

"Kirsten, it's okay, you're safe," he said in a calm, level voice. "I'm Pete Nimec."

She started to say something in response, but her throat had closed up, and her teeth were chattering too violently.

Instead, she strode over to him, put her face against his shoulder, put her arms around him, and started crying.

Noriko had gone to wait in the apartment with Kirsten while Nimec and Osmar took care of business in the parking court.

"Mr. Nimec," Osmar said. "There is something I must show you."

"Right."

Nimec finished flex-cuffing the wounded man, folded a blanket he'd gotten from the apartment under his head, then went over to Osmar.

Kneeling over the body of the one he'd dropped, the Malay lifted his motionless hand off the asphalt.

"You see kris tattoo?" he said, glancing up at Nimec.

Nimec nodded. "Guy I cuffed has exactly the same marking on him. What the hell is it, some kind of cult sign?"

Osmar shook his head.

"Is more like what you Americans call . . ." He made a low sound of concentration in his throat, as if groping hard for words. Then he snapped his fingers. "Ah," he said. *"Colors."*

"Gang colors, you mean," Nimec said. "As in the Crips and Bloods."

Osmar nodded, and placed his finger on the tattooed skin. "The kris, many pirate gangs have such marks. But you see designs on blade?"

Nimec squatted beside him for a closer look. He did indeed see them—grotesque anthropomorphic figures that reminded him a little of the paintings on Egyptian tombs.

"They are *rakasa,*" Osmar said. "Demons. Different for each brotherhood."

Sudden understanding spread across Nimec's features.

"These two punks . . . someone familiar with regional gang crime would be able tell their affiliation from the markings," he said

Osmar nodded again. "And this one, I know well from when I was with police," he said. "The men work for Khao Luan. He is Kuomintang."

The word rang a vague bell. Nimec searched his memory a few seconds.

"A heroin trader?" he said finally.

Another nod. "None are more powerful. The Thai army, they make him to flee during pacification program. Ten years ago, maybe more. Since then, he is in Indonesia."

Nimec gave him an imperative look. "Where? Does anybody know *where*?"

"Everyone knows, and everyone fears to touch him," Osmar said. "In parts of Banjarmasin, the Thai has longer arms than the government."

Nimec was quiet, letting it all sink in. What connection could a man like that have to Monolith? What on *earth* had Max stumbled onto?

After a moment he clapped a hand on Osmar's arm and nodded firmly.

"My friend, we're about to do some more island-hopping," he said. "And I promise you, if this guy's involved in Blackburn's disappearance, I'll cut his fucking arms off myself."

TWENTY-FIVE

THE SURVIVING MEMBER OF THE PAIR THAT GOT INTO the Sacramento vault hadn't talked—not to the Sword detail that apprehended him, not to the Feds after he'd been given into their custody. And it was anybody's guess whether he was *going* to talk.

Gordian, however, wasn't sure that was essential to determining who had been behind the act.

The main question for him, then, was of motive.

Back in San Jose now—he had booked reservations aboard a commuter flight while the A&P mechs continued their inspection of the Learjet in Washington—Gordian sat at his desk opposite Chuck Kirby, trying to put the pieces of a complex and profoundly troubling puzzle into place. They had already run through the whole thing a couple of times, but neither man felt it would hurt to bounce it around once more.

"Let's try it back to front," Gordian said. "Starting with the break-in at the Sacramento facility."

"Sure, why not," Kirby said. "Doing it the other way hasn't nailed it."

"I don't know whether it *can* be nailed, not with the fragmentary information we have," Gordian said. "But we can get closer, make some more important connections.''

Kirby nodded. ''The disc they took off the dead man, then,'' he said.

''The disc,'' Gordian repeated, sighing. ''The keycodes are used in communications systems UpLink has designed for a wide range of naval vessels. Obviously they would be of enormous value to any number of interests, both foreign and domestic.''

''Allies and enemies, for that matter,'' Kirby said. ''Everybody spies on everybody else. It's wide open until you look at how the thieves penetrated the vault.''

''Exactly.'' Gordian's face was sober. ''And if not for the surveillance videos capturing what happened after they killed poor Turner, the techies might've taken weeks, even months to find out. The wicked beauty of it is that the system defeated itself.''

''And that's still the part I can't quite grasp,'' Kirby said.

''It probably isn't vital that you do . . . although the concept isn't really that difficult,'' Gordian said. ''It involves basic computer file architecture, the way hard drives are set up. There's a minimum amount of space allocated for every file on a hard drive . . . the larger the drive, the larger the allocation. Regardless of how much data you have in a file, the computer reserves that minimum space.'' He thought a moment. ''Imagine a department store that only has gift boxes of a single size for their merchandise, no matter whether you're buying a ten-gallon hat or a gold forget-me-not for your wife's necklace. Since the box needs to be pretty big to contain the hat, that tiny charm's not going to be too visible when it's placed inside. In fact, it may even get lost.''

Kirby nodded. "The data-strings that let the thieves through the system's backdoor . . . you're saying they were too small to be noticed. Like the charm. And they slipped past your whiz kids when the software employed by the biometric scanner system was examined for backdoors prior to installation."

"And the techs can't even be held at fault," Gordian said, nodding. "Do a careful diagnostic of *any* hard drive, and you'll find the percentage of file-space being utilized out of whack with the actual number of stored bytes. You store one word-processing file with a couple of words on it, another with several pages of text, and it's probable both are grabbing the same amount of space. When the technicians are looking for Trojan horses, they typically sniff around for long, complex algorithms such as the type needed to match fingerprint or voice characteristics. In this case, the backdoor key was short and sweet . . . a basic geometric pattern . . . a small item in a big box."

"The star on the sapphire," Kirby said. "Incredible."

"To me, what's more incredible is that our security system's primary biometric software was produced by—and acquired from—Monolith Technologies, of all goddamn outfits under the sun," Gordian said. He shook his head. "Talk about an incomprehensible oversight . . ."

"Don't beat yourself over the head with it, Gord," Kirby said. "Their stuff's the best being made. And the system was implemented a while before the problems between you and Caine started brewing. Viewed as an isolated incident, the break-in wouldn't even necessarily place Caine under suspicion. There could be rogue hackers within his company—"

Gordian's face tightened.

"It isn't hackers who tried to steal UpLink out from

under me. Nor was it hackers who used Reynold Armitage as a point man in advance of the raid, or had my plane's landing-gear system sabotaged, or made Max Blackburn vanish into thin air."

Kirby released a breath. "We can't prove Caine's direct involvement with any of that. . . ."

"It's just the two of us here, Chuck. This isn't about what I can prove, but what I know," Gordian said. "Over the past seventy-two hours, the A&P team in D.C. has traced the plane's entire hydraulic circuit for leaks a half-dozen times. And found nothing. Also, the mechs here at home have paper checklists verifying they conducted the full preflight a day before we left, including eyeball inspections of the system's gauges and connections." He paused. "Somebody tampered with that plane after it was prepped. And the guard at the airport, a man named Jack McRea, fessed up to having left his post for several hours a couple nights ago."

"And has since been released from your employ, I hope," Kirby said.

Gordian nodded. "Far as he's been willing to admit, he was lured off to a motel by long legs and a miniskirt. Suckered into leaving the hangars wide open."

The room was silent a few moments.

"The logical jump still bothers me," Kirby said. "Tying Caine to an attempted murder without evidence, for godsakes."

"Mur*ders,* plural," Gordian said. "You were on that plane too, Chuck. As was Megan and Scull."

"Gord, my point is—"

"I know what it is. And again, I'm not talking about specific evidence, but getting a handle on the totality of events that have been wheeling around my head. Max is investigating Caine's business operations in Asia, Max drops out of sight. I take on the Morrison-Fiore Bill, Caine jumps into the ring as a challenger, then as a person who wants to devour my corporation. Somebody breaks into my encryption facility, they do it using a backdoor in Caine-designed software. And so on and so forth. There's too much coincidence. And now the whole thing seems to have taken on a sense of acceleration . . . almost desperation. . . ."

"Or urgency," Kirby said. "If we're going to walk the road you're inclined to lead us down, the keys on that disc they tried to snatch are at the heart of this."

Gordian nodded, his hands steepled under his chin.

The two men sat there quietly a while, thinking everything through.

Five minutes passed, then several more.

More thought, more silence.

Suddenly Gordian sat forward, his eyes widening.

Chuck looked at him. "Something the matter?"

"That word you used," he said. "*Urgency*. It's just that . . ."

He let the sentence trail off, moistened his lips.

Chuck kept looking at him.

"Oh, my God, how could I not have seen? That's why it's come to a head now. *My God,* the ceremony . . . the maiden run is today!"

"Gord, what the hell's *wrong*?"

Gordian shot his hand across the desk and gripped Kirby's wrist.

"The Seawolf," he said, speaking rapidly. "Its command and control systems . . . the systems that run the sub . . . they use UpLink encryption software. And the spare keys, the keys are on that disc."

Kirby was staring at him incredulously. "Gord, I'm not sure I'm reading you, or *want* to be reading you. But even if I am, the thing to remember is nobody got hold of them—"

Gordian sliced his right hand through the air to silence him, still digging the fingers of his left into Kirby's wrist.

"They aren't the only keys, Chuck," he said abruptly, his face white as a sheet. "You understand? We're talking about a nuclear submarine, a boat the President's going to be aboard. *And they aren't the only keys.*"

Watching his team ready themselves on the transportable dock, Omori was convinced he had done well, both in selecting his divers and finding a suitable launching area for the insertion. Notched into the coast of Pulau Ringitt—a small island less than five kilometers south of Sentosa—the saltwater inlet was protected by a zone of mud and marsh that made it the sort of place few people wanted to go sloshing around in.

Omori checked his watch. Not much longer now. Not much longer before his men climbed into the underwater delivery vehicle and the time for preparation was over at last.

He was eagerly looking forward to that moment.

Invisible beneath its camouflage netting, the delivery craft rested on a floating dock amid the thick rushes near the bank. Its bullet-shaped, fiberglass hull was windowless, and though this aided in reducing its detection signature, it also meant Omori's team would be navigating solely on their instruments once they lowered the canopy.

He regarded them from the stern of the speedboat which had towed the dock into position twenty-four hours earlier, and with which he would soon guide it back into deeper water. The four divers had already slipped into their wetsuits and Oxy-57 breathing apparatus. While these had not been designed for the depths at which they would be operating, Omori had been assured the closed-circuit gear would provide breathable air for the limited time their use would be required.

He glanced at his watch again, his frequent reading of its face the only outward sign of the pressure he was feeling. The act to which he had wholeheartedly committed himself would boost the *Inagawa-kai* to unchallenged dominance over competing Yakuza syndicates, and would guarantee him a personal status to surpass that of Oyabuns and Emperors. But even that did not begin to describe what it would mean. Nothing like it had ever been done. Nothing. It would be remembered forever.

The prospect of future glories pushing any thought of failure from his mind, Omori switched on his minicomputer and waited for Kersik's electronic message to appear.

The show was not turning out to be quite what Alec Nordstrum had expected.

No, scratch that, he thought. As a writer, it was his job to use language precisely. And as a member of the press, he had an ethical obligation to be fair.

The show was fine. A tour of the Keppel Harbor area, much fraternal camaraderie between President Ballard and his fellow heads of state, a beautifully organized and executed military parade composed of American, ASEAN, and JMSDF forces, and now the speechifying phase of the ceremony, held on the dock against the sleek, dark shape of the Seawolf. Soon Alex would be invited aboard the sub with the small party of invited journalists, and off they would slip into the octopus's garden for the signing of SEAPAC . . . at which point he'd probably be forced to sit in with the bilgewater.

And that, he supposed, got to the crux of his complaint.

The show was fine, but his seats were lousy. Whereas he'd thought he'd be getting a backstage pass, and had planned to watch the action from the wings, thus far he'd gotten the equivalent of general admission at a rock concert.

He stood in the crowded press area on the waterfront, listening to the Japanese Prime Minister's remarks, getting bumped, jostled, and elbowed by scores of his rude and disorderly international colleagues, thinking this was surely just the first foul taste of Encardi's revenge, and that pretty soon he would be made to drink long and deep of its bitter waters. Already the President had snubbed him. The President's coterie of advisors had blown him off. Perhaps he was being oversensitive, but once or twice he'd even thought that some members of the President's Secret Service detail—men Nordstrum knew by name, and in some cases worked out with at the gym—were shooting dirty looks his way.

He had dared to go with his conscience, to stand with Roger Gordian, and for that had become a marked man, banished from grace, cast among the rabble.

Politics, he mused. *Always politics.*

Nordstrum sighed, trying his best to follow Yamamoto's speech . . . which was not easy with some reporter from an Italian news organization shouting and blowing kisses across his face to a female news anchor from a French television show. *Questa sera, mi bella.*

Dear God, the price one paid for holding to convictions in this world.

He glanced disconsolately at his watch. Another forty minutes or so before he'd be able to make his path to the ramp with the others getting into the nuclear-attack submarine. Even if he *was* restricted to the waste-processing facilities, he'd be grateful to be aboard. Damned grateful.

As far as he could see, his situation couldn't get any worse than it already was.

The Chinese hovercraft had arrived at the atoll under cover of darkness, transported in the well decks of two civilian tankers that had been refitted for military usage. Nearly ninety feet long and half as wide, each amphibious landing craft was powered by four sixteen-thousand-horsepower turbines—two of which fed the shrouded air-screws that would thrust it along at better than fifty knots, the others driving the centrifugal fans that provided vertical lift, allowing the craft to float above sea and strand on a smooth cushion of air. Their decks bristled with pintle-mounted 12.7mm Type 77 machine guns and 40mm grenade launchers.

Standing on the beach of the lagoon, General Kersik Imman watched his men board their vessels in preparation for the Sandakan raid, most of them filing up the ramps onto the four lozenge-shaped flotation craft assembled at the tide line, the rest climbing into a swarm of slender aluminum-hulled cigarette boats. All were suited as he was, in woodland fatigues, their faces veiled by cammo netting, their rucksacks and load-bearing harnesses laden with combat equipment. In strict adherence to Kersik's specifications, the light-assault rifles slung over their shoulders were factory-new, and would make effective personal weapons. Zhiu Sheng had delivered as promised, and for that—as for many other qualities—Kersik deeply respected him.

Perhaps one day they would meet again in some civilized place, a place far from this wretched island where the mosquitos were as fat as grapes from the blood on which they endlessly gorged, a place where they could sit at tables and chairs instead of hard straw mats that cramped their buttocks, a place where they could comfortably reminisce about all they had seen and done since they'd first met as younger men, one an Indonesian general full of pride and aspiration, the other a spirited Communist builder seeking to give shape to Utopia. Both holding dreams of Asian unity and greatness.

Yes, Kersik thought, perhaps they would indeed meet at some future time, and discuss how their greatest dreams had been attained at stages of their lives when most men were snugly wrapped in soft blankets of contentment. And together they would recollect the monumental day the Japanese and Americans who sought to dominate the region—and the ASEAN *wayang kulit* puppets with whom they worked their intricate shadow plays—were swallowed by an underwater behemoth of their own creation.

For now, though, there was only the certain prospect of the attack about to be launched, and the soul-heaviness of an old warrior who knew in his weary heart that the basic equation of war was always out of balance, the accretion of violence always beyond control, the smallest of gains always bought and paid for with the blood of far too many irreplaceable human beings.

Adjusting his pack on his shoulders, Kersik strode

across the sand and boarded the vessel that would carry him to battle.

Khao Luan strode along the boardwalk toward his dwelling on the canal, popping fried, sugared pieces of *tempe goreng* into his mouth, thinking he'd been foolish not to have the canoe vender fill an extra container for him. At the rate he was going, there would be nothing left of the soybean cakes by the time he sat down at his table.

Stress always made him hungry, and he had awakened famished today. With good reason, too. This business he'd gotten into . . . Sandakan . . . the hijack of a nuclear submarine . . . the *hostage taking* of the President of the United States. . . .

For him, it had all been about keeping the sea routes open for his trade. SEAPAC represented a threat to that trade, a solidifying of cooperation between regional governments in matters relating to the patrol of their waters, a substantial impediment to the flow of contraband from Thailand and elsewhere. Disrupting the treaty signing, perhaps even suspending its implementation indefinitely, had seemed a reasonable and pragmatic aim, a sound business strategy for one intent on staying at the top of his game.

Ah, though, how it had evolved.

He walked on, tossing another bit of food into his mouth. Until this morning, he'd been able to concentrate on the particulars rather than the broad contours of the plan, doing his part, taking it a step at a time. Which was how he generally approached things. But with its realization at hand—less than an hour away, unbelievably— the full weight of what he and his allies had undertaken had begun pressing down on him. And while he'd decided that the best way to deal with that pressure was to pretend this was any other day . . . well, it was difficult, that was all.

Luan reached the ladder that climbed to his door, paused at its foot, and looked into his box of *tempe*. Two pieces left. Really, really, he would have to send the men out for more.

He shook both remaining cakes into his mouth, absently tossed the container over his shoulder into the water to his right, and gripped the ladder frame to hoist himself upward.

Inches from where the cardboard box had joined the other refuse floating along the canal, a young female vendor in a loose-fitting sarong hunched forward in her canoe, her head lowering behind mounds of fruit, her hand slipping under a natty hank of cloth.

When that hand reappeared a moment later, it was holding a flat, palm-sized radio.

"Empire State to South Philly, do you read?" the vendor said in a quiet voice, transmitting over a trunked digital channel.

"Loud and clear, Empire State. The rooster back in the barn?"

"Just strutted in, big and nasty in life as in pictures," she said.

A brief pause.

She bent lower, waiting, holding the radio out of sight.

"Sit tight, Empire State," the voice replied after a second. "We're on our way to pluck his feathers."

Jointly sponsored by the ASEAN republics from its original blueprints to its funding and final construction, the Sandakan cryptographic key-storage bank was the largest in Asia, and the second largest in the world, ranking only behind a subsequently built facility of its type in Europe. In terms of proportion, it was to most of the world's other key-recovery banks what Citibank was to a small-town S&L. Sprawling across many acres of shoreline, the concrete-and-steel structure gave a fortresslike impression, and was protected by a sophisticated array of alarm systems and guard units of chiefly Malaysian and Indonesian composition. All this security was in place for a simple reason: The spare key-codes stored within its vaults were those of the region's largest governmental, military, and financial institutions.

It had been regarded as a logical, convenient, and secure place for the Japanese and American governments to store the spare keys to many of Seawolf's encrypted operational systems, including those which controlled its Advanced SEAL Delivery System—or ASDS—docking hatches. These would allow a fully pressurized mini-sub containing from eight to twelve special-op divers to launch and recover its personnel during insertions requiring long-distance, deep-submergence transport. As planned, when the SEALS returned from a mission aboard the sixty-five-foot ASDS vehicle, the computers aboard their vessel would signal the Seawolf's control systems to open the ASDS hatch so that the crew and passengers—and their equipment—could reenter the submarine via its docking chamber, and move from there onto its main decks.

Nga Canbera did not know, and would never know, precisely which Japanese government official had passed this information on to the Inagawa-kai, which had in turn relayed it to him through Omori.

And what difference does it make? he thought, sitting in his den now, watching the SEAPAC ribbon-cutting ceremony on television. He had remained home from the office to watch it undistracted, putting on his finest silk robe for the occasion. So far—given his knowledge of what would happen once the dignitaries were under way—it was proving to be quite a source of amusement.

For him the challenge of the game was the important thing, and though Nga had experienced his moments of apprehension lately, he felt the play would have been meaningless without an edge of danger. Today he would put aside his worries and *enjoy* himself. Could the Seawolf be tricked into swallowing a poison pill? After all, it was in theory only a matter of putting the right keys in the wrong hands—wrong from the American and Japanese standpoint, that is. And while Marcus Caine's failure to deliver the command-and-control keys had been a setback, it had in a sense only added to the excitement. Once Kersik got his hands on the Sandakan keys, Omori's divers would still be able to open the ASDS hatch. After that, they would simply have to put greater reliance on force than finesse, and use guns and bullets rather than keystrokes and passwords to take the submarine.

And maybe, if he were very fortunate, there even would be a little bloodshed to make things more interesting.

His eyes wide with disbelief, U.S. Secretary of Defense Conrad Holden looked at the telephone receiver in his hand as if it had been invaded by an evil poltergeist . . . albeit one that possessed the voice and speech mannerisms of Roger Gordian, someone he'd known for many long years.

"Roger, are you certain?"

"I'm telling you it's going to be Sandakan, Conrad.

And it will roughly coincide with the sub's embarkation. They won't want to give us time to disable the key-codes.''

"But the sub's launching in a half an *hour*—''

"Then get off the phone with me and call somebody who can stop this from happening!''

Hotter and sweatier than he was accustomed to feeling, Luan was about to change his shirt when he heard it: the regular *thup-thup-thup* of rotors beating the air, rapidly getting louder and closer.

He looked across the room to where Xiang and his bodyguards had been throwing a pair of dice.

"What's that sound?'' he said, already knowing the answer. The army helicopters had been ubiquitous when he was driven from the hills of northern Thailand.

The pirate tossed down the dice and turned abruptly to his fellows.

"Get your weapons,'' he grunted. "We're being attacked.''

Leaning out the door of the Bell Jet Ranger chopper, Nimec extracted shells from his utility webbing, slapped them into his 12-gauge and pumped the forestock to chamber the first round. Like Osmar and the other three Sword ops in his team, he had on a pullover cowl, gas mask, and black Nomex Stealthsuit. The Zylon body armor underneath his shirt was both lighter and stronger than Kevlar.

Nimec gestured for the pilot to lower the chopper to a stabilized hover, and peered at the wooden structure below. There were a number of windows on all sides. He chose one of them as his target and pulled the trigger of his pump gun.

The finned CS bomblet disgorged from its muzzle in a train of propellent vapor, punched through the window, and burst open to release a cloud of tear gas.

Nimec chambered another round, fired, and loosed a third at the Thai's hideout. Billows of white smoke erupted from the windows.

He slung the weapon over his shoulder—he also had an MP5K against his side—donned his gloves, and signaled his companions to the door.

A moment later the rope line was dropped from its hoist bracket. One after another in quick succession, the men gripped the line and fast-roped to the boardwalk like firefighters sliding down a pole.

Submachine-gun volleys erupted on the ground almost the instant they alighted—stuttering from inside the house, from the dwellings around it, and from the wooden walkway that ran the length of the canal.

His head ducked low as his teammates laid down a lane of covering fire, Nimec raced around to the front of the hideout.

A man surged into his path from the gushing smoke of the building, bringing an FN P90 up in his direction. But he was half-blinded from the CS, and Nimec was quick to react. He jogged out of the way as the pirate released a stream of 9mm rounds. Nimec raked him across the middle with a burst from his MP5K, then kept dashing for the entrance without a backward glance.

He paused in front of the heavy plank door, sprayed the lock with bullets, and kicked it in with the flat of his foot. With his peripheral vision he could see Osmar running up on the left.

He looked over at him, signaled a crossover entry, and ticked off a three-count with his fingers.

Together they rushed forward into the house.

Minutes after the ribbon-cutting fanfare concluded, the delegation of world leaders was ushered across the gang, over the black anechoic tiles covering Seawolf's hull-like rubber flagstones, and then down into the sub by its executive officer. President Ballard dropped through the hatch first, followed by Prime Minister Yamamoto and the Malaysian and Indonesian heads-of-state.

The press contingent came next, Alex Norstrum at the back of the line, straining to see past a tall, broad-shouldered Canadian reporter who had been directed to board ahead of him.

As the group filed through a passageway toward the control room, Ballard felt as if he were about to step into the set of a Hollywood space opera, something about starships and wormholes in the space-time continuum. And in a sense he *was* entering a time machine, one which was capable of hurling him back through the accumulation of years and distance that had brought him to middle age, stripping the overlay of political cynicism and calculation from his face, and briefly revealing the excited countenance of a ten-year-old orphan from the Mississippi boondocks whose dreams had fueled a long, difficult journey from poverty to the Presidency. He goggled at the equipment and status boards filling up every corner of the brightly lit space with open wonder, his wide eyes no sooner landing on one piece of gadgetry than getting snagged by another of equal or greater fascination.

The sub's commanding officer, Commander Malcolm R. Frickes, USN, was saluting his guests from the control room entryway.

"It is my honor and privilege to welcome you all aboard," he said, stepping aside to let them enter.

Ballard enthusiastically returned the salute, swallowed, and gestured toward the periscopes on a raised platform in the center of the room.

"Do I get to look through one of *those*?" he asked.

Frickes smiled.

"Sir, you're the Commander-in-Chief," he said. "And that means you get to do anything you wish."

General Yussef Tabor, commanding officer of the Malaysian Army's 10th Parachute Brigade, could scarcely believe the orders that had just come down the line. He was to deploy his three airborne battalions—almost three thousand men—to Sandakan at once and assist the regular key-bank guard units in defending the beachhead.

Against *who* or *what* it was to be defended was unclear—but he at last saw an opportunity to be a true soldier. As the closest element of Malaysia's Rapid Deployment Force, stationed in Sabah less than thirty miles from the city, his would be the first of the support units to arrive. And that sat just fine with him.

After a decade of hunting illegal immigrants like a dogcatcher chasing down helpless puppies, it was high time for a mission he could be proud of.

Overcome with tear gas, his face tomato-red, Khao Luan was uncontrollably retching and coughing as Xiang tried to drag him into the barn. Gripping him under both arms from behind, the pirate opened the door and started to back his way through, but was still trying to maneuver his boss's weight when Nimec and Osmar burst into the house.

Osmar thrust his weapon out.

"Hold it!" he shouted in Bahasa. "Both of you!"

Breathing hard, Xiang stared at him a moment through thick braids of CS gas. Then, still partially supporting the Thai with one hand, he whipped the other behind his back and brought a donut-shaped P90 around on its strap.

The burst went wide, peppering a roof support, chewing out splinters of wood, Osmar got down into a crouch and fired back, intentionally aiming low. With Luan between him and the big man, he wanted to avoid shooting to kill, knowing the Thai might hold the answer to Blackburn's disappearance.

Luan sagged, clutching his meaty thigh, blood spraying from his femoral artery. Xiang tried to keep him erect, but was unable to manage it, and he went down with a crash. Retreating into the barn, the pirate triggered his weapon, sweeping it in an arc between Osmar and Nimec. Glass shattered somewhere in the house.

This time it was Nimec who fired back, squeezing off two crisp trigger pulls, *brrrat-brrrat*. He could hear sporadic exchanges of fire out on the walkway, and now and then a groan from one of the incapacitated pirates on the floor.

"Cuff Luan and the rest of these bastards!" he shouted to Osmar through his gas mask. *"I'm going after him!"*

Sea spray roiling up behind them, the four hovercraft scudded over the waves on pillows of air, flanked by dagger-shaped speedboats. They had covered nearly two thirds of the distance to the beach, and would be making landfall within a matter of minutes.

In the forward deckhouse of his vehicle, Kersik lifted his binoculars to his eyes to scan the LZ. He had mustered a force of close to three hundred men, outnumbering the key-bank guard by a third, and with the further advantage of surprise—

Kirsik blinked once, twice.

His eyes widened and widened against the lenses of the binoculars.

At first the dots he had seen against the fleecy backdrop of the cloud looked like insects. A sweeping, descending swarm of locusts.

But he knew all too well what they were.

Paratroopers.

Hundreds of them. *Thousands*. Alighting on the beachhead.

Had his ears not been filled with the deafening roar of the airscrews he might have heard the transports arriving sooner, heard them as he could now, *buzzing,* the buzz becoming a whine, the whine becoming a drone. . . .

He let the glasses drop from his trembling fingers and ran to the deckhouse radio, but by the time he'd transmitted his warning to the other vessels the incoming fire had begun, and the world was exploding all around him.

Omori had hardly seen the small email notice appear on his LCD before he realized the message was not from Kersik at all, but his contact in the Japanese Diet . . . a member of the Nationalist minority whose leaking of top-secret intelligence about the Seawolf had been at the core of the hijack plan since its initiation.

He opened the message and felt his stomach turn on itself.

Though there was only one word on his screen, it was sufficient to make him realize his plans had just come to an abrupt and crashing end:

YAMERU.

ABORT.

Omori dug his knuckles into his forehead and released a high mewl of anguish that instantly drew the attention of all four divers on the floating dock.

He did not look at them, or say anything to them. They would know what had happened just from looking at him.

Kersik, he thought, his fist pressing deeper into his brow.

Kersik had failed.

If he'd been holding a knife in his hand, Omori would have plunged it into his heart and brought the pain to an end then and there.

A blow to the rib cage almost dropped Nimec the instant he plunged through the door.

Stunned, scintillae whirling across his vision, he reeled against the wall of the barn, his MP5K sailing from his fingers.

He clamped his jaws around the pain in his chest. Whatever hit him had felt like an iron mallet, and if he'd been running straight rather than angling through the door, would have probably caught him below the diaphragm and made him lose consciousness. But the muscles of his chest had absorbed enough of its impact to keep him on his feet.

He gulped down a mouthful of air, struggling to get hold of himself—

And saw the giant's fist coming at him barely in the nick of time. He rolled sideways, twisting his head to avoid its pile-driver force, then slipped another blow as the pirate came charging in at him, his arms raised to get him in a squeeze hold, meaning to crush him against the wall with his bulk.

Nimec wasn't going to give him the chance. He could feel the strength flowing back into his legs and knew he had to move, stay out of the giant's reach, avoid going toe-to-toe with him at any cost. It had been his hand, his bare *hand,* that caught Nimec the first time. He'd have to make sure he didn't let it happen again.

Waiting until Xiang was almost on top of him, Nimec cocked his front leg and kicked it speedily up and out at his solar plexus. He heard the slam of his foot against the giant's flesh, saw him lurch backward, and followed through with a second snap kick to the same area.

Xiang staggered back another step and Nimec used the moment to scramble away from the wall, dancing on the balls of his feet like a boxer, getting a rhythm under him, working up some steam.

But the pirate was quicker on his feet than his size would have indicated. Rounding on Nimec, he lunged forward, rushing him head-on.

Nimec tried feinting sidweays, but was a hair too late. A sinewy forearm smashed across his lips and his head rocked back on his neck. He tasted blood, felt his knees weaken a little. Xiang hit him again, this time in the throat with his elbow. Nimec gagged, his eyes blurring.

And then, suddenly, Xiang's massive palms clapped down on either side of Nimec's head, his fingers forming a cage around his jaw and cheekbones. Nimec raised his own hands, wedged them up inside Xiang's forearms, gripped his wrists, and tried with all his strength to pry them apart. But the giant only held on and began steam-rolling forward, carrying Nimec along with him, backing Nimec across the floor of the barn then ramming him up against the wall opposite the door with an impact that jarred him to the bone.

He brought his face in close to Nimec, his features a quivering mask of rage, his breath gusting into his nostrils.

"You want to fight, I'll break your fucking neck right here!" he bellowed, shaking Nimec, battering his head against the wall. "Right here like I did to that other American!"

Nimec's eyes widened. His heart pounded and swelled within him until its beating seemed to fill the universe.

Like I did to that other American.

Groaning from exertion, he pushed against the pirate's wrists, pushed, pushed—

Right here.

That other American.

Pushed—

For an instant he thought the pirate's grip would never relent . . . and then, miraculously, it did.

Shoving off the wall, Nimec brought his knee up fast, driving it into his crotch. Xiang's hands fell away from his head. Nimec hit him again, hard to the face with his fist, kept pressing. Threw another jab, another, another.

The giant started to sag, but Nimec didn't let up. He just kept thinking that Max was dead, and this was the man who'd killed him.

Two, three, four more powerful jabs, and then Xiang surprised him. He fell forward heavily, lumbering into Nimec and knocking him backward.

In that moment, as the two men separated, Xiang lifted his bloody face, his lips twisted into a sneer, and pulled his kris from its sheath.

Nimec froze, staring at that long, wavy blade, but Xiang didn't give him time to react. The giant lunged forward, the knife flickering toward Nimec's throat.

Nimec moved back a half step, pivoting on the ball of his left foot, and reached out. His right hand caught the back of Xiang's knife hand. His left hand slapped the inside of the giant's elbow, then turned and lifted the elbow up and out. Without pausing, Nimec stepped forward, pulling the giant toward him, and buried the knife deep into Xiang's chest, directly below the rib cage and angling up toward the heart.

Xiang remained on his feet another few seconds, looked down at the knife jutting from the center of his rib cage with an expression of utter astonishment, and dropped onto his face.

Nimec stepped back, breathing hard, the pain of his wounds rising up within him, and looked down at the fallen giant.

It was, at last, over.

EPILOGUE

"JUST DAYS AGO, I SAT HERE AND EXPLAINED TO someone how I knew about Marcus Caine's crimes without being able to prove them," Gordian was saying. He placed his hand on the wallet-sized digital recorder on his desk. "Now I've got proof, thanks to you."

"And Max," Kirsten said from the seat opposite him. "If not for him, I'd never have gotten it. And to be honest about it, might have kidded myself into thinking nothing strange was going on at Monolith."

Gordian looked at her, his frank blue eyes meeting her brown ones.

"For a while, maybe," he said. "But sooner or later you'd have stopped kidding yourself. And you'd have done exactly what you did."

She shrugged. They were silent a moment, just the two of them in the office. Outside the window behind Gordian, Mount Hamilton rose through the late afternoon smog, massive and somehow benign in its fixed solidity.

"Maybe you're right," she said at last. "But I'd noticed a lot of unexplained payments to American lobbyists crossing my desk. Sums that went far beyond what they should have been receiving for their services. And as I started paying closer attention to them, I realized they always followed visits to my department head from someone who was with the Canbera bank in Indonesia.'' She shrugged again. ''Anyone with open eyes could have seen the money was graft to American politicians. The lobbying group to whom it was going was specifically hired to promote deregulation of cryptographic technology in Washington. But it wasn't until I mentioned it to Max that I allowed myself to see the truth.''

''And it was Max who convinced you to snoop around in the computer databases for financial discrepancies.''

''And plant the voice recorder in the Corporate Communications director's office.'' She shook her head. ''It's hard for me to believe how indiscreet they were. I mean, I walked right in there every day before my boss arrived, tucked it behind the sofa, and picked it up every evening between the time he left work and when the maintenance woman came to do her cleanup. Then I'd walk back to my own office and upload everything onto a computer disk before heading home. It went on like that for two months.''

''People get away with murder long enough, they get arrogant. They get arrogant, they start to think nothing can touch them. And as a result we've got half a dozen conversations about the payoffs between the director and Nga Canbera . . . and a couple with Marcus Caine's voice added to the mix. Coming over your former boss's speakerphone loud and clear.''

''The CEO of Monolith himself imparting his wisdom about which government officials to target for bribes,'' Kirsten said. ''Incredible, really.''

They were quiet again for a while. Then Gordian

leaned forward, meshed his fingers on the desk, and looked steadily at her face.

"Kirsten, I didn't ask you here to the States because I needed to have the voice recorder and disks hand-delivered," he said. "I wanted to tell you in person how deeply I appreciate what you've done. And also let you know that I'd be honored to have you working for UpLink—wherever in our organization you'd prefer—should you want a job with us."

She smiled a little. "That's a very generous offer . . . but I hope you won't be offended if I decline to accept it, at least for now. I'd like some time to myself. Time to . . . re-group. You understand?"

His eyes were still holding steady on her.

"Yes, yes, I do," he said. "As long as you understand that the offer stands if you ever change your mind. And that I never forget my friends."

She nodded, her smile growing larger. It was very gen-uine and very beautiful, and Gordian thought he knew what Blackburn must have seen in it.

"Is it back to Singapore for you, then?" he said.

She was quiet a moment, then nodded again.

"For a time, anyway. But there's one more thing I have to do here in America before I go."

Armitage sat by the answering machine in his office, his eyes staring out of his wasted features with a cold vitality which seemed to demand and consume all that was left of his life force—like small, mean creatures arising from detritus, feeding on decay.

There had been a number of messages from Marcus Caine waiting for him this morning, each more panicked and desperate than the one preceding it.

No more of that, he thought.

Bound to a failing body and his wheelchair, he was determined to cast off unnecessary ballast. It was hard enough to manage without the dead weight.

"Erase messages," he said, activating the device with a voice chip produced in one of Monolith's San Jose factories. He paused a moment, then set it to screen and disconnect any calls originating from Caine's home or office, verbally inputting the numbers to be blocked.

He did not want to be dragged down with Marcus as his role in the SEAPAC affair, the campaign finance scandal, and numerous other damning episodes became known. Indeed, any association with him at all would be a severe liability.

How quickly things changed. He had believed Caine a likely candidate to win Uplink International and forge a media/technology monopoly that would extend around the globe as no single entity of its type had done before . . . and as a plum for being instrumental in bringing that about, Armitage was to have been handed Uplink's biosciences division on a silver platter. Who could say what new treatments for his condition might have emerged with the company's resources at his disposal? Who could truly say?

But Marcus had disappointed him, *failed* him, and none of that was to be.

He pulled air through his throat and released it in a watery sigh. Perhaps the ALS would get him in the end. Almost certainly it would. But he would live long enough to see Marcus go down first. . . .

And no doubt write many interesting and widely read columns about his fall.

• • •

"There it is. You can check everything out if you'd like."

Marcus Caine sat on the leather-cushioned sofa in his study, a square of mahogany wall paneling pulled back on his right to reveal an open wall safe.

The man he'd spoken to stepped across the room and peered into the safe. He reached a hand inside, extracted a banded pack of bills, rifled their edges, then put them back and looked into the safe another minute.

"It contains over a million dollars in cash. And some trinkets . . . diamonds, my dear wife has always loved her diamonds . . . worth a great deal more."

The man shifted his gaze toward Caine. He was smallish with a pencil mustache and gray eyes that matched the color of his sport jacket.

"You sure you want me to do this?" he said.

Caine spread his arms over the top of the backrest, tilted his chin up, and laughed—a sound that reminded the man a little of crows.

"What's the problem? Are you afraid you'll screw up, the way your friends did at the airport? Or how about Sacramento—shall we discuss that merry fucking romp?"

"There's no reason to talk to me that way," the man said. "Those were tough assignments."

Caine laughed his harsh, cawing laugh again.

"Then let's see you tackle an easy one," he said. "Earn your money this time. And spare me the humiliation of becoming the poster boy for Court TV for a year or so, to be followed by a lifetime of prison interviews."

Silence.

The man walked across the room, stopped in front of Caine, and reached under his jacket. The weapon he brought out from underneath it was a Heckler & Koch .45 P9S.

A moment passed. Still standing there, he took a sound suppressor from his inside pocket and screwed it onto the barrel.

"You worried about how your wife finds you?" he asked.

Caine straightened, and brought his arms down off the backrest. The pained humor was gone from his face and his eyes were watery.

His mouth suddenly tightened.

"Earn your money," he snapped. "Make a fucking mess for her."

The man nodded, cocked the gun, and angled its bore up at Caine's head. There was the sound of Caine sucking in air, and then the muted thud of bullets leaving the gun as he pulled the trigger ten times, emptying the magazine.

When his job was finished, the man holstered the gun, walked back around the couch to the safe, and quickly emptied it, transferring everything that had been inside to his briefcase.

He paused briefly at the door on his way out. Looked at the body and the blood on the sofa and walls. And nodded to himself with satisfaction.

Got what you paid for, he thought.

The inscription on the gravestone was elegant, a quote from Wordsworth:

> *O joy! That in our embers*
> *Is something that doth live,*
> *That Nature yet remembers,*
> *What was so fugitive.*

Reading it, Kirsten wiped a hand across her eyes.

"I remember, too, Max," she said. "I remember."

Behind her, Pete Nimec waited quietly, standing in the shade of the Japanese maples that grew where Blackburn had been laid to rest, his body flown back from Malaysia soon after his identity was confirmed.

Kirsten knelt over the soil that filled the grave, still loose under her fingers.

"Atman and Brahman," she said. "Sometimes, Max, we need illusion to show us the truth in ways we can manage . . . and though I can't be sure, I sometimes think you didn't understand that, and sold yourself short because you didn't. That you felt guilty about asking me to make difficult choices, and let that guilt get in the way of your opening up to me." She felt moisture on her cheeks. "The thing is, Max, I believe Roger Gordian is right. That you were really showing me the way to my own conscience. To my own heart."

She tasted salt, touched her fingers to her lips, touched the place where Max's name was carved on the gravestone.

"You . . . what we had . . . it was *Brahman,* my sweet love," she whispered. "It was truth."

Kirsten lingered there a moment, her eyes closed as if in prayer or repose.

Then she rose, turned from the grave, and strode slowly to where Pete Nimec was waiting.

"You okay?" he asked softly.

She looked at him, smiled a little.

"I will be," she said.

Red Storm
ENTERTAINMENT

Red Storm Entertainment, Inc., was founded in November 1996 by best-selling author Tom Clancy and Virtus Corporation, the leader in 3-D multimedia authoring tools, to create and market multiple-media entertainment products. Red Storm Entertainment is privately held: Principal owners are Tom Clancy, Virtus Corporation, and Pearson plc, one of the world's largest and most respected media groups.

Red Storm Entertainment's objective is to lead the market in the development of entertainment products in multiple forms-interactive computer and console games, board games and related merchandise. To that end, the company is developing products that will satisfy hard-core gamers' appetites as well as appealing to a new, broader user community who is attracted to realistic and intelligent games.

Red Storm Entertainment released its first game, **Tom Clancy's Politika**, in November 1997, and will release five new products in 1998.

Tom Clancy's
ruthless.com

How Ruthless Can You Be?

Now you've seen how ruthless a modern CEO can be when pursuing an enemy. But that experience doesn't have to end when the novel does. The latest computer game from Red Storm Entertainment will challenge you to find the corporate raider lurking inside you.

Tom Clancy's ruthless.com is a bitter contest of economic growth and conquest set in the high-stakes world of modern corporate raiding. It combines the crushing grip of business expansion with the rapier strikes of deceit, dirty tricks, and outright crime. Each of the 1 to 6 players ruthlessly expands their empire, overrunning the others and grinding them into yesterday's dust until only one corporation alone wields true dominance. Special Activities are the spice of the game; players may invest time and money into Legal assaults, Dirty Tricks, and Hacking runs. Finally, Executive Orders involve the growth of the players' CEOs as well as subordinate Executives; these characters gain experience, skills, and personality traits throughout the game.

Tom Clancy's ruthless.com is a strategy game whose resource management and competition techniques carry the trappings of the business world, whose players are not concerned with spreadsheets and depreciation, but instead with the no-holds-barred actions their company takes in a global marketplace where greed is not good—it's great.

Features:
—Strong multiplayer component, including full chat, over a LAN, hot seat or the Internet
—Simultaneous turn-based strategy game
—Flexibility due to three modes of gameplay: Campaign, Scenario, Multiplayer
—Unprecedented dark graphic novel art
—Low system requirements: works on older computers

System Requirements:
OS: Windows 95 or later
CPU: 120 MHz Pentium or better
Network Play: Properly configured TCP/IP connection at 14.4 kbps or faster
RAM: 16 MB minimum, 32 MB preferred
Hard Disk: No specific requirements
CD-ROM: 4x speed or faster
Display: 800 x 600 Hi Color
3-D Acceleration: not required
Audio: DirectSound playback preferred

Tom Clancy's ruthless.com is available from the software retailers near you.

The Internet.

Parental discretion

included.

It's all within your reach.